KT-558-914

DIRK PITT® ADVENTURES BY CLIVE CUSSLER

CLIVE CUSSLER

POCKET
BOOKS

LONDON · SYDNEY · NEW YORK · TOKYO · SINGAPORE · TORONTO

SHOCK WAVE

A NOVEL

New York   London   Toronto   Sydney   Tokyo   Singapore

First published in Great Britain by Simon & Schuster UK Ltd, 1996
This edition first published by Pocket Books, 1997
An imprint of Simon & Schuster UK Ltd
A Viacom Company

3 5 7 9 10 8 6 4 2

Simon & Schuster UK Ltd
Africa House
64-78 Kingsway
London WC2B 6AH

Simon & Schuster Australia
Sydney

A CIP catalogue record for this book is available from the British Library

ISBN 0-671-85564-6

Designed by Levavi & Levavi
Illustrations by Errol Beauchamp

Printed and bound in Great Britain by Caledonian International Book
Manufacturing, Glasgow

With deep appreciation to
Dr. Nicholas Nicholas
Dr. Jeffrey Taffet
&
Robert Fleming

RAFT OF THE
GLADIATOR

THE GLADIATOR

Of the four clipper ships built in Aberdeen, Scotland, in 1854, one stood out from the others. She was the *Gladiator*, a big ship of 1,256 tons, 198 feet in length and a 34-foot beam, with three towering masts reaching for the sky at a rakish angle. She was one of the fleetest of the clippers ever to take to the water, but she was a dangerous ship to sail in rough weather because of her too fine lines. She was hailed as a *"ghoster,"* having the capability of sailing under the barest breath of wind. Indeed, the *Gladiator* was never to experience a slow passage from being becalmed.

Unfortunately, and unpredictably, she was a ship destined for oblivion.

Her owners fitted her out for the Australian trade and emigrant business, and she was one of the few clippers designed to carry passengers as well as cargo. But as they soon discovered, there weren't that many colonists who could afford the fare, so she was sailing with first- and second-class cabins empty. It was found to be far more lucrative to obtain government contracts for the transportation of convicts to the continent that initially served as the world's largest jail.

The *Gladiator* was placed under command of one of the hardest driving clipper captains, Charles "Bully" Scaggs. He was aptly named. Though Scaggs did not use the lash on shirking or insubordinate crewmen, he was ruthless in driving his men and ship on record runs between England and Australia. His aggressive methods produced results. On her third homeward voyage, *Gladiator* set a sixty-three-day record that still stands for sailing ships.

Scaggs had raced the legendary captains and clipper ships of his time, John Kendricks of the fleet *Hercules* and Wilson Asher in command of the renowned *Jupiter,* and never lost. Rival captains who left London within hours of the *Gladiator,* invariably found her comfortably moored at her dock when they arrived in Sydney Harbor.

The fast runs were a godsend to the prisoners, who endured the nightmarish voyages in appalling torment. Many of the slower merchant ships took as long as three and a half months to make the voyage.

Locked belowdecks, the convicts were treated like a cargo of cattle. Some were hardened criminals, some were political dissidents, all too many were poor souls who had been imprisoned for stealing a few pieces of cloth or scraps of food. The men were being sent to the penal colony for every offense from murder to pickpocketing. The women, separated from the men by a thick bulkhead, were mostly condemned for petty theft or shoplifting. For both sexes there were few conveniences of any kind. Skimpy bedding in small wooden berths, the barest of hygienic facilities and food with little nutrients was their lot for the months at sea. Their only luxuries were rations of sugar, vinegar and lime juice to ward off scurvy and a half-pint of port wine to boost their morale at night. They were guarded by a small detachment of ten men from the New South Wales Infantry Regiment, under the command of Lieutenant Silas Sheppard.

Ventilation was almost nonexistent; the only air came from hatchways with solidly built grills that were kept closed and heavily bolted. Once they entered the tropics, the air became stifling during the blazing hot days. They suffered even more during rough weather, cold and wet, thrown about by the waves crashing against the hull, living in a state of virtual darkness.

Doctors were required to serve on the convict ships, and the *Gladiator* was no exception. Surgeon-Superintendent Otis Gorman saw to the prisoners' general health and arranged for small groups of them to come on deck for fresh air and exercise whenever the weather permitted. It became a source of pride for surgeons to boast, when finally reaching the dock in Sydney, that they hadn't lost a prisoner. Gorman was a compassionate man who cared for his wards, bleeding them when required, lancing abscesses, dispensing treatment and advice on lacerations, blisters and purges, also overseeing the spreading of lime chloride in the water closets, the laundering of clothes and the scouring of the urine tubs. He seldom failed to receive a letter of thanks from the convicts as they filed ashore.

Bully Scaggs mostly ignored the unfortunates locked below his decks. Record runs were his stock in trade. His iron discipline and aggressiveness had paid off handsomely in bonuses from happy shipping owners while making him and his ship immortal in the legends of clipper ships.

This trip he smelled a new record and was relentless. Fifty-two days out of London, bound for Sydney with a cargo of trade goods and 192 convicts, 24 of them women, he pushed *Gladiator* to her absolute limits, seldom taking in sail during a heavy blow. His perseverance was rewarded with a twenty-four-hour run of an incredible 439 miles.

And then Scaggs' luck ran out. Disaster loomed over the astern horizon.

A day after *Gladiator*'s safe passage through the Bass Strait between Tasmania and the southern tip of Australia, the evening sky filled with ominous black clouds and the stars were blotted out as the sea grew vicious in proportion. Unknown to Scaggs, a full-blown typhoon was hurling itself upon his ship from the southeast beyond the Tasman Sea. Agile and stout as they were, the clipper ships enjoyed no amnesty from the Pacific's anger.

The tempest was to prove the most violent and devastating typhoon within memory of the South Sea islanders. The wind gained in velocity with each passing hour. The seas became heaving mountains that rushed out of the dark and pounded the entire length of the *Gladiator*. Too late, Scaggs gave the order to reef the sails. A vicious gust caught the exposed canvas and tore it to shreds, but not before snapping off the masts like toothpicks and pitching the shrouds and yards onto the deck far below. Then, as if attempting to clean up their mess, the pounding waves cleared the tangled wreckage of the masts overboard. A thirty-foot surge smashed into the stern and rolled over the ship, crushing the captain's cabin and tearing off the rudder. The deck was swept free of boats, helm, deckhouse and galley. The hatches were stove in, and water poured into the hold unobstructed.

This one deadly, enormous wave had suddenly battered the once graceful clipper ship into a helpless, crippled derelict. She was tossed like a block of wood, made unmanageable by the mountainous seas. Unable to fight the tempest, her unfortunate crew and cargo of convicts could only stare into the face of death as they waited in terror for the ship to take her final plunge into the restless depths.

Two weeks after the *Gladiator* failed to reach port, ships were sent out to retrace the known clipper passages through Bass Strait and the Tasman Sea, but they failed to turn up a trace of survivors, corpses or floating wreckage. Her owners wrote her off as a loss, the underwriters paid off, the relatives of the crew and convicts mourned their passing and the ship's memory became dimmed by time.

Some ships had a reputation as floating coffins or hell ships, but the rival captains who knew Scaggs and the *Gladiator* merely shook their heads and crossed off the vanished graceful clipper ship as a victim of her tender sailing qualities and Scaggs' aggressive handling of her. Two men who had once sailed on her suggested that she might have been abruptly caught in a following gust in unison with a wave that broke over the stern, the combined force pushing her bow beneath the water and sending her plummeting to the bottom.

In the Underwriting Room of Lloyd's of London, the famous maritime underwriters, the loss of the *Gladiator* was recorded in the logbook between the sinking of an American steam tugboat and the grounding of a Norwegian fishing boat.

Almost three years were to pass before the mysterious disappearance was solved.

Incredibly, unknown to the maritime world, the *Gladiator* was still afloat after the terrible typhoon had passed on to the west. Somehow the ravaged clipper ship had survived. But the sea was entering between sprung planks in the hull at an alarming rate. By the following noon, there were six feet of water in the hold, and the pumps were fighting a losing battle.

Captain Bully Scaggs' flinty endurance never wavered. The crew swore he kept the ship from foundering by sheer stubbornness alone. He issued orders sternly and calmly, enlisting those convicts who hadn't suffered major injuries from having been knocked about by the constant battering of the sea to man the pumps while the crew concentrated on repairing the leaking hull.

The rest of the day and night was spent in an attempt to lighten the ship, throwing overboard the cargo and any tool or utensil that was not deemed indispensable. Nothing helped. Much time was lost, and the effort achieved little. The water gained another three feet by the following morning.

By midafternoon an exhausted Scaggs bowed to defeat. Nothing he or anyone could do would save the *Gladiator*. And without boats there was only one desperate gamble to save the souls on board. He ordered Lieutenant Sheppard to release the prisoners and line them up on deck opposite the watchful eyes of his armed detachment of soldiers. Only those who worked the pumps and members of the crew feverishly attempting to caulk the leaks remained at their labor.

Bully Scaggs didn't need the lash or a pistol to have complete domination of his ship. He was a giant of a man with the physique of a stonemason. He stood six feet two inches tall, with eyes that were olive gray, peering from a face weathered by the sea and sun. A great shag of ink-black hair and a magnificent black beard that he braided on special occasions framed his face. He spoke with a deep, vibrant voice that enhanced his commanding presence. In the prime of life, he was a hard-bitten thirty-nine years old.

As he looked over the convicts he was startled by the number of injuries, the bruises, the sprains, the heads wrapped with blood-soaked bandages. Fear and consternation were revealed on every face. An uglier group of men and women he'd never laid eyes on. They tended to be short, no doubt due to a lifetime of insufficient diet. Their countenances were gaunt, their complexions, pallid. Cynical, impervious to the word of God, they were the dregs of British society, without expectation of seeing their homeland again, without hope of living out a fruitful life.

When the poor wretches saw the terrible damage above deck,

the stumps of the masts, the shattered bulwarks, the missing boats, they were overwhelmed with despair. The women began uttering cries of terror, all except one, Scaggs noted, who stood out from the rest.

His eyes briefly paused on the female convict, who was nearly as tall as most of the men. The legs showing beneath her skirt were long and smooth. Her narrow waist was shadowed by a nicely shaped bosom that spilled over the top of her blouse. Her clothes appeared neat and clean, and her waist-length yellow hair had a brushed luster to it, unlike that of the other women, whose hair was unkept and stringy. She stood poised, her fear masked by a show of defiance as she stared back at Scaggs through eyes as blue as an alpine lake.

This was the first time Scaggs had noticed her, and he idly wondered why he hadn't been more observant. He refocused his wandering thoughts on the emergency at hand and addressed the convicts.

"Our situation is not promising," Scaggs began. "In all honesty I must tell you the ship is doomed, and with the sea's destruction of our boats, we cannot abandon her."

His words were greeted with a mixed reaction. Lieutenant Sheppard's infantrymen stood silent and motionless, while many of the convicts began to wail and moan piteously. Expecting to see the ship go to pieces within moments, several of the convicts fell to their knees and begged the heavens for salvation.

Turning a deaf ear to the doleful cries, Scaggs continued his address. "With the help of a merciful God, I will attempt to save every soul on this ship. I intend to build a raft of sufficient size to carry everyone on board until we are saved by a passing ship or drift ashore on the Australian mainland. We'll load ample provisions of food and water, enough to last us for twenty days."

"If you don't mind me asking, Captain, how soon do you reckon before we'd be picked up?"

The question came from a huge man with a contemptuous expression who stood head and shoulders above the rest. Unlike his companions he was fashionably dressed, with every hair on his head fastidiously in place.

Before answering, Scaggs turned to Lieutenant Sheppard. "Who's that dandy?"

Sheppard leaned toward the captain. "Name is Jess Dorsett."

16

Scaggs' eyebrows raised. "Jess Dorsett the highwayman?"

The lieutenant nodded. "The same. Made a fortune, he did, before the Queen's men caught up with him. The only one of this motley mob who can read and write."

Scaggs immediately realized that the highwayman might prove valuable if the situation on the raft turned menacing. The possibility of mutiny was very real. "I can only offer you all a chance at life, Mr. Dorsett. Beyond that I promise nothing."

"So what do you expect of me and my degenerate friends here?"

"I expect every able-bodied man to help build the raft. Any of you who refuse or shirk will be left behind on the ship."

"Hear that, boys?" Dorsett shouted to the assembled convicts. "Work or you die." He turned back to Scaggs. "None of us are sailors. You'll have to tell us how to go about it."

Scaggs gestured toward his first officer. "I have charged Mr. Ramsey with drawing up plans and framing the raft. A work party drawn from those of my crew not required to keep us afloat will direct the construction."

At six feet four, Jess Dorsett seemed a giant when standing among the other convicts. The shoulders beneath the expensive velvet coat stretched broad and powerful. His copper-red hair was long and hung loose over the collar of the coat. His head was large nosed, with high cheekbones and a heavy jaw. Despite two months of hardship, locked in the ship's hold, he looked as though he'd just stepped out of a London drawing room.

Before they turned from each other, Dorsett and Scaggs briefly exchanged glances. First Officer Ramsey caught the intensity. The tiger and the lion, he thought pensively. He wondered who would be left standing at the end of their ordeal.

Fortunately, the sea had turned calm, since the raft was to be built in the water. The construction began with the materials being thrown overboard. The main framework was made up from the remains of the masts, lashed together with a strong rope. Casks of wine along with barrels of flour meant for the taverns and grocery stores of Sydney were emptied and tied within the masts for added buoyancy. Heavy planking was nailed across the top for a deck and then surrounded by a waist-high railing. Two spare topmasts were erected fore and aft and fitted with sails, shrouds and stays. When completed the raft measured eighty feet in length by forty feet wide, and though it looked quite large, by the time the provisions were loaded on board, it was a tight squeeze to pack in 192 convicts, 11 soldiers and the ship's crew, which numbered 28, including Bully Scaggs, for a total of 231. At what passed for the stern, a rudimentary rudder was attached to a makeshift tiller behind the aft mast.

Wooden kegs containing water, lime juice, brined beef and pork, as well as cheese, and several pots of rice and peas cooked in the ship's galley, were lowered on board between the masts and tied down under a large sheet of canvas that was spread over two thirds of the raft as an awning to ward off the burning rays of the sun.

The departure was blessed by clear skies and a sea as smooth as a millpond. The soldiers were disembarked first, carrying their muskets and sabers. Then came the convicts, who were all too happy to escape sinking with the ship, now dangerously down by the bow. The ship's ladder was inadequate to support them all, so most came over the side, dangling from ropes. Several jumped or fell into the water and were recovered by the soldiers. The badly injured were lowered by slings. Surprisingly, the exodus was carried off without incident. In two hours, all 203 were safely stationed on the raft in positions assigned by Scaggs.

The crew came next, Captain Scaggs the last man to leave the steeply slanting deck. He dropped a box containing two pistols, the ship's log, a chronometer, compass and a sextant into the arms of First Officer Ramsey. Scaggs had taken a position fix before dropping over the side and had told no one, not even Ramsey, that the storm had blown the *Gladiator* far off the normal shipping routes. They were drifting in a dead area of the Tasman Sea, three hundred miles from the nearest Australian shore, and what was worse, the current was carrying them even farther into nothingness where no ships sailed. He consulted his charts and determined their only hope was to take advantage of the adverse current and winds and sail east toward New Zealand.

Soon after settling in, everyone in their place on the crowded deck, the raft's passengers found to their dismay that there was only enough space for forty bodies to lie down at any one time. It was obvious to the seamen from the ship that their lives were in great jeopardy; the planked deck of the raft was only four inches above the water. If confronted with a rough sea, the raft and its unfortunate passengers would be immersed.

Scaggs hung the compass on the mast forward of the tiller. "Set sail, Mr. Ramsey. Steer a heading of one-fifteen degrees east-southeast."

"Aye, Captain. We'll not try for Australia, then?"

"Our best hope is the west coast of New Zealand."

"How far do you make it?"

"Six hundred miles," Scaggs answered as if a sandy beach lay just over the horizon.

Ramsey frowned and stared around the crowded raft. His eyes fell on a group of convicts who were in hushed conversation. Finally, he spoke in a tone heavy with gloom. "I don't believe any of us God-fearin' men will see deliverance while we're surrounded by this lot of scum."

The sea remained calm for the next five days. The raft's passengers settled into a routine of disciplined rationing. The cruel sun beat down relentlessly, turning the raft into a fiery hell. There was a desperate longing to drop into the water and cool their bodies, but already the sharks were gathering in anticipation of an easy meal. The seamen threw buckets of saltwater on the canvas awning, but it only served to heighten the humidity beneath.

Already the mood on the raft had begun to swing from melancholy to treachery. Men who had endured two months of confinement in the dark hold of the *Gladiator* now became troubled without the security of the ship's hull and with being encompassed by nothingness. The convicts began to regard the sailors and the soldiers with ferocious looks and mutterings that did not go unnoticed by Scaggs. He ordered Lieutenant Sheppard to have his men keep their muskets loaded and primed at all times.

Jess Dorsett studied the tall woman with the golden hair. She was sitting alone beside the forward mast. There was an aura of tough passivity about her, a manner of overlooking the hardships without expectations. She appeared not to notice the other female convicts, seldom conversing, choosing to remain aloof and quiet. She was, Dorsett decided, a woman of values.

He snaked toward her through the bodies packed on board the raft until he was stopped by the hard gaze of a soldier who motioned him back with a musket. Dorsett was a patient man and waited until the guards changed shifts. The replacement promptly began leering at the women, who quickly taunted him. Dorsett took advantage of the diversion to move until he was at the imaginary boundary line dividing the men from the women. The blond woman did not notice, her blue eyes were fixed on something only she could see in the distance.

"Looking for England?" he asked, smiling.

She turned and stared at him as if making up her mind whether to grace him with an answer. "A small village in Cornwall."

"Where you were arrested?"

"No, that was in Falmouth."

"For attempting to murder Queen Victoria?"

Her eyes sparkled and she laughed. "Stealing a blanket, actually."

"You must have been cold."

She became serious. "It was for my father. He was dying from the lung disease."

"I'm sorry."

"You're the highwayman."

"I was until my horse broke her leg and the Queen's men ran me down."

"And your name is Jess Dorsett." He was pleased that she knew who he was and wondered if she had inquired of him. "And you are . . .?"

"Betsy Fletcher," she answered without hesitation.

"Betsy," Dorsett said with a flourish, "consider me your protector."

"I need no fancy highwayman," she said smartly. "I can fend for myself."

He motioned around the horde jammed on the raft. "You may well need a pair of strong hands before we see hard ground again."

"Why should I put my faith in a man who never got his hands dirty?"

He stared into her eyes. "I may have robbed a few coaches in my time, but next to the good Captain Scaggs, I'm most likely the only man you can trust not to take advantage of a woman."

Betsy Fletcher turned and pointed at some evil-looking clouds scudding in their direction before a freshening breeze. "Tell me, Mr. Dorsett, how are you going to protect me from that?"

20

"We're in for it now, Captain," said Ramsey. "We'd better take down the sails."

Scaggs nodded grimly. "Cut short lengths of rope from the keg of spare cordage and pass them around. Tell the poor devils to fasten themselves to the raft to resist the turbulence."

The sea began to heap up uncomfortably, and the raft lurched and rolled as the waves began to sweep over the huddled mass of bodies, each passenger clutching their individual length of rope for dear life, the smart ones having tied themselves to the planks. The storm was not half as strong as the typhoon that did in the *Gladiator*, but it soon became impossible to tell where the raft began and the sea left off. The waves rose ever higher as the whitecaps blew off their crests. Some tried to stand to get their heads above water, but the raft was pitching and rolling savagely. They fell back on the planking almost immediately.

Dorsett used both his and Betsy's ropes to fasten her to the mast. Then he wrapped himself in the shroud lines and used his body to shield her from the force of the waves. As if to add insult to injury, rain squalls pelted them with the force of stones cast by devils. The disorderly seas struck from every direction.

The only sound that came above the fury of the storm was Scaggs' vehement cursing as he shouted orders to his crew to add more lines to secure the mound of provisions. The seamen struggled to lash down the crates and kegs, but a mountainous wave reared up at that moment and crashed down onto the raft and pushed it deep under the water. For the better part of a minute there was no one on that pathetic craft who didn't believe they were about to die.

Scaggs held his breath and closed his eyes and swore without opening his mouth. The weight of the water felt as though it was crushing the life out of him. For what seemed an eternity the raft sluggishly rose through a swirling mass of foam into the wind again. Those who hadn't been swept into the sea inhaled deeply and coughed out the saltwater.

The captain looked around the raft and was appalled. The entire mass of provisions had been carried away and had disappeared as if they had never been loaded aboard. What was even more horrendous was that the bulk of the crates and kegs had carved an avenue through the pack of convicts, maiming and thrusting them from the raft with the force of an avalanche. Their pathetic cries for help went unanswered. The savage sea made any attempt at rescue impossible, and the lucky ones could only mourn the bitter death of their recent companions.

The raft and its suffering passengers endured the storm through the night, pounded by the wash that constantly rolled over them. By the following morning the sea had begun to ease off, and the wind dwindled to a light southerly breeze. But they still kept an eye out for the occasional renegade wave that lurked out of sight before sweeping in and catching the half-drowned survivors off guard.

When Scaggs was finally able to stand and appraise the total extent of the damage, he was shocked to find that not one keg of food or water had been spared from the violence of the sea. Another disaster. The masts were reduced to a few shreds of canvas. He ordered Ramsey and Sheppard to take a count of the missing. The number came to twenty-seven.

Sheppard shook his head sadly as he stared at the survivors. "Poor beggars. They look like drowned rats."

"Have the crew spread what's left of the sails and catch as much rainwater as possible before the squall stops," Scaggs ordered Ramsey.

"We no longer have containers to store it," Ramsey said solemnly. "And what will we use for sails?"

"After everybody drinks their fill, we'll repair what we can of the canvas and continue on our east-southeast heading."

As life reemerged on the raft, Dorsett untied himself from the mast shrouds and gripped Betsy by the shoulders. "Are you harmed?" he asked attentively.

She peered at him through long strands of hair that were plastered against her face. "I won't be attending no royal ball looking like a drenched cat. Soaked as I am, I'm glad to be alive."

"It was a bad night," he said grimly, "and I fear it won't be the last."

Even as Dorsett comforted her, the sun returned with a vengeance. Without the awning, torn away by the onslaught of the wind and waves, there was no protection from the day's heat. The torment of hunger and thirst soon followed. Every morsel of food that could be found among the planks was quickly eaten. The little rainfall caught by the torn canvas sails was soon gone.

When their tattered remains were raised again, the sails had little effect and proved almost worthless for moving the raft. If the wind came from astern, the vessel was manageable. But attempting to tack only served to twist the raft into an uncontrollable position crosswise with its beam to the wind. The inability to command the direction of the raft only added to Scaggs' mounting frustrations. Having saved his precious navigational instruments by clutching them to his breast during the worst of the deluge, he now took a fix on the raft's position.

"Any nearer to land, Captain?" asked Ramsey.

"I'm afraid not," Scaggs said gravely. "The storm drove us north and west. We're farther away from New Zealand than we were at this time two days ago."

"We won't last long in the Southern Hemisphere in the dead of summer without fresh water."

Scaggs gestured toward a pair of fins cutting the water fifty feet from the raft. "If we don't sight a boat within four days, Mr. Ramsey, I fear the sharks will have themselves a sumptuous banquet."

The sharks did not have long to wait. The second day after the storm, the bodies of those who succumbed from injuries sustained during the raging seas were slipped over the side and quickly disappeared in a disturbance of bloody foam. One monster seemed particularly ravenous. Scaggs recognized it as a great white, feared as the sea's greediest murder machine. He estimated its length to be somewhere between twenty-two and twenty-four feet.

The horror was only beginning. Dorsett was the first to have a premonition of the atrocities that the poor wretches on the raft would inflict upon themselves.

"They're up to something," he said to Betsy. "I don't like the way they're staring at the women."

"Who are you talking about?" she asked through parched lips. She had covered her face with a tattered scarf, but her bare arms and her legs below the skirt were already burned and blistered from the sun.

"That scurvy lot of smugglers at the stern of the raft, led by the murderin' Welshman, Jake Huggins. He'd as soon slit your gullet as give you the time of day. I'll wager they're planning a mutiny."

Betsy stared vacantly around the bodies sprawled on the raft. "Why would they want to take command of this?"

"I mean to find out," said Dorsett as he began making his way over the convicts slouched about the damp planking, oblivious to everything around them while suffering from a burning thirst. He moved awkwardly, annoyed at how stiff his joints had become with no exercise except holding onto ropes. He was one of the few who dared approach the conspirators, and he muscled his way through Huggins' henchmen. They ignored him as they muttered to themselves in low tones and cast fierce looks at Sheppard and his infantrymen.

"What brings you nosin' around, Dorsett?" grunted Huggins.

The smuggler was short and squat with a barrel chest, long matted sandy hair, an extremely large flattened nose and an enormous mouth with missing and blackened teeth, which combined to give him a hideous leer.

"I figured you could use a good man to help you take over the raft."

"You want to get in on the spoils and live a while longer, do you?"

"I see no spoils that can prolong our suffering," Dorsett said indifferently.

Huggins laughed, showing his rotting teeth. "The women, you fool."

"We're all dying from thirst and the damnable heat, and you want sex?"

"For a famous highwayman, you're an idiot," Huggins said irritably. "We don't want to lay the little darlins. The idea is to cut them up and eat their tender flesh. We can save the likes of Bully Scaggs, his sailor boys and the soldiers for when we really gets hungry."

The first thought that struck Dorsett was that Huggins was making a disgusting joke, but the inspired evil that lurked in his eyes and the ghastly grin plainly demonstrated it was no play of words. The thought was so vile it filled Dorsett with horror and revulsion. But he was a consummate actor and gave an uncaring shrug.

"What's the hurry? We might be rescued by this time tomorrow."

"There won't be no ship or island on the horizon anytime

soon." Huggins paused, his ugly face contorted with depravity. "You with us, highwayman?"

"I've got nothing to lose by throwing in with you, Jake," Dorsett said with a tight smile. "But the big blond woman is mine. Do what you will with the rest."

"I can see you've taken a likin' to her, but my boys and I share and share alike. I'll let you have first claim. After that, she's divided up."

"Fair enough," Dorsett said dryly. "When do we make our move?"

"One hour after dark. At my signal we attack the soldier boys and go for their muskets. Once we're armed we'll have no trouble with Scaggs and his crew."

"Since I've already established a place by the forward mast, I'll take care of the soldier guarding the women."

"You want to be first in line for supper, is that it?"

"Just hearing you talk about it," said Dorsett sardonically, "makes me hungry."

Dorsett returned to Betsy's side but said nothing to her about the terror about to be unleashed by the convicts. He knew Huggins and his men were observing his every move, making certain he was not making a furtive effort to warn the *Gladiator*'s crew and the soldiers. His only opportunity would come with darkness, and he had to move before Huggins gave his signal to launch the horror. He lay as near to Betsy as the guard would allow and appeared to doze away the afternoon.

As soon as dusk covered the sea and the stars appeared, Dorsett left Betsy and snaked his way to within a few feet of First Officer Ramsey and hailed him in a hushed whisper.

"Ramsey, do not move or act as if you're listening to anyone."

"What is this?" Ramsey blurted under his breath. "What do you want?"

"Listen to me," Dorsett said softly. "Within the hour, the convicts, led by Jake Huggins, are going to attack the soldiers. If they are successful in killing them all, they will use their arms against you and your crew."

"Why should I believe the words of a common criminal?"

"You'll all be dead if you don't."

"I'll tell the captain," Ramsey said grudgingly.

"Just remind him it was Jess Dorsett who warned you."

Dorsett broke off and crawled back to Betsy. He removed his left boot, twisted off the sole and heel and removed a small knife with a four-inch blade. Then he sat back to wait.

A quarter-moon was beginning to rise over the horizon, giving the pitiful creatures on board the raft the look of ghostly wraiths, some of whom suddenly began rising to their feet and moving toward the prohibited area in the center.

"Kill the swine!" Huggins shouted, leaping forward and leading a surge of flesh toward the soldiers. Half out of their minds with thirst the mass of prisoners unleashed their hatred for authority and made a rush toward the middle of the raft from all sides.

A volley of musket fire cut holes in their ranks, and the unexpected resistance stunned them momentarily.

Ramsey had passed on Dorsett's alarm to Scaggs and Sheppard. The infantrymen, muskets loaded and bayonets fixed, waited along with Scaggs and his crew, who had been armed with the soldiers' sabers, the carpenter's hammers and hatchets, and any other weapon they could scrape up.

"Don't give 'em time to reload, boys!" Huggins roared. "Strike hard!"

The mass of maddened mutineers rushed forward again, met this time with thrusting bayonets and slashing sabers. Yet, nothing diminished their rage. They threw themselves against the cold steel, several of them grasping the sharpened blades in their bare hands. Desperate men grappled and sliced each other on a black sea under the eerie moonlight.

The soldiers and sailors fought furiously. Every inch of the raft was occupied by men fighting savagely to kill each other. The bodies piled up, entangling the feet of combatants. Blood flowed on the deck planking, making it difficult to stand if not impossible to rise after falling. In the darkness, now oblivious to their thirst and hunger, they blindly fought and slaughtered. The only sounds made by the combatants were the cries of the wounded and the moans of the dying.

The sharks, as if sensing a bounty, began circling ever closer. The high-pointed fin of the Executioner, the name the seamen gave the great white, silently carved through the water less than five feet from the raft. None of the unfortunates who fell in the water climbed on board again.

Pierced by five saber wounds, Huggins staggered toward Dorsett, a large splintered board in an upraised hand. "You bloody traitor!" he hissed.

Dorsett hunched and held the knife out in front of his body. "Step forward and die," he said calmly.

Infuriated, Huggins yelled back. "It is you who will feed the sharks, highwayman!" Then he put his head down and charged, swinging the board like a scythe.

At the instant Huggins lunged at him, Dorsett dropped to his hands and knees. Unable to check his momentum, the enraged Welshman stumbled over him and fell, crashing heavily to the deck. Before he could raise himself up, Dorsett had leaped on the immense back, reversed the knife in his hand and slashed Huggins' throat.

"You'll not be dining on the ladies this night," Dorsett said fiercely as Huggins' body stiffened before going limp in death.

Dorsett killed three more men that fateful night. At one stage of the battle he was assaulted by a small group of Huggins' followers who were set on ravaging the women. Foot to foot, man to man, they struggled and labored to murder each other.

Betsy appeared and fought at his side, screaming like a banshee and clawing at Dorsett's enemies like a tiger. Dorsett's only wound came from a man who gave out a fiendish yell before biting him cruelly in the shoulder.

The bloody brawl raged on for another two hours. Scaggs and his seamen, Sheppard and his infantrymen, fought desperately, beating off every assault and then counterattacking. Again and again the mad rush was pushed back by the ever-thinning ranks of the defenders who desperately clung to the center of the raft. Sheppard went down, garroted by two convicts. Ramsey suffered severe contusions and Scaggs had two ribs broken. Sadly, the convicts had managed to kill two of the women and toss them overboard during the melee. Then at last, having been decimated with dreadful casualties, one by one, two by two, the mutineers began ebbing back to the outer perimeter of the raft.

By daylight the dead were seen sprawling grotesquely around on the raft. The stage was set for the next hideous act of the macabre drama. As the surviving sailors and soldiers looked on incredulously, the convicts began cutting up and devouring their former comrades. It was a scene out of a nightmare.

Ramsey made a rough count of the remaining survivors and was shocked to see that only 78 out of the 231 were still alive. In the senseless battle, 109 convicts had perished. Five of Sheppard's soldiers had vanished, presumably thrown overboard, and Ramsey counted 12 of the *Gladiator*'s crewmen dead or missing. It seemed inconceivable that so few could have subdued so many, but the convicts were not trained for combat as were Sheppard's infantrymen, or as physically toughened by hard work at sea as Scaggs' crew.

The raft rode noticeably higher in the water now that its passenger list was sharply scaled down by 126 or so. Those parts of the corpses not eaten by the mob, crazed by the agony of hunger, were thrown to the waiting sharks. Unable to stop them, Scaggs restrained his revulsion and looked the other way as his crewmen, also maddened by the demands of shrinking stomachs, began cutting the flesh from three of the bodies.

Dorsett and Betsy and most of the other women, though weakened by the relentless torment of starvation, could not bring themselves to survive on the flesh of others. A rain squall came up in the afternoon and slaked their thirst, but the hunger pangs never let up.

Ramsey came over and spoke to Dorsett. "The captain would like a word with you."

The highwayman accompanied the first officer to where Scaggs was lying, his back against the aft mast. Surgeon-Superintendent Gorman was binding up the captain's rib cage with a torn shirt. Before the dead were rolled into the sea, the ship's surgeon stripped the bodies of their clothes to use as bandages. Scaggs looked up at Dorsett, his face taut with pain.

"I want to thank you, Mr. Dorsett, for your timely warning. I daresay the honest people who are still left on this hellish vessel owe their lives to you."

"I've led a wicked life, Captain, but I don't mingle with foul-smelling rabble."

"When we reach New South Wales, I'll do my best to persuade the governor to commute your sentence."

"I'm grateful to you, Captain. I'm under your orders."

Scaggs stared at the small knife that was shoved into Dorsett's belt-sash. "Is that your only weapon?"

"Yes, sir. It performed admirably last night."

"Give him a spare saber," Scaggs said to Ramsey. "We're not through with those dogs yet."

"I agree," said Dorsett. "They'll not have the same fury without Jake Huggins to lead them, but they're too unhinged by thirst to give up. They'll try again after dark."

His words were prophetic. For reasons known only to men deranged by lack of food and water, the convicts assaulted the defenders two hours after the sun set. The attack was not as fierce as the night before. Wraithlike figures reeled against each other, recklessly clubbing and slashing, the bodies of convicts, sailors and soldiers intermingling as they fell.

The convicts' resolve had been weakened by another day on the raft without food or drink, and their resistance suddenly faded and broke as the defenders counterattacked. The enfeebled convicts stopped and then stumbled back. Scaggs and his faithful seamen smashed into their center as Dorsett, along with Sheppard's few remaining infantrymen, struck from the flank. In another twenty minutes it was all over.

Fifty-two died that night. With the dawn, only twenty-five men and three women were left, out of the seventy-eight from the night before: sixteen convicts, including Jess Dorsett, Betsy Fletcher and two other women; two soldiers and ten of the *Gladiator*'s crew, including Captain Scaggs. First Officer Ramsey was among the dead. Surgeon-Superintendent Gorman was mortally wounded and passed on later that afternoon like a lamp that slowly runs out of oil. Dorsett had received a nasty gash in his right thigh, and Scaggs had suffered a broken collarbone to add to his broken ribs. Amazingly, Betsy had emerged with only minor bruises and cuts.

The convicts were thoroughly beaten; there wasn't one who didn't suffer from ugly wounds. The insane battle for the raft of the *Gladiator* was over.

By the tenth day of their grisly ordeal, another six had died. Two young lads, a cabin boy no more than twelve and a sixteen-year-old soldier, decided to seek death by throwing themselves into the sea. The other four were convicts who perished from their wounds. It was as if the rapidly dwindling number of survivors were watching a terrifying vision. The sun's blazing torment returned like a burning fever accompanied by delirium.

On day twelve they were down to eighteen. Those who could still move were in rags, their bodies covered with wounds from the massacre, faces disfigured by the burning sun, skin covered with sores from scraping against the constantly moving planking and immersion in saltwater. They were far beyond despondency, and their hollow eyes began to see visions. Two seamen swore they saw the *Gladiator*, dove off the raft and swam toward the imaginary ship until they went under or were taken by the ever present Executioner and his voracious friends.

Hallucinations conjured up every image from banquet tables laden with food and drink, to populated cities or homes none had visited since childhood. Scaggs fancied he was sitting in front of a fireplace with his wife and children in his cottage overlooking the harbor at Aberdeen.

He suddenly stared at Dorsett through strange eyes and said, "We have nothing to fear. I have signaled the Admiralty and they have sent a rescue ship."

In as much of a stupor as the captain, Betsy asked him, "Which pigeon did you use to send your message, the black or the gray?"

Dorsett's cracked and peeling lips curled in a painful smile. Amazingly, he had managed to keep his wits and had assisted the few seamen who could still move about in repairing damage to the raft. He found a few scraps of canvas and erected a small awning over Scaggs while Betsy tended to the captain's injuries and showed him the kindest attention. The sea captain, the highwayman and the thief struck up a friendship as the long hours dragged on.

His navigational instruments having been lost over the side during the fighting, Scaggs had no idea of their position. He ordered his men to make an attempt at catching fish using twine and nails for hooks. Bait was human flesh. The smaller fish completely ignored the offer of free food. Surprisingly, even the sharks failed to show an interest.

Dorsett tied a rope to the hilt of a saber and thrust it into the back of a large shark that swam close to the raft. Lacking his former strength to fight the monster of the deep, he wrapped the free end of the rope around a mast. Then he waited for the shark to die before dragging it on board. His only reward was an empty saber blade that was bent into a ninety-degree angle. Two sailors tried attaching bayonets to poles as spears. They punctured several sharks that did not seem at all disturbed by their wounds.

They had given up attempting to catch a meal when later that afternoon a large school of mullet passed under the raft. Between one and three feet long, they proved far easier to spear and throw on the deck of the raft than the sharks. Before the school swam past, seven cigar-shaped bodies with forked tails were flopping on the waterlogged planks.

"God hasn't forsaken us," mumbled Scaggs, staring at the silvery fish. "Mullet usually inhabit shallow seas. I've never seen them in deep water."

"It's as though he sent them directly to us," murmured Betsy, her eyes wide at the sight of her first meal in nearly two weeks.

Their hunger was so great and the number of fish so meager that they added the flesh of a woman who had died only an hour before. It was the first time Scaggs, Dorsett and Betsy had touched human flesh. Somehow eating one of their own seemed oddly justified when mixed with the fish. And since the taste was partially disguised it also seemed less disgusting.

Another gift arrived with a rain squall that took nearly an hour to pass over and provided them with a catch of two gallons of water.

Despite having their strength temporarily renewed, despondency was still painted on their faces. The wounds and contusions, irritated by the saltwater, caused unending agony. And there was still the sun, which continued to torture them. The air was stifling and the heat intolerable. The nights brought relief and cooler temperatures. But some of the raft's passengers could not endure the misery of one more day. Another five, four convicts and the last soldier, quietly slipped into the sea and perished quickly.

By the fifteenth day, only Scaggs, Dorsett, Betsy Fletcher, three sailors and four convicts, one a woman, were left alive. They were beyond caring. Death seemed unavoidable. The spark of self-preservation had all but gone out. The mullet was long gone, and although those who died had sustained the living, the lack of water and the torrid heat made it impossible to hold out for more than another forty-eight hours before the raft would float empty of life.

Then an event occurred that diverted attention from the unspeakable horrors of the past two weeks. A large greenish-brown bird suddenly appeared out of the sky, circled the raft three times and then lit with a flutter on a yardarm of the forward mast. It stared down through yellow eyes with beady black pupils at the pathetic humans on the raft, their clothes in shreds, limbs and faces scarred from combat and the scorching rays of the sun. The thought of trying to snare the bird for food instantly flooded everyone's mind.

"What kind of strange bird is that?" Betsy asked, her tongue so swollen her voice was like a whisper.

"It's a kea," Scaggs murmured. "One of my former officers kept one."

"Do they fly over the oceans like gulls?" asked Dorsett.

"No, they're a species of parrot that lives on New Zealand and the surrounding islands. I never heard of one flying over water unless . . ." Scaggs paused. "Unless it's another message from the Almighty." His eyes took on a distant look as he painfully rose to his feet and peered at the horizon. "Land!" he exclaimed with joy. "Land to the west of us."

Unnoticed in their apathy and lethargy until now, the raft was being pushed by the swells toward a pair of green mounds rising from the sea no more than ten miles distant. Everyone turned their eyes westward and saw a large island with two low mountains, one on each end, and a forest of trees between. For a long moment no one spoke, each suspended in expectation but fixed with a fear that they might be swept by the currents around their salvation. Almost all the haggard survivors struggled to their knees and prayed to be delivered on the beckoning shore.

Another hour passed before Scaggs determined that the island was growing larger. "The current is pushing us toward it," he announced gleefully. "It's a miracle, a bloody miracle. I know of no island on any chart in this part of the sea."

"Probably uninhabited," guessed Dorsett.

"How beautiful," Betsy murmured, staring at the lush green forest separating the two mounts. "I hope it has pools of cool water."

The unexpected promise of continued life revived what little strength they had left and inspired them to take action. Any desire of trapping the parrot for dinner quickly vanished. The feathered messenger was considered a good omen. Scaggs and his few seamen set a sail made from the tattered awning, while Dorsett and the remaining convicts tore up planks and feverishly used them as paddles. Then, as if to guide them, the parrot took wing and flew back toward the island.

The landmass rose and spread across the western horizon, drawing them like a magnet. They rowed like madmen, determined their sufferings should come to an end. A breeze sprang up from behind, pushing them ever faster toward sanctuary, adding to their delirium of hope. There would be no more waiting for death with resignation. Deliverance was down to less than three miles away.

With the last of his strength, one of the sailors climbed the mast shrouds to a yardarm. Shielding his eyes from the sun, he squinted over the sea.

"What do you make of the shoreline?" demanded Scaggs.

"Looks like we're coming to a coral reef surrounding a lagoon."

Scaggs turned to Dorsett and Fletcher. "If we can't make entry through a channel, the breakers will pile us up on the reef."

Thirty minutes later, the sailor on the mast called out. "I see a blue-water passage through the outer reef two hundred yards off to starboard."

"Rig a rudder!" Scaggs ordered his few crewmen. "Quickly!" Then he turned to the convicts. "Every man and woman who has the brawn, grab a plank and paddle for your life."

A dreadful fear appeared with the crashing of breakers onto the outer reef. The waves struck and burst in an explosion of pure white foam. The boom of water crashing into coral came like the thunder of cannon. The waves grew to a mountainous height as the seafloor rose when they neared land. Terror replaced desperation as the occupants of the raft envisioned the destruction that would occur if they were dashed against the reef by the crushing force of the breakers.

Scaggs took the jury-rigged tiller under one arm and steered toward the channel as his sailors worked the tattered sail. The convicts, looking like ragged scarecrows, paddled ineffectually. Their feeble efforts did very little to propel the raft. Only with everyone paddling on the same side at the same time, as Scaggs ordered, could they assist him in steering for the channel.

The raft was overtaken by a wall of churning froth that swept it forward at a terrible speed. For one brief moment it was elevated on the crest, the next it plunged into the trough. Two of the male convicts were swept into the blue-green turbulence and never seen again. The sea-worn raft was breaking up. The ropes, chafed and stretched by the constant rolling of the sea, began to fray and part. The framework of masts that supported the deck planking twisted and began splitting. The raft groaned when inundated by the following wave. To Dorsett, the immovable coral reef looked close enough to reach out and touch.

And then they were swept into the channel between the jagged edges of the reef. The surge carried them through, the raft spinning around, pieces of it whirling into the sun-sparkled sea like a Roman candle. As the main frame of the raft disintegrated around them, the survivors were thrown into the water.

Once past the barrier reef the blue, contorted sea became as gentle as a mountain lake and turned a bright turquoise. Dorsett came up choking, one arm locked around Betsy's waist.

"Can you swim?" he coughed.

She shook her head violently, sputtering out the seawater she'd swallowed. "Not a stroke."

He pulled her along as he swam toward one of the raft's masts, which was floating less than ten feet away. He soon reached it and draped Betsy's arms over the curved surface. He hung on beside her, gasping for breath, heart pounding, his weakened body exhausted from the exertion of the last hour. After taking a minute or two to recover, Dorsett looked about the floating wreckage and took count.

Scaggs and two of his sailors were a short distance away and still among the living, climbing aboard a small section of planking that was miraculously still tied together. Already they were ripping off boards to use as paddles. Of the convicts, he spotted two men and the woman floating in the water, clinging to various bits and pieces of what remained of the raft of the *Gladiator*.

Dorsett turned and looked toward the shore. A beautiful white sandy beach beckoned less than a quarter of a mile away. Then he heard a nearby shout.

"You and Betsy hang on," Scaggs hailed him. "We'll pick you and the others up and then work toward shore."

Dorsett waved in reply and gave Betsy a kiss on the forehead. "Mind you don't let me down now, old girl. We'll be walking dry land in half an hour—"

He broke off in sudden panic, his joy short lived.

The tall fin of a great white shark was circling the wreckage in search of new prey. The Executioner had followed them into the lagoon.

It wasn't fair, Dorsett screamed inside his mind. To have endured suffering beyond imagination only to have salvation snatched from their fingertips by the jaws of death was a foul injustice. Few were the men and women to have been more unfortunate. He clutched Betsy tightly in his arms and watched with morbid terror as the fin stopped circling, headed in their direction and slowly slipped beneath the surface. His heart froze as he waited helplessly for the jagged teeth to snap shut on his body.

Then, without warning, the second miracle occurred.

The calm waters of the lagoon under them abruptly turned into a boiling cauldron. Then a great fountainlike gush burst into the air, followed by the great white shark. The murderous beast thrashed about wildly, its awesome jaws snapping like a vicious dog's at a huge sea serpent that was coiled around it.

Everyone clutching the floating wreckage stared dumbstruck at the life-and-death struggle between the two monsters of the deep.

From his position on his scrap of raft, Scaggs had a good seat to observe the struggle. The body of the enormous eel-like creature stretched from a blunt head to a long, tapering tail. Scaggs estimated the length of the body to be sixty to sixty-five feet, with the circumference of a large flour barrel. The mouth on the end of the head opened and closed spasmodically, revealing short fanglike teeth. The skin appeared smooth and was a dark brown on the upper surface of the body, almost black, while the belly was an ivory white. Scaggs had often heard tales of ships sighting serpentine sea monsters, but had laughed them off as the visions of sailors after drinking too much rum in port. Frozen in awe, he was not laughing now as he watched the once-feared Executioner writhe violently in a futile attempt to shake off its deadly attacker.

The compact cartilaginous body of the shark prevented it from contorting its head and jaws far enough backward to bite into the serpent. Despite its tremendous strength and its frenzied convulsions, it could not shake the death grip. Revolving around in complete circles with great speed, shark and serpent writhed beneath the surface before reappearing in an explosion of spray that beat the water into froth again.

The serpent then began biting into the shark's gill slits. After another few minutes, the gargantuan combat faded, the shark's agonized struggle ceased and the two monsters slowly sank out of sight in the deepest part of the lagoon. The hunter had become the meal of another hunter.

Scaggs wasted no time after the epic battle in pulling the bedraggled convicts from the water onto the small piece of the raft that still hung together. Stunned by what they had witnessed, the pitifully few survivors finally reached the white sandy beach and staggered ashore, carried at last from their nightmare world to a Garden of Eden as yet unknown to European mariners.

A stream of pure water was soon found that ran from the volcanic mountain that rose above the southern end of the island. Five different varieties of tropical fruit grew in the forested area, and the lagoon was teeming with fish. Their perils over, only 8 out of the original 231 who set out on the raft of the *Gladiator* lived to tell about the horrors of their fifteen days adrift in the sweltering emptiness of the sea.

Six months after the tragic loss of the *Gladiator,* its memory was briefly revived when a fisherman, coming ashore to repair a leak in his small boat, discovered a hand gripping a sword protruding from the beach. Digging the object from the sand, he was surprised to find a life-sized image of an ancient warrior. He carried the wooden sculpture fifty miles north to Auckland, New Zealand, where it was identified as the figurehead of the lost clipper ship *Gladiator*.

Eventually cleaned and refinished, the warrior was placed in a small maritime museum, where onlookers often stared at it and pondered the mystery of the ship's disappearance.

The enigma of the clipper ship *Gladiator* was finally explained in July of 1858 by an article that ran in the *Sydney Morning Herald*.

RETURN FROM THE DEAD

The seas around Australia have witnessed many a strange sight, but none so strange as the sudden appearance of Captain Charles "Bully" Scaggs, reported missing and presumed dead when his clipper, the *Gladiator,* owners Carlisle & Dunhill of Inverness, vanished in the Tasman Sea during the terrible typhoon of January 1856 when only 300 miles southeast of Sydney.

Captain Scaggs astonished everyone by sailing into Sydney Harbor in a small vessel he and his only surviving crewman had constructed during their sojourn on an uncharted island.

The ship's figurehead, washed up on the west coast of New Zealand one and a half years ago, confirmed the loss of the ship. Until Captain Scaggs' miraculous return, no word on how his ship was lost or the fate of the 192 convicts being transported to the penal colony or the 11 soldiers and 28 crewmen was known.

According to Captain Scaggs, only he and two others were cast up on an uninhabited island, where they survived extreme hardships for over two years until they could build a vessel with tools and materials salvaged from the wreckage of another unfortunate ship that was driven ashore a year later with the loss of her entire crew. They constructed the hull of their craft from wood cut from the native trees they found growing on the island.

Captain Scaggs and his crewman, Thomas Cochran, the ship's carpenter, seemed remarkably fit after their ordeal and were anxious to board the next ship bound for England. They expressed their profound sorrow for the tragic deaths of the *Gladiator*'s passengers and their former shipmates, all of whom perished when the clipper sank during the typhoon. Incredibly, Scaggs and Cochran managed to cling to a piece of floating wreckage for several days before currents carried them onto the deserted island's beach, more dead than alive.

The tiny piece of land where the men existed for over two years cannot be precisely plotted since Scaggs lost all his navigational instruments at the time of the sinking. His best reckoning puts the uncharted island approximately 350 miles east-southeast of Sydney, an area other ships' captains claim is devoid of land.

Lieutenant Silas Sheppard, whose parents reside in Hornsby, and his detachment of ten men from the New South Wales Infantry Regiment, who were guarding the convicts, were also listed among the lost.

THE LEGACY

After Scaggs' return to England and a brief reunion with his wife and children, Carlisle & Dunhill offered him command of their newest and finest clipper ship, the *Culloden*, and sent him to engage in the China tea trade. After six more gruelling voyages, in which he set two records, Bully Scaggs retired to his cottage in Aberdeen, worn out at the early age of forty-seven.

The captains of clipper ships were men grown old before their time. The demands of sailing the world's fleetest ships took a heavy toll on body and spirit. Most died while still young. A great number went down with their ships. They were an elite breed, the famed iron men who drove wooden ships to unheard-of speeds during the most romantic era of the sea. They went to their graves, under grass or beneath the waves, knowing they had commanded the greatest sailing vessels ever built by man.

Tough as the beams inside his ships, Scaggs was taking his last voyage at fifty-nine. Having built up a tidy nest egg by investing in owners' shares on his last four voyages, he was providing his children with a sizable fortune.

Alone after the death of his beloved wife, Lucy, and his children grown with families of their own, he maintained his love for the sea by sailing in and around the firths of Scotland in a small ketch he'd built with his own hands. It was after a brief voyage through bitterly cold weather, to visit his son and grandchildren at Peterhead, that he took sick.

A few days before he died, Scaggs sent for his longtime friend and former employer, Abner Carlisle. A respected shipping magnate, who built a sizable fortune with his partner, Alexander Dunhill, Carlisle was a leading resident of Aberdeen. Besides his shipping company, he also owned a mercantile business and a bank. His favorite charities were the local library and a hospital. Carlisle was a thin, wiry man, completely bald. He had kindly eyes and walked with a noticeable limp, caused by a fall off a horse when he was a young man.

He was shown into Scaggs' house by the captain's daughter, Jenny, whom Carlisle had known since she was born. She embraced him briefly and took him by the hand.

"Good of you to come, Abner. He's been asking for you every half hour."

"How is the old sea dog?"

"I fear his days are numbered," she answered with a trace of sadness.

Carlisle looked around the comfortable house filled with nautical furniture, the walls holding charts marked with daily runs during Scaggs' record voyages. "I'm going to miss this house."

"My brothers say it is best for the family if we sell it."

She led Carlisle upstairs and through an open door into a bedroom with a large window that overlooked Aberdeen Harbor. "Father, Abner Carlisle is here."

"About time," Scaggs muttered grumpily.

Jenny gave Carlisle a peck on the cheek. "I'll go and make you some tea."

An old man, ravaged by three decades of a hard life at sea, lay unmoving on the bed. As bad as Scaggs looked, Carlisle couldn't help but marvel at the fire that still burned in those olive-gray eyes. "I've got a new ship for you, Bully."

"The hell you say," rasped Scaggs. "What's her rigging?"

"None. She's a steamer."

Scaggs' face turned red and he raised his head. "Goddamned stink pots, they shouldn't be allowed to dirty up the seas."

42

It was the response Carlisle had hoped for. Bully Scaggs may have been at death's door, but he was going out as tough as he lived.

"Times have changed, my friend. *Cutty Sark* and *Thermopylae* are the only clippers you and I knew that are still working the seas."

"I don't have much time for idle chatter. I asked you to come to hear my deathbed confession and do me a personal favor."

Carlisle looked at Scaggs and said sarcastically, "You thrash a drunk or bed a Chinese girl in a Shanghai brothel you never told me about?"

"I'm talking about the *Gladiator*," Scaggs muttered. "I lied about her."

"She sank in a typhoon," Carlisle said. "What was there to lie about?"

"She sank in a typhoon all right, but the passengers and crew didn't go down to the bottom with her."

Carlisle was silent for several moments, then he said carefully, "Charles Bully Scaggs, you're the most honest man I have ever known. In the half century we've known each other you've never betrayed a trust. Are you sure it isn't the sickness that's making you say crazy things?"

"Trust me now when I say I've lived a lie for twenty years in repayment of a debt."

Carlisle stared at him curiously. "What is it you wish to tell me?"

"A story I've told no one." Scaggs leaned back on his pillow and stared beyond Carlisle, far into the distance at something only he could see. "The story of the raft of the *Gladiator*."

Jenny returned half an hour later with tea. It was dusk, and she lit the oil lamps in the bedroom. "Father, you must try to eat something. I've made your favorite fish chowder."

"I've no appetite, Daughter."

"Abner must be starved, listening to you all afternoon. I'll wager he'll eat something."

"Give us another hour," ordered Scaggs. "Then make us eat what you will."

As soon as she was gone, Scaggs continued with the saga of the raft.

"When we finally got ashore there were eight of us left. Of the *Gladiator*'s crew, only myself, Thomas Cochran, the ship's carpenter, and Alfred Reed, an able seaman, survived. Among the convicts there was Jess Dorsett, Betsy Fletcher, Marion Adams, George Pryor and John Winkleman. Eight out of the 231 souls who set sail from England."

"You'll have to excuse me, dear old friend," said Carlisle, "if I appear skeptical. Scores of men murdering each other on a raft in the middle of the ocean, the survivors subsisting on human flesh and then being saved from being devoured by a man-eating shark through the divine intervention of a sea serpent that kills the shark. An unbelievable tale to say the least."

"You are not listening to the ravings of a dying man," Scaggs assured him weakly. "The account is true, every word of it."

Carlisle did not want to unduly upset Scaggs. The wealthy old merchant patted the arm of the sea captain who in no small way had helped to build the shipping empire of Carlisle & Dunhill and reassured him. "Go on. I'm anxious to hear the ending. What happened after the eight of you set foot on the island?"

For the next half hour, Scaggs told of how they drank their fill in a stream with sweet and pleasant water that ran from one of the small volcanic mountains. He described the large turtles that were caught in the lagoon, thrown on their backs and butchered with Dorsett's knife, the only tool among them. Then using a hard stone found at the water's edge and the knife as flint, they built a fire and cooked the turtle meat. Five different kinds of fruit that Scaggs had never seen before were picked from trees in the forest. The vegetation seemed oddly different from the plants he'd seen in Australia. He recounted how the survivors passed the next few days gorging themselves until they regained their strength.

"With our bodies on the mend, we set out to explore the island," Scaggs said, continuing his narration. "It was shaped like a fishhook, five miles in length and a little less than one wide. Two massive volcanic peaks, each about twelve to fifteen hundred feet high, stood at the extreme ends. The lagoon measured about three quarters of a mile long and was sheltered by a thick reef to seaward. The rest of the island was buttressed by high cliffs."

"Did you find it deserted?" asked Carlisle.

"Not a living soul did we see, nor animal. Only birds. We saw signs that Aborigines had once inhabited the island, but it appeared they had been gone a long time."

"Any evidence of shipwrecks?"

"Not at that time."

"After the calamity on the raft, the island must have seemed like paradise," said Carlisle.

"She was the most beautiful island I've seen in my many years at sea," Scaggs agreed, referring to his place of refuge in the feminine. "A magnificent emerald on a sapphire sea, she was." He hesitated as if envisioning the jewel rising out of the Pacific. "We soon settled into an idyllic way of life. I designated those to be in charge of certain services and appointed times for fishing, the construction and repair of shelter, the harvesting of fruit and other edibles, and the maintenance of a constant fire for cooking as well as to signal any ship that might pass by. In this manner we lived together in peace for several months."

"I'm keen to guess," said Carlisle. "Trouble flared between the women."

Scaggs shook his head feebly. "More like among the men *over* the women."

"So you experienced the same circumstances as the *Bounty* mutineers on Pitcairn Island."

"Exactly. I knew there would soon be trouble, and I designed a schedule for the women to be divided equally among the men. Not a scheme to everybody's liking, of course, especially the women. But I knew of no other way to prevent bloodshed."

"Under the circumstances, I would have to agree with you."

"All I succeeded in doing was hastening the inevitable. The convict John Winkleman murdered able-seaman Reed over Marion Adams, and Jess Dorsett refused to share Betsy Fletcher with anyone. When George Pryor attempted to rape Fletcher, Dorsett beat his brains in with a rock."

"And then you were six."

Scaggs nodded. "Tranquillity finally reigned on the island when John Winkleman married Marion Adams and Jess married Betsy."

"Married?" Carlisle snorted in righteous indignation. "How was that possible?"

"Have you forgotten, Abner?" Scaggs said with a grin cracking his thin lips. "As a ship's captain I was empowered to perform the ceremony."

"By not actually standing on the deck of your ship, I must say you stretched matters a bit."

"I have no regrets. We all lived in harmony until ship's carpenter Thomas Cochran and I sailed away."

"Did you and Cochran not have desire for the women?"

Scaggs' laughter turned into a brief coughing spell. Carlisle gave him a glass of water. When he recovered, Scaggs said, "Whenever my thoughts became carnal, I envisioned my sweet wife, Lucy. I vowed to her that I would always return from a voyage as chaste as I left."

"And the carpenter?"

"Cochran, as fate would have it, preferred the company of men."

It was Carlisle's turn to laugh. "You picked a strange lot to share your adventures."

"Before long we had built comfortable shelters out of rock and conquered boredom by constructing many ingenious devices to make our existence more enjoyable. Cochran's carpentry skill became particularly useful once we found proper woodworking tools."

"How did this come about?"

"After about fourteen months, a severe gale drove a French naval sloop onto the rocks at the southern end of the island. Despite our efforts to save them, the entire crew perished as the pounding of the breakers broke up their ship around them. When the seas calmed two days later, we recovered fourteen bodies and buried them next to George Pryor and Alfred Reed. Then Dorsett and I, who were the strongest swimmers, launched a diving operation to recover whatever objects from the wreck we might find useful. Within three weeks we had salvaged a small mountain of goods, materials and tools. Cochran and I now possessed the necessary implements to build a boat sturdy enough to carry us to Australia."

"What of the women? How did Betsy and Marion fare?" queried Carlisle.

Scaggs' eyes took on a sad look. "Poor Marion, she was kind and true, a modest servant girl who had been convicted of stealing food from her master's pantry. She died giving birth to a daughter. John Winkleman was horribly distraught. He went mad and tried to kill the baby. We tied him to a tree for four days until he finally got hold of his senses. But he was never quite the same again. He rarely spoke a word from that time until I left the island."

"And Betsy?"

"Cut from a different cloth, that one. Strong as a coal miner. She carried her weight with any man. Gave birth to two boys in as many years as well as nursing Marion's child. Dorsett and Betsy were devoted to each other."

"Why didn't they come with you?"

"Best they stayed on the island. I offered to plead for their release with the governor, but they didn't dare take the chance, and rightly so. As soon as they'd have landed in Australia, the penal constables would have grabbed the children and distributed them as orphans. Betsy's fate was probably to become a wool spinner in the filthy squalor of the female factory at Parramatta, while Jess was sure to end up in the convict barracks at Sydney. They'd likely never have seen their boys and each other again. I promised them that as long as I lived they'd remain forgotten along with the lost souls of the *Gladiator*."

"And Winkleman too?"

Scaggs nodded. "He moved to a cave inside the mountain at the north end of the island and lived alone."

Carlisle sat silent and reflected on the remarkable story Scaggs had related. "All these years you've never revealed their existence."

"I found out later that if I had broken my promise to remain silent, that bastard of a governor in New South Wales would have sent a ship to get them. He had a reputation for moving hell to regain an escaped prisoner." Scaggs moved his head slightly and stared through the window at the ships in the harbor. "After I returned home, I saw no reason to tell the story of the *Gladiator*'s raft."

"You never saw them again after you and Cochran set sail for Sydney?"

Scaggs shook his head. "A tearful good-bye it was, too, Betsy and Jess standing on the beach holding their baby boys and Marion's daughter, looking for all the world like a happy mother and father. They found a life that wasn't possible in the civilized world." He spat out the word "civilized."

"And Cochran, what was to stop him from speaking out?"

Scaggs' eyes glimmered faintly. "As I mentioned, he also had a secret he didn't want known, certainly not if he ever wished to go to sea again. He went down with the *Zanzibar* when she was lost in the South China Sea back in '67."

"Haven't you ever wondered how they made out?"

"No need to wonder," Scaggs replied slyly. "I know."

Carlisle's eyebrows raised. "I'd be grateful for an explanation."

"Four years after I departed, an American whaler sighted the island and stood in to fill her water casks. Jess and Betsy met the crew and traded fruits and fresh fish for cloth and cooking pots. They told the captain of the whaler that they were missionaries who were stranded on the island after their ship had been wrecked. Before long, other whalers began stopping by for water and food supplies. One of the ships traded Betsy seeds for hats she'd woven out of palms, and she and Jess began tilling several acres of arable land for vegetables."

"How do you know all this?"

"They began sending out letters with the whalers."

"They're still alive?" asked Carlisle, his interest aroused.

Scaggs' eyes saddened. "Jess died while fishing six years ago. A sudden squall capsized his boat. Betsy said it looked as if he struck his head and drowned. Her last letter, along with a packet, arrived only two days ago. You'll find it in the center drawer of my desk. She wrote that she was dying from some sort of disease of the stomach."

Carlisle rose and crossed the bedroom to a worn captain's desk that Scaggs had used on all his voyages after the *Gladiator* went down. He pulled a small packet wrapped in oilskin from the drawer and opened it. Inside he found a leather pouch and a folded letter. He returned to his chair, slipped on his reading glasses and glanced at the words.

"For a girl convicted of theft, she writes very well."

"Her earlier letters were full of misspellings, but Jess was an educated man, and under his tutelage, Betsy's grammar showed great improvement."

Carlisle began reading aloud.

My Dear Captain Scaggs,

I pray you are in good health. This will be my last letter to you as I have a malady of the stomach, or so the doctor aboard the whaling ship *Amie & Jason* tells me. So I will soon be joining my Jess.

I have a last request that I pray you will honor. In the

first week of April of this year, my two sons and Marion's daughter, Mary, departed the island on board a whaler whose captain was sailing from here to Auckland for badly needed repairs to his hull after a brush with a coral reef. There, the children were to book passage on a ship bound for England and then eventually make their way to you in Aberdeen.

I have written to ask you, dearest friend, to take them under your roof upon their arrival and arrange for their education at the finest schools England has to offer. I would be eternally grateful, and I know Jess would share the same sentiments, rest his dear departed soul, if you will honor my request.

I have included my legacy for your services and whatever cost it takes to see them through school. They are very bright children and will be diligent in their studies.

With deepest respect I wish you a loving farewell.

Betsy Dorsett

One final thought. The serpent sends his regards.

Carlisle peered over his glasses. " 'The serpent sends his regards.' What nonsense is that?"

"The sea serpent who saved us from the great white shark," answered Scaggs. "Turned out he lived in the lagoon. I saw him with my own eyes on at least four other occasions during my time on the island."

Carlisle looked at his old friend as if he were drunk, then thought better of pursuing the matter. "She sent young children alone on a long voyage from New Zealand to England?"

"Not so young," said Scaggs. "The oldest must be going on nineteen."

"If they left the island the early part of April, they may come knocking on your door at any time."

"Providing they did not have to wait long in Auckland to find a stout ship that made a fast passage."

"My God, man, you're in an impossible situation."

"What you really mean is, how can a dying man carry out an old friend's dying wish?"

"You're not going to die," said Carlisle, looking Scaggs in the eye.

"Oh yes I am," Scaggs said firmly. "You're a practical businessman, Abner. Nobody knows that better than me. That's why I asked to see you before I take my final voyage."

"You want me to wet-nurse Betsy's children."

"They can live in my house until you drop their anchor in the best educational institutions money can buy."

"The pitiful amount that Betsy made selling hats and food supplies to visiting whaling ships won't come close to covering the cost of several years of boarding at expensive schools. They'll need the proper clothes and private tutors to bring them up to proper learning levels. I hope you're not asking *me* to provide for total strangers."

Scaggs pointed to the leather pouch.

Carlisle held it up. "Is this what Betsy sent you to educate her children?"

Scaggs nodded slightly. "Open it."

Carlisle loosened the strings and poured the contents into his hand. He looked up at Scaggs incredulously. "Is this some sort of joke? These are nothing but ordinary stones."

"Trust me, Abner. They are not ordinary."

Carlisle held up one about the size of a prune in front of his spectacles and peered at it. The surface of the stone was smooth and its shape was octahedral, having eight sides. "This is nothing but some sort of crystal. It's absolutely worthless."

"Take the stones to Levi Strouser."

"The Jewish gem merchant?"

"Show the stones to him."

"Precious gems, they're not," said Carlisle firmly.

"Please . . ." Scaggs barely got the word out. The long conversation had tired him.

"As you wish, old friend." He pulled out his pocket watch and looked at the time. "I'll call on Strouser first thing in the morning and return to you with his appraisal."

"Thank you," Scaggs murmured. "The rest will take care of itself."

Carlisle walked under an early morning drizzle to the old business district near Castlegate. He checked the address and turned up the steps to one of the many inconspicuous gray houses built of local granite that gave the city of Aberdeen a solid if drab appearance. Small brass letters mounted beside the door read, simply,

Strouser & Sons. He pulled the bell knob and was shown into a Spartan furnished office by a clerk, offered a chair and a cup of tea.

A slow minute passed before a short man in a long frock coat, a salt-and-pepper beard down to his chest, entered through a side door. He smiled politely and extended his hand.

"I am Levi Strouser. What service can I perform for you?"

"My name is Abner Carlisle. I was sent by my friend Captain Charles Scaggs."

"Captain Scaggs sent a messenger who announced your coming. I am honored to have Aberdeen's most renowned merchant in my humble office."

"Have we ever met?"

"We don't exactly travel in the same social circles, and you are not the kind of man who buys jewelry."

"My wife died young and I never remarried. So there was no reason to purchase expensive baubles."

"I too lost a wife at an early age, but I was fortunate enough to find a lovely woman who bore me four sons and two daughters."

Carlisle had often done business with Jewish merchants over the years, but he had never had dealings in gemstones. He was on unfamiliar ground and felt uncomfortable with Strouser. He took out the leather pouch and laid it on the desk.

"Captain Scaggs requested your appraisal of the stones inside."

Strouser laid a sheet of white paper on the desktop and poured the contents of the pouch in a pile in the center. He counted the stones. There were eighteen. He took his time and carefully scrutinized each one through his loupe, a small magnifier used by jewelers. Finally, he held up the largest and the smallest stones, one in each hand.

"If you will kindly be patient, Mr. Carlisle, I would like to conduct some tests on these two stones. I'll have one of my sons serve you another cup of tea."

"Yes, thank you. I don't mind waiting."

Nearly an hour passed before Strouser returned to the room with the two stones. Carlisle was a shrewd observer of men. He had to be to have successfully negotiated over a thousand business ventures since he purchased his first ship at the tender age of twenty-two. He saw that Levi Strouser was nervous. There were no obvious signs, no shaking hands, little tics around the mouth, beads of sweat. It was there in the eyes. Strouser looked like a man who had beheld God.

"May I ask where these stones came from?" Strouser asked.

"I cannot tell you the exact location," Carlisle answered honestly.

"The mines of India are played out, and nothing like this has come out of Brazil. Perhaps one of the new diggings in South Africa?"

"It is not for me to say. Why? Is there a value to the stones?"

"You do not know what they are?" Strouser asked in astonishment.

"I am not an expert in minerals. My business is shipping."

Strouser held out his hands over the stones like an ancient sorcerer. "Mr. Carlisle, these are diamonds! The finest uncut stones I have ever seen."

Carlisle covered his amazement nobly. "I don't question your integrity, Mr. Strouser, but I can't believe you are serious."

"My family has dealt in precious stones for five generations, Mr. Carlisle. Believe me when I say you have a fortune lying on the desk. Not only do they have indications of perfect transparency and clearness, but they possess an exquisite and very extraordinary violet-rose color. Because of their beauty and rarity they command a higher price than the perfect colorless stones."

Carlisle came back on keel and cut away the cobwebs. "What are they worth?"

"Rough stones are almost impossible to classify for value since their true qualities do not become apparent until they are cut and faceted, to enhance the maximum optical effect, and polished. The smallest you have here weighs 60 carats in the rough." He paused to hold up the largest specimen. "This one weighs out at over 980 carats, making it the largest known uncut diamond in the world."

"I judge that it might be a wise investment to have them cut before I sell them."

"Or if you prefer, I could offer you a fair price in the rough."

Carlisle began to place the stones back in the leather pouch. "No, thank you. I represent a dying friend. It is my duty to provide him with the highest profit possible."

Strouser quickly realized that the canny Scotsman could not be influenced to part with the uncut stones. The opportunity to obtain the diamonds for himself, have them faceted and then sell them on the London market for an immense gain, was not in the cards. Better to make a good profit than none at all, he decided wisely.

"You need not go any farther than this office, Mr. Carlisle. Two of my sons apprenticed at the finest diamond-cutting house in Antwerp. They are as good if not better than any cutters in London. Once the stones are faceted and polished, I can act as your broker should you then wish to sell."

"Why should I not sell them on my own?"

"For the same reason I would come to you to ship goods to Australia instead of buying a ship and transporting them myself. I am a member of the London Diamond Exchange, you are not. I can demand and receive twice the price you might expect."

Carlisle was shrewd enough to appreciate a sound business offer when he heard one. He came to his feet and offered Strouser his hand. "I place the stones in your capable hands, Mr. Strouser. I trust it will prove to be a profitable arrangement for you and the people I represent."

"You can bank on it, Mr. Carlisle."

As the Scots shipping magnate was about to step from the office, he turned and looked back at the Jewish precious-stone dealer. "After your sons are finished with the stones, what do you think they will be worth?"

Strouser stared down at the ordinary-looking stones, visualizing them as sparkling crystals. "If these stones came from an unlimited source that can be easily exploited, the owners are about to launch an empire of extraordinary wealth."

"If you will forgive me for saying so, your appraisal sounds a bit fanciful."

Strouser looked across the desk at Carlisle and smiled. "Trust me when I say these stones, when cut and faceted, could sell in the neighborhood of one million pounds."*

"Good God!" Carlisle blurted. "That much?"

Strouser lifted the huge 980-carat stone to the light, holding it between his fingers as if it were the Holy Grail. When he spoke it was in a voice of adoring reverence. "Perhaps even more, much more."

* Approximately $7 million U.S. at that time, or close to $50 million on today's market.

PART I

DEATH FROM NOWHERE

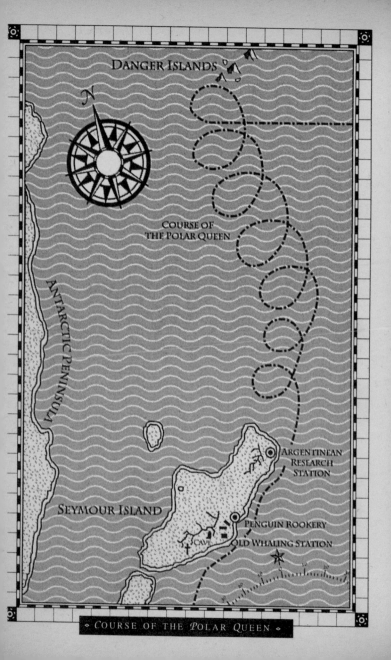

COURSE OF THE POLAR QUEEN

1

There was a curse of death about the island. A curse proven by the graves of men who set foot on the forbidding shore, never to leave. There was no beauty here, certainly nothing like the majestic ice-shrouded peaks, the glaciers that towered almost as high as the White Cliffs of Dover, or the icebergs that floated serenely like crystal castles that one might expect to see on and around the great landmass of the Antarctic and its offshore islands.

Seymour Island comprised the largest ice-free surface on or near the whole continent. Volcanic dust, laid down through the millennia, hastened the melting of ice, leaving dry valleys and mountains without a vestige of color and nearly devoid of all snow. It was a singularly ugly place, inhabited only by few varieties of lichen and a rookery of Adélie penguins who found Seymour Island an ample source for the small stones they use to build their nests.

The majority of the dead, buried in shallow pits pried from the rocks, came from a Norwegian Antarctic expedition after their ship was crushed in the ice in 1859. They survived two winters before their food supply ran out, finally dying off one by one from starvation. Lost for over a decade, their well-preserved bodies were not found until 1870, by the British while they were setting up a whaling station.

Others died and were laid beneath the rocks of Seymour Island. Some succumbed to disease, others to accidents that occurred during the whaling season. A few lost their lives when they wandered from the station, were caught by an unexpected storm and frozen by windchill. Surprisingly, their graves are well marked. Crews of whalers caught in the ice passed the winter until the spring melt by chiseling inscriptions on large stones, which they mounted over the burial sites. By the time the British closed the station in 1933, sixty bodies lay beneath the loathsome landscape.

The restless ghosts of the explorers and sailors that roamed the forsaken ground could never have imagined that one day their resting place would be crawling with accountants, attorneys, plumbers, housewives and retired senior citizens who showed up on luxurious pleasure ships to gawk at the inscribed stones and ogle the comical penguins that inhabited a piece of the shoreline. Perhaps, just perhaps, the island would lay its curse on these intruders too.

The impatient passengers aboard the cruise ship saw nothing ominous about Seymour Island. Safe in the comfort of their floating palace, they saw only a remote, unspoiled and mysterious land rising from a sea as blue as an iridescent peacock feather. They felt only excitement at a new experience, especially since they were among the first wave of tourists ever to walk the shores of Seymour Island. This was the third of five scheduled stops as the ship hopscotched among the islands along the peninsula, certainly not the most attractive, but one of the more interesting according to the cruise-line literature.

Many had traveled Europe and the Pacific, seen the usual exotic places travelers flock to around the world. Now they wanted something more, something different; a visit to a destination few had seen before, a remote place they could set foot on and brag about to friends and neighbors afterward.

As they clustered on the deck near the boarding ladder in happy anticipation of going ashore, aiming their telephoto lenses at the penguins, Maeve Fletcher walked among them, checking the bright orange insulated jackets passed out by the ship's cruise staff, along with life jackets for the short trip between the ship and shore.

Energetic and in constant motion, she moved about with a concentrated briskness in a lithe body that had seen more than its fair share of vigorous exercise. She towered above the women and stood taller than most of the men. Her hair, braided in two long pigtails, was as yellow as a summery iris. She stared through eyes as blue as the deep sea, from a strong face with high cheekbones. Her lips always seemed parted in a warm smile, revealing a tiny gap in the center of her upper teeth. Tawny skin gave her a robust outdoorsy look.

Maeve was three years shy of thirty, with a master's degree in zoology. After graduation she took a three-year sabbatical to gain field experience studying bird and animal life in the polar regions. After she returned to her home in Australia, she was halfway through her dissertation for a doctorate at the University of Melbourne when she was offered a temporary job as naturalist and expedition leader for passengers of Ruppert & Saunders, a cruise line based in Adelaide and specializing in adventure tours. It was an opportunity to earn enough money to finish her dissertation, so she dropped everything and set sail to the great white continent on board the company's ship *Polar Queen*.

This trip there were ninety-one paying passengers on board, and Maeve was one of four naturalists who were to conduct the excursions on shore. Because of the penguin rookery, the historic buildings still standing from the whaling operations, the cemetery and the site of the camp where the Norwegian explorers perished, Seymour Island was considered a historical site and a fragile environment. To reduce visitor impact, the passengers were guided ashore at staggered times and in separate groups for two-hour expeditions. They were also lectured on a code of behavior. They were not to step on lichens or moss, nor step within five meters of any bird or animal life. Nor could they sneak souvenirs, not so much as a small rock. Most of them were Australians, with a few New Zealanders mixed in.

Maeve was scheduled to accompany the first party of twenty-two visitors to the island. She checked off the list of names as the excited travelers stepped down the boarding ladder to a waiting Zodiac, the versatile rubber float craft designed by Jacques Cousteau. As she was about to follow the last passenger, the ship's first officer, Trevor Haynes, stopped her on the boarding ladder. Quiet and quite handsome in the lady's eyes, he was uncomfortable mingling with the passengers and rarely made an appearance away from the bridge.

"Tell your people not to be alarmed if they see the ship sailing off," he told her.

She turned and looked up the steps at him. "Where will you be going?"

"There is a storm brewing a hundred miles out. The captain doesn't want to risk exposing the passengers to any more rough water than necessary. Nor does he want to disappoint them by cutting short the shore excursions. He intends to steam twenty kilometers up the coast and drop off another group at the seal colony, then return in time to pick you up and repeat the process."

"Putting twice the number ashore in half the time."

"That's the idea. That way, we can pack up and leave and be in the relatively calm waters of the Bransfield Strait before the storm strikes here."

"I wondered why you didn't drop the anchor." Maeve liked Haynes. He was the only ship's officer who wasn't continually trying to sweet-talk her into his quarters after late-night drinks. "I'll expect you in two hours," she said with a wave.

"You have your portable communicator should you encounter a problem."

She held up the small unit that was attached to her belt. "You'll be the first to know."

"Say hello to the penguins for me."

"I shall."

As the Zodiac skimmed over water that was as flat and reflective as a mirror, Maeve lectured her little band of intrepid tourists on the history behind their destination. "Seymour Island was first sighted by James Clark Ross in 1842. Forty Norwegian explorers, castaway when their ship was crushed in the ice, perished here in 1859. We'll visit the site where they lived until the end and then take a short walk to the hallowed ground where they are buried."

"Are those the buildings they lived in?" asked a lady who must have been pushing eighty, pointing to several structures in a small bay.

"No," answered Maeve. "What you see are what remains of

an abandoned British whaling station. We'll visit it just before we take a short hike around that rocky point you see to the south, to the penguin rookery."

"Does anyone live on the island?" asked the same lady.

"The Argentineans have a research station on the northern tip of the island."

"How far away?"

Maeve smiled condescendingly. "About thirty kilometers." There's always one in every group who has the curiosity of a four-year-old, she mused.

They could see the bottom clearly now, naked rock with no growth to be seen anywhere. Their shadow followed them about two fathoms down as they cruised through the bay. No rollers broke on the shoreline, the sea ran smooth right up to the edge, lapping the exposed rock with the slight wash usually found around a small lake. The crewman shut off the outboard motor as the bow of the Zodiac skimmed onto the shore. The only sign of a living thing was a pure white snow petrel that glided through the sky above them like a large snowflake.

Only after she had helped everyone to disembark from the Zodiac and wade ashore onto the pebbled beach in the knee-high rubber boots supplied by the ship did Maeve turn and look at the ship as it gathered way and steamed northward.

The *Polar Queen* was quite small by cruise ship standards. Her length was only seventy-two meters, with a twenty-five hundred gross rated tonnage. She was built in Bergen, Norway, especially to cruise polar waters. She was as ruggedly constructed as an icebreaker, a function she could perform if the occasion arose. Her superstructure and the broad horizontal stripe below her lower deck were painted glacier white. The rest of her hull was a bright yellow. She could skirt the ice floes and icebergs with the agility of a rabbit due to her bow and stern thrusters. Her comfortable cabins were furnished in the style of a ski chalet, with picture windows facing the sea. Other amenities included a luxurious lounge and dining salon, hosted by a chef who turned out three-star culinary creations, a fitness center and a library filled with books and information on the polar regions. The crew was well trained and numbered twenty more than the passengers.

Maeve felt a tinge of regret she couldn't quite understand as the yellow-and-white *Polar Queen* grew smaller in the distance.

For a brief moment she experienced the apprehension the lost Norwegian explorers must have felt at seeing their only means of survival disappear. She quickly shook off any feelings of uneasiness and began leading her party of babbling travelers across the gray moonscape to the cemetery.

She allotted them twenty minutes to pick their way among the tombstones, shooting rolls of film of the inscriptions. Then she herded them around a vast pile of giant bleached whale bones near the old station while describing the methods the whalers used to process the whales.

"After the danger and exhilaration of the chase and kill," she explained, "came the rotten job butchering the huge carcass and rendering the blubber into oil. 'Cutting in' and 'trying out,' as the old-timers called it."

Next came the antiquated huts and rendering building. The whaling station was still maintained and monitored on an annual basis by the British and was considered a museum of the past. Furnishings, cooking utensils in the kitchen, along with old books and worn magazines, were still there just as the whalers left them when they finally departed for home.

"Please do not disturb any of the artifacts," Maeve told the group. "Under international law nothing may be removed." She took a moment to count heads. Then she said, "Now I'll lead you into the caves dug by the whalers, where they stored the oil in huge casks before shipping it to England."

From a box left at the entrance to the caves by expedition leaders from previous cruises, she passed out flashlights. "Is there anyone who suffers from claustrophobia?"

One woman who looked to be in her late seventies raised her hand. "I'm afraid I don't want to go in there."

"Anyone else?"

The woman who asked all the questions nodded. "I can't stand cold, dark places."

"All right," said Maeve. "The two of you wait here. I'll conduct the rest a short distance to the whale-oil storage area. We won't be more than fifteen minutes."

She led the chattering group through a long, curving tunnel carved by the whalers to a large storage cavern stacked with huge casks that had been assembled deep inside the rock and later left behind. After they entered she stopped and gestured at a massive rock at the entrance.

"The rock you see here was cut from inside the cavern and acts as a barrier against the cold and to keep competing whalers from pilfering surplus oil that remained after the station closed down for the winter. This rock weighs as much as an armored tank, but a child can move it, providing he or she knows its secret." She paused to step aside, placed her hand on a particular place on the upper side of the rock and easily pushed it to close the entrance. "An ingenious bit of engineering. The rock is delicately balanced on a shaft through its middle. Push in the wrong spot and it won't budge."

Everyone made jokes about the total darkness broken only by the flashlights as Maeve moved over to one of the great wooden casks. One had remained half full, and she held a small glass vial under a spigot and filled it with a small amount of oil. She passed the vial around, allowing the tourists to rub a few drops between their fingers.

"Amazingly, the cold has prevented the oil from spoiling, even after nearly a hundred and thirty years. It's still as fresh as the day it came from the cauldron and was poured into the cask."

"It feels as though it has extraordinary lubricating qualities," said a gray-haired man with a large red nose, common in a heavy drinker.

"Don't tell the oil companies," Maeve said with a thin smile. "Or the whales will become extinct before next Christmas."

One woman asked for the vial and sniffed it. "Can it be used as cooking oil?"

"Yes indeed," Maeve answered. "The Japanese are particularly fond of whale oil for cooking and margarine. In fact the old whalers used to dip their biscuits in saltwater and then fry them in the bubbling blubber. I tried it once and found it to have an interesting if slightly bland taste—"

Maeve was abruptly cut off by the scream of an elderly woman who frantically clutched the sides of her head. Six other people followed suit, the women crying out, the men groaning.

Maeve ran from one to the other, stunned at the look of intense pain in their eyes. "What is it?" she shouted. "What's wrong? Can I help you?"

Then suddenly it was her turn. A daggerlike thrust of pain plunged into her brain, and her heart began to pound erratically. Instinctively her hands pressed her temples. She stared dazedly at the excursion members. Through the hypnotic spell of agony and terror, all their eyes seemed to be bulging from their sockets. Then she was struck by a tidal wave of dizziness rapidly followed by great nausea. She fought an overwhelming urge to vomit before losing all balance and falling down.

No one could understand what was happening. The air became heavy and hard to breathe. The beams of the flashlights took on an unearthly bluish glow. There was no vibration, no shaking of the earth, and yet dust began to swirl inside the cavern. The only sounds were the screams of the tormented.

They began to sag and fall to the ground around Maeve. With horrified disbelief she found herself immersed in disorientation, caught in the grip of a crazy nightmare where her body was turning itself inside out.

One moment people stared at death from an unknown source. Then inexplicably, an instant later, the excruciating agony and vertigo began to ease. As quickly as it had come on, it faded and disappeared.

Maeve felt exhausted to her bones. She leaned weakly against the cask of whale oil, eyes closed, vastly relieved at being free of pain.

No one found the voice to speak for nearly two minutes. Finally, a man, who was cradling his stunned wife in his arms, looked up at Maeve. "What in God's name was that?"

Maeve slowly shook her head. "I don't know," she answered dully.

With great effort she made the rounds, greatly cheered at finding everyone still alive. They all appeared to be recovering with no lingering effects. Maeve was thankful that none of the more elderly had suffered permanent damage, especially heart attacks.

"Please wait here and rest while I check the two ladies at the entrance of the tunnel and contact the ship."

They were a good group, she thought. None questioned or blamed her for the unexplained event. They immediately began comforting each other, the younger ones helping the more elderly to restful positions. They watched as she swung open the massive door and walked through the portal until the beam of her flashlight vanished around a curve in the tunnel.

As soon as Maeve reached daylight again, she couldn't help wondering if it had all been a hallucination. The sea was still calm and blue. The sun had risen a little higher in a cloudless sky. And the two ladies who had preferred to remain in the open air were lying sprawled on their stomachs, each clutching at nearby rocks as if trying to keep from being torn away by some unseen force.

She bent down and tried to shake them awake but stiffened in horror when she saw the sightless eyes and the gaping mouths. Each had lost the contents of her stomach. They were dead, their skin already turning a dark purplish-blue.

Maeve ran down to the Zodiac, which was still sitting with its bow pulled onto the shoreline. The crewman who had brought them ashore was also lifeless, the same appalling expression on his face, with the same skin color. In numbed shock, Maeve lifted her portable communicator and began transmitting. "*Polar Queen*, this is land expedition one. We have an emergency. Please answer immediately. Over."

There was no reply.

She tried again and again to raise the ship. Her only response was silence. It was as if *Polar Queen* and her crew and passengers had never existed.

2

January is midsummer in Antarctica, and days are long with only an hour or two of twilight. Temperatures on the peninsula can reach as high as fifteen degrees Celsius (fifty-nine degrees Fahrenheit), but since the tour group had come ashore it had dropped to freezing. At the scheduled time for the *Polar Queen* to return there was neither word nor sign of her.

Maeve continued her futile attempts to make contact every half hour until eleven o'clock in the evening. As the polar sun dipped toward the horizon, she stopped hailing on the ship's channel to conserve the transmitter's batteries. The portable radio's range was limited to ten kilometers, and no other ship or passing aircraft was within five hundred kilometers of picking up her calls for help. The nearest source of relief was the Argentinean research station on the other end of the island, but unless freak atmospheric conditions stretched her signals, they would not have received them either. In frustration, she gave up and planned to try again later.

Where was the ship and crew? she wondered constantly. Was it possible they had encountered the same murderous phenomenon and suffered harm? She did not wish to dwell on pessimistic thoughts. For the time being she and her party were secure. But without food or bedding for warmth, she did not see how they could hold out very long. A few days at most. The ages of her excursion group were on the high side. The youngest couple were in their late sixties, while the rest ranged through the seventies to the oldest, a woman of eighty-three who wanted a taste of adventure before she went into a nursing home. A sense of hopelessness welled inside Maeve.

She noted with no small apprehension that dark clouds were beginning to drift in across the sea from the west, the vanguard of the storm that First Officer Trevor Haynes had warned Maeve to expect. She had enough experience with south polar weather conditions to know that coastal storms would be accompanied by fierce winds and blinding sleet. Little or no snow would fall. Debilitating windchill would be the primary danger. Maeve finally gave up hope of seeing the ship anytime soon and began to plan for the worst by making preparations for the excursion members to bed down for the next ten hours.

The still-standing huts and rendering shed were pretty well open to the elements. The roofs had caved in long ago, and high winds had broken the few windows as well as carrying off the doors. She decided her group would stand a better chance of surviving the bitter cold and life-threatening wind by remaining in the cavern. A fire using a stack of weathered lumber at the whaling station was a possibility, but it would have to be placed near the entrance. Farther back in the cave, and the smoke could cause asphyxiation.

Four of the younger men helped her place the bodies of the two women and crewman in the rendering shed. They also pulled the Zodiac farther ashore and tied it down to prevent it from being blown inland by the increasing winds. Next they sealed all but a small opening of the tunnel entrance with rocks to minimize any frigid gusts that might sweep through into the cavern. She did not want to seal them off completely from the outside by closing the rock door. Then she gathered everyone around and ordered them to huddle together for mutual warmth.

There was nothing left to do, and the hours of waiting for rescue seemed like an eternity. They tried to sleep but found it all but impossible. The numbing cold slowly began to penetrate their clothing, and the wind outside turned into a gale that shrieked like a banshee through the air hole in the stone barrier they'd erected at the tunnel entrance.

Only one or two complained. Most bore the ordeal stoically. Some were actually excited at experiencing a real adventure. Two of the Aussie husbands, big men who had made their fortune as partners in a construction firm, teased their wives and cracked sarcastic jokes to keep everyone's spirits up. They seemed as unconcerned as if they were waiting to board a plane. They were all good people in their twilight years, Maeve thought. It would be a shame, no, a crime, if they were to all die in that icy hellhole.

Her mind wandered, and she vaguely envisioned them all interred under the rocks with the Norwegian explorers and the British whalers. A delusion, she reminded herself firmly. Despite the fact that her father and sisters were violently hostile toward her, she could not bring herself to believe they would deny her proper burial in the family plot where her ancestors rested. And yet she knew it was a distinct possibility that her family would no longer admit that Maeve was of their own flesh and blood, not after the birth of her twin boys.

She lay there, staring at the fog that formed in the cavern from the heavy concentrated breathing, and tried to picture her sons, now only six years old, watched over by friends, while she earned badly needed money with the cruise line. What would become of them if she died? She prayed that her father would never get his hands on them. Compassion never entered into his reckonings. People's lives mattered little to him. Nor was money a driving force. He considered it merely a tool. Power to manipulate, that was his passion. Maeve's two sisters shared their father's callousness toward others. Fortunately, she took after her mother, a gentle lady who was driven to suicide by her cold and abusive husband when Maeve was twelve.

After the tragedy, Maeve never considered herself part of the family. None of them had forgiven her for leaving the fold and striking out on her own under a new name with nothing but the clothes on her back. It was a decision she had never regretted.

She awakened, listening for a sound, or rather the lack of it. The wind was no longer whistling into the tunnel from outside. The storm was still brewing, but there was a temporary break in the frigid wind. She returned and roused the two Australian contractors.

"I need you to accompany me to the penguin rookery," she told them. "They're not hard to capture. I'm breaking the law, but if we are to stay healthy until the ship returns, we must put nourishment in our stomachs."

"What do you think, mate?" boomed one of the men.

"I could use a taste of bird," replied the other.

"Penguins aren't candidates for gourmet dining," Maeve said, smiling. "Their meat is oily, but at least it's filling."

Before they left for the rookery, she prodded the others to their feet and sent them to steal wood from the whaling station to build a fire. "In for a penny, in for a pound. If I'm going to jail for killing protected creatures and destroying historic property, I might as well do a thorough job of it."

They made for the rookery, which was about two kilometers around the point encircling the north part of the bay. Though the wind had died, the sleet made their way miserable. They could hardly see more than three meters in front of them. It was as though they were looking at everything through a sheet of water. Sight was even more difficult without goggles. They were wearing only sunglasses, and the drifting sleet blew in around the rims of the lenses and caked their eyelashes. Only by keeping close to the edge of the water did they maintain a sense of direction. They added twenty minutes to the hike by not walking across the point as the crow flies, but at least the detour prevented them from becoming lost.

The wind howled in again, biting into their exposed faces. The thought of them all trekking to the Argentinean research station crossed Maeve's mind. But she quickly dismissed it. Few would survive the thirty-kilometer journey through the storm. Better than half the aged tourists would quickly perish along the way. Maeve had to consider all prospects, the feasible and the impractical. She might make it. She was young and strong. But she could not bring herself to desert the people who were depending on her. Sending the big Aussie men who trudged beside her was a possibility. The nagging problem as she saw it was what would they find when they arrived?

What if the Argentinean scientists had died under the same mysterious circumstances as the members of her own party? If the worst had occurred, then the only hard incentive for reaching the station was to use their powerful communications equipment. The decision was agonizing. Should she risk the two Australians' lives in a hazardous trek, or keep them at hand to help her care for the old and the weak? She decided against going for the research station. Her job did not involve putting the passengers of Ruppert & Saunders in life-threatening situations. It seemed inconceivable that they had been abandoned. They had no choice but wait it out until rescue came, from whatever source, and exist the best way they could until then.

The sleet had slackened, and their vision increased to nearly fifty meters. Overhead, the sun appeared as a dim orange ball with a halo of varied colors like a round prism. They rounded the spur of rock encompassing the bay and curved back to the shoreline containing the penguin rookery. Maeve did not relish the thought of killing penguins even as a means to stay alive. They were such tame and friendly creatures.

The *Pygoscelis adeliae* or Adélie penguins are one of seventeen true species. They sport a black-feathered back and hooded head and a white breast and stare through beady little eyes. As suggested by fossils found on Seymour Island, their ancestors evolved more than forty million years ago and were as tall as a man. Attracted to their almost human social behavior patterns, Maeve had spent one whole summer observing and studying a rookery and had begun a love affair with this most delightful of birds. In contrast with the larger emperor penguin, the Adélies can move as fast as five kilometers an hour and often faster when tobogganing over the ice on their chests. Give them a funny little derby and a cane to swing, she often mused, and they could have waddled along in a perfect imitation of Charlie Chaplin.

"I believe the bloody sleet is slackening," said one of the men. He was wearing a leather cap and puffing on a cigarette.

"About damned time," muttered the other, who had used a scarf to wrap his head, turban-style. "I feel like a damp rag."

They could clearly see out to sea for nearly half a kilometer. The once glasslike sea was now a turmoil of whitecaps agitated by the wind. Maeve turned her attention to the rookery. As far as she could see was a carpet of penguins, over fifty thousand of them. As she and the Aussies walked closer, it struck her as odd that none of the birds stood on their little feet, tail feathers extended as props to keep from falling over backward. They were scattered all about, most lying on their backs as if they had toppled over.

"Something's not right," she said. "None are standing."

"No fools those birds," said the man in the turban. "They know better than to stand against blowing sleet."

Maeve ran to the edge of the rookery and looked down at the penguins lying on the outer edge. She was struck by the absence of sound. None moved nor showed interest in her approach. She knelt and studied one. It lay limp on the ground, eyes staring sightless at her. Her face was stricken as she looked at the thousands of birds that showed no sign of life. She stared at two leopard seals, the natural predator of penguins, whose bodies washed back and forth in the small surge along the rock-strewn beach.

"They're all dead," she muttered in shock.

"Bloody hell," gasped the man in the leather cap. "She's right. Not one of the little buggers is breathin'."

This can't be real, Maeve thought wildly. She stood absolutely still. She could not see what caused the mass death, but she could feel it. The crazy idea that every living thing in the rest of the world had died from the mysterious malady suddenly struck her mind. Is it possible we're the only ones left alive on a dead planet? she wondered in near panic.

The man with the scarf-turban wrapped around his head bent over and picked up a penguin. "Saves us the trouble of having to slaughter them."

"Leave them be!" Maeve shouted at him.

"Why?" the man replied indignantly. "We've all got to eat."

"We don't know what killed them. They might have died from some sort of plague."

The man in the leather cap nodded. "The little lady knows what she's talking about. Whatever disease killed these birds could do us in too. I don't know about you, but I don't aim to be responsible for my wife's death."

"But it wasn't a disease," the other man argued. "Not what killed those little old ladies and that sailor lad. It was more like some fluke of nature."

Maeve stood her ground. "I refuse to gamble with lives. *Polar Queen* will be back. We haven't been forgotten."

"If the captain is trying to give us a good scare, he's doing a damned fine job of it."

"He must have a good reason for not returning."

"Good reason or not, your company better be heavily insured because they're going to get their ears sued off when we get back to civilization."

Maeve was in no mood to argue. She turned her back on the killing ground and set off toward the storage cavern. The two men followed, their eyes searching over a menacing sea for something that wasn't there.

3

To wake up after three days in a cave on a barren island in the middle of a polar storm and know you are responsible for three deaths and the lives of nine men and eleven women is not an enjoyable experience. Without any sign of the hoped-for arrival of the *Polar Queen*, the once-cheerful excursion that came ashore to experience the wondrous isolation of the Antarctic had become a nightmare of abandonment and despair for the vacation travelers. And to add to Maeve's desperation, the batteries of her portable communicator had finally gone dead.

Anytime now, Maeve knew she could expect the older members of the party to succumb to the harsh conditions inside the cave. They had lived their lives in warm and tropical zones and were not acclimated to the freezing harshness of the Antarctic. Young and hardy bodies might have lasted until help finally arrived, but these people lacked the strength of twenty- and thirty-year-olds. Their health was generally frail and vulnerable with age.

At first they joked and told stories, treating their ordeal as merely a bonus adventure. They sang songs, mostly "Waltzing

Matilda," and attempted word games. But soon lethargy set in, and they went quiet and unresponsive. Bravely, they accepted their suffering without protest.

Now, hunger overcame any fear of diseased meat, and Maeve stopped a mutiny by finally relenting and sending the men out to bring in several dead penguins. There was no problem of decomposition setting in since the birds had frozen soon after they were killed. One of the men was an avid hunter. He produced a Swiss army knife and expertly skinned and butchered the meat. By filling their bellies with protein and fat they would add fuel to maintain their body heat.

Maeve found some seventy-year-old tea in one of the whaler's huts. She also appropriated an old pot and a pan. Next she tapped the casks for a liter of the remaining whale oil, poured it in the pan and lit it. A blue flame rose, and everybody applauded her ingenuity at producing a workable stove. Then she cleaned out the old pot, filled it with snow and brewed the tea. Spirits were buoyed, but only for a short time. Depression soon recast its heavy net over the cavern. Their determination not to die was being sapped by the frigid temperature. They morbidly began to believe the end was inevitable. The ship was never returning, and any hope of rescue from another origin bordered on fantasy.

It no longer mattered if they expired from whatever unknown disease, if any, killed the penguins. None were dressed properly to resist for long sustained temperatures below freezing. The danger of asphyxiation was too great to use the whale oil to build a bigger fire. The small amount in the pan merely produced a feeble bit of warmth, hardly sufficient to prolong life. Eventually the fatal tentacles of the cold would encircle them all.

Outside, the storm went from bad to worse and it began to snow, a rare occurrence on the peninsula during summer. Hope of a chance discovery was destroyed as the storm mounted in intensity. Four of the elderly were near death from exposure, and Maeve suffered bleak discouragement as all control began to slip through her frozen fingers. She blamed herself for the three that were already dead, and it affected her badly.

The living looked upon her as their only hope. Even the men respected her authority and carried out her orders without question. "God help them," she whispered to herself. "I can't let them know I've come to the end of my rope."

She shuddered from an oppressive feeling of helplessness. A strange lethargy stole through her. Maeve knew she must see the terrible trial through to its final outcome, but she didn't think she had the strength to continue carrying twenty lives on her shoulders. She felt exhausted and didn't want to struggle anymore. Dimly, through her listlessness, she heard a strange sound unlike the cry of the wind. It came to her ears as though something were pounding the air. Then it faded. Only her imagination, she told herself. It was probably nothing but the wind changing direction and making a different howl through the air vent at the tunnel entrance.

Then she heard it again briefly before it died. She struggled to her feet and stumbled through the tunnel. A snowdrift had built up against the wind barrier and nearly filled the small opening. She removed several rocks to widen a passage and crawled outside into an icy world of wind and snow. The wind held steady at about twenty knots, swirling billows of snow like a tornado. Suddenly, she tensed and squinted her eyes into the white turbulence.

Something seemed to be moving out there, a vague shape with no substance and yet darker than the opaque veil that fell from the sky.

She took a step and pitched forward. For a long moment she thought of just lying there and going to sleep. The urge to give it all up was overwhelming. But the spark of life refused to diminish and blink out. She lifted herself to her knees and stared through the wavering light. She caught something moving toward her, and then a gust obliterated it. A few moments later it reappeared, but closer this time. Then her heart surged.

It was the figure of a man covered in ice and snow. She waved excitedly and called to him. He paused as if listening, then turned and began walking away.

This time she screamed, a high-pitched scream such as only a female could project. The figure turned and stared through the drifting snow in her direction. She waved both arms frantically. He waved back and began jogging toward her.

"Please don't let him be a mirage or a delusion," she begged the heavens.

And then he was kneeling in the snow beside her, cradling her shoulders in arms that felt like the biggest and strongest she had ever known. "Oh, thank God. I never gave up hoping you'd come."

He was a tall man, wearing a turquoise parka with the letters NUMA stitched over the left breast, and a ski mask with goggles. He removed the goggles and stared at her through a pair of incredible opaline green eyes that betrayed a mixture of surprise and puzzlement. His deeply tanned face seemed oddly out of place in the Antarctic.

"What in the world are you doing here?" he asked in a husky voice tinged with concern.

"I have twenty people back there in a cavern. We were on a shore excursion. Our cruise ship sailed off and never returned."

He looked at her in disbelief. "You were abandoned?"

She nodded and stared fearfully into the storm. "Did a worldwide catastrophe occur?"

His eyes narrowed at the question. "Not that I'm aware of. Why do you ask?"

"Three people in my party died under mysterious circumstances. And an entire rookery of penguins just north of the bay has been exterminated down to the last bird."

If the stranger was surprised at the tragic news, he hid it well. He helped Maeve to her feet. "I'd better get you out of this blowing snow."

"You're American," she said, shivering from the cold.

"And you're Australian."

"It's that obvious?"

"You pronounce *a* like *i*."

She held out a gloved hand. "You don't know how glad I am to see you, Mr. . . ?"

"My name is Dirk Pitt."

"Maeve Fletcher."

He ignored her objections, picked her up and began carrying her, following her footprints in the snow toward the tunnel. "I suggest we carry on our conversation out of the cold. You say there are twenty others?"

"That are still alive."

Pitt gave her a solemn look. "It would appear the sales brochures oversold the voyage."

Once inside the tunnel he set her on her feet and pulled off his ski mask. His head was covered by a thick mass of unruly black hair. His green eyes peered from beneath heavy dark eyebrows, and his face was craggy and weathered from long hours in the open but handsome in a rugged sort of way. His mouth seemed set in a casual grin. This was a man a woman could feel secure with, Maeve thought.

A minute later, Pitt was greeted by the tourists like a hometown football hero who had led the team to a big victory. Seeing a stranger suddenly appear in their midst had the same impact as winning a lottery. He marveled that they were all in reasonably fit shape, considering their terrible ordeal. The old women all embraced and kissed him like a son while the men slapped his back until it was sore. Everybody was talking and shouting questions at once. Maeve introduced him and related how they met up in the storm.

"Where did you drop from, mate?" they all wanted to know.

"A research vessel from the National Underwater & Marine Agency. We're on an expedition trying to discover why seals and dolphins have been disappearing in these waters at an astonishing rate. We were flying over Seymour Island in a helicopter when the snow closed in on us, so we thought it best to land until it blew over."

"There're more of you?"

"A pilot and a biologist who remained on board. I spotted what looked like a piece of a Zodiac protruding from the snow. I wondered why such a craft would be resting on an uninhabited part of the island and walked over to investigate. That's when I heard Miss Fletcher shouting at me."

"Good thing you decided to take a walk when you did," said the eighty-three-year-old great-grandmother to Maeve.

"I thought I heard a strange noise outside in the storm. I know now that it was the sound of his helicopter coming in to land."

"An incredible piece of luck we stumbled into each other in the middle of a blizzard," said Pitt. "I didn't believe I was hearing a woman's scream. I was sure it was a quirk of the wind until I saw you waving through a blanket of snow."

"Where is your research ship?" Maeve asked.

"About forty kilometers northeast of here."

"Did you by chance pass our ship, *Polar Queen?*"

Pitt shook his head. "We haven't seen another ship for over a week."

"Any radio contact?" asked Maeve. "A distress call, perhaps?"

"We talked to a ship supplying the British station at Halley Bay, but have heard nothing from a cruise ship."

"She couldn't have vanished into thin air," said one of the men in bewilderment. "Not along with the entire crew and our fellow passengers."

"We'll solve the mystery as soon as we can transport all you people to our research vessel. It's not as plush as *Polar Queen*, but we have comfortable quarters, a fine doctor and a cook who stands guard over a supply of very good wines."

"I'd rather go to hell than spend another minute in this freeze box," said a wiry New Zealand owner of a sheep station, laughing.

"I can only squeeze five or six of you at a time into the helicopter, so we'll have to make several trips," explained Pitt. "Because we set down a good three hundred meters away, I'll return to the craft and fly it closer to the entrance to your cave so you won't have to suffer the discomfort of trekking through the snow."

"Nothing like curbside service," Maeve said, feeling as if she had been reborn. "May I go with you?"

"Feel up to it?"

She nodded. "I think everyone will be glad to not have me ordering them about for a little while."

Al Giordino sat in the pilot's seat of the turquoise NUMA helicopter and worked a crossword puzzle. No taller than a floor lamp, he had a body as solid as a beer keg poised on two legs, with a pair of construction derricks for arms. His ebony eyes occasionally glanced into the snow glare through the cockpit windshield, then seeing nothing of Pitt, they refocused on the puzzle. Curly black hair framed the top of a round face, which was fixed with a perpetual sarcastic expression about the lips that suggested he was skeptical of the world and everyone in it, while the nose hinted strongly at his Roman ancestry.

A close friend of Pitt's since childhood, they had been inseparable during their years together in the Air Force before volunteering for an assignment to help launch the National Underwater & Marine Agency, a temporary assignment that had lasted the better part of fourteen years.

"What's a six-letter word for fuzzballed goondorpher that eats stinkweed?" he asked the man sitting behind him in the cargo bay of the aircraft, which was packed with laboratory testing equipment. The marine biologist from NUMA looked up from a specimen he'd collected earlier and raised his brows quizzically.

"There is no such beast as a fuzzballed goondorpher."

"You sure? It says so right here."

Roy Van Fleet knew when Giordino was sowing his cornfield with turnips. After three months at sea together, Van Fleet had become too savvy to fall for the stubby Italian's con jobs. "On second thought, it's a flying sloth from Mongolia. See if 'slobbo' fits."

Realizing he had lost his easy mark, Giordino looked up from the puzzle again and stared into the falling snow. "Dirk should have been back by now."

"How long has he been gone?" asked Van Fleet.

"About forty-five minutes."

Giordino screwed up his eyes as a pair of vague shapes took form in the distance. "I think he's coming in now." Then he added, "There must have been funny dust in that cheese sandwich I just ate. I'd swear he's got someone with him."

"Not a chance. There isn't another soul within thirty kilometers."

"Come see for yourself."

By the time Van Fleet had capped his specimen jar and placed it in a wooden crate, Pitt had thrown open the entry hatch and helped Maeve Fletcher climb inside.

She pushed back the hood on her orange jacket, fluffed out her long golden hair and smiled brightly. "Greetings, gentlemen. You don't know how happy I am to see you."

Van Fleet looked as if he had seen the Resurrection. His face registered total incomprehension.

Giordino, on the other hand, simply sighed in resignation. "Who else," he asked no one in particular, "but Dirk Pitt could tramp off into a blizzard on an uninhabited backwater island in the Antarctic and discover a beautiful girl?"

4

Less than an hour after Pitt alerted the NUMA research vessel *Ice Hunter*, Captain Paul Dempsey braved an icy breeze and watched as Giordino hovered the helicopter above the ship's landing pad. Except for the ship's cook busily preparing hot meals in the galley, and the chief engineer, who remained below, the entire crew, including lab technicians and scientists, had turned out to greet the first group of cold and hungry tourists to be airlifted from Seymour Island.

Captain Dempsey had grown up on a ranch in the Beartooth Mountains astride the Wyoming-Montana border. He ran away to sea after graduating from high school and worked the fishing boats out of Kodiak, Alaska. He fell in love with the icy seas above the Arctic Circle and eventually passed the examination to become captain of an ice-breaking salvage tug. No matter how high the seas or how strong the wind, Dempsey never hesitated to take on the worst storms the Gulf of Alaska could throw at him after he'd received a call from a ship in distress. During the next fifteen years, his daring rescues of innumerable fishing boats, six coastal freighters, two oil tankers and a Navy destroyer created a legend that resulted in a bronze statue beside the dock at Seward, a source of great embarrassment to him. Forced into retirement when the oceangoing salvage company became debt ridden, he accepted an offer from the chief director of NUMA, Admiral James Sandecker, to captain the agency's polar research ship, *Ice Hunter*.

Dempsey's trademark, a chipped briar pipe, jutted from one corner of his tight but good-humored mouth. He was a typical tugman, broad shouldered and thick waisted, habitually standing with legs wide set, yet he presented a distinguished appearance. Gray haired, clean shaven, a man given to telling good sea stories, Dempsey might have been taken for a jovial captain of a cruise ship.

He stepped forward as the wheels of the chopper settled onto the deck. Beside him stood the ship's physician, Dr. Mose Greenberg. Tall and slender, he wore his dark brown hair in a ponytail. His blue-green eyes twinkled, and he had about him that certain indefinable air of trustworthiness common to all conscientious, dedicated doctors around the world.

Dr. Greenberg, along with four crewmen bearing stretchers for any of the elderly passengers who found it difficult to walk on their own, ducked under the revolving rotor blades and opened the rear cargo door. Dempsey moved toward the cockpit and motioned to Giordino to open the side window. The stocky Italian obliged and leaned out.

"Is Pitt with you?" asked Dempsey loudly above the swoosh of the blades.

Giordino shook his head. "He and Van Fleet stayed behind to examine a pack of dead penguins."

"How many of the cruise ship's passengers were you able to carry?"

"We squeezed in six of the oldest ladies who had suffered the most. Four more trips ought to do it. Three to transport the remaining tourists and one to bring out Pitt, Van Fleet, the guide and the three dead bodies they stashed in an old whalers' rendering shed."

Dempsey motioned into the miserable mixture of snow and sleet. "Can you find your way back in this soup?"

"I plan to beam in on Pitt's portable communicator."

"How bad off are these people?"

"Better than you might expect for senior citizens who've suffered three days and nights in a frigid cave. Pitt said to tell Dr. Greenberg that pneumonia will be his main worry. The bitter cold has sapped the older folk's energy, and in their weakened condition, their resistance is real low."

"Do they have any idea what happened to their cruise ship?" asked Dempsey.

"Before they went ashore, their excursion guide was told by the first officer that the ship was heading twenty kilometers up the coast to put off another group of excursionists. That's all she knows. The ship never contacted her again after it sailed off."

Dempsey reached up and lightly slapped Giordino on the arm. "Hurry back and mind you don't get your feet wet." Then he moved around to the cargo door and introduced himself to the tired and cold passengers from the *Polar Queen* as they exited the aircraft.

He tucked a blanket around the eighty-three-year-old woman, who was being lifted to the deck on a stretcher. "Welcome aboard," he said with a warm smile. "We have hot soup and coffee and a soft bed waiting for you in our officers' quarters."

"If it's all the same to you," she said sweetly, "I'd prefer tea."

"Your wish is my command, dear lady," Dempsey said gallantly. "Tea it is."

"Bless you, Captain," she replied, squeezing his hand.

As soon as the last passenger had been helped across the helicopter pad, Dempsey waved off Giordino, who immediately lifted the craft into the air. Dempsey watched until the turquoise craft dissolved and vanished into the white blanket of sleet.

He relit the ever-present pipe and tarried alone on the helicopter pad after the others had hurried back into the comfort of the ship's superstructure to get out of the cold. He had not counted on a mission of mercy, certainly not one of this kind. Ships in distress on ferocious seas he could understand. But ship's captains who abandoned their passengers on a deserted island under incredibly harsh conditions he could not fathom.

The *Polar Queen* had sailed far more than 25 kilometers from the site of the old whaling station. He knew that for certain. The radar on *Ice Hunter*'s bridge could see beyond 120 kilometers, and there was no contact that remotely resembled a cruise ship.

· · ·

The gale had slackened considerably by the time Pitt, along with Maeve Fletcher and Van Fleet, reached the penguin rookery. The Australian zoologist and the American biologist had become friendly almost immediately. Pitt walked behind them in silence as they compared universities and colleagues in the field. Maeve plagued Van Fleet with questions pertaining to her dissertation, while he queried her for details concerning her brief observation of the mass decimation of the world's most beloved bird.

The storm had carried the carcasses of those nearest the shoreline out to sea. But by Pitt's best calculation a good forty thousand of the dead birds still lay scattered amid the small stones and rocks, like black-and-white gunnysacks filled with wet grain. With the easing of the wind and sleet, visibility increased to nearly a kilometer.

Giant petrels, the vultures of the sea, began arriving to feast upon the dead penguins. Majestic as they soared gracefully through the air, they were merciless scavengers of meat from any source. As Pitt and the others watched in disgust, the huge birds quickly disemboweled their lifeless prey, forcing their beaks inside the penguin carcasses until their necks and heads were red with viscera and gore.

"Not exactly a sight I care to remember," said Pitt.

Van Fleet was stunned. He turned to Maeve, his eyes unbelieving. "Now that I see the tragedy with my own eyes I find it hard to accept so many of the poor creatures dying within such a concentrated space in the same time period."

"Whatever the phenomenon," said Maeve, "I'm certain it also caused the death of my two passengers and the ship's crewman who brought us ashore."

Van Fleet knelt and studied one of the penguins. "No indication of injury, no obvious signs of disease or poison. The body appears fat and healthy."

Maeve leaned over his shoulder. "The only nonconformity that I found was the slight protrusion of the eyes."

"Yes, I see what you mean. The eyeballs seem half again as large."

Pitt looked at Maeve thoughtfully. "When I was carrying you to the cave, you said the three who died did so under mysterious circumstances."

She nodded. "Some strange force assaulted our senses, unseen and nonphysical. I have no idea what it was. But I can tell you that for at least a full five minutes it felt like our brains were going to explode. The pain was excruciating."

"From the blue coloring on the bodies you showed me in the rendering shed," said Van Fleet, "the cause of death appears to be cardiac arrest."

Pitt stared over the scene of so much annihilation. "Not possible that three humans, countless thousands of penguins and fifty or more leopard seals all expired together from a heart condition."

"There must be an interrelating cause," said Maeve.

"Any connection with the huge school of dolphins we found out in the Weddell Sea or the pod of seals washed up just across the channel on Vega Island, all deader than petrified wood?" Pitt asked Van Fleet.

The marine biologist shrugged. "Too early to tell without further study. There does, however, appear to be a definite link."

"Have you examined them in your ship's laboratory?" asked Maeve.

"I've dissected two seals and three dolphins and found no hook I can hang a respectable theory on. The primary consistency seems to be internal hemorrhaging."

"Dolphins, seals, birds and humans," Pitt said softly. "They're all vulnerable to this scourge."

Van Fleet nodded solemnly. "Not to mention the vast numbers of squid and sea turtles that have washed ashore throughout the Pacific and the millions of dead fish found floating off Peru and Ecuador in the past two months."

"If it continues unstopped there is no predicting how many species of life above and under the sea will become extinct." Pitt turned his gaze toward the sky at the distant sound of the helicopter. "So what do we know except that our mystery plague kills every living thing in air and liquid without discrimination?"

"All within a matter of minutes," added Maeve.

Van Fleet came to his feet. He appeared badly shaken. "If we don't determine whether the cause is from natural disturbances or human intervention of some kind, and do it damned quick, we may be looking at oceans devoid of all life."

"Not just oceans. You're forgetting this thing also kills on land," Maeve reminded him.

"I don't even want to dwell on that horror."

For a long minute no one said a word, each trying to comprehend the potential catastrophe that lay somewhere in and beyond the sea. Finally, Pitt broke the silence.

"It would appear," he said, a pensive look on his craggy face, "that we have our work cut out for us."

5

Pitt studied the screen of a large monitor that displayed a computer-enhanced satellite image of the Antarctic Peninsula and the surrounding islands. He leaned back, rested his eyes a moment and then stared through the tinted glass on the navigation bridge of *Ice Hunter* as the sun broke through the dissipating clouds. The time was eleven o'clock on a summer's evening in the Southern Hemisphere, and daylight remained almost constant.

The passengers from *Polar Queen* had been fed and bedded down in comfortable quarters charitably provided by the crew and scientists, who doubled up. Doc Greenberg examined each and every one and found no permanent damage or trauma. He was also relieved to find only a few cases of mild colds but no evidence of pneumonia. In the ship's biolaboratory, two decks above the ship's hospital, Van Fleet, assisted by Maeve Fletcher, was performing postmortem examinations on the penguins and seals they had airlifted from Seymour Island in the helicopter. The bodies of the three dead were packed in ice until they could be turned over to a professional pathologist.

Pitt ran his eyes over the huge twin bows of the *Ice Hunter*.

She was not your garden-variety research ship but one of a kind, the first scientific vessel entirely computer designed by marine engineers working with input from oceanographers. She rode high on parallel hulls that contained her big engines and auxiliary machinery. Her space-age rounded superstructure abounded with technical sophistication and futuristic innovations. The quarters for the crew and ocean scientists rivaled the staterooms of a luxury cruise ship. She was sleek and almost fragile looking, but that was a deception. She was a workhorse, born to ride smooth in choppy waves and weather the roughest sea. Her radically designed triangular hulls could cut through and crush an ice floe four meters thick.

Admiral James Sandecker, the feisty director of the National Underwater & Marine Agency, followed her construction from the first computerized design drawing to her maiden voyage around Greenland. He took great pride in every centimeter of her gleaming white superstructure and turquoise hulls. Sandecker was a master of obtaining funds from the new tightfisted Congress, and nothing had been spared in *Ice Hunter*'s construction nor her state-of-the-art equipment. She was without argument the finest polar research ship ever built.

Pitt turned and refocused his attention on the image beamed down from the satellite.

He felt almost no exhaustion. It had been a long and tiring day, but one filled with every emotion, happiness and satisfaction at having saved the lives of over twenty people and sorrow at seeing so many of nature's creatures lying dead almost as far as the eye could see. This was a catastrophe beyond comprehension. Something sinister and menacing was out there. A hideous presence that defied logic.

His thoughts were interrupted by the appearance of Giordino and Captain Dempsey as they stepped out of the elevator that ran from the observation wing above the navigation bridge down through fifteen decks to the bowels of the engine room.

"Any glimpse of *Polar Queen* from the satellite cameras?" asked Dempsey.

"Nothing I can positively identify," Pitt replied. "The snow is blurring all imaging."

"What about radio contact?"

Pitt shook his head. "It's as though the ship were carried away by aliens from space. The communications room can't raise a response. And while we're on the subject, the radio at the Argentinean research station has also gone dead."

"Whatever disaster struck the ship and the station," said Dempsey, "must have come on so fast none of the poor devils could get off a distress call."

"Have Van Fleet and Fletcher uncovered any clues leading to the cause of the deaths?" asked Pitt.

"Their preliminary examination shows that the arteries ruptured at the base of the creatures' skulls, causing hemorrhaging. Beyond that, I can tell you nothing."

"Looks like we have a thread leading from a mystery to an enigma to a dilemma to a puzzle with no solution in sight," Pitt said philosophically.

"If *Polar Queen* isn't floating nearby or sitting on the bottom of the Weddell Sea," Giordino said thoughtfully, "we might be looking at a hijacking."

Pitt smiled as he and Giordino exchanged knowing looks. "Like the *Lady Flamborough?*"

"Her image crossed my mind."

Dempsey stared at the deck, recalling the incident. "The cruise ship that was captured by terrorists in the port of Punta del Este several years ago."

Giordino nodded. "She was carrying heads of state for an economic conference. The terrorists sailed her through the Strait of Magellan into a Chilean fjord, where they moored her under a glacier. It was Dirk who tracked her down."

"Allowing for a cruising speed of roughly eighteen knots," Dempsey estimated, "terrorists could have sailed *Polar Queen* halfway to Buenos Aires by now."

"Not a likely scenario," Pitt said evenly. "I can't think of one solid reason why terrorists would hijack a cruise ship in the Antarctic."

"So what's your guess?"

"I believe she's either drifting or steaming in circles within two hundred kilometers of us." Pitt said it so absolutely he left little margin for doubt.

Dempsey looked at him. "You have a prognostication we don't know about?"

"I'm betting my money that the same phenomenon that struck

down the tourists and crewman outside the cave also killed everybody on board the cruise ship.''

"Not a pretty thought," said Giordino, "but that would explain why she never returned to pick up the excursionists."

"And let us not forget the second group that was scheduled to be put ashore twenty kilometers farther up the coast," Dempsey reminded them.

"This mess gets worse by the minute," Giordino muttered.

"Al and I will conduct a search for the second group from the air," Pitt said, contemplating the image on the monitor. "If we can't find any sign of their presence, we'll push on and check on the people manning the Argentinean research station. For all we know they could be dead too."

"What in God's name caused this calamity?" Dempsey asked no one in particular.

Pitt made a vague gesture with his hands. "The familiar causes for extermination of life in and around the sea do not fit this puzzle. Natural problems generally responsible for huge fish kills around the world, like fluctuations in temperatures of surface water or algal blooms such as red tides, do not apply here. Neither is present."

"That leaves man-made pollution."

"A possibility that also fails to measure up," Pitt argued. "There are no known industrial sources for toxic pollution within thousands of kilometers. And no radioactive and chemical wastes could have killed every penguin in such a short time span, certainly not those that were safely nesting on land clear of the water. I fear we have a threat no one has faced before."

Giordino pulled a massive cigar from the inside pocket of his jacket. The cigar was one of Admiral Sandecker's private stock, made expressly for his private enjoyment. And Giordino's too, since it was never discovered how he had helped himself to the admiral's private stock for over a decade without ever getting caught. He held a flame to the thick dark brown shaft of tobacco and puffed out a cloud of fragrant smoke.

"Okay," he said, enjoying the taste. "What's the drill?"

Dempsey wrinkled his nose at the cigar's aroma. "I've contacted officials of Ruppert & Saunders, the line that owns *Polar Queen*, and apprised them of the situation. They lost no time in initiating a massive air search. They've requested that we transport the survivors of the shore excursion to King George Island, where a British scientific station has an airfield. From there arrangements will be made to airlift them back to Australia."

"Before or after we look for *Polar Queen?*" Giordino put to him.

"The living come first," Dempsey replied seriously. As captain of the ship, the decisions belonged to him. "You two probe the coastline in your helicopter while I steer the *Hunter* on a course toward King George Island. After our passengers are safely ashore, we'll make a sweep for the cruise ship."

Giordino grinned. "By then, the Weddell Sea will be swarming with every salvage tug from here to Capetown, South Africa."

"Not our problem," said Dempsey. "NUMA isn't in the ship salvage business."

Pitt had tuned out of the conversation and walked over to a table where a large chart of the Weddell Sea was laid flat. He ignored any inclination to work by instinct and drove himself to think rationally, with his brain and not his gut. He tried to put himself onboard the *Polar Queen* when she was struck by the murdering scourge. Giordino and Dempsey went quiet as they stared at him expectantly.

After nearly a minute, he looked up from the chart and smiled. "Once we program the relevant data into the teleplotting analyzer, it should give us a ballpark location with a fighting chance for success."

"So what do we feed into the brain box?" Dempsey's term for any piece of electronics relating to the ship's computer systems.

"Every scrap of data on wind and currents from the last three and a half days, and their effects against a mass the size of *Polar Queen*. Once we calculate a drift pattern, we can tackle the problem of whether she continued making way with a dead crew at the helm, and in what direction."

"Suppose that instead of steaming around in circles, as you suggested, her rudder was set on a straight course?"

"Then she might be fifteen hundred kilometers away, somewhere in the middle of the South Atlantic and out of range of the satellite imaging system."

Giordino put it to Pitt. "But you don't think so."

"No," Pitt said quietly. "If the ice and snow covering this ship after the storm is any indication, *Polar Queen* has enough of the stuff coating her superstructure to make her nearly invisible to the satellite imaging system."

"Enough to camouflage her as an iceberg?" asked Dempsey.

"More like a snow-blanketed projection of land."

Dempsey looked confused. "You've lost me."

"I'll bet my government pension," said Pitt with cast-iron conviction, "we'll find the *Polar Queen* hard aground somewhere along the shore of the peninsula or beached on one of the outlying islands."

6

Pitt and Giordino took off at four o'clock in the morning, when most of the crew of *Ice Hunter* were still sleeping. The weather had returned to milder temperatures, calm seas and crystal-clear blue skies, with a light five-knot wind out of the southwest. With Pitt at the controls, they headed toward the old whaling station before swinging north in search of the second group of excursionists from *Polar Queen*.

Pitt could not help feeling a deep sense of sadness as they flew over the rookery's killing ground. The shore as far as the horizon seemed carpeted with the bodies of the comical little birds. The Adélie penguins were very territorial, and birds from other rookeries around the Antarctic Peninsula were not likely to immigrate to this particular breeding ground. The few survivors who might have escaped the terrible scourge would require twenty years or more to replenish the once numerous population of Seymour Island. Fortunately, the massive loss was not enough to critically endanger the species.

As the last of the dead birds flashed under the helicopter, Pitt leveled out at fifty meters and flew above the waterline, staring out the windscreen for any sign of the excursionists' landing site. Giordino gazed out his side window, scanning the open-water pack ice for any glimpse of *Polar Queen*, occasionally making a mark on a folded chart that lay across his lap.

"If I had a dime," Giordino muttered, "for every iceberg on the Weddell Sea, I could buy General Motors."

Pitt glanced past Giordino out the starboard side of the aircraft at a great labyrinth of frozen masses calved from the Larsen Ice Shelf and driven northwest by the wind and current into warmer water, where they split and broke up into thousands of smaller bergs. Three of them were as big as small countries. Some measured three hundred meters thick and rose as high as three-story buildings from just the water surface. All were dazzling white with hues of blue and green. The ice of these drifting mountains had formed from compacted snow in the ancient past, before breaking loose and plowing relentlessly over the centuries toward the sea and their slow but eventual meltdown.

"I do believe you could pick up Ford and Chrysler too."

"If *Polar Queen* struck any one of these thousands of bergs, she could have gone to the bottom in less time than it takes to tell about it."

"A thought I don't care to dwell on."

"Anything on your side?" asked Giordino.

"Nothing but gray, undistinguished rock poking through a blanket of white snow. I can only describe it as sterile monotony."

Giordino made another notation on his chart and checked the airspeed against his watch. "Twenty kilometers from the whaling station, and no sign of passengers from the cruise ship."

Pitt nodded in agreement. "Certainly nothing I can see that resembles a human."

"Maeve Fletcher said they were supposed to put the second party ashore at a seal colony."

"The seals are there all right," Pitt said, gesturing below. "Must be over eight hundred of them, all dead."

Giordino raised in his seat and peered out the port window as Pitt banked the helicopter in a gentle descending turn to give him a better view. The yellow-brown bodies of big elephant seals packed the shoreline for nearly a kilometer. From fifty meters in the air, they looked to be sleeping, but a sharp look soon revealed that not one moved.

"It doesn't look like the second excursion group left the ship," said Giordino.

There was nothing more to see, so Pitt swung the aircraft back on a course over the surf line. "Next stop, the Argentinean research station."

"It should be coming into view at any time."

"I'm not looking forward to what we might find," said Pitt uneasily.

"Look on the bright side." Giordino smiled tightly. "Maybe everybody said to hell with it, packed up and went home."

"Wishful thinking on your part," Pitt replied. "The station is highly important for its work in atmospheric sciences. It's one of five permanently occupied survey stations that measure the behavior and fluctuations of the Antarctic ozone hole."

"What's the latest news on the ozone layer?"

"Weakening badly in both Northern and Southern Hemispheres," Pitt answered seriously. "Since the large cavity over the Arctic pole has opened, the amoeba-shaped hole in the south, rotating in clockwise direction from polar winds, has traveled over Chile and Argentina as high as the forty-fifth parallel. It also passed across New Zealand's South Island as far as Christchurch. The plant and animal life in those regions received the most harmful dose of ultraviolet radiation ever recorded."

"Which means we'll have to pile on the suntan lotion," Giordino said sardonically.

"The least of the problem," said Pitt. "Small overdoses of ultraviolet radiation badly damage every agricultural product from potatoes to peaches. If the ozone values drop a few more percentage points, there will be a disastrous loss of food crops around the world."

"You paint a grim picture."

"That's only the background," Pitt continued. "Couple that with global warming and increasing volcanic activity, and the human race could see a rise in sea level of thirty to ninety meters in the next two hundred years. The bottom line is that we've altered the earth in a terrifying way we don't yet understand—"

"There!" Giordino abruptly cut in and pointed. They were coming over a shoulder of rock that sloped toward the sea. "Looks more like a frontier town than a scientific base."

The Argentinean research and survey station was a complex of ten buildings, constructed with solid steel portal frames that supported dome roofs. The hollow walls had been thickly filled with insulation against the wind and frigid cold. The antenna array for gathering scientific data on the atmosphere festooned the domed roofs like the leafless branches of trees in winter. Giordino tried one last time to raise somebody on the radio while Pitt circled the buildings.

"Still quiet as a hermit's doorbell," Giordino said uneasily as he removed the earphones.

"No outstretched hand from a welcome committee," Pitt observed.

Without a further word he settled the helicopter neatly beside the largest of the six buildings, the rotor blades whipping the snow into a shower of ice crystals. A pair of snowmobiles and an all-terrain tractor sat deserted, half buried in snow. There were no footprints to be seen, no smoke curled from the vents. No smoke or at least white vapor meant no inhabitants, none that were alive at any rate. The place looked eerily deserted. The blanket of white gave it a ghostly look indeed, thought Pitt.

"We'd better take along the shovels stored in the cargo bay," he said. "It looks like we're going to have to dig our way in."

It required no imagination at all to fear the worst. They exited the aircraft and trudged through snow up to their thighs until they reached the entrance to the central building. About two meters of snow had drifted against the door. Twenty minutes later they had removed enough to pull the door half ajar.

Giordino gave a slight bow and smiled grimly. "After you."

Pitt never doubted Giordino's fortitude for a minute. The little Italian was utterly fearless. It was an old routine they had practiced many times. Pitt led the way while Giordino covered any unexpected movement from the flanks and rear. One behind the other they stepped into a short tunnel ending at an interior door that acted as an additional cold barrier. Once through the inside door, they continued on down a long corridor that opened into a combination recreation and dining room. Giordino walked over to a thermometer attached to the wall.

"It's below freezing in here," he muttered.

"Somebody hasn't been tending the heat," Pitt acknowledged.

They did not have to go far to discover their first resident.

The odd thing about him was that he didn't look like he was dead. He knelt on the floor, clutching the top of a table, staring open-eyed and unwinkingly at Pitt and Giordino as if he had been expecting them. There was something unnaturally wrong and foreboding about his stillness. He was a big man, bald but for a strip of black hair running around the sides of his head and meeting in the back. Like most scientists who spent months and sometimes years in isolated outposts, he had ignored the daily male ritual of shaving, as evidenced by the elegantly brushed beard that fell down his chest. Sadly, the magnificent beard had been soiled when he retched.

The frightening part about him, the part that made the nape of Pitt's neck tingle, was the expression of abject fear and agony on the face that was frozen by the cold into a mask of white marble. He looked hideous beyond description.

The eyes bulged, and the mouth was oddly twisted open as if in a final scream. That this individual had died in extreme pain and terror was obvious. The fingernails of the white hands that dug into the tabletop were broken and split. Three of them had left tiny droppings of ice-crystalled blood. Pitt was no doctor and had never entertained the thought of becoming one, but he could tell this man was not stiffened by rigor mortis; he was frozen solid.

Giordino stepped around a serving counter and entered the kitchen. He returned within thirty seconds. "There are two more in there."

"Worst fears confirmed," said Pitt heavily. "Had just one of the station's people survived, he'd have maintained the auxiliary motors to run the generators for electrical heat and power."

Giordino looked down the corridors leading to the other buildings. "I'm not in the mood to hang around. I say we vacate this ice palace of the dead and contact *Ice Hunter* from the chopper."

Pitt looked at him shrewdly. "What you're really saying is that we pass the buck to Captain Dempsey and give him the thankless job of notifying the Argentinean authorities that the elite group of scientists manning their chief polar research station have all mysteriously departed for the great beyond."

Giordino shrugged innocently. "It seems the sensible thing to do."

"You could never live with yourself if you slunk off without making a thorough search for a possible survivor."

"Can I help it if I have an inordinate fondness for people who live and breathe?"

"Find the generating room, fuel the auxiliary motors, restart them and turn on the electrical power. Then head for the communications center and report to Dempsey while I check out the rest of the station."

Pitt found the rest of the Argentinean scientists where they had died, the same look of extreme torment etched on their faces. Several had fallen in the lab and instrument center, three grouped around a spectrophotometer that was used to measure the ozone. Pitt counted sixteen corpses in all, four of them women, sprawled in various compartments about the station. Everyone had protruding, staring eyes and gaping mouths, and all had vomited. They died frightened and they died in great pain, frozen in their agony. Pitt was reminded of the plaster casts of the dead from Pompeii.

Their bodies were fixed in odd, unnatural positions. None lay on the floor as if they had simply fallen. Most looked as if they had suddenly lost their balance and were desperately clinging to something to keep upright. A few were actually clutching carpeted flooring; one or two had hands tightly clasped against the sides of their head. Pitt was intrigued by the odd positions and tried to pry the hands away to see if they might have been covering any indications of injury or disease, but they were as rigid as if they had been grafted to the skin of the ears and temples.

The vomiting seemed an indication that death was brought about by virulent disease or contaminated food. And yet the obvious causes did not set right to Pitt's way of thinking. No plague or food poisoning is known to kill in a few short minutes. As he walked in deep contemplation toward the communications room, a theory began unfolding in his mind. His thoughts were rudely interrupted when he entered and was greeted by a cadaver perched on a desk like a grotesque ceramic statue.

"How did *he* get there?" Pitt asked calmly.

"I put him there," Giordino said matter-of-factly without looking up from the radio console. "He was sitting on the only chair in the room and I figured I needed it worse than he did."

"He makes a total of seventeen."

"The toll keeps adding up."

"You get through to Dempsey?"

"He's standing by. Do you want to talk to him?"

Pitt leaned over Giordino and spoke into the satellite telephone that linked him with almost any point of the globe. "This is Pitt. You there, skipper?"

"Go ahead Dirk, I'm listening."

"Has Al filled you in on what we've found here?"

"A brief account. As soon as you can tell me there are no survivors, I will alert Argentinean authorities."

"Consider it done. Unless I missed one or two in closets or under beds, I have a body count of seventeen."

"Seventeen," Dempsey repeated. "I read you. Can you determine the cause of death?"

"Negative," Pitt answered. "The apparent symptoms aren't like anything you'd find in your home medical guide. We'll have to wait for a pathologist's report."

"You might be interested to know that Miss Fletcher and Van Fleet have pretty well eliminated viral infections and chemical contamination as the cause of death for the penguins and seals."

"Everyone at the station vomited before they died. Ask them to explain that."

"I'll make a note of it. Any sign of the second shore party?"

"Nothing. They must still be on board the ship."

"Very strange."

"So what are we left with?"

Dempsey sighed defeatedly. "A big fat puzzle with too many missing pieces."

"On the flight here we passed over a seal colony that was wiped out. Have you determined how far the scourge extends?"

"The British station two hundred kilometers to the south of you on the Jason Peninsula and a U.S. cruise ship that's anchored off Hope Bay have reported no unusual events nor any evidence of mass creature destruction. By taking into account the area in the Weddell Sea where we discovered the school of dead dolphins, I put the death circle within a diameter of ninety kilometers, using the whaling station on Seymour Island as a center point."

"We're going to move on now," Pitt notified him, "and make a sweep for *Polar Queen*."

"Mind that you keep enough fuel in reserve to return to the ship."

"In the bank," Pitt assured Dempsey. "An invigorating swim in ice water I can do without."

Giordino closed down the research station's communications console, and then they stepped lively toward the entrance; jogged quickly was closer to the truth. Neither Pitt nor Giordino wished to spend another moment in that icy tomb. As they rose from the station, Giordino studied his chart of the Antarctic Peninsula.

"Where to?"

"The right thing to do is search in the area selected by *Ice Hunter*'s computer," Pitt replied.

Giordino gave Pitt a dubious look. "You realize, of course, that our ship's data analyzer did not agree with your idea of the cruise ship running aground on the peninsula or a nearby island."

"Yes, I'm well aware that Dempsey's brain box put *Polar Queen* steaming around in circles far out in the Weddell Sea."

"Do I detect a tone of conflict?"

"Let's just say a computer can only analyze the data that is programmed into it before offering an electronic opinion."

"So where to?" Giordino repeated.

"We'll check out the islands north of here as far as Moody Point at the tip of the peninsula. Then we'll curve east and work out to sea until we converge with the *Ice Hunter*."

Giordino well knew he was being baited and hooked by the biggest flimflam man in the polar seas, but he took the bait anyway. "You're not strictly following the computer's advice."

"Not one hundred percent, no."

Giordino could feel the jerk on the line. "I'd like a faint clue as to what's going on in your devious mind."

"We found no human bodies at the seal colony. So we now know the ship did not heave to for a shore excursion. Follow me?"

"Thus far."

"Picture the ship steering north from the whaling station. The scourge, plague or whatever you want to call it, strikes before the crew has a chance to send the passengers ashore. In these waters, with ice floes and bergs floating all around like ice cubes in a punch bowl, there is no way the captain would have set the ship on automated control. The risk of collision is too great. He would have taken the helm himself, probably steering the ship from one of the electronic steering consoles on the port and starboard bridge wings."

"Good as far as it goes," Giordino said mechanically. "Then what?"

"The ship was cruising along the coast of Seymour Island when the crew was stricken," Pitt explained. "Now take your chart and draw a line slightly north of east for two hundred kilometers and cross it with a thirty-kilometer arc. Then tell me where you are and what islands intersect the course."

Before Giordino complied, he stared at Pitt. "Why didn't the computer come to the same conclusion?"

"Because as a ship's captain, Dempsey was more concerned with winds and currents. He also assumed, and rightly so for a master mariner, that the last act of a dying captain would be to save his ship. That meant turning *Polar Queen* away from the danger of grounding on a rocky shore and steering her toward the relative safety of the sea and taking his chances with the icebergs."

"You don't think that was the way it was."

"Not after seeing the bodies at the research station. Those poor souls hardly had time to react much less carry out a sound decision. The captain of the cruise ship died in his own vomit while the ship was on a course parallel to the shore. With the rest of the ship's officers and the engine room crew stricken, *Polar Queen* sailed on until she either beached on an island, struck a berg and sank, or steamed out into the South Atlantic until her engines ran out of fuel and she became a drifting derelict far off the known sea lanes."

The absence of reaction to Pitt's divination was almost total. It was as if Giordino expected it. "Have you ever thought seriously of becoming a professional palm reader?"

"Not until five minutes ago," Pitt came back.

Giordino sighed and drew the course Pitt requested on the chart. After a few minutes he propped it against the instrument panel so Pitt could view his markings. "If your mystical intuition is on target, the only chance *Polar Queen* has for striking hard ground between here and the South Atlantic is on one of three small islands that are little more than pinnacles of exposed rock."

"What are they called?"

"Danger Islands."

"They sound like the setting of an adolescent pirate novel."

Giordino thumbed through a coastal reference manual. "Ships are advised to give them a wide berth," he said. "High basalt palisades rising sharply from rough waters. Then it lists the ships that have piled up on them." He looked up from the chart and reference manual and gave Pitt a very narrow look. "Not exactly a place where kids would play."

7

From Seymour Island to the mainland the sea was as smooth as a mirror and just as reflective. The rockbound mountains soared above the water and their snowy mantles were reproduced by the water in exacting detail. West of the islands the sea was calmed by a vast army of drifting icebergs that rose from marine-blue water like frosted sailing ships from centuries past. Not one genuine vessel was in sight, nothing of human manufacture marred the incredibly beautiful seascape.

They skirted Dundee Island, not far below the extreme tip of the peninsula. Directly ahead of them Moody Point curled toward the Danger Islands like the bony finger of the old guy with the scythe signifying his next victim. The calm waters ended off the point. As if they had walked from a warm comfortable room through a door into a storm outside, they found the sea suddenly transformed into an unbroken mass of white-capped swells marching in from the Drake Passage. A buffeting wind also sprang up and caused the helicopter to sway like a toy locomotive hurtling around a model train layout.

The peaks of the three Danger Islands came into view, their

rock escarpments rising out of a sea that writhed and thrashed around their base. They rose so steeply that even seabirds couldn't get a foothold on their sheer walls. They thrust angrily from the sea in contempt of the waves that broke against the unyielding rock in rapid explosions of foam and spray. The basalt formation was so hard that a million years of onslaught by a maddened sea produced little weathering. Their polished walls ran up to vertical peaks that possessed no flat spaces wider than a good-sized coffee table.

"No ship could live long in that bedlam," said Pitt.

"No shallow water around those pinnacles," Giordino observed. "The water looks to drop off a hundred fathoms within a stone's throw of the cliffs."

"According to the charts, it drops over a thousand meters in less than three kilometers."

They circled the first island in the chain, a wicked, brooding mass of ugly stone sitting amid the churning violence. There was no sign of floating debris on the tormented sea. They flew across the channel separating this island from the next, looking down on the rushing white-capped surge that reminded Pitt of the spring floodwaters gushing down the Colorado River through the Grand Canyon. No ship's captain would be crazy enough to take his vessel within a cannon shot of this place.

"See anything?" Pitt asked Giordino as he struggled to keep the helicopter stable against the unpredictable winds that tried to slam them against the towering cliffs.

"A seething mass of liquid only a white-water kayaker could love. Nothing more."

Pitt completed the circumference and dipped the craft toward the third and outermost island. This one looked dark and evil, and it took surprisingly little imagination to see that the peak was shaped in the likeness of an upturned face, much like that of the devil, with slitty eyes, small rock protrusions for horns and a sharp beard below smirking lips.

"Now that's what I call repugnant," said Pitt. "I wonder what name it goes by."

"No individual names are given on the chart," Giordino replied.

A moment later, Pitt swung the helicopter on a parallel course with the wave-swept palisades and began circling the barren island. Suddenly, Giordino stiffened and peered intently through the front windscreen. "Do you see that?"

Pitt turned briefly from the spectacular collision between water and rock and gazed forward and down. "I see no flotsam."

"Forget the water. Look over the top of that high ridge dead ahead."

Pitt studied the strange rock formation that trailed from the main mass and led into the sea like a man-made breakwater. "That blob of white snow beyond the ridge?"

"That ain't no blob of snow," Giordino said firmly.

Pitt suddenly realized what it was. "I've got it now!" he said with mounting excitement. It was smooth and white and shaped like a triangle with the top cut off. The upper rim was black, and there was some sort of painted emblem on the side. "A ship's funnel! And there's her radar mast sticking up forty meters forward. You made a good call, pal."

"If it's *Polar Queen*, she must have struck the cliffs on the other side of that spur."

But that was an illusion. When they flew over the natural seawall jutting into the sea it became apparent that the cruise ship was floating undamaged a good five hundred meters from the island. It was incredible, but there she was without a scratch.

"She's still clear!" Giordino shouted.

"Not for long," Pitt said. In an instant he took in the dire situation. The *Polar Queen* was steaming in large circles, her helm somehow jammed hard to starboard. They had arrived less than thirty minutes before her arc would bring her in collision with the sheer rocks, crushing her hull and sending everyone on board into deep, icy water.

"There are bodies on her deck," said Giordino soberly.

A few lay scattered about the bridge deck. Several had fallen on the sundeck near the stern. A Zodiac, still attached to the gangway, was dragged along through the swells, two bodies lying on its bottom. That no one was alive was obvious by the fact they were all covered with a thin coating of snow and ice.

"Two more revolutions and she'll kiss the rock," said Giordino.

"We've got to get down there and somehow turn her about."

"Not in this wind," said Giordino. "The only open space is the roof over the bridge-deck quarters. That's a tricky landing I wouldn't want to try. Once we dump airspeed and hover prior to setting down, we'll have as much control as a dry leaf. A sudden downdraft and we'll end up in the mess down there."

Pitt unsnapped his safety harness. "Then you drive the bus while I go down on the winch."

"There are people under restraint in rubber rooms who aren't that crazy. You'd be whipped around like a yo-yo on a string."

"You know any other way to get on board?"

"Only one. But it's not approved by the *Ladies Home Journal*."

"The battleship drop in the Vixen affair," said Pitt, recalling.

"One more occasion where you were damned lucky," said Giordino.

There was no doubt in Pitt's mind—the ship was going to pile up on the rocks. Once the bottom was torn out of her, she would sink like a brick. There was always the possibility that someone had survived the unknown plague as Maeve and her excursionists had in the cave. The cold, hard reality dictated that the bodies be examined in hopes of tracking down the cause of death. If there was the slightest chance of saving the *Polar Queen*, he had to take it.

Pitt looked at Giordino and smiled faintly. "It's time to cue the daring young man on the flying trapeze."

Pitt already wore thermal underwear made from heavy nylon pile to retain his body heat and shield him from frigid temperatures. Over this he pulled on a diver's dry suit, specially insulated for polar waters. The purpose of the dry suit was twofold. The first was to protect him from the windchill while he was dangling beneath the moving helicopter. The second, to keep him alive in cold water long enough for rescue, should he drop too soon or too late and miss the ship entirely.

He strapped on a quick-release harness and tightened the chin strap to the heavy crash-type helmet that contained his radio headset. He looked through the compartment that held Van Fleet's lab equipment and into the cockpit. "Do you read me okay?" he asked Giordino through the tiny microphone in front of his lips.

"A little fuzzy around the edges. But that should clear once you're free of the engine's interference. How about me?"

"Your every syllable is like a chime," Pitt jested.

"Because the upper superstructure is crowded with the funnel, forward mast and a batch of electronic navigation equipment, I can't risk dropping you amidships. It will have to be either the open bow or the stern."

"Make it the sundeck over the stern. The bow contains too much machinery."

"I'll start the run from starboard to port as soon as the ship turns and the wind comes from abeam," Giordino informed him. "I'll come in from the sea and attempt to take advantage of the calmer conditions on the lee side of the cliffs."

"Understood."

"You ready?"

Pitt adjusted his helmet's face mask and pulled on his gloves. He took the remote control unit to the winch motor in one hand, turned and pulled open the side entry hatch. If he hadn't been dressed for the abrupt blast of polar frigidity he would have been frozen into a Popsicle within a few seconds. He leaned out the door and gazed at *Polar Queen*.

She was circling in closer and closer to her death. Only fifty meters separated her from destruction on this pass. The uncompromising rock walls of the outermost Danger Island seemed to beckon to her. She looked like an uncaring moth serenely gliding toward a black spider, Pitt thought. There wasn't much time left. She was beginning her final circuit, which would bring her into collision with an immovable object. She would have died before but for the waves that crashed against the sheer rock and echoed back, delaying her trip to the bottom.

"Throttling back," Giordino said, announcing the start of his run over the ship.

"Exiting now," Pitt informed him. Pitt pressed the release button to reel out the cable. As soon as he had enough slack to clear the doorway he stepped into space.

The rush of wind took him in its grasp and strung his body out behind the underside of the helicopter. The rotor blades thumped above him, and the sound of the turbine exhaust came through his helmet and earphones. Whirling through the chilly air, Pitt felt the same sensation as that felt by a bungee jumper after the initial recoil. He focused his concentration onto the ship, which looked like a toy boat floating on a blanket of blue in the near distance.

The superstructure of the ship rapidly grew until it filled most of his vision.

"Coming up on her," Giordino's voice came over the earphones. "Mind you don't slam into the railing and slice yourself into little pieces."

He may have spoken as calmly as though he was parking a car in a garage, but there was a noticeable strain in Giordino's voice as he struggled to keep the slow-moving helicopter stable while heading through frenzied crosswinds.

"And don't you bloody your nose on those rocks," Pitt shot back.

Those were the last words between them. From now on it was all by sight and gut instinct. Pitt had let himself down until he was almost fifteen meters below and behind the chopper. He fought against the pull and momentum that worked to twist him in circles, using his outstretched arms like the wings and ailerons of an aircraft. He felt himself drop a few meters as Giordino reduced speed.

To Giordino it seemed *Polar Queen* churned the water with her screws as though it was business as usual and she was on a tropical pleasure cruise. He eased back on the throttle as far as he dared. One more notch and all control would belong to the winds. He was flying with every shred of experience he'd gained during many thousands of hours in the air, if being tossed about by fickle air currents could be called flying. Despite the wind buffeting, if he maintained his present course, he could drop Pitt dead center onto the sundeck. He later swore that he was pitched and yawed by winds coming at him from six different directions. From his position at the end of the winch cable, Pitt marveled that Giordino kept the craft on a straight line.

The black cliffs loomed up beyond the ship, ominous and menacing. If it was a sight to daunt the bravest of sea captains, it certainly daunted Giordino. It wouldn't do for him to make a spectacular head-on smash into the exposed rock, any more than it would do for Pitt to miscalculate and strike the side of the ship, breaking every bone in his body.

They were flying toward the lee side of the island, and the winds abated slightly. Not much, but enough for Giordino to feel he had firm control of the chopper and his destiny once more. One instant the cruise ship stretched in front of Giordino and the next the white superstructure and yellow hull swept out of sight beneath him. Then all he saw was ice-frozen rock that rose out of sight above his forward view. He could only hope Pitt was away as he abruptly threw the helicopter into a vertical ascent. The cliffs, wet from the billowing spray from the pounding waves, looked as if they were drawing him toward them like a magnet.

Then he was over the icy crest and was struck by the full force of the wind, which threw the aircraft on its tail, the rotor blades in a perpendicular position. Without any attempt at finesse, Giordino threw the helicopter around to a level position on a reverse course and beat back over the ship, his eyes darting as he looked out the window for a glimpse of Pitt.

Giordino did not know, could not have known, that Pitt had released his harness and made a perfect drop from a height of only three meters directly into the center of the sundeck's open swimming pool. Even from that short height it looked no larger than a postage stamp, but to Pitt it seemed as enticing as the cushiness of a haystack. He flexed his knees and stretched out his arms to lessen his momentum. The depth was only two meters in the deep end, and he made a tremendous splash, hurling a huge amount of water onto the deck. His feet, encased in dive boots, impacted solidly on the bottom, and he stopped dead, immersed in a stooped position.

With growing apprehension, Giordino circled the superstructure of the ship, searching for a glimpse of Pitt. He didn't spot him at first. He shouted into his microphone. "Did you make it down okay? Make yourself known, buddy."

Pitt waved his arms and replied. "I'm here in the swimming pool."

Giordino was dazed. "You fell in the pool?"

"I've a good notion to stay here," Pitt replied happily. "The heater is still on and the water is warm."

"I strongly suggest you get your butt to the bridge," Giordino said with deadly seriousness. "She's coming out of the backstretch and into the far turn. I give her no more than eight minutes before you hear a big scraping noise."

Pitt needed no further encouragement. He hoisted himself out of the pool and took off at a dead run along the deck to the forward companionway. The bridge was only one deck above. He took the companionway four steps at a time, threw open the door of the wheelhouse and rushed inside. A ship's officer was lying on the deck, dead, his arms clutching the base of the chart table. Pitt hurriedly scanned the ship's automated navigation systems console. He lost a precious few seconds searching for the digital course monitor. The yellow light indicated that the electronic control was on manual override. Feverishly he dashed outside onto the starboard bridge wing. It was empty. He turned and rushed back across the wheelhouse onto the port bridge wing. Two more ship's officers were lying in contorted positions on the deck, white and cold. Another ice-encrusted body hunched over the ship's exterior control panel on his knees, arms frozen underneath and around its pedestal. He wore a foul-weather jacket with no markings but a cap with enough gold braid to show that he was surely the captain.

"Can you drop the anchors?" asked Giordino.

"Easier said than done," Pitt replied irritably. "Besides, there is no flat bottom. The sides of the island probably drop at a near ninety-degree angle for a thousand fathoms. The rock is too smooth for the anchor flukes to dig in and grip."

Pitt saw in a glance why the ship maintained a direct track for nearly two hundred kilometers before initiating a circular course to port. A gold medal on a chain had fallen outside the captain's heavy jacket collar and hung suspended above the face of the control panel. Each gust of wind pushed it from side to side, and at the end of each pendulum swing, it struck against one of the toggle-type levers that controlled the movement of the ship, part of an electronics system almost all commanders of modern vessels use when docking in port. Eventually, the medal had knocked the directional lever into the half-port position, sending *Polar Queen* steaming around in corkscrewlike circles, ever closer to the Danger Islands.

Pitt lifted the medal and studied the inscription and image of a man engraved on one side. It was Saint Francis of Paola, the patron saint of mariners and navigators. Francis was revered for his miracles in saving sailors from resting in the deep. A pity Saint Francis had not rescued the captain, Pitt thought, but there was still a chance to save his ship.

If not for Pitt's timely appearance, the simplest of events, the freak circumstance of a tiny bit of metal tapping against a small lever, a twenty-five hundred gross ton ship and all its passengers and crew, alive or dead, would have crashed into unyielding rock and fallen into a cold and dispassionate sea.

"You'd better be quick," Giordino's anxious voice came over the earphones.

Pitt cursed himself for lingering and sneaked a fast glance in awe at the sinister walls that seemed to stretch above his head into the upper atmosphere. They were so flat and smooth from eons of wave action that it was as though some giant hand had polished their surface. The breakers rising out of the sea were roaring into the exposed cliff less than two hundred meters away. As *Polar Queen* narrowed the gap, the incoming swells slammed into her beam, shoving her hull ever closer to disaster. Pitt estimated that she would strike on her starboard bow in another four minutes.

Unimpeded, the relentless waves swept in from the deep reaches of the ocean and dashed into the cliff with the explosive concussion of a large bomb. The white sea burst and boiled in a huge witch's cauldron of blue water and white spray. It soared toward the top of the jagged rock island, hung there for a moment and then fell back, creating a return wave. It was this backwash that temporarily kept *Polar Queen* from being quickly swept against the palisades when she passed by.

Pitt tried to pull the captain away from the control panel, but he wouldn't budge. The hands clasped around the base refused to give. Pitt gripped the body under the armpits and heaved with all his strength. There was a sickening tearing sound that Pitt knew was the parting of frozen skin that had adhered to metal, then suddenly the captain was free. Pitt threw him off to the side, found the chrome lever that controlled the helm and pushed it hard against the slot marked PORT to increase the angle of turn away from calamity.

For nearly thirty seconds it seemed nothing was happening, then with agonizing slowness the bow began to swing away from the boiling surf. It was not nearly quick enough. A ship can't turn in the same radius as a big semitrailer. It takes almost a kilometer to come to a complete stop, much less cut a sharp inside turn.

He briefly considered throwing the port screw into reverse and swinging the ship on her axis, but he needed every knot of the ship's momentum to maintain headway through the quartering swell, and then there was the danger of the stern swinging too far to starboard and crashing into the cliff.

"She's not going to make it," Giordino warned him. "She's

caught by the rollers. You'd better jump while you still have a chance.''

Pitt didn't answer. He scanned the unfamiliar control panel and spotted the levers that controlled the bow and stern thrusters. There was also a throttle command unit that linked the panel to the engines. Holding his breath, Pitt set the thruster levers in the port position and pushed the throttles to full ahead. The response was almost instantaneous. Deep belowdecks, as if guided by an unseen hand, the engine revolutions increased. Momentary relief swelled within Pitt as he felt the throbbing vibration of engines at work under his feet. Now he could do little but stand and hope for the best.

Above the ship, Giordino looked down with a sinking sensation. From his vantage point it didn't seem the ship was turning. He saw no chance for Pitt to escape once the ship rammed into the island. Leaping into the boiling water meant only a futile struggle against the incredible power of a surging sea, an impossible situation at best.

"I'm coming in for you," he apprised Pitt.

"Stay clear," Pitt ordered. "You can't feel it up there, but the air turbulence this close to the precipice is murderous.''

"It's suicidal to wait any longer. If you jump now I can pick you up.''

"Like hell—" Pitt broke off in horror as the *Polar Queen* was caught broadside by a giant comber that rolled over her like an avalanche. For long moments she seemed to slide toward the cliff, nearer the frantic turmoil swirling around the rock. Then she was driving forward again, her icebreaker bow burying itself under the wave, the foaming crest curling as high as the bridge, spray streaming from it like a horse's mane in the breeze. The ship descended ever deeper as if she were continuing a voyage to the bottom far below.

8

The torrent came with a roar louder than thunder and flung Pitt to the deck. He instinctively held his breath as the icy water surged over and around him. He clung desperately to the pedestal of the control console to keep from being swept over the side into the maelstrom. He felt as if he had dropped over a towering cascade. All he could see through his face mask was a billow of bubbles and foam. Even in his arctic dry suit the cold felt like a million sharp needles stabbing his skin. He thought his arms were being pulled from their sockets as he clung for his life.

Then *Polar Queen* struggled up and burst through the back of the wave, her bow forging another ten meters to port. She was refusing to die, game to fight the sea to the bitter end. The water drained from the bridge in rivers until Pitt's head surfaced into the air again. He took a deep breath and tried to stare through the downpour of water that splashed back from the black rock of the cliffs. God, they seemed so close he could spit on them. So close that foam thrown upward by the horrendous collision of water against rock rebounded and fell over the ship like a cloudburst.

The ship was abeam of the chaos, and he eased back on the stern thruster in an attempt to quarter the surge.

The bow thruster dug in and shouldered the forward part of the ship into the flood as the stern screws thrashed the water into foam, pushing her on an angle away from the vertical rock face. Imperceptibly, but by the grace of God, her bow was edging out to sea.

"She's coming about!" Giordino yelled from above. "She's coming about!"

"We're not out of the woods yet." For the first time since the inundation, Pitt had the luxury of replying. He warily eyed the next sequence of waves that came rolling in.

The sea wasn't through with the *Polar Queen* yet. Pitt ducked as a huge sheet of spray crashed over the bridge wing. The next comber struck like an express train before colliding with the backwash from the last one. Bludgeoned by the impact from two sides, the ship was tossed upward until her hull was visible almost to the keel. Her twin screws rose into the air, throwing white water that reflected the sun like sparks of a fireworks pinwheel. She hung suspended for a terrible moment, finally dropping into a deep trough before she was struck by the next breaker in line. The bow was jerked to starboard, but the thruster battled her back on course.

Again and again the cruise ship heeled over as the waves rolled against the sides of her hull. There was no stopping her now. She was through the worst of it and shook off the endless swells as though she were a dog shaking water off its coat. The hungry sea might take her another time, but more likely she would end up at the scrappers thirty or more years from now. But this day she still sailed the brutal waters.

"You pulled it off! You really pulled it off!" shouted Giordino as though he didn't believe his eyes.

Pitt sagged against the bridge-wing railing and felt suddenly tired. It was then he became conscious of a pain in his right hip. He recalled striking against a stanchion that supported a night light when he was immersed by the giant wave. He couldn't see under the dry suit but he knew that his skin was forming a beautiful bruise.

Only after he set the navigation controls for a straight course south into the Weddell Sea did he turn and gaze at the pile of rock that towered above the sea like a jagged black column. There was an angry look about the cold face of the precipice, almost as if it were enraged at being cheated out of a victim. The barren island soon became little more than a pile of sea-ravaged rock as it receded in *Polar Queen*'s wake.

Pitt looked up as the turquoise helicopter hovered over the wheelhouse. "How's your fuel?" he asked Giordino.

"Enough to make *Ice Hunter* with a few liters to spare," Giordino answered.

"You'd better be on your way, then."

"Did you ever stop to think that if you board and sail an abandoned ship into the nearest port you'd make a few million bucks from the insurance underwriters on a salvage contract?"

Pitt laughed. "Do you really think Admiral Sandecker and the United States government would allow a poor but honest bureaucrat to keep the pay without screaming?"

"Probably not. Can I do anything for you?"

"Just give Dempsey my position and tell him I'll rendezvous at whatever position he chooses."

"See you soon," Giordino signed off. He was tempted to make a joke about Pitt's having an entire cruise ship to himself, but the reality of the situation quickly set in. There could be no joy at knowing you were the only one alive on a ship of the dead. He did not envy Pitt for even one second as he swung the helicopter into a turn and set a course for the *Ice Hunter*.

Pitt removed his helmet and watched as the turquoise helicopter flew low across the blue ice-cold sea. He watched until it became a speck on the golden-blue horizon. A fleeting sense of loneliness shrouded him as he gazed around the empty ship. How long he stood gazing across the decks devoid of life, he never recalled. He stood there as if stalling, his mind blank.

He was waiting for some sort of sound besides the slap of the waves against the bow and the steady beat of the engines. Maybe he waited for a sound that indicated the presence of people, voices or laughter. Maybe he waited for some sign of movement from something other than the ship's pennants flapping in the breeze. More likely he was seized by foreboding about what he would most certainly find. Already the scene at the Argentinean research station was being played out again. The dead passengers and crew, soaked through and sprawled on the upper decks, were only a sample of what he expected to find in the quarters and staterooms below.

At last he pulled his mind back on track and entered the wheelhouse. He set the engines on half speed and plotted an approximate course toward an interception point with *Ice Hunter*. Then he programmed the coordinates into the navigation computer and engaged the automated ship's control system, linking it with the radar to self-steer the ship around any passing icebergs. Assured the ship was in no further danger, he stepped from the wheelhouse.

Several of the bodies on the outer decks were crewmen who died in the act of maintaining the ship. Two were painting bulkheads, others had been working on the lifeboats. The bodies of eight passengers suggested that they had been admiring the unspoiled shoreline when they were struck down. Pitt walked down a passageway and looked in the ship's hospital. It was empty, as was the health club. He took the carpeted stairs down to the boat deck, which held the ship's six suites. They were all empty except one. An elderly woman lay as if sleeping. He touched her neck with his fingers. She was as cold as ice. He moved down to the salon deck.

Pitt began to feel like the Ancient Mariner on a ship of ghosts. The only thing missing was an albatross around his neck. The generators were still supplying electricity and heat, everything was orderly and everything in place. The interior warmth of the ship felt good after the inundation of icy water on the bridge wing. He was mildly surprised to find he had become immune to the dead bodies. He no longer bothered to closely examine them to see if there was a spark of life. He knew the tragic truth.

Though mentally prepared, he still found it hard to believe there was no life on board. That death had swept through the ship like a gust of wind was foreign to everything he'd ever experienced. It became most uncomfortable for him to intrude into the life of a ship that had known happier memories. He idly wondered what future passengers and crew would think, cruising on a jinxed ship. Would no one sail on her ever again, or would the tragedy attract sell-out crowds in search of adventure mixed with morbidness?

Suddenly he paused, cocked an ear and listened. Piano music was drifting from somewhere within the ship. He recognized the piece as an old jazz tune called "Sweet Lorraine." Then, as suddenly as the music began, it stopped.

Pitt began to sweat under the dry suit. He paused for a couple of minutes and stripped it off. The dead won't mind me walking around in my thermal underwear, he thought in grim humor. He pushed on.

He wandered into the kitchen. The area around the ovens and preparation tables was littered with the corpses of the chefs, ordinary kitchen help and waiters, lying two and three deep. There was a cold horror about the place. It looked like a charnel house but without the blood. Nothing but shapeless, lifeless forms frozen in their final act of clutching something tangible as if an unseen force were trying to drag them away. Pitt turned away, sickened, and rode the kitchen elevator up to the dining salon.

The tables were set for a meal unserved. Silverware, scattered by the ship's violent motion, still lay on immaculately clean tablecloths. Death must have arrived just prior to the seating for the lunchtime meal. He picked up a menu and studied the entrees. Sea bass, Antarctic ice fish, toothfish (a giant cod) and veal steak for those without a taste for fish. He laid the menu on the table and was about to leave when he spotted something that was out of place. He stepped over the body of a waiter and walked to a table by one of the picture windows.

Someone had eaten here. Pitt stared at the dishes that still had scraps of food on them. There was a nearly empty bowl of what looked like clam chowder, broken rolls smeared with butter and a half-consumed glass of ice tea. It was as though someone had just finished lunch and left for a stroll around the deck. Had they opened the dining salon early for someone? he wondered. He rejected any thought that suggested a passenger had eaten here after the death plague struck.

Pitt tried to write off the intriguing discovery with a dozen different logical solutions. But subconsciously, a fear began to grow. Unthinkingly, he began to look over his shoulder every so often. He left the dining salon and moved past the gift shop and worked forward into the ship's lounge. A Steinway grand piano was situated beside a small wooden dance floor. Chairs and tables were spaced around the lounge in a horseshoe arrangement. Besides the cocktail waitress who had fallen while carrying a tray of drinks, there was a party of eight men and women, mostly in their early seventies, who had been seated around a large table but now lay in grotesque positions on the carpet. As he studied the husbands and wives, some locked in a final embrace, Pitt experienced sadness and anguish at the same time. Overwhelmed with a sense of helplessness, he cursed the unknown cause of such a terrible tragedy.

Then he noticed another corpse. It was a woman, sitting on the carpet in one corner of the lounge. Her chin was on her knees, head cradled in her arms. Dressed in a fashionable short-sleeved leather jacket and wool slacks, she was not in a contorted position, nor did she appear to have vomited like all the others.

Pitt's nerves reacted by sending a cold shiver up his spine. His heart sprinted from a slow steady beat to a rapid pace. Gathering control over his initial shock, he moved slowly across the room until he stood looking down on her.

He reached out and touched her cheek with a light exploring fingertip, experiencing an incredible wave of relief as he felt warmth. He gently shook her by the shoulders and saw her eyelids quiver open.

At first she looked at him dazed and uncomprehending, and then her eyes flew wide, she threw her arms around him and gasped. "You're alive!"

"You don't know how happy I am to see you are too," Pitt said softly, his lips parted in a smile.

Abruptly, she pulled back from him. "No, no, you can't be real. You're all dead."

"You needn't be afraid of me," he said in a soothing tone.

She stared at him through wide brown eyes rimmed red from weeping, a sad enigmatic gaze. Her facial complexion was flawless, but there was an unmistakable pallor and just a hint of gauntness. Her hair was the color of red copper. She had the high cheekbones and full, sculptured lips of a fashion model. Their eyes locked for a moment, and then he dropped his stare slightly. From what he could tell about her in her curled position, she had a fashion model's figure. Her bared arms looked muscular for a woman. Only when she lowered her eyes and peered at his body did he suddenly feel embarrassed to be standing in front of a lady in his long johns.

"Why aren't you properly dressed?" she finally murmured.

It was an inconsequential question bred from a state of fear and trauma, not curiosity. Pitt didn't bother to explain. "Better yet, you tell me who you are and how you survived when the others died."

She looked as if she were about to fall over on her side, so he quickly bent down, circled his arm around her waist and lifted her into a leather chair next to a table. He walked over to the bar. He went behind the bar expecting to find the body of the bartender and was not disappointed. He took a bottle of Jack Daniel's Old No. 7 Tennessee sour mash whiskey from a mirrored shelf and poured a shot glass.

"Drink this," he said, holding the glass to her lips.

"I don't drink," she protested vaguely.

"Consider it medicinal. Just take a few sips."

She managed to consume the contents of the glass without coughing, but her face twisted into a sour expression as the whiskey, smooth as summer's kiss to a connoisseur, inflamed her tonsils. After she'd gasped a few breaths of air, she looked into his sensitive green eyes and sensed his compassion.

"My name is Deirdre Dorsett," she whispered nervously.

"Go on," he prompted. "That's a start. Are you one of the passengers?"

She shook her head. "An entertainer. I sing and play the piano in the lounge."

"That was you playing 'Sweet Lorraine.' "

"Call it a reaction from shock. Shock at seeing everyone dead, shock at thinking it would be my turn next. I can't believe I'm still alive."

"Where were you when the tragedy occurred?"

She peered at the four couples lying nearby in morbid fascination. "The lady in the red dress and the silver-haired man were celebrating their fiftieth anniversary with friends who accompanied them on the cruise. The night before their private party, the kitchen staff had carved a heart and cupid out of ice to sit in the middle of a bowl of champagne punch. While Fred, he's . . ." She corrected herself, "He was the bartender, opened the champagne, and Marta, the waitress, brought in a crystal bowl from the kitchen, I volunteered to bring the ice carving from the storage freezer."

"You were in the freezer?"

She nodded silently.

"Do you recall if you latched the door behind you?"

"It swings closed automatically."

"You could lift and carry the ice carving by yourself?"

"It wasn't very large. About the size of a small garden pot."

"Then what did you do?"

She closed her eyes very tightly, then pressed her hands against them and whispered. "I was only in there for a few minutes. When I came out I found everyone on the ship dead."

"Exactly how many minutes would you say?" Pitt asked softly.

She moved her head back and forth and spoke through her hands. "Why are you asking me all these questions?"

"I don't mean to sound like a prosecuting attorney. But please, it's important."

Slowly she lowered her hands and stared vacantly at the surface of the table. "I don't know, I have no way of knowing exactly how long I was in there. All I remember is it took me a little while to wrap the ice carving in a couple of towels so I could get a good grip on it and carry it without freezing my fingers."

"You were very lucky," he said. "Yours is a classic example of being in the right place at the right time. If you had stepped from the freezer two minutes before you did, you'd be as dead as all the others. You were doubly lucky I came on board the ship when I did."

"Are you one of the crew? You don't look familiar."

It was obvious to him she was not fully aware of the *Polar Queen*'s near brush with the Danger Islands. "I'm sorry, I should have introduced myself. My name is Dirk Pitt. I'm with a research expedition. We found your excursion party where they had been abandoned on Seymour Island and came looking for your ship after all radio calls went unanswered."

"That would have been Maeve Fletcher's party," she said quietly. "I suppose they're all dead too."

"Two passengers and the crewman who took them ashore," he answered. "Miss Fletcher and the rest are alive and well."

For a brief instant her face took on a series of expressions that would have done a Broadway actress proud. Shock was followed by anger culminating in a slow change to happiness. Her eyes brightened and she visibly relaxed. "Thank God Maeve is all right."

The sunlight came through the windows of the lounge and shone on her hair, which was loose and flowing about her shoulders, and he caught the scent of her perfume. Pitt sensed a strange mood change in her. She was not young but a confident woman in the prime of her early thirties, with strong inner qualities. He also felt a disconcerting desire for her that angered him. Not now, he thought, not under these circumstances. He turned away so she wouldn't see the rapt expression on his face.

"Why . . . ?" she asked numbly, gesturing around her. "Why did they all have to die?"

He stared at the eight friends who were enjoying a special moment before their lives were so cruelly stolen from them. "I can't be totally certain," he said in a voice solemn with rage and pity, "but I think I have a good idea."

9

Pitt was fighting fatigue when *Ice Hunter* sailed off the radar screen and loomed over the starboard bow. After searching the rest of the *Polar Queen* for other survivors, a lost cause as it turned out, he only allowed himself a short catnap while Deirdre Dorsett stood watch, ready to wake him lest the ship run down some poor trawler fishing for ice-water cod. There are those who feel refreshed after a brief rest. Not Pitt. Twenty minutes in dreamland was not enough to reconstitute his mind and body after twenty-four hours of stress and fatigue. He felt worse than when he lay down. He was getting too old to jump out of helicopters and battle raging seas, he mused. When he was twenty, he felt strong enough to leap over tall buildings with a single bound. At thirty, maybe a couple of one-story houses. How far back was that? Considering his sore muscles and aching joints, he was sure it must be eighty or ninety years ago.

He'd been working too long for the National Underwater & Marine Agency and Admiral Sandecker. It was time for a career move, something not as rigorous, with shorter hours. Maybe weaving hats out of palm fronds on a Tahiti beach, or something that stimulated the mind, like being a door-to-door contraceptive salesman. He shook off the silly thoughts brought on by weariness and set the automated control system to ALL STOP.

A quick radio transmission to Dempsey on board *Ice Hunter*, informing him that Pitt was closing down the engines and requesting a crew to come aboard and take over the cruise ship's operation, and then he picked up the phone and called Admiral Sandecker over a satellite link to give him an update on the situation.

The receptionist at NUMA headquarters put him straight through on Sandecker's private line. Though they were a third of the globe apart, Pitt's time zone in the Antarctic was only one hour ahead of Sandecker's in Washington, D.C.

"Good evening, Admiral."

"About time I heard from you."

"Things have been hectic."

"I had to get the story secondhand from Dempsey on how you and Giordino found and saved the cruise ship."

"I'll be happy to fill you in with the details."

"Have you rendezvoused with *Ice Hunter?*" Sandecker was short on greetings.

"Yes, sir. Captain Dempsey is only a few hundred meters off my starboard beam. He's sending a boat across to put a salvage crew on board and take off the only survivor."

"How many casualties?" asked Sandecker.

"After a preliminary search of the ship," answered Pitt, "I've accounted for all but 5 of the crew. Using a passenger list from the purser's office and a roster of the crew in the first officer's quarters, we're left with 20 passengers and 2 of the crew still among the living, out of a total of 202."

"That tallies to 180 dead."

"As near as I can figure."

"Since it is their ship, the Australian government is launching a massive investigation into the tragedy. A British research station with an airfield is situated not far to the southwest of your position, at Duse Bay. I've ordered Captain Dempsey to proceed there and transport the survivors ashore. The cruise line owners, Ruppert & Saunders, have chartered a Quantas jetliner to fly them to Sydney."

"What about the bodies of the dead passengers and crew?"

"They'll be packed in ice at the research station and flown to Australia on a military transport. Soon as they arrive, official investigators will launch a formal inquiry into the tragedy while pathologists conduct postmortem examinations on the bodies."

"Speaking of *Polar Queen*," said Pitt. He gave the admiral the particulars of its discovery by him and Giordino and the near brush with calamity in the ferocious breakers around the base of the Danger Islands. At the end he asked, "What do we do with her?"

"Ruppert & Saunders are also sending a crew to sail her back to Adelaide, accompanied by a team of Australian government investigators, who will examine her from funnel to keel before she reaches port."

"You should demand an open contract form for salvage. NUMA could be awarded as much as $20 million for saving the ship from certain disaster."

"Entitled to or not, we'll not charge one thin dime for saving their ship." Pitt detected the silky tone of satisfaction in Sandecker's voice. "I'll get twice that sum in favors and cooperation from the Aussie government for future research projects in and around their waters."

No one could ever accuse the admiral of being senile. "Niccolò Machiavelli could have taken lessons from you," Pitt sighed.

"You might be interested in learning that dead marine life in your area has tapered off. Fishermen and research-station support vessels have reported finding no unusual fish or mammal kills in the past forty-eight hours. Whatever the killer is, it has moved on. Now we're beginning to hear of massive amounts of fish and unusually high numbers of sea turtles being washed up on beaches around the Fiji Islands."

"Sounds suspiciously like the plague has a life of its own."

"It doesn't stay in one place," said Sandecker grimly. "The stakes are high. Unless our scientists can systematically eliminate the possible causes and home in on the one responsible damned quick, we're going to see a loss of sea life that can't be replenished, not in our lifetime."

"At least we can take comfort in knowing it's not a repeat of the explosive reproduction by the red tide from chemical pollution out of the Niger River."

"Certainly not since we shut down that hazardous waste plant in Mali that was the cause," added Sandecker. "Our monitors up and down the river have shown no further indications of the altered synthetic amino acid and cobalt that created the problem."

"Do our lab geniuses have any suspects on this one?" inquired Pitt.

"Not on this end," replied Sandecker. "We were hoping the biologists on board *Ice Hunter* might have come up with something."

"If they have, they're keeping it a secret from me."

"Do you have any notions on the subject?" asked Sandecker. There was a careful, almost cautious probing in his voice. "Something juicy that I can give the hounds from the news media who are parked in our lobby nearly two hundred strong."

A shadow of a smile touched Pitt's eyes. There was a private understanding between them that nothing of importance was ever discussed over a satellite phone. Calls that went through the atmosphere were as vulnerable to eavesdropping as an old farm-belt party line. The mere mention of the news media meant that Pitt was to dodge the issue. "They're drooling for a good story, are they?"

"The tabloids are already touting a ship of the dead from the Antarctic triangle."

"Are you serious?"

"I'll be happy to fax you the stories."

"I'm afraid they'll be disappointed by my hypothesis."

"Care to share it with me?"

There was a pause. "I think it might be an unknown virus that is carried by air currents."

"A virus," Sandecker repeated mechanically. "Not very original, I must say."

"I realize it has a queer sound to it," said Pitt, "about as logical as counting the holes in an acoustical ceiling when you're in the dentist's chair."

If Sandecker was puzzled by Pitt's nonsensical ramblings, he didn't act it. He merely sighed in resignation as if he was used to chatter. "I think we'd better leave the investigation to the scientists. They appear to have a better grip on the situation than you do."

"Forgive me, Admiral, I'm not thinking straight."

"You sound like a man wandering in a fog. As soon as Dempsey sends a crew on board, you head for *Ice Hunter* and get some sleep."

"Thank you for being so understanding."

"Simply a matter of appreciating the situation. We'll speak later." A click, and Admiral Sandecker was gone.

Deirdre Dorsett went out onto the bridge wing and waved wildly as she recognized Maeve Fletcher standing at the railing of *Ice Hunter*. Suddenly free of the torment of being the only person alive on a ship filled with cadavers, she laughed in sheer unaffected exhilaration, her voice ringing across the narrowing breach between the two ships.

"Maeve!" she cried.

Maeve stared across the water, searching the decks of the cruise ship for the female calling her name. Then her eyes locked on the figure standing on the bridge wing, waving. For half a minute she stared, bewildered. Then as she recognized Deirdre, her face took on the expression of someone walking in a graveyard at night who was suddenly tapped on the shoulder.

"Deirdre?" she shouted the name questioningly.

"Is that any way to greet someone close who's returned from the dead?"

"You . . . here . . . alive?"

"Oh, Maeve, you can't know how happy I am to see you alive."

"I'm shocked to see you too," said Maeve, slowly taking rein of her senses.

"Were you injured while ashore?" Deirdre asked as if concerned.

"A mild case of frostbite, nothing more." Maeve gestured to the *Ice Hunter* crewmen who were lowering a launch. "I'll hitch a ride and meet you at the foot of the gangway."

"I'll be waiting." Deirdre smiled to herself and stepped back into the wheelhouse, where Pitt was talking over the radio to Dempsey. He nodded and smiled at her before signing off.

"Dempsey tells me Maeve is on her way over."

Deirdre nodded. "She was surprised to see me."

"A fortunate coincidence," said Pitt, noting for the first time that Deidre was nearly as tall as he, "that two friends are the only members of the crew still alive."

Deirdre shrugged. "We're hardly what you'd call friends."

He stared curiously into brown eyes that glinted from the sun's rays that shone through the forward window. "You dislike each other?"

"A matter of bad blood, Mr. Pitt," she said matter-of-factly. "You see, despite our different surnames, Maeve Fletcher and I are sisters."

10

The sea was thankfully calm when *Ice Hunter*, trailed by *Polar Queen*, slipped under the sheltering arm of Duse Bay and dropped anchor just offshore from the British research station. From his bridge, Dempsey instructed the skeleton crew on board the cruise ship to moor her a proper distance away so the two ships could swing on their anchors with the tides without endangering each other.

Still awake and barely steady on his feet, Pitt had not obeyed Sandecker's order that he have a peaceful sleep. There were still a hundred and one details to be attended to after he turned over operation of *Polar Queen* to Dempsey's crew. First he put Deirdre Dorsett in the boat with Maeve and sent them over to *Ice Hunter*. Then he spent the better part of the sunlit night making a thorough search of the ship, finding the dead he had missed on his brief walk-through earlier. He closed down the ship's heating system to help preserve the bodies for later examination, and only when *Polar Queen* was safely anchored under the protecting arm of the bay did he hand over command and return to the NUMA research ship. Giordino and Dempsey waited in the wheelhouse to greet and congratulate him. Giordino took one look at Pitt's exhausted condition and quickly poured him a cup of coffee from a nearby pot that was kept brewing at all times in the wheelhouse. Pitt gratefully accepted, sipped the steaming brew and stared over the rim of the cup toward a small craft with an outboard motor that was chugging toward the ship.

Almost before the anchor flukes of *Ice Hunter* had taken bite of the bottom, representatives from Ruppert & Saunders had departed their aircraft and boarded a Zodiac for the trip from shore. Within minutes they climbed aboard the lowered gangway and quickly climbed to the bridge, where Pitt, Dempsey and Giordino awaited them. One man cleared the steps three at a time and pulled up short, surveying the three men standing before him. He was big and ruddy and wore a smile a yard wide.

"Captain Dempsey?" he asked.

Dempsey stepped forward and extended his hand. "I'm he."

"Captain Ian Ryan, Chief of Operations for Ruppert & Saunders."

"Happy to have you aboard, Captain."

Ryan looked apprehensive. "My officers and I are here to take command of *Polar Queen*."

"She's all yours, Captain," Dempsey said easily. "If you don't mind, you can send back my crew in your boat once you're aboard."

Relief spread across Ryan's weathered face. It could have been a delicate situation. Legally, Dempsey was salvage master of the cruise ship. Command had passed to him from the dead captain and the owners. "Am I to understand, sir, that you are relinquishing command in favor of Ruppert & Saunders?"

"NUMA is not in the salvage business, Captain. We make no claim on *Polar Queen*."

"The directors of the company have asked me to express our deepest thanks and congratulations for your efforts in saving our passengers and ship."

Dempsey turned to Pitt and Giordino and introduced them. "These are the gentlemen who found the survivors on Seymour Island and kept your company's ship from running onto the Danger Island rocks."

Ryan pumped their hands vigorously, his grasp strong and beefy. "A remarkable achievement, absolutely remarkable. I assure you that Ruppert & Saunders will prove most generous in their gratitude."

Pitt shook his head. "We have been instructed by our boss at NUMA headquarters, Admiral James Sandecker, that we cannot accept any reward or salvage monies."

Ryan looked blank. "Nothing, nothing at all?"

"Not one cent," Pitt answered, fighting to keep his bleary eyes open.

"How bloody decent of you," Ryan gasped. "That's unheard of in the annals of marine salvage. I've no doubt our insurance carriers will drink to your health every year on the anniversary of the tragedy."

Dempsey gestured toward the passageway leading to his quarters. "While we're on the subject of drinks, Captain Ryan, may I offer you one in my cabin?"

Ryan nodded toward his officers, who were grouped behind him. "Does that include my crew?"

"It most certainly does," Dempsey said with a friendly smile.

"You save our ship, rescue our passengers and then stand us a drink. If you don't mind my saying so," said Ryan in a voice that seemed to come from his boots, "you Yanks are damned odd people."

"Not really," Pitt said, his green eyes twinkling through the weariness. "We're just lousy opportunists."

Pitt's movements were purely out of habit as he took a shower and shaved for the first time since before he and Giordino took off to find *Polar Queen*. He came within an eye blink of sagging to his knees and drifting asleep under the soothing splash of the warm water. Too tired even to dry his hair, he tucked a bath towel around his waist and stumbled to his queen-sized bed—no tight bunk or narrow berth on this ship—pulled back the covers, stretched out, laid his head on the pillow and was gone.

His unconscious mind didn't register the knock on his cabin door. Normally alert to the tiniest peculiar sound, he did not awaken or respond when the knock came a second time. He was so dead to the world there wasn't the slightest change in his breathing. Nor was there a flutter of his eyelids when Maeve slowly opened the door, peered hesitantly into the small anteroom and softly called his name.

"Mr. Pitt, are you about?"

Part of her wanted to leave, but curiosity drew her on. She moved in cautiously, carrying two short-stemmed snifter glasses and a bottle of Rémy Martin XO cognac loaned to her by Giordino from his private traveling stock. The excuse for her barging in like this was to properly thank Pitt for saving her life.

Startled, she caught her reflection in a mirror above a desk that folded from the wall. Her cheeks were flushed like those of a young girl waiting for her date to the high school prom to show up. It was a condition she'd seldom experienced before. Maeve turned away, angry at herself. She couldn't believe she was entering a man's quarters without being invited. She hardly knew Pitt. He was little more than a stranger. But Maeve was a lady used to striking out on her own.

Her father, the wealthy head of an international mining operation, had raised Maeve and her sisters as if they were boys, not girls. There were no dolls or fancy dresses or debutante balls. His departed wife had given him three daughters instead of sons to continue the family's financial empire, so he simply ignored fate and trained them to be tough. By the time she was eighteen, Maeve could kick a soccer ball farther than most men in her college class, and she once trekked across the outback of Australia from Canberra to Perth with only a dog, a domesticated dingo, for company, an accomplishment her father rewarded her for by pulling her out of school and putting her to work in the family mines alongside of hard-bodied male diggers and blasters. She rebelled. This was no life for a woman with other desires. She ran away to Melbourne and worked her way through university toward a career in zoology. Her father made no attempt to bring her back into the family fold. He merely abolished her claim to any family investments and pretended she never existed after her twins were born out of wedlock six months after a wonderful year she spent with a boy she met in class. He was the son of a sheep rancher, beautifully dark from the harsh outback sun, with a solid body and sensitive gray eyes. They had laughed, loved and fought constantly. When they inevitably parted, she never told him she was pregnant.

Maeve set the bottle and glasses on the desk and stared down at the personal things casually thrown among a stack of papers and a nautical chart. She peeked furtively into a cowhide wallet fat with assorted credit cards, business and membership cards, two blank personal checks and $123 in cash. How strange, she thought, there were no pictures. She laid the wallet back on the desk and studied the other items strewn about. There was a well-worn, orange-faced Doxa dive watch with a heavy stainless-steel band, and a mixed set of house and car keys. That was all.

Hardly enough to give her an insight into the man who owned them, she thought. There had been other men who had entered her life and departed, some at her request, a few on their own. But they all left something of themselves. This seemed to be a man who walked a lonely path, leaving nothing behind.

She stepped through the doorway into his sleeping quarters. The mirror above the sink in the bathroom behind was still fogged with steam, a sign that the occupant had recently bathed. She smelled a small whiff of men's aftershave, and it produced a strange tingle in her stomach.

"Mr. Pitt," she called out again, but not loudly. "Are you here?"

Then she saw the body laid out full length on the bed, arms loosely crossed over the chest as though he were lying in a coffin. She breathed a sigh of relief at seeing that his loins were covered by a bath towel. "I'm sorry," she said very softly. "Forgive me for disturbing you."

Pitt slept on without responding.

Her eyes traveled from his head to his feet. The black mass of curly hair was still damp and tousled. His eyebrows were thick, almost bushy, and came close to meeting above a straight nose. She guessed he was somewhere in the neighborhood of forty, though the craggy features, the tanned and weathered skin and chiseled, unyielding jawline made him seem older. Small wrinkles around the eyes and lips turned up, giving him the look of a man who was perpetually smiling. It was a strong face, the kind of face women are drawn to. He looked like a man of strength and determination, the kind of man who had seen the best of times and worst of times but never sidestepped whatever life threw at him.

The rest of his body was firm and smooth except for a dark patch of hair on his chest. The shoulders were broad, the stomach flat, the hips narrow. The muscles of his arms and legs were pronounced but not thick or bulging. The body was not powerful but tended on the wiry side, even rangy. There was a tenseness that suggested a spring that was waiting to uncoil. And then there were the scars. She couldn't begin to imagine where they came from.

He did not seem cut from the same mold as the other men she had known. She hadn't really loved any of them, sleeping with them out of curiosity and rebellion against her father more than passionate desire. Even when she became pregnant by a fellow student, she refused an abortion to spite her father and carried her twin sons to birth.

Now, staring down at the sleeping man in the bed, she felt a strange pleasure and power at standing over his nakedness. She lifted the lower edge of the towel, smiled devilishly to herself, and let it fall back in place. Maeve found Pitt immensely attractive and wanted him, yes, feverishly and shamelessly wanted him.

"See something you like, little sister," came a quiet, husky voice from behind her.

Chagrined, Maeve spun and stared at Deirdre, who leaned casually against the doorway, smoking a cigarette.

"What are you doing here?" she demanded in a whisper.

"Keeping you from biting off more than you can chew."

"Very funny." In a motherly gesture, Maeve pulled the covers over Pitt's body and tucked them under the mattress. Then she turned and physically pushed Deirdre into the anteroom before softly closing the bedroom door. "Why are you following me? Why didn't you return to Australia with the other passengers?"

"I might ask the same of you, dear sister."

"The ship's scientists asked me to remain on board and make out a report of my experience with the death plague."

"And I remained because I thought we might kiss and make up," Deirdre said, drawing on her cigarette.

"There was a time I might have believed you. But not now."

"I admit there were other considerations."

"How did you manage to stay out of my sight during the weeks we were at sea?"

"Would you believe I remained in my cabin with an upset stomach."

"That's so much rot," snapped Maeve. "You have the constitution of a horse. I've never known you to be sick."

Deirdre looked around for an ashtray, and finding none, opened the cabin door and flipped her cigarette over the railing into the sea. "Aren't you the least bit amazed at my miraculous survival?"

Maeve stared into her eyes, confused and uncertain. "You told everyone you were in the freezer."

"Rather good timing, don't you think?"

"You were incredibly lucky."

"Luck had nothing to do with it," Deirdre contradicted. "What about yourself? Didn't it ever occur to you how you came to be in the whaling station caves at exactly the right moment?"

"What are you implying?"

"You don't understand, do you?" Deirdre said as if scolding a naughty child. "Did you think Daddy was going to forgive and forget after you stormed out of his office, swearing never to see any one of us again? He especially went mad when he heard that you had legally changed your name to that of our great-great-great-grandmother. Fletcher, indeed. Since you left, he's had your every movement observed from the time you entered Melbourne University until you were employed by Ruppert & Saunders."

Maeve stared at her with anger and disbelief that faded as something began to dawn slowly in her mind. "He was that afraid that I would talk to the wrong people about his filthy business operations?"

"Whatever unorthodox means Daddy has used to further the family empire was for your benefit as well as Boudicca and myself."

"Boudicca!" Maeve spat. "Our sister, the devil incarnate."

"Think what you may," Deirdre said impassively, "Boudicca has always had your best interests at heart."

"If you believe that, you're a bigger fool than I gave you credit for."

"It was Boudicca who talked Daddy into sparing your life by insisting I go along on the voyage."

"Sparing my life?" Maeve looked lost. "You're not making sense."

"Who do you think arranged for the ship's captain to send you ashore with the first excursion?"

"You?"

"Me."

"It was my turn to go ashore. The other lecturers and I worked in sequence."

Deirdre shook her head. "If they had stuck to the proper schedule, you'd have been placed in charge of the second shore party that never got off the ship."

"So what was your reasoning?"

"An act of timing," said Deirdre, suddenly turning cold. "Daddy's people calculated that the phenomenon would appear when the first shore party was safe inside the whaling station storage caves."

Maeve felt the deck reeling beneath her feet, and the color drained out of her cheeks. "No way he could have predicted the terrible event," she gasped.

"A smart man, our father," Deirdre said calmly as if she were gossiping with a friend over the telephone. "If not for his advance planning, how do you think I knew when to lock myself in the ship's freezer?"

"How could he possibly know when and where the plague would strike?" she asked skeptically.

"Our father," Deirdre said, baring her teeth in a savage smile, "is not a stupid man."

Maeve's fury seethed throughout her body. "If he had any suspicions, he should have given a warning and averted the slaughter," she snapped.

"Daddy has more important business than to fuss over a boat-load of dismal tourists."

"I swear before God I'll see that you all pay for your callousness."

"You'd betray the family?" Deirdre shrugged sarcastically, then answered her own question. "Yes, I believe you would."

"Bet on it."

"Never happen, not if you want to see your precious sons again."

"Sean and Michael are where Father will never find them."

"Call in the dogs if you have a mind to, but hiding the twins with that teacher in Perth was not really all that clever."

"You're bluffing."

"Your flesh-and-blood sister, Boudicca, merely persuaded the teacher and his wife, the Hollenders as I recall their name, to allow her to take the twins on a picnic."

Maeve trembled and felt she was going to be sick as the full enormity of the revelation engulfed her. "You have them?"

"The boys? Of course."

"The Hollenders, if she so much as hurt them—"

"Nothing of the sort."

"Sean and Michael, what have you done with them?"

"Daddy is taking very good care of them on our private island. He's even teaching them the diamond trade. Cheer up. The worst that can happen is that they suffer some type of accident. You know better than anybody the risks children run, playing around mining tunnels. The bright side is that if you stand with the family, your boys will someday become incredibly wealthy and powerful men."

"Like Daddy?" Maeve cried in outrage and fear. "I'd rather they die." She subdued the urge to kill her sister and sat heavily in a chair, broken and defeated.

"They could do worse," said Deirdre, gloating over Maeve's helplessness. "String along your friends from NUMA for a few days, and keep your mouth shut about what I've told you. Then we'll catch a flight for home." She walked to the door and turned. "I think you'll find Daddy most forgiving, providing you ask forgiveness and demonstrate your loyalty to the family." Then she stepped onto the outside deck and out of sight.

PART II

WHERE
DREAMS
COME FROM

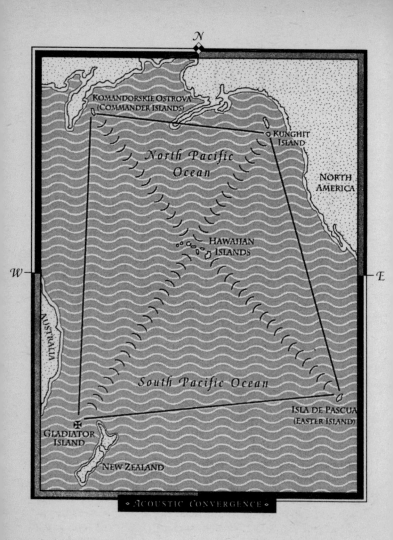

KOMANDORSKIE OSTROVA
(COMMANDER ISLANDS)

North Pacific
Ocean

KUNGHIT
ISLAND

NORTH
AMERICA

HAWAIIAN
ISLANDS

W

E

AUSTRALIA

South Pacific Ocean

ISLA DE PASCUA
(EASTER ISLAND)

GLADIATOR
ISLAND

NEW ZEALAND

◊ ACOUSTIC CONVERGENCE ◊

11

Admiral Sandecker seldom used the large board room for conferences. He reserved it mainly for visiting congressmen and -women, and respected scientists, foreign and American. For internal NUMA business, he preferred a smaller workroom just off his office. It was an extremely comfortable room, uniquely his own, sort of a hideaway for him to hold informal but confidential meetings with his NUMA directors. Sandecker often used it as an executive dining room, he and his directors relaxing in the soft leather chairs set around a three-meter-long conference table built from a section of a wooden hull salvaged from a schooner on the bottom of Lake Erie and solidly set in a thick turquoise carpet in front of a fireplace surrounded by a Victorian mantelpiece.

Unlike the modern design and decor of the other offices in the NUMA headquarters building, which were encased in soaring walls of green-tinted glass, this room looked as if it was straight out of an antiquated London gentlemen's club. All four walls and ceiling were richly paneled in a satiny teak, and there were paintings of United States naval actions hung in ornate frames.

There was a beautifully detailed painting of the epic battle between John Paul Jones in the woefully armed *Bonhomme Richard* and the new British fifty-gun frigate, *Serapis*. Next to it the venerable American frigate *Constitution* was demasting the British frigate *Java*. On the opposite wall the Civil War ironclads *Monitor* and *Virginia*, better known as the *Merrimac*, slugged it out. Commodore Dewey destroying the Spanish fleet in Manila Bay and a flight of dive bombers taking off from the carrier *Enterprise* to bomb the Japanese fleet during the Battle of Midway were mounted side by side. Only the painting above the fireplace lacked a sea battle. It was a portrait of Sandecker in casual uniform before he was promoted and thrown on the beach. Below the portrait, in a glass-enclosed case, sat a model of his last command, the missile cruiser *Tucson*.

After Sandecker's retirement, a former President of the United States picked him to organize and establish a newly funded government agency dedicated to research of the sea. Beginning in a rented warehouse with a staff of fewer than a dozen people, including Pitt and Giordino, Sandecker had built NUMA into a huge organization that was the envy of oceanographic institutions around the world, manned by two thousand employees, and with a huge budget rarely questioned and almost always approved by Congress.

Sandecker fought advancing age with a passion. Now in his early sixties, he was a fitness nut who jogged, lifted weights and engaged in any kind of exercise so long as it brought about sweat and an increased heartbeat. The results of strenuous workouts and a nutritious diet were readily apparent in his honed and trim shape. He was slightly under what would be called average height, and his flaming red hair was still full, cut close and slicked down, with a razor-edge part on the left side. The taut, narrow shape of his face was accented by piercing hazel eyes and a Vandyke beard that was an exact match in color for the hair on his head.

Sandecker's only vice was cigars. He loved to smoke ten grandly large cigars a day, specially selected and wrapped to his personal taste. He stepped into the conference room in a cloud of smoke as if he were a magician materializing on a fog-shrouded stage.

He walked to the head of the table and smiled benignly at the two men seated to his left and right. "Sorry to keep you so late, gentlemen, but I wouldn't have asked you to work overtime unless it was important."

Hiram Yaeger, the chief of NUMA's computer network and overseer to the world's most expansive data library on marine sciences, leaned his chair back on two legs and nodded toward Sandecker. Whenever a problem needed solving, Sandecker always started with Yaeger. Unperturbed in bib overalls and a ponytail, he lived with his wife and daughters in a ritzy section of the capital and drove a nonproduction BMW. "It was either respond to your request," he said with a slight twinkle in his eye, "or take my wife to the ballet."

"Either way, you lose," laughed Rudi Gunn, NUMA's executive director and second in command. If Dirk Pitt was Sandecker's ace troubleshooter, Gunn was his organizational wizard. Thin with slim hips and narrow shoulders, humorous as well as bright, he peered through thick horn-rimmed glasses from eyes that suggested an owl waiting for a field mouse to run under his tree.

Sandecker slid into one of the leather chairs, dropped an ash from his cigar into a dish made from an abalone shell and flattened a chart of the Weddell Sea and the Antarctic Peninsula on the surface of the table. He tapped his finger on a marked circle with a series of small red crosses drawn within its circumference and labeled by number. "Gentlemen, you're all familiar with the tragic situation in the Weddell Sea, the latest in a series of kill sites. Number one is the position where *Ice Hunter* found the dead dolphins. Two, the seal kills off South Orkney Island. Three, Seymour Island, the site of mass slaughter of men, women, penguins and seals. And four, the approximate position of *Polar Queen* when the scourge struck."

Yaeger studied the perimeter of the circle. "Looks to be about ninety kilometers in diameter."

"Not good," Gunn said, a deep frown creasing his forehead. "That's twice the size of the last kill zone, near Chirikof Island off the Aleutians."

"The count was over three thousand sea lions and five fishermen in that disaster," said Sandecker. He lifted a small remote control from the table, aimed it at a small panel in the far wall and pressed a button. A large screen slowly dropped from the ceiling. He pressed another button and a computer-generated chart of the

Pacific Ocean appeared in three-dimensional holograph. Several blue, neonlike globes, displaying animated fish and mammals, were projected seemingly from outside the screen and spaced in different areas of the chart. The globe over Seymour Island off the Antarctic Peninsula as well as one near Alaska included human figures. "Until three days ago," Sandecker continued, "all the reported kill zones have been in the Pacific. Now with the sea around Seymour Island, we have a new one in the South Atlantic."

"That makes eight appearances of the unknown plague in the past four months," said Gunn. "The occurrences seem to be intensifying."

Sandecker studied his cigar. "And not one lead to the source."

"Frustration is mine," Yaeger said holding his palms up in a helpless gesture. "I've tried a hundred different computer-generated projections. Nothing comes close to fitting the puzzle. No known disease or chemical pollution can travel thousands of miles, pop up out of the blue and kill every living thing within a limited area, before totally vanishing without a trace."

"I've got thirty scientists working on the problem," said Gunn, "and they have yet to stumble on a clue indicating a source."

"Anything from the pathologists on those five fishermen the Coast Guard found dead on their boat off Chirikof Island?" asked Sandecker.

"Preliminary postmortem examinations show no tissue damage from poison, inhaled or ingested, nor any fast-acting disease that's known to medical science. As soon as Colonel Hunt over at the Walter Reed Army Medical Center has completed his report, I'll have him call you."

"Dammit!" Sandecker burst out. "Something killed them. The skipper died in the wheelhouse, his hands gripped on the helm, while the crew went down on deck in the act of bringing in their nets. People just don't drop dead without cause, certainly not hardy men in their twenties and thirties."

Yaeger nodded in agreement. "Maybe we're looking in the wrong place. It has to be something we haven't considered."

Sandecker idly stared at his cigar smoke as it spiraled toward the paneled ceiling. He seldom laid his all cards on the table, preferring to turn them over slowly, one at a time. "I was talking to Dirk just before our meeting."

"Anything new at his end?" asked Gunn.

"Not from the biologists on board *Ice Hunter*, but Dirk has a theory, pretty farfetched he admits, but one none of us had thought of."

"I'd like to hear it," said Yaeger.

"He came up with a type of pollution."

Gunn looked at Sandecker, his eyes skeptical. "What type of pollution could he possibly suggest that we missed?"

Sandecker grinned like a sniper sighting through his scope. "Noise," he answered flatly.

"Noise," repeated Gunn. "What kind of noise?"

"He thinks there might be deadly sound waves that travel through water for hundreds, perhaps thousands of miles, before they surface and kill everything within a certain radius." Sandecker paused and studied his subordinates for their reaction.

Yaeger was not a cynical man, but he inclined his head and laughed. "I'm afraid old Pitt is hitting his special brand of tequila too hard and too fast."

Oddly, there was not a hint of doubt on Gunn's face. He peered intently at the projected image of the Pacific Ocean for a few moments. Then he said, "I think Dirk is onto something."

Yaeger's eyes narrowed. "You do?"

"I do," Gunn replied earnestly. "Rogue underwater acoustics might very well be our villain."

"I'm happy to hear another vote," said Sandecker. "When he first laid it on me, I thought Dirk's mind was sluggish from exhaustion. But the more I considered his theory, the more I came to believe in its possibilities."

"Word has it," said Yaeger, "that he single-handedly saved *Polar Queen* from running onto the rocks."

Gunn nodded. "It's true. After Al dropped him from a helicopter onto the ship, he steered it away from certain destruction."

"Back to the dead fishermen," Sandecker said, returning the conference to a more somber note. "How long before we have to turn their bodies over to local Alaskan authorities?"

"About five minutes after they learn we have them," replied Gunn. "The crewmen on the Coast Guard cutter that discovered the ship drifting in the Gulf of Alaska will surely talk once they dock at their station in Kodiak and come ashore."

"Even after their captain has ordered them to remain quiet," said Sandecker.

"We're not at war, Admiral. The Coast Guard is highly regarded in northern waters. They won't enjoy being party to a cover-up against men whose lives they are committed to saving. A couple of drinks at the Yukon Saloon and they'll break the news to anyone who will listen."

Sandecker sighed. "I suppose you're right. Commandant Mac-Intyre was not happy about the secrecy. It wasn't until he received a direct order from the secretary of defense that he caved in and turned the bodies over to NUMA scientists."

Yaeger gave Sandecker a knowing look. "I wonder who got to the secretary of defense?"

Sandecker smiled slyly. "After I explained the seriousness of the situation, he was most cooperative."

"Much hell will erupt," Yaeger prophesied, "once the local brotherhood of fishermen and the dead crew's family members discover that the bodies were found and autopsies performed a week before they were notified."

"Especially," Gunn added, "when they learn we shipped the bodies to Washington for the postmortem."

"We were too early in the hunt for the news media to play havoc with wild stories about how an entire crew and their pet parrot were found dead on a ship under mysterious circumstances. At the time, we didn't need another unexplained-phenomena blitz while we were groping in the dark ourselves."

Gunn shrugged. "The proverbial cat's out of the bag now. There's no hiding the *Polar Queen* disaster. After tonight it will be the lead news story on every TV news program around the world."

Sandecker nodded at Yaeger. "Hiram, you delve into your library and extract every piece of data dealing with underwater acoustics. Search out any experiments, commercial or military, involving high-energy sound waves through water, their cause and effects on humans and underwater mammals."

"I'll start on it immediately," Yaeger assured him.

Gunn and Yaeger rose from their chairs and left the conference room. Sandecker sat there, slouched in his chair and puffing on his cigar. His eyes moved from sea battle to sea battle, lingering for several moments on each before moving to the next. Then he closed his eyes tightly as he collected his thoughts.

It was the uncertainty of the dilemma that clouded his mind. After a while, he opened his eyes and stared at the computer-generated chart of the Pacific Ocean. "Where will it strike next?" he spoke aloud to the empty room. "Who will it kill?"

Colonel Leigh Hunt sat at his desk in his basement office—he disliked the more formal administration offices on the upper floors of Walter Reed—and contemplated a bottle of Cutty Sark. Out the window, darkness had settled over the District of Columbia, the streetlights had come on, and the rush-hour traffic was beginning to dwindle. The postmortems on the five fishermen fished from the cold waters of the Northwest were completed, and he was about to head home to his cat. The decision was whether to take a drink or make a final call before leaving. He decided to do both at the same time.

He punched the numbers on his telephone with one hand while he poured the scotch into a coffee cup. After two rings, a gruff voice answered.

"Colonel Hunt, I hope that's you."

"It is," replied Hunt. "How'd you know?"

"I had a gut feeling you'd call about now."

"Always a pleasure to talk to the Navy," said Hunt affably.

"What can you tell me?" asked Sandecker.

"First, are you sure these cadavers were found on a fishing boat in the middle of the sea?"

"They were."

"And the two porpoises and four seals you also sent over here?"

"Where else would you expect to find them?"

"I've never performed postmortem examinations on aquatic creatures before."

"Humans, porpoises and seals are all mammals under the skin."

"You, my dear admiral, have a very intriguing case on your hands."

"What did they die from?"

Hunt paused to empty half the cup. "Clinically, the deaths were caused by a disruption of the ossicular chain that consists of the malleus, incus and the stapes of the middle ear, which you may recall from your high school physiology class as the hammer, anvil and stirrup. The stapedial foot plate was also fractured. This caused debilitating vertigo and extreme tinnitus, or a roaring in the ears, all culminating in a rupture of the anterior inferior cerebellar artery and causing hemorrhaging into the anterior and middle cranial fossae inside the base of the skull."

"Can you break that down into simple English?"

"Are you familiar with the term 'infarction'?" asked Hunt.

"It sounds like slang."

"Infarction is a cluster of dead cells in organs or tissue that results from an obstruction, such as an air bubble, that cuts off circulating blood."

"Just where in the bodies did this thing take place?" inquired Sandecker.

"There was swelling of the cerebellum with compression of the brain stem. I also found that the vestibular labyrinth—"

"Come again?"

"Besides relating to other bodily cavities, 'vestibular' also pertains to the central cavity of the bony labyrinth of the ear."

"Please go on."

"The vestibular labyrinth appeared to be damaged by violent displacement. Somewhat as in a fall into deep water, where the hydraulic compression of air perforates the tympanic membrane as water is forced into the external ear canal."

"How did you arrive at this conclusion?"

"By applying a standard protocol to my investigation, I used magnetic resonance imaging and computer tomography, a diagnostic technique using X-ray photographs that eliminate the shadows of structures in front of and behind the section under scrutiny. Evaluation also included hematologic and serologic studies and lumbar puncture."

"What were the symptoms at the onset of the disorder?"

"I can't speak for the porpoises or seals," explained Hunt. "But the pattern among the humans was consistent. The sudden and intense vertigo, a dramatic loss of equilibrium, vomiting, extreme paroxysmal cranial pain and a sudden convulsion that lasted less than five minutes, all resulting in unconsciousness and then death. You might compare it to a stroke of monster proportions."

"Can you tell me what caused this trauma?"

Hunt hesitated. "Not with any degree of accuracy."

Sandecker was not to be put off. "Take a wild guess."

"Since you've put my back to the wall, I'd venture to say your fishermen, the porpoises and seals expired from extreme exposure to high-intensity sound."

12

To the crew lining the rails of *Mentawai*, an Indonesian freighter bound from Honolulu to her next port of call, Jayapura in New Guinea, the sight of an awkward-looking craft in the middle of the ocean was highly unusual if not downright remarkable. Yet the Ningpo-design Chinese junk sailed serenely through the one-meter-high swells that rolled against her bow from the east. She looked magnificent, her brightly colored sails filled with a southwesterly breeze, her varnished wood sparkling under a golden-orange rising sun. Two large eyes that crossed when sighted head-on were painted on her bows, born from the traditional faith that they would see her through fog and stormy seas.

The *Tz'u-hsi*, named after the last Chinese dowager empress, was the second home of Hollywood actor Garret Converse, never a nominee for an Academy Award but the biggest box-office action hero on the silver screen. The junk was twenty-four meters in length with a beam of six meters, built from top to bottom of cedar- and teakwood. Converse had installed every amenity for the crew's accommodations and the latest in navigational technology. No expense was spared. Few yachts were as luxuriously embellished. A master adventurer in the mode of Errol Flynn, Converse had sailed *Tz'u-hsi* from Newport Beach on a round-the-world cruise and was now running on the final leg across the Pacific, passing within fifty kilometers of Howland Island, Amelia Earhart's destination when she disappeared in 1937.

As the two ships plodded past each other on opposite courses, Converse hailed the freighter over the radio.

"Greetings from the junk *Tz'u-hsi*. What ship are you?"

The freighter's radio operator replied, "The freighter *Mentawai* out of Honolulu. Where are you bound?"

"Christmas Island, and then to California."

"I wish you clear sailing."

"The same to you," Converse answered.

The captain of *Mentawai* watched the junk slip astern and then nodded toward his first officer. "I never thought I'd see a junk this deep in the Pacific."

The first officer, a man of Chinese descent, nodded disapprovingly. "I crewed on a junk when I was a young boy. They're taking a great risk sailing through the breeding grounds of typhoons. Junks are not built for heavy weather. They ride too high and have a tendency to roll crazily. Their huge rudders are easily broken off by a rough sea."

"They're either very brave or very mad to tempt the fates," said the captain, turning his back on the junk as it grew smaller in the distance. "As for me, I feel more comfortable with a steel hull and the solid beat of engines under my decks."

Eighteen minutes after the freighter and junk crossed paths, a distress call was heard by the United States container carrier *Rio Grande,* bound for Sydney, Australia, with a cargo of tractors and agricultural equipment. The radio room was directly off the spacious navigation bridge, and the operator had only to turn to address the second officer, who stood the early morning watch.

"Sir, I have a distress signal from the Indonesian cargo freighter *Mentawai.*"

The second officer, George Hudson, picked up the ship's phone, punched a number and waited for an answering voice. "Captain, we've picked up a distress signal."

Captain Jason Kelsey was about to take his first forkful of breakfast in his cabin when the call came from the bridge. "Very well, Mr. Hudson. I'm on my way. Try and get her position."

146

Kelsey wolfed down his eggs and ham, gulped half a cup of coffee and walked through a short passageway to the navigation bridge. He went directly to the radio room.

The operator looked up, a curious look in his eyes. "Very strange signal, Captain." He handed Kelsey a notepad.

Kelsey studied it, then stared at the radio operator. "Are you sure this is what they transmitted?"

"Yes, sir. They came in quite clearly."

Kelsey read the message aloud. "All ships come quick. Freighter *Mentawai* forty kilometers south-southwest of Howland Island. Come quick. All are dying." He looked up. "Nothing more? No coordinates?"

The radio operator shook his head. "They went dead, and I haven't been able to raise them again."

"Then we can't use our radio direction-finding systems." Kelsey turned to his second officer. "Mr. Hudson, lay a course for *Mentawai*'s last reported position southwest off Howland Island. Not much to go on without exact coordinates. But if we can't make a visual sighting, we'll have to rely on our radar to spot them." He could have asked Hudson to run the course numbers through the navigation computer, but he preferred working by the old rules.

Hudson went to work on the chart table with parallel rulers, attached by swinging hinges, and a pair of dividers, and Kelsey signaled the chief engineer that he wanted *Rio Grande* to come to full speed. First Officer Hank Sherman appeared on the bridge, yawning as he buttoned his shirt.

"We're responding to a distress call?" he asked Kelsey.

The captain smiled and passed him the notepad. "Word travels fast on this ship."

Hudson turned from the chart table. "I make the distance to *Mentawai* approximately sixty-five kilometers, bearing one-three-two degrees."

Kelsey stepped over to the navigation console and punched in the coordinates. Almost immediately the big container ship began a slow swing to starboard as the computerized electronics system steered her onto a new course of 132 degrees.

"Any other ships responding?" he asked the radio operator.

"We're the only one who attempted a reply, sir."

Kelsey stared at the deck. "We should be able to reach her in a shade less than two hours."

Sherman continued staring at the message in bewilderment. "If this isn't some kind of hoax, it's very possible that all we'll find are corpses."

They found *Mentawai* a few minutes after eight in the morning. Unlike *Polar Queen,* which had continued steaming under power, the Indonesian freighter appeared to be drifting. She looked peaceful and businesslike. Smoke curled from her twin funnels, but no one was visible on the decks, and repeated hails through a loudspeaker from the bridge of *Rio Grande* brought no response.

"Quiet as a tomb," said First Officer Sherman ominously.

"Good Lord!" muttered Kelsey. "She's surrounded by a sea of dead fish."

"I don't much like the look of it."

"You'd better collect a boarding party and investigate," ordered Kelsey.

"Yes, sir. On my way."

Second Officer Hudson was peering at the horizon through binoculars. "There's another ship about ten kilometers off the port bow."

"Is she coming on?" asked Kelsey.

"No, sir. She seems to be moving away."

"That's odd. Why would she ignore a ship in distress? Can you make her out?"

"She looks like a fancy yacht, a big one with sleek lines. The design you see moored in Monaco or Hong Kong."

Kelsey moved to the threshold of the radio-room doorway and nodded to the operator. "See if you can raise that boat in the distance."

After a minute or two, the radio operator shook his head. "Not a peep. They've either closed down, or they're ignoring us."

The *Rio Grande* slackened speed and glided slowly toward the freighter rolling slowly in the low swells. They were very close to the lifeless ship now, and from the bridge wing of the big container ship, Captain Kelsey could look straight down on her decks. He saw two inert figures and what he took to be a small dog. He hailed the wheelhouse again, but all was silent.

The boat with Sherman's boarding party was lowered into the water and motored over to the freighter. They bumped and scraped alongside as they heaved a grappling hook over the railing and rigged it to pull up a boarding ladder. Within minutes, Sherman was over the side and bending over the bodies on the deck. Then he disappeared through a hatch below the bridge.

Four of the men had followed him while two remained in the boat and motored away from the hull a short distance, waiting for a signal to return and pick them up. Even after Sherman made certain the men lying on the deck were dead, he still half expected some of the freighter's crew to be waiting for him. After entering the hatch, he climbed a passageway to the bridge and was overwhelmed with a sense of unreality. All hands from the captain to the mess boy were dead, their corpses strewn about the deck where they fell. The radioman was found with his eyes bulging and his hands clasped around his set as if he were afraid of falling.

Twenty minutes passed before Sherman eased *Mentawai*'s radio operator to the floor and called over to the *Rio Grande*. "Captain Kelsey?"

"Go ahead, Mr. Sherman. What have you found?"

"All dead, sir, every one of them, including two parakeets found in the chief engineer's cabin and the ship's dog, a beagle with its teeth bared."

"Any clue as to the cause?"

"Food poisoning seems the most obvious. They look like they threw up before they died."

"Be careful of toxic gas."

"I'll keep my nostrils open," said Sherman.

Kelsey paused, contemplating the unexpected predicament. Then he said, "Send back the boat. I'll have it return with another five men to help you get the ship under way. The nearest major port is Apia in the Samoa Islands. We'll turn the ship over to authorities there."

"What about the bodies of the crew? We can't leave them lying around, certainly not in the tropical heat."

Without hesitation, Kelsey replied, "Stack them in the freezer. We want them preserved until they can be examined by—"

Kelsey was abruptly cut off in midsentence as *Mentawai*'s hull shuddered from an explosion from deep inside her bowels. The hatches above the cargo holds were thrown skyward as flame and smoke erupted from below. The ship seemed to heave herself out of the water before splashing back and taking on a sharp list to starboard. The roof of the wheelhouse collapsed inward. There was another deep rumble inside the freighter, followed by the screeching sound of tearing metal.

Kelsey watched in horror as the *Mentawai* began to roll over on her starboard side. "She's going down!" he shouted over the radio. "Get out of there before she goes under!"

Sherman was flat on the deck, stunned from the concussion of the blast. He looked around, dazed, as the deck slanted steeply. He slid into one corner of the shattered radio compartment and sat there in shock, staring dumbly as water surged through the open door to the bridge wing. It was an unreal picture that made no sense to his stunned mind. He took one long gasping breath that was the last he ever took, and tried feebly to rise to his feet, but it was too late. He was buried under the warm, green water of the sea.

Kelsey and the crew of *Rio Grande* stood frozen in shock as *Mentawai* rolled over with her hull showing above the water like some giant, rusting metal turtle. Except for the two men in the boat who were crushed by the hull, Sherman's boarding party was trapped inside the ship when the explosions occurred. None escaped to dive over the side. With a great roar of inrushing water and expelled air, the freighter dived beneath the surface as if anxious to become one more unsolved enigma of the sea.

No one on board *Rio Grande* could believe the freighter could go so quickly. They stared in horror at the wreckage mixed with wisps of smoke that swirled around her watery crypt, unable to believe their shipmates were locked inside a steel coffin hurtling toward eternal darkness at the bottom of the sea.

Kelsey stood there for nearly a full minute, the grief and outrage etched in his face. Somehow a tiny thought in the back of his mind finally mushroomed and emerged through the shock. He turned from the whirlpool of death, picked up a pair of binoculars and stared through the forward windows at the yacht vanishing in the distance. Now only a white speck against a blue sky and an azure sea, it was moving away at great speed. The mysterious vessel had not ignored the distress signal, he realized. It had come and gone and was now purposely running away from the disaster.

"Damn whoever you are," he spat in anger. "Damn you to hell."

•   •   •

Thirty-one days later, Ramini Tantoa, a native of Cooper Island in the Palmyra Atoll chain, awoke, and as was his usual routine went for a morning swim in the warm waters of the East Lagoon. Before he took two steps in the white sand outside his small bachelor hut, he was astonished to see what he recognized as a large Chinese junk that had somehow sailed through the outer reef channel during the night and was now grounded broadside on the beach. The port beam was already high and dry and imbedded in the sand, while the opposite side of the hull was lapped by the gentle waves of the lagoon.

Tantoa shouted a hello, but no one appeared on deck or echoed a reply. The junk looked deserted. All sails were set and fluttering under a light breeze, and the flag that flapped on the stern was the Stars and Stripes of the United States. The varnish on the teak sides looked shiny, as if it hadn't had time to fade under the sun. As he walked around the half-buried hull Tantoa felt as if the painted eyes on the bows followed him.

He finally worked up his nerve and climbed the huge rudder and over the stern railing onto the quarterdeck. He stood there disconcerted. From stem to stern the main deck was deserted. Everything seemed in perfect order, all lines coiled and in place, the rigging set and taut. Nothing lay loose on the deck.

Tantoa climbed below and walked fearfully through the interior of the junk, half expecting to find bodies. Thankfully he saw no signs of death or disorder. Not a single soul was on board.

No ship could sail from China, halfway across the Pacific Ocean, without a crew, Tantoa told himself. His imagination took hold, and he began to envision ghosts. A ship sailed by a spectral crew. Frightened, he rushed up the stairs onto the deck and leaped over the railing onto the warm sand. He had to report the derelict to the council of Cooper Island's little village. Tantoa ran up the beach to what he believed was a safe distance before staring over his shoulder to see if he was followed by some unspeakable horror.

The sand around the junk was deserted. Only the all-seeing eyes on the bows glared at him malevolently. Tantoa raced off toward his village and never looked back.

13

The atmosphere in the *Ice Hunter*'s dining room had a strange mood of subdued festivity. The occasion was a farewell party thrown by the crew and scientists for the survivors of the *Polar Queen* tragedy. Roy Van Fleet and Maeve had been working day and night, shoulder to shoulder, for the past three days, examining the remains of the penguins, seals and dolphins collected for study and filling notebooks full of observations.

Van Fleet had grown fond of her, but he stopped short of demonstrating any kind of affection; the vision of his pretty wife and three children was seldom out of his mind. He was sorry they couldn't have continued working together. The other scientists in the lab agreed that they made a great team.

The *Ice Hunter*'s chef did himself proud with an incredible gourmet dinner featuring filets of deep-sea cod with mushroom and wine sauce. Captain Dempsey looked the other way while the wine flowed. Only the officers standing watch over the operation of the ship had to remain dry, at least until they came off duty and it was their turn to party.

Dr. Mose Greenberg, the shipboard wit, made a long speech

laced with banal puns about everyone on board. He might have kept pontificating for another hour if Dempsey hadn't signaled for the chef to bring out a cake especially baked for the occasion. It was shaped like the continent of Australia, with icing picturing the more notable landmarks including Ayres Rock and Sydney Harbor. Maeve was truly touched, and tears moistened her eyes. Deirdre appeared bored with it all.

As captain, Dempsey sat at the head of the longest table, the women sitting in honor at his elbows. Because he was head of NUMA's special-projects division, Pitt was allotted the chair at the opposite end of the table. He tuned out the conversations flowing around him and focused his attention on the two sisters.

They couldn't have come out of the womb more unalike, he thought. Maeve was a warm and wild creature, a light brightly glowing with life. He fantasized her as a friend's untamed sister washing a car, clad in a tight T-shirt and cutoff shorts while displaying her girlish waist and shapely legs to great advantage. She had changed since he first met her. She talked exuberantly, her arms swaying for effect, vivacious and unpretentious. And yet her manner seemed oddly forced, as if her thoughts were elsewhere and she were under some unknown stress.

She wore a short-skirted red cocktail dress that fit her figure as if it were sewn on after she was in it. Pitt thought at first it was loaned to her by one of the women scientists on board who wore a smaller size, and then he recalled seeing her return with Deirdre from *Polar Queen* on *Ice Hunter*'s shore boat with their luggage stacked in the bow. She wore yellow coral earrings that matched the necklace around her bare neck. She glanced in his direction and their eyes met, but only for an instant. She was in the midst of describing her pet dingo in Australia, and she quickly looked back at her audience as if she hadn't recognized him.

Deirdre, on the other hand, exuded sensuality and sophistication, traits sensed by every man in the room. Pitt could easily picture her stretched out on a bed covered with silk sheets, beckoning. The only drawback was her imperious manner. She had seemed retiring and vulnerable when he'd found her on *Polar Queen*. But she too had transformed, into a cool and aloof creature. There was also a flinty hardness Pitt had not recognized before.

She sat in her chair straight-backed and regal in a brown sheath dress that stopped discreetly above her silk-stockinged knees.

She wore a scarf around her neck that accented her fawn eyes and copper hair, which was drawn severely back in a huge knot. As if sensing that Pitt was studying her, she slowly turned and stared back at him without expression, and then the eyes became cool and calculating.

Pitt found himself engaged in a game of wills. She was not about to blink even as she carried on a conversation with Dempsey. Her eyes seemed to look through him and, finding nothing of interest, continued on to a picture hanging on the wall behind. The brown eyes that were locked on opaline green never wavered. She obviously was a lady who held her own against men, Pitt reasoned. Slowly, very slowly, he began to cross his eyes. The comical ploy broke the spell and Deirdre's concentration. Thrusting her chin up in a haughty gesture, she dismissed Pitt as a clown and turned her attention back to the conversation at her end of the table.

Though Pitt felt a sensual desire for Deirdre, he felt himself drawn to Maeve. Perhaps it was her engaging smile with the slight gap between the teeth, or the beautiful mass of incredibly blond hair that fell in a cascade behind and in front of her shoulders. He wondered about her shift of manner since he first found her in the blizzard on Seymour Island. The ready smile and the easy laugh were no longer there. Pitt sensed that Maeve was subtly under Deirdre's control. It was also obvious, to him if to no one else, there was no love lost between them.

Pitt mused about the age-old choice faced by the sexes. Women were often torn between mister nice guy, who generally ended up as father of her kids, and the hell-raising jerk who represented offbeat romance and adventure. Men, for all their faults, were occasionally forced to choose between miss wholesome girl-next-door, who generally ended up as mother to his children, and the wild sexpot who couldn't keep her body off him.

For Pitt there could be no agonized decision. Late tomorrow evening, the ship would dock at the Chilean port of Punta Arenas in Tierra del Fuego, where Maeve and Deirdre would take a commuter flight to Santiago. From there they could book a direct flight to Australia. A waste of time, he thought, to allow his imagination to run amok. He did not dare to hope that he would ever lay eyes on either one of them again.

He slipped a hand below the table and touched the folded fax in his pants pocket. Overcome by curiosity, he had communicated with St. Julien Perlmutter, a close family friend who had accumulated the world's foremost library of shipwreck information. A well-known party-giver and gourmand, Perlmutter was well connected in Washington circles and knew where most of the skeletons were buried. Pitt had put in a call and asked his friend to check on the ladies' family background. Perlmutter faxed him a brief report in less than an hour with a promise of a more in-depth account within two days.

These were no ordinary women from common circumstances. If the unmarried men, and maybe even a few of the married, knew that Maeve and Deirdre's father, Arthur Dorsett, was head of a diamond empire second only to De Beers and the sixth richest man in the world, they might have pulled out all stops in begging the ladies' hand in marriage.

The section of the report that struck him as odd was a drawing of the Dorsett corporate hallmark that Perlmutter included. Instead of the obvious, a diamond on some sort of background, the Dorsett logotype was a serpent undulating through the water.

The ship's officer on duty came up alongside Pitt and spoke softly. "Admiral Sandecker is on the satellite phone and would like to talk to you."

"Thank you, I'll take the call in my cabin."

Unobtrusively, Pitt pushed back his chair, rose and left the dining room, unnoticed by all except Giordino.

Pitt exhaled a deep breath, removed his shoes and unlimbered in his leather chair. "Admiral, this is Dirk."

"About time," Sandecker grunted. "I could have written my next speech before a congressional budget committee."

"Sorry, sir, I was attending a party."

There was a pause. "A party on a NUMA vessel dedicated to scientific research?"

"A farewell get-together for the ladies we rescued from *Polar Queen*," Pitt explained.

"I'd better not hear of any questionable actions." Sandecker was as open and receptive as the next man, but discussing anything less than scientific procedure on board his fleet of research ships was not his strong point.

Pitt took great joy in needling the admiral. "Do you mean hanky-panky, sir?"

"Call it what you may. Just see that the crew plays it straight. We don't need any exposure in the scandal rags."

"May I ask the nature of this call, Admiral?" Sandecker never used the phone simply to reach out and touch someone.

"I require the services of you and Giordino here in Washington damned quick. How soon can you fly off *Ice Hunter* for Punta Arenas?"

"We're within the helicopter's range now," said Pitt. "We can lift off within the hour."

"I've arranged for a military jet transport to be waiting for your arrival at the airport."

Sandecker was never one to let the grass grow under his feet, Pitt thought. "Then Al and I will see you sometime tomorrow afternoon."

"We have much to discuss."

"Any new developments?"

"An Indonesian freighter was found off Howland Island with a dead crew."

"Did the bodies show the same symptoms as those on *Polar Queen?*"

"We'll never know," answered Sandecker. "It blew up and sank while a boarding party was investigating, killing them as well."

"That's a twist."

"And to add to the mystery," Sandecker continued, "a Chinese-junk luxury yacht owned and sailed by the movie actor Garret Converse is missing in the same area."

"His legion of fans won't be happy when they learn he died from unknown causes."

"His loss will probably get more coverage from the news media than all the dead on the cruise ship," Sandecker acknowledged.

"How has my theory on sound waves played?" Pitt asked.

"Yaeger's working it through his computers as we speak. With luck, he'll have gleaned more data by the time you and Al walk through the door. I have to tell you, he and Rudi Gunn think you may be onto something."

"See you soon, Admiral," Pitt said and hung up. He sat motionless and stared at the phone, hoping to God they were on the right track.

. . .

The dishes were cleared and the party in the ship's dining room had become loud with laughter as everyone competed in telling shaggy dog stories. As with Pitt, hardly anyone noticed that Giordino also had departed the festivities. Captain Dempsey entered into the humor of the evening with an old, old joke about a rich farmer who sends his ne'er-do-well son to college and makes him take along the old family dog, Rover. The kid then uses the old mangy dog to con his old man out of spending money by claiming he needs a thousand dollars because his professors claim they can make Rover read, write and talk. By the time he came to the punch line, everybody laughed more from sheer relief it was over than from the humor.

On one wall nearby, a ship's phone rang, and the first officer answered. Without a word, he nodded in Dempsey's direction. The captain caught the gesture, came over and took the call. He listened a moment, hung up the receiver and started for the open passageway leading to the stern deck.

"Are you all joked out?" Van Fleet called after him.

"I have to stand by for the helicopter's departure," he answered.

"What's the mission?"

"No mission. Pitt and Giordino have been ordered back to Washington by the admiral, posthaste. They're flying off to the mainland to catch a military transport."

Maeve overheard and grabbed Dempsey by the arm. "When are they leaving?"

He was surprised by the sudden strength of her grip. "They should be lifting off about now."

Deirdre came over and stood next to Maeve. "He must not care enough about you to say good-bye."

Maeve felt as if a giant hand had suddenly reached inside her and squeezed her heart. Anguish filled her body. She rushed out the door onto the deck. Pitt had only lifted the helicopter a scant three meters off the pad when she came running into view. She could clearly see both men through the helicopter's large windows. Giordino looked down, saw her and waved. Pitt had both hands busy and could only respond with a warm grin and a nod.

He expected to see her smile and wave in return, but her face seemed drawn in fear. She cupped her hands and cried out to him, but the noise of the turbine exhaust and thumping rotor blades drowned out her words. He could only shake his head and shrug in reply.

Maeve shouted again, this time with lowered hands as if somehow willing her thoughts into his mind. Too late. The helicopter shot into the air vertically and dipped over the side of the ship. She sagged to her knees on the deck, head in her hands, sobbing, as the turquoise aircraft flew over the endless marching swells of the sea.

Giordino looked back through his side window and saw Maeve slumped on the deck, Dempsey walking toward her. "I wonder what the fuss was all about," he said curiously.

"What fuss?" asked Pitt.

"Maeve . . . she acted like a Greek mourner at a funeral."

Concentrating on controlling the helicopter, Pitt had missed Maeve's unexpected display of grief. "Maybe she hates good-byes," he said, feeling a wave of remorse.

"She tried to tell us something," Giordino said vaguely, reliving the scene in his mind.

Pitt did not take a backward glance. He felt deep regret at not having said his farewells. It was rude to have denied Maeve the courtesy of a friendly hug and a few words. He had genuinely felt attracted to her. She had aroused emotions within him that he hadn't experienced since losing someone very dear to him in the sea north of Hawaii many years ago. Her name was Summer, and not a day passed that he didn't recall her lovely face and the scent of plumeria.

There was no way for him to tell if the attraction was mutual. There were a multitude of expressions in her eyes, but nothing he saw that indicated desire. And nothing in her conversation had led him to believe they were more than merely two people touching briefly before passing into the night.

He tried to remain detached and tell himself that their affair had nowhere to go. They were bound to lives on opposite sides of the world. It was best to let her fade into a pleasant memory of what might have been if the moon and stars had shone in the right direction.

"Weird," Giordino said, staring ahead at the restless sea as the islands north of Cape Horn grew in the distance.

" 'Weird'?" Pitt echoed in a tone of indifference.

"What Maeve yelled as we lifted off."

"How could you hear anything over the chopper's racket?"

"I couldn't. It was all in the way she formed the words with her mouth."

Pitt grinned. "Since when do you read lips?"

"I'm not kidding, pal," Giordino said in dead seriousness. "I know the message she tried to get across to us."

Pitt knew from long years of experience and friendship that when Giordino turned profound he worked purely from essentials. You didn't step into his circle, spar with him and step out unscathed. Pitt mentally remained outside the circle and peered in. "Spit it out. What did she say?"

Giordino slowly turned and looked at Pitt, his deep-set black eyes reflective and somber at the same time. "I could swear she said 'Help me.'"

14

The twin-engined Buccaneer jet transport touched down smoothly and taxied to a quiet corner of Andrews Air Force Base, southeast of Washington. Fitted out comfortably for high-ranking Air Force officers, the aircraft flew nearly as fast as the most modern fighter plane.

As the flight steward, in the uniform of an Air Force master sergeant, carried their luggage to a waiting car and driver, Pitt marveled at Admiral Sandecker's influence in the capital city. He wondered what general the admiral had conned into temporarily lending the plane to NUMA, and what manner of persuasion it took.

Giordino dozed during the drive, while Pitt stared unseeing at the low buildings of the city. The rush-hour traffic had begun streaming out of town, and the streets and bridges leading into the suburbs were jammed. Fortunately, their car was traveling in the opposite direction.

Pitt cursed his idiocy for not returning to *Ice Hunter* shortly after liftoff. If Giordino had interpreted her message correctly, Maeve was in some sort of trouble. The possibility that he had deserted her when she was calling out to him gnawed at his conscience.

The long arm of Sandecker reached through his melancholy and cast a shroud over his preoccupation with guilt. Never in Pitt's years with NUMA had he ever placed his personal problems above the vital work of the agency. During the flight to Punta Arenas, Giordino had provided the crowning touch.

"There's a time for being horny, and this isn't it. People and sea life are dying by the boatload out there on the water. The sooner we stop this evil, the more lives will be spared to pay taxes. Forget her for now. When this cauldron of crap is over you can take a year off and chase her Down Under."

Giordino might never have been hired to teach rhetoric at Oxford, but he seldom failed to fill a book with common sense. Pitt surrendered and reluctantly eased Maeve from his mind, not entirely successfully. The memory of her lingered like a portrait that became more beautiful with the passage of time.

His thoughts were broken as the car rolled over the driveway in front of the tall green, solar-glassed building that housed NUMA's headquarters. The visitors' parking lot was covered with television transmitter trucks and vans, emitting enough microwaves to launch a new chicken rotisserie franchise.

"I'll run you into the underground parking area," said the driver. "The vultures were expecting your arrival."

"You sure an ax murderer isn't roaming the building?" asked Giordino.

"No, the reception is for you. The news media are starved for details of the cruise ship massacre. The Australians tried to put a tight lid on it, but all hell broke loose after the surviving passengers talked when they reached Chile. They were glowing in their praise of how you guys rescued them and saved the cruise ship from going on the rocks. The fact that two of them were daughters of diamond king Arthur Dorsett naturally excited the exposé rags."

"So now they're calling it a massacre." Pitt sighed.

"Lucky for the Indians they can't blame this one on them," said Giordino.

The car stopped in front of a security guard stationed in front of a small alcove that led to a private elevator. They signed an entry form and took the elevator to the tenth floor. When the doors opened they stepped into a vast room that was Hiram Yaeger's electronics fiefdom from which the computer wizard directed NUMA's vast data systems network.

Yaeger looked up from a huge horseshoe-shaped desk in the middle of the room and smiled broadly. No bib overalls today, but he was wearing a faded Levi's jacket that looked like it had been dragged from Tombstone to Durango by a horse. He jumped to his feet and came from behind the desk, vigorously shaking Pitt's and Giordino's hands. "Good to see you two scoundrels back in the building. It's been as dull as an abandoned amusement park since you skipped to the Antarctic."

"Always good to be back on a floor that doesn't rock and roll," said Pitt.

Yaeger grinned at Giordino. "You look nastier than when you left."

"That's because my feet still feel cold as ice," Giordino replied in his usual burlesque tone.

Pitt glanced about the room crowded with electronic data systems and a crew of technicians. "Are the admiral and Rudi Gunn on hand?"

"Waiting for you in the private conference room," answered Yaeger. "We assumed you and Al would go there first."

"I wanted to catch you before we all sat down."

"What's on your mind?"

"I'd like to study your data on sea serpents."

Yaeger raised his eyebrows. "You did say *sea serpents?*"

Pitt nodded. "They intrigue me. I can't tell you why."

"It may surprise you to learn I have a mountain of material on sea serpents and lake monsters."

"Forget the legendary creatures swimming around in Loch Ness and Lake Champlain," said Pitt. "I'm only interested in the seagoing variety."

Yaeger shrugged. "Since most of the sightings are on inland waters, that cuts the search by eighty percent. I'll have a fat file on your desk tomorrow morning."

"Thank you, Hiram. I'm grateful as always."

Giordino peered at his watch. "We'd better move along before the admiral hangs us from the nearest yardarm."

Yaeger gestured to a nearby door. "We can take the stairway."

When Pitt and the others entered the conference room, San-

162

decker and Gunn were studying the region where the latest case of unexplained death was projected on the holographic chart. The admiral and Gunn stepped forward to greet them. For a few minutes they all stood in a tight little huddle and deliberated the turn of events. Gunn anxiously probed Pitt and Giordino for details, but they were both extremely tired, and they condensed the wild series of incidents into brief descriptions.

Sandecker knew better than to crowd them. Full reports could be written at a later time. He motioned to the empty chairs. "Why don't you sit down, and we'll get to work."

Gunn pointed toward one of the blue globes that seemed to float over one end of the table. "The latest kill zone," he said. "An Indonesian freighter called *Mentawai*, with a crew of eighteen."

Pitt turned to the admiral. "The vessel that exploded after another ship's crew had boarded her?"

"The same," said Sandecker, nodding. "As I told you aboard *Ice Hunter*, actor Garret Converse, his crew and his fancy junk were reported sailing in the same area by an oil tanker that went unscathed. The junk and everyone on board appear to have vanished."

"Nothing on satellite?" inquired Giordino.

"Too much cloud cover, and the infrared cameras won't pick out a vessel as small as a junk."

"There *is* something else to consider," said Gunn. "The captain of the American container ship that found *Mentawai* reported a luxury yacht speeding from the site. He can't swear to it in court, but he's certain the yacht closed with *Mentawai* before he arrived, after responding to the freighter's distress call. He also thinks the crew of the yacht are somehow responsible for the explosives that wiped out his boarding party."

"Sounds like the good captain has an overactive imagination," suggested Yaeger.

"To say this man is seeing demons is incorrect. Captain Jason Kelsey is a very responsible seaman with a solid history of skill and integrity."

"Did he get a description of the yacht?" asked Pitt.

"By the time Kelsey concentrated his attention on it, the yacht was too distant to identify. His second officer, however, observed it earlier through binoculars before it widened the gap. Fortunately, he's an amateur artist who enjoys sketching ships and boats while in port.''

"He drew a picture of it?"

"He admits to taking a few liberties. The yacht was pulling away from him, and his view was mostly of the stern quarter. But he managed to give us a good enough likeness to trace the hull design to her builders.''

Sandecker lit one of his cigars and nodded toward Giordino. "Al, why don't you act as lead investigator on this one?"

Giordino slowly pulled out a cigar, the exact mate of Sandecker's, and slowly rolled it between his thumb and fingers while warming one end with a wooden match. "I'll get on the trail after a shower and a change of clothes."

Giordino's slinky method of pilfering the admiral's private stock of cigars was a mystery that bewildered Sandecker. The cat-and-mouse game had gone on for years, with Sandecker unable to ferret out the secret and too proud to demand an answer from Giordino. What was particularly maddening to the admiral was that his inventory invariably failed to turn up a count of missing cigars.

Pitt was doodling on a notepad and spoke to Yaeger without looking up. "Suppose you tell me, Hiram. Did my idea of killer sound waves have any merit?"

"A great deal, as it turns out," replied Yaeger. "The acoustics experts are still working out a detailed theory, but it looks as if we're looking at a *killer* that travels through water and consists of several elements. There are multiple aspects to be examined. The first is a source for generating intense energy. The second, propagation, or how the energy travels from the source through the seas. Third, the target or structure that receives the acoustic energy. And fourth, the physiological effect on human and animal tissue.''

"Can you make a case for high-intensity sound waves that kill?" Pitt asked.

Yaeger shrugged. "We're on shaky ground, but this is the best lead we have at the moment. The only joker in the deck is that sound waves intense enough to kill could not come from an ordinary sound source. And even an intense source could not kill at any great distance unless the sound was somehow focused.''

"Hard to believe that after traveling great distances through water a combination of high-intensity sound and excessive resonance energy can surface and kill every living thing within thirty or more kilometers."

"Any idea where these sound rays originate?" asked Sandecker.

"Yes, as a matter of fact, we do."

"Can one sound source actually cause such a staggering loss of life?" asked Gunn.

"No, and that's the catch," replied Yaeger. "To produce wholesale murder above and under the sea of the magnitude we've experienced, we have to be looking at several different sources on opposite sides of the ocean." He paused, and shuffled through a stack of papers until he found the one he was looking for. Then he picked up a remote control and pressed a series of codes. Four green lights glowed on opposite corners of the holographic chart.

"By borrowing the global monitoring system of hydrophones placed by the Navy around the oceans to track the Soviet submarine fleet during the Cold War, we've managed to trace the source of the destructive sound waves to four different points in the Pacific Ocean." Yaeger paused to pass printed copies of the chart to everyone seated at the table. "Number one, by far the strongest, appears to emanate from Gladiator Island, the exposed tip of a deep ocean range of volcanic mountains that surfaces midway between Tasmania and New Zealand's South Island. Number two is almost on a direct line toward the Komandorskie Islands, off the Kamchatka Peninsula in the Bering Sea."

"That's a fair ways north," observed Sandecker.

"Can't imagine what the Russians have to gain," said Gunn.

"Then we head east across the sea to Kunghit Island, off British Columbia, Canada, for number three," Yaeger continued. "The final source as traced by a data pattern from the hydrophones is on the Isla de Pascua, or Easter Island as it is better known."

"Making the shape of a trapezium," commented Gunn.

Giordino straightened. "A what?"

"Trapezium, a quadrilateral with no two sides that are parallel."

Pitt rose from the table and moved until he was almost standing inside the three-dimensional chart of the ocean. "A bit unusual for the acoustic sources to all stem from islands." He turned and stared at Yaeger. "Are you sure of your data? There is no mistake, your electronic gear processed the tracking information from the hydrophone system correctly?"

Yaeger looked as though Pitt had stabbed him in the chest. "Our statistical analysis takes into account the acoustic network receptions and the alternative ray paths due to ocean variations."

"I stand humbled." Pitt bowed, making a gesture of apology. Then he asked, "Are the islands inhabited?"

Yaeger handed Pitt a small folder. "We've gleaned the usual encyclopedia of data on the islands. Geology, fauna, inhabitants. Gladiator Island is privately owned. The other three are leased from foreign governments for mineral exploration. These have to be considered forbidden zones."

"How can sound be propagated such great distances underwater?" inquired Giordino.

"High-frequency sound is rapidly absorbed by salts in seawater, but low-frequency acoustic waves ignore the molecular structure of the salts, and their signals have been detected at ranges reaching thousands of kilometers. The next part of the scenario gets hazy. Somehow, in a manner we've yet to understand, the high-intensity, low-frequency rays, radiating from the various sources, surface and focus in what is known as a 'convergence zone.' It's a phenomenon the scientists call 'caustics.' "

"Like in caustic soda?" asked Giordino.

"No, like an envelope formed when the sound rays meet and converge."

Sandecker held up a pair of reading spectacles to the light, checking for smudges. "And if we were all sitting on the deck of a ship that was in the middle of a convergence zone?"

"If struck by only one sound source," explained Yaeger, "we'd hear a soft hum and maybe suffer from nothing more than a mild headache. But if four waves converged in the same region at the same time, multiplying the intensity, the structure of the ship would ring or vibrate and the sonic energy would cause enough internal organ damage to kill all of us within a matter of minutes."

"Judging from the scattered sites of the disasters," said Giordino grimly, "this thing can run amok and strike anywhere in the sea."

"Or along shorelines," Pitt added.

"We're working on predicting where the ray channels converge," Yaeger said, "but it's difficult to come up with a set formula. For the moment, the best we can do is chart tides, currents, sea depths and water temperatures. They all can significantly alter the path of the sound rays."

"Since we have a vague notion of what we're dealing with," said Sandecker, "we can lay out a plan to pull the plug."

"The question is," Pitt commented, "except for the mineral exploration companies, what do the islands have in common?"

Giordino stared at his cigar. "Clandestine nuclear or conventional weapons testing?"

"None of the above," Yaeger replied.

"Then what?" demanded Sandecker.

"Diamonds."

Sandecker stared at Yaeger queerly. "Diamonds, you say?"

"Yes, sir." Yaeger checked his file. "The operations on all four islands are either owned or run by Dorsett Consolidated Mining Limited of Sydney, Australia. Second only to De Beers as the world's largest diamond producer."

Pitt felt as if someone had walked up and suddenly punched him in the stomach. "Arthur Dorsett," he said quietly, "the chairman of Dorsett Consolidated Mining, happens to be the father of the two women Al and I rescued in the Antarctic."

"Of course," said Gunn, suddenly seeing the light. "Deirdre Dorsett." Then a quizzical look came into his eyes. "But the other lady, Maeve Fletcher?"

"Deirdre's sister, who took an ancestral grandmother's name," explained Pitt.

Only Giordino saw the humor. "They went to an awful lot of trouble to meet us."

Sandecker shot him a withering look and turned to Pitt. "This strikes me as more than a mere coincidence."

Giordino came right back. "I can't help wondering what one of the world's richest diamond merchants will have to say when he learns his diggings came within a hair of killing off his darling daughters."

"We may have a blessing in disguise," said Gunn. "If Dorsett's mining operations are somehow responsible for an acoustic death plague, Dirk and Al have the credentials to walk up to his front door and ask questions. The man has every reason to act the role of a grateful father."

"From what I know of Arthur Dorsett," said Sandecker, "he's so reclusive, he won the hermit trophy from Howard Hughes. As with De Beers diamond mining operations, Dorsett's properties are heavily guarded against thievery and smuggling. He is never seen in public and he has never granted an interview to the news media. We're talking about a very private man. I doubt seriously that saving his daughters' lives will make a dent in this guy. He's as hard-nosed as they come."

Yaeger motioned toward the blue globes on the holographic chart. "People are dying out there. Surely he'll listen to reason should his operations be somehow responsible."

"Arthur Dorsett is a foreign national with an immense power base." Sandecker spoke slowly. "We have to consider him innocent of any wrongdoing until we have proof. For all we know at the moment, the scourge is a product of nature. As for us, we're committed to working through official channels. That's my territory. I'll start the ball rolling with the State Department and the Australian ambassador. They can set up a dialogue with Arthur Dorsett and request his cooperation in an investigation."

"That could take weeks," argued Yaeger.

"Why not save time," said Giordino, "cut through the red tape, and see if his mining technology is somehow behind the mass murders?"

"You could knock on the door of his nearest diamond mine and ask to see the excavating operation," Pitt suggested with the barest hint of sarcasm.

"If Dorsett is as paranoid as you make him out to be," Giordino said to Sandecker, "he's not the type of guy to play games with."

"Al is right," agreed Yaeger. "To stop the killing and stop it soon, we can't wait for diplomatic niceties. We'll have to go clandestine."

"Not a simple exercise, snooping around diamond mines," said Pitt. "They're notoriously well guarded against poachers and any intruders out for a quick buck scavenging for stones. Security around diamond-producing mines is notoriously heavy. Penetrating high-tech electronic systems will require highly trained professionals."

"A Special Forces team?" Yaeger put on the table.

Sandecker shook his head. "Not without presidential authority."

"What about the President?" asked Giordino.

"Too soon to go to him," answered the admiral. "Not until we can produce hard evidence of a genuine threat to national security."

Pitt spoke slowly as he contemplated the chart. "The Kunghit Island mine seems the most convenient of the four. Since it's in British Columbia and practically on our doorstep, I see no reason why we can't do a little exploring on our own."

Sandecker eyed Pitt shrewdly. "I hope you're not laboring under the impression our neighbors to the north might be willing to turn a blind eye to an intrusion?"

"Why not? Considering that NUMA found a very profitable oil site off Baffin Island for them several years ago, I figure they won't mind if we take a canoe trip around Kunghit and photograph the scenery."

"Is that what you think?"

Pitt looked at the admiral like a kid expecting a free ticket to the circus. "I may have overstated my case slightly, but yes, that's the way I see it."

Sandecker puffed meditatively on his cigar. "All right," he finally sighed. "Do your trespassing. But just remember, if you get caught by Dorsett's security people, don't bother to call home. Because nobody will answer the phone."

15

A Rolls-Royce sedan rolled soundlessly to a stop beside an ancient aircraft hangar that stood in a weed-grown field on the far perimeter of Washington's International Airport. Like an elegant dowager slumming on the wrong side of the tracks, the stately old car seemed out of place on a deserted dirt road during the night. The only illumination came from the dim yellow glow of a weathered streetlight that failed dismally at reflecting the silver and green metallic paint of the car.

The Rolls was a model known as the Silver Dawn. The chassis came out of the factory in 1955 and was fitted with a custom body by the coach-builders Hoopers & Company. The front fenders tapered gracefully into the body at the rear until the skirted wheels and sides were perfectly smooth. The engine was a straight six with overhead valves, which carried the car over the roads as quietly as the ticking of an electric clock. Speed with a Rolls-Royce was never a factor. When questioned about horsepower, the factory merely stated that it was adequate.

St. Julien Perlmutter's chauffeur, a taciturn character by the name of Hugo Mulholand, pulled on the emergency brake, switched off the ignition and turned to his employer, who filled most of the rear seat.

"I have never been comfortable driving you here," he said in a hollow bass voice that went with his bloodhound eyes. He stared at the rusting corrugated roof and walls that hadn't seen paint in forty years. "I can't see why anyone would want to live in such a disreputable shack."

Perlmutter weighed a solid 181 kilograms. Strangely, none of his body possessed more than a hint of flab. He was remarkably solid for a huge man. He held up the gold knob of a hollow cane that doubled as a brandy flask and rapped it on the walnut table that lowered from the rear of the front seat. "That disreputable shack, as you call it, happens to house a collection of antique automobiles and aircraft worth millions of dollars. The chances of being set upon by bandits are unlikely. They don't usually roam around airfields in the dead of night, and there are enough security systems to guard a Manhattan bank." Perlmutter paused to point his cane out the window at a tiny red light that was barely visible. "Even as we speak, we're being monitored by a video camera."

Mulholland sighed, stepped around the car and opened the door for Perlmutter. "Shall I wait?"

"No, I'm having dinner here. Enjoy yourself for a few hours. Then return and pick me up at eleven-thirty."

Mulholland helped Perlmutter from the car and escorted him to the entry door of the hangar. The door was stained and layered with dust. The camouflage was well conceived. Anyone who happened to pass the run-down–appearing hangar would assume it was simply a deserted building scheduled for demolition. Perlmutter rapped on the door with his cane. After a few seconds there was an audible click, and the door opened as if pulled by a ghostly hand.

"Enjoy your dinner," said Mulholland as he slid a cylindrical package under Perlmutter's arm and held up the handle of a briefcase for him to grasp. Then he turned and walked back to the Rolls.

Perlmutter stepped into another world. Instead of dust, grime and cobwebs, he was in a brilliantly lit, brightly decorated and spotless atmosphere of gleaming paint and chrome. Nearly four dozen classic automobiles, two aircraft and a turn-of-the-century railroad car sat in restored splendor on a highly polished concrete floor. The door closed silently behind him as he walked through the incredible display of exotic machinery.

Pitt stood on a balcony that extended from an apartment and which ran across one end of the hangar a good ten meters above the concrete floor. He gestured at the cylindrical package under Perlmutter's arm. "Beware of Greeks bearing gifts," he said, smiling.

Perlmutter looked up and gave him a scowl. "I am not Greek and this happens to be a bottle of French Dom Pérignon champagne," he said, holding up the package, "vintage 1983, to celebrate your return to civilization. I would imagine it's superior to anything in your cellar."

Pitt laughed. "All right, we'll test it against my Albuquerque, New Mexico, Gruet brut nonvintage sparkling wine."

"You can't be serious. Albuquerque? Gruet?"

"They beat out the best of the California sparkling wines in competition."

"All this talk about wine is making my stomach growl. Send down your lift."

Pitt sent down an antique freight elevator with ornate wrought-iron screens around it. As soon as it jangled to a stop, Perlmutter stepped in. "Will this thing take my weight?"

"I installed it myself to bring up the furniture. But this will be a true load-capacity test."

"That's a comforting thought," muttered Perlmutter as the elevator easily carried him up to Pitt's apartment.

At the landing they greeted each other like the old friends they were. "Good to see you, Julien."

"Always happy to dine with my tenth son." It was one of Perlmutter's running jokes. He was an old confirmed bachelor, and Pitt was the only son of Senator George Pitt of California.

"There are nine others just like me?" Pitt asked, feigning surprise.

Perlmutter patted his massive stomach. "Before this got in the way, you'd be amazed how many damsels succumbed to my suave manners and honeyed tongue." He paused to sniff the air. "Is that herring I smell?"

Pitt nodded. "You're eating basic German farmhand fare tonight. Corned beef hash with salt herring and steamed spiced sauerkraut preceded by lentil soup with pork liver sausage."

"I should have brought Munich beer instead of champagne."

"Be adventuresome," said Pitt. "Why follow the rules?"

"You're absolutely right," said Perlmutter. "Sounds wonderful. You'll make some woman a happy wife with your masterful cooking."

"I'm afraid a love of cooking won't make up for all my failings."

"Speaking of lovely ladies, what do you hear from Congresswoman Smith?"

"Loren is back in Colorado, campaigning to keep her seat in Congress," explained Pitt. "I haven't seen her in nearly two months."

"Enough of this idle talk," said Perlmutter impatiently. "Let's open the bottle of champagne and get to work."

Pitt provided an ice bucket, and they went through the Dom Pérignon before the main entree and finished the meal with the Gruet brut during desert. Perlmutter was mightily impressed with the sparkling wine from New Mexico. "This is quite good, dry and crisp," he said slyly. "Where can I buy a case?"

"If it was only 'quite good,' you wouldn't be interested in obtaining a case," said Pitt, grinning. "You're an old charlatan."

Perlmutter shrugged. "I never could fool you."

As soon as Pitt cleared the dishes, Perlmutter moved into the living room, opened his briefcase and laid a thick sheaf of papers on the coffee table. When Pitt joined him, he was glancing at the pages, checking his notations.

Pitt settled in a leather sofa beneath staggered shelves that held a small fleet of ship models, replicas of ships that Pitt had discovered over the years. "So what have you got on the renowned Dorsett family?"

"Would you believe this represents a shallow scratch on the surface?" Perlmutter replied, holding up the thick volume of over a thousand pages. "From what I've researched, the Dorsett history reads like a dynasty out of an epic novel."

"What about the current head of the family, Arthur Dorsett?"

"Extremely reclusive. Rarely surfaces in public. Obstinate, prejudiced and thoroughly unscrupulous. Universally disliked by all who remotely come in contact with him."

"But filthy rich," said Pitt.

"Disgustingly so," replied Perlmutter with the expression of a man who just ate a spider. "Dorsett Consolidated Mining Limited and the House of Dorsett chain of retail stores are wholly owned by the family. No stockholders, shareholders or partners. They also control a sister company called Pacific Gladiator that concentrates on the mining of colored gemstones."

"How did he get his start?"

"For that story we have to go back 144 years." Perlmutter held out his glass and Pitt filled it. "We begin with an epic of the sea that was recorded by the captain of a clipper ship and published by his daughter after he died. During a voyage in January of 1856, while he was transporting convicts, a number of them women, to the Australian penal colony at Botany Bay, an inlet south of the present city of Sydney, his ship ran afoul of a violent typhoon while beating north through the Tasman Sea. The ship was called the *Gladiator,* and she was skippered by one of the most famous clipper captains of the era, Charles 'Bully' Scaggs."

"Iron men and wooden ships," murmured Pitt.

"They were that," agreed Perlmutter. "Anyway, Scaggs and his crew must have labored like demons to save the ship from one of the worst storms of the century. But when the winds died and seas calmed, *Gladiator* was little more than a derelict. Her masts were swept over the side, her superstructure was destroyed and her hull was taking on water. The ship's boats were gone or smashed, and Captain Scaggs knew his ship had only hours to live, so he issued orders for the crew and any convicts handy as carpenters to dismantle what was left of the ship and build a raft."

"Probably the only option open to him," Pitt commented.

"Two of the convicts were Arthur Dorsett's ancestors," Perlmutter continued. "His great-great grandfather was Jess Dorsett, a convicted highwayman, and his great-great-grandmother was Betsy Fletcher, who was given a twenty-year sentence to the penal colony for stealing a blanket."

Pitt contemplated the bubbles in his glass. "Crime certainly didn't pay in those days."

"Most Americans don't realize that our own colonies were also a dumping ground for England's criminals until the Revolutionary War. Many families would be surprised to learn their ancestors landed on our shores as convicted criminals."

"Were the ship's survivors rescued from the raft?" asked Pitt.

Perlmutter shook his head. "The next fifteen days became a

saga of horror and death. Storms, thirst and starvation, and a mad slaughter between the sailors, a few soldiers and the convicts decimated the people clinging to the raft. When it finally drifted onto the reef of an uncharted island and went to pieces, legend has it the survivors were saved from a great white shark by a sea serpent while swimming to shore."

"Which explains the Dorsett hallmark. It came from the hallucinations of near-dead people."

"I wouldn't be surprised. Only 8 of the original 231 of the poor souls who left the ship staggered onto a beach—6 men and 2 women more dead than alive."

Pitt looked at Perlmutter. "That's 223 lost. A staggering figure."

"Of the 8," Perlmutter went on, "a seaman and a convict were later killed after fighting over the women."

"A replay of the mutiny on the *Bounty*."

"Not quite. Two years later, Captain Scaggs and his remaining seaman, luckily for him the *Gladiator*'s carpenter, built a boat out of the remains of a French naval sloop that was driven on the rocks by a storm with the loss of all hands. Leaving the convicts behind on the island, they sailed across the Tasman Sea to Australia."

"Scaggs deserted Dorsett and Fletcher?"

"For a very good reason. The enchantment of living on a beautiful island was preferred to the hell of the prison camps at Botany Bay. And because Scaggs felt he owed his life to Dorsett, he told the penal colony authorities that all the convicts had died on the raft so the survivors could be left in peace."

"So they built a new life and multiplied."

"Exactly," said Perlmutter. "Jess and Betsy were married by Scaggs and had two boys, while the other two convicts produced a girl. In time they built a little family community and began trading food supplies to whaling ships that began making Gladiator Island, as it later became known, a regular stopover during their long voyages."

"What became of Scaggs?" asked Pitt.

"He returned to the sea as master of a new clipper ship owned by a shipping company called Carlisle & Dunhill. After several more voyages to the Pacific, he retired and eventually died, twenty years later, in 1876."

"Where do diamonds enter the picture?"

"Patience," said Perlmutter like a schoolteacher. "A little background to better understand the story. To begin with, diamonds, though instigating more crime, corruption and romance than any other of the earth's minerals, are merely crystallized carbon. Chemically, they're sister to graphite and coal. Diamonds are thought to have been formed as long ago as three billion years, anywhere from 120 to 200 kilometers deep in the earth's upper mantle. Under incredible heat and pressure, pure carbon along with gases and liquid rock forced their way toward the surface through volcanic shafts commonly referred to as pipes. As this blend exploded upward, the carbon cooled and crystallized into extremely hard and transparent stones. Diamonds are one of the few materials to touch the earth's surface from remote depths."

Pitt stared at the floor, trying to picture nature's diamond-making process in his mind. "I assume a cross section of the ground would show a trail of diamonds swirling upward to surface in a circular shaft that widens at the surface like a raised funnel."

"Or a carrot," said Perlmutter. "Unlike pure lava, which raised high, peaked volcanos when it reached the surface, the mix of diamonds and liquid rock, known as kimberlite pipes after the South African city of Kimberly, cooled rapidly and hardened into large mounds. Some were worn down by natural erosion, spreading the diamonds into what are known as alluvial deposits. Some eroded pipes even formed lakes. The largest mass of crystallized stones, however, remained in the underground pipes or chutes."

"Let me guess. The Dorsetts found one of these diamond-laden pipes on their island."

"You keep getting ahead of me," Perlmutter muttered irritably.

"Sorry," Pitt said placatingly.

"The shipwrecked convicts unknowingly found not one, but two phenomenally rich pipes in volcanic mounds on opposite ends of Gladiator Island. The stones they found, which were freed from the rock by centuries of rain and wind, simply appeared to be 'pretty things,' as Betsy Fletcher referred to them in a letter to Scaggs. Actually, uncut and unpolished diamonds are dull-looking stones with almost no sparkle. They often feel and look like an oddly shaped bar of soap. It was not until 1866, after the American Civil War, that a U.S. Navy vessel on an exploratory voyage to find possible sites for deepwater ports throughout the South Pacific stopped at the island to take on water. On board was a geologist. He happened to see the Dorsett children playing a game with stones on the beach and became curious. He examined one of the stones and was amazed as he identified it as a diamond of at least twenty carats. When the geologist questioned Jess Dorsett as to where the stone came from, the cagey old highwayman told him he brought it with him from England."

"And that timely little event launched Dorsett Consolidated Mining."

"Not immediately," said Perlmutter. "After Jess died, Betsy sent her two boys, Jess Junior and Charles, no doubt named after Scaggs, and the daughter of the other two convicts, Mary Winkleman, to England to be educated. She wrote Scaggs for his help and included a pouch of uncut diamonds to pay for this undertaking, which the captain turned over to his friend and former employer, Abner Carlisle. Acting on behalf of Scaggs, who was on his deathbed, Carlisle had the diamonds faceted and polished, later selling them on the London exchange for nearly one million pounds, or about seven million dollars, in the currency of the time."

"A tidy sum for college tuition for those days," Pitt said consideringly. "The kids must have had a ball."

Perlmutter shook his head. "You're wrong this time. They lived frugally at Cambridge. Mary attended a proper girl's school outside of London. She and Charles married soon after he took his degree, and they returned to the island, where they directed the mining operations in the dormant volcanos. Jess Junior remained in England and opened the House of Dorsett in partnership with a Jewish diamond merchant from Aberdeen by the name of Levi Strouser. The London end of the business, which dealt in the cutting and sale of diamonds, had luxurious showrooms for retail sales, elegant offices on the upper floors for larger wholesale trading and a vast workshop in the basement, where the stones from Gladiator Island were cut and polished. The dynasty prospered, helped in no small measure by the fact that the diamonds that came out of the island pipes were a very rare violet-rose color and of the highest quality."

"The mines have never played out?"

"Not yet. The Dorsetts have been very shrewd in holding back much of their production in cooperation with the cartel to hold up the price."

"What about offspring?" asked Pitt.

"Charles and Mary had one boy, Anson. Jess Junior never married."

"Anson was Arthur's grandfather?" Pitt asked.

"Yes, he ran the company for over forty years. He was probably the most decent and honest of the lot. Anson was satisfied to run and maintain a profitable little empire. Never driven by greed like his descendants, he gave a great deal of money to charity. Any number of libraries and hospitals throughout Australia and New Zealand were founded by him. When he died in 1910, he left the company to a son, Henry, and a daughter, Mildred. She died young in a boating accident. She fell overboard during a cruise on the family yacht and was taken by sharks. Rumors circulated that she was murdered by Henry, but no investigations were made. Henry's money made sure of that. Under Henry, the family launched a reign of greed, jealousy, cruelty and ravenous power that continues to this day."

"I recall reading an article about him in the *Los Angeles Times*," said Pitt. "They compared Sir Henry Dorsett to Sir Ernest Oppenheimer of De Beers."

"Neither was exactly what you'd call a saint. Oppenheimer climbed over a multitude of obstacles to build an empire that reaches out to every continent and has diversified holdings in automobiles, paper and explosives manufacture, breweries, as well as the mining of gold, uranium, platinum and copper. De Beers' main strength, however, still lies with diamonds and the cartel that regulates the market from London to New York to Tokyo. Dorsett Consolidated Mining, on the other hand, remained totally committed to diamonds. And except for holdings in a number of colored gemstone mines—rubies in Burma, emeralds in Colombia, sapphires from Ceylon—the family never really diversified into other investments. All profits were plowed back into the corporation."

"Where did the name De Beers come from?"

"De Beers was the South African farmer who unknowing sold his diamond-laden land for a few thousand dollars to Cecil Rhodes, who excavated a fortune and launched the cartel."

"Did Henry Dorsett join Oppenheimer and the De Beers cartel?" asked Pitt.

"Although he participated in market price controls, Henry became the only large mine owner to sell independently. While eighty-five percent of the world's production went through the De Beers—controlled Central Selling Organization to brokers and dealers, Dorsett bypassed the main diamond exchanges in London, Antwerp, Tel Aviv and New York so he could market a limited production of fine stones direct to the public through the House of Dorsett, which now numbers almost five hundred stores."

"De Beers did not fight him?"

Perlmutter shook his head. "Oppenheimer formed the cartel to ensure a stable market and high prices for diamonds. Sir Ernest did not see Dorsett as a threat so long as the Australian didn't attempt to dump his supply of stones on the market."

"Dorsett must have an army of craftsmen to support such an operation."

"Over a thousand employees in three diamond-cutting facilities, two cleaving workshops and two polishing departments. They also have an entire thirty-story building in Sydney, Australia, that houses a host of artisans who create the House of Dorsett's distinctive and creative jewelry. While most of the other brokers hire Jews to cut and facet their stones, Dorsett hires mostly Chinese."

"Henry Dorsett died sometime in the late seventies, didn't he?"

Perlmutter smiled. "History repeated itself. At the age of sixty-eight, he fell off his yacht while in Monaco and drowned. It was whispered that Arthur got him drunk and shoved him into the bay."

"What's the story on Arthur?"

Perlmutter checked his file of papers, then peered over the lenses of his reading glasses. "If the diamond-buying public ever had any inkling of the dirty operations Arthur Dorsett has conducted over the past thirty years, they'd never buy another diamond till the day he dies."

"Not a nice man, I take it."

"Some men are two-faced, Arthur is at least five-faced. Born on Gladiator Island in 1941, the only child of Henry and Charlotte

Dorsett. He was educated by his mother, never going to school on the mainland until the age of eighteen, when he entered the Colorado School of Mines in Golden, Colorado. He was a big man, towering half a head above his classmates, yet he took no interest in sports, preferring to probe around the old ghost mines that are scattered throughout the Rocky Mountains. After graduation with a degree as a mining engineer, he worked the De Beers diggings in South Africa for five years before returning home and taking over as superintendent of the family mines on the island. During his frequent trips to the Dorsett headquarters building in Sydney, he met and married a lovely young girl, Irene Calvert, who was the daughter of a professor of biology at the university at Melbourne. She gave him three daughters."

"Maeve, Deirdre and . . ."

"Boudicca."

"Two Celtic goddesses and a legendary British queen."

"A feminine triad."

"Maeve and Deirdre are twenty-seven and thirty-one years of age. Boudicca is thirty-eight."

"Tell me more of their mother," said Pitt.

"Little to tell. Irene died fifteen years ago, again under mysterious circumstances. It wasn't until a year after she was buried on Gladiator Island that a Sydney newspaper reporter ferreted out the fact of her death. He ran an obituary on her before Arthur could bribe the managing editor to kill the piece. Otherwise, nobody would have known she was gone."

"Admiral Sandecker knows something of Arthur Dorsett and says he's impossible to reach," said Pitt.

"Very true. He is never seen in public, never socializes, has no friends. His entire life revolves around the business. He even has a secret tunnel for entering and leaving the Sydney headquarters building without being seen. He has cut Gladiator Island off from the outside world completely. To his way of thinking the less known about Dorsett mining operations the better."

"What about the company? He can't hide the dealings of a vast business forever."

"I beg to differ," said Perlmutter. "A privately owned corporation can get away with murder. Even the governments they operate under have an impossible time trying to probe company assets for tax purposes. Arthur Dorsett may be a reincarnation of

Ebenezer Scrooge, but he's never hesitated to spend big money to buy loyalty. If he thinks it's beneficial to make a government official an instant millionaire in order to gain leverage and power, Dorsett will go for it."

"Do his daughters work within the company?"

"Two of them are said to be employed by dear old Dad, the other one . . ."

"Maeve," Pitt offered.

"All right, Maeve, cut herself off from the family, put herself through university and came out a marine zoologist. Something of her mother's father must have come through in her genes."

"And Deirdre and Boudicca?"

"The gossipmongers claim the two are devils incarnate, and worse than the old man. Deirdre is the Machiavelli of the family, a conniving schemer with larceny in her veins. Boudicca is rumored to be quite ruthless and as cold and hard as ice from the bottom of a glacier. Neither seems to have any interest in men or high living."

A distant look reflected in Pitt's eyes. "What is it about diamonds that gives them so much allure? Why do men and women kill for them? Why have nations and governments risen and fallen because of them?"

"Besides their beauty after being cut and polished, diamonds have unique qualities. They happen to be the hardest known substance in the world. Rub one against silk and it produces a positive electrostatic charge. Expose it to the setting sun and it will later glow in the dark with an unearthly phosphorescence. No, my young friend. Diamonds are more than a myth. They are the ultimate creator of illusions." Perlmutter paused and lifted the champagne bottle from the ice bucket. He poured the final few drops in his glass almost sadly. Then he held it up. "Damn, it appears I've run dry."

16

After he left the NUMA building, Giordino signed out one of the agency's turquoise cars and drove to his recently purchased condominium in Alexandria, along the Potomac River. His rooms were an interior decorator's nightmare. None of the furniture or decor matched. Nothing conformed to the basic rules of taste and style. His succession of girlfriends who moved in and moved out all left their mark, and none of their redecorating blended with the judgment of his next companion. Happily, he stayed close friends with every one of them. They enjoyed his company, but none would have married him on a bet.

He wasn't a sloppy housekeeper, and he was a fair cook, but he was seldom at home. If he wasn't chasing around the world on undersea projects with Pitt, he was mounting expeditions to search for anything that was lost, be it ships, aircraft or people. He loved to hunt for the missing. He could never sit around his living room watching TV in the evenings or read a book. Giordino's mind was constantly traveling, and his thoughts were rarely trained on the lady by his side, a condition that frustrated the gentler sex no end.

He threw his dirty clothes in the washer and took a quick shower. Then he packed an overnight bag and drove to Dulles International, where he caught an early evening flight to Miami. Upon arrival, he rented a car, drove to the city's port area and checked into a dockside motel. Next he checked the Yellow Pages for marine architects, copying the names, addresses and phone numbers of those who specialized in private motor yachts. Then he began to call.

The first four, who had already left for home, responded with answering machines, but the fifth picked up the call. Giordino was not surprised. He had expected that one of them would be conscientiously working late, creating the construction plans for some rich man's floating home away from home.

"Mr. Wes Wilbanks?" inquired Giordino.

"Yes, this is Wes. What can I do for you this time of night?" The voice had a soft Southern drawl.

"My name is Albert Giordino. I'm with the National Underwater & Marine Agency. I need your help in identifying the manufacturer of a boat."

"Is it docked here in Miami?"

"No, sir. It could be anywhere in the world."

"Sounds mysterious."

"More than you know."

"I'll be in the office tomorrow at around ten."

"This is a matter of some urgency," Giordino said with quiet authority.

"Okay, I'll be wrapping up in about an hour. Why don't you drop by then? Do you have the address?"

"Yes, but I'm a stranger to Miami."

Wilbanks gave Giordino directions. The architect's office was only a few blocks away, so Giordino grabbed a fast dinner at a small Cuban café and set off on foot, following the directions he'd received over the phone.

The man who opened the door was in his early thirties, quite tall and dressed in shorts and a flowered shirt. Giordino's head barely came to Wilbanks' shoulder, and he had to look up. The handsome face was framed by an abundance of fashionably slicked-back hair that was graying at the temples. He definitely had the look of someone who belonged to the yachting set, Giordino decided.

"Mr. Giordino, Wes Wilbanks. I'm real pleased to meet you."

"Thank you for seeing me."

"Come on in. Would you like some coffee? Made this morning, but the chicory keeps it flavorful."

"Love some."

Wilbanks led him into an office with a hardwood floor, shelves covering one wall stacked with books on yacht and small-boat design. The other wall was filled with half-hull models that Giordino assumed were built from Wilbanks' plans. The middle of the room contained a large antique drafting table. A desk with a computer sat nestled on a bench in front of a picture window overlooking the port.

Giordino accepted a cup of coffee and laid the sketches from the second officer of the container ship *Rio Grande* on the drafting table. "I know this isn't much to go on, but I'm hoping you might point me toward the manufacturer."

Wilbanks studied the drawings, tilting his head from side to side. After a solid minute, he rubbed his chin and peered over the sketch paper. "At first glance it looks like a basic design from any one of a hundred boatbuilders. But I do believe whoever observed the boat and sketched it was fooled by the angle from which he viewed it. Actually, I believe there are two hulls, not one, mounting a futuristic pod that gives it a space-age look. I've always wanted to create something like this but have yet to find a customer willing to stray very far from conventional designs."

"You sound like you're talking about a craft for flying to the moon."

"Not far from it." Wilbanks sat down at his computer and turned it on. "Let me show you with computer graphics what I mean." He rummaged through a drawer, retrieved a disk and inserted it into his machine. "Here's a concept I created purely for fun and out of frustration at knowing I'll never get paid to build it."

The image of a sleek sport cruiser without any sharp lines or edges filled the monitor. Gone was the traditional angular bow. The entire hull and pod that covered the cockpit were smooth and rounded. Nothing conservative about this craft. It looked like something from fifty years in the future. Giordino was impressed. Through the use of computer graphics, Wilbanks gave him a tour through the interior of the boat, focusing on the bold and unusual design of the appliances and furniture. This was truly imagination and innovation at work.

"You visualize all this from a couple of rough drawings?" Giordino asked in awe.

"Hold on and you'll see," said Wilbanks. He ran the sketches through an electronic scanner that transferred the images to his computer monitor. Then he overlaid the images with his own plans and compared them. Except for minor differences in design and dimensions, they were a very close match.

"All in the eyes of the beholder," Giordino murmured.

"I'm insanely envious that one of my peers got there first," Wilbanks said. "I'd have sold my kids for a contract to do this baby."

"Can you give me an idea as to the size and power source?"

"Of mine or yours?"

"The boat in the sketches," replied Giordino.

"I should say the overall length is somewhere around thirty meters. The beam, just under ten meters. As to power plants, if it were me I would have specified a pair of Blitzen Seastorm turbodiesels. Most likely BAD 98s, which combined could produce more than twenty-five hundred horsepower. Estimated cruising speed with these engines could easily push a boat this size through calm seas at seventy knots or more, much more depending upon the efficiency of the twin hulls."

"Who has the facilities to build such a boat?"

Wilbanks leaned back and thought a moment. "A boat of this size and configuration calls for pretty radical fiberglass forming. Glastec Boats in San Diego could do the job, as could Heinklemann Specialty Boat Builders in Kiel, Germany."

"What about the Japanese?"

"They're not players in the yacht industry. Hong Kong has a number of small boatyards, but they primarily build in wood. Most fiberglass-boat builders stick to tried and proven concepts."

"Then in your judgment it's either Glastec or Heinklemann," said Giordino.

"Those are the two I'd call in to bid on my design," Wilbanks assured him.

"What about the architect?"

"I can think of at least twenty off the top of my head who specialize in radical design."

Giordino smiled. "I was lucky in stumbling onto number twenty-one."

"Where are you staying?"

"The Seaside Motel."

"NUMA doesn't exactly splurge with their expense accounts, do they?"

"You should meet my boss, Admiral James Sandecker. He and Shylock were bosom buddies."

Wilbanks laughed. "Tell you what, drop back by my office about ten in the morning. I should have something for you."

"I'm grateful for your help."

Giordino shook Wilbanks' hand, then took a long walk along the waterfront before returning to his motel room, where he read a mystery novel before finally falling asleep.

At ten o'clock on the nose, Giordino entered Wilbanks' studio. The boat architect was studying a set of plans. He held them up and grinned.

"After you left last night," he said, "I refined the sketches you gave me and ran off scaled plans. Then I reduced the size and faxed them to San Diego and Germany. Because of the difference in time, Heinklemann had responded before I came in this morning. Glastec replied to my inquiry only twenty minutes before you walked in."

"Were they familiar with the boat in question?" asked Giordino impatiently.

"Bad news on that end, I'm afraid," Wilbanks said deadpan. "Neither designed or built your boat."

"Then it's back to square one."

"Not really. The good news is that one of Heinklemann's engineers saw and studied your boat when it was moored in Monaco about nine months ago. He reports the manufacturer was a French firm, a new one in the industry I wasn't aware of. Jusserand Marine out of Cherbourg."

"Then we can fax them a set of your plans," said Giordino, his hopes on the rise again.

"No need." Wilbanks waved him off. "Though the subject never came up, I assumed your real reason for tracing the boat manufacturer was to learn the identity of the owner."

"I have no reason to deny it."

"The Heinklemann engineer who spotted the boat in Monaco was also kind enough to include the owner's name in the fax. He mentioned that he inquired only after he noticed that the crew looked more like a band of Mafia toughs than polished seamen maintaining and sailing a luxury yacht."

"Mafia toughs?"

"He claimed they all packed guns."

"The name of the owner?"

"A woman, a wealthy Australian. Her family made a fortune in diamond mining. Her name is Boudicca Dorsett."

17

While Pitt was on a flight to Ottawa, Canada, Giordino called his plane and briefed him on the mystery yacht.

"There is no doubt?" asked Pitt.

"Not in my book," replied Giordino. "It's almost a dead certainty the boat that fled the death scene belongs to the Dorsett family."

"The plot thickens."

"You might also be interested in learning that the admiral asked the Navy to conduct a satellite search of the central and eastern belt of the Pacific Ocean. The yacht was discovered and tracked. It made a brief layover in Hawaii and then continued on toward your goal."

"Kunghit Island? Then I can kill two stones with one bird."

"You're just full of pathetic clichés this morning."

"What does the yacht look like?"

"Unlike any boat you've ever seen before. Strictly a space-age design."

"I'll keep an eye out for it," Pitt promised.

"I know it's a waste of breath saying this," Giordino said cynically, "but stay out of trouble."

"I'll wire if I need money." Pitt laughed as he hung up, thankful that he had a caring friend like Albert Cassius Giordino.

After landing and renting a car, Pitt took the bridge across the Rideau River into Ottawa, the Canadian capital city. The weather was colder than the inside of a refrigerator, and the landscape appeared ugly and barren without leaves on the trees. The only havens of color that sprang from a thick sheet of snow covering the ground were scattered stands of green pines. He glanced over the railing at the river below. The river, which ran into the Ottawa River and thence to the mighty St. Lawrence, was flowing under a coating of ice. Canada was an incredibly beautiful country, thought Pitt, but its harsh winters should be sent far to the north, never to return.

As he drove across the bridge over the Ottawa River and into the small city of Hull, he glanced at his map and memorized the streets leading to a group of three upscale buildings that housed several government offices. The one he was looking for was Environment Canada, a department of the government that corresponded to the U.S. Environmental Protection Agency in Washington.

A security guard at a gatehouse gave him directions and waved him through. Pitt slipped the car into a slot in the visitors' parking lot and entered the building. A quick glance at the building directory, and he was into the elevator and on his way up to Environment Canada's offices.

A receptionist nearing retirement looked up and forced a thin smile. "May I help you?"

"My name is Pitt. I have an appointment with Mr. Edward Posey."

"One moment." She dialed a number, announced his arrival and then nodded. "Please take the hallway down to the doorway at the end."

Pitt thanked her and did as he was told. A pretty red-haired secretary met him at the door and ushered him into Posey's office.

A short man with glasses and a beard rose from his chair, leaned over the desk and pressed Pitt's extended hand. "A pleasure to see you again, Dirk. How long has it been?"

"Eleven years ago, during the spring of 1989."

"Yes, the Doodlebug Project. We met at the conference when

you gave a report on your discovery of the oil field near Baffin Island."

"I need a favor, Ed."

Posey nodded to a chair. "Sit down, sit down. What exactly can I do for you?"

"I'd like your permission to investigate the mining activities being conducted at Kunghit Island."

"You talking about Dorsett Consolidated's operations?"

Pitt nodded. "The same. NUMA has reason to believe their excavating technology is having a devastating effect on sea life as far away as the Antarctic."

Posey gave him a thoughtful look. "This have anything to do with that Australian cruise ship and its dead passengers?"

"Any connection is purely circumstantial at this date."

"But you have your suspicions?" Posey inquired.

"We do."

"Natural Resources Canada is who you should talk to."

"I don't think so. If your government operates anything like mine, it would take an act of Parliament to allow an investigation onto land that is legally leased by a mining company. Even then, Arthur Dorsett is too powerful to allow that to happen."

"It would seem you've crawled into a pipe with no outlet," said Posey.

"There *is* a way out," Pitt said, smiling, "providing you cooperate."

Posey looked uneasy. "I can't authorize you to snoop around Dorsett's diamond mine, certainly not without hard evidence of unlawful damage to the environment."

"Maybe, but you can hire my services to check out the spawning habits of cauliflower-nosed salmon."

"Spawning season is almost over. Besides, I've never heard of a cauliflower-nosed salmon."

"Neither have I."

"You'll never fool security at the mine. Dorsett hires the best in the business, British ex-commandos and American Special Forces veterans."

"I don't have to climb the fence onto mining property," explained Pitt. "I can find all I require with instruments while sailing around the inlets of Kunghit Island."

"In a survey boat?"

"I was thinking of a canoe, local color and all."

"Forget the canoe. The waters around Kunghit are treacherous. The waves roll in out of the Pacific and pound the rocky shores like you wouldn't believe."

"You make it sound unsafe."

"If the sea doesn't get you," Posey said seriously, "Dorsett's goon squad will."

"So I'll use a bigger boat and carry a harpoon," Pitt said cynically.

"Why don't you simply go on the property with a bona fide team of Canadian environmental engineers and blow the whistle on any shady operations?"

Pitt shook his head. "A waste of time. Dorsett's foreman would only close down the mine until they left. Better to investigate when their guard isn't up."

Posey stared past Pitt out the window for several seconds. Then he shrugged. "Okay, I'll arrange for you to work under contract with Environment Canada to investigate the kelp forest around Kunghit Island. You're to study any possible damage to the kelp from chemicals running into the sea from the mining operations. How does that sound?"

"Thank you," Pitt said sincerely. "How much do I get paid?"

Posey picked up on the joke. "Sorry, you're not in the budget. But I might be persuaded to buy you a hamburger at the nearest fast-food joint."

"Done."

"One more thing."

"Are you going it alone?"

"One does not look as suspicious as two."

"Not in this case," said Posey grimly. "I strongly advise you take along one of the local Indians as a guide. That will give you more of an official look. Environment Canada works closely with the tribes to prevent pollution and save forested land. A researcher and a local fisherman working on a project for the government should dilute any doubts by Dorsett security."

"Do you have a name in mind?" asked Pitt.

"Mason Broadmoor. A very resourceful guy. I've hired him before on a number of environmental projects."

"An Indian with the name of Mason Broadmoor?"

"He's a member of the Haida who live on the Queen Charlotte

Islands of British Columbia. Most of them took British names generations ago. They're excellent fishermen and are familiar with the waters around Kunghit Island."

"Is Broadmoor a fisherman?"

"Not really. But he's very creative."

"Creative at what?

Posey hesitated for a few moments, straightened some papers on his desk and then stared at Pitt rather sheepishly.

"Mason Broadmoor," he said finally, "carves totem poles."

18

Arthur Dorsett stepped out of the private elevator to his pent-house suite as he did every morning at precisely seven o'clock, like a bull charging into the ring at Seville, huge, menacing, invincible. He was a giant of a man, brawny shoulders brushing the sides of the door frame as he ducked under the lintel. He had the hairy, muscular build of a professional wrestler. Coarse and wiry sandy hair swirled about his head like a thicket of brambles. His face was ruddy and as fierce as the black eyes that stared from beneath heavy, scraggly brows. He walked with a odd rocking motion, his shoulders dipping up and down like the walking beam of a steam engine.

His skin was rough and tanned by long days in the sun, working in the open mines, driving his miners for higher production, and he could still fill a muck bucket with the best of them. A huge mustache curled downward past the corners of lips that were constantly stretched open like a moray eel's, revealing teeth yellowed from long years of pipe smoking. He radiated contempt and supreme arrogance. Arthur Dorsett was an empire unto himself who followed no laws but his own.

Dorsett shunned the limelight, a difficult feat with his incredible wealth and the $400 million jewelry trade building he built in Sydney. Paid for without bank loans, out of his own coffers, the Trump Towers–like building housed the offices of diamond brokers, traders and merchants, cutting and faceting laboratories and a polishing factory. Known as a major player among diamond producers, Arthur Dorsett also played a highly secret role behind the scenes of the colored gemstone market.

He strode into the large anteroom, past four secretaries without acknowledging their presence, into an office that was located in the center of the building, with no windows to allow a magnificent panoramic view of modern Sydney sprawling outward from its harbor. Too many men who had been crossed in business deals with Dorsett gladly would have hired a sniper to take him out. He entered through a steel door into an office that was plain, even Spartan, with walls two meters thick. The entire room was one gigantic vault where Dorsett directed the family mining ventures and where he had collected and now displayed the largest and most opulent stones dug from his mines and faceted by his cutting workshops. Hundreds of incredibly beautiful stones were laid out on black velvet in glass cases. It was estimated this one room alone held diamonds worth close to $1.2 billion.

Dorsett didn't need a millimeter gauge to measure stones and a diamond scale to weigh them, nor a loupe to detect the flaws or dark spots of carbon within. There was no more practiced eye in the business. Of all the incredible diamonds arrayed for his personal satisfaction, he always came and stared down at the largest, most precious and perhaps the most highly-prized gem in the world.

It was D-grade flawless with tremendous luster, perfect transparency, strong refraction and a fiery dispersion of light. An overhead light beam excited a burst of radiant fire in an eye-dazzling display of the stone's violet-rose color. Discovered by a Chinese worker at the Gladiator mine in 1908, it was the largest diamond ever found on the island, originally weighing in at 1130 carats when rough. Cutting reduced it to 620. The stone was double rose-cut in ninety-eight facets to bring out its brilliance. If any diamond ignited the imagination with thoughts of romance and adventure, it was the Dorsett Rose, as Arthur had modestly named it. The value was inestimable. Few even knew of its existence. Dorsett well knew there were a good fifty men somewhere around the world who would dearly love to murder him in order to gain ownership of the stone.

Reluctantly, he turned away and sat down behind his desk, a huge monstrosity built of polished lava rock with mahogany drawers. He pressed a button on a console that alerted his head secretary that he was now in his office.

She came back over the intercom almost immediately. "Your daughters have been waiting nearly an hour."

Indifferent, Dorsett replied with a voice that was as hard as the diamonds in the room. "Send the little darlin's in." Then he sat back to watch the parade, never failing to enjoy the physical and personal differences of his daughters.

Boudicca, a statuesque giantess, strode through the doorway with the self-assurance of a tigress entering an unarmed village. She was dressed in a ribbed-knit cardigan with matching sleeveless tunic and truffle-and-parchment striped pants stuffed inside a pair of calfskin riding boots. Far taller than her sisters, she towered over all but a very few men. Staring up at her Amazon beauty never failed to inspire expressions of awe. Only slightly shorter than her father, she had his black eyes, but more ominous and veiled than fierce. She wore no makeup, and a flood of reddish-blond hair fell to her hips, loose and flowing. Her body was not given to fat but well proportioned. Her expression was half contemptuous, half evil. She easily dominated anyone in her presence except, of course, her father.

Dorsett saw Boudicca as a son he had lost. Over the years he had begrudgingly accepted her secret lifestyle, because all that truly mattered to him was that Boudicca was as strong willed and unyielding as he was.

Deirdre seemed to float into the room, poised and nonchalant, fashionable in a simple but elegant claret wool double-breasted coatdress. Undeniably glamorous, she was not a woman who invented herself. She knew exactly what she was capable of doing. There was no pretense about her. Delicate facial features and supple body aside, she had definite underlying masculine qualities. She and Boudicca dutifully sat down in two of three chairs placed in front of Dorsett's desk.

Maeve followed her sisters, moving as gracefully as pond reeds in a light breeze, and wearing an indigo plaid wool zip-front shirt with matching skirt over a white ribbed turtleneck. Her long blond hair was soft and glowing, her skin flushed red and her blue eyes blazing with anger. She moved in a straight line between her seated sisters, chin up firmly, staring deeply into her father's eyes, which reflected intrigue and corruption.

"I want my boys!" she snapped. It was not a plea but a demand.

"Sit down, girl." her father ordered, picking up a briar pipe and pointing it like a gun.

"No!" she shouted. "You abducted my sons, and I want them back or by God I'll turn you and these two conniving bitches over to the police, but not before I've exposed you all to the news media."

He looked at her steadily, calmly appraising her defiance. Then he called his secretary over the intercom. "Will you please connect me with Jack Ferguson?" He smiled at Maeve. "You remember Jack, don't you?"

"That sadistic ape you call your superintendent of mines. What about him?"

"I thought you'd like to know. He's baby-sitting the twins."

The anger fled from Maeve's face and was replaced with alarm. "Not Ferguson?"

"A little discipline never hurt growing boys."

She started to say something, but the intercom buzzed and Dorsett held up his hand for silence. He spoke through a speaker phone on his desk. "Jack, you there?"

There was the sound of heavy equipment in the background as Ferguson replied over his portable phone. "I'm here."

"Are the boys nearby?"

"Yes, sir. I've got them loading muck that's spilled from the cars."

"I'd like you to arrange an accident—"

"No!" Maeve screamed. "My God, they're only six years old. You can't murder your own grandchildren!" She was horrified to see that Deirdre had an expression of complete indifference on her face, while Boudicca wore a look as cold as a granite tomb.

"I don't consider those bastards my grandchildren," Dorsett roared back.

Maeve was overcome with sickening fear. It was a battle she could not win. Her sons were in deadly danger, and she saw clearly that her only hope of saving them was to submit to her father's will. She was achingly aware of her helplessness. Somehow she had to stall for time until she devised a plan to save her boys. Nothing else mattered. If only she had gotten her plight across to the man from NUMA. He might have thought of a way to help her. But he was thousands of kilometers away.

She sagged into an empty chair, beaten but still defiant, her emotions in upheaval. "What do you want from me?"

Her father relaxed and pushed a button on the phone, ending the call. The deep creases that ran from the corners of his eyes widened. "I should have beaten you when you were young."

"You did, Daddy dear," she said, remembering. "Many times."

"Enough sentiment," he growled. "I want you to return to the United States and work with their National Underwater & Marine Agency. Watch them carefully. Observe their methods in attempting to discover the cause of the unexplained deaths. If they begin to get close to an answer, do what you can to stall them. Sabotage or murder, whatever it takes. Fail me and those dirty little urchins you whelped in the gutter will surely die. Do well, and they'll live in wealth."

"You're mad," she gasped, stunned at what she'd heard. "You'd murder your own flesh and blood as if it meant nothing—"

"Oh, but you've very wrong, dear sister," Boudicca interrupted. "Twenty billion dollars is far more than nothing."

"What insane scheme have you hatched?" asked Maeve.

"If you hadn't run away from us, you'd know," said Deirdre nastily.

"Daddy is going to collapse the world diamond market," revealed Boudicca as unruffled as if she were describing a new pair of shoes.

Maeve stared at him. "That's impossible. De Beers and the rest of the cartel will never permit a drastic fall in the price of diamonds."

Dorsett seemed to bulk even larger behind his desk. "Despite their usual manipulation of the laws of supply and demand, in another thirty days the collapse will be a reality, when a tidal wave of stones hits the market at prices any child can afford from his or her allowance."

"Even you can't dictate the diamond market."

"You're dead wrong, Daughter," said Dorsett smugly. "The overhyped prices on diamonds have traditionally depended on manufactured scarcity. To exploit the myth of diamond rarity, De Beers has propped up the values by buying into new mines in Canada, Australia, Africa, and then stockpiling the production. When Russia opened up their mines in Siberia and filled a five-story warehouse with thousands of tons of stones, De Beers could hardly allow them to flood the market. So they worked out a deal together. De Beers makes billion-dollar trade loans to the new state of Russia and is paid back in diamonds, thus maintaining high prices in the best interests of the producers and dealers. Many are the mines the cartel has purchased, then closed to keep the supply down. The American pipe in the state of Arkansas is a case in point. If mined, it has every potential of becoming one of the world's leading producers of diamonds. Instead, De Beers bought the property and turned it over to the U.S. Park Service, which only allows tourists to dig around the surface for a small charge."

"They used the same methods with the owners of mining companies from Tanzania to Brazil," said Deirdre. "You taught us well, Daddy. We're all familiar with the behind-the-scenes intrigues of the diamond cartel."

"I'm not," snapped Maeve at Dorsett. "I was never interested in the diamond trade."

"A pity you turned a deaf ear to Daddy's lectures," said Boudicca, "It would have been in your best interests to have been more attentive."

"What has all this to do with causing the market to fall?" asked Maeve. "A collapse in prices would wipe out Dorsett Consolidated Mining too. How could you possibly profit from such a disaster?"

"Better you not know until after the event," Dorsett said, clamping his stained teeth on the stem of the empty pipe. "Unlike Boudicca and Deirdre, you can't be trusted to keep silent."

"Thirty days. That's your timetable?"

Dorsett sat back, folded his huge hands across his chest and nodded. "I've had our mining crews working three shifts, twenty-four hours a day for the past ten years. In another month I will have accumulated a stockpile of over $2 billion worth of stones.

With the worldwide economy flat, diamond sales to consumers have temporarily stagnated. All of the enormous sums the cartel has spent in advertising have failed to push sales. If my instincts are right, the market will reach bottom in thirty days before it rebounds. I intend to attack when it's down.''

"What are you doing in the mines that causes death throughout the ocean?'' demanded Maeve.

"About a year ago, my engineers developed a revolutionary excavator using high-energy pulsed ultrasound to carve through the blue clay that contains the major deposits of diamonds. Apparently, the subterranean rock under the islands we mine creates a resonance that channels into the surrounding water. Though a rare event, it occasionally converges with the resonance from our other mining operations, near Siberia, Chile and Canada. The energy intensifies to a level that can kill animals and humans. However unfortunate, I cannot allow these aberrant side effects to throw off my time schedule.''

"Don't you understand?'' pleaded Maeve. "Don't you care about the sea life and hundreds of people your greed has killed? How many more must die before this madness is satisfied?''

"Only after I have destroyed the diamond market will I stop,'' Dorsett said coldly. He turned to Boudicca. "Where is the yacht?''

"I sent it on to Kunghit Island after I debarked in Honolulu and flew home. My chief of security there has informed me that the Canadian Mounties are becoming suspicious. They've been flying over the island, taking photographs and asking questions of the nearby inhabitants. With your permission, I would like to rejoin the yacht. Your geophysicists are also predicting another convergence approximately five hundred kilometers east of Seattle. I should be standing by to remove any possible wreckage to frustrate investigation by the American Coast Guard.''

"Take the company jet and return as soon as possible.''

"You know where the deaths will occur next?'' Maeve demanded in dismay. "You must warn ships to stay out of the area.''

"Not a practical idea,'' Boudicca answered, "letting the world in on our secret. Besides, Daddy's scientists can only give rough estimates for where and when the sound waves will strike.''

Maeve stared at her sister, her lips slowly tightening. "You had a pretty good idea when you put Deirdre on the *Polar Queen* to save my life.''

Boudicca laughed. ''Is that what you think?''

''That's what she told me.''

''I lied to keep you from informing the NUMA people,'' said Deirdre. ''Sorry, sister dear, father's engineers made a slight miscalculation in time. The acoustic plague was estimated to strike the ship three hours earlier.''

''Three hours earlier . . .'' Maeve murmured as the awful truth slowly dawned on her. ''I would have been on the ship.''

''And you would have died with the others,'' said Deirdre as if disappointed.

''You meant for me to die!'' Maeve gasped, contempt and horror in her expression.

Her father looked at her as if he were examining a stone he'd picked up at his mine. ''You turned your back on your sisters and me. To us, you no longer existed. You still don't.''

19

A strawberry-red floatplane with Chinook Cargo Carriers painted in white block letters on the side of the fuselage rocked gently in the water beside a refueling dock near the Shearwater Airport in British Columbia. A short, brown-haired man with an unsmiling face, dressed in an old-fashioned leather flight suit, was holding a gas nozzle in one of the wing tanks. He looked down and examined the man who walked casually along the dock, carrying a backpack and a large black case. He was dressed in jeans with a skier's down vest. A cowboy hat was set square on his head. When the stranger stopped beside the aircraft and looked up, the pilot nodded at the wide-brimmed hat.

"A Stetson?"

"No, it was custom-made by Manny Gammage out of Austin, Texas."

The stranger studied the floatplane. It looked to have been built prior to 1970. "A de Havilland, isn't she?"

The pilot nodded. "De Havilland Beaver, one of the finest bush planes ever designed."

"An oldie but goody."

"Canadian-built in 1967. She'll lift over four thousand kilograms off a hundred meters of water. Revered as the workhorse of the North. Over a hundred of them are still flying."

"Don't see big radial engines much anymore."

"You a friend of Ed Posey?" the pilot asked abruptly.

"I am," answered Pitt without introducing himself.

"A bit breezy today."

"About twenty knots, I should judge."

"You a flyer?"

"I have a few hours in the air."

"Malcolm Stokes."

"Dirk Pitt."

"I understand you want to fly to Black Water Inlet."

Pitt nodded. "Ed Posey told me that's where I could find a totem carver by the name of Mason Broadmoor."

"I know Mason. His village sits at the lower end of Moresby Island, across the Houston Stewart Channel from Kunghit Island."

"How long a flight?"

"An hour and a half across Hecate Strait. Should get you there in time for lunch."

"Sounds good," said Pitt.

Stokes gestured at the black case. "What you got in there, a trombone?"

"A hydrophone, an instrument for measuring underwater sound."

Without further discussion, Stokes capped the fuel tank and inserted the nozzle back into the gas pump as Pitt loaded his gear on board. After untying the mooring lines and pushing the plane away from the dock with one foot, Stokes made his way to the cockpit.

"Care to ride up front?" he asked.

Pitt smiled inwardly. He saw no passenger seats in the cargo section. "Don't mind if I do."

Pitt strapped himself into the copilot's seat as Stokes started and warmed up the big single radial engine and checked his gauges. Already the receding tide had carried the aircraft three meters from the dock. After a visual check of the channel for other boats or planes, Stokes eased the throttle forward and took off, banking the Beaver over Campbell Island and heading west.

As they climbed, Pitt recalled the report Hiram Yaeger had given him before leaving Washington.

The Queen Charlotte Islands are made up of about 150 islands running parallel to the Canadian mainland 160 kilometers to the east. The total area of the islands comes to 9,584 square kilometers. The population of 5,890 is made up mostly of Haida Indians, who invaded the islands in the eighteenth century. The Haida used the abundant red cedars to build huge dugout canoes and multifamily plank houses supported by massive portal poles, and to carve splendid totem poles as well as masks, boxes and dishes.

The economy is based on lumber and fishing as well as the mining of copper, coal and iron ore. In 1997, prospectors working for Dorsett Consolidated Mining Ltd., found a kimberlite pipe on Kunghit Island, the southernmost island in the Queen Charlotte chain. After drilling a test hole, 98 diamonds were found in one 52-kilogram sample. Although Kunghit Island was part of the South Moresby National Park Reserve, the government allowed Dorsett Consolidated to file a claim and lease the island. Dorsett then launched an extensive excavation operation and closed off the island to all visitors and campers. It was estimated by New York brokers C. Dirgo & Co. that the mine could bring out as much as $2 billion in diamonds.

Pitt's thoughts were interrupted by Stokes. "Now that we're away from prying eyes, how do I know you're Dirk Pitt with the National Underwater & Marine Agency?"

"Do you have the authority to ask?"

Stokes took a leather case from his breast pocket and flipped it open. "Royal Canadian Mounted Police, Criminal Intelligence Directorate."

"So I'm addressing *Inspector* Stokes."

"Yes, sir, that is correct."

"What would you like to see, credit cards, driver's license, NUMA ID, a blood donor card?"

"Just answer one question," said Stokes, "dealing with a shipwreck."

"Go ahead."

"The *Empress of Ireland?*"

Pitt slouched in his seat and grinned. "She was a Canadian & Pacific transatlantic liner that went down after a collision with a collier in the St. Lawrence River a couple of miles from the town of Rimouski in the year 1914. The death toll was over a thousand, many of them from a contingent of the Salvation Army that was going to England for a convention. The ship lies in about fifty meters of water. NUMA surveyed her in May of 1989."

"Very good. You must be who you say you are."

"Why the Mounties?" asked Pitt. "Posey didn't mention anything about a criminal investigation."

"It wasn't Ed's job. Your request to nose around Kunghit Island crossed my desk as a matter of routine. I'm one of a team of five men who have had the Dorsett diamond mine under surveillance for the past nine months."

"Any particular reason?"

"Illegal immigration. We suspect Dorsett smuggles Chinese onto the island to work the mine."

"Why Chinese? Why not hire local Canadian citizens?"

"We believe Dorsett buys workers from criminal syndicates and then uses them as slave labor. Think what he saves in taxes, employee insurance, pensions and union wages."

"You represent Canadian law enforcement. What's stopping you from going in and checking out the workers for proper papers?"

"Dorsett has bought off a raft of bureaucrats and members of Parliament to protect his operations. Every time we attempt to investigate the premises, we run into a battery of high-priced attorneys who throw up a mile of legal roadblocks. Without some kind of documented proof, the CID hasn't a leg to stand on."

"Why do I have this foolish notion that I'm about to be used?" Pitt muttered.

"Your appearance was most opportune, Mr. Pitt. For the Mounties, anyway."

"Let me guess. You expect me to go where no Mounties dare go."

"Well, you're an American. If you get caught trespassing the worst you can expect is to be deported. With us, it could prove a bit of a political mess. My team and I, of course, have our pensions to look forward to."

"Of course," said Pitt sardonically.

"I'll be happy to oblige if you wish to reconsider and order me to return you to the airport at Shearwater."

"As much as I'd like to change my destination for some good

fishing in a stream filled with salmon, there are people dying out there on the sea. I'm here to find out how and if Dorsett Consolidated's mining operations are somehow responsible.''

''I was briefed on the ships struck by an unknown acoustic plague,'' said Stokes. ''It appears we're after the same quarry for different reasons.''

''The trick is to nail Dorsett before more innocent people die.''

''May I ask about your game plan?''

''Nothing complex,'' Pitt answered. ''I hope to infiltrate the mine, hiring Mason Broadmoor as a guide to get me on the island, providing he's willing.''

''If I know Mason, he'll jump at the chance. His brother was fishing near the island about a year ago. One of Dorsett Consolidated's security boats ordered him away. Since the family had been fishing those waters for generations, he refused. They beat him pretty badly and burned his boat. When we investigated, Dorsett's security people claimed that Broadmoor's boat exploded and they rescued him.''

''His word against twenty of them.''

''More like eight, but you get the picture.''

''Now it's your turn,'' said Pitt kindly. ''How am I supposed to help you?''

Stokes pointed out his window at a forested island with a great dirt scar in the middle of it. ''Kunghit Island. They carved a small runway for air transport to ferry in men and supplies. I'll fake engine trouble and we'll drop in. While I tinker under the cowling, you regale the security guards with your tales of derring-do under the sea.''

Pitt stared at Stokes dubiously. ''What do you hope to accomplish besides antagonizing Dorsett's security enforcers?''

''I have my reasons for wanting to land. Reason one. To allow the cameras encased in the floats to take close-up pictures during landing and takeoff.''

''Somehow I have the impression they hate uninvited visitors. What makes you think we won't be stood against a privy and shot?''

''Reason two,'' said Stokes, brushing off Pitt's objections. ''My superiors are hoping for just such an event. Then they can come swooping in here and close the bastards down.''

''Naturally.''

"Reason three. We have an undercover agent working in the mines. We're hoping he can pass me information while we're on the ground."

"We're just full of devious little plots, aren't we?" said Pitt.

"In a more serious vein, if worse comes to worst, I'll let Dorsett's security people know I'm a Mountie before they offer us a cigarette and a blindfold. They're not so stupid as to risk invasion by a small army of law officers running about the place searching for the body of one of their finest."

"You *did* notify your team and superiors we'd be dropping in?"

Stokes looked hurt. "Any disappearance is timed to make the evening newspapers. Not to worry, Dorsett's mine executives abhor bad publicity."

"When exactly do we pull off this marvel of Royal Mounted Police planning?"

Stokes pointed down to the island again. "I should begin my descent in about five minutes."

Pitt could do little but sit back and enjoy the view. Below he could see the great volcanic cone with its central pipe of blue ground that contained the rough diamonds. What looked like a giant bridge of steel girders stretched over the open core, with a myriad of steel cables that raised and lowered the excavated debris. Once they reached the top, the buckets then moved horizontally like ski gondolas across the open pit to buildings where the diamonds were extracted from the tailings, which were then dumped onto a huge mound that enclosed the diggings. The mound also acted as an artificial barrier to discourage anyone from entering or leaving, a reality Pitt found obvious from the total absence of any entrances except one, a tunnel that opened to a road that led to a dock on a small bay. He knew from his map that the bay was called Rose Harbour. As he watched, a tug with an empty barge in tow was pulling away from the dock and heading toward the mainland.

A series of prefabricated buildings grouped between the mound and the pit were apparently used for offices and living quarters for the miners. The enclosure, easily two kilometers in diameter, also accommodated the narrow airstrip with a hangar. The entire mining operation looked like a gigantic scar on the landscape from the air.

"That's one big pockmark," said Pitt.

Without looking down, Stokes said, "That pockmark, as you call it, is where dreams come from."

Stokes leaned out his fuel mixture and starved his big 450-horsepower Pratt & Whitney R-985 Wasp engine until it began to miss and backfire. Already, a voice was coming over the radio warning him away from the property, but he ignored it. "I have a fuel blockage and must borrow your airstrip for an emergency landing. Sorry for the inconvenience, but it can't be helped." Then he switched off the radio.

"Don't you just hate dropping in unannounced?" said Pitt.

Stokes was concentrating on landing the plane, with the engine coughing and barely turning over, and did not reply. He lowered a pair of small wheels through the forward center of the two large pontoons and lined up with the runway. A crosswind caught the plane, and Stokes overcompensated. Pitt tensed slightly as he observed that Stokes lacked full control. The Mountie was reasonably competent but hardly an expert pilot. The landing was rough, and he almost ground-looped.

Before the plane rolled to a stop in front of the airstrip's hangar, it was surrounded by nearly ten men in blue combat fatigues, holding Bushmaster customized M-16 assault rifles with suppressors. A tall, gaunt man in his early thirties and wearing a combat helmet stepped up on one of the floats and opened the door. He entered the aircraft and made his way to the cockpit. Pitt noticed the guard rested his hand on a holstered nine-millimeter automatic.

"This is private property, and you are trespassing," he said in a perfectly friendly voice.

"Sorry," said Stokes. "But the fuel filter clogged. The second time this month. It's this damned stuff they're passing off as gas nowadays."

"How soon can you make repairs and be on your way?"

"Twenty minutes, no more."

"Please hurry," said the security official. "You'll have to remain by your plane."

"May I borrow a bathroom?" Pitt asked politely.

The security guard studied him for a moment, then nodded. "There's one in the hangar. One of my men will escort you."

"You don't know how grateful I am," Pitt said as if in minor agony. He jumped out of the plane and set off toward the hangar with a security guard close at his heels. Once inside the metal structure, he turned as if waiting expectantly for the guard to direct him to the door leading to the bathroom. It was a ploy; he'd already guessed the correct door, but it gave him a brief instant to glance at the aircraft resting on the hangar floor.

A Gulfstream V, the latest development in business jets, was an imposing aircraft. Unlike the earlier Learjet—so eagerly purchased and flown by the rich and famous—whose interior barely had enough room to turn around in, the G V was spacious, giving passengers plenty of elbowroom and enough height for most tall men to stand up straight. Capable of cruising 924 kilometers per hour at an altitude of just under 11,000 meters, with a range of 6,300 nautical miles, the aircraft was powered by a pair of turbofan jets built by BMW and Rolls-Royce.

Dorsett spared no expense for his transportation fleet, thought Pitt. An aircraft like this cost upward of $33 million.

Parked just in front of the main hangar door, menacing and sinister in dark blue-black paint, were a pair of squat looking helicopters. Pitt recognized them as McDonnell Douglas 530 MD Defenders, a military aircraft designed for silent flying and high stability during abnormal maneuvers. A pair of 7.62 millimeter guns were mounted in pods under the fuselage. An array of tracking gear sprouted from the underside of the cockpit. These were scout models specially modified for tracking diamond smugglers or other unwelcome intruders on the ground.

After he came out of the bathroom, he was motioned by the guard into an office. The man who sat at a desk was small, thin, fastidiously attired in a business suit, suave, cool and completely satanic. He turned from a computer monitor and studied Pitt, his deep-set eyes gray and unreadable. Pitt found the man slimy and repellant.

"I am John Merchant, chief of security for this mine," he said with a distinctive Australian accent. "May I see some identification, please?"

Silently, Pitt handed over his NUMA ID and waited.

"Dirk Pitt." Merchant rolled the name on his tongue and repeated it. "Dirk Pitt. Aren't you the chap who found an immense cache of Inca treasure in the Sonoran Desert a few years ago?"

"I was only one member of the team."

"Why have you come to Kunghit?"

"Better you ask the pilot. He's the one who landed the plane on your precious mining property. I'm only a passenger along for the ride."

"Malcolm Stokes is an inspector with the Royal Canadian Mounted Police. He's also a member of the Criminal Investigation Directorate." Merchant gestured toward his computer. "I have an entire data file on him. It's you who are in question."

"You're very thorough," said Pitt. "Taking into account your close contacts in the Canadian government, you probably already know I'm here to study the effects of chemical pollution on the local kelp and fish populations. Would you care to see my documents?"

"I already have copies."

Pitt was tempted to believe Merchant, but he knew Posey well enough to trust his confidence. He decided Merchant was lying. It was an old Gestapo ploy, to make the victim think the accuser knew all there was to know. "Then why bother to inquire?"

"To find if you are in the habit of inaccurate statements."

"Am I under suspicion for some hideous crime?" asked Pitt.

"My job is to apprehend smugglers of illicit diamonds before they traffic their stones to European and Middle Eastern clearinghouses. Because you came here uninvited, I have to consider your motives."

Pitt observed the reflection of the guard in the windows of a glass cabinet. He was standing slightly behind Pitt, to his right, automatic weapon held across his chest. "Since you know who I am and claim to have bona fide documentation for my purpose for coming to the Queen Charlotte Islands, you cannot seriously believe that I'm a diamond smuggler." Pitt rose to his feet. "I've enjoyed the conversation, but I see no reason to hang around."

"I regret that you must be detained temporarily," Merchant said, brisk and businesslike.

"You have no authority."

"Because you are a trespasser on private property under false pretenses, I have every right to make a citizen's arrest."

Not good, Pitt thought. If Merchant dug deeper and connected him to the Dorsett sisters and the *Polar Queen,* then no lies, no matter how creative, could explain his presence here. "What about Stokes? Since you claim you know he's a Mountie, why not turn me over to him?"

"I prefer turning you over to his superiors," Merchant said

almost cheerfully, "but not before I can investigate this matter more thoroughly."

Pitt didn't doubt now that he would not be allowed off the mining property alive. "Is Stokes free to leave?"

"The minute he finishes his unnecessary repairs to the aircraft. I enjoy observing his primitive attempts at surveillance."

"It goes without saying that he'll report my seizure."

"A foregone conclusion," said Merchant dryly.

Outside the hangar came the popping sound of an aircraft engine firing up. Stokes was being forced to take off without his passenger. If he was going to act, Pitt figured that he had less than thirty seconds. He noted an ashtray on the desk with several cigarette butts and assumed Merchant smoked. He threw up his hands in a gesture of defeat.

"If I'm to be detained against my wishes, do you mind if I have a cigarette?"

"Not at all," said Merchant, pushing the ashtray across the desk. "I may even join you."

Pitt had stopped smoking years before, but he made a slow movement as if to reach in the open breast pocket of his shirt. He doubled up his right hand into a fist and clasped it with his left. Then in a lightning move, pulling with one arm and pushing with the other for extra strength, he jammed his right elbow into the security guard's stomach. There came an explosive gasp of agony as the guard doubled over.

Merchant's reaction time was admirable. He pulled a small nine-millimeter automatic from a belt holster and unsnapped the safety in one well-practiced motion. But before the muzzle of the gun could clear the desktop, he found himself staring down the barrel of the guard's automatic rifle, now cradled in Pitt's steady hands, lined up on Merchant's nose. The security chief felt as though he were staring through a tunnel with no light at the other end.

Slowly, he placed his pistol on the desk. "This will do you no good," he said acidly.

Pitt grabbed the automatic and dropped it in his coat pocket. "Sorry I can't stay for dinner, but I don't want to lose my ride."

Then he was through the door and sprinting across the hangar floor. He threw the rifle in a trash receptacle, cleared the door and slowed to a jog as he passed through the ring of guards.

They stared at him suspiciously, but assumed their boss had allowed Pitt to leave. They made no move to stop him as Stokes opened the throttle and the floatplane began moving down the runway. Pitt leaped onto a float, yanked open the door against the wash from the propeller and threw himself inside the cargo bay.

Stokes looked dumbfounded as Pitt slipped into the copilot's seat. "Good Lord! Where did you come from?"

"The traffic was heavy on the way to the airport," Pitt said, catching his breath.

"They forced me to take off without you."

"What happened to your undercover agent?"

"He didn't show. Security around the plane was too tight."

"You won't be happy to learn that Dorsett's security chief, a nasty little jerk called John Merchant, has you pegged as a snooping Mountie from the CID."

"So much for my cover as a bush pilot," Stokes muttered as he pulled back on the control column.

Pitt slid open the side window, stuck his head into the prop blast and looked back. The security guards appeared to be wildly scurrying about like ants. Then he saw something else that caused a small knot in his stomach. "I think I made them mad."

"Could it be something you said?"

Pitt pulled the side window closed. "Actually, I beat up a guard and stole the chief of security's side arm."

"That would do it."

"They're coming after us in one of those armed helicopters."

"I know the type," Stokes said uneasily. "They're a good forty knots faster than this old bus. They'll overhaul us long before we can make it back to Shearwater."

"They can't shoot us down in front of witnesses," said Pitt. "How far to the nearest inhabited community on Moresby Island?"

"Mason Broadmoor's village. It sits on Black Water Inlet, about sixty kilometers north of here. If we get there first, I can make a water landing in the middle of the village fishing fleet."

His adrenaline pumping, Pitt gazed at Stokes through eyes flashing with fire. "Then go for it."

20

Pitt and Stokes quickly became aware they were in a no-win situation from the very start. They had little choice but to take off toward the south before banking on a 180-degree turn for Moresby Island to the north. The McDonnell Douglas Defender helicopter, manned by Dorsett's security men, had merely to lift vertically off the ground in front of the hangar, turn northward and cut in behind the slower floatplane even before the chase shifted into first gear. The de Havilland Beaver's airspeed indicator read 160 knots, but Stokes felt as if he were flying a glider as they crossed the narrow channel separating the two islands.

"Where are they?" he asked without taking his eyes from a low range of cedar- and pine-covered hills directly ahead and the water only a hundred meters below.

"Half a kilometer back of our tail and closing fast," Pitt answered.

"Just one?"

"They probably decided knocking us down was a piece of cake and left the other chopper home."

"But for the extra weight and air drag of our floats, we might be on equal footing."

"Do you carry any weapons in this antique?" asked Pitt.

"Against regulations."

"A pity you didn't hide a shotgun in the floats."

"Unlike your American peace officers, who think nothing of packing an arsenal, we're not keen to wave guns around unless there is a life-threatening situation."

Pitt glanced at him incredulously. "What do you call this mess?"

"An unforeseen difficulty," Stokes answered stoically.

"Then all we have is the nine-millimeter automatic I stole, against two heavy machine guns," said Pitt resignedly. "You know, I downed a chopper by throwing a life raft into its rotor blades a couple of years ago."

Stokes turned and stared at Pitt, unable to believe the incredible calm. "Sorry. Except for a pair of life vests, the cargo bay is bare."

"They're swinging around on our starboard side for a clear shot. When I give the word, drop the flaps and pull back the throttle."

"I'll never pull out if I stall her at this altitude."

"Coming down in treetops beats a bullet in the brain and crashing in flames."

"I never thought of it quite like that," Stokes said grimly.

Pitt watched intently as the blue-black helicopter pulled parallel to the floatplane and seemed to hang there, like a hovering falcon eyeing a pigeon. They were so close that Pitt could discern the expressions on the faces of the pilot and copilot. They were both smiling. Pitt opened his side window and held the automatic out of sight under the frame.

"No warning over the radio?" said Stokes disbelievingly. "No demand we return to the mine?"

"These guys play tough. They wouldn't dare kill a Mountie unless they've got orders from someone high up in Dorsett Consolidated."

"I can't believe they expect to get away with it."

"They're sure as hell going to try," Pitt said quietly, his eyes locked on the gunner. "Get ready." He was not optimistic. Their only advantage, which was really no advantage at all, was that the 530 MD Defender was better suited for ground attack than air-to-air combat.

Stokes held the control column between his knees as one hand embraced the flap levers and the other gripped the throttle. He found himself wondering why he placed so much trust in a man he had known less than two hours. The answer was simple. In all his years with the Mounties he had seen few men who were in such absolute control of a seemingly hopeless situation.

"Now!" Pitt shouted, raising and firing off the automatic in the same breath.

Stokes rammed the flaps to the full down position and slapped back the throttle. The old Beaver, without the power of its engine and held by the wind resistance against the big floats, slowed as abruptly as if it had entered a cloud of glue.

At almost the same instant, Stokes heard the rapid-fire stammer of a machine gun and the thump of bullets on one wing. He also heard the sharp crack of Pitt's automatic. This was no fight, he thought as he frantically threw the near-stalling plane around in the air, this was a high school quarterback facing the entire defensive line of the Phoenix Cardinal football team. Then suddenly, for some inexplicable reason the shooting stopped. The nose of the plane was dropping, and he pushed the throttle forward again to regain a small measure of control.

Stokes stole a glance sideways as he leveled out the floatplane and picked up speed. The helicopter had veered off. The copilot was slumped sideways in his seat behind several bullet holes in the plastic bubble of the cockpit. Stokes was surprised to find that the Beaver still responded to his commands. What surprised him even more was the look on Pitt's face. It was sheer disappointment.

"Damn!" Pitt muttered. "I missed."

"What are you talking about? You hit the copilot."

Pitt, angry at himself, stared at him. "I was aiming at the rotor assembly."

"You timed it perfectly," Stokes complimented him. "How did you know the exact instant to give me the signal and then shoot?"

"The pilot stopped smiling."

Stokes let it go. They weren't out of the storm yet. Broadmoor's village was still thirty kilometers away.

"They're coming around for another pass," said Pitt.

"No sense in attempting the same dodge."

Pitt nodded. "I agree. The pilot will be expecting it. This time pull back on the control column and do an Immelmann."

"What's an Immelmann?"

Pitt looked at him. "You don't know? How long have you been flying, for God's sake?"

"Twenty-one hours, give or take."

"Oh, that's just great," Pitt groaned. "Pull up in a half loop and then do a half roll at the top, to end up going in the opposite direction."

"I'm not sure I'm up for that."

"Don't the Mounties have qualified professional pilots?"

"None who were available for this assignment," Stokes said stiffly. "Think you might hit a vital part of the chopper this time?"

"Not unless I'm amazingly lucky," Pitt replied. "I'm down to three rounds."

There was no hesitating on the part of the Defender's pilot. He angled in for a direct attack from above and to the side of his helpless quarry. A well-designed attack that left little room for Stokes to maneuver.

"Now!" Pitt yelled. "Put your nose down to gain speed and then pull up into your loop."

Stokes' inexperience caused hesitation. He was barely coming to the top of the loop in preparation for the half roll when the 7.62 millimeter shells began smashing into the floatplane's thin aluminum skin. The windshield burst into a thousand pieces as shells hammered the instrument panel. The Defender's pilot altered his aim and raked his fire from the cockpit across the fuselage. It was an error that kept the Beaver in the air. He should have blasted the engine.

Pitt fired off his final three rounds and hurled himself forward and down to make himself as small a target as possible in an act that was pure illusion.

Remarkably, Stokes had completed the Immelmann, late to be sure, but now the Beaver was headed away from the helicopter before its pilot could swing his craft around 180 degrees. Pitt shook his head in dazed incredulity and checked his body for wounds. Except for a rash of small cuts on his face from slivers that had flown off the shattered windshield, he was unscathed. The Beaver was in level flight, and the radial engine was still roaring smoothly at full revolutions. The engine was the only part of the plane that hadn't been riddled with bullets. He looked at Stokes sharply.

"Are you okay?"

Stokes slowly turned and gazed at Pitt through unfocused eyes. "I think the bastards just shot me out of my pension," he murmured. He coughed and then his lips were painted with blood that seeped down his chin and trickled onto his chest. Then he slumped forward against his shoulder harness, unconscious.

Pitt took the copilot's control wheel in his hands and immediately threw the floatplane around into a hard 180-degree bank until he was heading back on a course toward Mason Broadmoor's village. His snap turn caught the helicopter's pilot off guard, and a shower of bullets sprayed the empty air behind the floatplane's tail.

He wiped away the blood that had trailed into one eye and took stock. Most of the aircraft was stitched with over a hundred holes, but the control systems and surfaces were undamaged and the big 450 Wasp engine was still pounding away on every one of its cylinders.

Now what to do?

The first plan that ran through his mind was to make an attempt at ramming the helicopter. The old take 'em with you routine, Pitt mused. But that's all it could have been, an attempt. The Defender was far more nimble in the air than the lumbering Beaver with its massive pontoons. He'd stand as much chance as a cobra against a mongoose, a fight the mongoose never failed to win against the slower cobra. Only when it came up against a rattlesnake did the mongoose go down to defeat. The crazy thought running through Pitt's mind became divine inspiration as he sighted a low ridge of rocks about half a kilometer ahead and slightly to his right.

There was a path toward the rocks through a stand of tall Douglas fir trees. He dove between the trees, his wingtips brushing the needles of the upper branches. To anyone else it would have seemed like a desperate act of suicidal madness. The gambit misled the Defender's pilot, who broke off the third attack and followed slightly above and behind the floatplane, waiting to observe what looked like a certain crash.

Pitt kept the throttle full against its stop and gripped the control wheel with both hands, eyes focused on the wall of rocks that loomed ahead. The airstream blasted through the shattered windshield, and he was forced to turn his head sideways in order to see. Fortunately, the gale swept away the trickling blood and the tears that it pried from his squinting eyes.

He flew on between the trees. There could be no misjudgment, no miscalculation. He had to make the right move at the exact moment in time. A tenth of a second either way would spell certain death. The rocks were rushing toward the plane as if driven from behind. Pitt could clearly see them now, gray-and-brown jagged boulders with black streaks. He didn't have to look to see the needle on the altimeter registering on zero or the needle on the tachometer wavering far into the red. The old girl was hurtling toward destruction just as fast as she could fly.

"Low!" he shouted into the wind rushing through the smashed windshield. "Two meters low!"

He barely had time to compensate before the rocks were on him. He gave the control column a precisely measured jerk, just enough to raise the plane's nose, just enough so the tips of the propeller whipped over the ridge, missing the crest by centimeters. He heard the sudden crunch of metal as the aluminum floats smashed into the rocks and tore free of the fuselage. The Beaver shot into the air, as graceful as a soaring hawk released from its tether. Unburdened by the weight of the bulky floats, which lay smashed against the rocks, and with the drag on the aircraft decreased by nearly half, the ancient plane became more maneuverable and gained another thirty knots in airspeed. She responded to Pitt's commands instantly, without a trace of sluggishness as she chewed the air, fighting for altitude.

Now, he thought, a satanic grin on his lips, I'll show you an Immelmann. He threw the aircraft into a half loop and then snapped it over in a half roll, heading on a direct course toward the helicopter. "Write your will, sucker!" he shouted, his voice drowned out by the rush of wind and the roar of the engine's exhaust. "Here comes the Red Baron."

Too late the chopper's pilot read Pitt's intentions. There was nowhere to dodge, nowhere to hide. The last thing he expected was an assault by the battered old floatplane. But here it was closing on a collision course at almost two hundred knots. It came roaring at him at a speed he didn't believe possible. He made a series of violent maneuvers, but the pilot of the old floatplane anticipated his moves and kept coming on. He angled the helicopter's nose toward his opponent in a wild attempt to blast the punctured Beaver out of the sky before the imminent crash.

Pitt saw the helicopter turn head-on, saw the flash from the guns in the pods, heard the shells punching into the big radial engine. Oil suddenly spurted from under the cowling, streaming onto the exhaust stacks and causing a dense trail of blue smoke to streak behind the plane. Pitt held up a hand to shield his eyes from the hot oil splattering against his face in stinging torrents from the airstream.

The sight that froze in his memory a microsecond before the impact was the expression of grim acceptance on the face of the helicopter's pilot.

The prop and engine of the floatplane smashed squarely into the helicopter just behind the cockpit in an explosion of metal and debris that sheared off the tail rotor boom. Deprived of its torque compensation, the main body of the helicopter was thrown into a violent lateral drift. It spun around crazily for several revolutions before plummeting like a stone, five hundred meters to the ground. Unlike special-effects crashes in motion pictures, it didn't immediately burst into flames after crumpling into an unrecognizable mass of smoldering wreckage. Nearly two minutes passed before flames flickered from the debris and a blinding sheet of flame enveloped it.

Pieces of the Beaver's shattered propeller spun into the sky like a fireworks pinwheel. The cowling seemed to burst off the engine and fluttered like a wounded bird into the trees. The engine froze and stopped as quickly as if Pitt had turned off the ignition switch. He wiped the oil from his eyes, and all he could see over the exposed cylinder heads was a carpet of treetops. The Beaver's airspeed fell off, and she stalled as he braced himself for the crash. The controls were still functioning, and he tried to float the plane down into the upper tree limbs.

He almost made it. But the outer edge of the right wing collided with a seventy-meter-tall red cedar, throwing the aircraft into an abrupt ninety-degree turn. Now totally out of control and dead in what little sky was left, the plane plunged into a solid mass of trees. The left wing wrapped itself around another towering cedar and was torn away. Green pine needles closed over the red plane, blotting it out from any view from above. The trunk of a fir tree, half a meter wide, rose in front of the battered aircraft. The propeller hub struck the tree head-on and punched right through it. The engine was pulled from its mountings as the upper half of the tree fell across the careening aircraft and knocked off the tail section. What remained of the wreckage plowed into the moist compost earth of the forest floor before finally coming to a dead stop.

For the next few minutes the ground below the trees was as silent as a cemetery. Pitt sat there, too stunned to move. He stared dazedly through the opening that was once the windshield. He noticed for the first time that the entire engine was gone and wondered vaguely where it went. At last his mind began to come level again, and he reached over and examined Stokes.

The Mountie shuddered in a fit of coughing, then shook his head feebly and regained a small measure of consciousness. He stared dumbly over the instrument panel at the pine branches that hung into the cockpit. "How did we come down in the forest?" he mumbled.

"You slept through the best part," Pitt muttered, as he tenderly massaged a gang of bruises.

Pitt didn't require eight years of medical school to know Stokes would surely die if he didn't get to a hospital. Quickly, he unzipped the old flying suit, ripped opened the Mountie's shirt and searched for the wound. He found it to the left of the breastbone, below the shoulder. There was so little blood and the hole was so small, he almost missed it. This wasn't made by a bullet, was Pitt's first reaction. He gently probed the hole and touched a sharp piece of metal. Puzzled, he looked up at the frame that once held the windshield. It was smashed beyond recognition. The impact of a bullet had driven a splinter from the aluminum frame into Stokes' chest, penetrating the left lung. Another centimeter and it would have entered the heart.

Stokes coughed up a wad of blood and spit it out the open window. "Funny," he murmured, "I always thought I'd get shot in a highway chase or in a back alley."

"No such luck."

"How bad does it look?"

"A metal splinter in your lung," Pitt explained. "Are you in pain?"

"More of a throbbing ache than anything else."

Pitt stiffly rose out of his seat and came around behind Stokes. "Hang on, I'll get you out of here."

Within ten minutes, Pitt had kicked open the crumpled entry door and carefully manhandled Stokes' deadweight outside, where he gently laid him on the soft ground. It took no small effort, and he was panting heavily by the time he sat next to the Mountie to catch his breath. Stokes' face tightened in agony more than once, but he never uttered so much as a low moan. On the verge of slipping into unconsciousness, he closed his eyes.

Pitt slapped him awake. "Don't black out on me, pal. I need you to point the way to Mason Broadmoor's village."

Stokes' eyes fluttered open, and he looked at Pitt questioningly, as if recalling something. "The Dorsett helicopter," he said between coughs. "What happened to those bastards who were shooting at us?"

Pitt stared back at the smoke rising above the forest and grinned. "They went to a barbecue."

21

Pitt had expected to trudge through snow in January on Kunghit Island, but only a light blanket of the white stuff had fallen on the ground, and much of that had melted since the last storm. He pulled Stokes along behind him on a travois, a device used for hauling burdens by American Plains Indians. He couldn't leave Stokes, and to attempt carrying the Mountie on his back was inviting internal hemorrhaging, so he lashed two dead-branch poles together with cargo tie-down straps he scrounged in the wreckage of the aircraft. Rigging a platform between the poles and a harness on one end, he strapped Stokes to the middle of the travois. Then throwing the harness end over his shoulders, Pitt began dragging the injured Mountie through the woods. Hour followed hour, the sun set and night came on as he struggled north through the darkness, setting his course by the compass he'd removed from the aircraft's instrument panel, an expedient he had used several years previously when trekking across the Sahara Desert.

Every ten minutes or so Pitt asked Stokes, "You still with me?"

"Hanging in," the Mountie repeated weakly.

"I'm looking at a shallow stream that runs to the west."

"You've come to Wolf Creek. Cross it and head northwest."

"How much farther to Broadmoor's village?"

Stokes replied in a hoarse murmur. "Two, maybe three kilometers."

"Keep talking to me, you hear?"

"You sound like my wife."

"You married?"

"Ten years, to a great lady who gave me five children."

Pitt readjusted the harness straps, which were cutting into his chest, and pulled Stokes across the stream. After plodding through the underbrush for a kilometer, he came to a faint path that led in the direction he was headed. The path was grown over in places, but it offered relatively free passage, a godsend to Pitt after having forced his way through woods thick with shrubs growing between the trees.

Twice he thought he'd lost the path, but after continuing on the same course for several meters, he would pick it up again. Despite the freezing temperature, his exertions were making him sweat. He dared not allow himself to stop and rest. If Stokes was to live to see his wife and five children again, Pitt had to keep going. He kept up a one-way conversation with the Mountie, fervently trying to keep him from drifting into a coma from shock. Concentrating on keeping one foot moving ahead of the other, Pitt failed to recognize anything strange.

Stokes whispered something, but Pitt couldn't make it out. He turned his head, cocked an ear and paused. "You want me to stop?" Pitt asked.

"Smell it . . . ?" Stokes barely whispered.

"Smell what?"

"Smoke."

Then Pitt had it too. He inhaled deeply. The scent of wood smoke was coming from somewhere ahead. He was tired, desperately tired, but he leaned forward against the harness and staggered on. Soon his ears picked up the sound of a small gas engine, of a chain saw cutting into wood. The wood smell became stronger, and he could see smoke drifting over the tops of the trees in the early light of dawn. His heart was pounding under the strain, but he wasn't about to quit this close to his destination.

The sun rose but remained hidden behind dark gray clouds. A light drizzle was falling when he stumbled into a clearing that touched the sea and opened onto a small harbor. He found himself staring at a small community of log houses with corrugated metal roofs. Smoke was rising out of their stone chimneys. Tall cylindrical totem poles were standing in different parts of the village, carved with the features of stacked animal and human figures. A small fleet of fishing boats rocked gently beside a floating dock, their crews working over engines and repairing nets. Several children, standing under a shed with open sides, were observing a man carving a huge log with a chain saw. Two women chatted as they hung wash on a line. One of them spotted Pitt, pointed and began shouting at the others.

Overcome by exhaustion, Pitt sank to his knees as a crowd of a dozen people rushed toward him. One man, with long straight black hair and a round face, knelt down beside Pitt and put an arm around his shoulder. "You're all right now," he said with concern. He motioned to three men who gathered around Stokes and gave them an order. "Carry him into the tribal house."

Pitt looked at the man. "You wouldn't by chance be Mason Broadmoor?"

Coal-black eyes stared at him curiously. "Why, yes, I am."

"Boy," said Pitt as he sagged bone weary to the soft ground, "am I ever glad to see you."

The nervous giggle of a little girl roused Pitt from a light sleep. Tired as he was, he'd only slept four hours. He opened his eyes, stared at her a moment, gave her a bright smile and crossed his eyes. She ran out of the room, yelling for her mother.

He was in a cozy room with a small stove radiating wondrous heat, lying in a bed made up of bear and wolf hides. He smiled to himself at the recollection of Broadmoor standing in the middle of an isolated Indian village with few modern conveniences, calling over his satellite phone for an air ambulance to transport Stokes to a hospital on the mainland.

Pitt had borrowed the phone to contact the Mountie office at Shearwater. At the mention of Stokes' name, he was immediately put through to an Inspector Pendleton, who questioned Pitt in detail about the events commencing the previous morning. Pitt ended the briefing by giving Pendleton directions to the crash site so the Mounties could send in a team to retrieve the cameras inside the pontoons, if they had survived the impact.

A seaplane arrived before Pitt had finished a bowl of fish soup that was thrust on him by Broadmoor's wife. Two paramedics and a doctor examined Stokes and assured Pitt the Mountie had every chance of pulling through. Only after the seaplane had lifted off the water on its flight back to the mainland and the nearest hospital had Pitt gratefully accepted the loan of the Broadmoor family bed and fallen dead asleep.

Broadmoor's wife entered from the main living room and kitchen. A woman of grace and poise, stout yet supple, Irma Broadmoor had haunting coffee eyes and a laughing mouth. "How are you feeling, Mr. Pitt? I didn't expect you to wake up for another three hours at least."

Pitt checked and made sure he still wore his pants and shirt before he threw back the covers and dropped his bare feet to the floor. "I'm sorry to have put you and your husband out of your bed."

She laughed, a light musical laugh. "The time is a little past noon. You've only been asleep since eight o'clock."

"I'm most grateful for your hospitality."

"You must be hungry. That bowl of fish soup wasn't enough for a big man like you. What would you like to eat?"

"A can of beans will be fine."

"People sitting around a campfire eating canned beans in the north woods is a myth. I'll grill some salmon steaks. I hope you like salmon."

"I do indeed."

"While you're waiting, you can talk to Mason. He's working outside."

Pitt pulled on his socks and hiking boots, ran his hands through his hair and faced the world. He found Broadmoor in the open shed, chiseling away on a five-meter-long red cedar log that lay horizontal on four heavy-duty sawhorses. Broadmoor was attacking it with a round wooden mallet shaped like a bell and a concave chisel called a fantail gouge. The carving was not far enough along for Pitt to visualize the finished product. The faces of animals were still in the rough stage.

Broadmoor looked up as Pitt approached. "Have a good rest?"

"I didn't know bearskins were so soft."

Broadmoor smiled. "Don't let the word out or they'll be extinct within a year."

"Ed Posey told me you carved totem poles. I've never seen one in the works before."

"My family have been carvers for generations. Totems evolved because the early Indians of the Northwest had no written language. Family histories and legends were preserved by carving symbols, usually animals, on red cedar trees."

"Do they have religious significance?" asked Pitt.

Broadmoor shook his head. "They were never worshiped as icons of gods, but respected more as guardian spirits."

"What are the symbols on this pole?"

"This is a mortuary pole, or what you might call a commemorative column. The pole is in honor of my uncle, who passed away last week. When I finish the carvings, they will illustrate his personal crest, which was an eagle and a bear, along with a traditional Haida figure of the deceased. After completion it will be erected, during a feast, at the corner of his widow's house."

"As a respected master carver, you must be booked up for many months in advance."

Broadmoor shrugged modestly. "Almost two years."

"Do you know why I'm here?" Pitt asked, and the abrupt question caught Broadmoor with the mallet raised to strike the fantail gouge.

The wood-carver laid his tools aside and motioned for Pitt to follow him to the edge of the harbor, where he stopped beside a small boathouse that extended into the water. He opened the doors and stepped inside. Two small craft floated within a U-shaped dock.

"Are you into Jet Skis?" asked Pitt.

Broadmoor smiled. "I believe the term is now watercraft."

Pitt studied the pair of sleek Duo 300 WetJets by Mastercraft Boats. High-performance craft that could seat two people, they were vividly painted with Haida animal symbols. "They look like they can almost fly."

"Over water, they do. I modified their engines to gain another fifteen horsepower. They move along at almost fifty knots." Broadmoor suddenly changed the subject. "Ed Posey said you wanted to circle Kunghit Island with acoustic measuring equipment. I thought the watercraft might be an efficient means of conducting your project."

"They'd be ideal. Unfortunately, my hydrophone gear was badly damaged when Stokes and I crashed. The only other avenue left open to me is to probe the mine itself."

"What do you hope to discover?"

"The method of excavation Dorsett is using to retrieve the diamonds."

Broadmoor picked up a pebble at the waterline and threw it far out into the deep green water. "The company has a small fleet of boats patrolling the waters around the island," he said finally. "They're armed and have been known to attack fishermen who venture too close."

"It seems Canadian government officials didn't tell me all I needed to know," said Pitt, cursing Posey under his breath.

"I guess they figured since you were under their license to do field research, you wouldn't be harassed by the mine's security."

"Your brother. Stokes mentioned the assault and burning of his boat."

He pointed back toward the partially carved totem pole. "Did he also tell you they killed my uncle?"

Pitt shook his head slowly. "No. I'm sorry."

"I found his body floating eight kilometers out to sea. He had lashed himself to a pair of fuel cans. The water was cold, and he died of exposure. All we ever found of his fishing boat was a piece of the wheelhouse."

"You think Dorsett's security people murdered him."

"I know they murdered him," Broadmoor said, anger in his eyes.

"What about the law?"

Broadmoor shook his head. "Inspector Stokes only represents a token investigative force. After Arthur Dorsett sent his prospecting geologists swarming all over the islands until they found the main diamond source on Kunghit, he used his power and wealth to literally take over the island from the government. Never mind that the Haida claim the island as tribal sacred ground. Now it is illegal for any of my people to set foot on the island without permission or to fish within four kilometers of its shore. We can be arrested by the Mounties who are paid to protect us."

"I see why the mine's chief of security has so little regard for the law."

"Merchant, 'Dapper John' as he's called," Broadmoor said, pure hatred in his round face. "Lucky you escaped. Chances are you'd have simply disappeared. Many men have attempted to search for diamonds in and around the island. None were successful and none were ever seen again."

"Has any of the diamond wealth gone to the Haida?" Pitt asked.

"So far we've been screwed," answered Broadmoor. "Whether wealth from the diamonds will come to us has become more a legal than a political issue. We've negotiated for years in an attempt to get a piece of the action, but Dorsett's attorneys have stalled us in the courts."

"I can't believe the Canadian government allows Arthur Dorsett to dictate to them."

"The country's economy is on the ropes, and the politicians close their eyes to payoffs and corruption while embracing any special interest that slips money into the treasury." He paused and stared into Pitt's eyes as if trying to read something. "What is your interest, Mr. Pitt? Do you want to shut the mine down?"

Pitt nodded. "I do, providing I can prove their excavation is causing the acoustic plague responsible for the mass killing of humans and sea life."

He looked at Pitt. "I will take you inside the mining property."

Pitt considered the offer briefly. "You have a wife and children. No sense in risking two lives. Put me on the island and I'll figure a way to get over the mound without being seen."

"Can't be done. Their security systems are state-of-the-art. A squirrel can't get past them, as proven by their little bodies that litter the mound, along with those of hundreds of other animals that inhabited the island before Dorsett's mining operation gutted what was once a beautiful environment. And then there are the Alsatian police dogs that can smell out a diamond-smuggling intruder at a hundred meters."

"There's always the tunnel."

"You'll never get through it alone."

"Better that than your wife becoming another widow."

"You don't understand," Broadmoor said patiently; his eyes burned with consuming flames of revenge. "The mine pays my tribal community to keep their kitchen stocked with fresh fish. Once a week my neighbors and I sail to Kunghit and deliver our catch. At the docks we load it on carts and transport the fish through the tunnel to the office of the head cook. He serves us breakfast, pays us in cash—not nearly what the catch is worth—and then we leave. You've got black hair. You could pass for a Haida if you wear fisherman's work clothes and keep your head down. The guards are more concerned with diamonds smuggled out of camp than fish coming in. Since we only deliver and take nothing, we're not suspect."

"Are there no good paying jobs for your people at the mine?"

Broadmoor shrugged. "To forget how to fish and hunt is to forget independence. The monies we make stocking their kitchen goes toward a new school for our children."

"There's a small problem. Dapper John Merchant. We've met and struck up a mutual dislike. He had a close look at my face."

Broadmoor waved a hand airily. "Merchant recognizing you is not a problem. He'd never soil his expensive Italian shoes by hanging around the tunnel and kitchens. In this weather he seldom shows his face outside his office."

"I won't be able to gather much information from the kitchen help," said Pitt. "Do you know any miners you can trust to describe the excavation procedures?"

"All the mine workers are Chinese, illegally brought in by criminal syndicates. None speak English. Your best hope is an old mining engineer who hates Dorsett Consolidated with a passion."

"Can you contact him?"

"I don't even know his name. He works the graveyard shift and usually eats breakfast about the same time we deliver our fish. We've talked a few times over a cup of coffee. He's not happy about the working conditions. During our last conversation, he claimed that in the past year over twenty Chinese workers have died in the mines."

"If I can get ten minutes alone with him, he might be of great help in solving the acoustics enigma."

"No guarantee he'll be there when we make the delivery," said Broadmoor.

"I'll have to gamble," Pitt said thoughtfully. "When do you deliver your next catch?"

"The last of our village fleet should be docking within a few hours. We'll ice and crate the catch later this evening and be ready to head for Kunghit Island at first light."

Pitt wondered if he was physically and mentally primed to lay his life on the line again. Then he thought of the hundreds of dead bodies he'd seen on the cruise ship, and there wasn't the slightest doubt about what he must do.

22

Six small fishing boats, painted in a variety of vivid colors, sailed into Rose Harbour, their decks stacked with wooden crates filled with fish packed in ice. The diesel engines made a soft chugging sound through tall exhaust stacks as they turned the shafts to the propellers. A low mist covered the water and turned it a gray green. The sun was half a globe on the eastern horizon, and the wind was less than five knots. The waves showed no whitecaps, and the only foam came from the prop wash and the bows of the boats as they shouldered their way through gentle swells.

Broadmoor came up to Pitt, who was sitting in the stern, watching the gulls that dipped and soared over the boat's wake in hope of a free meal. "Time to go into your act, Mr. Pitt."

Pitt could never get Broadmoor to call him Dirk. He nodded and pretended to carve a nose on a half-finished mask the Haida had loaned him. He was dressed in yellow oilskin pants with suspenders that were slung over a heavy woolen sweater knitted by Irma Broadmoor. He wore a stocking cap pulled down over his thick, black eyebrows. Indians are not known for five o'clock shadows so he had given his face a close shave. He did not look up as he lightly scraped the dull side of the knife over the mask, staring out of the corners of his eyes at the long dock—not a small pier but a true landing stage for big ships, with anchored pilings—that loomed larger as the boats entered the harbor. A tall crane moved on rails along one side of the dock to unload heavy equipment and other cargo from oceangoing ships.

A large craft with unusually smooth lines and a globular-shaped superstructure, unlike any luxury yacht Pitt had ever seen, lay moored to the dock. Her twin high-performance fiberglass hulls were designed for speed and comfort. She looked capable of skimming the sea at over eighty knots. Going by Giordino's description of a seagoing, space-age design, this was the boat seen running from the freighter *Mentawai*. Pitt looked for the name and port, normally painted across the transom, but no markings marred the beauty of the yacht's sapphire-blue hull.

Most owners are proud of their pet name for their boat, Pitt thought, and its port of registry. He had a pretty good idea why Arthur Dorsett didn't advertise his yacht.

His interest kindled, he stared openly at the windows with their tightly drawn curtains. The open deck appeared deserted. None of the crew or passengers were about this early in the morning. He was about to turn his attention from the yacht and focus on half a dozen uniformed security guards standing on the dock, when a door opened and a woman stepped out onto the deck.

She was incredibly stunning, Amazon tall, strikingly beautiful. Shaking her head, she tossed a long, unbrushed mane of red-blond hair out of her face. She was wearing a short robe and looked as if she had just risen from bed. Her breasts looked plump but oddly out of proportion, and were completely covered by the robe that shielded any hint of cleavage. Pitt perceived an untamed, ferocious look about her, as undaunted as a tigress surveying her domain. Her gaze swept over the little fishing fleet, then fell on Pitt when she caught him openly staring at her.

The everyday, devil-may-care Pitt would have stood up, swept off his stocking cap and bowed. But he had to play the role of an Indian, so he looked at her expressionless and merely nodded a respectful greeting. She turned away and dismissed him as if he were simply another tree in the forest, while a uniformed steward approached and held out a cup of coffee on a silver tray. Shivering in the cold dawn, she returned inside the main salon.

"She's quite impressive, isn't she?" said Broadmoor, smiling at the look of awe on Pitt's face.

"I have to admit she's unlike any woman I've ever seen."

"Boudicca Dorsett, one of Arthur's three daughters. She shows up unexpectedly several times a year on that fancy yacht of hers."

So this was the third sister, Pitt mused. Perlmutter had described her as ruthless and as cold and hard as ice from the bottom of a glacier. Now that he had laid eyes on Dorsett's third daughter, Pitt found it hard to believe Maeve had come out of the same womb as Deirdre and Boudicca. "No doubt to demand higher production from her slave laborers and count the take."

"Neither," said Broadmoor. "Boudicca is director of the company's security organization. I'm told she travels from mine to mine, inspecting the systems and personnel for any weaknesses."

"Dapper John Merchant will be particularly vigilant while she's probing for cracks in his security precautions," said Pitt. "He'll take special pains to ensure his guards look alert to impress his boss."

"We'll have to be extra cautious," Broadmoor agreed. He nodded toward the security guards on the dock, waiting to inspect the fishing boats. "Look at that. Six of them. They never sent more than two on any other delivery. The one with the medallion around his neck is in charge of the dock. Name is Crutcher. He's a mean one."

Pitt gave the guards a cursory glance to see if he recognized any that had gathered around the floatplane during his intrusion with Stokes. The tide was out, and he had to stare up at the men on the dock. He was especially apprehensive about being recognized by the guard he'd laid out in John Merchant's office. Luckily, none looked familiar.

They carried their weapons slung over one shoulder, muzzle pointing forward in the general direction of the Indian fishermen. It was all for show and intimidation, Pitt quickly perceived. They weren't about to shoot anyone in front of observing seamen on a nearby cargo ship. Crutcher, a cold-faced, arrogant young man of no more than twenty-six or -seven, stepped up to the edge of the dock as Broadmoor's helmsman eased the fishing boat along the pilings. Broadmoor cast a line that fell over the guard's combat boots.

"Hi there, friend. How about tying us up?"

The cold-faced guard kicked the rope off the dock back onto the boat. "Tie up yourself," he snapped.

A dropout from a Special Forces team, that one, Pitt thought as he caught the line. He scrambled up a ladder onto the dock, and purposely brushed against Crutcher as he looped the line around a small bollard.

Crutcher lashed out with his boot and kicked Pitt upright, then grabbed him by his suspenders and shook him violently. "You stinking fish head, mind your manners."

Broadmoor froze. It was a trick. The Haida were a quiet people, not prone to quick anger. He thought with fearful certainty that Pitt would shake himself loose and punch the contemptuous guard.

But Pitt didn't bite. He relaxed his body, rubbed a hand over a blossoming bruise on his buttocks and stared at Crutcher with an unfathomable gaze. He pulled off his stocking cap as if in respect, revealing a mass of black hair whose natural curls had been greased straight. He shrugged with a careless show of deference.

"I was not careful. I'm sorry."

"You don't look familiar," said Crutcher coldly.

"I make this trip twenty times," Pitt said quietly. "I've seen you lots before. Your name is Crutcher. Three deliveries back, you punched my gut for unloading the fish too slow."

The guard studied Pitt for a moment, then gave a short laugh, a jackal laugh. "Get in my way again, and I'll boot your ass across the channel."

Pitt registered a look of friendly resignation and jumped back onto the deck of the fishing boat. The rest of the fishing fleet was slipping into the openings at the dock between the supply ships. Where there was no room, the boats tied together parallel, end to end, the crew of the outer boat transferring their cargo of fish across the deck of the one moored to the dock. Pitt joined the fishermen and began passing crates of salmon up to one of Broadmoor's crew, who stacked them on flatbed trailers that were hitched to a small tractor vehicle with eight drive wheels. The crates were heavy, and Pitt's biceps and back soon ached in protest. He gritted his teeth, knowing the guards would suspect he didn't belong if he couldn't heave the ice-filled fish crates around with the ease of the Haida.

Two hours later the trailers were loaded, then four of the guards and the crews of the fishing boats piled aboard as the train set off toward the mining operation's mess hall. They were stopped at the tunnel entrance, herded into a small building and told to strip to their underwear. Then their clothes were searched and they were individually X-rayed. All passed scrutiny except one Haida who absentmindedly carried a large fishing knife in his boot. Pitt found it strange that instead of merely confiscating the knife, it was returned and the fisherman sent back to his boat. The rest were allowed to dress and reboard the trailers for the journey to the excavation area.

"I would think they'd search you for concealed diamonds when you came out rather than entering," said Pitt.

"They do," explained Broadmoor. "We go through the same procedure when we exit the mine. They X-ray you going in as a warning that it doesn't pay to smuggle out a handful of diamonds by swallowing them."

The arched concrete tunnel that penetrated the mound of mine tailings was about five meters high by ten wide, ample room for large trucks to transport men and equipment back and forth from the loading dock. The length stretched nearly half a kilometer, the interior brightened by long rows of fluorescent lighting. Side tunnels yawned about halfway through, each about half the size of the main artery.

"Where do those lead?" Pitt asked Broadmoor.

"Part of the security system. They circle the entire compound and are filled with detection devices."

"The guards, the weapons, the array of security systems. Seems like overkill, just to prevent a few diamonds from being smuggled off the property."

"Only the half of it. They don't want the illegal laborers escaping to the mainland. It's part of the deal with corrupt Canadian officials."

They emerged at the other end of the tunnel amid the busy activity of the mining operation. The driver of the tractor curled the train of trailers onto a paved road that circled the great open pit that was the volcanic chute. He pulled up beside a loading dock that ran along a low concrete building in the shape of a quonset hut, and stopped.

A man wearing the white attire of a chef under a fur-trimmed overcoat opened a door to a warehouse where foodstuffs were stored. He threw a wave of greeting to Boardmoor. "Good to see you, Mason. Your arrival is timely. We're down to two cases of cod."

"We've brought enough fish to grow scales on your workers." Broadmoor turned and said in a low voice to Pitt, "Dave Anderson, the head cook for the miners. A decent guy but he drinks too much beer."

"The frozen-food locker is open," said Anderson. "Mind how you stack the crates. I found salmon mixed in with flounder your last trip. It screws up my menus."

"Brought you a treat. Fifty kilos of moose steaks."

"You're okay, Mason. You're the reason I don't buy frozen fish from the mainland," the cook replied with a wide smile. "After you've stored the crates, come on into the mess hall. My boys will have breakfast waiting for your people. I'll write a check as soon as I've inventoried your catch."

The wooden crates of fish were stacked in the frozen-food locker, and the Haida fishermen, followed by Pitt, thankfully tramped into the warmth of the mess hall. They walked past a serving line and were dished up eggs, sausages and flapjacks. As they helped themselves to coffee out of a huge urn, Pitt looked around at the men sitting at the other tables. The four guards were conversing under a cloud of cigarette smoke near the door. Close to a hundred Chinese miners from the early morning graveyard shift filled up most of the room. Ten men who Pitt guessed to be mining engineers and superintendents sat at a round table that was set off in a smaller, private dining room.

"Which one is your disgruntled employee?" he asked Broadmoor.

Broadmoor nodded toward the door leading into the kitchen. "He's waiting for you outside by the garbage containers."

Pitt stared at the Indian. "How did you arrange that?"

Broadmoor smiled shrewdly. "The Haida have ways of communicating that don't require fiber optics."

Pitt did not question him. Now was not the time. Keeping a wary eye on the guards, he casually walked into the kitchen. None of the cooks or dishwashers looked up as he moved between the ovens and sinks through the rear door and dropped down the steps outside. The big metal garbage containers reeked of stale vegetables in the sharp, crisp air.

He stood there in the cold, not sure what to expect.

A tall figure moved from behind a container and approached him. He was wearing a yellow jumpsuit. The bottoms of the legs were smeared with mud that had a strange bluish cast to it. A miner's hard hat sat on his head, and his face was covered by what Pitt took for a mask with a breathing filter. He clutched a bundle under one arm. "I understand you're interested in our mining operation," he said quietly.

"Yes. My name is—"

"Names are unimportant. We don't have much time if you are to leave the island with the fishing fleet." He unfolded a jumpsuit, a respirator mask and a hard hat and handed them to Pitt. "Put these on and follow me."

Pitt said nothing and did as he was told. He did not fear a trap. The security guards could have taken him anytime since he set foot on the dock. He dutifully zipped up the front of the jumpsuit, tightened the chin strap of the hard hat, adjusted the respirator mask over his face and set out after a man he hoped could show him the source behind the violent killings.

23

Pitt followed the enigmatic mining engineer across a road into a modern prefabricated building that housed a row of elevators that transported the workers to and from the diggings far below. Two larger ones carried the Chinese laborers but the smaller one on the end was for the use of company officials only. The lift machinery was the latest in Otis elevator technology. The elevator moved smoothly, without sound or sensation of dropping.

"How deep do we go?" asked Pitt, his voice muffled by the breathing mask.

"Five hundred meters," replied the miner.

"Why the respirators?"

"When the volcano we're standing in erupted in the distant past, it packed Kunghit Island with pumice rock. The vibration that results from the excavating process can churn up pumice dust, which raises hell with the lungs."

"Is that the only reason?" asked Pitt slyly.

"No," replied the engineer honestly. "I don't want you to see my face. That way, if security gets suspicious, I can pass a lie-detector test, which our chief of security uses with the frequency of a doctor giving urine tests."

"Dapper John Merchant," Pitt said, smiling.

"You know John?"

"We've met."

The older man shrugged and accepted Pitt's claim without comment.

As they neared the bottom of the run, Pitt's ears were struck by a weird humming sound. Before he could ask what it was, the elevator stopped and the doors slid open. He was led through a mine shaft that opened onto an observation platform perched fifty meters above the vast excavation chamber below. The equipment at the bottom of the pit was not the typical type of machinery one might expect to encounter in a mine. No cars filled with ore pulled over tracks by a small engine, no drills or explosives, no huge earth-moving vehicles. This was a well-financed, carefully designed and organized operation that was run by computers aided in a small way by human labor. The only obvious mechanization was the huge overhead bridge with the cables and buckets that lifted the diamond-bearing blue rock-clay to the surface and carried it to the buildings where the stones were extracted.

The engineer turned and stared at him through green eyes over the mask. "Mason did not tell me who you are or who you represent. And I don't want to know. He merely said you were trying to trace a sound channel that travels underwater and kills."

"That's true. Untold thousands of various forms of sea life and hundreds of people have already died mysteriously in the open sea and along shorelines."

"You think the sound originates here?"

"I have reason to believe the Kunghit Island mine is only one of four sources."

The engineer nodded knowingly. "Komandorskie in the Bering Sea, Easter Island, Gladiator Island in the Tasman Sea, being the other three."

"You guessed?"

"I know. They all use the same pulsed ultrasound excavation equipment as we do here." The engineer swept his hand over the open pit. "We used to dig shafts, in an attempt to follow the largest concentration of diamonds. Much like miners following a vein of gold. But after Dorsett scientists and engineers perfected a new method of excavating that produced four times the production in one third the time, the old ways were quickly abandoned."

Pitt leaned over the railing and stared at the action across the bottom of the pit. Large robotic vehicles appeared to ram long shafts into the blue clay. Then came an eerie vibration that traveled up Pitt's legs to his body. He gazed questioningly at the engineer.

"The diamond-bearing rock and clay are broken up by high-energy pulsed ultrasound." The engineer paused and pointed to a large concrete structure with no obvious windows. "See that building on the south side of the pit?"

Pitt nodded.

"A nuclear generating plant. It takes an enormous amount of power to produce enough energy at ten to twenty bursts a second to penetrate the rock-hard clay and break it apart."

"The crux of the problem."

"How so?" asked the engineer.

"The sound generated by your equipment radiates into the sea. When it converges with the energy pulses from the other Dorsett mines scattered around the Pacific, its intensity increases to a level that can kill animal life within a large area."

"An interesting concept as far as it goes, but a piece is missing."

"You don't find it plausible?"

The engineer shook his head. "By itself, the sound energy produced down below could not kill a sardine three kilometers from here. The ultrasound drilling equipment uses sound pulses with acoustic frequencies of 60,000 to 80,000 hertz, or cycles per second. These frequencies are absorbed by the salts in the sea before they travel very far."

Pitt stared into the eyes of the engineer, trying to read where he was coming from, but other than the eyes and a few strands of graying hair that trailed from under the hard hat, all he could readily see was that the stranger was the same height and a good twenty pounds heavier. "How do I know you're not trying to throw me off the track?"

Pitt could not see the tight smile behind the respirator mask, but he guessed it was there. "Come along," said the engineer. "I'll show you the answer to your dilemma." He stepped back into the elevator, but before he pushed the next button on the panel, he handed Pitt an acoustic-foam helmet. "Take off your hard hat and set this over your head. Make certain it's snug or you'll get a case of vertigo. It contains a transmitter and receiver so we can converse without shouting.''

"Where are we headed?" asked Pitt.

"An exploratory tunnel, cut beneath the main pit to survey the heaviest deposit of stones."

The doors opened and they stepped out into a mine shaft carved from the volcanic rock and shored up with heavy timbers. Pitt involuntarily lifted his hands and pressed them against the sides of his head. Though all sound was muffled, he felt a strange vibration in his eardrums.

"Do you hear me all right?" asked the engineer.

"I hear you," answered Pitt through the tiny microphone. "But through a humming sound."

"You'll get used to it."

"What is it?"

"Follow me a hundred meters up the shaft and I'll show you your missing piece."

Pitt trailed in the engineer's footsteps until they reached a side shaft, only this one held no shoring timbers. The volcanic rock that made up its rounded sides was almost as smooth as if it had been polished by some immense boring tool.

"A Thurston lava tube," Pitt said. "I've seen them on the big island of Hawaii."

"Certain lavas such as those basaltic in composition form thin flows called pahoehoe that run laterally, with smooth surfaces," clarified the engineer. "When the lava cools closer to the surface, the deeper, warmer surge continues until it flows into the open, leaving chambers, or tubes as we call them. It is these pockets of air that are driven to resonate by the pulsed ultrasound from the mining operation above."

"What if I remove the helmet?"

The engineer shrugged. "Go ahead, but you won't enjoy the results."

Pitt lifted the acoustic-foam helmet from his ears. After half a minute he became disoriented and reached out to the wall of the tube to keep from losing his balance. Next came a mushrooming sensation of nausea. The engineer reached over and replaced the helmet on Pitt's head. Then he circled an arm around Pitt's waist to hold him upright.

"Satisfied?" he asked.

Pitt took a long breath as the vertigo and nausea quickly passed. "I had to experience the agony. Now I have a mild idea of what those poor souls suffered before they died."

The engineer led him back to the elevator. "Not a pleasant ordeal. The deeper we excavate, the worse it becomes. The one time I walked in here without protecting my ears, my head ached for a week."

As the elevator rose from the lava tube, Pitt fully recovered except for a ringing in his ears. He knew it all now. He knew the source of the acoustic plague. He knew how it worked to destroy. He knew how to stop it—and was buoyed by the knowledge.

"I understand now. The air chambers in the lava resonate and radiate the high-intensity sound pulses down through rock and into the sea, producing an incredible burst of energy."

"There's your answer." The engineer removed his helmet and ran a hand through a head of thinning gray hair. "The resonance added to the sound intensity creates incredible energy, more than enough to kill."

"Why did you risk your job and maybe your life showing me this?"

The engineer's eyes burned, and he shoved his hands deep into the pockets of his jumpsuit. "I do not like working for people I cannot trust. Men like Arthur Dorsett create trouble and tragedy —if you two should ever meet, you can smell it on him. This whole operation stinks, as do all his other mining operations. These poor Chinese laborers are driven until they drop. They're fed well but paid nothing and forced to slave in the pit eighteen hours a day. Twenty have died in the past twelve months from accidents, because they were too exhausted to react and move out of the way of the equipment. Why the need to dig diamonds twenty-four hours a day when there is a worldwide surplus of the damned stones? De Beers may head a repugnant monopoly, but you have to give them credit. They hold production down so prices remain high. No, Dorsett has a rotten scheme to harm the market. I'd give a year's pay to know what's going on in his diabolic mind. Someone like you, who understands the horror we're causing here, can now work to stop Dorsett before he kills another hundred innocent souls."

"What's stopping you from blowing the whistle?" asked Pitt.

"Easier said than done. Every one of the scientists and engineers who direct the digging signed ironclad contracts. No performance, no pay. Dorsett's attorneys would throw up a smoke screen so thick you couldn't cut it with a laser if we sued. Just as bad, if the Mounties learned of the carnage among the Chinese laborers, and the coverup, Dorsett would claim ignorance and make damned certain we'd all stand trial for conspiracy. As it is, we're scheduled to leave the island in four weeks. Our orders are to shut down the mine the week before. Only then are we to be paid off and sent on our way."

"Why not get on a boat and leave now?"

"The thought crossed our minds until the chief superintendent tried exactly that," said the engineer slowly. "According to letters we received from his wife, he never arrived home and was never seen again."

"Dorsett runs a tight ship."

"As tight as any Central American drug operation."

"Why shut down the mine when it still produces?"

"I have no idea. Dorsett set the dates. He obviously has a plan he doesn't intend to share with the hired help."

"How does Dorsett know none of you will talk once you're on the mainland?"

"It's no secret that if one of us talks, we all go to jail."

"And the Chinese laborers?"

He stared at Pitt over the respirator clamped around the lower part of his face, his eyes expressionless. "I have a suspicion they'll be left inside the mine."

"Buried?"

"Knowing Dorsett, he wouldn't bat an eye when he gave the order to his security flunkies."

"Have you ever met the man?" asked Pitt.

"Once was enough. His daughter, The Emasculator, is as bad as he is."

"Boudicca." Pitt smiled thinly. "She's called The Emasculator?"

"Strong as an ox, that one," said the engineer. "I've seen her lift a good-sized man off the ground with one arm."

Before Pitt could ask any more questions, the elevator reached the surface level and stopped in the main lift building. The engineer stepped outside, glancing at a Ford van that drove past. Pitt followed him around the corner of the mess hall and behind the garbage containers.

The engineer nodded at Pitt's jumpsuit. "Your gear belongs to a geologist who's down with the flu. I'll have to return it before he discovers it missing and wonders why."

"Great," Pitt muttered. "I probably contacted his flu germs from the respirator."

"Your Indian friends have returned to their boats." The engineer gestured at the food-storage loading dock. The tractor and trailers were gone. "The van that just passed by the elevator building is a personnel shuttle. It should return in a couple of minutes. Hail the driver and tell him to take you through the tunnel."

Pitt stared at the old engineer dubiously. "You don't think he'll question why I didn't leave with the other Haida?"

The old engineer took a notebook and a pencil from a pocket of his jumpsuit and scribbled a few words. He tore off the sheet of paper, folded it and passed it to Pitt. "Give him this. It will guarantee your safe passage. I have to return to work before Dapper John's muscle boys begin to ask questions."

Pitt shook his hand. "I'm grateful for your help. You took a terrible risk by revealing Dorsett Consolidated secrets to a perfect stranger."

"If I can prevent future deaths of innocent people, any risk on my part will have been well worth it."

"Good luck," said Pitt.

"The same to you." The engineer began to walk away, thought of something and turned back. "One more thing, out of curiosity. I saw the Dorsett gunship take off after a floatplane the other day. It never returned."

"I know," said Pitt. "It ran into a hill and burned."

"You know?"

"I was on the floatplane."

The engineer looked at him queerly. "And Malcolm Stokes?"

Pitt quickly realized that this was the undercover man Stokes had mentioned. "A metal splinter in one lung. But he'll live to enjoy his pension."

"I'm glad. Malcolm is a good man. He has a fine family."

"A wife and five children," said Pitt. "He told me after we crashed."

"Then you got clear only to jump back in the fire."

"Not very bright of me, was it?"

The engineer smiled. "No, I guess it wasn't." Then he turned and headed back into the elevator building, where he disappeared from Pitt's view.

Five minutes later, the van appeared and Pitt waved it to a stop. The driver, in the uniform of a security guard, stared at Pitt suspiciously. "Where did you come from?" he asked.

Pitt handed him the folded note and shrugged wordlessly.

The driver read the note, wadded it up, tossed it on the floor and nodded. "Okay, take a seat. I'll run you as far as the search house at the other end of the tunnel."

As the driver closed the door and shifted the van into drive, Pitt took a seat behind him and casually leaned down and picked up the crumpled note.

It read,

This Haida fisherman was in the john when his friends unknowingly left him behind. Please see that he gets to the dock before the fishing fleet departs.

C. Cussler
Chief Foreman

24

The driver stopped the van in front of the security building, where Pitt was explored from head to feet by X ray for the second time that morning. The doctor in charge of anatomical search nodded as he completed a checklist.

"No diamonds on you, big boy," he said, stifling a yawn.

"Who needs them?" Pitt grunted indifferently. "You can't eat stones. They're a curse of the white man. Indians don't kill each other over diamonds."

"You're late, aren't you? Your tribesmen came through here twenty minutes ago."

"I fell asleep," said Pitt, hurriedly throwing on his clothes.

He took off at a dead run and rushed onto the dock. Fifty meters from the end he came slowly to a stop. Concern and misgiving coursed through him. The Haida fishing fleet was a good five kilometers out in the channel. He was alone with nowhere to go.

A large freighter was unloading the last of its cargo across the dock from the Dorsett yacht. He dodged around the big containers that were hoisted from the cargo holds on wooden skids and tried to lose himself amid the activity while moving toward the gangway in an attempt to board the ship. One hand on the railing and one foot on the first step was as far as he got.

"Hold it right there, fisherman." The calm voice spoke from directly behind him. "Missed your boat, did you?"

Pitt slowly turned around and froze as he felt his heart double its beat. The sadistic Crutcher was leaning against a crate containing a large pump as he casually puffed on the stub of a cigar. Next to him stood a guard with the muzzle of his M-1 assault rifle wavering up and down Pitt's body. It was the same guard Pitt had struck in Merchant's office. Pitt's heart went on triple time as Dapper John Merchant himself stepped from behind the guard, staring at Pitt with the cold authority of one who holds men's lives in the palms of his hands.

"Well, well, Mr. Pitt, you are a stubborn man."

"I knew he was the same one who punched me the minute I saw him board the shuttle van." The guard grinned wolfishly as he stepped forward and thrust the gun barrel into Pitt's gut. "A little payback for hitting me when I wasn't ready."

Pitt doubled over in sharp pain as the narrow, round muzzle jabbed deeply into his side, badly bruising but not quite penetrating the flesh. He looked up at the grinning guard and spoke through clenched teeth. "A social misfit if I've ever seen one."

The guard lifted his rifle to strike Pitt again, but Merchant stopped him. "Enough, Elmo. You can play games with him after he's explained his persistent intrusion." He looked at Pitt apologetically. "You must excuse Elmo. He has an instinctive drive to hurt people he doesn't trust."

Pitt desperately tried to think of some way to escape. But except for jumping in the icy water and expiring from hypothermia or—and this was the more likely option of the two—being blasted into fish meal by Elmo's automatic rifle, there was no avenue open.

"You must have an active imagination if you consider me a threat," Pitt muttered to Merchant as he stalled for time.

Merchant leisurely removed a cigarette from a gold case and lit it with a matching lighter. "Since we last met, I've run an in-depth check on you, Mr. Pitt. To say you are a threat to those you oppose is a mild understatement. You are not trespassing on Dorsett property to study fish and kelp. You are here for another, more ominous purpose. I rather hope you'll explain your presence in vivid detail without prolonged theatrical resistance."

"A pity to disappoint you," said Pitt, between deep breaths. "I'm afraid you won't have time for one of your sordid interrogations."

Merchant was not easily fooled. But he knew that Pitt was no garden-variety diamond smuggler. A tiny alarm went off in the back of his mind when he saw the utter lack of fear in Pitt's eyes. He felt curious yet a trifle uneasy. "I freely admit I thought more highly of you than to expect a cheap bluff."

Pitt stared upward and scanned the skies. "A squadron of fighters from the aircraft carrier *Nimitz,* bristling with air-to-surface missiles, should be whistling over at any moment."

"A bureaucrat with an obscure governmental agency with the power to order an attack on Canadian soil? I don't believe so."

"You're right about me," said Pitt. "But my boss, Admiral James Sandecker, has the leverage to order an air strike."

For an instant, a brief eye blink in time, Pitt thought Merchant was going to buy it. Hesitation clouded the security chief's face. Then he grinned, stepped forward and wickedly backhanded Pitt across the mouth with a gloved hand. Pitt staggered backward, feeling the blood springing from his lips.

"I'll take my chances," Merchant said drily. He wiped a speck of blood from his leather glove with a bored expression of distaste. "No more stories. You will speak only when I ask for answers to my questions." He turned to Crutcher and Elmo. "Escort him to my office. We'll continue our discussion there."

Crutcher pushed a flat-handed palm into Pitt's face and sent him staggering across the dock. "I think we'll walk instead of ride to your office, sir. Our nosy friend could use a little exercise to soften him up . . ."

"Hold on there!" came a sharp voice from the deck of the yacht. Boudicca Dorsett was leaning against the rail, watching the drama below on the dock. She was wearing a wool cardigan over a white turtleneck and a short pleated skirt. Her white-stockinged legs were encased in a pair of high calfskin riding boots. She tossed her long hair over her shoulders and gestured to the gangway leading from the dock to the yacht's promenade deck. "Bring your intruder on board."

Merchant and Crutcher exchanged indulgent glances before

hustling Pitt on board the yacht. Elmo prodded him viciously in the lower back with the assault rifle, forcing him through a teak doorway into the main salon.

Boudicca sat on one edge of a desk carved from driftwood with an Italian-marble top. Her skirt, taut under her legs, rose to mid-thigh. She was a robust woman, almost masculine in her movements, yet exuding sensuality and an unmistakable aura of wealth and polish. She was used to intimidating men, and she frowned when she saw Pitt clinically appraising her.

A first-class performance, Pitt observed. Most men would have been awed and cowed. Merchant, Crutcher and Elmo couldn't keep their eyes off her. But Pitt refused to play on her turf. He ignored Boudicca's obvious charms and forced his eyes to travel over the luxurious furnishings and decor of the yacht's salon.

"Nice place you have here," he said impassively.

"Shut your mouth in front of Ms. Dorsett," Elmo snapped, raising the butt of his weapon to strike Pitt again.

Pitt whirled on his feet, knocked away the approaching rifle with one hand and rammed his other fist into Elmo's gut just above the groin. The guard groaned in pain and anger and doubled over, dropping the rifle, both hands clutched at the point of impact.

Pitt scooped up the rifle from the salon's thick carpet before anyone could react and calmly handed the weapon to a stunned Merchant. "I'm tired of being on the receiving end of this cretin's sadistic habits. Please keep him under control." Then he turned to Boudicca. "I realize it's early, but I could use a drink. Do you stock tequila on board this floating villa?"

Boudicca remained calm and aloof, staring at Pitt with renewed curiosity. She looked at Merchant. "Where did he come from?" she demanded. "Who is this man?"

"He penetrated our security by posing as a local fisherman. In reality he's an American agent."

"Why is he snooping around the mine?"

"I was taking him back to my office for the answers when you called us to come aboard," replied Merchant.

She rose to her full height and stood taller than any man in the salon. Her voice became incredibly deep and sensuous, and her eyes were cool as they flicked over Pitt. "Your name, please, and your business here."

Merchant began to answer. "His name is—"

"I want *him* to tell me," she cut Merchant off.

"So you're Boudicca Dorsett," Pitt said, brushing off her question and returning her gaze. "Now I can say I know all three."

She searched his face for a moment. "All three?"

"Arthur Dorsett's lovely daughters," answered Pitt.

Anger at being toyed with flashed in her eyes. She took two steps, reached out, grasped Pitt's upper arms and squeezed as she leaned forward, crushing him against one wall of the salon. There was no expression in the giantess' black eyes as they stared unblinkingly into Pitt's, almost nose to nose. She said nothing, only stood there increasing the pressure and pushing upward until his feet were barely touching the carpet.

Pitt resisted by tensing his body and flexing his biceps, which felt as if they were clamped in ever-tightening vises. He could not believe any man, much less a woman, could be so strong. His muscles began to feel as if they were mashed to pulp. He clenched his teeth and bleeding lips together to fight the rising pain. The restricted blood flow was numbing and turning his hands white when Boudicca finally released her grip and stepped back.

"Now then, before I encircle your throat, tell me who you are and why you're prying into my family's mining operation."

Pitt stalled for a minute while the pain subsided and feeling returned to his lower arms and hands. He was stunned by the woman's inhuman strength. Finally, he gasped out, "Is that any way to treat the man who rescued your sisters from certain death?"

Her eyes widened questioningly, and she stiffened. "What are you talking about? How do you know my sisters?"

"My name is Dirk Pitt," he said slowly. "My friends and I saved Maeve from freezing to death and Deirdre from drowning in the Antarctic."

"You?" The words seemed to boil from her lips. "You're the one from the National Underwater & Marine Agency?"

"The same." Pitt walked over to a lavish bar with a copper surface and picked up a cocktail napkin to dab away the blood that dripped from a cut lip. Merchant and Crutcher looked as stunned as if a horse they had bet their life savings on had run out of the money.

Merchant gazed blankly at Boudicca. "He must be lying."

"Would you like me to describe them in detail?" asked Pitt carelessly. "Maeve is tall, blond, with incredibly blue eyes. Strictly a camp-on-the-beach type." He paused to point at a portrait of a young blond woman, wearing an old-fashioned dress with a diamond the size of a quail's egg set in a pendant around her neck. "That's her in the painting."

"Not even close." Boudicca smirked. "That happens to be a portrait of my great-great-great-grandmother."

"Neither here nor there," Pitt said with feigned indifference, unwilling to tear his eyes away from the incredible likeness of Maeve. "Deirdre, on the other hand, has brown eyes and red hair and walks like a runway model."

After a long pause, Boudicca said, "He must be who he says he is."

"That doesn't explain his presence here," Merchant persisted.

"I told you during our last meeting," said Pitt. "I came here to study the effects of the chemicals and pollution flowing into the sea from the mine."

Merchant smiled thinly. "An inventive story, but far from the truth."

Pitt could not relax for a moment. He was in the company of dangerous people, cunning and shrewd. He had felt his way, assessing the reaction to his line of approach, but he realized it was only a matter of a minute or two before Boudicca figured out his game. It was inevitable. She had enough pieces to fill in the borders of the puzzle. He decided he could better control the situation by telling the truth.

"The gospel you want, the gospel you'll get. I'm here because the pulsed ultrasound you use to excavate for diamonds causes an intense resonance that channels great distances underwater. When undersea conditions are optimal these pulses converge with those from your other mining operations around the Pacific and kill any living organism in the area. But of course I'm not telling you anything you don't already know."

He'd caught Boudicca off balance. She stared at Pitt as if he had stepped off an alien spaceship. "You're quite good at creating a scene," she said hesitantly. "You should have gone into the movies."

"I've considered it," said Pitt. "But I don't have James Woods' talent or Mel Gibson's looks." He discovered a bottle of

Herradura silver tequila behind the bar on a glass shelf backed by a gold-tinted mirror and poured himself a shot glass. He also found a lime and a salt shaker. He let Boudicca and the others stand there and watch as he dabbed his tongue on the flap of skin between his thumb and forefinger before sprinkling salt on it. Then he downed the tequila, licked the salt and sucked on the lime. "There, now I feel ready to face the rest of the day. As I was saying, you know more about the horrors of the acoustic plague, as it's come to be called, than I do, Ms. Dorsett. The same killer that came frighteningly close to killing your sisters. So it would be foolish of me to waste my time attempting to enlighten you."

"I don't have the vaguest idea of what you're talking about." She turned to Merchant and Crutcher. "This man is dangerous. He is a menace to Dorsett Consolidated Mining. Get him off my boat and do with him whatever you think is necessary to ensure he doesn't bother us again."

Pitt made one last toss of the dice. "Garret Converse, the actor, and his Chinese junk, the *Tz'u-hsi*. David Copperfield would be proud of the way you made Converse, his entire crew and boat disappear." The expected reaction was all there. The strength and the arrogance evaporated.

Boudicca suddenly looked lost. Then Pitt threw in the clincher. "Surely you haven't forgotten the *Mentawai*. Now there was a sloppy job. You mistimed your explosives and blew up the boarding party from the *Rio Grande* who were investigating what appeared to be an abandoned ship. Unfortunately for you, your yacht was seen fleeing the scene and later identified."

"A most intriguing tale." There was scorn in Boudicca's voice, but a scorn disputed by a deep foreboding in her face. "You might almost say spellbinding. Are you quite finished, Mr. Pitt, or do you have an ending?"

"An ending?" Pitt sighed. "It hasn't been written yet. But I think it's safe to say that very soon Dorsett Consolidated Mining Limited will be only a memory."

He had gone one step too far. Boudicca began to lose control. Her anger swelled, and she came close to Pitt, her face tight and cold. "My father can't be stopped. Not by any legal authority or any government. Not in the next twenty-seven days. By then, we'll have closed down the mines of our own accord."

"Why not do it now and save God only knows how many lives?"

"Not one minute before we're ready."

"Ready for what?"

"A pity you can't ask Maeve."

"Why Maeve?"

"Deirdre tells me that she became quite friendly with the man who saved her."

"She's in Australia," said Pitt.

Boudicca shook her head and showed her teeth. "Maeve is in Washington, working as an agent for our father, feeding him whatever information NUMA has collected on the deathly sound waves. Nothing like having a trusted relative in the enemy camp to keep one out of trouble."

"I misjudged her," Pitt said brusquely. "She led me to believe that protecting sea life was her life's work."

"Any moral indignation flew out the window when she learned my father was holding her twin sons as insurance."

"Don't you mean hostages?" The mist began to lift. Pitt began to see that Arthur Dorsett's machinations went far beyond mere greed. The man was a bloodthirsty cutthroat, a predator who thought nothing of using his own family as pawns.

Boudicca disregarded Pitt's remark and nodded at John Merchant. "He's yours to dispose of as you will."

"Before we bury him with the others," said Crutcher with seeming anticipation, "we'll persuade him to fill in any details he might have purposely left out."

"So I'm to be tortured and then executed," Pitt said nonchalantly, helping himself to another shot of tequila while his mind desperately created and discarded a dozen useless plans for escape.

"You've condemned yourself by coming here," said Boudicca. "If, as you say, officials of NUMA suspected our excavation operations were responsible for sending deadly sound waves throughout the ocean, there would have been no need for you to clandestinely spy on Dorsett property. The truth is, you have learned the answers within the past hour and have yet to pass them on to your superiors in Washington. I compliment you, Mr. Pitt. Slipping through our security and entering the mine was a masterstroke. You could not have done it alone. Explanations will be forthcoming after Mr. Merchant motivates you to share your secrets."

She nailed me good, Pitt thought in defeat. "You *will* give Maeve and Deirdre my best wishes."

"Knowing my sisters, they've probably already forgotten you."

"Deirdre maybe, not Maeve. Now that I've met all of you, it's evident that she's the most virtuous of the three."

Pitt was surprised at the look of hatred that flashed in Boudicca's eyes. "Maeve is the outcast. She has never been close to the family."

Pitt grinned, a natural grin, mischievous and challenging. "It's easy to see why."

Boudicca stood up, looking even taller due to the heels of her boots, and stared down at Pitt, enraged at the laughter she read in his opaline green eyes. "By the time we close the mine, Maeve and her bastard sons will be gone." She spun around and glared at Merchant. "Get this scum off my boat," she said. "I don't want to see him again."

"You won't, Ms. Dorsett," said Merchant, motioning for Crutcher to push Pitt from the salon. "I promise, this will be your last look at him."

With Pitt between them and Elmo bringing up the rear, Merchant and Crutcher escorted their captive down the gangway and walked across the dock toward a waiting van. As they passed by the large containers of supplies and equipment that had been off-loaded from the cargo ship, the loud exhaust from the diesel engines operating the cranes drowned out a dull thud. Only when Crutcher suddenly crumpled to the planking of the dock did Pitt spin around in a defensive crouch, just in time to see Merchant's eyes roll up into his head before he dropped like a sack of sand. Several steps behind them, Elmo lay stretched out like a dead man, which he was.

The whole operation hadn't taken ten seconds from the killing blow to the back of Elmo's neck to the concussion of John Merchant's skull.

Mason Broadmoor grabbed Pitt's arm with his left hand, his right still gripping a massive steel wrench. "Quick, jump!"

Confused, Pitt hesitated. "Jump where?"

"Off the dock, you idiot."

Pitt needed no further urging. Five running steps and they both flew through the air and landed in the water a few meters in front of the bow of the cargo ship. The ice-cold water shocked every nerve ending in Pitt's body before his adrenaline took over and he found himself swimming beside Broadmoor.

"Now what?" he gasped, breathing steam over the icy water while shaking the water from his face and hair.

"The watercraft," answered Broadmoor after snorting water from his nose. "We sneaked them off the fishing boat and hid them under the pier."

"They were on the boat? I didn't see them."

"A hidden compartment I built myself," Broadmoor said, grinning. "You never know when you'll need to skip town ahead of the sheriff." He reached one of the Duo 300 WetJets that were floating beside a concrete piling and climbed aboard. "You know how to ride a watercraft?"

"Like I was born on one," said Pitt, pulling himself aboard and straddling the seat.

"If we keep the cargo ship between us and the dock, we should be blocked from their line of fire for a good half kilometer."

They punched the starters, the modified engines roared to life, and with Broadmoor less than a meter in the lead, they burst from under the dock as if shot from a cannon. They stuck the noses of their watercraft in a hard turn and sliced around the bows of the cargo ship, using the hull as a shield. The engines accelerated with no hint of hesitation. Pitt never looked back. He hunched over the handlebars and pressed the trigger throttle to its stop, half expecting a hail of gunfire to pepper the water around him at any second. But their getaway was clean, they were far out of range before the rest of John Merchant's security team was alerted.

For the second time in nearly as many days, Pitt was making a wild escape from the Dorsett mine for Moresby Island. The water sped past in a blue-green blur. The bright colors and the Haida designs on the watercraft glittered radiantly in the bright sun. Pitt's senses sharpened at the danger, and his reactions quickened.

From the air the channel between the islands seemed little more than a wide river. But from the surface of the sea, the inviting safety of the trees and rocky hills of Moresby appeared like a speck on the far horizon.

Pitt was awed by the stability of the WetJet's V-hull and the torque of its modified big-bore, long-stroke engine, which drove the craft with a ferocious low snarl through the low swells with hardly a bounce. Fast, agile, the variable-pitch impeller delivered incredible thrust. These were truly machines with muscle. Pitt couldn't know with any certainty, but he estimated he was whipping over the sea at close to sixty knots. It was almost like riding a high-performance motorcycle over water.

He jumped Broadmoor's wake, pulled even until they were hurtling across the water virtually side by side and shouted, "We'll be dead meat if they come after us!"

"Not to worry!" Broadmoor yelled back. "We can outrun their patrol boats!"

Pitt turned and peered over his shoulder at the rapidly receding island. He cursed under his breath as he spotted the remaining Defender helicopter rising above the mound surrounding the mine. In less than a minute it was sweeping across the channel, taking up the chase and following their wakes.

"We can't outrun their helicopter," Pitt informed Broadmoor loudly.

In contrast to a grim-faced Pitt, Mason Broadmoor looked as enthusiastic and bright eyed as a boy warming up for his first track meet. His brown features were flushed with excitement. He stood on the footrests and glanced back at the pursuing aircraft. "The dumb bastards don't stand a chance," he said grinning. "Follow in my wake."

They were rapidly overhauling the homeward-bound fishing fleet, but Broadmoor made a hard turn toward Moresby Island, giving the boats a wide berth. The shore was only a few hundred meters away, and the helicopter had pulled to within a kilometer. Pitt could see waves sluicing and heaving in constant motion as they hurled against the rocks below a shore of steep, jagged cliffs, and he wondered if Broadmoor had a death wish as he aimed his watercraft toward the swirling breakers. Pitt turned his attention from the approaching helicopter and put his faith in the Haida totem carver. He stuck the nose of his watercraft into the rooster tail shooting up behind the front-runner and hung in the foaming wake, as they ran flat out through a cauldron of waves thrashing against a fortress of offshore rocks.

To Pitt it looked as if they were on a direct course toward the wave-hammered cliffs. He gripped the handlebars, braced his feet in the padded footwells and hung on to keep from being pitched off. The rumble of the breakers came like thunderclaps, and all he could see was a gigantic curtain of spray and foam. The image of the *Polar Queen,* drifting helpless toward the barren rock island in the Antarctic flickered through his mind. But this time, he was aboard a speck in the sea instead of an ocean liner. He plunged on despite a growing certainty that Broadmoor was certifiably insane.

Broadmoor cut around a huge rock. Pitt followed, instantly setting up the turn, shifting his body back and outside to slightly weight the front inside of the hull, then hanging on, the hull biting into the water as he carved the turn in Broadmoor's wake. They rocketed over the crest of a huge roller and smashed down in the trough before ascending on the back of the next one.

The helicopter was almost upon them, but the pilot stared in dumb fascination at the suicidal course set by the two men on the watercraft. Astonished, he failed to line up and fire his twin 7.62 guns. Wary of his own danger, he pulled the aircraft up in a steep vertical climb and swept over the palisades. He banked sharply to come around for another look but the watercraft had already been out of sight for a critical ten seconds. When he circled back over the water, his quarry had vanished.

Some inner instinct told Pitt that in another hundred meters he would be pulped against the unyielding wall rising out of the water and that would be the end of it. The choice was to veer off and take his chances with the firepower from the helicopter, but he remained inflexibly on course. His life was passing in front of him. Then he saw it.

A tiny crevice in the lower face of the cliffs suddenly yawned open like the eye of a needle, no wider than two meters. Broadmoor swept into the narrow opening and was gone.

Pitt grimly followed, swearing that the ends of his handlebars brushed the sides of the entrance, and abruptly found himself in a deep grotto with a high, inverted V-shaped ceiling. Ahead of him, Broadmoor slowed and glided to a stop beside a small rock landing, where he jumped off his machine, tore off his coat and began stuffing it with a bundle of dead kelp that had washed into the grotto. Pitt immediately saw the wisdom of the Indian's scheme. He hit the stop switch on the handlebar and matched Broadmoor's actions.

Once the coats were filled to simulate headless torsos, they were thrown in the water at the entrance to the grotto. Pitt and Broadmoor stood there watching as the dummies were swept back and forth before being carried by the backwash into the maelstrom outside.

"You think that will fool them?" asked Pitt.

"Guaranteed," answered Broadmoor confidentially. "The wall of the cliff slants out, making the opening to the grotto impossible to see from the air." He cocked an ear at the sound of the helicopter outside. "I'll give them another ten minutes before they head back to the mine and tell Dapper John Merchant, if he's regained consciousness, that we bashed our brains out on the rocks."

Broadmoor was prophetic. The sound of the helicopter echoing into the grotto gradually died and faded away. He checked the fuel tanks of the watercraft and nodded comfortably. "If we run at half speed we should have just enough fuel to reach my village."

"I suggest we relax till after sunset," said Pitt. "No sense in showing our faces in case the pilot of the helicopter has a suspicious disposition. Can you navigate home in the dark?"

"Blindfolded in a straitjacket," Broadmoor said indisputably. "We'll leave at midnight and be in bed by 3:00 A.M."

For the next several minutes, worn out from the excitement of the hard run across the channel and the near brush with death, they sat in silence, listening to the reverberating roar of the surf outside the grotto. Finally, Broadmoor reached into a small compartment on his WetJet and retrieved a canvas-covered half-gallon canteen. He pulled out a cork stopper and handed the canteen to Pitt.

"Boysenberry wine. Made it myself."

Pitt took a long swallow and made a strange face. "You mean boysenberry brandy, don't you?"

"I admit that it does have a nice kick." He smiled as Pitt passed back the canteen. "Did you find what you were looking for at the mine?"

"Yes, your engineer led me to the source of the problem."

"I am glad. Then it has all been worth it."

"You paid a high price. You'll not be selling any more fish to the mining company."

"I felt like a whore taking Dorsett money anyway," said Broadmoor with a disgusted expression.

"As a consolation, you'll also be interested to learn that Boudicca Dorsett claimed her daddy was going to close down the mine a month from now."

"If it's true, my people will be happy to hear it," said Broadmoor, handing back the canteen. "That calls for another drink."

"I owe you a debt I can't repay," said Pitt quietly. "You took a great risk to help me escape."

"It was worth it to bash Merchant and Crutcher's skulls," Broadmoor laughed. "I've never felt this good before. It is I who must thank *you* for the opportunity."

Pitt reached out and shook Broadmoor's hand. "I'm going to miss your cheery disposition."

"You're going home?"

"Back to Washington with the information I've gathered."

"You're okay for a mainlander, friend Pitt. If you ever need a second home, you're always welcome in my village."

"You never know," said Pitt warmly. "I just might take you up on that offer someday."

They departed the grotto long after dark as insurance against chance discovery by Dorsett security patrol boats. Broadmoor draped the chain of a small shaded penlight around his neck so that it was hanging on his back.

Fortified by the boysenberry wine, Pitt followed the tiny beam through the surf and around the rocks, amazed at the ease with which Broadmoor navigated in the dark without mishap.

The image of Maeve, forced to work as a spy under the boot of her father, blackmailed by his seizure of her twin sons, made him boil with anger. He also felt a stab in his heart, a feeling that had not coursed through him in years. His emotions stirred with the memories of another woman. Only then did he realize it was possible to feel the same love for two different women from different times, one living, one dead.

Driven and torn by conflicting emotions of love and hate and a determination to stop Arthur Dorsett no matter the cost and consequences, he gripped the handlebars till his knuckles gleamed white under the light from a quarter-moon as he forged through the cataract from Broadmoor's wake.

25

For most of the afternoon the wind blew steadily out of the northeast. A brisk wind, but not enough to raise more than an occasional whitecap on the swells that topped out at one meter. The wind brought with it a driving rain that fell in sheets, cutting visibility to less than five kilometers and striking the water as if its surface was churned by millions of thrashing herring. To most sailors it was miserable weather. But to British seamen like Captain Ian Briscoe, who spent their early years walking the decks of ships plowing through the damp of the North Sea, this was like old home week.

Unlike his junior officers, who remained out of the gusting spray and stayed dry, Briscoe stood on the bridge wing of his ship as if recharging the blood in his veins, staring out over the bow as if expecting to see a ghost ship that didn't appear on radar. He noted that the mercury was holding steady and the temperature was several degrees above freezing. He felt no discomfort in his oilskins except that caused by the occasional drops of water that snaked their way through the strands of his precisely cut red beard and trickled down his neck.

After a two-week layover in Vancouver, where she participated in a series of naval exercises with ships of the Canadian Navy, Briscoe's command, the Type 42 destroyer HMS *Bridlington,* was en route home to England via Hong Kong, a stopover for any British naval ship that was sailing across the Pacific. Although the ninety-nine-year lease had run out and the British Crown Colony was returned to China in 1996, it became a matter of pride to occasionally show the Cross of Saint George and to remind the new owners of who were the founders of the financial Mecca of Asia.

The door to the wheelhouse opened, and the second officer, Lieutenant Samuel Angus, leaned out. "If you can spare a few moments from defying the elements, sir, could you please step inside?"

"Why don't you come out, my boy?" Briscoe roared over the wind. "Soft. That's the trouble you young people. You don't appreciate foul weather."

"Please, Captain," Angus pleaded. "We have an approaching aircraft on radar."

Briscoe walked across the bridge wing and stepped into the wheelhouse. "I see nothing unusual in that. You might say it's routine. We've had dozens of aircraft fly over the ship."

"A helicopter, sir? Over twenty-five hundred kilometers from the American mainland and no military vessels between here and Hawaii."

"The bloody fool must be lost," Briscoe growled. "Signal the pilot and ask if he requires a position fix."

"I took the liberty of contacting him, sir," replied Angus. "He speaks only Russian."

"Who do we have who can understand him?"

"Surgeon Lieutenant Rudolph. He's fluent in Russian."

"Call him up to the bridge."

Three minutes later, a short man with blond hair stepped up to Briscoe, who was sitting in the elevated captain's chair, peering into the rain. "You sent for me, Captain?"

Briscoe nodded curtly. "There's a Russian helicopter muddling about in the storm. Get on the radio and find out why he's flying around an empty sea."

Lieutenant Angus produced a headset, plugged it into a communications console and handed it to Rudolph. "The frequency is set. All you have to do is talk."

Rudolph placed the earphones over his ears and spoke into the tiny microphone. Briscoe and Angus waited patiently while he carried on what seemed a one-way conversation. Finally, he turned to the captain. "The man is terribly upset, almost incoherent. The best I can make of it, is that he's coming from a Russian whaling fleet."

"Then he's only doing his job."

Rudolph shook his head. "He keeps repeating, 'they're all dead' and wants to know if we have helicopter landing facilities on the *Bridlington*. If so, he wants to come aboard."

"Impossible," Briscoe grunted. "Inform him that the Royal Navy does not allow foreign aircraft to land on Her Majesty's ships."

Rudolph repeated the message just as the helicopter's engines became audible and it suddenly materialized out of the falling rain, half a kilometer off the port bow at a height of no more than twenty meters above the sea. "He sounds on the verge of hysteria. He swears that unless you shoot him down, he's going to set down on board."

"Damn!" The oath fairly exploded from Briscoe's lips. "All I need is for some terrorist to blow up my ship."

"Not likely any terrorists are roaming about this part of the ocean," said Angus.

"Yes, yes, and the Cold War's been over for ten years. I know all that."

"For what it's worth," said Rudolph, "I read the pilot as scared out of his wits. I detect no indication of threat in his tone."

Briscoe sat silent for a few moments, then flicked a switch on the ship's intercom. "Radar, are your ears up?"

"Yes, sir," a voice answered. "Any ships in the area?"

"I read one large vessel and four smaller ones, bearing two-seven-two degrees, distance ninety-five kilometers."

Briscoe broke off and pressed another switch. "Communications?"

"Sir?"

"See if you can raise a fleet of Russian whaling ships ninety-five kilometers due west of us. If you need an interpreter, the ship's doc can translate."

"My thirty-word Russian vocabulary should get me by," the communications officer answered cheerfully.

Briscoe looked at Rudolph. "All right, tell him permission is granted to set down on our landing pad."

Rudolph passed on the word, and they all watched as the helicopter angled in from the starboard beam and began a shallow power-glide approach over the landing pad just forward of the stern in readiness for a hovering descent.

To Briscoe's practiced eyes, the pilot was handling the aircraft erratically, failing to compensate for the brisk wind. "That idiot flies like he's got a nervous disorder," snapped Briscoe. He turned to Angus. "Reduce speed and order an armed reception committee to greet our visitor." Then as an afterthought. "If he so much as scratches my ship, shoot him."

Angus grinned amiably and winked at Rudolph behind the captain's back as he ordered the helmsman at the ship's console to reduce speed. There was no insubordination intended in their shared humor. Briscoe was admired by every man of the crew as a gruff old sea dog who watched over his men and ran a smooth ship. They were well aware that few ships in the Royal Navy had a captain who preferred sea duty to promotion to flag rank.

The visitor was a smaller version of the Ka-32 Helix Russian Navy helicopter, which was used for light transport duty and air reconnaissance. This one, used by a fishing fleet for locating whales, looked badly in need of maintenance. Oil streaked from the engine cowlings and the paint on the fuselage was badly chipped and faded.

The British seamen waiting under the protection of steel bulkheads cringed as the helicopter flared out barely three meters above the pitching deck. The pilot sharply decreased his engine rpms too early, and the craft dropped heavily to the deck, bounced drunkenly back into the air and then smacked down hard on its wheels before finally settling like a chastised collie into motionless submission. The pilot shut down his engines, and the rotor blades swung to a stop.

The pilot slid open an entry door and stared up at the *Bridlington*'s huge radar dome before turning his eyes to the five advancing seamen, automatic weapons firmly clutched in their hands. He jumped down to the deck and peered at them curiously before he was taken roughly by the arms and hustled through an open hatch. The seamen escorted him up three decks through a wide

261

companionway before turning into a passageway that led to the officers' wardroom.

The ship's first officer, Lieutenant Commander Roger Avondale, had joined the reception committee and stood off to one side with Lieutenant Angus. Surgeon Lieutenant Rudolph waited at Briscoe's elbow to interpret. He studied the Russian pilot's eyes and read terror numbed by fatigue in the wide pupils.

Briscoe nodded at Rudolph. "Ask him what in hell made him assume he can board a foreign naval vessel any time he chooses."

"You might also inquire as to why he was flying alone," added Avondale. "Not likely he'd scout for whales by himself."

Rudolph and the pilot began a rapid-fire exchange that lasted for a solid three minutes. Finally the ship's doctor turned and said, "His name is Fyodor Gorimykin. He is chief pilot in command of locating whales for a whaling fleet from the port of Nikolayevsk. According to his story, he and his copilot and an observer were out scouting for the catcher ships—"

"Catcher ships?" inquired Angus.

"Swift-moving vessels about sixty-five meters in length that shoot explosive harpoons into unsuspecting whales," explained Briscoe. "The whale's body is then inflated with air to keep it afloat, marked with a radio beacon that sends out homing signals and left while the catcher continues its killing spree. Later, it returns to its catch and tows it back to the factory ship."

"I had drinks with a captain of a factory ship in Odessa a few years ago," said Avondale. "He invited me aboard. It was an enormous vessel, nearly two hundred meters in length, totally self-sufficient, with high-tech processing equipment, laboratories and even a well-staffed hospital. They can winch a hundred-ton blue whale up a ramp, strip the blubber like you'd peel a banana and cook it in a rotating drum. The oil is extracted and everything else is ground and bagged as fish- or bonemeal. The whole process takes little more than half an hour."

"After being hunted to near extinction, it's a wonder there are any whales left to catch," muttered Angus.

"Let's hear the man's story." Briscoe demanded impatiently.

"Failing to locate a herd," Rudolph continued, "he returned to his factory ship, the *Aleksandr Gorchakov*. After landing, he swears they found the entire crew of the vessel, as well as the crews on the nearby catcher ships, dead."

"And his copilot and observer?" Briscoe persisted.

"He says he panicked and took off without them."

"Where did he intend to go?"

Rudolph questioned the Russian and waited for the answer to pour out. "Only as far away from the mass death as his fuel would take him."

"Ask him what killed his shipmates."

After an exchange, Rudolph shrugged. "He doesn't know. All he knows is that they had expressions of agony on their faces and appeared to have died in their own vomit."

"A fantastic tale, to say the least," observed Avondale.

"If he didn't look as if he'd seen a graveyard full of ghosts," said Briscoe, "I'd think the man was a pathological liar."

Avondale looked at the captain. "Shall we take him at his word, sir?"

Briscoe thought for a moment, then nodded. "Lay on another ten knots, then signal Pacific Fleet Command. Apprise them of the situation and inform them we are altering course to investigate."

Before action could be taken, a familiar voice came over the bridge speaker system. "Bridge, this is radar."

"Go ahead, radar," acknowledged Briscoe.

"Captain, those ships you ordered us to track."

"Yes, what about them?"

"Well, sir, they're not moving, but they're beginning to disappear off the scope."

"Is your equipment functioning properly?"

"Yes, sir, it is."

Briscoe's face clouded in bafflement. "Explain what you mean by 'disappearing.' "

"Just that, sir," answered radar officer. "It looks to me as if those ships out there are sinking."

The *Bridlington* arrived at the Russian fishing fleet's last known position and found no ships floating on the surface. Briscoe ordered a search pattern, and after steaming back and forth a large oil slick was spotted, surrounded by a widely scattered sea of flotsam, some of it in localized clusters. The Russian helicopter pilot rushed to a deck railing, gestured at an object in the water and began crying out in anguish.

"Why is he babbling?" Avondale shouted to Rudolph from the bridge wing.

"He's saying his ship is gone, all his friends are gone, his copilot and observer are gone."

"What is he pointing at?" asked Briscoe.

Rudolph peered over the side and then looked up. "A flotation vest with *Aleksandr Gorchakov* stamped on it."

"I have a floating body," announced Angus, peering through binoculars. "Make that four bodies. But not for long. There are shark fins circling the water around them."

"Throw a few shells from the BOFORS at the bloody butchers," Briscoe ordered. "I want the bodies in one piece so they can be examined. Send out boats to retrieve whatever debris they can find. Somebody, somewhere, is going to want as much evidence as we can collect."

As the twin forty-millimeter BOFORS guns opened up on the sharks, Avondale turned to Angus. "Damned queer goings on, if you ask me. What do you make of it?"

Angus turned and gave the first officer a slow grin. "It would seem that after being slaughtered for two centuries, the whales finally have their revenge."

26

Pitt sat behind the desk in his office for the first time in nearly two months, his eyes distant, his hand toying with a Sea Hawk dive knife he used as a letter opener. He said nothing, waiting for a response from Admiral Sandecker who sat across from him.

He had arrived in Washington early that morning, a Sunday, and gone directly to the empty NUMA headquarters building, where he spent the next six hours writing up a detailed report on his discoveries on Kunghit Island and offering his suggestions on how to deal with the underwater acoustics. The report seemed anticlimactic after the exhausting rigors of the past few days. Now he resigned himself to allowing other men, more qualified men, to deal with the problem and come up with the proper solutions.

He swung around in his chair and gazed out the window at the Potomac River and envisioned Maeve standing on the deck of *Ice Hunter*, the look of fear and desperation in her face. He felt furious with himself for deserting her. He was certain Deirdre had divulged the kidnapping of Maeve's children by her father on board *Ice Hunter*. Maeve had reached out to the only man she could trust, and Pitt had failed to recognize her distress. That part of the story Pitt had left out of his report.

Sandecker closed the report and laid it on Pitt's desk. "A remarkable bit of fancy footwork. A miracle you weren't killed."

"I had help from some very good people," Pitt said seriously.

"You've gone as far as you can go on this thing. I'm ordering you and Giordino to take ten days off. Go home and work on your antique cars."

"You'll get no argument from me," said Pitt, massaging the bruises on his upper arms.

"Judging from your narrow escape, Dorsett and his daughters play tough."

"All except Maeve," said Pitt quietly. "She's the family outcast."

"You know, I assume, that she is working with NUMA in our biology department along with Roy Van Fleet."

"On the effects of the ultrasound on sea life, yes, I know."

Sandecker studied Pitt's face, examining every line in the weathered yet still youthful-looking features. "Can we trust her? She could be passing along data on our findings to her father."

Dirk's green eyes registered no sign of subtlety. "Maeve has nothing in common with her sisters."

Sensing Pitt's reluctance to discuss Maeve, Sandecker changed the subject. "Speaking of sisters, did Boudicca Dorsett give you any indication as to why her father intends to shut down his operations in a few weeks?"

"Not a clue."

Sandecker rolled a cigar around in his fingers pensively. "Because none of Dorsett's mining properties are on U.S. soil, there is no rapid-fire means to stop future killings."

"Close one mine out of the four," said Pitt, "and you drain the sound waves' killing potency."

"Short of ordering in a flight of B-1 bombers, which the President won't do, our hands are tied."

"There must be an international law that applies to murder on the high seas," said Pitt.

Sandecker shook his head. "Not one that covers this situation. The lack of an international law-enforcement organization plays in Dorsett's favor. Gladiator Island belongs only to the family, and it would take a year or more to talk the Russians into closing the mine off Siberia. Same with Chile. As long as Dorsett pays off high-ranking government officials, his mines stay open.''

"There's the Canadians," said Pitt. "If given the reins, the Mounties would go in and close the Kunghit Island mine tomorrow, because of Dorsett's use of illegal immigrants for slave labor.''

"So what's stopping them from raiding the mine?''

Pitt recalled Inspector Stokes' words about the bureaucrats and members of Parliament in Dorsett's wallet. "The same barriers; paid cronies and shrewd lawyers.''

"Money makes money," Sandecker said heavily. "Dorsett is too well financed and well organized to topple by ordinary methods. The man is an incredible piece of avaricious machinery.''

"Not like you to embrace a defeatist attitude, Admiral. I can't believe you're about to forfeit the game to Arthur Dorsett.''

Sandecker's eyes took on the look of a viper about to strike. "Who said anything about forfeiting the game?''

Pitt enjoyed prodding his boss. He didn't believe for an instant that Sandecker would walk away from a fight. "What do you intend to do?''

"Since I can't order an armed invasion of commercial property and possibly kill hundreds of innocent civilians in the process, or drop a Special Forces team from the air to neutralize all Dorsett mining excavations, I'm forced to take the only avenue left open for me.''

"And that is?" Pitt prompted.

"We go public," Sandecker said without a flicker or change in his expression. "First thing tomorrow I call a press conference and blast Arthur Dorsett as the worst monster unleashed on humanity since Attila the Hun. I'll reveal the cause of the mass killings and lay the blame on his doorstep. Next I'll stir up members of Congress to lean on the State Department, who in turn will lean on the governments of Canada, Chile and Russia to close all Dorsett operations on their soil. Then we'll sit back and see where the chips fall.''

Pitt looked at Sandecker in long, slow admiration, then he smiled. The admiral was sailing in stormy waters without giving a damn for the torpedoes or the consequences. "You'd take on the devil if he looked cross-eyed at you.''

"Forgive me for blowing off steam. You know as well as I there will be no press conference. Without solid, presentable evidence I would gain nothing but a quick trip into a mental institution. Men like Arthur Dorsett are self-regenerating. You cannot simply destroy them. They are created by a system of greed that leads to power. The pathetic thing about such men is that they don't know how to spend their wealth nor give it away to the needy.'' Sandecker paused and lit his cigar with a flourish. Then he said coldly, ''I don't know how, but I swear by the Constitution I'm going to nail that slime bag to the barn so hard his bones will rattle.''

Maeve put on a good face through her ordeal. At first she had wept whenever she was alone in the small colonial house in Georgetown that her father's aides had leased for her. Panic swept her heart at thoughts of what might be happening to her twin boys on Gladiator Island. She wanted to rush to their sides and sweep them away to safety, but she was powerless. She actually saw herself with them in her dreams. But the dreams of sleep became nightmares on awakening. There wasn't the least hope of fighting the incredible resources of her father. She never detected anyone, but she knew without doubt that his security people were watching her every move.

Roy Van Fleet and his wife, Robin, who had taken Maeve under her wing, invited her to join them in attending a party thrown by a wealthy owner of an undersea exploration company. She was loath to go, but Robin had pushed her, refusing to take no for an answer and insisting she put a little fun in her life, never realizing the torment Maeve was going through.

''Loads of capital bigwigs and politicians will attend,'' Robin gushed. ''We can't miss it.''

After applying her makeup and pulling her hair tightly back in a bun, Maeve put on a brown Empire-waist dress of silk chiffon and embroidered net with beaded bodice and a short three-tier skirt that came to several inches above her knees. She had splurged on the outfit in Sydney, thinking it quite stylish at the time. Now she wasn't so sure. She suddenly suffered pangs of shyness at showing too much leg at a Washington party.

''The devil with it,'' she said to herself in front of a full-length mirror. ''Nobody knows me anyway.''

She peered through the curtains at the street outside. There was a light layer of snow on the ground, but the streets were clear. The temperature was cold but not frigid. She poured herself a short glass of vodka on ice, put on a long black coat that came down to her ankles and waited for the Van Fleets to pick her up.

Pitt showed the invitation he'd borrowed from the admiral at the door of the country club and was passed through the beautiful wooden doors carved with the likenesses of famous golfers. He dropped off his topcoat at the cloakroom and was directed into a spacious ballroom paneled in dark walnut. One of Washington's elite interior decorators had created a stunning undersea illusion in the room. Cleverly designed paper fish hung from the ceiling, while hidden lighting gave off a soft wavering blue-green glow that provided an eye-pleasing watery effect.

The host, president of Deep Abyss Engineering, his wife and other company officials stood in a receiving line to greet the guests. Pitt avoided them and dodged the line, heading straight for one dim corner of the bar, where he ordered a tequila on the rocks with lime. Then he turned, leaned his back against the bar and surveyed the room.

There must have been close to two hundred people present. An orchestra was playing a medley from motion picture musical scores. He recognized several congressmen and four or five senators, all on committees dealing with the oceans and the environment. Many of the men wore white dinner jackets. Most were in the more common black evening clothes, some with vividly patterned cummerbunds and bow ties. Pitt preferred the old look. His tux sported a vest with a heavy gold chain draped across the front, attached to a pocket watch that had once belonged to his great-grandfather, who had been a steam locomotive engineer on the Santa Fe Railroad.

The women, mostly wives with a few mistresses mixed in, dressed elegantly, some in long dresses, some in shorter skirts complemented by brocaded or sequined jackets. He could always tell the married from the single couples. The married stood beside each other as if they were old friends; the single couples were constantly touching each other.

Pitt wall-flowered at cocktail parties and did not enjoy mingling to make small talk. He was easily bored and seldom stayed more than a hour before heading back to the apartment above his aircraft hangar. Tonight was different. He was on a quest. Sandecker had informed him that Maeve was coming with the Van Fleets. His eyes wandered the tables and the crowded dance floor but found no sign of her.

Either she changed her mind at the last minute or hadn't arrived yet, he figured. Never one to compete for the attention of a gorgeous girl surrounded by admirers, he picked out a plain woman in her thirties who weighed as much as he. She was sitting alone at a dinner table and was thrilled when a good-looking stranger walked up and asked her to dance. The women other men ignored, the ones who lost out in the natural-born beauty department, Pitt discovered to be the smartest and most interesting. This one turned out to be a ranking official at the State Department, who regaled him with inside gossip on foreign relations. He danced with two other ladies who were considered by some to be unattractive, one a private secretary to the party's host and the other a chief aide to a senator who was chairman of the Oceans Committee. Having performed his pleasurable duty, Pitt returned to the bar for another tequila.

It was then that Maeve walked into the ballroom.

Just looking at her, Pitt was pleasantly surprised to find a warm glow settling over his body. The entire room seemed to blur, and everyone in it faded into a gray mist, leaving Maeve standing alone in the center of a radiant aura.

He came back down to earth as she stepped away from the receiving line ahead of the Van Fleets and paused to gaze at the crowded mass of partygoers. Her long blond hair, pulled back in a bun to reveal every detail of her face, highlighted her fabulous cheekbones. She self-consciously raised a hand and held it to her, between her breasts, fingers slightly spread. The short dress showed off her long, tapered legs and enhanced the perfect molding of her body. She was majestic, he thought with a trace of lust. There was no other word to describe her. She was poised with the grace of an antelope on the edge of flight.

"Now there's a lovely sweet young thing," said the bartender, staring at Maeve.

"I couldn't agree more," said Pitt.

Then she was walking with the Van Fleets to a table, where they all sat down and ordered from a waiter. Maeve was no sooner settled in her chair when men, both young and old enough to be her grandfather, came up and asked her to dance. She politely turned down every request. He was amused to see that no appeals moved her. They quickly gave up and moved on, feeling boyishly rejected. The Van Fleets excused themselves to dance while they waited for the first course. Maeve sat alone.

"She's choosy, that one," observed the bartender.

"Time to send in the first team," Pitt said as he set his empty glass on the bar.

He walked directly across the dance floor through the swaying couples without stepping left or right. A portly man Pitt recognized as a senator from the state of Nevada brushed against him. The senator started to say something, but Pitt gave him a withering stare that cut him off.

Maeve was people-watching out of sheer boredom when she became vaguely aware of a man striding purposefully in her direction. At first she paid him little notice, thinking he was only another stranger who wanted to dance with her. In another time, another place, she might have been flattered by the attention, but her mind was twenty thousand kilometers away. Only when the intruder approached her table, placed his hands on the blue tablecloth and leaned toward her did she recognize him. Maeve's face lit with inexpressible joy.

"Oh, Dirk, I thought I'd never see you again," she gasped breathlessly.

"I came to beg your forgiveness for not saying good-bye when Al and I abruptly left the *Ice Hunter*."

She was both surprised and pleased at his behavior. She thought he held no affection for her. Now it was written in his eyes. "You couldn't have known how much I needed you," she said, her voice barely audible above the music.

He came around the table and sat beside her. "I know now," he said solemnly.

Her face turned to avoid his gaze. "You could not begin to understand the scrape I'm in."

Pitt took Maeve's hand in his. It was the first time he had deliberately touched her. "I had a nice chat with Boudicca," he said with a slight sardonic grin. "She told me everything."

Her poise and grace seemed to crumble. "You? Boudicca? How is that possible?"

He stood and gently pulled her from her chair. "Why don't we dance, and I'll tell you all about it later."

As if by magic, here he was, holding her tightly, pressing her close as she responded and burrowed into his body. He closed his eyes momentarily as he inhaled the aroma of her perfume. The scent of his masculine aftershave, no cologne for Pitt, spread through her like ripples on a mountain lake. They danced cheek to cheek as the orchestra played Henry Mancini's "Moon River."

Maeve softly began singing the words. "Moon River, wider than a mile. I'm crossing you in style someday." Suddenly, she stiffened and pushed him back slightly. "You know about my sons?"

"What are their names?"

"Sean and Michael."

"Your father is holding Sean and Michael hostage on Gladiator Island so he can extort from you information on any breakthroughs by NUMA on the slaughter at sea."

Maeve stared up at him in confusion, but before she could ask any further questions, he pulled her close again. After a few moments he could feel her body sag as she began to cry softly. "I feel so ashamed. I don't know where to turn."

"Think only of the moment," he said tenderly. "The rest will work itself out."

Her relief and pleasure at being with him pushed aside her immediate problems, and she began murmuring the lyrics of "Moon River" again. "We're after the same rainbow's end, waitin' round the bend, my huckleberry friend, Moon River and me." The music faded and came to an end. She leaned back against his arm, which was around her waist, and smiled through the tears. "That's you."

He gave her a sideways look. "Who?"

"My huckleberry friend, Dirk Pitt. You're the perfect incarnation of Huckleberry Finn, always rafting down the river in search of something, you don't know what, around the next bend."

"I guess you could say that old Huck and I have a few things in common."

They kept moving around the dance floor, still holding each other as the band took a break and the other couples drifted back to their tables. Neither was the least bit self-conscious at the amused stares. Maeve started to say, "I want to get out of here," but her mind lost control of her tongue and it came out, "I want you."

As soon as she spoke the words a wave of embarrassment

swept over her. Blood flushed her neck and face, darkening the healthy tan of her complexion. What must the poor man think of me? she wondered, mortified.

He smiled broadly. "Say good night to the Van Fleets. I'll get my car and meet you outside the club. I hope you dressed warm."

The Van Fleets exchanged knowing looks when she said she was leaving with Pitt. With her heart pounding madly, she hurried across the ballroom, checked out her coat and ran through the doors to the steps outside. She spotted him standing by a low red car, tipping the valet parking attendant. The car looked like it belonged on a racetrack. Except for the twin bucket seats, there was no upholstery. The small curved racing windscreen offered the barest protection from the airstream. There were no bumpers, and the front wheels were covered by what Maeve thought were motorcycle fenders. The spare tire was hung on the right side of the body between the fender and the door.

"Do you actually drive this thing?" she asked.

"I do," he answered solemnly.

"What do you call it?"

"A J2X Allard," Pitt answered, holding open a tiny aluminum door.

"It looks old."

"Built in England in 1952, at least twenty-five years before you were born. Installed with big American V-8 engines, Allards cleaned up at the sports car races until the Mercedes 300 SL coupes came along."

Maeve slipped into the Spartan cockpit, her legs stretched out nearly parallel to the ground. She noticed that the dashboard did not sport a speedometer, only four engine gauges and tachometer. "Will it get us where we're going?" she asked with trepidation.

"Not in drawing room comfort, but she comes close to the speed of sound," he said, laughing.

"It doesn't even have a top."

"I never drive it when it rains." He handed her a silk scarf. "For your hair. It gets pretty breezy sitting in the open. And don't forget to fasten your seat belt. The passenger door has an annoying habit of flying open on a sharp left turn."

Pitt eased his long frame behind the wheel, as Maeve knotted the ends of the scarf under her chin. He turned the ignition-starter key, depressed the clutch and shifted into first gear. There was no ear-shattering roar of exhaust, or scream of protesting tires. He eased out into the country club's driveway as quietly and smoothly as if he were driving in a funeral procession.

"How do you pass NUMA information to your father?" he asked in casual conversation.

She was silent for a few moments, unable to meet his eyes. Finally, she said, "One of Father's aides comes by my house, dressed as a pizza delivery boy."

"Not brilliant, but clever," Pitt said, eyeing a late-model Cadillac STS sedan parked by the side of the drive, just inside the main gate of the country club. Three dark figures were sitting in it, two in front, one in the rear seat. He watched in the rearview mirror as the Cadillac's headlights blinked on and it began following the Allard, keeping a respectable distance. "Are you under surveillance?"

"I was told I'd be closely watched, but I have yet to catch anyone at it."

"You're not very observant. We have a car following us now."

She clutched his arm tightly. "This looks like a fast car. Why don't you simply speed away from them."

"Speed away from them?" he echoed. He glanced at her, seeing the excitement flashing in her eyes. "That's a Cadillac STS behind us, with a three-hundred-plus-horsepower engine that will hurl it upwards of 260 kilometers an hour. This old girl also has a Cadillac engine, with dual four-throat carburetors and an Iskenderian three-quarter cam."

"Which means nothing to me," she said flippantly.

"I'm making a point," he continued. "This was a very fast car forty-eight years ago. It's still fast, but it won't go over 210 kilometers an hour, and that's with a tailwind. The bottom line is that he's got us outclassed in horsepower and top speed."

"You must be able to do something to lose them."

"There is, but I'm not sure you're going to like it."

Pitt waited until he had climbed a sharp hill and dropped down the other side before he mashed the accelerator against its stop. Momentarily out of sight, he gained a precious five-second lead over the driver of the Cadillac. With a surge of power, the little red sports car abruptly leaped over the asphalt road. The trees lining the shoulder of the pavement, their leafless branches stretching over the road like skeletal latticework, became a mad blur under the twin headlight beams. The sensation was one of falling down a well.

Peering into the tiny rearview mirror perched on a small shaft mounted on the cowling, Pitt judged that he had gained a good 150 meters on the Cadillac before the driver crested the hill and realized his quarry had sprinted away. Pitt's total lead was now about a third of a kilometer. Allowing for the Cadillac's superior speed, Pitt estimated that he would be overtaken in another four or five minutes.

The road was straight and rural, running through a swanky region of Virginia just outside of Washington that was occupied by horse farms. Traffic was almost nonexistent this time of night, and Pitt had no trouble passing two slower cars. The Cadillac was pressing hard and gaining with every kilometer. Pitt's grip on the steering wheel was loose and relaxed. He felt no fear. The men in the pursuing car were not out to harm either him or Maeve. This was not a life-or-death struggle. What he did feel was exhilaration as the tach needle crept into the red, a nearly empty road stretched out in front of him, and the wind roared in his ears in concert with the deep, throaty exhaust that blasted out of big twin pipes mounted under the sides of the Allard.

He took his eyes off the road for an instant and glanced at Maeve. She was pressed back in the seat, her head tilted up slightly as if to inhale the air rushing over the windscreen. Her eyes were half closed and her lips partly open. She looked almost as if she were in the throes of sexual ecstasy. Whatever it was, the thrill, the fury of the sounds, the speed, she was not the first woman to fall under the exciting spell of adventure. And what such women desired on the side was a good man to share it with.

Until they came into the outskirts of the city, there was little Pitt could do but crush the accelerator pedal with his foot and keep the wheels aimed alongside the painted line in the center of the road. Without a speedometer, he could only estimate his speed by the tachometer. His best guess was between one-ninety and two hundred kilometers per hour. The old car was giving it everything she had.

Held by the safety belt, Maeve twisted around in the bucket seat. "They're gaining!" she shouted above the roar.

Pitt stole another quick peek in the rearview mirror. The chase car had pulled up to within a hundred meters. The driver was no slouch, he thought. His reflexes were every bit as fast as Pitt's. He turned his attention back on the road.

They were coming into a residential area now. Pitt might have tried to lose the Cadillac on the house-lined streets, but it was too dangerous to even consider. He could not risk running down a family and their dog out for a late night stroll. He wasn't about to cause a fatal accident involving innocent people.

It was only a matter of another minute or two before he would have to slow down and merge with the increased traffic for safety's sake. But for the moment the road ahead was deserted, and he maintained his speed. Then a sign flashed past that warned of construction on a county road leading west at the next junction. The road, Pitt knew, was winding with numerous sharp curves. It ran about five kilometers through open country before ending on the highway that ran by the CIA headquarters at Langley.

He jerked his right foot off the accelerator and jammed it on the brake pedal. Then he spun the steering wheel to the left, snapping the Allard broadside before tearing down the middle of the road, the tires smoking and screaming across the asphalt. Before the car drifted to a stop, the rear wheels were spinning and the Allard leaped onto the county road, which led into the pitch-black of the countryside.

Pitt had to focus every bit of his concentration on the curves ahead. The old sealed-beam headlights did not illuminate the road as far ahead as the more modern halogen units, and he had to use his sixth sense to prepare for the next bend. Pitt loved corners, ignoring the brakes, throwing the car into a controlled skid, then maneuvering into setting up for a straight line until the next curve.

The Allard was in its element now. The heavier Cadillac was stiffly sprung for a road car, but its suspension was no match for the lighter sports car, which was built for racing. Pitt had a love affair with the Allard. He had an exceptional sense of the car's balance and gloried in its simplicity and big, pounding engine. A taut grin stretched his lips as he threw the car into the curves, driving like a demon without touching the brakes, downshifting only on the hairpin turns. The driver of the Cadillac fought on relentlessly but rapidly lost ground with every turn.

Yellow warning lights were flashing on barricades ahead. A ditch opened up beside the road where a pipeline was in the midst of being laid. Pitt was relieved to see that the road carried through and was not blocked completely. The road turned to dirt and gravel for a hundred meters, but he never took his foot off the accelerator. He reveled at the huge cloud of dust he left in his wake, knowing it would slow their pursuer.

After another two minutes of her exciting breakneck ride, Maeve pointed ahead and slightly to her right. "I see headlights," she said.

"The main highway," Pitt acknowledged. "Here is where we lose them for good."

Traffic was clear at the intersection, no cars approaching from either direction for nearly half a kilometer. Pitt burned rubber in a hard turn to the left, away from the city.

"Aren't you going the wrong way?" Maeve cried above the screeching tires.

"Watch and learn," Pitt said as he snapped the wheel back, gently braked and eased the Allard around in a U-turn and drove in the opposite direction. He crossed the junction with the county road before the lights of the Cadillac were in view and picked up speed as he drove toward the glow of the capital city.

"What was that all about?" asked Maeve.

"It's called a red herring," he said conversationally. "If the hounds are as smart as I think they are, they'll follow my tire marks in the opposite direction."

She squeezed his arm and snuggled against him. "What do you do for your finale?"

"Now that I've dazzled you with my virtuosity, I'm going to arouse you with my charm."

She gave him a sly look. "What makes you think I haven't been frightened out of any desire for intimacy?"

"I can climb into your mind and see otherwise."

Maeve laughed. "How can you possibly read my thoughts?"

Pitt shrugged cavalierly and said, "It's a gift. I have Gypsy blood running in my veins."

"You, a Gypsy?"

"According to the family tree, my paternal ancestors, who migrated from Spain to England in the seventeenth century, were Gypsies."

"And now you read palms and tell fortunes."

"Actually, my talents run in other directions, like when the moon is full."

She looked at him warily but took the bait. "What happens when the moon is full?"

He turned and said with the barest hint of a grin, "That's when I go out and steal chickens."

27

Maeve stared warily into the blackness as Pitt drove along a darkened dirt road on the edge of Washington's International Airport. He approached what looked like an ancient, deserted aircraft hangar. There was no other building nearby. Her uneasiness swelled and she instinctively crouched down in the seat as Pitt pulled the Allard to a stop under dim, yellowed lights on a tall pole.

"Where are you taking me?" she demanded.

He looked down at her as if bemused. "Why, my place, of course."

Her face took on an expression of womanly distaste. "You live in this old shed?"

"What you see is a historic building, built in 1936 as a maintenance hangar for an early airline long since demised."

He pulled a small remote transmitter from his coat pocket and punched in a code. A second later a door lifted, revealing what seemed to Maeve a yawning cavern, pitch-black and full of evil. For effect, Pitt turned off the headlights, drove into the darkness, sent a signal to close the door and then sat there.

"Well, what do you think?" he teased in the darkness.

"I'm ready to scream for help," Maeve said with growing confusion.

"Sorry." Pitt punched in another code and the interior of the hangar burst into bright light from rows of fluorescent lamps strategically set around the hangar's arched ceiling.

Maeve's jaw dropped in awe as she found herself looking at priceless examples of mechanical art. She could not believe the glittering collection of classic automobiles, the aircraft and early American railroad car. She recognized a pair of Rolls-Royces and a big convertible Daimler, but she was unfamiliar with the American Packards, Pierce Arrows, Stutzes, Cords and the other European cars on display, including a Hispano-Suiza, Bugatti, Isotta Fraschini, Talbot Lago and a Delahaye. The two aircraft that hung from the ceiling were an old Ford Trimotor and a Messerschmitt 262 World War II fighter aircraft. The array was breathtaking. The only exhibit that seemed out of place was a rectangular pedestal supporting an outboard motor attached to an antique cast-iron bathtub.

"Is this all yours?" she gasped.

"It was either this or a wife and kids," he joked.

She turned and tilted her head coquettishly. "You're not too old to marry and have children. You just haven't found the right woman."

"I suppose that's true."

"Unlucky in love?"

"The Pitt curse."

She gestured to a dark blue Pierce Arrow travel trailer. "Is that where you live?"

He laughed and pointed up. "My apartment is up those circular iron stairs, or if you're lazy, you can take the freight elevator."

"I can use the exercise," she said softly.

He showed her up the ornate wrought-iron spiral staircase. The door opened into a living room–study filled with shelves stacked with books about the sea and glass-encased models of ships Pitt had discovered and surveyed while working for NUMA. A door on one side of the room led into a large bedroom decorated like the captain's cabin of an old sailing ship complete with a huge wheel as a backboard for the bed. The opposite end of the living room opened into a kitchen and dining area. To Maeve, the apartment positively reeked of masculinity.

280

"So this is where Huckleberry Finn moved after leaving his houseboat on the river," she said, kicking off her shoes, settling onto a leather couch and curling up her legs on the cushions.

"I'm on water most of the year as it is. These rooms don't see me as often as I'd like." He removed his coat and untied his bow tie. "Can I offer you a drink?"

"A brandy might be nice."

"Come to think of it, I carried you away from the party before you had a chance to eat. Let me whip you up something."

"The brandy will do just fine. I can gorge tomorrow."

He poured Maeve a Rémy Martin and sat down on the couch beside her. She wanted him desperately, wanted to press herself into his arms, to just touch him, but inside herself she was seething with turmoil. A sudden wave of guilt swept over her as she visualized her children suffering under the brutal hand of Jack Ferguson. She could not push aside the enormity of it. Her chest felt tight, and the rest of her body, numb and weak. She ached for Sean and Michael, who were to her still babies. To allow herself to fall into a sensual adventure was little short of a crime. She wanted to scream with despair. She set the brandy on the coffee table and abruptly began to weep uncontrollably.

Pitt held her tightly. "Your children?" he asked.

She nodded between sobs. "I'm sorry, I didn't mean to mislead you."

Strangely, female emotions had never been a big mystery with Pitt as with most men, and he was never confused or mystified when the tears came. He looked upon women's sometimes emotional behavior more with compassion than discomfort. "Put a woman's concern for her offspring against her sex drive, and motherly concern wins every time."

Maeve would never comprehend how Pitt could be so understanding. To her, he didn't seem human. He certainly was unlike any man she'd ever known. "I'm so lost and afraid. I've never been more helpless in my life."

He rose from the couch and came back with a box of tissues. "Sorry I can't offer you a handkerchief, but I don't carry them much anymore."

"You don't mind . . . my disappointing you?"

Pitt smiled as Maeve wiped her eyes and blew her nose with a loud snort. "The truth is, I had ulterior motives."

Her eyes widened questioningly. "You don't want to go to bed with me?"

"I'd turn in my testosterone card if I didn't. But that's not entirely why I brought you here."

"I don't understand."

"I need your help in consolidating my plans."

"Plans for what?"

He looked at her as if he was surprised she asked. "To sneak onto Gladiator Island, of course, snatch your boys and make a clean getaway."

Maeve made nervous gestures of incomprehension with her hands. "You'd do that?" she gasped. "You'd risk your life for me?"

"And your sons," Pitt added firmly.

"But why?"

He had an overpowering urge to tell her she was lithe and lovely and that he harbored feelings of deep affection for her, but he couldn't bring himself to sound like a lovesick adolescent. True to form, he swerved to the light side.

"Why? Because Admiral Sandecker gave me ten days off, and I hate to sit around and not be productive."

A smile returned to her damp face, and she pulled him against her. "That's not even a good lie."

"Why is it," he said just before he kissed her, "that women always see right through me?"

PART III

DIAMONDS . . . THE GRAND ILLUSION

◦ MARVELOUS MAEVE ◦

28

The Dorsett manor house sat in the saddle of the island, between the two dormant volcanos. The front overlooked the lagoon, which had become a bustling port for the diamond mining activities. Two mines in both volcanic chutes had been in continuous operation almost from the day Charles and Mary Dorsett returned from England after their marriage. There were those who claimed the family empire began then, but those who knew better held that the empire was truly launched by Betsy Fletcher when she found the unusual stones and gave them to her children to play with.

The original dwelling, mostly built from logs, with a palm frond or palapa roof, was torn down by Anson Dorsett. It was he who designed and built the large mansion that still stood after being remodeled by later generations until eventually taken over by Arthur Dorsett. The style was based on the classical layout—a central courtyard surrounded by verandas from which doors opened onto thirty rooms, all furnished in English colonial antiques. The only visible modern convenience was a large satellite dish, rising from a luxuriant garden, and a modern swimming pool in the center courtyard.

Arthur Dorsett hung up the phone, stepped out of his office-study and walked over to the pool where Deirdre was languidly stretched on a lounge chair, in a string bikini, carefully absorbing the tropical sun into her smooth skin.

"You'd better not let my superintendents see you like that," he said gruffly.

She slowly raised her head and looked down over a sea of skin. "I see no problem. I have my bra on."

"And women wonder why they're raped."

"Surely you don't want me to go around wearing a sack," she said mockingly.

"I have just gotten off the phone with Washington," he said heavily. "It seems your sister has vanished."

Deirdre sat up, startled, and lifted a hand to shade her eyes from the sun. "Are your sources reliable? I personally hired the best investigators, former Secret Service agents, to keep her under surveillance."

"It's confirmed. They bungled their assignment and lost her after a wild ride through the countryside."

"Maeve isn't smart enough to lose professional investigators."

"From what I've been told, she had help."

Her lips twisted into a scowl. "Let me guess: Dirk Pitt."

Dorsett nodded. "The man is everywhere. Boudicca had him in her grasp at our Kunghit Island mine, but he slipped through her fingers."

"I sensed he was dangerous when he saved Maeve. I should have known *how* dangerous when he interrupted my plans to be airlifted off the *Polar Queen* by our helicopter after I set the ship on a collision course toward the rocks. I thought we were rid of him after that. I never imagined he would pop up without warning at our Canadian operation."

Dorsett motioned to a pretty little Chinese girl who was standing by a column supporting the roof over the veranda. She was dressed in a silk dress with long slits up the sides. "Bring me a gin," he ordered. "Make it a tall one. I don't like skimpy drinks."

Deirdre held up a tall, empty glass. "Another rum collins."

The girl hurried off to bring the drinks. Deirdre caught her father eyeing the girl's backside and rolled her eyes. "Really, Daddy. You should know better than to bed the hired help. The world expects better from a man of your wealth and status."

"There are some things that go beyond class," he said sternly.

"What do we do about Maeve? She's obviously enlisted Dirk Pitt and his friends from NUMA to help her retrieve the twins."

Dorsett pulled his attention from the departing Chinese servant. "He may be a resourceful man, but he won't find Gladiator Island as easy to penetrate as our Kunghit Island property."

"Maeve knows the island better than any of us. She'll find a way."

"Even if they make it ashore"—he lifted a finger and pointed through the arched door of the courtyard in the general direction of the mines—"they'll never get within two hundred meters of the house."

Deirdre smiled diabolically. "Preparing a warm welcome seems most appropriate."

"No warm welcome, my darling daughter, not here, not on Gladiator Island."

"You have an ulterior plan." It was more statement than question.

He nodded. "Through Maeve, they will, no doubt, devise a scheme to infiltrate our security. Unfortunately for them, they won't have the opportunity of exercising it."

"I don't understand."

"We cut them off at the pass, as the Americans are fond of saying, before they touch our shore."

"A perceptive man, my father." She stood up and hugged him, inhaling his smell. Even when she was a little girl he had smelled of expensive cologne, a special brand he imported from Germany, a musky, no-nonsense smell that reminded her of leather briefcases, the indefinable scent of a corporation boardroom and the wool of an expensive business suit.

He reluctantly pushed her away, angry at a growing feeling of desire for his own flesh and blood. "I want you to coordinate the mission. As usual, Boudicca will expedite."

"I'll bet my share of Dorsett Consolidated you know where to find them." She smiled archly at him. "What is our timetable?"

"I suspect that Mr. Pitt and Maeve have already left Washington."

Her eyes squinted at him under the sun. "So soon?"

"Since Maeve hasn't been seen at her house, nor has Pitt set foot in his NUMA office for the past two days, it goes without saying that they are together and on their way here for the twins."

"Tell me where to set a trap for them," she said, a sparkle of the feline hunter in her eyes, certain her father had the answer. "An airport or hotel in Honolulu, Auckland or Sydney?"

He shook his head. "None of those. They won't make it easy for us by flying on commercial flights and staying at secluded inns. They'll take one of NUMA's small fleet of jet transports and use the agency's facilities as a base."

"I didn't know the Americans had a permanent base for oceanographic study in either New Zealand or Australia."

"They don't," replied Dorsett. "What they do have is a research ship, the *Ocean Angler,* which is on a deep-sea survey project in the Bounty Trough, west of New Zealand. If all goes according to plan, Pitt and Maeve will arrive in Wellington and rendezvous with the NUMA ship at the city docks this time tomorrow."

Deirdre stared at her father with open admiration. "How could you know all this?"

He smiled imperiously. "I have my own source in NUMA, who I pay very well to keep me informed of any underwater discoveries of precious stones."

"Then our strategy is to have Boudicca and her crew intercept and board the research ship and arrange for it to disappear."

"Not wise," Dorsett said flatly. "Boudicca has learned that Dirk Pitt somehow traced the cleanup of the derelict ships to her and our yacht. We send one of NUMA's research ships and its crew to the bottom and they'll know damned well we were behind it. No, we'll treat that matter more delicately."

"Twenty-four hours isn't much time."

"Leave after lunch and you can be in Wellington by supper. John Merchant and his security force will be waiting for you at our warehouse outside of the city."

"I thought Merchant had his skull fractured on Kunghit Island."

"A hairline crack. Just enough to make him insane for revenge. He insisted on being in on the kill."

"And you and Boudicca?" asked Deirdre.

"We'll come across in the yacht and should arrive by midnight," answered Dorsett. "That still leaves us ten hours to firm up our preparations."

"That means we'll be forced into seizing them during daylight."

Dorsett gripped Deirdre by the shoulders so hard she winced. "I'm counting on you, Daughter, to overcome any obstacles."

"A mistake, thinking we could trust Maeve," Deirdre said reproachfully. "You should have guessed she would come chasing after her brats the first chance she got."

"The information she passed on to us before disappearing was useful," he insisted, angrily. Excuses for miscalculation did not come easily to Arthur Dorsett.

"If only Maeve had died on Seymour Island, we wouldn't have this mess."

"The blame is not entirely hers," said Dorsett. "She had no prior knowledge of Pitt's intrusion on Kunghit. He's cast out a net, but any information he might have obtained cannot hurt us."

Despite the minor setback, Dorsett was not overly concerned. His mines were on islands whose isolation was a barrier to any kind of organized protest. His vast resources had shifted into gear. Security was tightened to keep any reporters from coming within several kilometers of his operations. Dorsett attorneys worked long hours to keep any legal opposition at bay while the public relations people labeled the stories of deaths and disappearances throughout the Pacific Ocean as products of environmentalist rumor mills and attempted to throw the blame elsewhere, the most likely target being secret American military experiments.

When Dorsett spoke it was with renewed calm. "Twenty-three days from now any storm raised by Admiral Sandecker will die a natural death when we close the mines."

"We can't make it look as though we're admitting guilt by shutting down our operations, Daddy. We'd open ourselves to a mountain of lawsuits by environmentalists and families of those who were killed."

"Not to worry, Daughter. Obtaining evidence that proves our mining methods cause underwater ultrasonic convergence that kills organic life is next to impossible. Scientific tests would have to be conducted over a period of months. In three weeks' time, scientists will have nothing to study. Plans have been made to remove every nut and bolt from our diamond excavations. The acoustic plague, as they insist on calling it, will be yesterday's headlines."

The little Chinese girl returned with their drinks and served them from a tray. She retreated into the shadows of the veranda as soundlessly as a wraith.

"Now that their mother has betrayed us, what will you do with Sean and Michael?"

"I'll arrange for her never to see them again."

"A great pity," Deirdre said as she rolled the icy glass over her forehead.

Dorsett downed the gin as if it were water. He lowered the glass and looked at her. "Pity? Who am I supposed to pity, Maeve or the twins?"

"Neither."

"Who then?"

Deirdre's exotic-model features wore a sardonic grin. "The millions of women around the world, when they find out their diamonds are as worthless as glass."

"We'll take the romance out of the stone," Dorsett said, laughing. "*That,* I promise you."

29

Wellington, observed Pitt through the window of the NUMA aircraft, couldn't have rested in a more beautiful setting. Enclosed by a huge bay and a maze of islands, low mountains with Mount Victoria as the highest peak, and lush, green vegetation, the port boasted one of the finest harbors in the world. This was his fourth trip in ten years to the capital city of New Zealand, and he had seldom seen it without scattered rain showers and gusting winds.

Admiral Sandecker had given Pitt's mission his very reluctant blessing with grave misgivings. He considered Arthur Dorsett a very threatening man, a greedy sociopath who killed without a shred of remorse. The admiral cooperated by authorizing a NUMA aircraft for Pitt and Giordino to fly, with Maeve, to New Zealand and take command of a research ship as a base of operations for the rescue, but with the strict condition that no lives be risked in the attempt. Pitt gladly agreed, knowing the only people at risk, once the *Ocean Angler* stood a safe distance off Gladiator Island, would be the three of them. His plan was to use an underwater submersible to slip into the lagoon, then land and help Maeve reclaim her sons before returning to the ship. It was, Pitt thought bemusedly, a plan without technicalities. Once on shore, everything hinged on Maeve.

He looked across the cockpit at Giordino, who was piloting the executive Gulfstream jet. His burly friend was as composed as if he were lounging under a palm tree on a sandy beach. They had been close friends since that first day they had met in elementary school and gotten into a fistfight. They played on the same high school football team, Giordino as a tackle, Pitt as quarterback, and later at the Air Force Academy. Blatantly using his father's influence—George Pitt happened to be the senior Senator from California—to keep them together, Dirk and Al had trained in the same flight school and flown two tours with the same tactical squadron in Vietnam. When it came to the ladies, however, they differed. Giordino reveled in affairs, while Pitt felt more comfortable with relationships.

Pitt rose from his seat, moved back into the main cabin and stared down at Maeve. She had slept fitfully during the long and tedious flight from Washington, and her face looked tired and drawn. Even now her eyes were closed, but the way she constantly changed position on the narrow couch indicated she had not yet crossed over the threshold into unconscious slumber. He reached over and gently shook her. "We're about to land in Wellington," he said.

Her indelible blue eyes fluttered open. "I'm awake," she murmured sleepily.

"How do you feel?" he asked with gentleness and concern.

She roused herself and nodded gamely. "Ready and willing."

Giordino flared the aircraft, dropping smoothly till the tires touched and smoked briefly on contact with the ground. He taxied off the runway onto the flight line toward the parking area for transient and privately owned aircraft. "You see a NUMA vehicle?" he shouted over his shoulder at Pitt in the back.

The familiar turquoise and white colors were not in sight. "Must be late," said Pitt. "Or else we're early."

"Fifteen minutes early by the old timepiece on the instrument panel," replied Giordino.

A small pickup truck with a flight-line attendant in the bed motioned for Giordino to follow them to an open parking space between a line of executive jet aircraft. Giordino rolled to a stop when his wingtips were even with the planes on either side of him and began the procedure for shutting down the engines.

Pitt opened the passenger door and set a small step at the end of the stairs. Maeve followed him out and walked back and forth to stretch her joints and muscles, stiff and tensed after the long flight. She looked around the parking area for their transportation. "I thought someone from the ship was going to meet us," she said between yawns.

"They must be on their way."

Giordino passed out their traveling bags, locked up the aircraft and took cover with Pitt and Maeve under one wing while a sudden rain squall passed over the airport. Almost as quickly as it appeared, the storm moved across the bay, and the sun broke through a rolling mass of white clouds. A few minutes later, a small Toyota bus with the words HARBOR SHUTTLE painted on the sides splashed through the puddles and stopped. The driver stepped to the ground and jogged over to the aircraft. He was slim with a friendly face and dressed like a drugstore cowboy.

"One of you Dirk Pitt?"

"Right here," Pitt acknowledged.

"Carl Marvin. Sorry I'm running late. The battery went dead in the shore van we carry aboard the *Ocean Angler,* so I had to borrow transportation from the harbormaster. I do hope you weren't inconvenienced."

"Not at all," said Giordino sourly. "We enjoyed the typhoon during intermission."

The sarcasm flew over the driver's head. "You haven't been waiting long, I hope."

"No more than ten minutes," said Pitt.

Marvin loaded their bags in the back of the shuttle bus and drove away from the aircraft as soon as his passengers were seated. "The dock where the ship is moored is only a short drive from the airport," he said cordially. "Just sit back and enjoy the trip."

Pitt and Maeve sat together, held hands like teenagers and talked in low tones. Giordino settled into the seat in front of them and directly behind the driver. He spent most of the drive studying an aerial photo of Gladiator Island that Admiral Sandecker had borrowed from the Pentagon.

Time passed quickly and they soon turned off the main road into the bustling dock area, which was quite close to the city. A fleet of international cargo vessels, representing mostly Asian shipping lines, were moored beside long piers flanked by huge storage buildings. No one paid any attention to the wandering course taken by the driver around the buildings, ships and huge cargo cranes. His eyes watched the passengers in the rearview mirror almost as often as they were turned on the piers ahead.

"The *Ocean Angler* is just on the other side of the next warehouse," he said, vaguely gesturing at some unseen object through the windshield.

"Is she ready to cast off when we board?" asked Pitt.

"The crew is standing by for your arrival."

Giordino stared thoughtfully at the back of the driver's head. "What's your duty on the ship?" he asked.

"Mine?" said Marvin without turning. "I'm a photographer with the film crew."

"How do you like sailing under Captain Dempsey?"

"A fine gentlemen. He is most considerate of the scientists and their work."

Giordino looked up and saw Marvin peering back in the rearview mirror. He smiled until Marvin refocused his attention on his driving. Then, shielded by the backrest of the seat in front of him, he wrote on a receipt for aircraft fuel that was pumped aboard in Honolulu before they headed toward Wellington. He wadded up the paper and casually flipped it over his shoulder on Pitt's lap.

Talking with Maeve, Pitt had not picked up on the words that passed between Giordino and the driver. He casually unfolded the note and read the message:

THIS GUY IS A PHONY.

Pitt leaned forward and spoke conversationally without staring suspiciously at the driver. "What makes you such a killjoy?"

Giordino turned around and spoke very softly. "Our friend is not from the *Ocean Angler*."

"I'm listening."

"I tricked him into saying Dempsey is the captain."

"Paul Dempsey skippers the *Ice Hunter*. Joe Ross is captain of the *Angler*."

"Here's another inconsistency. You and I and Rudi Gunn went over NUMA's scheduled research projects and assigned personnel before we left for the Antarctic."

"So?"

"Our friend up front not only has a bogus Texas accent, but he claims to be a photographer with the *Ocean Angler*'s film crew. Get the picture?''

"I do," Pitt murmured. "No film crew was recruited to go on the project. Only sonar technicians and a team of geophysicists went on board, to survey the ocean floor."

"And this character is driving us straight into hell," said Giordino, looking out the window and toward a dockside warehouse just ahead with a large sign across a pair of doors that read DOR-SETT CONSOLIDATED MINING LTD.

True to their fears, the driver swung the bus through the gaping doors and between two men in the uniforms of Dorsett Consolidated security guards. The guards quickly followed the bus inside and pushed the switch to close the warehouse doors.

"In the final analysis, I'd have to say we've been had," said Pitt.

"What's the plan of attack?" asked Giordino, no longer speaking in a hushed voice.

There wasn't time for any drawn-out conference. The bus was passing deeper into the darkened warehouse. "Dump our buddy Carl and let's bust out of here."

Giordino did not wait for a countdown. Four quick steps and he had a choke hold on the man who called himself Carl Marvin. With unbelievable speed, Giordino swung the man from behind the steering wheel, opened the entry door of the bus and heaved him out.

As if they had rehearsed, Pitt jumped into the driver's seat and jammed the accelerator to the carpeted floorboard. Not an instant too soon, the bus surged forward through a knot of armed men, scattering them like leaves in the wake of a tornado. Two pallets holding cardboard boxes of electrical kitchen appliances from Japan sat directly in front of the bus. Pitt's expression gave no hint that he was aware of the approaching impact. Boxes, bits and pieces of toasters, blenders and coffeemakers burst into the air as though they were shrapnel from an exploding howitzer shell.

Pitt swung a broadside turn down a wide aisle separating tiers of stacked crates of merchandise, took aim at a large metal door and crouched over the steering wheel. With a metallic clatter that sent the door whirling from its mountings, the Toyota bus roared out of the warehouse onto the loading dock, Pitt twisting the wheel rapidly to keep from clipping one leg of a towering loading crane.

This part of the dockyard was deserted. No ships were moored alongside, loading and unloading their cargo holds. A party of workers repairing a section of the pier were taking a break, sitting elbow to elbow in a row on a long wooden barricade that stretched across an access road leading from the pier as they ate their lunch. Pitt lay on the horn, spinning the wheel violently to avoid striking the workers, who froze at the sight of the vehicle bearing down on them. As the bus slewed around the barricade, Pitt almost missed it entirely, but a piece of the rear bumper caught a vertical support and spun the barricade around, slinging the dockworkers about the pier as if they were on the end of a cracked whip.

"Sorry about that!" Pitt yelled out the window as he sped past.

He regretted not having been more observant, and belatedly realized the phony driver had purposely taken a roundabout route to confuse them. A ploy that worked all too well. He had no idea which way to turn for the entrance to the highway leading into the city.

A long truck and trailer pulled in front of him, blocking off his exit. He frantically cramped the steering wheel in a crazy zigzag to avoid smashing into the huge truck. There was a loud metallic crunch, followed by the smashing of glass and the screech of tortured metal as the bus sideswiped the front end of the truck. The bus, its entire right side gouged and smashed, bounced wildly out of control. Pitt corrected and fishtailed the shattered vehicle until it straightened. He pounded the steering wheel angrily at seeing fluid spraying back over the newly cracked windshield. The impact had sprung the radiator from its mounts and loosened the hoses to the engine. That wasn't the only problem. The right tire was blown and the front suspension knocked out of alignment.

"Do you have to hit everything that comes across your path?" Giordino asked irritably. He sat on the floor on the undamaged side of the bus, his huge arms circled around Maeve.

"Thoughtless of me," said Pitt. "Anyone hurt?"

"Enough bruises to win an abuse lawsuit," said Maeve bravely.

Giordino rubbed a swelling knot on one side of his head and

gazed at Maeve woefully. "Your old man is a sneaky devil. He knew we were coming and threw a surprise party."

"Someone at NUMA must be on his payroll." Pitt spared Maeve a brief glance. "Not you, I hope."

"Not me," Maeve said firmly.

Giordino made his way to the rear of the bus and stared out the window for signs of pursuit. Two black vans careened around the damaged truck and took up the chase. "We have hounds running up our exhaust pipe."

"Good guys or bad?" asked Pitt.

"I hate to be the bearer of sad tidings, but they ain't wearing white hats."

"You call that a positive identification?"

"How about, they have Dorsett Consolidated Mining logos painted on their doors."

"You sold me."

"If they come any closer, I could ask for their driver's license."

"Thank you, I have a rearview mirror."

"You'd think we'd have left enough wreckage to have a dozen cop cars on our tails by now," grumbled Giordino. "Why aren't they doing their duty and patrolling the docks? I think it only fitting they arrest you for reckless driving."

"If I know Daddy," said Maeve, "he paid them to take a holiday."

With no coolant, the engine rapidly heated up and threw clouds of steam from under the hood. Pitt had almost no control over the demolished vehicle. The front wheels, both splayed outward, fought to travel in opposite directions. A narrow alleyway between two warehouses suddenly yawned in front of the bus. Down to the final toss of the dice, Pitt hurled the bus into the opening. His luck was against him. Too late he realized the alleyway led onto a deserted pier with no exit except the one he passed through.

"The end of the trail," Pitt sighed.

Giordino turned and looked to the rear again. "The posse knows it. They've stopped to gloat over their triumph."

"Maeve?"

Maeve walked to the front of the bus. "Yes?" she said quietly.

"How long can you hold your breath?"

"I don't know; maybe a minute."

"Al? What are they doing?"

"Walking toward the bus, holding nasty-looking clubs."

"They want us alive," said Pitt. "Okay, gang, take a seat and hold on tight."

"What are you going to do?" asked Maeve.

"*We*, love of my life, are going for a swim. Al, open all the windows. I want this thing to sink like a brick."

"I hope the water's warm," said Giordino as he unlatched the windows. "I hate cold water."

To Maeve, Pitt said, "Take several deep breaths and get as much oxygen as you can into your bloodstream. Exhale and then inhale as we go over the side."

"I bet I can swim underwater farther than you," she said with gutsy resolve.

"Here's your chance to prove it," he said admiringly. "Don't waste time waiting for an air pocket. Go out the windows on your right and swim under the pier as soon as the water stops surging inside the bus."

Pitt reached behind the driver's seat, unzipped his overnight bag, retrieved a nylon packet and stuffed it down the front of his pants, leaving a larger-than-life bulge.

"What in the world are you doing?" asked Maeve.

"My emergency goody bag," explained Pitt. "I never leave home without it."

"They're almost on us," Giordino announced calmly.

Pitt slipped on a leather coat, zipped it to his collar, turned and gripped the wheel. "Okay, let's see if we can get high marks from the judges."

He revved up the engine and shifted the automatic transmission into LOW. The battered bus jerked forward, right front tire flapping, steam billowing so thick he could hardly see ahead, gathering speed for the plunge. There was no railing along the pier, only a low, wooden horizontal beam that acted as a curb for vehicles. The front wheels took the brunt of the impact. The already weakened front suspension tore away as the wheelless chassis ground over it, the rear tires tearing rubber as they spun, pushing what was left of the Toyota bus over the side of the pier.

The bus seemed to fall in slow motion before the heavier front end dropped and struck the water with a great splash. The last thing Pitt remembered before the windshield fell inward and the seawater surged through the open passenger door was the loud hiss of the overheated engine as it was inundated.

The bus bobbed once, hung for an instant and then sank into the green water of the bay. All Dorsett's security people saw when they ran to the edge of the dock and looked down, was a cloud of steam, a mass of gurgling bubbles and a spreading oil slick. The waves created by the impact spread and rippled into the pilings beneath the pier. They waited expectantly for heads to appear, but no indication of life emerged from the green depths.

Pitt guessed that if the docks could accommodate large cargo ships the water depth had to be at least fifteen meters. The bus sank, wheels down, into the muck on the bottom of the harbor, disturbing the silt, which burst into a rolling cloud. Pushing away from the wheel, he stroked toward the rear of the bus to make sure Maeve and Giordino were not injured and had exited through a window. Satisfied they had escaped, he snaked through the opening and kicked into the blinding silt. When he burst into the clear, visibility was better than he had expected, the water temperature a degree or two colder. The incoming tide brought in fairly clean water, and he could easily distinguish the individual pilings under the pier. He estimated visibility at twenty meters.

He recognized the indistinct shapes of Maeve and Giordino about four meters in front, swimming strongly into the void ahead. He looked up, but the surface was only a vague pattern of broken light from a cloudy sky. And then suddenly the water darkened considerably as he swam under the pier and between the pilings. He temporarily lost the others in the shadowy murk, and his lungs began to tighten in complaint from the growing lack of air. He swam on an angle toward the surface, allowing the buoyancy of his body to carry him upward, one hand raised above his head to ward off imbedding something hard and sharp in his scalp. He finally surfaced in the midst of a small sea of floating litter. He sucked in several breaths of salty air and swung around to find Maeve and Giordino bobbing in the water a short distance behind him.

They swam over, and his regard for Maeve heightened when he saw her smiling. "Show-off," she whispered, aware that voices could be heard by the Dorsett men above. "I bet you almost drowned trying to outdistance me."

"There's life in the old man yet," Pitt murmured.

"I don't think anyone saw us," muttered Giordino. "I was almost under the dock before I broke free of the silt cloud."

Pitt motioned in the general direction of the main dock area. "Our best hope is to swim under the pier until we can find a safe place to climb clear."

"What about boarding the nearest ship we can find?" asked Giordino.

Maeve looked doubtful. Her long blond hair floated in the water behind her like golden reeds on a pond. "If my father's people picked up our trail, he'd find a way to force the crew to turn us over to him."

Giordino looked at her, "You don't think the crew would hold us until we were under the protection of local authorities?"

Pitt shook his head, flinging drops of water in a spiral. "If you were the captain of a ship or the commander in charge of dock police, would you believe a trio of half-drowned rats or the word of someone representing Arthur Dorsett?"

"Probably not us," Giordino admitted.

"If only we could reach the *Ocean Angler.*"

"That would be the first place they'd expect us to go," said Maeve.

"Once we were on board, Dorsett's men would have a fight on their hands if they tried to drag us off," Pitt assured her.

"A moot point," Giordino said under his breath. "We haven't the foggiest idea where the *Ocean Angler* is berthed."

Pitt stared at his friend reproachfully. "I hate it when you're sober minded."

"Has she a turquoise hull and white on the cabins above like the *Ice Hunter?*" asked Maeve.

"All NUMA ships have the same color scheme," Giordino answered.

"Then I saw her. She's tied to Pier 16."

"I give up. Where's Pier 16 from here?"

"The fourth one north of here," replied Pitt.

"How would you know that?"

"The signs on the warehouses. I noticed number 19 before I drove off of Pier 20."

"Now that we've fixed our location and have a direction, we'd best get a move on," Giordino suggested. "If they have half a brain they'll be sending down divers to look for bodies in the bus.''

"Stay clear of the pilings," cautioned Pitt. "Beneath the surface, they're packed with colonies of mussels. Their shells can cut through flesh like a razor blade.''

"Is that why you're swimming in a leather jacket?" asked Maeve.

"You never know who you'll meet," Pitt said drily.

Without a visual sighting, there was no calculating how far they had to go before reaching the research ship. Conserving their strength, they breaststroked slowly and steadily through the maze of pilings, out of sight of Dorsett's men on the dock above. They reached the base of Pier 20, then passed beneath the main dockyard thoroughfare, which connected to all the loading docks, before turning north toward Pier 16. The better part of an hour crept by before Maeve spotted the turquoise hull reflected in the water beneath the pier.

"We made it," she cried out happily.

"Don't count your prize money," Pitt warned her. "The dock might be crawling with your father's muscle patrol.''

The ship's hull was only two meters from the pilings. Pitt swam until he was directly beneath the ship's boarding ramp. He reached up, locked his hands around a cross member that reinforced the pilings and pulled himself out of the water. Climbing the slanting beams until he reached the upper edge of the dock, he slowly raised his head and scanned the immediate vicinity.

The area around the boarding ramp was deserted, but a Dorsett security van was parked across the nearest entry onto the pier. He counted four men lined across an open stretch between stacks of cargo containers and several parked cars alongside the ship moored in front of the *Ocean Angler*.

He ducked below the edge of the dock and spoke to Maeve and Giordino. "Our friends are guarding the entrance to the pier about eighty meters away, too far to stop us from making it on board.''

No more conversation was necessary. Pitt pulled both of them onto the beam he was standing on. Then, at his signal, they all climbed over the beam that acted as a curb, dodged around a huge bollard that held the mooring lines of the ship, and with Maeve in the lead, dashed up the boarding ramp to the open deck above.

When he reached the safety of the ship, Pitt's instincts began working overtime. He had erred badly, and the mistake couldn't be undone. He knew when he saw the men guarding the dock begin walking slowly and methodically toward the *Ocean Angler* as if they were out for a stroll through the park. There was no shouting or confusion. They acted as though they had expected their quarry to suddenly appear and reach the sanctuary of the ship. He knew when he looked over decks devoid of human activity that something was very, very wrong. Someone on the crew should have been in evidence on a working ship. The robotic submersibles, the sonar equipment, the great winch for lowering survey systems into the depths were neatly secured. Rare was the occasion when an engineer or scientist wasn't fussing with his prized apparatus. And he knew when a door opened from a companionway leading to the bridge and a familiar figure stepped out onto the deck that the unthinkable had happened.

"How nice to see you again, Mr. Pitt," said John Merchant, snidely. "You never give up, do you?"

30

Pitt, in those first few moments of bitter frustration, felt an almost tangible wave of defeat wash over him. The fact that they had been effortlessly and completely snared, that Maeve was trapped in the arms of her father, that there was every likelihood that he and Giordino would be murdered, was a heavy pill to swallow.

It was all too painfully obvious that with advance warning from their agent inside NUMA, Dorsett's men had arrived at the *Ocean Angler* first, and through some kind of subterfuge had temporarily subdued the captain and crew and taken over the ship just long enough to trap Pitt and the others. It had all been so predestined, so transparent that Arthur Dorsett had been certain to do something beyond the bounds of the ordinary, as a backup strategy in the event that Pitt and Giordino had slipped through his fingers and somehow come on board. Pitt felt he should have predicted it and come up with an alternate plan, but he'd underestimated the shrewd diamond tycoon. Pirating an entire ship while it was docked within stone's throw of a major city had not crossed Pitt's mind.

When he saw a small army of uniformed men appear from their

hiding places, some with police clubs, a few leveling rubber-pellet guns, he knew hope was lost. But not irretrievably lost. Not so long as he had Giordino at his side. He looked down at Giordino to see how he was reacting to the terrible shock. As far as he could tell, Giordino looked as though he was enduring a boring classroom lecture. There was no reaction at all. He stared at Merchant as though measuring the man for a coffin, a stare, Pitt observed, that was strangely like the one with which Merchant was appraising Giordino.

Pitt put his arm around Maeve, whose brave front began to crumble. The blue eyes were desolate, the wide, waxen eyes of one who knows her world is ending. She bowed her head and placed it in her hands as her shoulders sagged. Her fear was not for herself but for what her father would do to her boys now that it was painfully obvious she had deceived him.

"What have you done with the crew?" Pitt demanded of Merchant, noting the bandage on the back of his head.

"The five men left on board were persuaded to remain in their quarters."

Pitt looked at him questioningly. "Only five?"

"Yes. The others were invited to a party in their honor by Mr. Dorsett, at Wellington's finest hotel. Hail to the brave explorers of the deep, that sort of thing. As a mining company, Dorsett Consolidated has a vested interest in whatever minerals are discovered on the seafloor."

"You were well prepared," said Pitt coldly. "Who in NUMA told you we were coming?"

"A geologist, I don't know his name, who keeps Mr. Dorsett informed of your underwater mining projects. He's only one of many who provide the company with inside information from businesses and governments around the world."

"A corporate spy network."

"And a very good one. We've tracked you from the minute you took off from Langley Field in Washington."

The guards who surrounded the three made no move to restrain them. "No shackles, no handcuffs?" asked Pitt.

"My men have been commanded to assault and maim only Miss Dorsett should you and your friend attempt to escape." Merchant's teeth fairly gleamed under the sun between his thin lips. "Not my wish, of course. The orders came direct from Ms. Boudicca Dorsett."

"A real sweetheart," Pitt said acidly. "I'll bet she tortured her dolls when she was little."

"She has some very interesting plans for you, Mr. Pitt."

"How's your head?"

"Not nearly injured enough to keep me from flying over the ocean to apprehend *you*."

"I can't stand the suspense. Where do we go from here?"

"Mr. Dorsett will arrive shortly. You will all be transferred to his yacht."

"I thought his floating villa was at Kunghit Island."

"It was, several days ago." Merchant smiled, removed his glasses and meticulously polished the lenses with a small cloth. "The Dorsett yacht has four turbocharged diesel engines connected to water jets that produce a total of 18,000 horsepower that enable the 80-ton craft to cruise at 120 kilometers an hour. You will find Mr. Dorsett is a man of singularly high taste."

"In reality, he probably has a personality about as interesting as a cloistered monk's address book," said Giordino readily. "What does he do for laughs besides count diamonds?"

Just for a moment, Merchant's eyes blazed at Giordino and his smile faded, then he caught himself and the lifeless look returned as if it had been applied by a makeup artist.

"Humor, gentlemen, has its price. As Miss Dorsett can tell you, her father lacks a fondness for satiric wit. I venture to say that by this time tomorrow you will have precious little to smile about."

Arthur Dorsett was nothing like Pitt had pictured him. He expected one of the richest men in the world, with three beautiful daughters, to be reasonably handsome, with a certain degree of sophistication. What Pitt saw before him in the salon of the same yacht he'd stood in at Kunghit Island was a troll from Teutonic folklore who'd just crawled from an underworld cave.

Dorsett stood a half a head taller than Pitt and was twice as broad from hips to shoulders. This was not a man who was comfortable sitting behind a desk. Pitt could see from whom Boudicca had gotten the black, empty eyes. Dorsett had weathered lines in his face, and the rough, scarred hands indicated that he wasn't afraid of getting them dirty. The mustache was long and scraggly with a few bits of his lunch adhering to the strands of hair. But the thing that struck Pitt as hardly befitting a man of Dorsett's international stature was the teeth that looked like the ivory keys of an old piano, yellowed and badly chipped. Closed lips should have covered the ugliness, but oddly, they never seemed to close, even when Dorsett was not talking.

He was positioned in front of the driftwood desk with the marble top, flanked by Boudicca, who stood on his left, wearing denim pants and a shirt that was knotted at her midriff but, oddly, buttoned at the neck, and Deirdre, who sat in a patterned-silk chair, chic and fashionably dressed in a white turtleneck under plaid shirt and skirt. Crossing his arms and sitting on his desk with one foot on a carpeted deck, Dorsett smiled like a monstrous old hag. The sinister eyes examined every detail of Pitt and Giordino like needles, probing every centimeter from hair to shoelaces. He turned to Merchant, who was standing behind Maeve, his hand resting inside a tweed sport coat on a holstered automatic slung under one arm.

"Nicely done, John." He beamed. "You anticipated their every move." He lifted a matted eyebrow and stared at the two men standing before him, wet and bedraggled, turned his eyes to Maeve, stringy damp hair sticking to her forehead and cheeks, grinned hideously and nodded at Merchant. "Not all went as you expected, perhaps? They look like they fell in a moat."

"They delayed the inevitable by trying to escape into the water," Merchant said airily. The self-assurance, the pomposity, were mirrored in his eyes. "In the end they walked right into my hands."

"Any problems with the dockyard security people?"

"Negotiations and compensation came off smoothly," Merchant said buoyantly. "After your yacht came alongside the *Ocean Angler*, the five crewmen we detained were released. I'm confident that any formal complaint filed by NUMA officials will be met with bureaucratic indifference by local authorities. The country owes a heavy debt to Dorsett Consolidated for its contribution to the economy."

"You and your men are to be commended." Dorsett nodded approvingly. "A liberal bonus will be forthcoming to all involved."

"That is most kind of you, sir," Merchant purred.

"Please leave us now."

Merchant stared at Pitt and Giordino warily. "They are men

who should be watched carefully," he protested mildly. "I do not advise taking chances with them."

"You think they're going to try and take over the yacht?" Dorsett laughed. "Two defenseless men against two dozen who are armed? Or are you afraid they might jump overboard and swim to shore?" Dorsett motioned through a large window at the narrow tip of Cape Farewell, on New Zealand's South Island, which was rapidly disappearing in the wake behind the yacht. "Across forty kilometers of sea infested with sharks? I don't think so."

"My job is to protect you and your interests," said Merchant as he slid his hand from the gun, buttoned his sport coat and stepped quietly toward the door. "I take it seriously."

"Your work is appreciated," Dorsett said, abruptly becoming curt with impatience.

As soon as Merchant was gone, Maeve lashed out at her father. "I demand you tell me if Sean and Michael are all right, unharmed by your rotten mine superintendent."

Without a word, Boudicca stepped forward, reached out her hand in what Pitt thought was a show of affection, but brought it viciously across Maeve's cheek, a blow with such force it almost knocked her sister off her feet. Maeve stumbled and was caught by Pitt as Giordino stepped between the two women.

Shorter by half, Giordino had to look up into Boudicca's face as if he were staring up at a tall building. The scene became even more ludicrous, because he had to peer up and over Boudicca's bulbous breasts. "There's a homecoming for you," he said drolly.

Pitt was familiar with the look in his friend's eye. Giordino was a keen judge of faces and character. He saw something, some infinitesimal oddity that Pitt missed. Giordino was taking a risk that in his estimation was justified. He grinned slyly as he looked Boudicca up and down. "I'll make you a wager," he said to her.

"A wager?"

"Yes. I'll bet you don't shave your legs or your armpits."

There was a moment of silence, not borne by shock but more from curiosity. Boudicca's face suddenly twisted with fury, and she pulled back her fist to strike. Giordino stood complacently, expecting the blow but making no move to dodge or ward it off.

Boudicca hit Giordino hard, harder than most Olympic boxers. Her balled fist caught Giordino on the side of the cheek and the jaw. It was a savage blow, a damaging roundhouse blow, not one that was expected from a woman, and it would have knocked most men off their feet, cold. Most men would have been unconscious for twenty-four hours, most, that is, that Boudicca had ever struck in ungoverned fury. Giordino's head snapped to one side and he took a step backward, shook his head as if to clear it and then spat out a tooth onto the expensive carpet. Incredibly, against all comprehension, he stepped forward until he was under Boudicca's protruding bosom again. There was no animosity, no expression of vengeance in his eyes. Giordino simply gazed at her reflectively. "If you had any sense of decency and fair play, you'd let me have a turn."

Boudicca stood in confused amazement, massaging a sore hand. Uncontrolled outrage was slowly replaced with cold animosity. The look came into her eye of a rattlesnake about to strike with deadly purpose. "You are one stupid man," she said coldly.

Her hands lashed out and clamped around Giordino's neck. He stood with his fists clenched at his sides, making no move to stop her. His face drained of all color and his eyes began to bulge and still he made no effort to defend himself. He stared at her without any malice at all.

Pitt well remembered the strength in Boudicca's hands; he still had the bruises on his arms to attest to it. At a loss as to Giordino's out-of-character display of passivity, he moved away from Maeve in readiness to kick Boudicca in a kneecap, when her father shouted.

"Release him!" Arthur Dorsett snapped. "Do not soil your hands on a rat."

Giordino still stood like a statue in a park, when Boudicca released her grip around his throat and stepped back, rubbing the knuckles she had scraped on his face.

"Next time," she snarled, "you won't have my father to save your filthy hide."

"Did you ever think of turning professional?" Giordino rasped hoarsely, tenderly touching the growing discoloration marks around his neck. "I know this carnival that could use a geek—"

Pitt put his hand on Giordino's shoulder. "Let's hear what Mr. Dorsett has to say before you sign up for a rematch."

"You're wiser than your friend," said Dorsett.

"Only when it comes to averting pain and associating with criminals."

"Is that what you think of me? That I'm a common criminal?"

"Considering that you're responsible for murdering hundreds of people, an unqualified yes."

Dorsett shrugged imperviously and sat down behind his desk. "Regrettably, it was necessary."

Pitt felt feverish with anger against Dorsett. "I can't recall a single justification for cold-bloodedly cutting short the lives of innocent men, women and children."

"Why should you lose sleep over a few deaths, when millions in the third world die every year from famine, disease and war?"

"It was the way I was brought up," said Pitt. "My mother taught me life was a gift."

"Life is a commodity, nothing more." Dorsett scoffed. "People are like old tools that are used and then thrown away or destroyed when they have no more purpose. I pity men like you who are burdened with morals and principles. You are doomed to chase a mirage, a perfect world that never was and never will be."

Pitt found himself staring at stark, unfettered madness. "You'll die chasing a mirage too."

Dorsett smiled humorlessly. "You're wrong, Mr. Pitt. I will grasp it in my hands before my time comes."

"You have a sick, warped philosophy of life."

"So far it has served me very well."

"What's your excuse for not stopping the mass killing caused by your ultrasonic mining operations?"

"To mine more diamonds, what else?" Dorsett stared at Pitt as though he were studying a specimen in a jar. "In a few weeks I will make millions of women happy by providing them with the most precious of stones at a cost a beggar can afford."

"You don't strike me as the charitable type."

"Diamonds are really nothing but bits of carbon. Their only practical asset is they happen to be the hardest substance known to man. This alone makes them essential for the machining of metals and drilling through rock. Did you know the name 'diamond' comes from the Greek, Mr. Pitt? It means indomitable. The Greeks, and later the Romans, wore them as protection from wild beasts and human enemies. Their women, however, did not adore diamonds as women do now. Besides driving off evil spirits, they were used as a test for adultery. And yet when it comes to beauty, you can get the same sparkle from crystal."

As Dorsett spoke of diamonds his stare didn't falter, but the throbbing pulse in the side of his neck gave away his deep feeling on the subject. He talked as if he had suddenly risen to a higher plane that few could experience.

"Are you also aware that the first diamond engagement ring was given by Archduke Ferdinand of Austria to Mary of Burgundy in the year 1477, and the belief that the 'vein of love' runs directly from the brain to the third finger of the left hand was a myth that came out of Egypt?"

Pitt stared back with unconcealed contempt. "What I'm aware of is the current glut of uncut stones being held in warehouses throughout South Africa, Russia and Australia to inflate false values. I also know the cartel, essentially a monopoly directed by De Beers, fixes the price. So how is it possible for one man to challenge the entire syndicate and cause a sudden, drastic drop of prices on the diamond market?"

"The cartel will play right into my hands," said Dorsett contemptuously. "Historically, whenever a diamond-producing mining company or nation tried to go around them and merchandise their stones on the open market, the cartel slashed prices. The maverick, failing to compete and finding itself in a no-win situation, eventually returned to the fold. I'm counting on the cartel to repeat their act. By the time they realize that I'm dumping millions of diamonds at two cents on the dollar with no regard for earnings, it will be too late for them to react. The market will have collapsed."

"What percentage is there in dominating a depressed market?"

"I'm not interested in dominating the market, Mr. Pitt. I want to kill it for all time."

Pitt noticed that Dorsett didn't gaze right at him but fixed his eyes impassively on a point behind Pitt's head as if seeing a vision only he could see. "If I read you correctly, you're cutting your own throat."

"It sounds that way, doesn't it?" Dorsett lifted a finger at Pitt. "Exactly what I wanted everyone to think, even my closest associates and my own daughters. The truth of the matter is that I expect to make a great sum of money."

"How?" Pitt asked, his interest aroused.

Dorsett allowed a satanic grin to display his grotesque teeth. "The answer lies not in diamonds but in the colored gemstone market."

"My God, I see what this is all about," said Maeve as if witnessing a revelation. "You're out to corner the market on colored stones."

She began to shiver from her wet clothing and a sweeping dread. Pitt removed his soggy leather jacket and draped it around her shoulders.

Dorsett nodded. "Yes, Daughter. During the last twenty years, your wise old father has stockpiled his diamond production while quietly buying up claims to the major colored gemstone mines around the world. Through a complex formation of front corporations I now secretly control eighty percent of the market."

"By colored gemstones," said Pitt, "I assume you mean rubies and emeralds."

"Indeed, and a host of other precious stones, including sapphire, topaz, tourmaline and amethyst. Almost all are far more scarce than diamonds. The deposits of tsavorite, red beryl or red emerald, and the Mexican fire opal, for example, are becoming increasing difficult to find. A number of colored gemstones are so rare they are sought by collectors and are very seldom made into jewelry."

"Why haven't the prices of colored stones matched that of diamonds?" asked Pitt.

"Because the diamond cartel has always managed to push color into the shadows," Dorsett told him with the fervor of a zealot. "For decades, De Beers has spent enormous sums of money in high-powered research to study and survey international markets. Millions were spent advertising diamonds and creating an image of eternal value. To keep prices fixed, De Beers created a demand for diamonds to keep pace with the mushrooming supply. And so the web of imagery capturing a man showing his love for a woman through the gift of a diamond was spun through a shrewd advertising campaign that reached its peak with the slogan, 'Diamonds are forever.' " He began to pace the room, gesturing with his hands for effect. "Because colored gemstone production is fragmented by thousands of independent producers, all competing and selling against each other, there has been no unified organization to promote colored stones. The trade has suffered from a lack of consumer awareness. I intend to change all that after the price of diamonds plunges."

"So you've jumped in with both feet."

"Not only will I produce colored stones from the mines," declared Dorsett, "but unlike De Beers, I will cut and merchandise them through the House of Dorsett, my chain of stores on the retail market. Sapphires, emeralds and rubies may not be eternal, but when I'm through they will make any woman who wears them feel like a goddess. Jewelry will have achieved a new splendor. Even the famous Renaissance goldsmith Benvenuto Cellini proclaimed the ruby and emerald more glorious than diamonds."

It was a staggering concept, and Pitt carefully considered the possibilities before he asked, "For decades women have bought the idea that diamonds have an undeniable tie to courtship and a lifetime relationship. Do you really think you can switch their desire from diamonds to colored stones?"

"Why not?" Dorsett was surprised that Pitt could express doubt. "The notion of a diamond engagement ring did not take hold until the late 1800s. All it takes is a strategy to revamp social attitudes. I have a top creative advertising agency with offices in thirty countries ready to launch an international promotional campaign in unison with my operation to send the cartel down the drain. When I'm finished, colored stones will be the prestige gems for jewelry. Diamonds will merely be used for background settings."

Pitt's gaze traveled from Boudicca to Deirdre and then Maeve. "Like most men, I'm a poor judge of women's inner thoughts and emotions, but I know it won't be easy convincing them that diamonds are not a girl's best friend."

Dorsett laughed drily. "It's the men who buy precious stones for women. And as much as they want to impress their true love, men have a higher regard for value. Sell them on the fact that rubies and emeralds are fifty times more rare than diamonds, and they'll buy them."

"Is that true?" Pitt was skeptical. "That an emerald is fifty times more rare than a comparable diamond?"

Dorsett nodded solemnly. "As the deposits of emeralds dry up, and they will in time, the gap will become much higher. Actually, it could safely be said of the red emerald, which comes only

312

from one or two mines in the state of Utah, that it is over a million times as rare."

"Cornering one market while destroying another, there has to be more in it for you than mere profit."

"Not 'mere profit,' my dear Pitt. Profits on a level unheard of in history. We're talking tens of billions of dollars."

Pitt was incredulous at the staggering sum. "You couldn't achieve that kind of money unless you doubled the price of colored gemstones."

"Quadrupled would be closer to the truth. Of course, the raise would not take place overnight, but in graduated price hikes over a period of years."

Pitt moved until he was standing directly in front of Dorsett, peering up closely at the taller man. "I have no quarrel with your desire to play King Midas," he said with quiet steadiness. "Do what you will with the price of diamonds. But for God's sake shut down the ultrasonic excavation of your mines. Call your superintendents and order them to stop all operations. Do it now before another life is lost."

There came a strange stillness. Every pair of eyes turned toward Dorsett in expectation of an outburst of wrath at being challenged. He stared at Pitt for long seconds before turning to Maeve.

"Your friend is impatient. He does not know me, does not recognize my determination." Then he again faced Pitt. "The assault on the diamond cartel is set for February twenty-second, twenty-one days from now. To make it work I need every gram, every carat, my mines can produce until then. Worldwide press coverage, advertising space in newspapers and time on television is purchased and scheduled. There can be no change, there *will* be no change in plans. If a few rabble die, so be it."

Mental derangement, Pitt thought, those were the only words to describe the eerie malignity in Dorsett's coal-black eyes. Mental derangement and total indifference to any thought of remorse. He was a man totally without conscience. Pitt felt his skin crawl from just looking at him. He wondered how many deaths Arthur Dorsett was accountable for. Long before he began excavating diamonds with ultrasound, how many men had died who stood in his way to becoming rich and powerful? He felt a sharp chill at knowing the man was a sociopath on the same level as a serial killer.

"You will pay for your crimes, Dorsett," Pitt said calmly but with a cold edge in his voice. "You will surely pay for the unbearable grief and agony you have caused."

"Who will be the angel of my retribution?" Dorsett sneered. "You, maybe? Mr. Giordino here? I do not believe there will be ordained retaliation from the heavens. The possibility is too remote. The only certainty I can bank on, Mr. Pitt, is that you won't be around to see it."

"Execute the witnesses by shooting them in the head and throwing their bodies overboard, is that your policy?"

"Shoot you and Mr. Giordino in the head?" There was no trace of emotion, of any feeling in Arthur Dorsett's voice. "Nothing so crude and mundane, nor so merciful. Thrown in the sea? Yes, you may consider that a foregone conclusion. In any event, I will guarantee you and your friend a slow but violent death."

31

After thirty hours of pounding through the sea at incredible speeds, the powerful turbodiesels fell off to a muffled throb, and the yacht slowed and began to drift amid a sea of gentle swells. The last sight of the New Zealand shoreline had long since disappeared in the yacht's wake. To the north and west dark clouds were laced with forks of lightning, the thunder rumbling dully across the horizon. To the south and east there were no clouds and thunder. The skies were blue and clear.

Pitt and Giordino had spent the night and half the next day locked in a small supply compartment aft of the engine room. There was barely enough room to sit on the deck with knees drawn up to their chins. Pitt kept awake most of the time, the clarity of his mind heightened, listening to the revolutions of the engines, the thump of the swells. Casting aside all thoughts of restraint, Giordino had wrenched the door off its hinges only to be confronted by four guards with the muzzles of their automatic weapons pushed into his navel. Defeated, he promptly dropped off to sleep before the door was rehung.

Angered and blaming only himself for their predicament, Pitt was very self-critical, but no fault could really be attached to him. He should have out-thought John Merchant. He had been caught with his guard down because he miscalculated their fanatic desire to lure Maeve back into their clutches. He and Giordino were mere sideline pawns. Arthur Dorsett considered them little more than a minor annoyance in his insane crusade for an absurd accumulation of wealth.

There was something weird and ominous about their unmoving concentration on such a complex plan to ensnare a daughter and eliminate the men from NUMA. Pitt wondered dimly why he and Giordino had been kept alive, and he had no sooner done so when the damaged door creaked open and John Merchant stood leering on the threshold. Pitt automatically checked his Doxa watch at seeing his nemesis. It was eleven-twenty in the morning.

"Time to board your vessel," Merchant announced pleasantly.

"We're changing boats?" asked Pitt.

"In a manner of speaking."

"I hope the service is better than on this one," said Giordino lazily. "You will, of course, take care of our luggage."

Merchant dismissed Giordino with a brisk shrug. "Please hurry, gentlemen. Mr. Dorsett does not like to be kept waiting."

They were escorted out onto the stern deck, surrounded by a small army of guards armed with a variety of weapons designed to inflict bodily harm but not kill. Both men blinked in the fading sunlight just as the first few raindrops fell, carried ahead of the advancing clouds by a light breeze.

Dorsett sat protected under an overhang in a chair at a table laden with several savory dishes laid out in silver serving bowls. Two uniformed attendants stood at his elbow, one ready to pour at the slightest indication that his wineglass required refilling, the other to replace used silverware. Boudicca and Deirdre, seated on their father's left and right, didn't bother looking up from their food as Pitt and Giordino were brought into their divine presence. Pitt glanced around for Maeve, but she wasn't to be seen.

"I regret that you must leave us," said Dorsett between bites of toast heaped with caviar. "A pity you couldn't have stayed for brunch."

"Don't you know you're supposed to boycott caviar?" said Pitt. "Poachers have nearly driven sturgeon to extinction."

Dorsett shrugged apathetically. "So it costs a few dollars more."

Pitt turned, his eyes staring over the empty sea, starting to look ugly from the approaching storm. "We were told we were to board another boat."

"And so you shall."

"Where is it?"

"Floating alongside."

"I see," Pitt said quietly. "I see indeed. You plan to set us adrift."

Dorsett rubbed food from his mouth with a napkin with the savoir-faire of an auto mechanic wiping his greasy hands. "I apologize for providing such a small craft, one without an engine, I might add, but it's all I have to offer."

"A nice sadistic touch. You enjoy the thought of our suffering."

Giordino glanced at two high-performance powerboats that were cradled on the upper deck of the yacht. "We're overwhelmed by your generosity."

"You should be grateful that I'm giving you a chance to live."

"Adrift in a part of the sea devoid of maritime traffic, directly in the path of a storm." Pitt scowled. "The least you should do is supply pen and paper to make out our last wills and testaments."

"Our conversation has ended. Good-bye, Mr. Pitt, Mr. Giordino, bon voyage." Dorsett nodded at John Merchant. "Show these NUMA scum to their craft."

Merchant pointed to a gate in the railing that was swung open.

"What, no confetti and streamers?" muttered Giordino.

Pitt stepped to the edge of the deck and stared down at the water. A small semi-inflatable boat bobbed in the water beside the yacht. Three meters in length by two meters wide, it had a fiberglass V-hull that appeared sturdy. The center compartment, however, would barely hold four people, the neoprene outer flotation tube taking up half the boat. The craft had mounted an outboard engine at one time, but that had been removed. The control cables still dangled from a center console. The interior was empty except for a figure in Pitt's leather jacket huddled in one end.

Cold rage swept Pitt. He took Merchant by the collar of his yachting jacket and cast him aside as easily as if he'd been a straw scarecrow. He stormed back to the dining table before he could be stopped. "Not Maeve too," he said sharply.

Dorsett smiled, but it was an expression completely lacking in humor. "She took her ancestor's name, she can suffer as her ancestor did."

"You bastard!" Pitt snarled with animal hate. "You fornicating scab—!" That was as far as he got. One of Merchant's guards rammed the butt of his automatic rifle viciously in Pitt's side, just above the kidney.

A tidal wave of agony consumed Pitt, but sheer wrath kept him on his feet. He lurched forward, grabbed the tablecloth in both hands, gave a mighty jerk and wrenched it into the air. Glasses, knives, forks, spoons, serving dishes and plates filled with gourmet treats exploded over the deck with a great clatter. Pitt then threw himself across the table at Dorsett, not with the mere intent to strike him or choke him to death. He knew he'd have one, and only one, chance at maiming the man. He extended his index fingers and jabbed just as he was smothered in guards. A maddened Boudicca slung her hand down in a ferocious chop to Pitt's neck, but she missed and caught him on the shoulder. One of Pitt's fingers missed its target and scraped over Dorsett's forehead. The other struck home, and he heard an agonized primeval scream. Then he felt the blows raining on him in every bone of his body, then nothing as the crazy melee snapped into blackness.

Pitt woke and thought he was in some bottomless pit or a cave deep in the earth. Or at least in the depths of some underground cavern where there was only eternal darkness. Desperately, he tried to feel his way out, but it was like stumbling through a labyrinth. Lost in the throes of a nightmare, doomed to wander forever in a black maze, he thought vaguely. Then suddenly, for no more than the blink of an eye, he saw a dim light far ahead. He reached out for it and watched it grow into dark clouds scudding across the sky.

"Praise be, Lazarus is back from the dead." Giordino's voice seemed to come from a city block away, partially drowned out by the rumble of traffic. "And just in time to die again, by the look of the weather."

As he became fully conscious, Pitt wished he could return to the forbidding labyrinth. Every square centimeter of his body throbbed with pain. From his skull to his knees, it seemed every bone was broken. He tried to sit up, but stopped in mid-motion and groaned in agony. Maeve touched his cheek and cradled his shoulders with one arm. "It will hurt less if you don't try to move."

He looked up into her face. The sky-blue eyes were wide with caring and affection. As if she were weaving a spell, he could feel her love falling over him like gossamer, and the agony slipped away as if drawn from his veins.

"Well, I certainly made a mess of things, didn't I?" he murmured.

She slowly shook her head, the long blond hair trailing across his cheeks. "No, no, don't think that. You wouldn't be here if it wasn't for me."

"Merchant's boys worked you over pretty good before throwing you off the yacht. You look like you were used for batting practice by the Los Angeles Dodgers."

Pitt struggled to a sitting position. "Dorsett?"

"I suspect you may have fixed one of his eyes so he'll look like a real pirate when he slips on his eye patch. Now all he needs is a dueling scar and a hook."

"Boudicca and Deirdre carried him inside the salon during the brawl," said Maeve. "If Merchant had realized the full extent of Father's injury, there is no telling what he might have done to you."

Pitt's gaze swept an empty and ominous sea through eyes that were swollen and half closed "They're gone?"

"Tried to run us over before they cut and ran to beat the storm," said Giordino. "Lucky for us the neoprene floats on our raft, and without an engine that's all you can call it, rebounded off the yacht's bows. As it was, we came within a hair of capsizing."

Pitt refocused his eyes on Maeve. "So they left us to drift like your great-great-great-grandmother, Betsy Fletcher."

She stared at him oddly. "How did you know about her? I never told you."

"I always investigate the women I want to spend the rest of my life with."

"And a short life it'll be," said Giordino, pointing grimly to the northwest. "Unless my night-school class in meteorology steered me wrong, we're sitting in the path of what they call in these parts a typhoon, or maybe a cyclone, depending how close we are to the Indian Ocean."

The sight of the dark clouds and the streaks of lightning followed by the threatening rumble of thunder was enough to make Pitt lose heart as he peered across the sea and listened to the increasing wind. The margin between life and death had narrowed to a paper's thickness. Already the sun was blotted out and the sea turned gray. The tiny boat was minutes away from being swallowed in the maelstrom.

Pitt hesitated no longer. "The first order of the day is to rig a sea anchor." He turned to Maeve. "We'll need my leather jacket and some line and anything that will help create a drag to keep us from capsizing in heavy seas."

Without a word, she slipped out of the coat and handed it to him while Giordino rummaged in a small storage locker under a seat. He came up with a rusty grappling hook attached to two sections of nylon line, one five meters, the other, three meters. Pitt laid open the jacket and filled it with everyone's shoes and the grappling hook, along with some old engine parts and several corroded tools Giordino had scrounged from the storage locker. Then he zipped it up, knotted the sleeves around the open waistband and collar and tied the makeshift bundle to the shorter nylon line. He cast it over the side and watched it sink before tying the other end of the line solidly to the walk-around console mounted with the useless controls for the missing outboard engine.

"Lie on the floor of the boat," ordered Pitt, tying the remaining line around the center console. "We're in for a wild ride. Loop the line around your waists and tie off the end so we won't lose the boat if we capsize and are thrown in the sea."

He took one last look over the neoprene buoyancy tubes at the menacing swells that swept in from a horizon that lifted and dropped. The sea was ugly and beautiful at the same time. Lightning streaked through the purple-black clouds, and the thunder came like the roll from a thousand drums. The tumult fell on them without pity. The full force of the gale, accompanied by a torrential rain, a drenching downpour that blocked out the sky and turned the sea into a boiling broth of foam, struck them less then ten minutes later. The drops, whipped by a wind that howled like a thousand banshees, pelted them so hard it stung their skin.

Spray was hurled from wave crests that rose three meters

above the troughs. All too quickly the waves reached a height of seven meters, broken and confused, striking the boat from one direction and then another. The wind increased its shrieking violence as the sea doubled its frightening onslaught against the frail boat and its pitiful passengers. The boat was slewing and corkscrewing violently as it was tossed up on the wave crests before being plunged into the troughs. There was no sharp dividing line between air and sea. They couldn't tell where one began and the other left off.

Miraculously, the sea anchor was not torn away. It did its duty and exerted its drag, preventing the sea gone berserk from capsizing the boat and throwing everyone into the murderous waters from which there was no return. The gray waves curled down upon them, filling the boat's interior with churning foam, soaking them all to the skin, but tending to pull the center of gravity deeper in the water, giving an extra fraction of stability. The twisting motion and the choppy rise and fall of the boat whirled their cargo of seawater around their bodies, making them feel they were being whipped inside a juice blender.

In a way, the size of the tiny craft was a blessing. The neoprene tubes around the sides made it as buoyant as a cork. No matter how violent the tempest, the durable hull would not burst into pieces, and if the sea anchor held, it would not capsize. Like the palms that leaned in the wind from gale-force winds, it would endure. The next twenty-four minutes passed like twenty-four hours, and as they hung on grimly to stay alive, Pitt found it hard to believe the storm had not overwhelmed them. There was no word, no description for the misery.

The never-ending walls of water poured into the boat, leaving the three of them choking and gasping until the boat was thrust up and onto the crest of the next swell. There was no need for bailing. The weight of the water filling the interior helped keep them from capsizing. One second they were struggling to keep from floating over the sides of the tubes, the following second preparing for the next frenzied motion, as they fell into a trough, to keep from being slung into the air.

With Maeve between them, each with one arm protectively draped over her body, Pitt and Giordino braced their feet against the sides for support. If one of them was thrown from the boat, there could be no chance of rescue. No soul could survive alone in the writing sea. The downpour cut visibility to a few meters, and they would quickly be lost to view.

During a flash of lightning, Pitt looked over at Maeve. She looked convinced that she had been dropped into hell and must have been suffering the torment of the damned from seasickness. Pitt wished he could have consoled her with words, but she could never have heard him over the howl of the wind. He cursed the name of Dorsett. God, how terrible it was to have a father and sisters who hated her enough to steal away her children and then try to murder her because she was good and kind and refused to be a part of their criminal acts. It was horribly wrong and unfair. She could not die, he told himself, not as long as he still lived. He gripped her shoulder and gave it an affectionate squeeze. Then he stared at Giordino.

Giordino's expression was stoic. His apparent nonchalance under such hell reassured Pitt. Whatever will be, will be, was written in his eyes. There was no limit to the man's endurance. Pitt knew that Giordino would push himself beyond the depths of understanding, even die, long before he would let loose his grip on the boat and Maeve. He would never surrender to the sea.

Almost as if their minds worked together simultaneously, Giordino looked to see how Pitt was faring. There were two kinds of men, he thought. There were those who saw the devil waiting for their soul and were deathly afraid of him. And there were those who mired themselves in hopelessness and looked upon him as a relief from their worldly misery. Pitt was of neither kind. He could stare at the devil and spit in his eye.

Giordino's friend of thirty years looked as though he could go on forever. Giordino ceased to be amazed by Pitt's fortitude and love for adversity. Pitt thrived on disaster and calamity. Oblivious to the frenzied pounding by the swells, he did not look like a man waiting for the end, a man who felt there was nothing he could do against the furies of the sea. His eyes gazed into the sheets of rain and froth that lashed his face, strangely remote. Almost as if he were sitting high and dry in his hangar apartment, his mind seemed concentrated elsewhere, disembodied and in a vacuum. Pitt was, Giordino had thought on more than one occasion while they were in or under the sea, a man utterly at home in his own element.

Darkness came and passed, a night of torment that never

seemed to end. They were numbed by the cold and constantly soaked. The chill cut through their flesh like a thousand knives. Dawn was a deliverance from hearing the waves roar and break without seeing them. With a sunrise shrouded by the convulsive clouds, they still grimly hung onto life by the barest of threads. They longed for daylight, but it finally came in a strange gray light that illuminated the terrible sea like an old black-and-white motion picture.

Despite the savagery of the turbulence, the atmosphere was hot and oppressive, a salty blanket that was too thick to breathe. The passage of time had no relation to the dials of their wristwatches. Pitt's old Doxa and Giordino's newer Aqualand Pro were watertight to two hundred meters deep and kept on ticking, but saltwater had seeped into Maeve's little digital watch and it soon stopped.

Not long after the sea went on its rampage, Maeve buried her head against the bottom of a flotation tube and prayed that she might live to see her boys again, prayed that she would not die without giving them fond memories of her, not some vague recollection that she was lost and buried in an uncaring sea. She agonized over their fate in the hands of her father. At first she had been more frightened than at any other moment in her life, the fear like a cold avalanche of snow that smothered her. Then gradually it began to subside as she realized the arms of the men about her back and shoulders never let up their pressure. Their self-control seemed extraordinary, and their strength seemed to flow inside her. With men such as these protecting her, a spark grew and nurtured the imperceptible but growing belief that she just might still be alive to see another dawn.

Pitt was not nearly so optimistic. He was well aware that his and Giordino's energy was waning. Their worst enemies were the unseen threats of hypothermia and fatigue. Something had to give, their tenacity or the storm's violence. The constant effort to keep from drowning had taken all they had to give. The fight had been against all odds, and total exhaustion was just around the corner. And yet, he refused to see the futility of it all. He clung to life, drawing on his dwindling reserve of strength, holding tight as the next wave engulfed them, knowing their time to die was fast approaching.

32

But Pitt, Maeve and Giordino did not die.

By early evening, there was an easing of the wind, and the jumbled seas began to diminish shortly after. Unknown to them, the typhoon had veered off its earlier course from the northwest and suddenly headed southeast toward the Antarctic. The wind velocity noticeably slackened, down from over 150 kilometers to a little below 60, and the seas curtailed their madness, the distance between the wave crests and the troughs decreasing to no more than 3 meters. The rain thinned into a light drizzle that became a mist, hovering over the flattened swells. Overhead, a lone gull materialized from nowhere, before darkness swept the seas again, and circled the little boat, screaming as if in stunned surprise at seeing it still afloat.

In another hour, the sky was clear of clouds, and the wind was hardly strong enough to sail a sloop in. It was as if the storm were a bad dream that struck in the night and vanished with the soft light of day. They had won only one battle in a war with the elements. The savage seas and the cruel winds had failed to take them into the depths. What the great whirling storm could not destroy with its murderous fury, it rewarded with clemency.

It seemed almost mystical, Maeve thought. *If they were destined to die, they never would have lived through the storm. We were kept alive for a purpose,* she decided staunchly.

No word passed among the fatigued and battered trio huddled in the boat. Consoled by the calm in the wake of the departed tempest, exhausted beyond endurance, they entered a region of utterly uncaring indifference to their circumstances and fell into deep sleep.

The swells retained a mild chop until the next morning, a legacy of the storm, before the seas became as liquid smooth as a millpond. The mist had long since faded, and visibility cleared to the far reaches of empty horizons. Now the sea settled down to achieve by attrition what it had failed to achieve by frenzied intensity. They slowly awoke to a sun they had sorely missed for the last forty-eight hours but that now burned down on them with unrelenting severity.

An attempt to sit up sent waves of pain through Pitt's body. The battering from the sea was added to the injuries he had suffered from John Merchant's men. Blinking against the dazzling glare of the sun's reflection on the water, he very slowly eased himself to a sitting position. There was nothing to do now but lie in the boat and wait. But wait for what? Wait in the forlorn hope that a ship might appear over the horizon on a direct course toward them? They were drifting in a dead part of the sea, far from the shipping lanes, where ships rarely sailed.

Arthur Dorsett had picked their drop-off point cleverly. If through some divine miracle they survived the typhoon, then thirst and starvation would take them. Pitt would not let them die, not after what they had been through. He took an oath of vengeance, to live for no other reason but to kill Arthur Dorsett. Few men deserved to die more. Pitt swore to overlook his normal codes and standards of ethics and morality should he and Dorsett ever meet again. Nor did he forget Boudicca and Deirdre. They too would pay for their depraved treatment of Maeve.

"It's all so quiet," said Maeve. She clung to Pitt, and he could feel her trembling. "I feel like the storm is still raging inside my head."

Pitt rubbed caked salt from his eyes, comforted in a small degree at feeling that the swelling had gone down. He looked down into the intensely blue eyes, drugged with fatigue and misted by deep sleep. He watched as they stared at him, and they began to shine. "Venus arising from the waves," he said softly.

She sat up and fluffed out her salt-encrusted blond hair. "I don't feel like Venus," she said, smiling. "And I certainly don't look like her." She pulled up her sweater and gently touched the red weals around her waist, put there by the constant friction of the safety line.

Giordino slipped open an eye. "If you two don't quiet up and let a man sleep, I'm going to call the manager of this hotel and complain."

"We're going for a dip in the pool and then have some break-fast on the lanai," said Maeve with intrepid brightness. "Why don't you join us?"

"I'd rather call room service," Giordino drawled, seemingly exhausted by the mere act of speaking.

"Since we're all in such a lively mood," said Pitt, "I suggest we get on about the business of survival."

"What are our chances of rescue?" asked Maeve innocently.

"Nil," answered Pitt. "You can bet your father dropped us in the bleakest part of the sea. Admiral Sandecker and the gang at NUMA have no idea what happened to us. And if they did, they wouldn't know where to look. If we're to reach our normal life expectancy, we'll have to do it without outside help."

Their first task was to pull in the steadfast sea anchor and remove their shoes and the tools and other items from Pitt's jacket. Afterward, they took an inventory of every single item, seemingly useless or not, that might come in handy for the long haul ahead. At last, Pitt removed the small packet that he had shoved down his pants just before driving the bus over the side of the dock.

"What did you find with the boat?" he asked Giordino.

"Not enough hardware to hang a barn door. The storage com-partment held a grand total of three wrenches of various sizes, a screwdriver, a fuel pump, four spark plugs, assorted nuts and bolts, a couple of rags, a wooden paddle, a nylon boat cover and a handy-dandy little number that's going to add to the enjoyment of the voyage."

"Which is?

Giordino held up a small hand pump. "This, for pumping up the flotation tubes."

"How long is the paddle?"

"A little over a meter."

"Barely tall enough to raise a sail," said Pitt.

"True, but by tying it to the console, we can utilize it as a tent pole to stretch the boat cover over us for shade."

"And lest we forget, the boat cover will come in handy for catching water should we see rain again," Maeve reminded them.

Pitt looked at her. "Do you have anything on your person that might prove useful?"

She shook her head. "Clothes only. My Frankenstein sister threw me on the raft without so much as my lipstick."

"Guess who *she's* talking about," Giordino muttered.

Pitt opened the small waterproof packet and laid out a Swiss army knife, a very old and worn Boy Scout compass, a small tube of matches, a first aid kit no larger than a cigarette package, and a vest-pocket .25 caliber Mauser automatic pistol with one extra clip.

Maeve stared at the tiny gun. "You could have shot John Merchant and my father."

"Pickett stood a better chance at Gettysburg than I did with that small army of security guards."

"I thought you looked awfully well endowed," she said with a sly smile. "Do you always carry a survival kit?"

"Since my Boy Scout days."

"Who do you intend to shoot in the middle of nowhere?"

"Not who, but what. A bird, if one comes close enough."

"You'd shoot a defenseless bird?"

Pitt looked at her. "Only because I have this strange aversion to starving to death."

While Giordino pumped air into the flotation tubes before working on a canopy, Pitt examined every square centimeter of the boat, checking for any leaks or abrasions in the neoprene floats and structural damage to the fiberglass hull. He dove overboard and ran his hands over the bottom but found no indication of damage. The craft appeared to be about four years old and had apparently been used as a shore boat when Dorsett's yacht moored off a beach without a dock. Pitt was relieved to find it slightly worn but in otherwise excellent shape. The only flaw was the missing outboard engine that no longer hung on the transom of the boat.

Climbing back on board, he kept them busy all day with odd little jobs to take their minds off their predicament and growing thirst. Pitt was determined to keep their spirits up. He had no illusions as to how long they could last. He and Giordino had once trekked through the Sahara Desert without water for nearly seven days. That was a dry heat; here the heavy humidity sucked the life out of them.

Giordino rigged the nylon cover as shield from the burning rays of the sun, draping it over the paddle he had mounted on the control console and tying it down over the high sides of the flotation tubes with short lengths cut from the nylon line. He sloped one edge so that any rainwater it caught would flow and drop into an ice chest Maeve had found under one seat. She cleaned the grime from the long unused ice chest and did her best to straighten up the interior of the boat to make it liveable. Pitt used his time to separate the strands from a section of nylon line and knot them into a fishing line.

The only food source within two thousand kilometers or more was fish. If they didn't catch any, they would starve. He fashioned a hook from the prong of his belt buckle and tied it to the line. The opposite end was attached to the center of one of the wrenches so he could grip it in both hands. The quandary was how to catch them. There were no earthworms, trout flies, bass plugs or cheese around here. Pitt leaned over the flotation tubes, cupped his hands around his eyes to shut out the sunlight and stared into the water.

Already, inquisitive guests were congregating under the shadow of the raft. Those who plow through the sea on ships and boats powered by big engines with roaring exhausts and thrashing propellers often complain that there is no life to be seen in the open ocean. But for those who float close to the surface of the water, drifting soundlessly, it soon becomes a window, opening on the other side on citizens of the deep, who are far more numerous and varied than the animals who roam the solid earth.

Schools of herringlike fish, no larger than Pitt's little finger, darted and wiggled under the boat. He recognized pompano, dolphins, not to be confused with the porpoise and their larger cousins, the dorado, with their high foreheads and long fin running down the top of their multicolored iridescent bodies. A couple of large mackerel glided in circles, occasionally striking at one of the smaller fish. There was also a small shark, a hammerhead, one of the strangest inhabitants of the sea, each of his eyes perched on the end of a wing that looked like it was jammed into his head.

"What are you going to use as bait?" asked Maeve.

"Me," said Pitt. "I'm using myself as a gourmet delight for the little fisheys."

"Whatever do you mean?"

"Watch and learn."

Maeve stared in undisguised awe as Pitt took his knife, rolled up a pant leg, and calmly carved off a small piece of flesh from the back of his thigh. Then he imbedded it on the improvised hook. It was done so matter-of-factly that Giordino did not notice the act until he saw a few drops of blood on the floor of the boat.

"Where's the pleasure in that?" he asked.

"You got that screwdriver handy?" Pitt inquired.

Giordino held it up. "You want me to operate on you too?"

"There's a small shark under the boat," Pitt explained. "I'm going to entice it to the surface. When I grab it, you ram the screwdriver into the top of his head between the eyes. Do it right and you might stick his pea-sized brain."

Maeve wanted no part of this business. "Surely you're not bringing a shark on board?"

"Only if we get lucky," Pitt said, tearing off a piece of his T-shirt and wrapping it around the small gouge in his leg to staunch the bleeding.

She crawled to the stern of the boat and crouched behind the console, happy to get out of the way. "Mind you don't offer him anything to bite on."

With Giordino kneeling beside him, Pitt slowly lowered the human bait into the water. The mackerel circled it, but he jiggled the line to discourage them. A few of the tiny scavenger fish darted in for a quick nibble, but they quickly left the scene as the shark, sensing the small presence of blood, homed in on the bait. Pitt hauled in on the line every time the shark came close.

As Pitt worked the hook and bait slowly toward the boat, Giordino, his upraised arm poised with the screwdriver held dagger-fashion, peered into the deep. Then the shark was alongside, ashen gray on the back, fading to white on the belly, his dorsal fin coming out of the sea like a submarine raising its periscope. The screwdriver swung in an arc and struck the tough head of the shark as he rubbed his side against the flotation tubes. In the hand of most other men, the shaft would never have penetrated the cartilaginous skeleton of the shark, but Giordino rammed it in up to the hilt.

Pitt leaned out, clamped his arm under the shark's belly behind the gills and heaved just as Giordino struck again. He fell backward into the boat, cradling the one-and-a-half-meter hammerhead shark in his arms like a child. He grabbed the dorsal fin, wrapped his legs around the tail and hung on.

The savage jaws were snapping but found only empty air. Maeve cringed behind the console and screamed as the bristling triangular teeth gnashed only centimeters away from her drawn-up legs.

As if he were wrestling an alligator, Giordino threw all his weight on the thrashing beast from the sea, holding down the body on the floor of the boat, scraping the inside of his forearms raw on the sandpaperlike skin.

Though badly injured, the hammerhead displayed an incredible vitality. Unpredictable, it was aggressive one minute and oddly docile the next. Finally, after a good ten minutes of futile thrashing, the shark gave up and lay still. Pitt and Giordino rolled off and caught their breath. The writhing fight had aggravated Pitt's bruises, and he felt like he was swimming in a sea of pain.

"You'll have to cut him," he gasped to Giordino. "I feel as weak as a kitten."

"Rest easy," Giordino said. There was a patience, a warm understanding in his voice. "After the beating you took on the yacht and the pounding from the storm, it's a wonder you're not in a coma."

Although Pitt had honed the blades on his Swiss army knife to a razor edge, Giordino still had to grip the handle with both hands and exert a great deal of muscle in slicing through the tough underbelly of the shark. Under Maeve's guidance as a professional marine zoologist, he expertly cut out the liver and made an incision in the stomach, finding a recently eaten dorado and several herring. Then Maeve showed him how to slice the flesh from inside the skin efficiently.

"We should eat the liver now," she advised. "It will begin decaying almost immediately, and it is the most nutritious part of the fish."

"What about the rest of the meat?" asked Giordino, swishing

the knife and his hands in the water to remove the slime. "It won't take long to spoil in this heat."

"We've got a whole ocean of salt. Slice the meat into strips. Then string it up around the boat. As it dries, we take the salt that has crystallized on the canopy and rub it into the meat to preserve it."

"I hated liver when I was a kid," said Giordino, somewhat green around the gills at the thought. "I don't think I'm hungry enough to eat it raw."

"Force yourself," said Pitt. "The idea is to keep physically fit while we can. We've proven we can supply our stomachs. Our real problem now is lack of water."

Nightfall brought a strange quiet. A half-moon rose and hung over the sea, leaving a silvery path toward the northern horizon. They heard a bird squawking in the star-streaked sky, but couldn't see it. The cold temperatures common to the southern latitudes came with the disappearance of the sun and eased their thirst a little, and their minds turned to other things. The swells beat rhythmically against the boat and lulled Maeve into thoughts of a happier time with her children. Giordino imagined himself back in his condominium in Washington, sitting on a couch, an arm draped around a pretty woman, one hand holding a frosty mug of Coors beer and his feet propped on a coffee table as they watched old movies on television.

After resting most of the afternoon, Pitt was wide awake and felt revitalized enough to work out their drift and forecast the weather by observing the shape of the clouds, the height and run of the waves and the color of the sunset. After dusk he studied the stars and attempted to calculate the boat's approximate position on the sea. Using his old compass while locked in the storage compartment during the voyage from Wellington, he noted that the yacht had maintained a southwest heading of two-four-zero degrees for twenty minutes short of thirty hours. He recalled John Merchant saying the yacht could cruise at 120 kilometers an hour. Multiplying the speed and time gave him a rough distance traveled of 3,600 kilometers from the time they left Wellington until they were set adrift. This he estimated would put them somewhere in the middle of the south Tasman Sea, between the lower shores of Tasmania and New Zealand.

The next puzzle to solve was how far were they driven by the storm? This was next to impossible to estimate with even a tiny degree of accuracy. All Pitt knew for certain was that the storm blew out of the northwest. In forty-eight hours it could have carried them a considerable distance to the southeast, far from any sight of land. He knew from experience on other projects that the currents and the prevailing winds in this part of the Indian Ocean moved slightly south of east. If they were drifting somewhere between the fortieth and fiftieth parallels, their drift would carry them into the desolate vastness of the South Atlantic, where no ship traveled. The next landfall would be the southern tip of South America, nearly thirteen thousand kilometers away.

He stared up at the Southern Cross, a constellation that was not visible above thirty degrees north latitude, the latitude running across North Africa and the tip of Florida. Described since antiquity, its five bright stars had steered mariners and fliers across the immense reaches of the Pacific since the early voyages of the Polynesians. Millions of square miles of loneliness, dotted only by the islands, which were the tips of great mountains that rose unseen from the ocean floor.

However he figured it, no matter how strong their desire to survive, and despite any good luck they might receive, the odds were overwhelming against their ever setting foot on land again.

33

Hiram Yaeger swam deep in the blue depths of the sea, the water rushing past in a blur as if he were in a jet aircraft flying through tinted clouds. He swept over the edge of seemingly bottomless chasms, soared through valleys of vast mountain ranges that climbed from the black abyss to the sun-glistened surface. The seascape was eerie and beautiful at the same time. The sensation was the same as flying through the void of deep space.

It was Sunday and he worked alone on the tenth floor of the deserted NUMA building. After nine straight hours of staring steadily at his computer monitor, Yaeger leaned back in his chair and rested his tired eyes. He had finally put the finishing touches on a complex program he had created using image-synthesis algorithms to show the three-dimensional propagation of sound waves through the sea. With the unique technology of computer graphics, he had entered a world few had traveled before. The computer-generated drama of high-intensity sound traveling through water had taken Yaeger and his entire staff a week to calculate. Using special-purpose hardware and a large database of sound-speed variations throughout the Pacific, they had perfected a photorealistic model that traced the sound rays to where convergence zones would occur throughout the Pacific Ocean.

The underwater images were displayed in extremely rapid sequence to create the illusion of motion in and around actual three-dimensional sound-speed contour maps that had been accumulated over a thirty-year study period from oceanographic data. It was computer imaging taken to its highest art form.

He kept an eye on a series of lights beginning with yellow and advancing through the oranges before ending in deep red. As they blinked on in sequence, they told him how close he was coming to the point where the sound rays would converge. A separate digital readout gave him the latitude and longitude. The pièce de résistance of his imagery was the dynamic convergence-zone display. He could even program the image to raise his viewpoint above the surface of the water and show any ships whose known courses were computed to bisect that particular sector of the ocean at a predictable time.

The red light farthest to his right flashed, and he punched in the program to bring the image out of the water, revealing a surface view of the convergence point. He expected to see empty horizons of water, but the image on the viewing screen was hardly what he'd imagined. A mountainous landmass with vegetation filled the screen. He ran through the entire sequence again, beginning from the four points around the ocean that represented Dorsett Consolidated's island mines. Ten, twenty, thirty times he reran the entire scenario, tracing the sound rays to their ultimate meeting place.

Finally satisfied there was no mistake, Yaeger sagged wearily in his chair and shook his head. "Oh my God," he murmured, "Oh my God."

Admiral Sandecker had to force himself not to work on Sundays. A hyper-workaholic, he ran ten kilometers every morning and performed light workouts after lunch to work off excess energy. Sleeping but four hours a night, he put in long, grueling days that would inflict burnout on most other men. Long divorced, with a daughter living with her husband and three children on the other side of the world in Hong Kong, he was far from lonely. Considered a prime catch by the older single women of Washington, he was inundated by invitations to intimate dinners and parties of the social elite. As much as he enjoyed the company of ladies, NUMA was his love, his passion. The marine science agency took the place of a family. It was spawned by him and bred into a giant institution revered and respected around the world.

Sundays, he cruised along the shores of the Potomac River in an old Navy double-ender whaleboat he had bought surplus and rebuilt. The arched bow brushed aside the murky brown water as he cut the wheel to dodge a piece of driftwood. There was history attached to the little eight-meter vessel. Sandecker had documented her chronology from the time she was built in 1936 at a small boatyard in Portsmouth, Maine, and then transported to Newport News, Virginia, where she was loaded on board the newly launched aircraft carrier *Enterprise*. Through the war years and many battles in the South Pacific, she served as Admiral Bull Halsey's personal shore boat. In 1958, when the *Enterprise* was decommissioned and scrapped, the aging double-ender was left to rot in a storage area behind the New York Shipyard. It was there Sandecker found and bought the worn remains. He then beautifully restored her with loving care until she looked like the day she came out of that boatyard in Maine.

As he listened to the soft chugging from the ancient four-cylinder Buda diesel engine, he reflected on events of the past week and contemplated his actions for the week to follow. His most pressing concern was Arthur Dorsett's greed-inspired acoustic plague, which was devastating the Pacific Ocean. This problem was closely followed by the unanticipated abduction of Pitt and Giordino and their subsequent disappearance. He was deeply troubled that neither dilemma was blessed with even a clue toward a solution.

The members of Congress he had approached had refused his pleas to take drastic measures to stop Arthur Dorsett before his guilt was ironclad. In their minds there simply was not enough evidence to tie him to the mass deaths, reasoning that was fueled by Dorsett's highly paid lobbyists. Par for the course, thought a frustrated Sandecker. The bureaucrats never acted until it was too late. The only hope left was to persuade the President to take action, but without the support of two or more prominent members of Congress, that was also a lost cause.

A light snow fell over the river, coating the barren trees and winter-dead growth on the ground. His was the only boat in sight on the water that wintry day. The afternoon sky was ice blue and the air sharp and quite cold. Sandecker turned up the collar of a well-worn Navy peacoat, pulled a black stocking cap down over his ears and swung the whaleboat toward the pier along the Maryland shore where he kept it docked. As he approached from upriver, he saw a figure get out of the warm comfort of a four-wheel-drive Jeep and walk across the dock. Even at a distance of five hundred meters he easily recognized the strange hurried gait of Rudi Gunn.

Sandecker slipped the whaleboat across the current and slowed the old Buda diesel to a notch above idle. As he neared the dock, he could see the grim expression on Gunn's bespectacled face. He suppressed a rising chill of dread and dropped the rubber bumpers over the port side of the hull. Then he threw a line to Gunn, who pulled the boat parallel to the dock before tying off the bow and stern to cleats bolted to the gray wood.

The admiral removed a boat cover from a locker, and Gunn helped him stretch it over the boat's railings. When they finished and Sandecker stepped onto the dock, neither man had yet spoken. Gunn looked down at the whaleboat.

"If you ever want to sell her, I'll be the first in line with a checkbook."

Sandecker looked at him and knew Gunn was hurting inside. "You didn't drive out here just to admire the boat."

Gunn stepped to the end of the dock and gazed grimly out over the murky river. "The latest report since Dirk and Al were snatched from the *Ocean Angler* in Wellington is not good."

"Let's have it."

"Ten hours after Dorsett's yacht vanished off our satellite cameras—"

"The reconnaissance satellites lost them?" Sandecker interrupted angrily.

"Our military intelligence networks do not exactly consider the Southern Hemisphere a hotbed of hostile activity," Gunn replied acidly. "Budgets being what they are, no satellites with the ability to photograph the earth in detail are in orbits able to cover the seas south of Australia."

"I should have considered that," Sandecker muttered in disappointment. "Please go on."

"The National Security Agency intercepted a satellite phone

call from Arthur Dorsett aboard his yacht to his superintendent of operations on Gladiator Island, a Jack Ferguson. The message said that Dirk, Al and Maeve Fletcher were set adrift in a small, powerless boat in the sea far below the fiftieth parallel, where the Indian Ocean meets the Tasman Sea. The exact position wasn't given. Dorsett went on to say that he was returning to his private island."

"He placed his own daughter in a life-threatening situation?" Sandecker muttered, incredulous. "I find that unthinkable. Are you sure the message was interpreted correctly?"

"There is no mistake," said Gunn.

"That's cold-blooded murder," muttered Sandecker. "That means they were cast off on the edge of the Roaring Forties. Gale-force winds sweep those latitudes most of the year."

"It gets worse," said Gunn solemnly. "Dorsett left them drifting helplessly in the path of a typhoon."

"How long ago?"

"They've been adrift over forty-eight hours."

Sandecker shook his head. "If they survived intact, they'd be incredibly difficult to find."

"More like impossible when you throw in the fact that neither our Navy nor the Aussies' have any ships or aircraft available for a search."

"Do you believe that?"

Gunn shook his head. "Not for a minute."

"What are their chances of being spotted by a passing ship?" asked Sandecker.

"They're nowhere near any shipping lanes. Except for the rare vessel transporting supplies to a subcontinent research station, the only other ships are occasional whalers. The sea between Australia and Antarctica is a virtual wasteland. Their odds of being picked up are slim."

There was something tired, defeated about Rudi Gunn. If they were a football team with Sandecker as coach, Pitt as quarterback and Giordino as an offensive tackle, Gunn would be their man high in the booth, analyzing the plays and sending them down to the field. He was indispensable, always spirited; Sandecker was surprised to see him so depressed.

"I take it you don't give them much chance for survival."

"Three people on a small raft adrift, besieged by howling winds and towering seas. Should they miraculously survive the typhoon, then comes the onslaught of thirst and hunger. Dirk and Al have come back from the dead on more than one occasion in the past, but I fear that this time the forces of nature have declared war on them.''

"If I know Dirk," Sandecker said irrefutably, "he'll spit right in the eye of the storm and stay alive if he has to paddle that raft all the way to San Francisco." He shoved his hands deep in the pockets of his old peacoat. "Alert any NUMA research vessels within five thousand kilometers and send them into the area."

"If you'll forgive me for saying so, Admiral, it's a case of too little, too late."

"I'll not stop there." Sandecker's eyes blazed with intent. "I'm going to demand that a massive search be launched, or by God I'll make the Navy and the Air Force wish they never existed."

Yaeger tracked down Sandecker at the admiral's favorite restaurant, a little out-of-the-way ale and steak house below Washington, where he was having a somber dinner with Gunn. When the compact Motorola Iridium wireless receiver in his pocket beeped, Sandecker paused, washed down a bite of filet mignon with a glass of wine and answered the call. "This is Sandecker."

"Hiram Yaeger, Admiral. Sorry to bother you."

"No need for apologies, Hiram. I know you wouldn't contact me outside the office if it wasn't urgent."

"Is it convenient for you to come to the data center?"

"Too important to tell me over the phone?"

"Yes, sir. Wireless communication has unwanted ears. Without sounding overdramatic, it is critical that I brief you in private."

"Rudi Gunn and I will be there in half an hour." Sandecker slipped the phone back into the pocket of his coat and resumed eating.

"Bad news?" asked Gunn.

"If I read between the lines correctly, Hiram has gathered new data on the acoustic plague. He wants to brief us at the data center."

"I hope the news is good."

"Not from the tone of his voice," Sandecker said soberly. "I suspect he discovered something none of us wants to know."

Yaeger was slouched in his chair, feet stretched out, contemplating the image on an oversized video display computer terminal when Sandecker and Gunn walked into his private office. He turned and greeted them without rising from his chair.

"What do you have for us?" Sandecker asked, not wasting words.

Yaeger straightened and nodded at the video screen. "I've arrived at a method for estimating convergence positions for the acoustic energy emanating from Dorsett's mining operations."

"Good work, Hiram," said Gunn, pulling up a chair and staring at the screen. "Have you determined where the next convergence will be?"

Yaeger nodded. "I have, but first, let me explain the process." He typed in a series of commands and then sat back. "The speed of sound through seawater varies with the temperatures of the sea and the hydrostatic pressure at different depths. The deeper you go and the heavier the column of water above, the faster sound travels. There are a hundred other variables I could go into, dealing with atmospheric conditions, seasonal differences, convergence-zone propagation access and the formation of sound caustics, but I'll keep it simple and illustrate my findings."

The image on the viewing screen displayed a chart of the Pacific Ocean, with four green lines, beginning at the locations of the Dorsett mines and intersecting at Seymour Island in the Antarctic. "I began by working backward to the source from the point where the acoustic plague struck. Tackling the hardest nut to crack, Seymour Island, because it actually sits around the tip of the Antarctic Peninsula in the Weddell Sea, which is part of the South Atlantic, I determined that deep ocean sound rays were reflected by the mountainous geology on the seafloor. This was kind of a fluke and didn't fit the normal pattern. Having established a method, I calculated the occurrence of a more elementary event, the one that killed the crew of the *Mentawai*."

"That was off Howland Island, almost dead center in the Pacific Ocean," commented Sandecker.

"Far simpler to compute than the Seymour convergence," said Yaeger as he typed in the data that altered the screen to show four blue lines beginning from Kunghit, Gladiator, Easter and the Komandorskie Islands and meeting off Howland Island. Then he added four additional lines in red. "The intersection of convergence zones that wiped out the Russian fishing fleet northeast of Hawaii,'' he explained.

"So where do you fix the next convergence-zone intersection?'' asked Gunn.

"If conditions are stable for the next three days, the latest death spot should be about here.''

The lines, this time in yellow, met nine hundred kilometers south of Easter Island.

"Not much danger of it striking a passing ship in that part of the ocean,'' mused Sandecker. "Just to be on the safe side, I'll issue a warning for all ships to detour around the area.''

Gunn moved in closer to the screen. "What is your degree of error?''

"Plus or minus twelve kilometers,'' answered Yaeger.

"And the circumference where death occurs?''

"We're looking at a diameter anywhere from forty to ninety kilometers, depending on the energy of the sound rays after traveling great distances.''

"The numbers of sea creatures caught in such a large area must be enormous.''

"How far in advance can you predict a convergence-zone intersection?'' Sandecker queried.

"Ocean conditions are tricky to predict as it is,'' replied Yaeger. "I can't guarantee a reasonably accurate projection beyond thirty days into the future. After that, it becomes a crapshoot.''

"Have you calculated any other convergence sites beyond the next one?''

"Seventeen days from now.'' Yaeger glanced at a large calendar with a picture of a lovely girl in a tight skirt sitting at a computer. "February twenty-second.''

"That soon.''

Yaeger looked at the admiral, a polar-cold expression on his face. "I was saving the worst till last.'' His fingers played over the keyboard. "Gentlemen, I give you February twenty-second and a catastrophe of staggering magnitude.''

They were not prepared for what flashed on the screen. What Sandecker and Gunn saw on the video screen was an unthinkable event they had no control over, an encircling web of disaster that they could see no way to stop. They stared in sick fascination at the four purple lines that met and crossed on the screen.

"There can be no mistake?" asked Gunn.

"I've run my calculations over thirty times," said Yaeger wearily, "trying to find a flaw, an error, a variable that will prove me wrong. No matter how I shake and bake it, the result always comes out the same."

"God, no," whispered Sandecker. "Not there, not of all places in the middle of a vast and empty ocean."

"Unless some unpredictable upheaval of nature alters the sea and atmosphere," said Yaeger quietly, "the convergence zones will intersect approximately fifteen kilometers off the city of Honolulu."

34

This President, unlike his predecessor, made decisions quickly and firmly without vacillating. He refused to take part in advisory meetings that took forever and accomplished little or nothing, and he particularly disliked aides running around lamenting or cheering the latest presidential polls. Conferences to build defenses against criticism from the media or the public failed to shake him. He was set on accomplishing as much as possible in four years. If he failed, then no amount of rhetoric, no sugar-coated excuses or casting the blame on the opposing party would win him another election. Party hacks tore their hair and pleaded with him to present a more receptive image, but he ignored them and went about the business of governing in the nation's interest without giving a second thought to whose toes he stepped on.

Sandecker's request to see the President hadn't impressed White House Chief of Staff Wilbur Hutton. He was quite impervious to such requests from anyone who wasn't one of the party leaders of Congress or the Vice President. Even members of the President's own cabinet had difficulty in arranging a face-to-face meeting. Hutton pursued his job as Executive Office gatekeeper overzealously.

Hutton was not a man who was easily intimidated. He was as big and beefy as a Saturday night arena wrestler. He kept his thinning blond hair carefully trimmed in a crewcut. With a head and face like an egg dyed red, he stared from limpid smoke-blue eyes that were always fixed ahead and never darted from side to side. A graduate of Arizona State with a doctorate in economics from Stanford, he was known to be quite testy and abrupt with anyone who bragged of coming from an Ivy League school.

Unlike many White House aides, he held members of the Pentagon in great respect. Having enlisted and served as an infantryman in the Army and with an enviable record of heroism during the Gulf War, he had a fondness for the military. Generals and admirals consistently received more courteous recognition than dark-suited politicians.

"Jim, it's always good to see you." He greeted Sandecker warmly despite the fact that the admiral showed up unannounced. "Your request to see the President sounded urgent, but I'm afraid he has a full schedule. You needn't have made a special trip for nothing."

Sandecker smiled, then turned serious. "My mission is too delicate to explain over the phone, Will. There is no time to go through channels. The fewer people who know about the danger, the better."

Hutton motioned Sandecker to a chair as he walked over and closed the door to his office. "Forgive me for sounding cold and heartless, but I hear that story with frequent regularity."

"Here's one you haven't heard. Sixteen days from now every man, woman and child in the city of Honolulu and on most of the island of Oahu will be dead."

Sandecker felt Hutton's eyes delving into the back of his head. "Oh, come now, Jim. What is this all about?"

"My scientists and data analysts at NUMA have cracked the mystery behind the menace that's killing people and devastating the sea life in the Pacific Ocean." Sandecker opened his briefcase and laid a folder on Hutton's desk. "Here is a report on our findings. We call it the acoustic plague because the deaths are caused by high-intensity sound rays that are concentrated by refraction. This extraordinary energy then propagates through the sea until it converges and surfaces, killing anyone and anything within a radius up to ninety kilometers."

Hutton said nothing for a few moments, wondering for a brief instant if the admiral had slipped off the deep end, but only for an instant. He had known Sandecker too long not to take him as a serious, no-nonsense man dedicated to his job. He opened the cover of the report and scanned the contents while the admiral sat patiently. At last he looked up.

"Your people are sure of this?"

"Absolutely," Sandecker said flatly.

"There is always the possibility of a mistake."

"No mistake," Sandecker said firmly. "My only concession is a less than five percent chance the convergence could take place a safe distance away from the island."

"I hear through the congressional grapevine that you've approached Senators Raymond and Ybarra on this matter but were unable to get their backing for a military strike against Dorsett Consolidated property."

"I failed to convince them of the seriousness of the situation."

"And now you've come to the President."

"I'll go to God if I can save two million lives."

Hutton stared at Sandecker, head tilted to the side, his eyes dubious. He tapped a pencil on his desktop for a few moments, then nodded and stood, convinced that the admiral could not be ignored.

"Wait right here," he commanded. He stepped through a doorway that led to the Oval Office and disappeared for a solid ten minutes. When he reappeared, Hutton motioned Sandecker inside. "This way, Jim. The President will see you."

Sandecker looked at Hutton. "Thank you, Will. I owe you one."

As the admiral entered the Oval Office, the President graciously came from around President Roosevelt's old desk and shook his hand. "Admiral Sandecker, this is a pleasure."

"I'm grateful for your time, Mr. President."

"Will says this is an urgent matter concerning the cause of all those deaths on the *Polar Queen*."

"And many more."

"Tell the President what you told me," said Hutton, handing the report on the acoustic plague to the President to read while the admiral explained the threat.

Sandecker presented his case with every gun blazing. He was forceful and vibrant. He believed passionately in his people at

NUMA, their judgments and conclusions. He paused for emphasis, then wound up by requesting military force to stop Arthur Dorsett's mining operations.

The President listened intently until Sandecker finished, then continued reading in silence for a few more minutes before looking up. "You realize, of course, Admiral, that I cannot arbitrarily destroy personal property on foreign soil."

"Not to mention the taking of innocent lives," Hutton added.

"If we can stop the operations of only one of the Dorsett Consolidated mines," said Sandecker, "and prevent the acoustic energy from traveling from its source, we could weaken the convergence enough to save nearly two million men, women and children who live in and around Honolulu from an agonizing death."

"You must admit, Admiral, acoustic energy is not a threat the government is prepared to guard against. This is completely new to me. I'll need time for my advisers on the National Science Board to investigate NUMA's findings."

"The convergence will occur in sixteen days," said Sandecker darkly.

"I'll be back to you in four," the President assured him.

"That still leaves us plenty of time to carry out a plan of action," said Hutton.

The President reached out his hand. "Thank you for bringing this matter to my attention, Admiral," he said in official jargon. "I promise to give your report my fullest attention."

"Thank you, Mr. President," said Sandecker. "I couldn't ask for more."

As Hutton showed him out of the Oval Office, he said, "Don't worry, Jim. I'll personally shepherd your warning through the proper channels."

Sandecker fixed him with a blistering glare. "Just make damned sure the President doesn't let it fall through the cracks, or there won't be anyone left in Honolulu to vote for him."

35

Four days without water. The sun's unrelenting heat and the constant humidity sucked the perspiration from their bodies. Pitt would not let them dwell on the empty vastness that could depress all physical energy and creative thought. The monotonous lapping of the waves against the boat nearly drove them mad until they became immune to it. Ingenuity was the key to survival. Pitt had studied many shipwreck accounts and knew that too many shipwrecked mariners expired from lethargy and hopelessness. He drove Maeve and Giordino, urging them to sleep only at night and keep as busy as possible during daylight hours.

The prodding worked. Besides serving as the ship's butcher, Maeve tied lines to a silk handkerchief and trailed it over the stern of the boat. Acting as a finely meshed net, the handkerchief gathered a varied collection of plankton and microscopic sea life. After a few hours, she divided her specimens into three neat piles on a seat lid, as if it were some sort of salad-of-the-sea.

Giordino used the harder steel of the Swiss army knife to notch barbs into the hook fashioned from Pitt's belt buckle. He took over the fishing duties, while Maeve put her knowledge of biology and zoology to work, expertly cleaning and dissecting the day's catch. Most shipwrecked sailors would have simply lowered the hook into the sea and waited. Giordino skipped preliminary fish seduction. After baiting the hook with the choicer, more appetizing, to fish at any rate, morsels from the shark's entrails, he began casting the line as if he were a cowboy roping a calf, slowing reeling it in over his elbow and the valley between his thumb and forefinger, jiggling it every meter to give life to the bait. Apparently, finding a moving dinner acted as an enticement to his prey, and soon Giordino hooked his first fish. A small tuna bit the lure, and less than ten minutes later the bonito was reeled on board.

The annals of shipwrecked sailors were rife with tales of those who died of starvation while surrounded by fish, because they lacked the basic skills to catch them. Not Giordino. Once he got the hang of it and sharpened his system to a fine science, he began to pull in fish with the virtuosity of a veteran fisherman. With a net, he could have filled the entire boat in a matter of hours. The water around and beneath the little craft looked like an aquarium. Fish of every size and luminescent color had congregated to escort the castaways. The smallest, vibrantly colored fish came and drew the larger fish that in turn attracted the larger sharks that made an ominous nuisance of themselves by bumping against the boat.

Menacing and graceful at the same time, the killers of the deep glided back and forth beside the boat, their triangular fins cutting the water surface like a cleaver. Accompanied by their entourage of legendary pilot fish, the sharks would roll on their sides as they slid under the boat. Rising on the crest of a swell when the boat was in a trough, they could actually stare down at their potential victims through catlike eyes as lifeless as ice cubes. Pitt was reminded of a Winslow Homer painting, a print of which had hung in a classroom of his elementary school. It was called the *Gulf Stream*. In the scene a black man was shown floating on a demasted sloop surrounded by a school of sharks, with a waterspout in the background. It was Homer's interpretation of man's uneven struggle against natural forces.

The old tried-and-true method devised by castaways and early navigators of chewing the moisture out of the raw fish was a feature of meals, along with the shark meat dried into jerky by the sun. Their sushi bar was also enhanced by two fair-sized flying fish they found flopping in the bottom of the boat during the night. The oily flavor of fresh, raw fish did not win any gourmet awards with their taste buds, but it went a long way in diminishing the agony of hunger and thirst. Their empty stomachs were appeased after only a few bites.

The need to replenish their body fluids was also lessened by dropping briefly over the side every few hours while the others kept a sharp eye out for sharks. The cooling sensation generated by lying in wet clothes under the shade of the boat cover helped fight the misery of dehydration as well as the torment of sunburn. It also helped to dissolve the coating of salt that rapidly accumulated on their bodies.

The elements made Pitt's job of navigating fairly simple. The westerly winds out of the Roaring Forties were carrying them east. The current cooperated and flowed in the same direction. For determining his approximate position, a rough estimate at best, he relied on the sun and stars while using a cross-staff he'd fashioned of two slivers of wood cut from the paddle.

The cross-shaft was a method of determining latitude devised by ancient mariners. With one end of the shaft held to the eye, a crosspiece was calibrated by sliding it back and forth until one end fit exactly between either the sun or star and the horizon. The angle of latitude was then read on notches carved on the staff. Once the angle was established, the mariner was able by crude reckoning to establish a rough latitude without published tables for reference. To determine his longitude—in Pitt's case, how far east they were being driven—was another matter.

The night sky blazed with stars that became glittering points on a celestial compass that revolved from east to west. After a few nights of fixing their positions, Pitt was able to record a rudimentary log by inscribing his calculations on one end of the nylon boat cover with a small pencil Maeve had fortuitously discovered stuffed under a buoyancy tube. His primary obstacle was that he was not as familiar with the stars and constellations this far south as he was with the ones found north of the equator, and he had to grope his way.

The light boat was sensitive to the wind's touch and often swept over the water as if it were under sail. He measured their speed by tossing one of his rubber-soled sneakers in front of the boat that was tied to a five-meter line. Then he counted the seconds it took the boat to pass the shoe, pulling it from the water before it drifted astern. He discovered that they were being pushed along by the westerly wind at a little under three kilometers an hour. By rigging the nylon boat cover as a sail and using the paddle as a short mast, he found they could increase their speed to five kilometers, or an easy pace if they could have stepped out of the boat and walked alongside.

"Here we are drifting rudderless like jetsam and flotsam over the great sea of life," Giordino muttered through salt-caked lips. "Now all we have to do is figure out a way to steer this thing."

"Say no more," said Pitt, using the screwdriver to remove the hinges on a fiberglass seat that covered a storage compartment. In less than a minute, he held up the rectangular lid, which was about the same size and shape as a cupboard door. "Every move a picture."

"How do you plan to attach it?" asked Maeve, becoming immune to Pitt's continuing display of inventiveness.

"By using the hinges on the remaining seats and attaching them to the lid, I can screw it to the transom that held the outboard motor so that it can swing back and forth. Then by attaching two ropes to the upper end, we can operate it the same as any rudder on a ship or airplane. It's called making the world a better place to live."

"You've done it," Giordino said stoically. "Artistic license, elementary logic, idle living, sex appeal, it's all there."

Pitt looked at Maeve and smiled. "The great thing about Al is that he is almost totally theatrical."

"So now that we've got a particle of control, great navigator, what's our heading?"

"That's up to the lady," said Pitt. "She's more familiar with these waters than we are."

"If we head straight north," Maeve answered, "we might make Tasmania."

Pitt shook his head and gestured at the makeshift sail. "We're not rigged to sail under a beam wind. Because of our flat bottom, we'd be blown five times as far east as north. Making landfall on the southern tip of New Zealand is a possibility but a remote one. We'll have to compromise by setting the sail to head slightly north of east, say a heading of seventy-five degrees on my trusty Boy Scout compass."

"The further north the better," she said, holding her arms

around her breasts for warmth. "The nights are too cold this far south."

"Do you know if there are landfalls on that course?" Giordino asked Maeve.

"Not many," she answered flatly. "The islands that lie south of New Zealand are few and far apart. We could easily pass between them without sighting one, especially at night."

"They may be our only hope." Pitt held the compass in his hand and studied the needle. "Do you recall their approximate whereabouts?"

"Stewart Island just below the South Island. Then come the Snares, the Auckland Islands, and nine hundred kilometers farther south are the Macquaries."

"Stewart is the only one that sounds vaguely familiar," said Pitt thoughtfully.

"Macquarie, you won't care for." Maeve gave an instinctive shiver. "The only inhabitants are penguins, and it often snows."

"It must be swept by colder currents out of the Antarctic."

"Miss any one of them and it's open sea all the way to South America," Giordino said discouragingly.

Pitt shielded his eyes and scanned the empty sky. "If the cold nights don't get us, without rain we'll dehydrate long before we step onto a sandy beach. Our best approach is to keep heading toward the southern islands in hopes of hitting one. You might call it putting all our eggs in several baskets to lower the odds."

"Then we make a stab for the Macquaries," said Giordino.

"They're our best hope," Pitt agreed.

With Giordino's able help, Pitt soon set the sail for a slight tack on a magnetic compass bearing of seventy-five degrees. The rudimentary rudder worked so well that they were able to increase their heading to nearly sixty degrees. Buoyed by the realization that they had a tiny grip on their destiny, they felt a slight optimism begin to emerge, heightened by Giordino's sudden announcement.

"We have a squall heading our way."

Black clouds had materialized and were sweeping out of the western sky as quickly as if some giant above were unrolling a carpet over the castaways. Within minutes drops of moisture began pelting the boat. Then they came heavier and more concentrated until the rain fell in a torrential downpour.

"Open every locker and anything that resembles a container," ordered Pitt as he frantically lowered the nylon sail. "Hold the sail on a slant with one end over the side of the boat for a minute to wash away the salt accumulation, before we form it into a trough to funnel the rainwater into the ice chest."

As the rain continued to pour down, they all tilted their faces toward the clouds, opening wide and filling their mouths, swallowing the precious liquid like greedy young birds demanding a meal from their winged parents. The pure fresh smell and pure taste came as sweet as honey to parched throats. No sensation could have been more pleasing.

The wind rushed over the sea, and for the next twelve minutes they reveled in a blinding deluge. The neoprene flotation tubes rumbled like drums as the raindrops struck their skintight sides. Water soon filled the ice chest and overflowed on the bottom of the boat. The life-giving squall ended as abruptly as it had begun. Hardly a drop was wasted. They removed their clothes and wrung the water from the cloth into their mouths before storing any excess from the bottom of the boat in every receptacle they could devise. With the passing of the squall and the intake of fresh water, their spirits rose to new heights.

"How much do you figure we collected?" Maeve wondered aloud.

"Between ten and twelve liters," Giordino guessed.

"We can stretch it another three liters by mixing it with seawater," said Pitt.

Maeve stared at him. "Aren't you inviting disaster? Drinking water laced with salt isn't exactly a cure for thirst."

"On hot, sultry days in the tropics, humans have a tendency to pour a stream of water down their throats until it comes out their ears and still feel thirsty. The body takes in more liquid than it needs. What your system really needs after sweating a river, is salt. Your tongue may retain the unwanted taste of seawater, but trust me, adding it to fresh water will quench your thirst without making you sick."

After a meal of raw fish and a replacement of their body liquids, they felt almost human again. Maeve found a small amount of grease where the engine controls once attached under the console and mixed it with oil she had squeezed from the caught fish to make a sunburn lotion. She laughingly referred to her concoction as Fletcher's Flesh Armour and pronounced the Skin Protection Factor a minus six. The only affliction they could not remedy was the sores that were forming on their legs and backs, caused by chafing from the constant motion of the boat. Maeve's improvised suntan lotion helped but did not correct the growing problem.

A stiff breeze sprang up in the afternoon, which boiled the sea around them as they were flung to the northeast, caught in the whim of the unpredictable waves. The leather jacket sea anchor was thrown out, and Pitt lowered the sail to keep it from blowing away. It was like racing down a snowy hill on a giant inner tube, completely out of control. The blow lasted until ten o'clock the next morning before finally tapering off. As soon as the seas calmed, the fish came back. They were seemingly maddened by the interruption, thrashing the water and butting up against the boat. The more voracious fish, the bullies on the block, had a field day with their smaller cousins. For close to an hour the water around the raft turned to blood as the fish acted out their never-ending life-or-death struggle that the sharks always won.

Tired beyond measure from being thrown about in the boat, Maeve quickly fell asleep and dreamed of her children. Giordino also took a siesta, his dreams conjuring up a vision of an all-you-can-eat restaurant buffet. For Pitt there were no dreams. He brushed all feelings of weariness aside and rehoisted the sail. He took a sighting of the sun with his cross-staff and set a course with the compass. Settling into a comfortable position in the stern, he steered the boat toward the northeast with the ropes attached to the rudder.

As so often when the sea was calm, he felt aloof from the problems of staying alive and the sea around him. After thinking and rethinking the situation, his thoughts always returned to Arthur Dorsett. He stirred himself to summon up his anger. No man could visit unspeakable horrors on innocent people, even his own daughter, and not suffer a form of retribution. It mattered more than ever now. The leering faces of Dorsett and his daughters Deirdre and Boudicca beckoned to him.

There was no room in Pitt's mind for the suffering of the past five days, for any emotion revolving around the torment of near death, no thought of anything but the primeval obsession for revenge. Revenge or execution, there was no distinction in Pitt's mind. Dorsett would not, could not be permitted to continue his reign of evil, certainly not after so many deaths. He had to be held accountable.

Pitt's mind was fixed on not one but two objectives—the rescue of Maeve's two sons and the killing of the evil diamond merchant.

36

Pitt steered the tiny craft over the vast sea throughout the eighth day. At sunset, Giordino took over the navigation duties while Pitt and Maeve dined on a combination of raw and dried fish. A full moon rose over the horizon as a great amber ball before diminishing and turning white as it crossed the night sky above them. After several swallows of water to wash down the taste of fish, Maeve sat nestled in Pitt's arms and stared at the silver shaft in the sea that led to the moon.

She murmured the words from "Moon River." "Two drifters off to see the world." She paused, looked up into Pitt's strong face and studied the hard line of his jaw, the dark and heavy brows and the green eyes that glinted whenever the light struck them right. He had a well-shaped nose, for a man, it but showed evidence of having been broken on more than one occasion. The lines around his eyes and the slight curl of the lips gave him the appearance of someone who was humorous and always smiling, a man a woman could be comfortable with, who posed no threat. There was a strange blend of hardness and sensitivity that she found incredibly appealing.

She sat quietly, mesmerized by him, until he looked down suddenly, seeing the expression of fascination on her face. She made no movement to turn away.

"You're not an ordinary man," she said without knowing why.

He stared quizzically. "What makes you say that?"

"The things you say, the things you do. I've never known anybody who was so in tune with life."

He grinned, his pleasure apparent. "Those are words I've never heard from a woman."

"You must have known many?" she asked with girlish curiosity.

"Many?"

"Women."

"Not really. I always wanted to be a lecher like Al here, but seldom found the time."

"Married?"

"No, never."

"Come close?"

"Maybe once."

"What happened?"

"She was killed."

Maeve could see that Pitt had never quite bridged the chasm separating sorrow and bittersweet memory. She regretted asking the question and felt embarrassed. She was instinctively drawn to him and wanted to burrow into his mind. She guessed that he was the kind of man who longed for something deeper than a casual physical relationship, and she knew that insincere flirting held no attraction for him.

"Her name was Summer," he continued quietly. "It was a long time ago."

"I'm sorry," said Maeve softly.

"Her eyes were gray and her hair red, but she looked much like you."

"I'm flattered."

He was about to ask her about her boys but stopped himself, realizing it would spoil the intimacy of the moment. Two people alone, well, almost alone, in a world of moon, stars and a black restless sea. Devoid of humans and solid ground, thousands of kilometers of fluid nothingness surrounded them. It was all too easy to forget where they were and imagine themselves sailing across the bay of some tropical island.

"You also bear an incredible resemblance to your great-great-great-grandmother," he said.

She raised her head and gazed at him. "How could you possibly know I look like her?"

"The painting on the yacht, of Betsy Fletcher."

"I must tell you about Betsy sometime," said Maeve, curling up in his arms like a cat.

"No need," he said smiling. "I feel I know her almost as well as you. A very heroic woman, arrested and sent to the penal colony at Botany Bay, survivor of the raft of the *Gladiator*. She helped save the lives of Captain 'Bully' Scaggs and Jess Dorsett, a convicted highwayman who became her husband and your great-great-great-grandfather. After landing on what became known as Gladiator Island, Betsy discovered one of the world's largest diamond mines and founded a dynasty. Back in my hangar I have an entire dossier on the Dorsetts, beginning with Betsy and Jess and continuing through their descendants down to you and your reptilian sisters."

She sat up again, a sudden anger in her snapping blue eyes. "You had me investigated, you rat, probably by your CIA."

Pitt shook his head. "Not you so much as the chronicles of the Dorsett family of diamond merchants. My interest comes under the heading of research, which was conducted by a fine old gentleman who would be very indignant if he knew you referred to him as an agent with the CIA."

"You don't know as much about my family as you might think," she said loftily. "My father and his forefathers were very private men."

"Come to think of it," he said soothingly, "there is one member of your cast who intrigues me more than the others."

She looked at him lopsidedly. "If not me, who then?"

"The sea monster in your lagoon."

The answer took her completely by surprise. "You can't mean Basil?"

He looked blank a moment. "Who?"

"Basil is not a sea monster, he's a sea serpent. There's a distinct difference. I've seen him on three different occasions with my own eyes."

Then Pitt broke out laughing. "Basil? You call him Basil?"

"You wouldn't laugh if he got you in his jaws," she said waspishly.

Pitt shook his head. "I can't believe I'm listening to a trained zoologist who believes in sea serpents."

"To begin with, sea serpent is a misnomer. They are not true serpents, like snakes."

"There have been wild stories from tourists claiming to have seen strange beasties in every lake from Loch Ness to Lake Champlain, but I haven't heard of any sightings in the oceans since the last century."

"Sightings at sea do not receive the publicity they used to. Wars, natural disasters and mass murders have pushed them out of the headlines."

"That wouldn't stop the tabloids."

"Sea routes for powered ships are fairly well fixed," Maeve explained patiently. "The early sailing ships moved in unfrequented waters. Whaling ships, which sailed after whales rather than the shortest distance between ports, often reported sightings. Wind-driven ships also sailed silently and were able to approach a serpent on the surface, while a modern diesel vessel can be heard underwater for kilometers. Just because they're large doesn't mean they aren't shy, retiring creatures, indefatigable ocean voyagers who refuse to be captured."

"If they aren't illusions or snakes, then what are they, leftover dinosaurs?"

"Okay, Mr. Skeptic," she said seriously, a touch of defiant pride in her tone. "I'm writing my Ph.D. thesis on the subject of cryptozoology, the science of legendary beasts. For your information there are 467 sightings confirmed after faulty vision, hoaxes and secondhand reports have been eliminated. I have them all categorized in my computer at the university; nature of sightings, including weather and sea conditions in which sightings took place; geographical distribution, distinguishing characteristics, color, shape and size. Through graphics-rendering techniques I can backtrack the beasts' evolution. To answer your question, they've probably evolved from dinosaurs in a manner similar to alligators and crocodiles. But they are definitely not 'leftovers.' The Plesiosaurs, the species most often thought to have survived as present-day sea serpents, never exceeded sixteen meters, far smaller than Basil, for example."

"All right, I'll reserve judgment until you convince me they truly exist."

"There are six primary species," she lectured. "The most sightings have been of a long-necked creature with one main hump and with head and jaws similar to that of a large dog. Next is one that is always described as having the head of a horse with a mane and saucer-shaped eyes. This creature is also reported to have goatlike whiskers under its lower jaw."

" 'Goat whiskers,' " Pitt repeated cynically.

"Then there is the variety with a true serpentine body like that of an eel. Another has the appearance of a giant sea otter, while yet another is known for its row of huge, triangular fins. The kind most often pictured has many dorsal humps, an egg-shaped head and big doglike muzzle. This serpent is almost always reported as being black on top and white on the bottom. Some have seal- or turtlelike flippers or fins, some do not. Some grow enormously long tails, others a short stub. Many are described as having fur, most others are silky smooth. The colors vary from yellow-gray to brown to black. Almost all witnesses agree that the lower part of the bodies are white. Unlike most true sea and land snakes, which propel themselves by wiggling side-to-side, the serpent moves by making vertical undulations. It appears to dine on fish, only shows itself in calm weather and has been observed in every sea except the waters around the Arctic and Antarctic."

"How do you know all these sightings were not misinterpreted?" asked Pitt. "They could have been basking sharks, clumps of seaweed, porpoises swimming in single file, or even a giant squid."

"In most cases there was more than one observer," retorted Maeve. "Many of the viewers were sea captains of great integrity. Captain Arthur Rostron was one."

"I know the name. He was captain of the *Carpathia*, the ship that picked up the *Titanic* survivors."

"He witnessed a creature that appeared in great distress, as if it were injured."

"Witnesses may be completely honest, but mistaken," Pitt insisted. "Until a serpent, or a piece of one, is handed over to scientists to dissect and study, there is no proof."

"Why can't reptiles twenty to fifty meters in length, with snakelike features, still live in the seas as they did during the Mesozoic era? The sea is not a crystal windowpane. We cannot see into its depths and scan far horizons as on land. Who knows how many giant species, still unknown to science, roam the seas?"

"I'm almost afraid to ask," Pitt said, his eyes smiling. "What category does Basil fall into?"

"I've classified Basil as a mega-eel. He has a cylindrical body thirty meters long, ending in a tail with a point. His head is slightly blunt like the common eel's but with a wide canine mouth filled with sharp teeth. He is bluish with a white belly, and his jet-black eyes are as large as a serving dish. He undulates in the horizontal like other eels and snakes. Twice I saw him raise the front part of his body a good ten meters out of the water before falling back with a great splash."

"When did you first see him?"

"When I was about ten," Maeve answered. "Deirdre and I were sailing about the lagoon in a little cutter our mother had given us, when suddenly I had this strange sensation of being watched. A cold shiver shot up my spine. Deirdre acted as if nothing was happening. I slowly turned around. There, about twenty meters behind our stern, was a head and neck rising about three meters out of the water. The thing had two glistening black eyes that were staring at us."

"How thick was the neck?"

"A good two meters in diameter, as big as a wine vat, as Father often described it."

"He saw it too?"

"The whole family observed Basil on any number of occasions, but usually when someone was about to die."

"Go on with your description."

"The beast looked like a dragon out of a child's nightmare. I was petrified and couldn't say a word or scream, while Deirdre kept staring over the bow. Her attention was focused on telling me when to tack so we wouldn't run onto the outer reef."

"Did it make a move toward you?" Pitt asked.

"No. It just stared at us and made no attempt to molest the boat as we sailed away from it."

"Deirdre never saw it."

"Not at that time, but she later sighted it on two different occasions."

"How did your father react when you told him what you had seen?"

"He laughed and said, 'So you've finally met Basil.' "

"You said the serpent made itself known when there was a death?"

"A family fable with some kernel of truth. Basil was seen in the lagoon by the crew of a visiting whaler when Betsy Fletcher was buried, and later when my great-aunt Mildred and my mother died, both in violent circumstances."

"Coincidence or fate?"

Maeve shrugged. "Who can say? The only thing I can be sure of is that my father murdered my mother."

"Like Grandfather Henry supposedly killed his sister Mildred."

She gave him a strange look. "You know about that too."

"Public knowledge."

She stared over the black sea to where it met the stars, the bright moon illuminating her eyes, which seemed to grow darker and sadder. "The last three generations of Dorsetts haven't exactly set virtuous standards."

"Your mother's name was Irene."

Maeve nodded silently.

"How did she die?" Pitt asked gently.

"She would have eventually died, brokenhearted from the abuse heaped upon her by the man she desperately loved. But while walking along the cliffs with my father, she slipped and fell to her death in the surf below." An expression of hatred became etched on her delicate face. "He pushed her," she said coldly. "My father pushed her to her death as sure as there are stars in the universe."

Pitt held her tightly and felt her shudder. "Tell me about your sisters," he said, changing the subject.

The look of hatred faded, and her features became delicate again. "Not much to tell. I was never very close to either of them. Deirdre was the sneaky one. If I had something she wanted, she simply stole it and pretended it was hers all along. Of the three, Deirdre was Daddy's little girl. He lavished most of his affection on her, I guess because they were kindred spirits. Deirdre lives in a fantasy world created by her own deceit. She can't tell the truth even when there is no reason to lie."

"Has she ever married?"

"Once, to a professional soccer player who thought he was going to live out his life as a member of the jet set with his own set of toys. Unfortunately for him, when he wanted a divorce and demanded a settlement that equaled Australia's national budget, he conveniently fell off one of the family yachts. His body was never found."

"It doesn't pay to accept invitations to go sailing with the Dorsetts," Pitt said caustically.

"I'm afraid to think about all the people Father has eliminated who stood in his way in fact or in his imagination."

"And Boudicca?"

"I never really knew her," she said distantly. "Boudicca is eleven years older than me. Soon after I was born, Daddy enrolled her in an exclusive boarding school, or so I was always told. It sounds odd to say my sister was a total stranger to me. I was nearly ten years old when I met her for the first time. All I really know about her is that she has a passion for handsome young men. Daddy isn't pleased, but he does little to stop her from sleeping around."

"She's one strong lady."

"I saw her manhandle Daddy once, when he was striking our mother during a drunken rampage."

"Odd that they all have such a murderous dislike for the only member of the family who is loving and decent."

"When I escaped the island, where my sisters and I were kept virtual prisoners after Mother died, Daddy could not accept my independence. My earning my own way through university without tapping the Dorsett fortune angered him. Then, when I was living with a young man and became pregnant, instead of opting for an abortion I decided to go the whole nine months after the doctor told me I was having twins. I refused to marry the boy, so Daddy and my sisters severed all my ties to the Dorsett empire. It all sounds so mad, and I can't explain it. I legally changed my name to that of my great-great-great-grandmother and went on with my life, happy to be free of a dysfunctional family."

She had been racked by wicked forces over which she had no control, and Pitt pitied her while respecting her fortitude. Maeve was a loving woman. He looked into the guileless blue eyes of a child. He swore to himself that he would move heaven and earth to save her.

He started to say something, but out of the blackness he caught sight of the seething crest of a huge wave bearing down on them.

The giant swell appeared to break across his entire field of vision. A cold dread gripped the nape of his neck as he saw three similar waves rolling behind the first.

He gave a warning shout to Giordino and flung Maeve to the floor. The swell curled down on top of the boat, inundating it with foam and spray, rolling over and pressing down the starboard quarter as it struck. The opposite side was flung into the air, and the boat twisted sideways as it fell into a deep trough, broadside to the next wall of water.

The second wave rose and touched the stars before surging over them with the force of a freight train. The boat plunged under the black tempest, completely submerged. Overwhelmed by the maddened sea, Pitt's only option for staying alive was to grip a buoyancy tube as tightly as possible in a replay of the earlier typhoon. To be cast overboard was to stay overboard. Any legitimate bookmaker would have preferred the odds covering the sharks over drowning.

The little boat had somehow struggled to the surface when the final two waves struck it violently in succession. They wrenched it around in a writhing inferno of raging water. The helpless passengers were plummeted under the liquid wall and immersed again. Then they were sliding down the smooth back of the final wave, and the sea went as calm as if nothing had happened. The tumultuous combers raced past and swept into the night.

"Another precision display of the sea's temper," sputtered Giordino, his arms locked in a death grip around the console. "What did we do to make her so mad?"

Pitt immediately released Maeve and lifted her to a sitting position. "Are you all right?"

She coughed for several seconds before gasping, "I expect . . . I'll live. What in God's name hit us?"

"I suspect a seismic disturbance on the sea bottom. It doesn't take a quake of great magnitude to set off a series of rogue waves."

Maeve wiped the wet strands of blond hair out of her eyes. "Thankfully, the boat didn't capsize and none of us was thrown out."

"How's the rudder?" Pitt asked Giordino.

"Still hanging. Our paddle-mast survived in good shape, but our sail has a few rips and tears."

"Our food and water supply also came through in good shape," volunteered Maeve.

"Then we came through nearly unscathed," said Giordino, as though he didn't quite believe it.

"Not for long, I fear," Pitt said tautly.

Maeve stared around the seemingly uninjured boat. "I don't see any obvious damage that can't be repaired."

"Nor I," Giordino agreed after examining the integrity of the buoyancy tubes.

"You didn't look down."

In the bright moonlight they could see the grim tension that was reflected on Pitt's face. They stared in the direction he gestured and suddenly realized that any hope of survival had rapidly vanished.

There, running the entire length of the bottom hull, was a crack in the fiberglass that was already beginning to seep water.

37

Rudi Gunn was not into sweat and the thrill of victory. He relied on his mental faculties, a regimen of disciplined eating habits and his metabolism to keep him looking young and trim. Once or twice a week, as today, when the mood struck him, he rode a bicycle during his lunch hour, along side Sandecker, who was a jogging nut. The admiral's daily run took him ten kilometers over one of several paths that ran through Potomac Park. The exercise was by no means conducted in silence. As one man ran and the other rode, the affairs of NUMA were discussed as if they were conversing in an office.

"What is the record for someone adrift at sea?" asked Sandecker as he adjusted a sweat band around his head.

"Steve Callahan, a yachtsman, survived 76 days after his sloop sank off the Canary Islands," answered Gunn, "the longest for one man in an inflatable raft. The Guinness World Record holder for survival at sea is held by Poon Lim, a Chinese steward who was set adrift on a raft after his ship was torpedoed in the South Atlantic during World War Two. He survived 133 days before being picked up by Brazilian fishermen."

"Was either adrift during a force ten blow?"

Gunn shook his head. "Neither Callahan nor Poon Lim was hit with a storm near the intensity of the typhoon that swept over Dirk, Al and Miss Fletcher."

"Going on two weeks since Dorsett abandoned them," said Sandecker between breaths. "If they outlasted the storm, they must be suffering badly from thirst and exposure to the elements."

"Pitt is a man of infinite resourcefulness," said Gunn indisputably. "Together with Giordino, I wouldn't be surprised if they washed up on a beach in Tahiti and are relaxing in a grass shack."

Sandecker stepped to the side of the path to allow a woman pushing a small child in a three-wheeled carrier to jog past in the other direction. After he resumed running, he murmured, "Dirk always used to say, The sea does not give up its secrets easily."

"Things might have been resolved if Australian and New Zealand search-and-rescue forces could have joined NUMA's efforts."

"Arthur Dorsett has a long reach," Sandecker said, irate. "I received so many excuses as to why they were busy on other rescue missions I could have papered a wall with them."

"There's no denying the man wields incredible power." Gunn stopped pedaling and paused beside the admiral. "Dorsett's bribe money reaches deep into the pockets of friends in the United States Congress and the parliaments of Europe and Japan. Astounding, the famous people who work for him."

Sandecker's face turned crimson, not from exertion but from hopelessness. He could not restrain his anger and resentment. He came to a stop, leaned down and gripped his knees, staring at the ground. "I'd close down NUMA in a minute for the chance to get my hands around Arthur Dorsett's neck."

"I'm sure you're not alone," said Gunn. "There must be thousands who dislike, distrust and even hate him. And yet they never betray him."

"Small wonder. If he doesn't arrange fatal accidents for those who stand in his way, he buys them off by filling their Swiss bank safety deposit boxes with diamonds."

"A powerful persuader, diamonds."

"He'll never influence the President with them."

"No, but the President *can* be misled by bad advice."

"Surely not when the lives of over a million people are at stake."

"No word yet?" asked Gunn. "The President said he'd be back to you in four days. It's been six."

"The urgency of the situation wasn't lost on him—"

Both men turned at the honk of a horn from a car with NUMA markings. The driver pulled to a stop in the street opposite the jogging path. He leaned out the passenger's window and shouted. "I have a call from the White House for you, Admiral."

Sandecker turned to Gunn and smiled thinly. "The President must have big ears."

As the admiral stepped over to the car, the driver handed him a portable phone. "Wilbur Hutton on a safe line, sir."

"Will?"

"Hello, Jim, I'm afraid I have discouraging news for you."

Sandecker tensed. "Please explain."

"After due consideration, the President has postponed any action regarding your acoustic plague."

"But why?" Sandecker gasped. "Doesn't he realize the consequences of no action at all?"

"Experts on the National Science Board did not go along with your theory. They were swayed by the autopsy reports from Australian pathologists at their Center for Disease Control in Melbourne. The Aussies conclusively proved that the deaths on board the cruise ship were caused by a rare form of bacterium similar to the one causing Legionnaires' disease."

"That's impossible!" Sandecker snapped.

"I only know what I was told," Hutton admitted. "The Aussies suspect that contaminated water in the ship's heating system humidifiers was responsible."

"I don't care what the pathologists say. It would be folly for the President to ignore my warning. For God's sake, Will, beg, plead or do whatever it takes to convince the President to use his powers to shut down Dorsett's mining operations before it's too late."

"Sorry, Jim. The President's hands are tied. None of his scientific advisers thought your evidence was strong enough to run the risk of an international incident. Certainly not in an election year."

"This is insane!" Sandecker said desperately. "If my people

are right, the President won't be able to get elected to clean public bathrooms.''

"That's your opinion," said Hutton coldly. "I might add that Arthur Dorsett has offered to open his mining operations to an international team of investigators."

"How soon can a team be assembled?"

"These things take time. Two, maybe three weeks."

"By then you'll have dead bodies stacked all over Oahu."

"Fortunately or unfortunately, depending on how you look at it, you're in a minority in that belief."

Sandecker muttered darkly, "I know you did your best, Will, and I'm grateful."

"Please contact me if you come upon any further information, Jim. My line is always open to you."

"Thank you."

"Good-bye."

Sandecker handed the phone back to the driver and turned to Gunn. "We've been sandbagged."

Gunn looked shocked. "The President is ignoring the situation?"

Sandecker nodded in defeat. "Dorsett bought off the pathologists. They turned in a phony report claiming the cause of death of the cruise ship passengers was contamination from the heating system."

"We can't give up," Gunn said, furious at the setback. "We must find another means of stopping Dorsett's madness in time."

"When in doubt," Sandecker said, the fire returning to his eyes, "bank on somebody who is smarter than you are." He retrieved the phone and punched in a number. "There is one man who might have the key."

Admiral Sandecker bent down and teed up at the Camelback Golf Club in Scottsdale, Arizona. It was two o'clock in the afternoon under a cloudless sky, only five hours after he had jogged with Rudi Gunn in Washington. After landing at the Scottsdale airport, he borrowed a car from a friend, an old retired Navy man, and drove directly to the golf course. January in the desert could be cool, so he wore slacks and a long-sleeve cashmere sweater. There were two courses, and he was playing on the one called Indian Bend.

He sighted on the green 365 meters away, took two practice swings, addressed his ball and swung effortlessly. The ball soared nicely, sliced a bit to the right, bounced and rolled to a stop 190 meters down the fairway.

"Nice drive, Admiral," said Dr. Sanford Adgate Ames. "I made a mistake talking you into a friendly game of golf. I didn't suspect old sailors took a ground sport seriously." Behind a long, scraggly gray beard that covered his mouth and came down to his chest, Ames looked like an old desert prospector. His eyes were hidden behind blue-tinted bifocals.

"Old sailors do many strange things," Sandecker retorted.

Asking Dr. Sanford Adgate Ames to come to Washington for a high-level conference was no different from praying to God to conjure up a sirocco wind to melt the polar ice cap. Neither was likely to respond. Ames hated New York and Washington with equal passion and absolutely refused to visit either place. Offers of testimonial dinners and awards wouldn't budge him from his hideaway on Camelback Mountain in Arizona.

Sandecker needed Ames, needed him urgently. Biting the bullet, he requested a meeting with the soundmeister, as Ames was called among his fellow scientists. Ames agreed, but with the strict provision Sandecker bring his golf clubs, as all discussion would take place on the links.

Highly respected in the scientific community, Ames was to sound what Einstein was to time and light. Blunt, egocentric, brilliant, Ames had written more than three hundred papers on almost every known aspect of acoustical oceanography. His studies and analyses over the course of forty-five years covered phenomena ranging from underwater radar and sonar techniques to acoustic propagation to subsurface reverberation. Once a trusted adviser with the Defense Department, he was forced to resign after his fervent objections to ocean noise tests being conducted around the world to measure global warming. His caustic attacks on the Navy's underwater nuclear test projects was also a source of animosity at the Pentagon. Representatives of a host of universities trooped to his doorstep in hopes of getting him to join their faculties, but he refused, preferring to do research with a small staff of four students he paid out of his own pocket.

"What do you say to a dollar a hole, Admiral? Or are you a true betting man?"

"You're on, Doc," said Sandecker agreeably.

Ames stepped up to the tee, studied the fairway as if aiming a rifle and swung. He was a man in his late sixties, but Sandecker noted that his backswing reach was only a few centimeters off that of a man much younger and more nimble. The ball soared and dropped into a sand trap just past the 200-meter marker.

"How quickly the mighty fall," said Ames philosophically.

Sandecker was not conned easily. He knew he was being stroked. Ames had been notorious in Washington circles as a golf hustler. It was agreed by those on his sting list that if he hadn't gone into physics he'd have entered the PGA tour as a professional.

They stepped into a golf cart and started off after their balls with Ames at the wheel. "How can I help you, Admiral?" he asked.

"Are you aware of NUMA's efforts to track down and stop what we call an acoustic plague?" responded Sandecker.

"I've heard rumors."

"What do you think?"

"Pretty farfetched."

"The President's National Science Board agrees," Sandecker growled.

"I can't say I really blame them."

"You don't believe sound can travel thousands of kilometers underwater, then surface and kill?"

"Output from four different high-intensity acoustical sources converging in the same area and causing death to every mammal within hearing distance? Not a hypothesis I'd recommend advancing, not if I wished to retain my standing among my peers."

"Hypothesis be damned!" Sandecker burst out. "The dead already total over four hundred. Colonel Leigh Hunt, one of our nation's finest pathologists, has proven conclusively that the cause of death is intense sound waves."

"That's not what I heard from the postmortem reports out of Australia."

"You're an old fake, Doc," said Sandecker, smiling. "You've been following the situation."

"Any time the subject of acoustics is mentioned, I'm interested."

They reached Sandecker's ball first. He selected a number

three wood and knocked his ball into a sand trap twenty meters in front of the green.

"You too seem to have an affinity for sand traps," said Ames offhandedly.

"In more ways than one," Sandecker admitted.

They stopped at Ames' ball. The physicist pulled a three iron from his golf bag. His game appeared more mental than physical. He took no practice swings nor went through any wiggling motions. He simply stepped up to the ball and swung. There was a shower of sand as the ball lofted and dropped on the green within ten meters of the cup.

Sandecker needed two strokes with his sand wedge to get out of the trap, then two putts before his ball rolled into the cup for a double bogey. Ames putted out in two for a par. As they drove to the second tee, Sandecker began to outline his findings in a detailed narrative. The next eight holes were played under heavy discussion as Ames questioned Sandecker relentlessly and brought up any number of arguments against acoustic murder.

At the ninth green, Ames used his pitching wedge to lay his ball within a club's length of the hole. He watched with amusement as Sandecker misread the green and curled his putt back into the surrounding grass.

"You might be a pretty fair golfer if you got out and played more often, Admiral."

"Five times a year is enough for me," Sandecker replied. "I don't feel I'm accomplishing anything by chasing a little ball for six hours."

"Oh, I don't know. I've developed some of my most creative concepts while relaxing on a golf course."

After Sandecker finally laid a putt in the hole, they returned to the cart. Ames pulled a can of Diet Coke from a small ice chest and handed it to the admiral. "What exactly do you expect me to tell you?" he asked.

Sandecker stared at him. "I don't give a damn what ivory tower scientists think. People are dying out there on the sea. If I don't stop Dorsett, more people are going to die, in numbers I don't care to think about. You're the best acoustics man in the country. I'm hoping you can steer me on a course to end the slaughter."

"So I am your final court of appeals." The subtle change in

Ames' friendly tone was to one that could hardly be called dead sober, but it was unmistakable. "You want me to come up with a practical solution to your problem."

"Our problem," Sandecker gently corrected him.

"Yes," Ames said heavily, "I can see that now." He held a can of Diet Coke in front of his eyes and stared at it curiously. "Your description of me is quite correct, Admiral. I am an old fake. I worked out a blueprint of sorts before you left the ground in Washington. It's far from perfect, mind you. The chance of success is less than fifty-fifty, but it's the best I can devise without months spent in serious research."

Sandecker looked at Ames, masking his excitement, his eyes alight with a hope that wasn't there before. "You've actually conceived a plan for terminating Dorsett's mining operations?" he asked expectantly.

Ames shook his head. "Any kind of armed force is out of my territory. I'm talking about a method for neutralizing the acoustic convergence."

"How is that possible?"

"Simply put, sound-wave energy can be reflected."

"Yes, that goes without saying," said Sandecker.

"Since you know the four separate sound rays will propagate toward the island of Oahu and you have determined the approximate time of convergence, I assume your scientists can also accurately predict the exact position of the convergence."

"We have a good fix, yes."

"There's your answer."

"That's it?" Any stirrings of hope that Sandecker had entertained vanished. "I must have missed something."

Ames shrugged. "Occam's razor, Admiral. Entities should not be multiplied unnecessarily."

"The simplest answer is preferred over the complex."

"There you have it. My advice, for what it's worth, is for NUMA to build a reflector similar to a satellite dish, lower it into the sea at the point of convergence and beam the acoustic waves away from Honolulu."

Sandecker kept his face from showing any emotion, but his heart pounded against his ribs. The key to the enigma was ridiculously uncomplicated. True, the execution of a redirection project would not be easy, but it *was* feasible.

"If NUMA can build and deploy a reflector dish in time," he asked Ames, "where should the acoustic waves be redirected?"

A wily smile crossed Ames' face. "The obvious choice would be to some uninhabited part of the ocean, say south to Antarctica. But since the convergence energy slowly diminishes the farther it travels, why not send it back to the source?"

"The Dorsett mine on Gladiator Island," Sandecker said, tempering the awe in his voice.

Ames nodded. "As good a choice as any. The intensity of the energy would not have the strength to kill humans after making a round trip. But it should put the fear of God in them and give them one hell of a headache."

38

This was the end of the line, Pitt thought bitterly. This was as far as any human was expected to go. This was the conclusion of the valiant effort, the future desires and loves and joys of each one of them. Their end would come in the water as food for the fish, the pitiful remains of their bodies sinking a thousand fathoms to the desolate bottom of the sea. Maeve never to see her sons again, Pitt mourned by his mother and father and his many friends at NUMA. Giordino's memorial service, Pitt mused with a last vestige of humor, would be well attended, with an impressive number of grieving women, any one of whom could have been a beauty queen.

The little boat that had carried them so far through so much chaos was literally coming apart at the seams. The crack along the bottom of the hull lengthened fractionally with every wave that carried the boat over its crest. The buoyancy tubes would keep them afloat, but when the hull parted for good and the pieces went their separate ways, they would all be thrown in the merciless water, clinging helplessly to the wreckage and vulnerable to the ever-present sharks.

For the moment the sea was fairly calm. From crest to trough, the waves rolled just under a meter. But if the weather suddenly became unsettled and the sea kicked up, death would do more than merely stare them in the eyes. The old man with the scythe would embrace them quickly without further hesitation.

Pitt hunched over the rudder in the stern, listening to the now familiar scrape and splash of the bailer. His intense green eyes, sore and swollen, scanned the horizon as the orb of the morning sun flushed from a golden-orange glow to flaming yellow. He searched, hoping against hope that a hint of land might rise above the clean straight horizon of the sea surrounding them. He searched in vain. No ship, aircraft or island revealed itself. Except for a few small clouds trailing to the southeast a good twenty kilometers away, Pitt's world was as empty as the plains of Mars, the boat little more than a pinprick on a vast seascape.

After catching enough fish to start a seafood restaurant, hunger was not an anxiety. Their water supply, if conserved, was good for at least another six or seven days. It was the fatigue and lack of sleep caused by the constant bailing to keep the boat afloat that was taking a toll. Every hour was misery. Without a bowl or a bottle of any kind, they were forced to splash the incoming water overboard with their cupped hands until Pitt devised a container from the waterproof packet that held the accessories he had smuggled past the Dorsetts. When tied to a pair of wrenches to form a concave receptacle, it could expel a liter of seawater with one scoop.

At first they labored in four-hour shifts, because Maeve demanded she carry her share of the exertion. She worked gamely, fighting the stiffness that soon attacked the joints of her arms and wrists, followed by agonizing muscle aches. The grit and guts were there, but she did not have the natural strength of either man. The shifts soon were divided and allocated by stamina. Maeve bailed for three hours before being spelled by Pitt, who struggled for five. Giordino then took over and refused any relief until he had put in a full eight hours.

As the seam split farther and farther apart, the water no longer seeped, but rather spurted like a long fountain. The sea pried its way in faster than it could be cast out. With their backs against the wall and no trace of relief in sight, they slowly began to lose their steadfastness.

"Damn Arthur Dorsett," Pitt shouted in his mind. "Damn Boudicca, damn Deirdre!" The murderous waste, the uselessness of it all made no sense. He and Maeve were no major threat to Dorsett's fanatical dreams of empire. Alone, they never could have stopped him, or even slowed him down. It was a pure act of sadism to set them adrift.

Maeve stirred in her sleep, murmuring to herself, then lifted her head and stared, semiconscious, at Pitt. "Is it my turn to bail?"

"Not for another five hours," he lied with a smile. "Go back to sleep."

Giordino paused from bailing for a moment and stared at Pitt, sickness in his heart from knowing without question that Maeve would soon be torn limb from limb and devoured by the murder machines of the deep. Grimly, he went back to his work, laboring ceaselessly, throwing a thousand and more containerfuls of water over the side.

God only knew how Giordino could keep going. His back and arms must have been screaming in protest. The steel willpower to endure went far beyond the limits of comprehension. Pitt was stronger than most men, but alongside Giordino, he felt like a child watching an Olympic weight lifter. When Pitt had yielded the container in total exhaustion, Giordino took it up as if he could go on forever. Giordino, he knew, would never accept defeat. The tough, stocky Italian would probably die trying to get a stranglehold on a hammerhead.

Their peril sharpened Pitt's mind. In a final desperate attempt, he lowered the sail, laid it flat in the water, then slipped it under the hull and tied the lines to the buoyancy tubes. The nylon sheet, pressed against the crack by the pressure of the water, slowed the advance of the leakage by a good fifty percent, but at best it was only a stopgap measure that bought them a few extra hours of life. Unless the sea became perfectly calm, the physical breakdown of the crew and the splitting apart of the boat, Pitt figured, would occur shortly after darkness fell. He glanced at his watch and saw that sunset was only four and a half hours away.

Pitt gently grabbed Giordino's wrist and removed the container from his hand. "My turn," he said firmly. Giordino did not resist. He nodded in appreciation and fell back against a buoyancy tube, too exhausted to sleep.

The sail held back the flow of water enough so that Pitt actually stayed even for a short time. He bailed into the afternoon, mechanically, losing all sense of time, barely noting the passage of the brutal sun, never wilting under its punishing rays. He bailed like a robot, not feeling the pain in his back and arms, his senses completely numbed, going on and on as if he were caught in a narcotic stupor.

Maeve had roused herself out of a state of lethargy. She sat up and peered dully at the horizon behind Pitt's back. "Don't you think palm trees are pretty," she murmured softly.

"Yes, very pretty," Pitt agreed, giving her a tight smile, believing her to be hallucinating. "You shouldn't stand under them. People have been killed by falling coconuts."

"I was in Fiji once," she said, shaking her hair loose. "I saw one drop through the windshield of a parked car."

To Pitt, Maeve looked like a little girl, lost and wandering aimlessly in a forest, who had given up all hope of ever finding her way home. He wished there was something he could do or say that would comfort her. But there was nothing on God's sea that anyone could do. His sense of compassion and utter inadequacy left him embittered.

"Don't you think you should steer more to starboard?" she said listlessly.

"Starboard?"

She stared as if in a trance. "Yes. You don't want to miss the island by sailing past it."

Pitt's eyes narrowed. Slowly, he turned and peered over his shoulder. After nearly sixteen days of taking position sightings from the sun and suffering from the glare on the water, his eyes were so strained that he could only focus in the distance for a few seconds before closing them. He cast his eyes briefly across the bow but saw only blue-green swells.

He turned back. "We can no longer control the boat," he explained softly. "I've taken down the sail and placed it under the hull to slow the leakage."

"Oh, please," she pleaded. "It's so close. Can't we land and walk around on dry ground if only for a few minutes?"

She said it so calmly, so rationally in her Australian twang, that Pitt felt his spine tingle. Could she actually be seeing something? Reason dictated that Maeve's mind was playing tricks on her. But a still-glowing spark of hope mixed with desperation made him rise to his knees while clutching a buoyancy tube for stability. At that moment the boat rose on the crest of the next swell and he had a brief view of the horizon.

But there were no hills with palm trees rising above the sea.

Pitt circled his arm around Maeve's shoulders. He remembered her as robust and spirited. Now she looked small and frail, and yet her face glowed with an intensity that wasn't there before. Then he saw that she was not staring across the sea but into the sky.

For the first time he noticed the bird above the boat, wings outspread, hovering in the breeze. He cupped his hands over his eyes and gazed at the winged intruder. The wingspan was about a meter, the feathers a mottled green with specks of brown. The upper beak curled and came to a sharp point. To Pitt the bird appeared to be an ugly cousin of the more colorful parrot family.

"You see it too," said Maeve excitedly. "A kea, the same one that led my ancestors to Gladiator Island. Sailors shipwrecked in southern waters swear the kea shows the way to safe harbors."

Giordino peered upward, regarding the parrot more as a meal than a divine messenger sent by ghosts to guide them toward dry land. "Ask Polly to recommend a good restaurant," he muttered wearily. "Preferably one that doesn't have fish dishes on the menu."

Pitt did not reply to Giordino's survivalist humor. He studied the kea's movements. The bird hovered as if resting and made no attempt at aimlessly circling the boat. Then, apparently catching its second breath, it began to wing away in a southeasterly direction. Pitt immediately took a compass bearing on the bird's course, keeping it in sight until it became a speck and disappeared.

Parrots are not water birds like the gulls and petrels that range far over the seas. Perhaps it was lost, Pitt thought. But that didn't play well. For a bird that preferred to sink its claws on something solid, it made no attempt to land on the only floating object within sight. That meant that it was not tired of flying on instinct toward some unknown mating ground. This bird knew exactly where it was and where it was going. It flew with a plan. Perhaps, just perhaps, it was in the midst of flying from one island to another. Pitt was certain it could see something from a higher altitude that the miserable people in the dilapidated boat below could not.

He moved to the control console and pulled himself to his feet, clutching the stand with both hands to keep from being pitched overboard. Again he squinted through swollen eyes toward the southeast.

He had become all too familiar with clouds on the horizon that gave the illusion of land rising from the sea. He was too used to seeing white tufts of cotton drifting over the outer edge of the sea, their uneven shapes and dark gray colors raising false hopes before altering form and gliding onward, driven by winds out of the west.

This time it was different. One solitary cloud on the horizon remained stationary while the others moved past it. It rose from the sea faintly but without any signature of mass. There was no indication of green vegetation because the cloud itself was not a piece of an island. It was formed by vapor rising from sun-baked sand before condensing in a colder level of air.

Pitt restrained any feelings of excitement and delight when he realized the island was still a good five hours' sail away. There wasn't a prayer of reaching it, even with the sail spread once more on the mast while the sea poured into the boat. Then his dashed hopes began to reassemble as he recognized it not as the top of an undersea mount that had thrust above the sea after a million years of volcanic activity and then nurtured lush green hills and valleys. This was a low, flat rock that supported a few unidentifiable trees that somehow survived the colder climate this far south of the tropic zone.

The trees, clearly visible, were clustered on the small areas of sand that filled the cracks of the rocks. Pitt now realized the island was much closer than it had seemed at first view. It lay no more than eight or nine kilometers away, the tops of the trees giving the impression of a shaggy rug being pulled over the horizon.

Pitt took a bearing on the island, noting that it precisely matched the kea's course. Next he checked the wind direction and drift, and determined that the current would carry them around the northern tip. They would have to sail southeast on a starboard tack as Maeve had, amazingly, pictured in her imagination.

"The little lady wins a prize," Pitt announced. "We're within sight of land."

Both Maeve and Giordino struggled to their feet, clung to Pitt and gazed at their distant hope of refuge. "She's no mirage," said Giordino with a big grin.

"I told you the kea would lead us to a safe harbor," Maeve whispered softly in Pitt's ear.

Pitt did not allow himself to be carried away by elation. "We're not there yet. We'll have to replace the sail and bail like hell if we're to land on its shore."

Giordino judged the distance separating them from the island, and his expression sobered considerably. "Our home-away-from-home won't make it," he predicted. "She'll split in two before we're halfway."

39

The sail was raised, and any length of line that could be spared was used to tie the splitting hull together. With Maeve at the rudder, Giordino bailing like a crazy man and Pitt sloshing the water in sheets over the side with his bare hands, the ruptured boat set its bow directly toward the small, low-lying island a few kilometers distant. At long last they had visible proof that Pitt's navigation had paid off.

The mind-drugging fatigue, the overwhelming exhaustion had dropped from Pitt and Giordino like a heavy rock. They entered a zone where they were no longer themselves, a psychological zone where another world of stress and suffering had no meaning. It didn't matter that their bodies would pay heavily in agony later, as long as their sheer determination and refusal to accept defeat carried them across the gap separating the boat from the beckoning shore. They were aware of the pain screaming from their shoulders and backs, but the awareness was little more than an abstract protest from the mind. It was as if the torment belonged elsewhere.

The wind filled the sail, shoving the boat on a course for the solitary outcrop on the horizon. But the heartless sea was not about to release them from its grip. The current fought them, forking as it ran up against the shore and flowing in a loop past the outer limits of the island, threatening to push them back into the vast nothingness of the Pacific.

"I think we're being swept around it," Maeve said fearfully.

Facing forward as he frantically scooped the surging water out of the boat, Pitt seldom took his eyes off the nearing island. At first he thought they were seeing only one island, but as they approached within two kilometers he saw it was two. An arm of the sea, about a hundred meters in width, separated one from the other. He could also make out what appeared to be a tidal current running through the gap between the islands.

By the wind streaks on the surface and the spraying foam, Pitt could tell that the following breeze had shifted even more in their favor, blowing the boat on a sharper angle across the unfriendly current. That was a plus, he thought optimistically. The fact that the water this far south was too cold for coral reefs to form and wait in ambush to tear them to shreds didn't hurt either.

As he and Giordino fought the incoming water, they became conscious of a sullen thunder that seemed to grow louder. A quick pause, and their eyes locked as they realized that it was the unique sound of surf pounding against rock cliffs. The waves had turned murderous and were drawing the boat ever closer into a fatal embrace. The castaways' happy anticipation of setting foot on dry land again suddenly turned to a fear of being crushed in a thrashing sea.

Instead of a safe haven, what Pitt saw was a forbidding pair of rocks jutting abruptly from the sea, surrounded and struck by the onslaught of massive breakers. These were not tropical atolls with inviting white sand beaches and waving friendly natives, the stuff of Bali Ha'i, blessed by heaven and lush plant life. There was no sign of habitation on either island, no smoke, no structures of any kind to be seen. Barren, windswept and desolate they seemed a mysterious outpost of lava rock, their only vegetation a few clusters of low nonflowering plants and strange-looking trees whose growth appeared stunted.

He could not believe that he was in a war with unyielding stone and water for the third time since he had found and rescued Maeve on the Antarctic Peninsula. For a brief instant his thoughts raced back to the near escape of the *Polar Queen* and the flight from Kunghit Island with Mason Broadmoor. Both times he had mechanical power to carry him clear. Now he was fighting a watery burial on a little waterlogged boat with a sail not much bigger than a blanket.

The master seaman's first consideration when encountering rough seas, he recalled reading somewhere, was the preservation of the stability of his boat. The good sailor should not allow his boat to take on water, which would affect her buoyancy. He wished that whoever wrote that was sitting beside him.

"Unless you see a stretch of beach to land on," Pitt shouted at Maeve, "steer for the breach between the islands."

Maeve's lovely features, drawn and burned from the sun, became set and tense. She nodded silently, tightly gripped the rudder lines and focused every bit of her strength on the task.

The jagged walls that climbed above the crashing surf looked more menacing with each passing minute. Water was pouring alarmingly into the boat. Giordino ignored the approaching upheaval and concentrated on keeping the boat from sinking under them. To stop bailing now could have fatal consequences. Ten seconds of uninterrupted flow of seawater through the damaged boat and they would sink five hundred meters from shore. Struggling helpless in the water, if the sharks didn't get them, the surge and rocks would. He kept bailing, never missing a beat, his faith and trust entirely in the hands of Pitt and Maeve.

Pitt studied the cadence of the waves as friction with the bottom slope caused them to rise and slow down, measuring the break of the crests ahead and astern and timing their speed. The wave period shortened to roughly nine seconds and was moving at approximately twenty-two knots. The swells were beating in on an oblique angle to that of the rugged shoreline, causing the waves to break sharply as they refracted in a wide turn. Pitt did not need an old clipper ship captain to tell him that with their extremely limited sail power, there was little opportunity for maneuvering their way into the slot. His other fear was that of backwash swinging off the shoreline of both islands and turning the channel entrance into a maelstrom.

He could feel the pressure of the next wave surging beneath his knees, which were pressed into the bottom of the hull, and he judged its mass by the vibrations as it rumbled under him. The poor boat was being cruelly thrust into a tumult her designers never intended. Pitt did not dare put out the makeshift sea anchor as demanded by most sailor's manuals when traveling through violent seas. With no engine he believed it in their best interests to run with the waves. The drag of the anchor would most certainly pull the boat apart as the immense pressure from the waves drove them forward.

He turned to Maeve. "Try and keep us in the darkest blue of the water."

"I'll do my best," she replied bravely.

The roar of the breakers came with a steady, rolling beat, and soon they saw as well as heard the hiss of the spray as it burst into the sky. Without direct and manual control, they were helpless; the whims of the restless sea took them wherever it desired. The surge was building ever higher now. On closer inspection the slot between the rock outcroppings seemed like an insidious trap, a silent siren beckoning them to a false refuge. Too late to sail out to sea and around the islands. They were committed and there could be no turning back.

The islands and the frothing witches' cauldron along their malevolent shores became hidden behind the backs of the waves that passed under the boat. A fresh gust of wind sprang up and thrust them toward a rock-walled cleft that offered their only chance at survival.

The seas became more nervous the nearer they approached. So did Pitt when he calculated the crest of the waves to be almost ten meters in height when they curled and broke. Maeve struggled with the rudder to control their course, but the boat did not answer her helm and quickly became unmanageable. They were totally caught in the surge.

"Hold on!" Pitt shouted.

He took a quick glance astern and noted their position in regard to the sea's vertical movement. He knew that wave speed was highest just before reaching its crest. The breakers were rolling in like huge trucks in a convoy. The boat dropped into a trough, but their luck held as the swell broke just after passing them, and then they were riding on the back of the following wave at what seemed like breakneck speed. The surf was torn up and hurled in every direction as the wind whipped off the crests. The boat fell back only to be struck by the next sea as it rose under them to a height of eight meters, curled and collapsed over their heads. The boat did not broach nor did it pitchpole or even capsize. It landed flat and was thrown downward, crashing into the trough with a huge splash.

They were under a literal wall of hydraulic pressure. It felt as though the boat were being transported underwater by an out-of-control elevator. The total submersion seemed to take minutes, but it could not have lasted more than a few seconds. Pitt kept his eyes open and saw Maeve blurred and looking like a surreal vision in the liquid void, her face remarkably serene, her blond hair flowing up and out behind her. As he watched, she suddenly became lucent and distinct as they broke into the sunshine again.

Three or more seas rolled over them with diminishing force, and then they were through the breakers and into calmer water. Pitt snapped his head around, spitting out the saltwater he had taken in by not closing his mouth tightly, his wavy black hair whipping off the water droplets in glistening streaks.

"We're through the worst!" he yelled happily. "We've gained the channel!"

The surge that swept into the channel had been reduced to rolling waves no higher than the average doorway. Amazingly, the boat was still afloat and in one piece. Through the grinding ferocity of the crashing breakers it still somehow held together. The only apparent damage was to the sail and paddle-mast, which had been torn away but were floating nearby, still attached to the boat by a line.

Giordino had never stopped bailing, even when he was sitting in water up to his chest. He sputtered and wiped the salt from his eyes and continued throwing water over the side like there was no tomorrow.

The hull was now completely cracked in two and barely held together by the hurriedly attached nylon lines and the clamps connecting the buoyancy floats. Giordino finally conceded defeat as he found himself sitting up to his armpits in seawater. He looked around dazedly, his breath labored, his mind deadened by exhaustion. "What now?" he mumbled.

Before Pitt answered, he dipped his face in the water and peered at the bottom of the channel. The visibility was exceptional, though blurred without a face mask, and he could see sand and rock only ten meters below. Schools of vividly colored fish swam about leisurely, taking no notice of the strange creature floating overhead.

"No sharks in here," he said thankfully.

"They seldom swim through breakers," said Maeve through a spasm of coughing. She was sitting with her arms stretched out and draped over the stern buoyancy tube.

The current through the channel was carrying them closer to the northern island. Solid ground was only thirty meters away. Pitt looked at Maeve and broke into a crooked grin. "I'll bet you're a strong swimmer."

"You're talking to an Aussie," she said coolly, and then added, "Remind me sometime to show you my butterfly and backstroke medals."

"Al is played out. Can you tow him to shore?"

"The least I can do for the man who kept us out of the mouths of sharks."

Pitt gestured toward the nearest shoreline. There was no sandy beach, but the rock flattened out into a shelf as it met the water. "The way looks clear to climb on firm ground."

"And you?" She pulled back her hair with both hands, wringing away the water. "Do you want me to come back for you?"

He shook his head. "I saved myself for a more important effort."

"What effort?"

"Club Med hasn't built a resort here yet. We still need all the food supplies we have in hand. I'm going to tow what's left of the boat and the goodies therein."

Pitt helped roll Giordino over the half-sunken buoyancy tubes into the water, where he was grasped under the chin lifeguard-style by Maeve. She stroked strongly to shore, pulling Giordino behind her. Pitt watched for a moment until he saw Giordino grin shiftily and lift one hand in a 'bye wave. The nefarious little devil, Pitt thought. He's enjoying a free ride.

Splicing and knotting the rigging back into one long nylon line, Pitt attached it to the half-sunken boat and tied the other end around his waist. Then he swam toward shore. The deadweight was too much to simply drag behind him. He would stop in the water, heave on the line, gain a short distance and then repeat the process. The current helped by nudging the boat around in an arc toward shore. After traveling twenty meters, he finally felt firm ground beneath his feet. Now he could use the added leverage to pull the boat onto the rock shelf. He was wearily grateful when Maeve and Giordino both waded in and helped him tow it ashore.

"You recovered quickly," he said to Giordino.

"My recuperative powers are the marvel of doctors everywhere."

"I think he suckered me," said Maeve, feigning hostility.

"Nothing like the feel of terra firma to rejuvenate one's soul."

Pitt sat down and rested, too tired to dance for joy at being off the water. He slowly rose to his knees before standing up. For a few moments he had to hold onto the ground to steady himself. The motion of nearly two weeks bobbing about in a small boat had affected his balance. The world spun, and the entire island rocked as if it floated on the sea. Maeve immediately sat back down, while Giordino planted both feet firmly on the rock and clutched a nearby tree with thick foliage. After a few minutes, Pitt rose shakily to his feet and made a few faltering steps. Not having walked since the abduction in Wellington, he found his legs and ankles were unfeeling and stiff. Only after he'd staggered about twenty meters and back did his joints begin to loosen and operate as they should.

They hauled the boat farther onto the rocks and rested for a few hours before dining on their dried fish, washed down by rainwater they found standing in several concave impressions in the rock. Their energies restored, they began to survey the island. There was precious little to see. The whole island and its neighbor across the channel had the appearance of solid piles of lava rock that had exploded from the ocean floor, building over the eons until reaching the surface before being eroded into low mounds. If the water had been fully transparent and the islands viewed down to their base on the seafloor, they might have been compared to the great dramatic spires of Monument Valley, Arizona, rising like islands in a desert sea.

Giordino paced off the width from shore to shore and announced that their refuge was only 130 meters across. The highest point was a flattened plateau no more than 10 meters in height. The landmass curved into a tear shape that stretched north and south, with the windward arc facing the west. From rounded end to spiked point, the length was no more than a kilometer. Surrounded by natural seawalls that defied the swells, the island had the appearance of a fortress under constant attack.

A short distance away, they discovered the shattered remains of a boat that lay high and dry in a small inlet that was carved out of the rock by the sea, evidently driven there by large storm waves. She was a fair-sized sailboat, rolled over on her port side, half her hull and keel torn away from an obvious collision with rocks. She must have been a pretty boat at one time, Pitt imagined. Her upperworks had been painted light blue with orange undersides. Though the masts were gone, the deckhouse looked undamaged and intact. The three of them approached and studied it before peering inside.

"A grand, seaworthy little boat," observed Pitt, "about twelve meters, well built, with a teak hull."

"A Bermuda ketch," said Maeve, running her hands over the worn and sun-bleached teak planking. "A fellow student at the marine lab on Saint Croix had one. We used to island-hop with it. She sailed remarkably well."

Giordino stared at the paint and caulking on the hull appraisingly. "Been here twenty, maybe thirty years, judging by her condition."

"I hope whoever became marooned on this desolate spot was rescued," Maeve said quietly.

Pitt swept a hand around the barrenness. "Certainly no sane sailor would go out of his way to visit here."

Maeve's eyes brightened, and she snapped her fingers as if something deep in her memory had surfaced. "They're called the Tits."

Pitt and Giordino glanced at each other as if not believing what they had heard. "You did say 'tits'?" Giordino inquired.

"An old Australian tale about a pair of islands that look like a woman's breasts. They're said to disappear and reappear, like Brigadoon."

"I hate to be a debunker of Down Under myths," said Pitt facetiously, "but this rock pile hasn't gone anywhere for the last million years."

"They're not shaped like any mammary glands I've ever seen," muttered Giordino.

She gave both men a pouty look. "I only know what I heard, about a pair of legendary islands south of the Tasman Sea."

Hoisted by Giordino, Pitt climbed aboard the canted hull and crawled through the hatch into the deckhouse. "She's been stripped clean," he called out from the inside. "Everything that wasn't screwed down has been removed. Check the transom and see if she has a name.''

Maeve walked around to the stern and stared up at the faded letters that were barely readable. *"Dancing Dorothy.* Her name was *Dancing Dorothy.''*

Pitt climbed down from the yacht's cockpit. ''A search is in order to locate the supplies taken from the boat. The crew may have left behind articles we can put to use.''

Resuming their exploration, it took little more than half an hour to skirt the entire coast of the tear-shaped little island. Then they worked their way inland. They separated and strung out in a loose line to cover more territory. Maeve was the first to spot an axe half buried in the rotting trunk of a grotesquely shaped tree.

Giordino pulled it loose and held it up. ''This should come in handy.''

''Odd-looking tree,'' said Pitt, eyeing its trunk. ''I wonder what it's called.''

''Tasmanian myrtle,'' Maeve clarified. ''Actually, it's a species of false beech. They can grow as high as sixty meters, but there isn't enough sandy loam here to support their root system, so all the trees we see on the island look like they've been dwarfed.''

They continued to search around carefully. A few minutes later Pitt stumbled onto a small ravine that opened onto a flat ledge on the lee side of the island. Lodged in one side of a rock wall, he spied the head of a brass gaff for landing fish. A few meters beyond, they came to a jumbled stack of logs in the form of a hut, with a boat's mast standing beside it. The structure was about three meters wide by four meters long. The roof of logs intermixed with branches was undamaged by the elements. The unknown builder had raised a sound dwelling.

Outside the hut was a wealth of abandoned supplies and equipment. A battery and the corroded remains of a radio-telephone, a direction-finding set, a wireless receiver for obtaining weather bulletins and time signals for rating a chronometer, a pile of rusty food cans that had been opened and emptied, an intact teakwood dingy equipped with a small outboard motor and miscellaneous nautical hardware, dishes and eating utensils, a few pots and pans, a propane stove and other various and sundry items from the wrecked boat. Strewn around the stove, still discernible, were bones of fish.

"The former tenants left a messy campground," said Giordino, kneeling to examine a small gas-driven generator for charging the boat's batteries, which had operated the electronic navigational instruments and radio equipment scattered about the campsite.

"Maybe they're still in the hut," murmured Maeve.

Pitt smiled at her. "Why don't you go in and see?"

She shook her head. "Not me. Entering dark and creepy places is man's work."

Women are indeed enigmatic creatures, Pitt thought. After all the dangers Maeve had encountered in the past few weeks, she couldn't bring herself to walk into the hut. He bent under the low doorway and stepped inside.

40

After being exposed to bright light for days on end, Pitt's eyes took a minute or two to become accustomed to the interior darkness of the hut. Except for the shaft of sun through the doorway, the only illumination came from the light seeping through the cracks between the logs. The air was heavy and damp with the musty smell of dirt and rotted logs.

There were no ghosts or phantoms lurking in the shadows, but Pitt did find himself staring into the empty eye sockets of a skull attached to a skeleton.

It lay on its back in a berth salvaged from the sailboat. Pitt identified the remains as a male from the heavy brow above the eye sockets. The dead man had lost teeth. All but three were missing. But rather than having been knocked out of their sockets, they appeared to have fallen out.

A tattered pair of shorts covered the pelvis, and the bony feet still wore a pair of rubber-soled deck shoes. There was no flesh evident. The tiny creatures that crawled out of the dampness had left a clean set of bones. The only indication of the dead man's former appearance was a tuft of red hair that lay beneath the skull. The skeletal hands were crossed above the rib cage and clutched a leather log book.

A quick look around the interior of the hut showed that the proprietor had set up housekeeping in an efficient manner, utilizing the fixtures from his stranded boat. The sails from the *Dancing Dorothy* had been spread across the ceiling to keep out any wind and rain that penetrated the branches laced in the roof. A writing desk held British Admiralty charts, a stack of books on piloting, tide tables, navigation lights, radio signals and a nautical almanac. Nearby there was a standing shelf stuffed with brochures and books filled with technical instructions on how to operate the boat's electronic instruments and mechanical gear. A finely finished mahogany box containing a chronometer and a sextant sat on a small wooden table beside the bunk. Sitting beneath the table was a hand bearing compass and a steering compass that had been mounted on the sailboat. The steering helm was leaning against a small folding dining table, and a pair of binoculars was tied to a spoke.

Pitt leaned over the skeleton, gently removed the logbook and left the hut.

"What did you find?" asked Maeve with burning curiosity.

"Let me guess," said Giordino. "A humongous chest full of pirate treasure."

Pitt shook his head. "Not this trip. What I found was the man who sailed the *Dancing Dorothy* onto the rocks. He never made it off the island."

"He's dead?" queried Maeve.

"Since long before you were born."

Giordino stepped to the doorway and peered inside the hut at the remains. "I wonder how he came to be so far off the beaten track."

Pitt held up the logbook and opened it. "The answers should be in here."

Maeve stared at the pages. "Can you make out the writing after all this time?"

"Yes. The log is well preserved, and the hand wrote boldly." Pitt sat down on a rock and scanned several pages before looking up. "His name was Rodney York, and he was one of twelve yachtsmen entered in a solo nonstop race around the world, beginning in Portsmouth, England, and sponsored by a London newspaper. First prize was twenty thousand pounds. York departed Portsmouth on April the twenty-fourth, 1962.''

"Poor old guy has been lost for thirty-eight years," said Giordino solemnly.

"On his ninety-seventh day at sea, he was catching a few hours' sleep when the *Dancing Dorothy* struck"—Pitt paused to glance up at Maeve and smile—"what he calls the 'Miseries.' ''

"York must not have studied Australian folklore," said Giordino.

"He quite obviously made up the name," Maeve said righteously.

"According to his account," Pitt continued, "York made good time during his passage of the southern Indian Ocean after rounding the Cape of Good Hope. He then took advantage of the Roaring Forties to carry him on a direct course across the Pacific for South America and the Strait of Magellan. He figured he was leading the race when his generator gave out and he lost all contact with the outside world."

"That explains a lot of things," said Giordino, staring over Pitt's shoulder at the logbook. "Why he was sailing in this part of the sea and why he couldn't send position coordinates for a rescue party. I checked his generator when we came on site. The two-cycle engine that provides its power is in sad shape. York tried to repair it and failed. I'll give it a try, but I doubt if I can do any better."

Pitt shrugged. "So much for borrowing York's radio to call for help."

"What does he write after being marooned?" demanded Maeve.

"Robinson Crusoe, he was not. He lost most of his food supplies when the yacht struck the rocks and capsized. When the boat was later washed up on shore after the storm, he recovered some canned goods, but they were soon gone. He tried to fish, but caught barely enough to stay alive, even with whatever rock crabs he could find and five or six birds he managed to snare. Eventually, his body functions began to give out. York lasted on this ugly pimple in the ocean for a hundred and thirty-six days. His final entry reads: 'Can no longer stand or move about. Too weak to do anything but lie here and die. How I wish I could see another sunrise over Falmouth Bay in my native Cornwall. But it

392

is not to be. To whoever finds this log and the letters I've written separately to my wife and three daughters, please see they get them. I ask their forgiveness for the great mental suffering I know I must have caused them. My failure was not from fault so much as bad luck. My hand is too tired to write more. I pray I didn't give up too soon.' "

"He needn't have worried about being found soon after he died," said Giordino. "Hard to believe he lay here for decades without a curious crew from a passing ship or a scientific party coming ashore to set up some kind of weather data gathering instruments."

"The dangers of landing amid the breakers and the unfriendly rocks are enough to outweigh any curiosity, scientific or otherwise."

Tears rolled down Maeve's cheeks as she wept unashamedly. "His poor wife and children must have wondered all these years how he died."

"York's last land bearing was the beacon on the South East Cape of Tasmania." Pitt stepped back into the hut and reappeared a minute later with an Admiralty chart showing the South Tasman Sea. He laid it flat on the ground and studied it for a few moments before he looked up. "I see why York called these rocks the Miseries," said Pitt. "That's how they're labeled on the Admiralty chart."

"How far off were your reckonings?" asked Giordino.

Pitt produced a pair of dividers he'd taken from the desk inside and measured off the approximate position he had calculated with his cross-staff. "I put us roughly 120 kilometers too far to the southwest."

"Not half bad, considering you didn't have an exact fix on the spot where Dorsett threw us off his yacht."

"Yes," Pitt admitted modestly, "I can live with that."

"Where exactly are we?" asked Maeve, now down on her hands and knees, peering at the chart.

Pitt tapped his finger on a tiny black dot in the middle of a sea of blue. "There, that little speck approximately 965 kilometers southwest of Invercargill, New Zealand."

"It seems so near when you look at it on a map," said Maeve wistfully.

Giordino pulled off his wristwatch and rubbed the lens clean against his shirt. "Not near enough when you think that no one bothered to drop in on poor Rodney for almost forty years."

"Look on the bright side," said Pitt with an infectious grin. "Pretend you've pumped thirty-eight dollars in quarters into a slot machine in Las Vegas without a win. The law of averages is bound to catch up in the next two quarters."

"A bad analogy," said Giordino, the perennial killjoy.

"How so?"

Giordino looked pensively inside the hut. "Because there is no way we can come up with two quarters."

41

"Nine days and counting," declared Sandecker, gazing at the unshaven men and weary women seated around the table in his hideaway conference room. What was a few days previously a neat and immaculate gathering place for the admiral's closest staff members, now resembled a war room under siege. Photos, nautical charts and hastily drawn illustrations were taped randomly to the teak-paneled walls; the turquoise carpet was littered with scraps of paper and the shipwreck conference table cluttered with coffee cups, notepads scribbled with calculations, a battery of telephones and an ashtray heaped with Sandecker's cigar butts. He was the only one who smoked, and the air-conditioning was turned to the maximum setting to draw off the stench.

"Time is against us," said Dr. Sanford Adgate Ames. "It is physically impossible to construct a reflector unit and deploy it before the deadline."

The sound expert and his student staff in Arizona intermingled with Sandecker's NUMA people in Washington as if they were sitting at the same table in the same room. The reverse was also true. Sandecker's experts appeared to be sitting amid the student staff in Ames' work quarters. Through the technology of video holography, their voices and images were transmitted across the country by photonics, the transference of sound and light by fiber optics. By combining photonics with computer wizardry, time and space limitations disappeared.

"A valid deduction," Sandecker agreed. "Unless we can utilize an existing reflector."

Ames removed his blue-tinted bifocals and held them up to the light as he inspected the lenses for specks. Satisfied they were clean, he remounted them on his nose. "According to my calculations, we're going to require a parabolic reflector the size of a baseball diamond or larger, with an air gap between the surfaces to reflect the sound energy. I can't imagine who you can find to manufacture one in the short time before the time window closes."

Sandecker looked across the table at a tired Rudi Gunn, who stared back through the thick lenses of his glasses, which magnified eyes reddened from lack of sleep. "Any ideas, Rudi?"

"I've run through every logical possibility," Gunn answered. "Dr. Ames is right, it is out of the question to consider fabricating a reflector in time. Our only prospect is to find an existing one and transport it to Hawaii."

"You'll have to break it down, ship it in pieces and then put it back together," said Hiram Yaeger, turning from a laptop computer that was linked to his data library on the tenth floor. "No known aircraft can carry something of such a large surface area through the air in one piece."

"If one is shipped from somewhere within the United States, supposing it is found," insisted Ames, "it would have to go by boat."

"But what kind of ship is large enough to hold a thing that size?" asked Gunn of no one in particular.

"An oil supertanker or an aircraft carrier," said Sandecker quietly, as if to himself.

Gunn picked up on the statement immediately. "An aircraft carrier's flight deck is more than large enough to carry and deploy a reflector shield the size Doc Ames has proposed."

"The speed of our latest nuclear carriers is still classified, but Pentagon leaks indicate they can cut the water at fifty knots. Ample time to make the crossing between San Francisco and Honolulu before the deadline."

"Seventy-two hours," said Gunn, "from departure to deployment at the site."

Sandecker stared at a desk calendar with the previous dates crossed out. "That leaves exactly five days to find a reflector, get it to San Francisco and deploy it at the convergence zone."

"A tight schedule, even if you had a reflector in hand," said Ames steadily.

"How deep does it have to be rigged?" Yaeger asked Ames' image.

Almost as if she were cued, a pretty woman in her mid-twenties handed Ames a pocket calculator. He punched a few numbers, rechecked his answer and then looked up. "Allowing for the overlapping convergence zones to meet and surface, you should place the center of the reflector at a depth of 170 meters."

"Current is our number one problem," said Gunn. "It'll prove a nightmare trying to keep the reflector in place long enough to bounce the sound waves."

"Put our best engineers on the problem," ordered Sandecker. "They'll have to design some kind of rigging system to keep the reflector stable."

"How can we be sure that by refocusing the converging sound waves we can return them on a direct channel back to the source on Gladiator Island?" Yaeger asked Ames.

Ames impassively twisted the ends of the mustache that extended beyond his beard. "If the factors that propagated the original sound wave, such as salinity, water temperature and the sound speed, remain constant, the reflected energy should return to the source along its original path."

Sandecker turned to Yaeger. "How many people are on Gladiator Island?"

Yaeger consulted his computer. "The intelligence reports from satellite photos suggest a population of around 650 people, mostly miners."

"Slave labor imported from China," muttered Gunn.

"If not kill, won't we injure every living thing on the island?" Sandecker asked Ames.

Another of Ames' students unhesitantly passed a sheet of paper into the acoustics expert's hands. He scanned it for a moment before looking up. "If our analysis is close to the mark, the overlapping convergence zones from the four separated mining operations scattered throughout the Pacific will drop to an energy factor of twenty-eight percent when they strike Gladiator Island, not enough to maim or cause harm to human or animal.''

"Can you estimate the physical reaction?''

"Headaches and vertigo along with mild nausea should be the only discomforts.''

"A moot point if we can't set a reflector on site before the convergence,'' Gunn said, staring at a chart on the wall.

Sandecker drummed his fingers on the table thoughtfully. "Which puts us back in the starter's gate before the race.''

A woman in her forties, fashionably dressed in a conservative blue suit, stared contemplatively at one of the admiral's paintings, the one illustrating the famous World War II aircraft carrier *Enterprise* during the battle for Midway. Her name was Molly Faraday, and she was a former analyst with the National Security Agency who had jumped over to NUMA at Sandecker's urging, to be his intelligence agency coordinator. With soft toffee-colored hair and brown eyes, Molly was all class. Her gaze swiveled from the painting to Sandecker and fixed him with a somber look.

"I think I might have the solution to our problems,'' she said in a quiet monotone.

The admiral nodded. "You have the floor, Molly.''

"As of yesterday,'' she lectured, "the Navy's aircraft carrier *Roosevelt* was docked at Pearl Harbor, taking on supplies and making repairs to one of her flight-deck elevators before joining the Tenth Fleet off Indonesia.''

Gunn looked at her curiously. "You know that for certain?''

Molly smiled sweetly. "I keep my toes dipped in the offices of the Joint Chiefs.''

"I know what you're thinking,'' said Sandecker. "But without a reflector, I fail to see how a carrier at Pearl Harbor can solve our dilemma.''

"The carrier is a side bonus,'' explained Molly. "My primary thought was a recollection of an assignment at a satellite information collection center on the Hawaiian island of Lanai.''

"I didn't know Lanai had a satellite facility,'' said Yaeger. "My wife and I honeymooned on Lanai and drove all over the island without seeing a satellite downlink facility.''

"The buildings and parabolic reflector are inside the extinct Palawai volcano. Neither the natives, who always wondered what was going on in there, nor the tourists could ever get close enough to check it out.''

"Besides tuning in on passing satellites," asked Ames, "what was its purpose?"

"Passing *Soviet* satellites," Molly corrected him. "Fortunately, the former Soviet military chiefs had a fetish for guiding their spy satellites over the military bases on the Hawaiian Islands after they orbited the U.S. mainland. Our job was to penetrate their transponders with powerful microwave signals and foul up their intelligence photos. From what the CIA was able to gather, the Russians never did figure out why their satellite reconnaissance photos always came back blurred and out of focus. About the time the Communist government disintegrated, newer space communications facilities made the Palawai facility redundant. Because of its immense size, the antenna was later utilized to transmit and receive signals from deep-space probes. Now I understand that its dated technology has made the facility's equipment obsolete, and the site, though still guarded, is pretty much abandoned."

Yaeger jumped right to the heart of the matter. "How large is the parabolic reflector?"

Molly buried her head in her hands a moment before looking up. "I seem to recall that it was eighty meters in diameter."

"More than the surface area we require," said Ames.

"Do you think the NSA will let us borrow it?" asked Sandecker.

"They'd probably pay *you* to carry it away."

"You'll have to dismantle it and airlift the pieces to Pearl Harbor," said Ames, "providing you can borrow the carrier *Roosevelt* to reassemble and lower it on the convergence area."

Sandecker looked squarely at Molly. "I'll use my powers of persuasion with the Navy Department if you'll work on the National Security Agency end."

"I'll get on it immediately," Molly assured him.

A balding man with rimless glasses, sitting near the end of the table, raised a hand.

Sandecker nodded at him and smiled. "You've been pretty quiet, Charlie. Something must be stirring around in your brain."

Dr. Charlie Bakewell, NUMA's chief undersea geologist, removed a wad of gum from his mouth and neatly wrapped it in paper before dropping it in a wastebasket. He nodded at the image of Dr. Ames in the holograph. "As I understand this thing, Dr. Ames, the sound energy alone can't destroy human tissue, but enhanced by the resonance coming from the rock chamber which is under assault by the acoustic mining equipment, its frequency is reduced so that it can propagate over vast distances. When it overlaps in a single ocean region, the sound is intense enough to damage human tissue."

"You're essentially correct," admitted Ames.

"So if you reflect the overlapping convergence zones back through the ocean, won't some energy reflect from Gladiator Island?"

Ames nodded. "Quite true. As long as the energy force strikes the submerged level of the island without surfacing and is scattered in diverse directions, any prospect of carnage is dramatically decreased."

"It's the moment of impact against the island that concerns me," said Bakewell conversationally. "I've reviewed the geological surveys on Gladiator Island by geologists hired by Dorsett Consolidated Mining nearly fifty years ago. The volcanos on the opposite ends of the island are not extinct but dormant. They have been dormant for less than seven hundred years. No human was present during the last eruption, but scientific analysis of the lava rock dates it some time in the middle of the twelfth century. The ensuing years have been followed by alternating periods of passivity and minor seismic disturbances."

"What is your point, Charlie?" asked Sandecker.

"My point, Admiral, is that if a catastrophic force of acoustical energy slams into the base of Gladiator Island it just might set off a seismic disaster."

"An eruption?" asked Gunn.

Bakewell merely nodded.

"What in your estimation are the odds of this happening?" inquired Sandecker.

"There is no way of absolutely predicting any level of seismic or volcanic activity, but I know a qualified vulcanologist who will give you a bet of one in five."

"One chance of eruption out of five," Ames said, his holographic image gazing at Sandecker. "I am afraid, Admiral, that Dr. Bakewell's theory puts our project into the category of unacceptable risk."

Sandecker did not hesitate a second with his reply. "Sorry, Dr. Ames, but the lives of a million or more residents of Honolulu, along with tens of thousands of tourists and military personnel stationed at bases around Oahu, take priority over 650 miners."

"Can't we warn Dorsett Consolidated management to evacuate the island?" said Yaeger.

"We have to try," Sandecker said firmly. "But knowing Arthur Dorsett, he'll simply shrug off any warning off as a hollow threat."

"Suppose the acoustic energy is deflected elsewhere?" suggested Bakewell.

Ames looked doubtful. "Once the intensity deviates from its original path, you run the risk of it retaining its full energy and striking Yokohama, Shanghai, Manila, Sydney or Auckland, or some other heavily populated coastal city."

There was a brief silence as everyone in the room turned to face Sandecker, including Ames, who was sitting at a desk thirty-two hundred kilometers to the west. Abstractedly, Sandecker toyed with an unlit cigar. What most did not know was that his mind wasn't on the possible destruction of Gladiator Island. His mind was saddened and angered at the same time over the abandonment of his best friends in a raging sea by Arthur Dorsett. In the end, hate won out over any humane consideration.

He stared at the image of Sanford Ames. "Compute your calculations, Doc, for aiming the reflector at Gladiator Island. If we don't stop Dorsett Consolidated, and stop them in the shortest time possible, no one else will."

42

Arthur Dorsett's private elevator in the jewelry trade center rose noiselessly. The only evidence of ascent was the progression of blinking floor levels over the doors. When the car eased to a gentle stop at the penthouse suite, Gabe Strouser stepped out into an entryway that led to the open courtyard where Dorsett stood waiting to greet him.

Strouser did not relish his meeting with the diamond maverick. They had known each other since they were children. The close association between the Strousers and the Dorsetts had lasted well over a century, until Arthur cut off any future dealings with Strouser & Sons. The break was not amicable. Dorsett coldly ordered his attorneys to inform Gabe Strouser that his family's services were no longer required. The axe fell, not with a personal confrontation but over the telephone. It was an insult that badly stung Strouser, and he never forgave Dorsett.

To save his family's venerable old firm, Strouser had switched his allegiance to the cartel in South Africa, eventually moving his company headquarters from Sydney to New York. In time he rose to become a respected director of the board. Because the cartel was barred from doing business in the United States due to national antitrust laws, they operated behind the coattails of the respected diamond merchants of Strouser & Sons, who acted as their American arm.

He would not be here now if the other board directors had not panicked at the rumors of Dorsett Consolidated Mining's threat to bury the market in an avalanche of stones at sharply discounted prices. They had to act decisively and fast if they were to avert a disaster. A deeply scrupulous man, Strouser was the only cartel member the board of directors could trust to persuade Dorsett not to shatter the established price levels of the market.

Arthur Dorsett stepped forward and shook Strouser's hand vigorously. "It's been a long time, Gabe, too long."

"Thank you for seeing me, Arthur." Strouser's tone was patronizing, but with an indelible tinge of aversion. "As I recall, your attorneys ordered me never to contact you again."

Dorsett shrugged indifferently. "Water under the bridge. Let's forget it happened and talk old times over lunch." He motioned to a table, set under an arbor shielded by bulletproof glass, with a magnificent view of Sydney's harbor.

The complete opposite of the crude, earthy mining tycoon, Strouser was a strikingly attractive man in his early sixties. With a thick head of well-groomed silver hair, a narrow face with high cheekbones and finely shaped nose that would be the envy of most Hollywood movie actors, he was trim and athletically built with evenly tanned skin. Several centimeters shorter than the hulking Dorsett, he had dazzling white teeth and a friendly mouth. He gazed at Dorsett through the blue-green eyes of a cat ready to spring away from the attack of a neighbor's dog.

His suit was beautifully cut of the finest wool, conservative but with a few subtle touches that made him look fashionably up-to-date. The tie was expensive silk, the shoes custom-made Italian and polished just short of a mirror shine. His cuff links, contrary to what people expected, were not diamonds but made from opals.

He was mildly surprised at the friendly reception. Dorsett seemed to be playing a character in a bad play. Strouser had expected an uncomfortable confrontation. He certainly had not anticipated being indulged. He no sooner sat down than Dorsett motioned to a waiter, who lifted a bottle of champagne from a sterling-silver ice bucket and poured Strouser's glass. He noted with some amusement that Dorsett simply drank from a bottle of Castlemaine beer.

"When the cartel's high muck-a-mucks said they were sending a representative to Australia for talks," said Dorsett, "it never occurred to me they would send you."

"Because of our former long-standing association, the directors thought I could read your mind. So they asked me to inquire about a rumor circulating within the trade that you are about to sell stones cheaply in an effort to corner the market. Not industrial-grade diamonds, mind you, but quality gem stones."

"Where did you hear that?"

"You head an empire of thousands, Arthur. Leaks from disgruntled employees are a way of life."

"I'll have my security people launch an investigation. I don't cotton to traitors, not on my payroll."

"If what we hear has substance, the diamond market is facing a profound crisis," explained Strouser. "My mission is make you a substantial offer to keep your stones out of circulation."

"There is no scarcity of diamonds, Gabe, there never was. You know you can't buy me. A dozen cartels couldn't keep my stones out of circulation."

"You've been foolish for operating outside the Central Selling Organization, Arthur. You've lost millions by not cooperating."

"A long-term investment is about to pay enormous dividends," Dorsett said irrefutably.

"Then it's true?" Strouser asked casually. "You've been stockpiling for the day when you could turn a fast profit."

Dorsett looked at him and smiled, showing his yellowed teeth. "Of course it's true. All except for the part about a fast profit."

"I'll give you credit, Arthur, you're candid."

"I have nothing to hide, not now."

"You cannot continue to go your own way as if the network didn't exist. Everybody loses."

"Easy for you and your pals at the cartel to say when you hold monopolistic control over world diamond production."

"Why exploit the market on a whim?" said Strouser. "Why systematically cut each other's throat? Why disrupt a stable and prosperous industry?"

Dorsett held up a hand to interrupt. He nodded to the waiter, who served a lobster salad from a cart. Then he stared at Strouser steadily.

"I am not operating on a whim. I have over a hundred metric tons of diamonds stored in warehouses around the world, with another ten tons ready to ship from my mines as we speak. A few days from now, when fifty percent of them are cut and faceted, I intend to sell them through the House of Dorsett retail stores at ten dollars a carat, on average. The rough stones, I'll sell to dealers at fifty cents a carat. When I'm finished, the market will tumble and diamonds will lose their luster as a luxury and an investment."

Strouser was stunned. His earlier impression was that Dorsett's marketing strategy was for a temporary dip in prices to make a quick profit. Now he saw the enormity of the grand design. "You'll impoverish thousands of retailers and wholesalers, yourself included. What can you possibly gain by putting a rope around your neck and kicking over the stool?"

Dorsett ignored his salad, swilled his beer and gestured for another before continuing. "I'm sitting where the cartel has sat for a hundred years. They control eighty percent of the world's diamond market. I control eighty percent of the world's colored gemstone market."

Strouser felt as if he were teetering on a trapeze. "I had no idea you owned so many colored gemstone mines."

"Neither does anyone else. You're the first outside my family to know. It was a long and tedious process, involving dozens of interlocking corporations. I bought into every one of the major colored stone producing mines in the world. After I orchestrate the demise of diamond values, I plan to move colored stones into the limelight at discounted prices, thereby spiraling the demand. Then I slowly raise the retail price, take the profits and expand."

"You always were a snatch and trash artist, Arthur. But even you can't destroy what took a century to build."

"Unlike the cartel, I don't plan to suppress competition at the retail level. My stores will compete fairly."

"You are making a fight nobody can win. Before you can collapse the diamond market, the cartel will break you. We'll use every international financial and political maneuver ever devised to stop you in your tracks."

"You're blowin' in the wind, mate," Dorsett came back heatedly. "Gone are the days when buyers have to grovel in your high-and-mighty selling offices in London and Johannesburg. Gone are the days of licking boots to be a registered buyer who has to take what you offer him. No more sneaking through back streets to bypass your well-oiled machinery to purchase uncut stones. No more will international police and your hired security organizations fight sham battles with people you label criminals because they engage in your artificially created myth of smuggling and selling on what your little playmates have concocted as the great and terrible illicit diamond market. No more restrictions to create an enormous demand. You've brainwashed governments into passing laws that confine diamond traffic to your channels and your channels only. Laws that forbid a man or woman from legitimately selling a rough stone they found in their own backyard. Now, at long last, the illusion of diamonds as a valued object is only days away from being pronounced dead."

"You cannot outspend us," said Strouser, fighting to remain calm. "We think nothing of spending hundreds of millions to advertise and promote the romance of diamonds."

"Don't you think I've considered that and planned for it?" Dorsett laughed. "I'll match your advertising campaign budget with my own, pushing the chameleon quality of colored gemstones. You'll promote the sale of a single diamond for an engagement ring, while I'll promote the spectrum, a world of fashion touched by colored jewelry. My campaign is based around the theme 'Color her with love.' But that's only the half of it, Gabe. I also plan to educate the great unwashed public about the true rarity of colored gemstones versus the cheap, overabundant supply of diamonds. The end result is that I will significantly shift the buyer's attitude away from diamonds."

Strouser rose to his feet and threw his napkin on the table. "You're a menace that will destroy thousands of people and their livelihood," he said uncompromisingly. "You must be prevented from disrupting the market."

"Don't be a fool," said Dorsett, showing his teeth. "Climb aboard. Switch your allegiance from diamonds to colored stones. Get smart, Gabe. Color is the wave of the future in the jewelry market."

Strouser fought to control the anger that was seething to the surface. "My family have been diamond merchants for ten generations. I live and breathe diamonds. I will not be the one to turn my back on tradition. You have dirty hands, Arthur, even if they are well manicured. I will personally fight you up and down the line until you are no longer a factor in the market."

"Any fight comes too late," Dorsett said coldly. "Once colored gemstones take over the market, the diamond craze will disappear overnight."

"Not if I can help it."

"What do you intend to do when you leave here?"

"Alert the board of directors of what you have up your sleeve so they can plan an immediate course of action to knock the wind out of your scheme before it can be realized. It's not too late to stop you."

Dorsett remained sitting and looked up at Strouser. "I don't think so."

Strouser missed his meaning and turned to leave. "Since you won't listen to reason, I have nothing more to say. Good day to you, Arthur."

"Before you leave, Gabe, I have a present for you."

"I want nothing from you!" Strouser snapped angrily.

"This, you will appreciate." Dorsett laughed uncharitably. "On second thought, perhaps you won't." He motioned with one hand. "Now, Boudicca, now."

In one swift motion, the big woman suddenly appeared behind Strouser and pinned his arms to his sides. The diamond merchant instinctively struggled for a minute, then relaxed, staring dazedly at Dorsett.

"What is the meaning of this? I demand that you unhand me."

Dorsett looked at Strouser and spread his hands disarmingly. "You neglected to eat your lunch, Gabe. I can't allow you to leave hungry. You might get the idea that I'm inhospitable."

"You're crazy if you think you can intimidate me."

"I'm not going to intimidate you," Dorsett said with sadistic amusement. "I'm going to feed you."

Strouser looked lost. He shook his head in disgust and began an unequal struggle to break free of Boudicca's embrace.

At a nod of Dorsett's head, Boudicca manhandled Strouser back to the table, grasped him under the chin with one hand and bent his head backward, face up. Then Dorsett produced a large plastic funnel and stuffed the lower end between Strouser's lips and teeth. The expression in the diamond merchant's eyes transformed from rage to shock to bulging terror. His muffled cries were ignored as Boudicca tightened her hold around him.

"Ready, Daddy," she said, leering in cruel anticipation.

"Since you live and breathe diamonds, my old friend, you can eat them too," said Dorsett as he lifted a small canister shaped like a teapot that had been sitting on the table and began pouring a stream of flawless D-grade, one-carat diamonds down Strouser's throat while using one hand to pinch the nostrils of his victim shut. Strouser thrashed wildly, his legs kicking in the air, but his arms were locked as tightly as if he were trapped by a python.

Out of sheer terror, Strouser tried desperately to swallow the stones, but there were too many. Soon his throat could hold no more and his body's convulsions became less frantic as he choked for air and quickly suffocated.

The glaze of death froze his open eyes into an unseeing stare as the glittering stones slowly spilled from the corners of his mouth, rattled across the table and fell to the floor.

43

Two days off the sea and everyone felt as if raised from the dead. York's campsite was tidied up and every article and object inventoried. Maeve refused to go in the hut even after they buried Rodney York in a small ravine that was partially filled with sand. A tentlike shelter was built from the old Dacron sails found inside the hut, and they settled down to the day-to-day routine of existence.

To Giordino, the greatest prize was a toolbox. He immediately went to work on the radio and the generator but finally gave up in frustration after nearly six hours of futile labor.

"Too many parts broken or too badly corroded to repair. After sitting all these years, the batteries are deader than fossilized dinosaur dung. And without a generator to charge them, the radio-telephone, direction-finding set and wireless receiver are useless."

"Can replacements be fabricated with what we've got lying about?" asked Pitt.

Giordino shook his head. "General Electric's chief engineer couldn't fix that generator, and even if he could, the engine to turn it over is completely shot. There's a crack in the crankcase. York must not have seen it and run the engine after the oil leaked out, burning the bearings and freezing the pistons. It would take an automotive machine shop to put it back in running order.''

Pitt's first project as resident handyman was to find three small blocks of wood that were straight grained. These he split from a side board on the berth that had served as Rodney York's final resting place. Next, he made a template of everyone's forehead just above the eyebrows from the stiff paper jackets of novels he found on York's bookshelf. He marked the template lines on the edge of the wood blocks and trimmed accordingly, cutting out an arched slot for the nose. Holding the blocks tightly between his knees he gouged and smoothed hollows on the inner curl of the wood. Then he removed the excess outer wood and cut two horizontal slits in the hollowed walls. With oil from a can sitting beside the outboard engine, he stained the thinly curled finished product before cutting two holes in the ends and attaching nylon cord.

''There you are, ladies and gentlemen,'' he said, passing them out. ''Colonel Thadeus Pitt's spectacular sun goggles, from a secret design revealed on the lips of a dying Eskimo just before he rode off across the Arctic Ocean on the back of a polar bear.''

Maeve adjusted hers over her eyes and tied the cord behind her head. ''How clever, they really shut out sun.''

''Damned clever, those Inuits,'' said Giordino peering through the eye slits. ''Can you make the slits a tad wider? I feel like I'm staring through a crack under a door.''

Pitt smiled and handed Giordino his Swiss army knife. ''You may customize your goggles to your personal taste.''

''Speaking of taste,'' Maeve announced beside a small fire she had started with matches from Pitt's survival kit. ''Come and get it. Tonight's menu is grilled mackerel with cockles I found buried in sand pockets below the tide line.''

''Just when my stomach got used to eating fish raw,'' joked Giordino.

Maeve dished the steaming fish and cockles onto York's old plates. ''Tomorrow night's fare, if there is a marksman in our little group, will be something on the wing.''

''You want us to shoot defenseless little birds?'' asked Giordino in mock horror.

''I counted at least twenty frigate birds, sitting on the rocks,'' she said, pointing to the north shore. "If you build a blind, they'll walk by close enough for you to hit them with your little popgun."

"Roasted bird sounds good to my shrinking stomach. I'll bring back tomorrow night's supper or you can hang me by the thumbs," Pitt promised.

"Can you pull any other tricks out of your hat besides the goggles?" asked Maeve whimsically.

Pitt lay back on the sand with his hands behind his head. "I'm glad you brought that up. After a strenuous afternoon of intense thought, I've arrived at the conclusion that we should move on to a more receptive climate."

Maeve gave him a look of utter skepticism. "Move on?" She glanced at Giordino for moral support, but he gave her a you-never-learn look and continued nibbling on his mackerel. "We have two badly damaged boats that can't sail across a swimming pool. Just what do you suggest we use for our all-expenses-paid cruise to nowhere?"

"Elementary, my dear Fletcher," he said expansively. "We build a third boat."

"Build a boat," she said, her voice on the edge of laughter.

Conversely, Giordino's expression was intense and serious. "You think there's a Chinaman's chance of repairing York's sail-boat?"

"No. The hull is damaged beyond any possibility of repairing with our limited resources. York was an experienced sailor, and he obviously didn't see any way it could be refloated. But we can, however, utilize the upper deck."

"Why not make the best of it right here?" Maeve argued. "We're more resourceful than poor Rodney. Our survival skills are far greater than his. We can catch enough fish and fowl to keep us going until a ship comes by."

"That's the problem," said Pitt. "We *can't* survive on what we can catch alone. If Rodney's missing teeth are any indication, he died from scurvy. A dietary lack of vitamin C and a dozen other nutrients I can think of weakened him until he could no longer function. At that stage of physical erosion, death was just around the corner. If a ship does eventually arrive and put a landing party on shore, they'll find four skeletons instead of one. I strongly believe it is in our best interests to make every effort to push on while we're still physically capable."

"Dirk is right," Giordino said to Maeve. "Our only chance at seeing city lights again is to leave the island."

"Build a boat?" demanded Maeve. "With what materials?"

She stood, firmly, gracefully, her arms and legs slim and tan, the flesh taut and young, her head cocked like a wary lynx. Pitt was as captivated as he had been when they were together on board the *Ice Hunter*.

"A flotation tube from our boat here, the upper works from York's boat there, throw in a few logs, and pretty soon you've got a vessel fit for an ocean voyage."

"This I have to see," said Maeve.

"As you wish," Pitt replied airily. He began drawing a diagram in the sand. "The idea is to connect our boat's buoyancy tubes under the deck cabin from York's boat. Then we fashion a pair of beech tree trunks into outriggers for stability and we've got ourselves a trimaran."

"Looks practical to me," Giordino agreed.

"We need over 130 square meters of sail," Pitt continued. "We have a mast and a rudder."

Giordino pointed over to the tent. "York's old Dacron sails are brittle and rotten with forty years of mildew. The first stiff breeze will crack and blow them into shreds."

"I've considered that," said Pitt. "The Polynesian mariners wove sails from palm fronds. I see no reason why we can't weave fully leafed branches from the beech trees to accomplish the same purpose. And we have plenty of extra rigging from the sailboat for shrouds and to lash outriggers to the center hull."

"How long will it take us to build your trimaran?" asked Maeve, doubt becoming replaced by growing interest.

"I figure we can knock together a vessel and shove off in three days if we put in long hours."

"That soon?"

"The construction is not complicated, and thanks to Rodney York, we have the tools to complete the job."

"Do we continue sailing east or head northeast for Invercargill?" asked Giordino.

Pitt shook his head. "Neither. With Rodney's navigational instruments and Admiralty charts, I see no reason why I can't lay a reasonably accurate course for Gladiator Island."

Maeve looked at him as if he had turned mad, her hands hanging limply at her sides. "That," she said in bewilderment, "is the craziest notion you've come up with yet."

"May be," he said, his eyes set and fixed. "But I think it only appropriate that we finish what we set out to do . . . rescue your boys."

"Sounds good to me," Giordino put in without hesitation. "I'd like a rematch with King Kong, or whatever your sister calls herself when she isn't crushing car bodies at a salvage yard."

"I'm indebted to you enough as it is. But—"

"No buts," said Pitt. "As far as we're concerned it's a done deal. We build our hermaphrodite boat, sail it to Gladiator Island, snatch your boys and escape to the nearest port of safety."

"Escape to safety! Can't you *understand?*" Her voice was imploring, almost despairing. "Ninety percent of the island is surrounded by vertical cliffs and precipices impossible to climb. The only landing area is the beach circling the lagoon, and it's heavily guarded. No one can cross through the reef without being shot. My father has built security defenses a well-armed assault force couldn't penetrate. If you attempt it, you will surely die."

"Nothing to be alarmed about," Pitt said subtly. "Al and I flit on and off islands with the same finesse as we do in and out of ladies' bedrooms. It's all in selecting the right time and spot."

"That and a lot of wrist action," Giordino added.

"Father's patrol boats will spot you long before you can enter the lagoon."

Pitt shrugged. "Not to worry. I have a homespun remedy for dodging nasty old patrol boats that never fails."

"And dare I ask what it is?"

"Simple. We drop in where they least expect us."

"Both your brains were boiled by the sun." She shook her head in defeat. "Do you expect Daddy to ask us in for tea?" Maeve had one remorseful moment of guilt. She saw clearly that she was responsible for the terrible dangers and torment inflicted on these two incredible men who were willing to give up their lives for her twin sons, Michael and Sean. She felt a wave of despondency sweep over her that quickly turned to resignation. She came over and knelt between Pitt and Giordino, placing an arm around each of their necks. "Thank you," she murmured softly. "How could I be so lucky as to find men as wonderful as you?"

"We make a habit of helping maidens in distress." Giordino saw the tears welling in her eyes and turned away, genuinely embarrassed.

Pitt kissed Maeve on the forehead. "It's not as impossible as it sounds. Trust me."

"If only I had met you what seems like a hundred years ago," she whispered with a catch in her voice. She looked as if she were about to say more, rose to her feet and quickly walked away to be by herself.

Giordino stared at Pitt curiously. "Can I ask you something?"

"Anything."

"Do you mind sharing how we're going to get on and off the island once we arrive offshore?"

"We get on with a kite and a grappling hook I found among York's gear."

"And off again?" Giordino prompted, totally confused but unwilling to pursue the subject.

Pitt threw a dried beech log on the fire and watched the sparks swirl upward. "That," he said, as relaxed as a boy waiting for his bobber to sink at a fishing hole, "that part of the plan I'll worry about when the time comes."

44

Their vessel to escape the island was built on a flat section of rock in a small valley protected from the breeze, thirty meters from the water. They laid out rail-like ways of beech logs to slide their weird creation into the relatively calm waters between the two islands. The demands were not cruel or exacting. They were in better condition than when they arrived and found themselves able to work through the nights, when the atmosphere was coldest, and rest for a few hours during the heat of the day. For the most part, construction went smoothly without major setbacks. The closer they got to completion, the more their fatigue fell away.

Maeve threw herself into weaving two sails from the leafy branches. For simplicity, Pitt had decided to step the mast York had salvaged from his ketch, to take a spanker on the mizzen and a square sail on the mainmast. Maeve wove the larger sail for the mainmast first. The first few hours were spent experimenting, but by late afternoon she began to get the hang of it and could weave a square meter in thirty minutes. By the third day, she was down to twenty minutes. Her matting was so strong and tight, Pitt asked her to make a third sail, a triangular jib to set forward of the mainmast.

Together, Pitt and Giordino unbolted and lifted the ketch's upper deckhouse and mounted it over the forward part of the steering cockpit. This abbreviated section of the ketch was then lashed on top of the buoyancy tubes from their little boat, which now served as the center hull. The next chore was to step the tall aluminum masts, which were reduced in height to compensate for the shorter hull and lack of a deep keel. Since no chain plates could be attached to the neoprene buoyancy tubes, the shrouds and stays to support the masts were slung under the hull and joined at a pair of turnbuckles. When finished, the hybrid craft had the appearance of a sailboat perched on a hovercraft.

The following day, Pitt reset the ketch's rudder to ride higher in the water, rigging it to a long tiller, a more efficient system for steering a trimaran. Once the rudder was firmly in place and swung to his satisfaction, he attacked the forty-year-old outboard engine, cleaning the carburetor and fuel lines before overhauling the magneto.

Giordino went to work on the outriggers. He chopped down and trimmed two sturdy beech trees whose trunks curved near their tops. Next he placed the logs alongside the hull and extended them out with the curved sections facing forward like a pair of skis. The outriggers were then lashed to cross-member logs that ran laterally across the hull near the bow and just aft of the cockpit and were braced fore and aft. Giordino was quite pleased with himself, after he put a shoulder against the outriggers and heaved mightily, proclaiming them solid and rigid with no indication of give.

As they sat around the fire at dawn, warding off the early morning chill of the southern latitudes, Pitt pored over York's navigational and plotting charts. At noon he took sights of the sun with the sextant, and later, at night, he shot several stars. Then with the aid of the nautical almanac and the "Short Method" tables that cut trigonometry calculations to bare bones, he practiced fixing his position until his figures accurately matched the known latitude and longitude of the Misery Islands on the chart.

"Think you can hit Gladiator Island on the nose?" Maeve asked him over dinner on the second evening before the launch.

"If not the nose, then the chin," Pitt said cheerfully. "Which reminds me, I'll need a detailed map of the island."

"How detailed?"

"Every building, every path and road, and I'd like it all to scale."

"I'll draw you a map from memory as accurately as I can," Maeve promised.

Giordino chewed on a small thigh from a frigate bird Pitt had managed to shoot with his miniature automatic pistol. "What do you make the distance?"

"Precisely 478 kilometers as the crow flies."

"Then it's closer than Invercargill."

"That's the beauty of it."

"How many days will it take to arrive?" asked Maeve.

"Impossible to say," answered Pitt. "The first leg of the voyage will be the hardest, tacking to windward until we pick up friendly currents and easterly breezes blowing off New Zealand. With no keel to carve the water and prevent them being blown sideways, trimarans are notoriously inept when it comes to sailing into the wind. The real challenge will come after we set off. Without a shakedown cruise we're in the dark as to her sailing qualities. She may not tack to windward at all, and we may end up being blown back toward South America."

"Not a comforting thought," said Maeve, her mind clouded with the appalling implications of a ninety-day endurance trial. "When I think about it, I'd just as soon remain on dry land and end up like Rodney York."

The day before the launch was one of feverish activity. Final preparations included the manufacture of Pitt's mystery kite, which was folded and stowed in the deckhouse along with 150 meters of light nylon line from York's boat that had retained its integral strength. Then their meager supplies of foodstuffs were loaded on board along with the navigational instruments, charts and books. Cheers erupted over the barren rocks when the outboard motor coughed to life after four decades and nearly forty pulls on the starter rope by Pitt, who felt as if his arm was about to fall off.

"You did it!" Maeve shouted delightedly.

Pitt spread his hands in a modest gesture. "Child's play for somebody who restores antique and classic automobiles. The main problems were a clogged fuel line and a gummed-up carburetor."

"Nice going, pal," Giordino congratulated him. "A motor will come in handy during our approach to the island."

"We were lucky the fuel cans were airtight and none of the contents evaporated after all these years. As it is, the gas has almost turned to shellac, so we'll have to keep a sharp eye on the fuel filter. I'm not keen on flushing out the carburetor every thirty minutes."

"How many hours of fuel did York leave us?"

"Six hours, maybe seven."

Later, with Giordino's help, Pitt mounted the outboard motor to brackets on the stern section of the cockpit. For a final touch, the steering compass was installed just forward of the tiller. After the woven-mat sails were attached to the mast, gaffs and booms with spiral lacing, the sails were raised and lowered with only a minor bind or two. Then they all stood back and stared at their creation. The boat looked reasonably businesslike, but by no stroke of the imagination could she be called pretty. She sat squat and ugly, the outriggers adding to her look of awkwardness. Pitt doubted whether any boats that ever sailed the seven seas were as bizarre as this one.

"She's not exactly what you'd call sleek and elegant," mused Giordino.

"Nor will she ever be entered in the America's Cup Race," added Pitt.

"You men fail to see her inner beauty," said Maeve fancily. "She must have a name. It wouldn't be fitting if she wasn't christened. What if we call her the *Never Say Die?*"

"Fitting," said Pitt, "but not in keeping with mariners' superstitions of the sea. For good luck she should have a woman's name."

"How about the *Marvelous Maeve?*" offered Giordino.

"Oh, I don't know," said Pitt. "It's corny but cute. I'll vote for it."

Maeve laughed. "I'm flattered, but modesty dictates something more proper, say like *Dancing Dorothy II.*"

"Then it's two against one," Giordino said solemnly. "*Marvelous Maeve* she is."

Giving in, Maeve found an old rum bottle cast off by Rodney York and filled it with seawater for the launching. "I christen thee *Marvelous Maeve,*" she said, laughing, and broke the bottle

418

against one of the beech logs lashed to the buoyancy tubes. "May you swim the seas with the speed of a mermaid."

"Now comes our fitness exercise," said Pitt. He passed out lines attached to the forward section of the middle hull. Everyone looped one end of a line around their waist, dug in their feet and leaned forward. Slowly, stubbornly, the boat began to slide over the tree trunks laid on the ground like railroad tracks. Still weakened from a lack of proper food and their ordeal, the three quickly used up their depleted strength dragging the boat toward a two-meter precipice rising from the water.

Maeve, as was to be expected by now, pulled her heart out until she could go no further and sagged to her hands and knees, heart pounding, lungs heaving for air. Pitt and Giordino hauled the great deadweight another ten meters before casting off the lines and dropping to the ground ahead of Maeve. Now the boat teetered on the edge of the ends of two beech-log ways that angled down and under the low rolling waves.

Several minutes passed. The sun was a quarter of the way past the eastern horizon, and the sea was innocent of any sign of turbulence. Pitt slipped the rope loop from around his waist and threw it on the boat. "I guess there's no reason to put off the inevitable any longer." He climbed into the cockpit, swung the outboard motor down on its hinges and pulled at the starter rope. This time it popped to life on the second try.

"Are you two up to giving our luxury yacht a final nudge over the edge?" he said to Maeve and Giordino.

"After having gone to all this work to stir up my hormones," Giordino grumbled, "what's in it for me?"

"A tall gin and tonic on the house," Pitt replied.

"Promises, promises. That's sadism of the worst kind," Giordino groused. He slipped a muscled arm around Maeve's waist, pulled her to her feet and said, "Push, lovely lady, it's time to bid a fond farewell to this rockbound hell."

The two of them moved aft, stiffened their arms, hands against the stern, and shoved with all their remaining strength. The *Marvelous Maeve* moved reluctantly, then picked up speed as the forward section dipped over the edge onto the ways, and the stern lifted. She hung poised for two seconds, then dove into the water with a heavy splash that flew to the sides, before settling flat on the surface. Pitt's rationale for starting the outboard motor now became apparent as he had instant control of the boat against the flow of the current. He quickly circled it back to the edge of the low cliff. As soon as the bow gently bumped against the sheer rock, Giordino held Maeve by her wrists and gently lowered her down onto the roof of the deckhouse. Then he jumped and landed on his feet, as agile as a gymnast, beside her.

"That concludes the entertainment part of the program," said Pitt, reversing the outboard.

"Shall we raise my sails?" asked Maeve, personalizing the pride of her accomplishment.

"Not yet. We'll motor around to the leeward side of the island where the sea is calmer before we test the wind."

Giordino helped Maeve step past the deckhouse and into the cockpit. They sat down to rest a moment while Pitt steered the boat through the channel and into the swells sweeping around the north and south end of the two deserted islands. They no sooner reached the open sea than the sharks appeared.

"Look," said Giordino, "our friends are back. I'll bet they missed our company."

Maeve leaned over the side and peered at the long gray shapes moving under the surface. "A new group of followers," she said. "These are makos."

"The species with the jagged and uneven teeth only an orthodontist could love?"

"The same."

"Why do they plague me?" Giordino moaned. "I've never ordered shark in a restaurant."

Half an hour later, Pitt gave the order. "Okay, let's try the sails and see what kind of a boat we've concocted."

Giordino unfolded the woven-mat sails, which Maeve had carefully reefed in accordion pleats, and hoisted the mainsail successfully while Maeve raised the mizzen. The sails filled, and Pitt eased over the tiller, skidding the boat on a tack, heading northwest against a brisk west wind.

Any yachtsman would have rolled on his deck in laughter if he had seen the *Marvelous Maeve* bucking the seas. A boat designer of professional standing would have whistled the Mickey Mouse Club anthem. But the peculiar looking sailboat had the last laugh. The outriggers dug into the water and maintained her stability. She responded to her helm amazingly well and kept her bow on course without being swept sideways. To be sure, there were problems to be ironed out with her rigging. But remarkably, she took to the sea as if she had been born there.

Pitt took a final look at the Miseries. Then he looked at the packet wrapped in a piece of Dacron sail that held Rodney York's logbook and letters. He vowed that if he somehow lived through the next several days he would get York's final testament to his living relatives, trusting that they would mount an expedition to bring him home again to be buried beside Falmouth Bay in his beloved Cornwall.

45

On the tenth floor of a modernistic all-glass structure built in the shape of a pyramid on the outskirts of Paris, a group of fourteen men sat around a very long ebony conference table. Impeccably dressed, wielding enormous power, immensely wealthy and unsmiling, the directors of the Multilateral Council of Trade, known simply to insiders as the Foundation, an institution dedicated to the development of a single global economic government, shook hands and engaged in small talk before sitting down to business. Normally, they met three times a year, but this day they met in an emergency session to discuss the latest unexpected threat to their widespread operations.

The men in the room represented vast international corporations and high levels of government. Only one top-ranking member from the South African cartel was entirely involved with the selling of quality diamonds. A Belgian industrialist from Antwerp and a real-estate developer from New Delhi, India, acted as the Foundation's middlemen for the huge illicit flow of industrial diamonds to the Islamic Fundamentalist Bloc, which was struggling to create its own nuclear destruction systems. Millions of these smaller industrial diamonds were sold underground to the bloc to make the precision instruments and equipment necessary to construct such systems. The larger, more exotic quality diamonds were used to finance unrest in Turkey, Western Europe, Latin America and several of the South Asian countries, or any other hot spot where subversive political organizations could play into the hands of the Foundation's many other interests, including the sale of arms.

All these men were known by the news media, all were celebrities in their chosen fields, but none were identified with membership in the Foundation. That was a secret known only to the men in the room and their closest associates. They flew across oceans and continents, weaving their webs in all sorts of strange places, taking a toll while amassing unheard-of profits.

They listened with close attention in silence as their chosen chairman, the billionaire head of a German banking firm, reported on the current crisis facing the diamond market. A regal man with a bald head, he spoke slowly in fluent English, a language every national around the table understood.

"Gentlemen, because of Arthur Dorsett we are facing a profound crisis in a vital area of our operations. An appraisal of his conduct by our intelligence network points to a diamond market headed into dark waters. Make no mistake about it, if Dorsett dumps over a hundred metric tons of diamonds on the retail market at street-beggar prices, as he is reported ready to do, this sector of the Foundation will totally collapse."

"How soon will this take place?" asked the sheik of an oil-rich country on the Red Sea.

"I have it on good authority that eighty percent of Dorsett's inventory will be on sale in his chain of retail stores in less than a week," answered the chairman.

"What do we stand to lose?" asked the Japanese head of a vast electronics empire.

"Thirteen billion Swiss francs for starters."

"Good God!" The French leader of one of the world's largest women's fashion houses rapped his fist on the table. "This Australian Neanderthal has the power to do such a thing?"

The chairman nodded. "From all accounts, he has the inventory to back him."

"Dorsett should never have been allowed to operate outside the cartel," said the American former secretary of state.

"The damage is done," agreed the diamond cartel member.

"The world of gems as we know it may never quite be the same again."

"Is there no way we can cut him off before his stones are distributed to his stores?" asked the Japanese businessman.

"I sent an emissary to make him a generous offer to buy his stock in order to keep it out of circulation."

"Have you heard back?"

"Not yet."

"Who did you send?" inquired the chairman.

"Gabe Strouser of Strouser & Sons, a respected international diamond merchant."

"A good man and a hard bargainer," said the Belgian from Antwerp. "We've had many dealings together. If anyone can bring Dorsett to heel, it's Gabe Strouser."

An Italian who owned a fleet of container ships shrugged unemotionally. "As I recall, diamond sales dropped drastically in the early eighties. America and Japan suffered severe recessions and demand dropped, kindling a glut in supply. When the economy turned around in the nineties, prices shot up again. Is it not possible for history to repeat itself?"

"I understand your point," acknowledged the chairman, leaning back in his chair and folding his arms. "But this time a chill wind is blowing, and anyone who depends on diamonds for a living will be frozen out. We've discovered that Dorsett has budgeted over $100 million in advertising and promotion in all the major diamond-buying countries. If, as we have come to believe he will, he sells for pennies on the dollar, high diamond values will be a thing of the past, because the public is about to be brainwashed into thinking they are worth little more than glass."

The Frenchman sighed heavily. "I know my models would certainly look at other luxurious baubles as an eternal investment. If not diamond jewelry, I would have to buy them expensive sports cars."

"What is behind Dorsett's odd strategy?" asked the CEO of a major Southeast Asian airline. "Surely, the man isn't stupid."

"Stupid like a hyena waiting for a lion to fall asleep after eating only half its kill," replied the German chairman. "My paid agents throughout the world banking network have learned that Dorsett has bought up seventy, perhaps as high as eighty percent of the major colored gemstone producing mines."

There was a collective murmur of awareness as the latest information sank in. Every man at the table immediately recognized and assimilated Arthur Dorsett's grand plan.

"Diabolically simple," muttered the Japanese electronics magnate. "He pulls the rug from under diamonds before driving the price of rubies and emeralds through the roof."

A Russian entrepreneur, who ran up a vast fortune by buying shut-down aluminum and copper mines in Siberia for next to nothing and then reopening them using Western technolgy, looked doubtful. "It sounds to me like—what is that saying in the West?—Dorsett is robbing Peter to pay Paul. Does he really expect to make enough on colored gemstones to make up for his losses on diamonds?"

The chairman nodded to the Japanese, who replied, "At the request of our chairman, I asked my financial analysts to run the figures through our data systems. Astounding as it seems, Arthur Dorsett, the House of Dorsett chain of retail stores and Dorsett Consolidated Mining Limited stands to make a minimum of $20 billion American. Perhaps as high as $24 billion, depending on a predicted rising economy."

"Good Lord," exclaimed a British subject who owned a publishing empire. "I can't begin to imagine what I would do with a profit of $24 billion."

The German laughed. "I would use it to buy out your holdings."

"You could send me packing to my Devonshire farm for a fraction of that amount."

The United States member spoke up. A former secretary of state and the acknowledged head of one of America's wealthiest families, he was the founding father of the Foundation. "Do we have any idea where Dorsett's diamond inventory is at the present time?"

"With his deadline only a few days away," answered the South African, "I should guess that the stones not being currently cut are in transit to his stores."

The chairman looked from the Italian shipping-fleet baron to the Asian airline magnate. "Either of you gentlemen have any knowledge of Dorsett's shipping procedures?"

"I seriously doubt he would transport his diamonds by sea," said the Italian. "Once a ship docked in port, he'd still have to arrange transport inland."

"If I were Dorsett, I'd ship my stones by air," agreed the

Asian. "That way he could distribute immediately in almost any city in the world."

"We might stop one or two of his planes," said the Belgian industrialist, "but without knowing flight schedules, it would impossible to close off the shipments entirely."

The Asian shook his head negatively. "I think intercepting even one flight is optimistic. Dorsett has probably chartered a fleet of aircraft in Australia. I fear we're closing the gate after the cows have escaped."

The chairman turned to the South African representing the diamond cartel. "It appears the great masquerade is over. The artificially created value of diamonds is not *forever* after all."

Rather than display any feelings of disillusionment, the South African actually smiled. "We've been counted out before. My board of directors and I consider this a minor setback, nothing more. Diamonds really are *forever,* gentlemen. Mark my words, the price on quality stones will rise again when the luster of sapphires, emeralds and rubies wears off. The cartel will fulfill its obligations to the Foundation through our other mineral interests. We'll not sit on our thumbs patiently awaiting for the market to return."

The chairman's private secretary entered the room and spoke to him softly. He nodded and looked at the South African. "I'm told a reply from your emissary to negotiate with Arthur Dorsett has arrived in the form of a package."

"Odd that Strouser didn't contact me directly."

"I've asked that the package be sent in," said the chairman. "I think we're all anxious to see if Mr. Strouser was successful in his negotiations with Arthur Dorsett."

A few moments later the secretary returned, holding in both hands a square box tied with a red-and-green ribbon. The chairman gestured toward the South African. The secretary stepped over and set the box on the table in front of the him. A card was attached to the ribbon. He opened the envelope and read it aloud:

> *There is limestone and soapstone,*
> *and there is hailstone and flagstone.*
> *But behind Strouser's tongue*
> *is one now cheap as dung,*
> *the gemstone worthless as brimstone.*

The South African paused and stared at the box gravely. "That does not sound like Gabe Strouser. He is not a man noted for his levity."

"I can't say he's good at writing limericks, either," commented the French fashion designer.

"Go ahead, open the box," pressed the Indian.

The ribbon was untied, the lid lifted and then the South African peered inside. His face blanched and he jumped to his feet so abruptly his chair crashed over backward. He ran, stumbling, over to a window, threw it open and retched.

Stunned, everyone around the table rushed over and inspected the hideous contents of the box. A few reacted like the South African, some reflected shocked horror, others, the ones who had ordered brutal killings during their rise to wealth, stared grimly without displaying emotion at the bloody head of Gabe Strouser, the grotesquely widened eyes, the diamonds spilling from his mouth.

"It seems Strouser's negotiations were unsuccessful," said the Japanese, fighting the bile that rose in his throat.

After taking a few minutes to recover, the chairman called in the chief of the Foundation's security and ordered him to remove the head. Then he faced the members, who had slowly recovered and returned to their chairs. "I ask that you keep what we've just seen in the strictest secrecy."

"What about that butcher Dorsett?" snapped the Russian, anger reddening his face. "He cannot go unpunished for murdering people representing the Foundation."

"I agree," said the Indian. "Vengeance must take the highest priority."

"A mistake to act harshly," cautioned the chairman. "Not a wise move to call attention to ourselves by getting carried away with revenge. One miscalculation in executing Dorsett and our activities will become open to scrutiny. I think it best to undermine Arthur Dorsett from another direction."

"Our chairman has a point," said the Dutchman, his English slow but sufficient. "The better course of action for the present would be to contain Dorsett and then move in when he falters, and make no mistake, a man of his character cannot help but make a grand mistake sometime in the near future."

"What do you suggest?"

"We stand on the sidelines and wait him out."

The chairman frowned. "I don't understand. I thought the idea was to go on the offensive."

"Unloading his diamond supply will obliterate Dorsett's reserve assets," explained the Dutchman. "It will take him at least a year before he can raise gemstone prices and take his profits. In the meantime we keep a grip on the diamond market, maintain our stockpiles and follow Dorsett's lead by buying up control of the remaining colored gemstone production. Compete with him. My industrial spies inform me that Dorsett has concentrated on gems better known to the public while overlooking the rarer stones."

"Can you give us an example of rarer stones?"

"Alexandrite, tsavorite, and red beryl come to mind."

The chairman glanced at the others around the table. "Your opinions, gentlemen?"

The British publisher leaned forward with clenched fists. "A bloody sound idea. Our diamond expert has hit on a way to beat Dorsett at his own game while turning temporarily decreased diamond values to our advantage."

"Then do we agree?" asked the chairman with a smile that was far from pleasant.

Every hand went up, and fourteen voices gave an affirmative yea.

PART IV

CATASTROPHE IN PARADISE

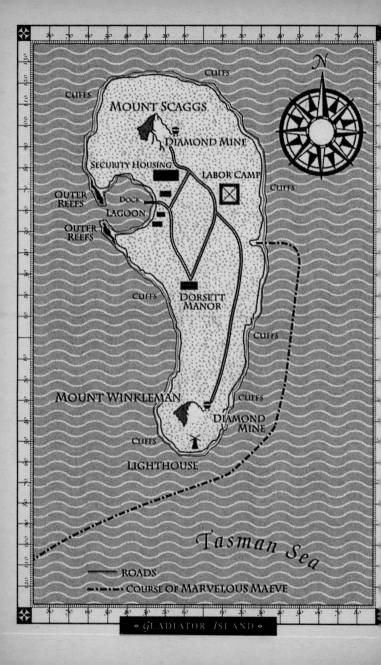

46

A sandy-haired marine sergeant sat in a pair of sun-bleached shorts and a red-flowered aloha shirt and drank a can of beer while a movie cassette tape in the VCR played on a television set. He slouched sumptuously on a couch that he had scrounged from one of the two luxury hotels on the Hawaiian island of Lanai that was being remodeled. The movie was an early John Wayne epic, *Stagecoach*. A virtual-reality headset that he had purchased from a Honolulu electronics store encompassed his head. After connecting the headset into the VCR, he could "enter" the television screen and mingle with the actors during scenes from the movie. He was lying beside John Wayne on the top of the stagecoach during the climactic chase scene, shooting at the pursuing Indians, when a loud buzzer cut into the action. Reluctantly, he removed the set from his head and scanned four security monitors that viewed strategic areas of the classified facility he guarded. Monitor three showed a car approaching over a dirt road leading through a pineapple field to the entry gate. The late morning sun glinted off its front bumper while the rear bumper pulled a trail of dust.

After several months of bleak duty, the sergeant had his routine down to a fine science. In the three minutes it took for the car to travel up the road, he changed into a neatly pressed uniform and was standing at attention beside the gate that barred access through a tunnel into the open core of the long-extinct volcano.

On closer scrutiny he saw that it was a Navy staff car. He stooped and peered in the side window. "This is a restricted area. Do you have permission to enter?"

The driver, in the whites of a Navy enlisted man, motioned a thumb over his shoulder. "Commander Gunn in the back has the necessary entry papers."

Proficient, businesslike, Rudi Gunn had wasted no precious time in seeking permission to dismantle the huge dish antenna in the middle of the Palawai volcano on Lanai. Unraveling the convoluted thread through the bureaucracy to track down the agency that held jurisdiction over the antenna and then confronting the department that operated the space communications facility would be a month-long expedition in itself. The next chore, an impossible one, would be to find a bureaucrat willing to take responsibility for allowing the dish to be taken down and temporarily loaned to NUMA.

Gunn eliminated the useless red tape by merely having NUMA's printing department dummy up an official-looking requisition form in triplicate, authorizing NUMA to relocate the antenna to another site on the Hawaiian island of Oahu for a secret project. The document was then signed by several workers in the printing department, on lines under lofty fictitious titles. What normally would have taken the better part of a year, before being officially denied, took less than an hour and a half, time mostly spent in setting the type.

When Gunn, wearing his uniform as a commander in the Navy, was driven up to the gate outside the tunnel entrance and produced his authorization to dismantle and remove the antenna, the sergeant in command of the deserted facility was dutifully cooperative. He was even more cooperative after assessing the exquisite form of Molly Faraday sitting next to Gunn in the backseat. If he had any thought of calling a superior officer for official confirmation it quickly melted as he stared at a convoy of large flatbed trucks and a portable crane that followed in the tracks of the staff car. Authority for an operation of this magnitude must have come from the top of the ladder.

"Good to have some company," the sergeant said with a wide smile. "It gets pretty boring up here with nary a soul to talk to while I'm on duty."

"How many are you?" asked Molly sweetly through the rear window.

"Only three of us, ma'am, one for each eight-hour shift."

"What do you do when you're not on guard duty?"

"Lay on the beach mostly, or try and pick up single girls at the hotels."

She laughed. "How often are you able to leave the island?"

"Every thirty days. Then five days leave in Honolulu, before returning to Lanai."

"When was the last time an outsider visited the facility?"

If the sergeant realized he was being interrogated, he didn't show it. "Some guy with National Security Agency credentials came and poked around about four months ago. Hung around less than twenty minutes. You're the first to visit since him."

"We should have the antenna down and out of here sometime late tonight," said Gunn.

"May I inquire, sir, where it's going to be reassembled?"

"What if I told you it was going to be scrapped?"

"Wouldn't surprise me in the least," said the sergeant. "With no repair or maintenance in the last few years, the old dish is beginning to look like it's been worked over by the elements."

Gunn was amused at seeing the marine stalling while enjoying the opportunity to talk to a stranger. "May we pass through and get to work, Sergeant?"

The sergeant snapped a salute and quickly pressed a button that electrically swung open the gate. After the staff car passed out of sight into the tunnel, he watched and waved to the drivers of the trucks and crane. When the last vehicle disappeared inside the volcano, he closed the gate, entered the guard compound and changed back into his shorts and aloha shirt before releasing the pause button on his VCR. He adjusted his virtual-reality headset and reversed the cassette tape until he rejoined John Wayne in blasting away at the Indians.

"So far so good," Gunn said to Molly.

"Shame on you for telling that nice young boy you were junking the antenna," she chided him.

"I merely said, 'what if?' "

"We get caught forging official documents, painting a used

car to look like an official Navy vehicle and stealing government property . . ." Molly paused and shook her head in wonder. "They'll hang us from the Washington Monument."

"I'll gladly pay the price if we save nearly two million people from a horrible death," said Gunn without regret.

"What happens after we deflect the acoustic wave?" she asked. "Do we return the antenna and reassemble it?"

"I wouldn't have it any other way." He stared at her, as if surprised she asked the question, before smiling devilishly. "Unless, of course, there's an accident and we drop it on the bottom of the sea."

Sandecker's end of the project was not going one-tenth as well. Despite relying heavily on the Navy's old admiral buddy system, he could not convince anyone with command authority to temporarily loan him the aircraft carrier *Roosevelt* and her crew. Somewhere along the chain of command between the President and the Admiral in Command of Pacific Fleet Operations someone had spiked his request.

The admiral was pacing the office of Admiral John Overmeyer at Pearl Harbor with the ferocity of a bear who'd lost its cub to a zoo. "Damn it, John!" snapped Sandecker. "When I left Admiral Baxter of the Joint Chiefs, he assured me that approval to use the *Roosevelt* for the deployment of an acoustic reflector was a done deal. Now you sit there and tell me I can't have her."

Overmeyer, looking as sturdy and vigorous as an Indiana farmer, threw up his hands in exasperation. "Don't blame me, Jim. I can show you the orders."

"Who signed them?"

"Admiral George Cassidy, Commanding Officer of the San Francisco Naval District."

"What in hell does some desk jockey who operates ferryboats have to do with anything?"

"Cassidy does not operate ferryboats," Overmeyer said wearily. "He's in command of the entire Pacific Logistics Command."

"He's not over you," stated Sandecker sharply.

"Not directly, but if he decided to get nasty, every transport carrying supplies for all my ships between here and Singapore might be inexplicably delayed."

"Don't stroke me, John. Cassidy wouldn't dare drag his feet, and you damn well know it. His career would go down the drain if he allowed petulance to stand in the way of supplying your fleet."

"Have it your way," said Overmeyer. "But it doesn't alter the situation. I cannot let you have the *Roosevelt*."

"Not even for a lousy seventy-two hours?"

"Not even for seventy-two seconds."

Sandecker suddenly halted his pacing, sat down in a chair and stared Overmeyer in the eye. "Level with me, John. Who put the handcuffs on me?"

Obviously flustered, Overmeyer could not hold the stare and looked away. "That's not for me to say."

"The fog begins to clear," said Sandecker. "Does George Cassidy know he's being cast as a villain?"

"Not to my knowledge," Overmeyer answered honestly.

"Then who in the Pentagon is stonewalling my operation?"

"You didn't hear this from me."

"We served together on the *Iowa*. You've never known me to expose a friend's secrets."

"I'd be the last man to doubt your word," Overmeyer said without hesitation. This time he returned Sandecker's stare. "I don't have absolute evidence, mind you, but a friend at the Naval Weapons Testing Center hinted that it was the President himself who dropped the curtain on you, after some unnamed snitch at the Pentagon let your request for an aircraft carrier slip to the White House. My friend also suggested that scientists close to the President thought your acoustic plague theory was off the wall."

"Can't they get it through their collective academic heads that people and untold numbers of sea life have already died from it?"

"Apparently not."

Sandecker sagged in his chair and expelled a long breath. "Stabbed in the back by Wilbur Hutton and the President's National Science Board."

"I'm sorry, Jim, but word has gone out in Washington circles that you're some kind of fanatical kook. It may well be that the President wants to force you to resign from NUMA so he can put a political crony in your place."

Sandecker felt as if the executioner's axe was rising. "So what? My career is unimportant. Can't I get through to anyone?

Can't I get it across to you, Admiral, that you and every man under your command on the island of Oahu will be dead in three days?''

Overmeyer looked at Sandecker with great sadness in his eyes. It is a difficult thing for a man to believe another is breaking down, especially if that man is his friend. "Jim, to be honest, you terrify me. I want to trust your judgment, but there are too many intelligent people who think your acoustic plague has as much chance of actually occurring as the end of the world.''

"Unless you give me the *Roosevelt*," said Sandecker evenly, "your world will cease to exist on Saturday at eight o'clock in the morning.''

Overmeyer shook his head grimly. "I'm sorry, Jim, my hands are tied. Whether I believe your prediction of doom or not, you know damned well I can't disobey orders that come down from my Commander-in-Chief.''

"If I can't convince you, then I guess I'd better be on my way." Sandecker came to his feet, started for the door and turned. "Do you have family here at Pearl?''

"My wife and two visiting granddaughters.''

"I hope to God I'm wrong, but if I were you, my friend, I'd get them off the island while you still can.''

The giant dish was only half dismantled by midnight. The interior of the volcano was illuminated by incandescent brilliance and echoed with the sounds of generators, the clank of metal against metal and the curses of the dismantling crew. The pace remained frantic from start to finish. The NUMA men and women sweated and fought bolted connections that were rusted together from lack of upkeep and repair. Sleep was never considered, nor were meals. Only coffee as black as the surrounding sea was passed around.

As soon as a small section of the steel-reinforced fiberglass dish was removed from the main frame, the crane picked it up and set it on the flatbed of a waiting truck. After five sections were stacked one on top of the other and tied down, the truck exited the interior of the volcano and drove toward the port of Kaumala-pau on the west coast, where the antenna parts were loaded on board a small ship for transport to Pearl Harbor.

Rudi Gunn was standing shirtless, sweating from the humidity of a steamy night, directing a team of men laboring strenuously to disconnect the main hub of the antenna from its base. He was constantly consulting a set of plans for the same type of antenna used in other space tracking facilities. The plans came from Hiram Yaeger, who had obtained them by breaking into the corporate computer system of the company that had originally designed and constructed the huge dishes.

Molly, who had changed into a more comfortable khaki blouse and shorts, sat nearby in a small tent, manning the communications and fielding any problems that arose during the dismantling operation and transportation of parts to the loading dock. She stepped out of the tent and handed Gunn a cold bottle of beer.

"You look like you could use a little something to wet your tonsils," she said.

Gunn nodded thankfully and rolled the bottle across his forehead. "I must have consumed twenty liters of liquid since we got here."

"I wish Pitt and Giordino were here," she said sadly. "I miss them."

Gunn stared absently at the ground. "We all miss them. I know the admiral's heart is torn out."

Molly changed the subject. "How's it look?"

He tilted his head toward the half-dismantled antenna. "She's fighting us every step of the way. Things are going a little faster now that we know how to attack her."

"A shame," she decided after a thoughtful survey of the thirty men and four women who struggled so long and hard to tear apart and move the antenna, their dedication and tireless efforts now seemingly wasted in a magnificent attempt to save so many lives, "that all this may very well come to nothing."

"Don't give up on Jim Sandecker," said Gunn. "He may have been blocked by the White House in securing the *Roosevelt*, but I'll bet you a dinner with soft lights and music that he'll come up with a replacement."

"You're on," she said, smiling thinly. "That's a bed I'll gladly lose."

He looked up curiously. "I beg your pardon?"

"A Freudian slip." She laughed tiredly. "I meant 'bet.' "

At four in the morning, Molly received a call from Sandecker. His voice showed no trace of fatigue.

"When do you expect to wrap up?"

"Rudi thinks we'll have the final section loaded on board the *Lanikai*—"

"The what?" Sandecker interrupted.

"The *Lanikai*, a small interisland freighter I chartered to haul the antenna to Pearl Harbor."

"Forget Pearl Harbor. How soon before you'll be out of there?"

"Another five hours," replied Molly.

"We're running tight. Remind Rudi we have less than sixty hours left."

"If not Pearl Harbor, where do we go?"

"Set a course for Halawa Bay, on the island of Molokai," answered Sandecker. "I found another platform for deploying the reflector."

"Another aircraft carrier?"

"Something even better."

"Halawa Bay is less than a hundred kilometers across the channel. How did you manage that?"

"They who await no gifts from chance, conquer fate."

"You're being cryptic, Admiral," Molly said, intrigued.

"Just tell Rudi to pack up and get to Molokai no later than ten o'clock this morning."

She had just switched off the portable phone when Gunn entered the tent. "We're breaking down the final section," he said wearily. "And then we're out of here."

"The admiral called," she informed Gunn. "He's ordered us to take the antenna to Halawa Bay."

"On Molokai?" Gunn asked, his eyes narrowed questioningly.

"That was the message," she said flatly.

"What kind of ship do you suppose he's pulled out of his hat?"

"A fair question. I have no idea."

"It'd better be a winner," Gunn muttered, "or we'll have to close the show."

47

There was no moon, but the sea flamed with spectral blue-green phosphorescence under the glint of the stars that filled the sky from horizon to horizon like unending city lights. The wind had veered and swept in from the south, driving the *Marvelous Maeve* hard to the northwest. The green-and-yellow beech-leaf sail filled out like a woman's tattooed breast, while the boat leaped over the waves like a mule running with thoroughbreds. Pitt had never imagined that the ungainly looking craft could sail so well. She would never win a trophy, but he could have closed his eyes and envisioned himself on a first-class yacht, skimming over the sea without a care in the world.

The swells no longer had the same hostile look nor did the clouds look as threatening. The nightly chill also diminished as they traveled north into warmer waters. The sea had tested them with cruelty and harshness, and they had passed with flying colors. Now the weather was cooperating by remaining constant and charitable.

Some people tire of looking at the sea from a tropical beach or the deck of a cruise ship, but Pitt was not among them. His restless soul and the capricious water were one, inseparable in their shifting moods.

Maeve and Giordino no longer felt as though they were struggling to stay alive. Their few moments of warmth and pleasure, nearly drowned by adversity, were becoming more frequent. Pitt's unshakable optimism, his contagious laughter, his unrelenting grasp of hope, his strength of character sustained and helped them face the worst that nature could throw at them. Never did they perceive a bare hint of depression in his perspective, whatever the situation. No matter how strained he appeared as he sighted his sextant on the stars or warily watched for a sudden change of the wind, he was always smiling.

When she realized she was falling deeply in love with him, Maeve's independent spirit fought against it. But when she finally accepted the inevitable, she gave in to her feelings completely. She continually found herself studying his every move, his every expression as he jotted down their position on Rodney York's chart of the southern sea.

She touched him on the arm. "Where are we?" she asked softly.

"At first light I'll mark our course and figure the distance separating us from Gladiator Island."

"Why don't you give it a rest? You haven't slept more than two hours since we left the Miseries."

"I promise I'll take a nice long siesta when we're on the last leg of the voyage," he said, peering through gloom at the compass.

"Al never sleeps either," she said, pointing at Giordino, who never ceased examining the condition of the outriggers and the rigging holding the boat together.

"If the following wind holds and my navigating is anywhere near the mark, we should sight your island sometime early morning on the day after tomorrow."

She looked up at the great field of stars. "The heavens are lovely tonight."

"Like a woman I know," he said, eyes going from compass to the sails to Maeve. "A radiant creature with guileless blue eyes and hair like a shower of golden coins. She's innocent and intelligent and was made for love and life."

"She sounds quite appealing."

"That's only for starters. Her father happens to be one of the richest men in the solar system."

She arched her back and snuggled against his body, feeling its hardness. She brushed her lips against the mirth lines around his eyes and his strong chin. "You must be very smitten with her."

"Smitten, and why not?" he said slowly. "She is the only girl in this part of the Pacific Ocean who makes me mad with passionate desire."

"But I'm the only girl in this part of the Pacific Ocean."

He kissed her lightly on the forehead. "Then it's your solemn duty to fulfill my most intimate fantasies."

"I'd take you up on that if we were alone," she said in a sultry voice. "But for now, you'll just have to suffer."

"I could tell Al to take a hike," he said with a grin.

She pulled back and laughed. "He wouldn't get far." Maeve secretly sensed a flow of happiness at knowing no flesh-and-blood woman stood between them. "You're a special kind of man," she whispered. "The kind every woman longs to meet."

He laughed easily. "Not so. I've seldom swept the fair sex off their feet."

"Maybe it's because they see that you're unreachable."

"I can be had if they play their cards right," he said jokingly.

"Not what I mean," she said seriously. "The sea is your mistress. I could read it in your face through the storm. It was not as if you were fighting the sea as much as you were seducing it. No woman can compete with a love so vast."

"You have a deep affection for the sea too," he said tenderly, "and the life that lives in it."

Maeve breathed in the night. "Yes, I can't deny devoting my life to it."

Giordino broke the moment by emerging from the deckhouse and announcing that one of the buoyancy tubes was losing air. "Pass the pump," he ordered. "If I can find the leak, I'll try and patch it."

"How is *Marvelous Maeve* holding up?" Pitt asked.

"Like a lady in a dance contest," Giordino replied. "Limber and lithe, with all her body joints working in rhythm."

"She hangs together until we reach the island and I'll donate her to the Smithsonian to be displayed as the boat most unlikely to succeed."

"We strike another storm," said Giordino warily, "and all bets are off." He paused and casually glanced around the black horizon where the stars melted into the sea. Suddenly, he stiffened. "I see a light off to port."

Pitt and Maeve stood and stared in the direction Giordino indicated with his hand. They could see a green light, indicating a ship's starboard side, and white range masthead lights. It looked to be passing far in their wake toward the northeast.

"A ship," Pitt confirmed. "About five kilometers away."

"She'll never see us," said Maeve anxiously. "We have no lights of our own."

Giordino disappeared in the deckhouse and quickly reappeared. "Rodney York's last flare," he said, holding it up.

Pitt gazed at Maeve. "Do you want to be rescued?"

She looked down at the black sea rolling under the boat and slowly shook her head. "It's not my decision to make."

"Al, how say you? A hearty meal and a clean bed strike you as tempting?"

Giordino grinned. "Not half as inviting as a second go-around with the Dorsett clan."

Pitt circled an arm around Maeve's shoulder. "I'm with him."

"Two days," Maeve murmured thankfully. "I can't believe I'll actually see my boys again."

Pitt said nothing for a moment, thinking of the unknown that lay ahead of them. Then he said gently, "You'll see them, and you'll hold them in your arms. I promise you."

There was never any real inclination to turn from their established goal. Pitt and Giordino's minds ran as one. They had entered a zone where they were indifferent and uncaring of their own lives. They were so wrapped up in their determination to reach Gladiator Island that neither man bothered to watch as the lights of the passing ship grew smaller and gradually disappeared in the distance.

48

When the interisland cargo ship carrying the dismantled antenna steamed into Halawa Bay on Molokai, all hands lined the railings and stared in rapt fascination at the peculiar vessel moored in the harbor. The 228-meter-long ship, with its forest of cranes and twenty-three-story derrick rising in the middle of its hull, looked like it had been designed and constructed by an army of drunken engineers, spastic welders and Oklahoma oil riggers.

An expansive helicopter pad hung over the stern by girders as if it was an add-on accessory. The high bridge superstructure rose on the aft end of the hull, giving the ship the general look of an oil tanker, but that's where any similarity ended. The center section of hull was taken up by an enormous conglomeration of machinery with the appearance of a huge pile of scrap. A veritable maze of steel stairways, scaffolding, ladders and pipes clustered around the derrick, which reached up and touched the sky like a gantry used to launch heavy rockets into space. The raised house on the forecastle showed no sign of ports, only a row of skylightlike windows across the front. The paint was faded and chipped with streaks of rust showing through. The

443

hull was a marine blue, while the superstructure was white. The machinery had once been painted myriad colors of gray, yellow and orange.

"Now I can die happy after having seen it all," Gunn exclaimed at the sight.

Molly stood beside him on the bridge wing and stared in awe. "How on earth did the admiral ever conjure up the *Glomar Explorer?*"

"I won't even venture to guess," Gunn muttered, gazing with the wonder of a child seeing his first airplane.

The captain of the *Lanikai* leaned from the door of the wheelhouse. "Admiral Sandecker is on the ship-to-ship phone, Commander Gunn."

Gunn raised a hand in acknowledgment, stepped from the bridge wing and picked up the phone.

"You're an hour late," were the first words Gunn heard.

"Sorry, Admiral. The antenna was not in pristine shape. I ordered the crew to perform routine repair and maintenance during disassembly so that it will go back together with less hassle."

"A smart move," Sandecker agreed. "Ask your captain to moor his ship alongside. We'll begin transferring the antenna sections as soon as his anchors are out."

"Is that the famous Hughes *Glomar Explorer* I'm seeing?" asked Gunn.

"One and the same with a few alterations," answered Sandecker. "Lower a launch and come aboard. I'll be waiting in the captain's office. Bring Ms. Faraday."

"We'll be aboard shortly."

Originally proposed by Deputy Director of Defense David Packard, formerly of Hewlett-Packard, a major electronics corporation, and based on an earlier deep-ocean research ship designed by Willard Bascom and called the *Alcoa Seaprobe*, the *Glomar Explorer* became a joint venture of the CIA, Global Marine Inc. and Howard Hughes, through his tool company that eventually became the Summa Corporation.

Construction was commenced by the Sun Shipbuilding & Dry Dock Company at their shipyard facilities in Chester, Pennsylvania, and the huge vessel was immediately wrapped in secrecy, with the aid of misleading information. She was launched forty-one months later in the late fall of 1972, a remarkable achievement in technology for a vessel completely innovative in concept.

She then became famous for her raising of a Russian Golf-class submarine from a depth of five kilometers in the middle of the Pacific. Despite news stories to the contrary, the entire sub was raised in pieces and examined, a colossal feat of intelligence that paid great dividends in knowledge about Soviet submarine technology and operation.

After her brief moment of fame, no one quite knew what to do with the *Explorer,* so she eventually wound up in the hands of the United States government and was included in the Navy's mothball program. Until recently, she had languished for over two decades in the backwash of Suisan Bay, northeast of San Francisco.

When Gunn and Molly stepped onto the deck of the immense vessel, they felt as though they were standing in the center of an electric generating plant. Seen close up, the scope of the machinery was staggering. None of the tight security that surrounded the vessel during her first voyage was visible. They were met at the top of the boarding ramp by the ship's second officer and no one else.

"No security guards?" asked Molly.

The officer smiled as he showed them up a stairway leading to a deck below the wheelhouse. "Since this is a commercial operation and we're not on a secret mission to steal foreign naval vessels from the seafloor, no security measures are necessary."

"I thought the *Explorer* was in mothballs," said Gunn.

"Until five months ago," replied the officer. "Then she was leased to Deep Abyss Engineering to mine copper and manganese from the deep ocean two hundred kilometers south of the Hawaiian Islands."

"Have you begun operations?" asked Molly.

"Not yet. Much of the ship's equipment is ancient by today's standards and we've had to make some major changes, especially to the electronics. At the moment, the main engines are acting up. Soon as they're repaired, we'll be on our way."

Gunn and Molly exchanged questioning looks without voicing their concern. As if tuned to the same wavelength, they wondered how a ship that was dead in the water could get them where they had to be in time to deflect the acoustic plague.

The ship's officer opened the door to a spacious, elegant stateroom. "These quarters were reserved for Howard Hughes in the event he ever visited the ship, an event that is not known to have taken place."

Sandecker stepped forward and greeted them. "An extraordinary piece of work. I compliment you both. I take it the dismantling turned out to be a tougher job than we estimated."

"Corrosion was the enemy," Gunn admitted. "The grid connections fought us every step of the way."

"I never heard so much cursing," said Molly with a smile. "The engineers turned the air blue, believe you me."

"Will the antenna serve our purpose?" asked Sandecker.

"If the sea doesn't get too nasty and tear it apart at the seams," replied Gunn, "it should get the job done."

Sandecker turned and introduced a short plump man a few years over forty. "Captain James Quick, my aides Molly Faraday and Commander Rudi Gunn."

"Welcome aboard," said Quick, shaking hands. "How many of your people are coming with you?"

"Counting Ms. Faraday and me, I have a team of thirty-one men and five women," Gunn answered. "I hope our numbers don't cause a problem."

Quick leisurely waved a hand. "No bother. We have more empty quarters than we know what do with and enough food to last two months."

"Your second officer said you had engine problems."

"A stacked deck," said Sandecker. "The captain tells me a sailing time is indefinite."

"So it was a case of hurry up and wait," muttered Gunn.

"A totally unforeseen obstacle, Rudi, I'm sorry."

Quick set his cap on his head and started for the door. "I'll gather up my crane operators and order them to begin transferring the antenna from your ship."

Gunn followed him. "I'll come along and manage the operation from the *Lanikai*."

As soon as they were alone, Molly gazed at Sandecker with canny regard. "How on earth did you ever convince the government to loan you the *Glomar Explorer?*"

"I bypassed official Washington and made Deep Abyss Engineering an offer they couldn't refuse."

Molly stared at him. "You purchased the *Glomar Explorer?*"

"I chartered her," he corrected her. "Cost me an arm and half a leg."

"Is there room in NUMA's budget?"

"Circumstances demanded a quick deal. I wasn't about to haggle with so many lives in the balance. If we're proven right about the deadly acoustic convergence, I'll shame Congress out of the funds. And to be on the safe side, I hammered out a performance clause."

"Finding the *Explorer* nearby after the Navy refused the *Roosevelt* was like stumbling on a gold mine."

"What luck giveth, luck taketh away." Sandecker shook his head slowly. "The *Explorer* is in Molokai because of propeller shaft bearing failure during the voyage from California. Whether she can get under way and put us on site before it's too late is open to question."

The big starboard cranes used to lift machinery were soon extended outward over the open cargo deck of *Lanikai*. Hooks attached to the boom cables were lowered and coupled to the antenna sections before hoisting and swinging them on board the *Glomar Explorer*, where they were stacked on an open area of the deck in numbered sequence for reassembly.

Within two hours, the transfer was completed and the antenna sections tied down on board the *Explorer*. The little cargo ship pulled up her anchors, gave a farewell blast of her air horn and began moving out of the harbor, her part of the project finished. Gunn and Molly waved as the *Lanikai* slowly pushed aside the green waters of the bay and headed out into the open sea.

The NUMA team members were assigned quarters and enjoyed a well-deserved meal from the *Explorer*'s expansive galley before bedding down in staterooms that had gone unused since the ship wrestled the Soviet sub from the deep waters of the Pacific. Molly had taken over the role of housemother and circulated among the team to make sure none had come down sick or had injured themselves during the antenna breakdown.

Gunn returned to the former VIP quarters once reserved for the eccentric Howard Hughes. Sandecker, Captain Quick and another man, who was introduced as Jason Toft, the ship's chief engineer, were seated around a small game table.

"Care for a brandy?" asked Quick.

"Yes, thank you."

Sandecker sat wreathed in cigar smoke and idly sipped the golden liquid in his glass. He did not look like a happy camper. "Mr. Toft has just informed me that he can't get the ship under way until critical parts are delivered from the mainland."

Gunn knew the admiral was churning inside, but he looked as cool as a bucket of ice on the exterior. He looked at Toft. "When do you expect the parts, Chief?"

"They're in flight from Los Angeles now," answered Toft, a man with a huge stomach and short legs. "Due to land in four hours. Our ship's helicopter is waiting on the ground at the Hilo airport on the big island of Hawaii to ferry the parts directly to the *Explorer*."

"What exactly is the problem?" asked Gunn.

"The propeller shaft bearings," Toft explained. "For some strange reason, because the CIA rushed construction, I guess, the propeller shafts were not balanced properly. During the voyage from San Francisco the vibration cracked the lubricating tubes, cutting off the flow of oil to the shaft bearings. Friction, metal fatigue, overstress, whatever you want to call it, the port shaft froze solid about a hundred miles off Molokai. The starboard shaft was barely able to carry us here before *her* bearings burned out."

"As I told you earlier, we're working under a critical deadline." ·

"I fully understand the scope of your dilemma, Admiral. My engine-room crew will work like madmen to get the ship under way again, but they're only human. I must warn you, the shaft bearings are only part of the problem. The engines may not have many hours on them, having only taken the ship from the East Coast to the middle of the Pacific and then back to California, back in the 1970s, but without proper attention for the last twenty years, they are in a terrible state of neglect. Even if we should get one shaft to turn, there is no guarantee we'll get past the mouth of the harbor before breaking down again."

"Do you have the necessary tools to do the job?" Sandecker pressed Toft.

"The caps on the starboard shaft have been torn down and the bearings removed. Replacement should go fairly smoothly. The port shaft, however, can only be repaired at a shipyard."

Gunn addressed himself to Captain Quick. "I don't understand why your company didn't have the *Explorer* refitted at a local shipyard after she came out of mothballs in San Francisco."

"Blame it on the bean-counters." Quick shrugged. "Chief Toft and I strongly recommended a refit before departing for Hawaii, but management wouldn't hear of it. The only time spent at the shipyard was for removal of much of the early lifting equipment and the installation of the dredging system. As for standard maintenance, they insisted it was a waste of money and that any mechanical failures could be repaired at sea or after we reached Honolulu, which obviously we failed to do. And on top of that, we're way undermanned. The original crew was 172 men, I have 60 men and women on board, mostly maritime crewmen, crane and equipment operators and mechanics to maintain the machinery. Twelve of that number are geologists, marine engineers and electronics experts. Unlike your NUMA projects, Commander Gunn, ours is a bare-bones operation."

"My apologies, Captain," said Gunn. "I sympathize with your predicament."

"How soon can you get us under way?" Sandecker asked Toft, trying to keep the fatigue of the past few weeks from showing.

"Thirty-six hours, maybe more."

The room went silent as every eye was trained on Sandecker. He fixed the chief engineer with a pair of eyes that went as cold as a serial killer's. "I'll explain it to you one more time," he offered sharply, "as candidly as I can put it. If we are not on station at the convergence site with our antenna positioned in the water thirty-five hours from now, more people will die than inhabit most small countries. This is not a harebrained fantasy or the script for a Hollywood science-fiction movie. It's real life, and I for one do not want to stand there looking at a sea of dead bodies and say 'If only I'd made the extra effort, I might have prevented it.' Whatever magic it takes, Chief, we must have the antenna in the water and positioned before 8:00 A.M. the day after tomorrow."

"I'll not promise the impossible," Toft came back sternly. "But if we can't make your schedule, it won't be for the lack of my engine-room people working themselves to death." He drained his glass and walked from the room, closing the door heavily behind him.

"I'm afraid you upset my chief engineer," Quick said to Sandecker. "A bit harsh, weren't you, laying the blame on him if we fail?"

Sandecker stared at the closed door thoughtfully. "The stakes are too high, Captain. I didn't plan it this way, certainly not for the burden to sit on Chief Toft's shoulders. But like it or not, that man holds the fate of every human being on the island of Oahu in his hands."

At 3:30 P.M. the following afternoon, a haggard and grimy Toft stepped into the wheelhouse and announced to Sandecker, Gunn and Captain Quick, "The bearings in the port shaft have been replaced. I can get us under way, but the best speed I can give you is five knots with a little edge to spare."

Sandecker pumped Toft's hand. "Bless you, Chief, bless you."

"What is the distance to the convergence site?" asked Quick.

"Eighty nautical miles," Gunn answered without hesitation, having worked the course out in his mind over a dozen times.

"A razor-edge margin," Quick said uneasily. "Moving at five knots, eighty nautical miles will take sixteen hours, which will put us on your site a few minutes before oh-eight hundred hours."

"Oh-eight hundred hours," Gunn repeated in a tone slightly above a whisper. "The precise time Yaeger predicted the convergence."

"A razor-thin margin," Sandecker echoed, "but Chief Toft has given us a fighting chance."

Gunn's face became drawn. "You realize, I hope, Admiral, that if we reach the area and are hit by the convergence, we all stand a good chance of dying."

Sandecker looked at the other three men without a change of expression. "Yes," he said quietly. "A very good chance."

49

Shortly after midnight, Pitt took his final sighting of the stars and marked his chart under the light of a half-moon. If his calculations were in the ballpark, they should be sighting Gladiator Island within the next few hours. He instructed Maeve and Giordino to keep a lookout ahead while he allowed himself the luxury of an hour's sleep. It seemed to him that he had barely drifted off when Maeve gently shook him awake.

"Your navigation was right on the button," she said, excitement in her tone. "The island is in sight."

"A beautiful job of navigating, old buddy," Giordino congratulated him. "You beat your estimated time of arrival."

"Just under the wire too," Maeve said, laughing. "Dead leaves are beginning to fall off the sails."

Pitt stared into the night but only saw the splash of stars and moon on the sea. He opened his mouth to say he couldn't see anything when a shaft of light swung across the western horizon, followed by a bright red glow. "Your island has a beacon?" he asked Maeve.

"A small lighthouse on the rim of the southern volcano."

"At least your family did something to aid marine navigation."

Maeve laughed. "Thoughts of lost sailors never entered my great-grandfather's mind when he built it. The purpose has always been to warn ships to steer clear of the island and not to come ashore."

"Have many vessels come to grief on the island's coast?"

She looked down at her hands and clasped them. "When I was little, Daddy often talked about ships that were cast on the rocks."

"Did he describe survivors?"

She shook her head. "There was never talk of rescue attempts. He always said that any man who stepped foot on Gladiator Island without an invitation had a date with Satan."

"Meaning?"

"Meaning, the badly injured were murdered and any able-bodied survivor was put to work in the mines until he died. No one has ever escaped from Gladiator to tell of the atrocities."

"You escaped."

"A lot of good it did the poor miners," she said sadly. "No one ever took my word over my family's. When I tried to explain the situation to authorities, Daddy merely bought them off."

"And the Chinese laborers working the mines today? How many of them leave the island in one piece?"

Maeve's face was grim. "Almost all eventually die from the extreme heat in the bottom of the lower mine pits."

"Heat?" There was curiosity in Pitt's face. "From what source?"

"Steam vents through cracks in the rock."

Giordino gave Pitt a pensive look. "A perfect place to organize a union."

"I make landfall in about three hours," said Pitt. "Not too late to change our minds, skip the island and try for Australia."

"It's a violent, unrelenting world," Giordino sighed. "Absolutely worthless without a good challenge now and then."

"There speaks the backbone of America," Pitt said with a smile. He stared up at the moon as if appraising it. "I figure we have just enough light to do the job."

"You still haven't explained how we're going to come ashore unobserved by Daddy's security guards," said Maeve.

"First, tell me about the cliffs surrounding Gladiator Island."

She looked at him queerly for a moment, then shrugged. "Not much to tell. The cliffs encircle the whole landmass except for the lagoon. The western shore is pounded by huge waves. The eastern side is calmer but still dangerous."

"Are there any small inlets on the eastern shore with a sandy beach and natural rock chimneys cut into the cliffs?"

"There are two that I remember. One has a good entrance but a tiny beach. The other is more narrow but with a broader stretch of sand. If you're thinking of landing at either one, you can forget it. Their bluffs rise steeply for a good hundred meters. A first-rate professional rock climber using all the latest techniques and equipment wouldn't think of attempting that climb in the dead of night."

"Can you guide us into the narrow channel with the roomy beach?" asked Pitt.

"Didn't you hear me?" Maeve said flatly. "You might as well climb Mount Everest with an ice pick. And then there are the security guards. They patrol the bluffs every hour."

"At night too?"

"Daddy leaves no door open for diamond smugglers," she said as if explaining to a schoolchild.

"How large is the patrol?"

"Two men, who make one complete circuit of the island during their shift. They're followed by another patrol on the hour."

"Is it possible for them to see the beach from the edge of the bluff?" Pitt grilled her.

"No. The cliff is too steep to see straight down." She looked at Pitt, her eyes in the moonlight wide and questioning. "Why all the interrogation about the backside of the island? The lagoon is the only way in."

He exchanged scheming looks with Giordino. "She has the luscious body of a woman but the mind of a skeptic."

"Don't feel bad," Giordino said, yawning. "Women never believe me either."

Pitt gazed on the rocks that had had a long roll of fatalities, rocks where the shipwrecked men who survived wished they had drowned rather than suffer untold miseries as slaves in the Dorsett diamond mines. For a long time, as the cliffs of Gladiator Island loomed up out of the darkness, no one on the *Marvelous*

Maeve moved or spoke. Pitt saw Maeve's back as she lay in the bow, acting as lookout for any offshore rocks. He glanced at Giordino and caught the white blur of his friend's face and the slow nod as he stood poised to start the outboard motor.

The light from the half-moon was more than he dared hope for. It was enough to illuminate the steeply angled palisades, but sufficiently meager to prevent the *Marvelous Maeve* from being observed by probing eyes on the bluffs. As if the partial moon wasn't blessing enough, the sea cooperated with a fairly smooth surface of low, passive swells, and there was a following wind. Without an easterly breeze, Pitt's best laid plans for infiltrating the island would go down the drain. He turned the trimaran on a course parallel to the island's shoreline. At seventy meters a white horizontal blur, trimmed with phosphorescence, grew out of the darkness, accompanied by the low drumming of seas rolling against the cliffs.

Until they sailed around the tip of the island, and the back of the volcano shielded the little boat from the sweeping beam of the Gladiator lighthouse, Pitt felt like a convict in an old prison movie, trying to escape over a wall with searchlights playing all around. Strangely, all conversation dropped to hushed tones as if they could be heard over the soft boom of the surf.

"How far to the inlet?" he called to Maeve softly.

"I think it's about a kilometer up the shore from the lighthouse," she answered without turning.

The boat had lost considerable way after swinging east to north along the shoreline, and Pitt was finding it difficult to maintain a steady course. He raised a hand as a signal to Giordino to start the outboard motor. Three heartbeats slowed and then suddenly increased as Giordino pulled on the starter rope, ten, twenty, thirty times without success.

Giordino paused, massaged his tiring arm, stared menacingly at the ancient motor and began talking to it. "You don't start on the next pull, I will attack and unnecessarily mutilate every bolt in your crankcase." Then he took a firm grip on the pull handle and gave a mighty heave. The motor snorted and its exhaust puffed a few moments before settling down to a steady snarl. Giordino wiped the sweat from his face and looked pleased. "One more manifestation of Giordino's law," he said, catching his breath. "Deep down, every mechanical contrivance has a fear of being junked."

Now that Giordino steered the craft with the outboard, Pitt lowered the sails and removed his kite from the deckhouse. He deftly looped a coil of thin line on the deck of the boat. Then he tied a small grappling hook, found at York's campsite, to the line slightly below where it attached to the kite. Then he sat and waited, knowing in his heart of hearts that what he had in mind had only one chance of succeeding out of too many to count.

"Steer port," warned Maeve, gesturing to her left. "There is a pinnacle of rocks about fifty meters dead ahead."

"Turning to port," Giordino acknowledged as he pulled the steering handle of the outboard toward him, swinging the bows around on a twenty-degree angle toward shore. He kept a cautious eye on the white water swirling around several black rocks that rose above the surface until they were safely astern.

"Maeve, see anything yet?" asked Pitt.

"I can't be certain. I never had to find the bloody inlet in the dark before," she replied testily.

Pitt studied the swells. They were growing steeper and closer together. "The bottom is coming up. Another thirty meters and we'll have to turn for open water."

"No, no," Maeve said in an excited voice. "I think I see a break in the cliffs. I'm sure of it. That's the inlet that leads to the largest beach."

"How far?" Pitt demanded.

"Sixty or seventy meters," she answered, rising to her knees and pointing toward the cliffs.

Then Pitt had it too. A vertical opening in the face of the palisades that ran dark in the shadows out of the moonlight. Pitt wetted his finger and tested the wind. It held steady out of the east. "Ten minutes," he begged under his breath. "All I need is ten minutes." He turned to Giordino. "Al, can you hold us in a steady position about twenty meters from the entrance?"

"It won't be easy in the surge."

"Do your best." He turned to Maeve. "Take the tiller and aim the bow head-on into the swells. Combine your efforts with Al's on the outboard to keep the boat from swinging broadside."

Pitt unfolded the struts on his homemade kite. When extended, the Dacron surface measured nearly two and half meters high. He held it up over the side of the boat, pleased to see it leap up out of his hands as the breeze struck its bowed surface. He payed out the line as the kite rose and dipped in the predawn sky.

Maeve suddenly saw the genius behind Pitt's mad plan. "The grappling hook," she blurted. "You're trying to snag it on the top of the bluffs and use the line to climb the cliffs."

"That's the idea," he replied as he focused his gaze on the obscure shape of the kite, just slightly visible under the half-light from the moon.

Adroitly jockeying the throttle of the outboard and the Forward/Reverse lever, Giordino performed a masterful job of keeping the boat in one spot. He neither spoke nor took his eyes off the sea to observe Pitt's actions.

Pitt had prayed for a steady wind, but he got more than he bargained for. The onshore breeze, meeting resistance from the rising palisades, curved and rushed up their steep face before sweeping over the summit. The big kite was nearly pulled from his grip. He used a sleeve of his battered leather jacket as a protective glove, holding it around the line to keep the friction from burning his hands. The immense drag was nearly pulling his arms out of their sockets. He clamped his teeth together and hung on, mentally plagued by any number of things that could go wrong, any one of which would end their undertaking: a sudden shift in the wind smashing the kite against the rocks, Giordino losing the boat to the incoming surge, the grappling hook unable to find a grip on the rocks, a patrol appearing at the wrong time and discovering them.

He brushed off all thoughts of failure as he taxed his depth perception to the limit. In the black of night, even with the moon's help, he could not begin to accurately judge when the grappling hook had risen beyond the top of the bluffs. He felt the knot he'd tied to indicate when the line had payed out a hundred meters slip under the leather jacket. He roughly figured another twenty meters before loosening his grip on the line. Released from its resistance to the wind, the kite began to seesaw and fall.

Pitt felt as if a great pressure was released from his mind and body as he gave a series of tugs on the line and felt it go taut. The grappling hook had dug its points into the rock on the first attempt and was holding firm. "Take her in, Al. We've got our way to the top."

Giordino had been waiting for the word. His struggle to keep the trimaran in a fixed position under the steady onslaught of the waves was a study in skill and finesse. Gladly, he eased the motor into Forward, opened the throttle and threaded the *Marvelous Maeve* between the rocks into the eye of the cove under the cliffs.

Maeve returned to the bow and acted as lookout, guiding Giordino through the black water that seemed to grow calmer the deeper they penetrated the inlet. "I see the beach," she informed them. "You can just make out a light strip of sand fifteen meters ahead and to starboard."

In another minute the bow and outriggers touched the strip of beach and ran up onto the soft sand. Pitt looked at Maeve. The cliffs shadowed the light from the moon, and he saw her features only vaguely. "You're home," he said briefly.

She tilted her head and gazed up between the cliffs at the narrow slot of sky and stars that looked light-years away. "Not yet, I'm not."

Pitt had never let the line to the grappling hook out of his hands. Now, he slipped the leather jacket over Maeve's shoulders and gave the line a hard tug. "We'd better get moving before a patrol comes along."

"I should go first," said Giordino. "I'm the strongest."

"That goes without saying," Pitt said, smiling in the dark. "I believe it's your turn anyway."

"Ah, yes," Giordino said, remembering. "Payback time for watching like an impotent snail when that terrorist cut your safety line while you were swimming around that sinkhole in the Andes."

"I had to climb out using nothing but a pair of screwdrivers."

"Tell me the story again," said Giordino sarcastically. "I never tire of hearing it."

"On your way, critic, and keep an eye peeled for a passing patrol."

With only a nod, Giordino grabbed at the thin line and gave it a sharp pull to test its immovability. "This thing strong enough to take my weight?"

Pitt shrugged. "We'll have to hope so, won't we?"

Giordino gave him a sour look and started up the side of the cliff. He quickly vanished in the blackness while Pitt grasped the end of the line and held it taut to take up the slack.

"Find a couple of protruding rocks and tie off the boat fore and aft," Pitt ordered Maeve. "If worse comes to worst, we may have to rely on *Marvelous Maeve* to carry us away from here.''

Maeve looked at him curiously. "How else did you expect to escape?''

"I'm a lazy sort. I had it in the back of my mind that we could steal one of your father's yachts, or maybe an aircraft.''

"Do you have an army I'm not aware of?''

"You're looking at half of it.''

Further conversation died as they gazed unseeing in the darkness, speculating on Giordino's progress. Pitt's only awareness of his friend's movements was the quivering on the line.

After thirty minutes, Giordino stopped to catch his breath. His arms ached like a thousand devils were stabbing them. His ascent had been fairly rapid considering the unevenness of the rocks. Climbing without the line would have been impossible. Even with the proper gear, having to make his way in the dark a meter at a time, groping for toeholds, driving in pitons and securing ropes, the climb would have taken the better part of six hours.

One minute of rest, no more, then it was hand over hand again. Wearily but still powerfully he pulled himself upward, kicking around the overhangs, taking advantage of the ledges. The palms of his hands were rubbed raw from the never-ending clutching and heaving on the thin nylon line salvaged from Rodney York's boat. As it was, the old line was hardly strong enough to take his bulk. But it had had to be light in weight for the kite to carry the grappling hook over the top. Any heavier and it would have been a lost cause.

He paused to look upward at the shadowy lip of the summit, lined against the stars. Five meters, he estimated, five meters to go. His breath was heaving in aching gasps, his chest and arms bruised from scraping against unseen rock in the darkness. His immense strength was down to the bottom of its reserves. He was climbing the last few meters on guts alone. Indestructible, as hard and gritty as the rock on which he climbed, Giordino kept going, refusing to stop again until he could climb no more. Then suddenly the ground at the top of the cliff opened before his eyes and spread out on a horizontal level. One final heave over the edge and he lay flat, listening to his heart pound, his lungs pumping like bellows, sucking air in and out.

For the next three minutes Giordino lay without moving, elated that the agonizing exertion was over. He surveyed his immediate surroundings and found himself stretched across a path that traveled along the edge of the cliffs. A few paces beyond, a wall of trees and underbrush loomed dark and uninviting. Seeing no sign of lights or movement, he traced the line to the grappling hook and saw that it was firmly imbedded in a rock outcropping.

Pitt's zany idea had worked incredibly well.

Satisfied the hook wasn't going anywhere, he rose to his feet. He untied the kite and hid it in the vegetation opposite the path before returning to the edge of the bluff and giving two sharp tugs on the rope that vanished into the darkness.

Far below, Pitt turned to Maeve. "Your turn."

"I don't know if I'm up to this," she said nervously. "Heights scare me."

He made a loop, dropped it over her shoulders and cinched it tight around her waist. "Hold tight to the line, lean back from the cliff and walk up the side. Al will haul you up from above."

He answered Giordino's signal by jerking three times on the line. Maeve felt the slack taken up, followed by the pressure around her waist. Clamping her eyes tightly shut, she began walking like a fly up the vertical face of the cliff.

Far above, his arms too numb to elevate Maeve by hand, Giordino had discovered a smooth slot in the rock that would not damage or cut into the nylon fibers. He inserted the line and laid it over his shoulders. Then he bent forward and staggered across the path, dragging Maeve's weight up the cliff behind him.

In twelve minutes, Maeve appeared over the edge, eyes tightly closed. "Welcome to the top of the Matterhorn," Giordino greeted her warmly.

"Thank God that's behind me," she moaned gratefully, opening her eyes for the first time since leaving the beach. "I don't think I could ever do it again."

Giordino untied Maeve. "Keep watch while I hoist Dirk. You can see a fair distance along the cliffs to the north, but the path south is hidden by a big group of rocks about fifty meters away."

"I remember them," said Maeve. "They have a hollow interior with natural ramparts. My sister Deirdre and I used to play there and pretend we were royalty. It's called the Castle. There's a small rest station and a telephone inside for the guards."

"We've got to bring Dirk up before the next patrol comes along," said Giordino, carefully dropping the line again.

To Pitt, it felt as if he were being hauled topside in the time it took to fry an egg. But less than ten meters from the rim, his ascent abruptly stopped. No word of warning, no word of encouragement, only silence. It could only mean one thing. His timing was unlucky. A patrol must be approaching. Unable to see what was occurring on the ledge above, he pressed his body into a small crevice, lying rigid and still, listening for sounds in the night.

Maeve had spotted the beam of light as it swung around one wall of the Castle and immediately alerted Giordino. Quickly, he secured the line around a tree to maintain tension so Pitt wouldn't be dropped back onto the beach. He brushed dirt and dead leaves over the section of rope that showed but had no time to conceal the grappling hook.

"What about Dirk?" Maeve whispered frantically. "He might wonder what happened and call up to us."

"He'll guess the plot and be as quiet as a mouse," Giordino answered with certainty. He shoved her roughly into the underbrush beside the path. "Get in there and stay low till the guards pass by."

Inexorably, the unswerving single beam of light grew larger as it approached. After having walked their circuit a hundred times in the past four months without seeing so much as a strange footprint, the two-man patrol should have been lax and careless. Routine inaction leads to boredom and indifference. They should have walked right on past, seeing only the same rocks, the same bends in the path, hearing the same faint beat of the surf pounding the rocks far below. But these men were highly trained and highly paid. Bored, yes, lethargic, no.

Giordino's pulse jumped at seeing that the guards were studying every inch of the path as they walked. He could not have known that Dorsett paid a twenty-five thousand dollar bonus for the severed hand of every diamond smuggler that was caught. What became of the rest of the body was never known, much less discussed. These men took their work seriously. They spied something and stopped directly in front of Maeve and Giordino.

"Hello, here's something the last patrol missed, or wasn't here an hour ago."

"What do you see?" asked his partner.

"Looks like a grappling hook off a boat." The first guard dropped to one knee and brushed away the hurried camouflage. "Well, well, it's attached to a line that drops down the cliff."

"The first attempt to enter the island from the bluffs since that party of Canadian smugglers we caught three years ago." Afraid to stand too close to the edge, the guard beamed his light down the cliff face, but saw nothing.

The other guard pulled out a knife and made ready to cut the line. "If any are waiting to come up from below, they're about to be awfully disappointed."

Maeve sucked in her breath as Giordino stepped out of the bushes onto the path. "Don't you characters have anything better to do than wander around at night?"

The first guard froze, his knife hand raised in the air. The second guard spun around and leveled his Bushmaster M-16 assault rifle at Giordino. "Freeze in your position or I'll fire."

Giordino did as he was told, but tensed his legs in preparation to spring. Fear and temporary shock gripped him at realizing it was only a matter of seconds before Pitt would be hurtling toward the sea and rocks below. But the guard's face went blank and he lowered his weapon.

His partner looked at him. "What's wrong with you?"

He broke off, peered behind Giordino and saw a woman step into the beam of light. There was no fear in her expression, rather it was one of anger. "Put away your silly guns and behave as you were trained!" she snapped.

The guard with the flashlight beamed it at Maeve. He stood in silent surprise, peering intently into her face before finally mumbling, "Miss Dorsett?"

"Fletcher," she corrected him. "Maeve Fletcher."

"I . . . we were told you drowned."

"Do I look like I've been floating in the sea?" Maeve, in her ragged blouse and shorts, wasn't sure how she appeared to the guards. But she knew without doubt that she didn't look like the daughter of a billionaire diamond tycoon.

"May I ask what you're doing here this time of the morning?" the guard asked politely but firmly.

"My friend and I decided to take a walk."

The guard with the knife wasn't buying it. "You'll excuse me," he said, grabbing the line in his free hand in readiness to slice it with his left, "but there is something very wrong here."

Maeve stepped over and abruptly slapped the man with the leveled rifle across the cheek. The startling display of supremacy surprised both guards, and they hesitated. Swift as a coiled rattler, Giordino sprang at the nearer guard, brushing away the assault rifle and smashing his head into the man's stomach. The guard grunted in a violent convulsion before crashing to the ground on his back. Giordino, losing his footing, toppled across the fallen guard.

In the same instant, Maeve threw herself at the guard poised to cut Pitt's lifeline, but he swung a vicious backhand that caught her on the side of the head and stopped her in her tracks. Then he dropped the knife and threw up his assault rifle, the index finger of his right hand sliding against the trigger as he aimed the barrel at Giordino's chest.

Giordino knew he was dead. Entangled with the other guard, he had no time for any defensive move. He knew it was impossible to reach the guard before he saw the flash from the muzzle. He could do nothing but stiffen his body in expectation of the bullet's impact.

But no shot rang out and no bullet struck Giordino's flesh.

Unnoticed, a hand with an arm attached snaked over the edge of the cliff, reached up and snatched the rifle, jerking it out of the guard's hands. Before the guard drew another breath, he was yanked into space. His final scream of terror echoed throughout the black void until it became muffled and died as if covered by a funeral shroud.

Then Pitt's head, lit by the flashlight on the ground, raised above the cliff's edge. The eyes blinked in the glare of the light and then the lips turned up in a slight grin.

"I believe that's what you call *flying* in the face of adverse opinion."

50

Maeve hugged Pitt. "You couldn't have arrived at a more opportune moment."

"How come you didn't blast away with your little popgun?" asked Giordino.

Pitt pulled the tiny automatic out of his back pocket and held it in the palm of his hand. "After the guard with the flashlight failed to find me hiding in a crevasse, I waited a minute and then pulled myself up to the edge of the cliff to see what was happening. When I saw you were within an instant of being shot, there was no time to draw and aim. So I did the next best thing."

"Lucky he did," Maeve said to Giordino, "or you wouldn't be here."

Giordino was not one to display maudlin sentiment. "Next chance I get, I'll carry out his trash." He glanced down at the guard who was writhing on the ground in the fetal position, clutching his abdomen. He picked up the M-16 and checked the ammo clip. "A nice addition to our arsenal."

"What do we do with him?" asked Maeve. "Chuck him over the cliff?"

"Nothing so drastic," answered Pitt. Instinctively, he glanced in both directions along the path leading along the ledge. "He can't hurt us now. Better to gag and tie him up and leave him for his buddies to find. When he and his partner don't show up to check in at the next guard station, they're certain to come searching for them."

"The next patrol won't show up for another fifty minutes," said Giordino, rapidly pulling the nylon line over the cliff's edge onto the path. "Time enough for a good head start."

Minutes later the guard, his eyes wide with fright and clothed only in his underwear, hung in space from the grappling hook, ten meters below the rim of the clifftop. The nylon line was wrapped around his body tightly, like a cocoon.

With Maeve as a guide, they set off along the cliff path. Giordino packed the diminutive automatic pistol, while Pitt, now clad in the guard's uniform, carried the Bushmaster M-16. They no longer felt exposed and helpless. Irrational, Pitt knew, for there must have been no less than a hundred other security guards standing watch over the mines and the island's shoreline. That wasn't the worst of their problems. Now that there was no returning to the *Marvelous Maeve,* they would have to seek other means of transport, a plan Pitt had always held in the back of his mind without the foggiest notion of how to carry it out. That wasn't a primary concern just yet. What mattered now was finding Maeve's boys and stealing them out of the hands of their crazy grandfather.

After traveling about five hundred meters, Maeve held up a hand and gestured into the thick underbrush. "We'll cross the island here," she informed them. "A road curves to within thirty meters of where we stand. If we're careful and remain out of sight of any traffic, we can follow the road into the central housing area for Dorsett employees."

"Where are we in relation to the volcanos that anchor each end of the island?" asked Pitt.

"We're about half way between and opposite the lagoon."

"Where do you think your boys might be held?" Giordino put to her.

"I wish I knew," she said distantly. "My first guess is the manor house, but I wouldn't put it past my father to keep them under guard in the security compound, or worse, they're kept by Jack Ferguson."

"Not a good idea to wander around like tourists looking for a restaurant," said Pitt.

"I'm with you," Giordino agreed. "The proper thing to do is find someone in authority with the answers and twist his arm."

Pitt fastidiously straightened the jacket of his stolen uniform and brushed off the shoulders. "If he's on the island, I know just the man."

Twenty minutes later, after traveling over a road that wound in a series of hairpin turns over the spine of the island, they approached the compound that housed the mining engineers and the security guards. Keeping in the sheltered gloom of the underbrush, they skirted the detention camp for the Chinese laborers. Bright lights illuminated the barracks and open grounds, surrounded by a high electrified fence that was topped by rows of circular razor wire. The area was so heavily secured by electronic surveillance systems that no guards were walking around the perimeter.

In another hundred meters, Maeve stopped and gestured for Pitt and Giordino to drop behind a low hedge that bordered a concrete thoroughfare. One end of the road ended at a driveway that passed through a large arched gate to the Dorsett family manor house. A short distance in the opposite direction, the road split. One broad avenue trailed down a slope to the port in the center of the lagoon, where the docks and warehouses reflected a weird appearance under the eerie yellow glow of sodium-vapor lamps. Pitt took an extra minute to study the big boat tied beside the dock. Even at this distance, there was no mistaking the Dorsett yacht. Pitt was especially pleased to see a helicopter sitting on the upper deck.

"Does the island have an airstrip?" he asked Maeve.

She shook her head. "Daddy refused to construct one, preferring all his transportation by sea. He uses a helicopter to carry him back and forth from the Australian mainland. Why do you want to know?"

"A process of elimination. Our getaway bird sits yonder on the yacht," Pitt said.

"You clever man, you had that in mind all along."

"I was merely swept up in a orgy of inspiration," Pitt said artfully, then asked, "How many men guard the yacht?"

"Only one, who monitors the dock security systems."

"And the crewmen?"

"Whenever the boat is docked at the island, Daddy requires the crew to stay in quarters ashore."

Pitt took note that the other fork in the road curved toward the main compound. The mines inside the volcanos were alive with activity, but the central area of the Dorsett Consolidated Mining community was deserted. The dock beside the yacht appeared totally deserted under the floodlights mounted on a nearby warehouse. Everyone else, it seemed, was asleep in bed, a not uncommon circumstance at four o'clock in the morning.

"Point out the chief of security's house," Pitt said to Maeve.

"The mining engineers and my father's servants live in the cluster of buildings closest to the lagoon," answered Maeve. "The house you want sits on the southeast corner of the security guards' compound. Its walls are painted gray."

"I see it." Pitt drew a sleeve across his forehead to wipe away the sweat. "Is there a way to reach it other than the road?"

"A walkway runs along the rear."

"Let's get moving. We don't have a whole lot of time before daylight."

They stayed in the shadows behind the hedge and the neatly trimmed trees that stretched alongside the paved shoulders of the road. Tall streetlights were spaced every fifty meters, the same as most city streets. Except for the soft rustle of wild grass and scattered leaves beneath their feet, the three of them moved quietly toward the gray house at the corner of the compound.

When they reached a clump of bushes outside the rear door, Pitt put his mouth to Maeve's ear. "Have you ever been inside the house before?"

"Only once or twice when I was a little girl and Daddy asked me to deliver a message to the man who headed his security a long time ago," she replied in a soft murmur.

"Can you say whether the house has an alarm system to detect intruders?"

Maeve shook her head. "I can't imagine who would want to break into the security chief's diggings."

"Any live-in help?"

"They're housed in a different compound."

"The back door it is," Pitt whispered.

"I hope we find a well-stocked kitchen," muttered Giordino.

"I'm not comfortable sneaking around in the dark on an empty stomach, a very empty stomach, I might add."

"You can have first crack at the refrigerator," Pitt promised.

Pitt stepped out of the shadows and slipped up to one side of the back door and peered through a window. The interior was lit only by a dim light over a hallway that ended at a stairwell leading to the second floor. Cautiously, he reached over and gently twisted the latch. There was a barely audible click as the shaft slipped from its catch. He took a deep breath and cracked the door ever so slightly. It swung on its hinges noiselessly, so he pushed it wide open and stepped into a rear entryway that opened into a small kitchen. He stepped across the kitchen and quietly closed a sliding door leading to a hallway. Then he turned on the light. At the signal, Maeve and Giordino followed him in.

"Oh, thank you, God," muttered Giordino in ecstasy at seeing a beautifully decorated kitchen over whose counters and oven hung expensive cooking utensils fit for a gourmet chef.

"Warm air," Maeve whispered happily. "I haven't felt warm air in weeks."

"I can taste the ham and eggs already," said Giordino.

"First things first," Pitt said quietly.

Turning the light out again, he slipped the hallway door open, leveled the assault rifle and stepped into the hallway. He cocked his head and listened, hearing only the soft noise of a heater fan. Flattening himself against the wall, he moved along the hallway under the muted light before starting up the carpeted stairway, testing each step for a squeak before setting his weight on it.

At the landing at the top of the stairs, he found two closed doors, one on either side. He tried the one to his right. The room was furnished as a private office with computer, telephones and file cabinets. The desk was incredibly orderly and free of clutter, the same as the kitchen. Pitt smiled to himself. He expected no less from the inhabitant. Sure of himself now, he stepped over to the left door, kicked it open and switched on the light.

A beautiful Asian girl, no more than eighteen, with long black silken hair falling over the side of the bed to the floor, stared in bulging-eyed fright at the figure standing in the doorway with an assault rifle. She opened her mouth as if to scream but emitted a muted gurgling sound.

The man next to her was a cool customer. He lay on his side, eyes closed, and made no attempt to turn and look at Pitt. Pitt would have missed the fractional movement but for the apparent indifference of the man. He lightly pulled the trigger, sending two quick shots into the pillow. The muzzle blast was muffled by the gun's suppressor and came like a pair of hand claps. Only then did the man in bed bolt upright and stare at a hand that was bleeding from a bullet through the palm.

Now the girl shrieked, but neither man seemed to care. They both waited patiently until she froze into silence.

"Good morning, Chief," said Pitt cheerfully. "Sorry to inconvenience you."

John Merchant blinked in the light and focused his eyes on his intruder. "My guards will have heard the screams and come on the run," he said calmly.

"I doubt that. Knowing you, I should judge that feminine screams coming from your living quarters are considered a nightly occurrence by your neighbors."

"Who are you? What do you want?"

"How quickly they forget."

Merchant squinted and then his mouth dropped open in recognition. His face registered abject disbelief. "You can't be . . . you can't be . . . Dirk Pitt!"

As if prompted, Maeve and Giordino came into the room. They stood there behind Pitt, saying nothing, looking at the two people in bed as if watching a staged drama.

"This has to be a nightmare," Merchant gasped.

"Do you bleed in your dreams?" asked Pitt, slipping his hand under Merchant's pillow, retrieving the nine-millimeter automatic the security chief was reaching for and throwing it to Giordino. He thought the slimy little man would come around to accepting the situation, but Merchant was too stunned at seeing the ghosts of three people he thought were dead.

"I saw you cast adrift with my own eyes, before the storm struck," Merchant said in a dull monotone. "How is it possible you all survived?"

"We were swallowed by a whale," said Giordino, pulling the window curtains closed. "We upset his tummy, and you can guess what happened next."

"You people are crazy. Give up your weapons. You'll never get off the island alive."

Pitt placed the muzzle of his assault rifle against Merchant's forehead. "The only words I want to hear from you concern the location of Miss Fletcher's sons. Where are they?"

A spark of defiance gleamed in Merchant's eyes. "I won't tell you anything."

"Then you will surely die," said Pitt coldly.

"Strange words from a marine engineer and an oceanographer, a man who sets women and children on a pedestal, and who is respected for his word and integrity."

"I applaud your homework."

"You won't kill me," said Merchant, regaining control of his emotions. "You are not a professional assassin, nor a man who has the stomach for murder."

Pitt gave a casual shrug. "I'd venture to say that one of your guards, the one I threw over the cliffs about half an hour ago, would disagree."

Merchant stared at Pitt impassively, not certain whether to believe him. "I do not know what Mr. Dorsett has done with his grandsons."

Pitt moved the rifle barrel from Merchant's head to one knee. "Maeve, count to three."

"One," she began, as composed as if she were counting lumps of sugar in a cup of tea. "Two . . . three."

Pitt pulled the trigger and a bullet smashed through Merchant's kneecap. Merchant's mistress went into another fit of screaming until Giordino clamped his hand over her mouth.

"Can we please have some quiet? You're cracking the plaster."

A complete transformation came over Merchant. The evil malignity of the repellant little man was suddenly replaced with a demeanor marked by pain and terror. His mouth twisted as he spoke. "My knee, you've shattered my knee!" he rasped in horror.

Pitt placed the muzzle against one of Merchant's elbows. "I'm in a hurry. Unless you wish to be doubly maimed, I suggest you speak, and speak the truth or you'll have a tough time brushing your teeth from now on."

"Miss Fletcher's sons work in the mines with the other laborers. They're kept with the others in the guarded camp."

Pitt turned to Maeve. "It's your call."

Maeve looked into Merchant's eyes, her face taut with emotion. "He's lying. Jack Ferguson, my father's overseer, is in charge of the boys. They would never be out of his sight."

"Where does he hang out?" asked Giordino.

"Ferguson lives in a guest house beside the mansion so he can be at my father's beck and call," said Maeve.

Pitt smiled coldly at Merchant. "Sorry, John, wrong answer. That will cost you an elbow."

"No, please, no!" Merchant muttered through teeth clenched from the pain. "You win. The twins are kept in Ferguson's quarters when they're not working in the mines."

Maeve stepped forward until she was standing over Merchant, distraught and grieved at envisioning the suffering her sons were enduring. Her self-control crumbled as she slapped him sharply, several times across the face. "Six-year-old boys forced to work in the mines! What kind of sadistic monsters are you?"

Giordino wrapped his arms gently around Maeve's waist and pulled her back into the center of the room, as she broke into anguished sobbing.

Pitt's face reflected sorrow and anger. He moved the muzzle to within a millimeter of Merchant's left eye. "One more question, friend John. Where sleeps the helicopter's pilot?"

"He's in the mining company's medical clinic with a broken arm," Merchant answered sullenly. "You can forget about forcing him to fly you from the island."

Pitt nodded and smiled knowingly at Giordino. "Who needs him?" He looked about the room and nodded toward the closet. "We'll leave them in there."

"Do you intend to murder us?" asked Merchant slowly.

"I'd sooner shoot skunks," Pitt pointed out. "But since you brought it up, you and your little friend will be tied up, gagged and locked in the closet."

Merchant's fear was obvious from the tic at one corner of his mouth. "We'll suffocate in there."

"I can shoot you both now. Take your pick."

Merchant said no more and offered no resistance as he and the girl were bound with the bed sheets, torn into strips, and unceremoniously dumped into the closet. Giordino moved half the furniture in the bedroom against the door to keep it from being forced open from the inside.

"We've got what we came for," said Pitt. "Let's be on our way to the old homestead."

"You said I could raid the refrigerator," protested Giordino. "My stomach is going through rejection pains."

"No time for that now," said Pitt. "You can gorge later."

Giordino shook his head sorrowfully as he stuffed Merchant's nine-millimeter automatic inside his belt. "Why do I feel as though there's a conspiracy afoot to deplete my body sugar?"

51

Seven o'clock in the morning. A blue sky, unlimited visibility and a sea with low swells rolling like silent demons toward unseen shores where they would crash and die. It was a normal day like most days in the tropical waters off the Hawaiian Islands, warm with more than a trace of humidity and a light breeze, generally referred to as the trade winds. It was a Saturday, a day when the beaches at Waikiki and the windward side of the island were slowly coming alive with early birds awake for an early morning dip. Soon they would be followed by thousands of local residents and vacationers looking forward to leisurely hours of swimming in surf subdued by offshore reefs, and sunbathing on heated sand later in the day. Lulled by the relaxing atmosphere, none were remotely aware that this might be their last day on earth.

The *Glomar Explorer*, only one of her big twin screws driving under full power, pushed steadily toward the site of the deadly acoustic convergence, the sound waves already hurtling through the sea from the four sources. She should have been running a good half hour late, but Chief Engineer Toft had pushed his crew to and beyond the edge of exhaustion. He cursed and pleaded with the engine that strained against its mounts, bound to the only operating shaft, and coaxed another half knot out of it. He swore to get the ship to its meeting with destiny with time to spare, and by God he was doing it.

Up on the starboard wing of the bridge, Sandecker peered through binoculars at a commercial version of the Navy's SH-60B Sea Hawk helicopter, with NUMA markings, as it approached the ship from bow-on, circled once and dropped on the big ship's stern landing pad. Two men hurried from the aircraft and entered the aft superstructure. A minute later, they joined Sandecker on the bridge.

"Did the drop go well?" Sandecker asked anxiously.

Dr. Sanford Adgate Ames nodded with a slight smile. "Four arrays of remote acoustical sensing instruments have been deployed under the surface at the required locations thirty kilometers distant from the convergence zone."

"We laid them directly in the four estimated paths of the sound channels," added Gunn, who had made the flight with Ames.

"They're set to measure the final approach and intensity of the sound?" Sandecker asked.

Ames nodded. "The telemetry data from the underwater modems will be relayed by their surface flotation satellite link to the onboard processor and analyst terminal here on board the *Explorer*. The system works similarly to submarine acoustic locating programs."

"Fortunately, we have a weather and current window working in our favor," said Gunn. "All things considered, the sound waves should come together as predicted."

"Warning time?"

"Sound travels underwater at an average of fifteen hundred meters per second," replied Ames. "I figure twenty seconds from when the sound waves pass the modems until they strike the reflector dish under the ship."

"Twenty seconds," Sandecker repeated. "Damned little time to mentally prepare for the unknown."

"Since no one without some kind of protection has survived to describe the full intensity of the convergence, my best estimate of its duration before it is totally deflected toward Gladiator Island is approximately four and a half minutes. Anyone on board the ship who does not reach the dampened shelter will surely die horribly."

Sandecker turned and gestured at the vivid green mountains of Oahu, only fifteen kilometers distant. "Will any effects reach the people on shore?"

"They might feel a brief but sharp pain inside their heads, but no permanent harm should come to them."

Sandecker stared out the bridge windows at the huge mass of machinery soaring skyward in the middle of the ship. Infinite miles of cable and hydraulic lines ranged over the deck from the derrick and cranes. Teams of men and women, sitting and standing on platforms suspended in the air like those used by skyscraper window cleaners, worked at reconnecting the seemingly unending number of links on the enormous reflector shield. The giant derrick held the main frame of the shield, while the surrounding cranes lifted the smaller numbered pieces into their slots where they were then joined. Thanks to Rudi Gunn's foresight in cleaning and oiling the connectors, all parts fit quickly and smoothly. The operation was going like clockwork. Only two more parts were left to install.

The admiral turned his gaze toward the jewel of the Pacific, easily distinguishing details of Diamond Head, the hotels strung along Waikiki Beach, the Aloha Tower in Honolulu, the homes fading into the clouds that always seemed to hover over Mount Tantalus, the jetliners landing at the international airport, the facilities at Pearl Harbor. There could be no room for error. Unless the operation went according to plan, the beautiful island would become a vast killing field.

At last he looked at the man studying the digital numbers on the ship's computerized navigation system. "Captain Quick."

The master of the *Glomar Explorer* looked up. "Admiral Sandecker."

"How far to the site?"

Quick smiled. It was only the twentieth time the admiral had asked the same question since departing Halawa Bay. "Less than five hundred meters and another twenty minutes until we begin pinpointing the ship over the numbers your people computed for the Global Positioning System."

"Which leaves us only forty minutes to deploy the reflector shield."

"Thanks to Chief Toft and his engine-room crew, otherwise we never could have made it on schedule."

"Yes," Sandecker agreed. "We owe him big."

474

The long minutes passed with everyone in the wheelhouse keeping one eye on the clock and the other on the red digital numbers of the Global Positioning System as they diminished finally to a row of zeros, indicating the ship was over the precise site where the sound rays were calculated to converge and explode with unparalleled intensity. The next project was to hold the ship in the exact spot. Captain Quick focused on programming the coordinates into the automated ship's control system, which analyzed sea and weather conditions and controlled the thruster jets on the bow and stern. In an incredibly short time span, the *Glomar Explorer* had achieved station and was able to hover motionless in the water, resisting wind and current within a deviation factor of less than a meter.

Several other systems, each critical to the operation, also came into play. The pitch was feverish. Teams of engineers and technicians, electronics systems experts and scientists worked simultaneously to put the reflector shield in the precise path of the sound waves. The NUMA team, working on platforms far above the deck, made the final connections and attached the shield to the drop hook of the derrick.

Far below, one of the most unique sections of the ship stirred to life. Taking up the middle third of the ship, the 1,367 square meter Moon Pool, as it was called, filled with water as two sections of the center hull, one fore, the other aft, retracted into specially designed sleeves. The true heart of the seafloor dredging system and what had been the recovery operation of the Russian submarine, the Moon Pool was where it all came together, where the dredging hose would be extended thousands of meters deep to the minerals carpeting the ocean's bottom and where the vast reflector shield would be lowered into the sea.

The engineering systems on board the *Glomar Explorer* were originally constructed to raise heavy objects from the seafloor, not to lower lighter but more expansive objects downward. Procedures were hurriedly modified for the complex operation. Minor glitches were quickly overcome. Every move was coordinated and performed with precision.

The tension on the lowering cable was increased by the derrick operator until the reflector hung free in the air. The appropriate signal by the NUMA team was given, indicating that the reflector assembly was "all completed." The entire unit was then lowered diagonally through the rectangular Moon Pool into the sea with centimeters to spare. It was that close. The immersion time ran ten meters a minute. Full deployment by the cables securing the dish at the precise angle and depth to ricochet the sound waves to Gladiator Island took fourteen minutes.

"Six minutes and ten seconds to convergence," Captain Quick's voice droned over the ship's loudspeakers. "All ship's personnel will go to the engine-room storage compartment at the aft end of the ship and enter as you have been instructed. Do this immediately. I say immediately. Run, do not walk."

Suddenly, everyone was dropping down ladders and scaffolding, hurrying in unison like a pack of marathon runners toward the propulsion and pump room deep in the bowels of the ship. Here, twenty ship's crew members had been busily sound-isolating the supply compartment with every piece of dampening material they could lay their hands on. The ship's towels, blankets, bedding and mattresses, along with all cushions from lounge chairs and any scraps of lumber they could scrounge were placed against ceiling, deck and bulkheads to deaden all intruding sound.

As they rushed down the passageways belowdecks, Sandecker said to Ames, "This is the agonizing part of the operation."

"I know what you're thinking," Ames replied, agilely descending two steps at a time. "The anxiety of wondering if we made a tiny miscalculation that put us in the wrong place at the wrong time. The frustration of not knowing whether we succeeded if we don't live through the convergence. The unknown factors are mind boggling."

They reached the engine room storage compartment, which had been selected to ride out the convergence because of its watertight door and its total lack of air ducts. They were checked in by two ship's officers who were counting heads and handing out sound-deadening headgear that fit over the ears. "Admiral Sandecker, Dr. Ames, please place these over your ears and try not to move around."

Sandecker and Ames found the NUMA team members settled in one corner of the compartment and joined them, moving beside Rudi Gunn and Molly Faraday, who had preceded them. They immediately gathered around monitoring systems that were integrated with the warning modems and other underwater sensors. Only the admiral, Ames and Gunn held off using the sound deadeners so they could confer right up to the final few seconds.

The compartment quickly filled amid a strange silence. Unable to hear, no one spoke. Captain Quick stood on a small box so he could be observed by all in the room. He held up two fingers as a two minute warning. The derrick operator, who had the farthest to travel, was the last man to enter. Satisfied that every person on the ship had been accounted for, the captain ordered that the door be sealed. Several mattresses were also pressed against the exit to muffle any sound that seeped into the confined compartment. Quick held up one finger, and the tension began to build until it lay like a mantle over the people packed closely together. All stood. There wasn't enough room to sit or recline.

Gunn had calculated that the ninety-six men and women had less than fifteen minutes in the tight quarters before their breathable air stagnated and they were overwhelmed by the effects of asphyxiation. Already the atmosphere was beginning to grow stale. The only other immediate danger was claustrophobia rearing its ugly head. The last thing they needed was unbridled hysteria. He gave Molly an encouraging wink and began monitoring the time while almost everyone else watched the ship's captain as if he were a symphony orchestra conductor with poised baton.

Quick raised both hands and curled them into fists. The moment of truth had arrived. Everything now hinged on the data analyzed by Hiram Yaeger's computer network. The ship was on station exactly as directed, the shield was in the precise position calculated by Yaeger and cross-checked by Dr. Ames and his staff. The entire operation down to the slightest detail was acted upon. Nothing less than a sudden and unusual change in sea temperature or an unforeseen seismic occurrence that significantly altered the ocean's current could spell disaster. The enormous consequences of failure were blanked from the minds of the NUMA team.

Five seconds passed, then ten. Sandecker began to feel the prickle of disaster in the nape of his neck. Then suddenly, ominously, the acoustic sensors, thirty kilometers distant, began registering the incoming sound waves along their predicted paths.

"Good Lord!" muttered Ames. "The sensors have gone off the scale. The intensity is greater than I estimated."

"Twenty seconds and counting!" snapped Sandecker. "Get your ear mufflers on."

The first indication of the convergence was a small resonance that rapidly grew in magnitude. The dampened bulkheads vibrated in conjunction with a hum that penetrated the sound-deadening ear protectors. The crowded people in the confined room sensed a mild form of disorientation and vertigo. But no one was struck by nausea and none panicked. The discomfort was borne stoically. Sandecker and Ames stared at each other, fulfillment swamping them in great trembling waves.

Five long minutes later it was all over. The resonance had faded away, leaving an almost supernatural silence behind it.

Gunn was the first to react. He tore off his sound deadeners, waved his arms and shouted at Captain Quick. "The door. Open the door and let some air in here."

Quick got the message. The mattresses were cast aside and the door undogged and thrown open. The air that filtered into the room reeked with oil from the ship's engine room but was welcomed by all as they slowly removed the sound deadeners from their heads. Vastly relieved the threat was over, they shouted and laughed like fans celebrating a win of their favorite football team. Then slowly, in an orderly manner, they filed from the storage room, up the companionways and into the fresh air.

Sandecker's reaction time was almost inhuman. He ran up the companionways to the wheelhouse in a time that would have broken any existing record, if there had been one. He snatched up a pair of binoculars and rushed out onto the bridge wing. Anxiously, he focused the lenses on the island, only fifteen kilometers distant.

Cars were traveling routinely on the streets, and busy crowds of sunseekers moved freely about the beaches. Only then did he expel a long sigh and sag in relief over the railing, totally drained of emotion.

"An utter triumph, Admiral," Ames said, pumping Sandecker's hand. "You proved the best scientific minds in the country wrong."

"I was blessed with your expertise and support, Doc," Sandecker said as if a great weight had been lifted from his shoulders. "I'd have accomplished nothing but for you and your staff of bright young scientists."

Overcome with exhilaration, Gunn and Molly both hugged Sandecker, an act considered unthinkable on any other occasion. "You did it!" said Gunn. "Nearly two million lives saved, thanks to your stubbornness."

"*We* did it," Sandecker corrected him. "From beginning to end it was a team effort."

Gunn's expression suddenly turned sober. "A great pity Dirk wasn't here to see it."

Sandecker nodded solemnly. "His concept was the spark that ignited the project."

Ames studied the array of instruments he had set up during the voyage from Molokai.

"The reflector positioning was perfect," he said happily. "The acoustic energy was reversed exactly as intended."

"Where is it now?" asked Molly.

"Combined with the energy from the other three island mining operations, the sound waves are traveling back to Gladiator Island faster than any jet plane. Their combined force should strike the submerged base in roughly ninety-seven minutes."

"I'd love to see his face."

"Whose face?" asked Ames innocently.

"Arthur Dorsett's," answered Molly, "when his private island starts to rock and roll."

52

The two men and the woman crouched in a clump of bushes off to one side of the great archway that broke the middle of a high, lava-rock wall enclosing the entire Dorsett estate. Beyond the archway, a brick driveway circled around a large, well-trimmed lawn through a grand port cochere, a tall structure extending from the front of the house to shelter people getting in and out of cars. The entire driveway and house were illuminated by bright lamps strategically spaced about the landscaped grounds. Entry was barred by a thick iron gate that looked like it came from a castle out of the Middle Ages. Nearly five meters thick, the archway itself housed a small office for the security guards.

"Is there another way in?" Pitt asked Maeve softly.

"The arched gate is the only way in or out," she whispered back.

"No drainage pipe or small ravine conveniently running beneath the wall?"

"Believe me, when I think of all the times I wanted to run away from my father when I was a young girl, I'd have found a passage leading from the grounds."

"Security detectors?"

"Laser beams along the top of the wall with infrared body-heat sensors installed at different intervals about the grounds. Anything larger than a cat will cause an alarm to sound in the security office. Television cameras automatically come on and aim their lenses at the intruder."

"How many guards?"

"Two at night, four during the day."

"No dogs?"

She shook her head in the darkness. "Father hates animals. I never forgave him for stomping on a small bird with a broken wing I was trying to nurse back to health."

"Old Art certainly creates an image of barbarity and viciousness," said Giordino. "Does he do cannibalism too?"

"He's capable of anything, as you very well found out," said Maeve.

Pitt stared at the gate thoughtfully, carefully gauging visible activity by the guards. They seemed content to stay inside and monitor the security systems. Finally, he rose to his feet, rumpled his uniform and turned to Giordino.

"I'm going to bluff my way inside. Hang loose until I open the gate."

He slung the assault rifle over his shoulder and pulled his Swiss army knife from a pocket. Extending a small blade he made a small cut in one thumb, squeezed out the blood and smeared it over his face. When he reached the gate, Pitt dropped to his knees and gripped the bars in both hands. Then he began to shout in a low moaning tone, as if in pain.

"Help me. I need help!"

A face appeared around the door, then disappeared. Seconds later, both guards ran out of the security office and opened the gate. Pitt fell forward into their waiting arms.

"What happened?" demanded a guard. "Who did this to you?"

"A gang of Chinese tunneled out of the camp. I was coming up the road from the dock when they jumped me from behind. I think I killed two of them before I got away."

"We'd better alert the main security compound," blurted one of the guards.

"Help me inside first," Pitt groaned. "I think they fractured my skull."

The guards lifted Pitt to his feet and slung his arms over their shoulders. They half carried, half dragged him into the security office. Slowly, Pitt moved his arms inward until the guards' necks were in the crooks of his elbows. As they pressed together to pass through the doorway, he took a convulsive step backwards, hooked the guards' necks in a tight grip and exerted every bit of strength in his biceps and shoulder muscles. The sound of their bared heads colliding was an audible thud. They both crashed to the floor, unconscious for at least the next two hours.

Safe from detection, Giordino and Maeve hurried through the opened gate and joined Pitt inside the office. Giordino picked up the guards as if they were straw scarecrows and sat them in chairs around a table facing a row of video monitors. "To anyone walking by," he said, "it'll look like they fell asleep during the movie."

A quick scan of the security system, and Pitt closed down the alarms, while Giordino bound the guards with their own ties and belts. Then Pitt looked at Maeve. "Where's Ferguson's quarters?"

"There are two guest houses in a grove of trees behind the manor. He lives in one of them."

"I don't suppose you know which one?"

She shrugged. "This is the first time I've returned to the island since I ran away to Melbourne and the university. If I remember correctly, he lives in the one nearest the manor."

"Time to repeat our break-in act," said Pitt. "Let's hope we haven't lost our touch."

They moved up the driveway at a steady, unhurried pace. They were too weakened from an inadequate diet and the hardships of the past weeks to run. They reached what Maeve believed was the living quarters of Jack Ferguson, superintendent of Dorsett's mines on Gladiator Island.

The sky was beginning to lighten in the east as they approached the front door. The search was taking too long. With the coming of dawn, their presence would most certainly be discovered. They had to move fast if they wanted to find the boys, reach the yacht and escape in Arthur Dorsett's private helicopter before the remaining darkness was lost.

There was no stealth this time, no slinking quietly into the house. Pitt walked up to the front door, kicked it in with a splintering crunch and walked inside. A quick look around with the flashlight taken from the guards at the cliff told him all he needed to know. Ferguson lived there all right. There was a stack of mail on a desk that was addressed to him and a calendar with notations. Inside a closet, Pitt found neatly pressed men's pants and coats.

"Nobody home," he said. "Jack Ferguson has gone. No sign of suitcases, and half the hangars in the closet are empty."

"He's got to be here," said Maeve in confusion.

"According to dates he's marked on his calendar, Ferguson is on a tour of your father's other mining properties."

She stared at the vacant room in futility and growing despair. "My boys are gone. We're too late. Oh God, we're too late. They're dead."

Pitt put his arm around her. "They're as alive as you and I."

"But John Merchant—"

Giordino stood in the doorway. "Never trust a man with beady eyes."

"No sense in wasting time here," said Pitt, pushing past Giordino. "The boys are in the manor house, always have been, as a matter of fact."

"You couldn't have known Merchant was lying," Maeve challenged Pitt.

He smiled. "Ah, but Merchant didn't lie. You were the one who said the boys lived with Jack Ferguson in a guest house. Merchant merely went along with you. He guessed we were suckers enough to buy it. Well, maybe we did, but only for a second."

"You knew?"

"It goes without saying that your father wouldn't harm your sons. He may threaten, but a dime will get you a quarter they're sequestered in your old room, where they've been all along, playing with a room full of toys, courtesy of their old granddad."

Maeve looked at him in confusion. "He didn't force them to work in the mines?"

"Probably not. He turned the screws on your maternal instincts to make you think your babies were suffering so he could make you suffer. The dirty bastard wanted you to go to your death believing he would enslave the twins, place them in the care of a sadistic foreman and work them until they died. Face facts. With Boudicca and Deirdre childless, your boys are the only heirs he's got. With you out of the way, he figured he could raise and mold them into his own image. In your eyes a fate worse than death.''

Maeve looked at Pitt for a long moment, her expression turning from disbelief to understanding, then she shivered. "What kind of fool am I?''

"A great song title," said Giordino. "I hate to dampen good news, but this time the people of the house are stirring about.'' He gestured at lights shining in the windows of the manor house.

"My father always rises before dawn," said Maeve. "He never allowed my sisters and me to sleep after sunrise.''

"What I wouldn't give to join them for breakfast," moaned Giordino.

"Not to sound like an echo chamber," said Pitt, "but we need a way in without provoking the inhabitants.''

"All rooms of the manor open onto interior verandas except one. Daddy's study has a side door that leads onto a squash court.''

"What's a squash court?" inquired Giordino.

"A court where they play squash," answered Pitt. Then to Maeve. "In what direction is your old bedroom?''

"Across the garden and past the swimming pool to the east wing, second door on the right.''

"That's it then. You two go after the boys.''

"What will you do?''

"Me, I'm going to borrow Daddy's phone and stick him with a long-distance call.''

53

The atmosphere on board the *Glomar Explorer* was relaxed and partylike. The NUMA team and the ship's personnel that were gathered in the spacious lounge next to the galley celebrated their success in repelling the acoustic plague. Admiral Sandecker and Dr. Ames were sitting opposite each other, sipping champagne poured from a bottle produced by Captain Quick from his private stock for special occasions.

After further consideration, it was decided to reclaim the antenna/reflector from the water and dismantle it again in case Dorsett Consolidated's disastrous mining operations could not be terminated and it became essential to stop another acoustic convergence in order to save lives. The reflector shield was raised, and the hull below the Moon Pool was sealed off and the sea pumped from its cavernous interior. Within an hour, the historic ship was on its return course to Molokai.

Sandecker heaved himself out of his chair after being informed by the ship's communications officer that he had an important call from his chief geologist, Charlie Bakewell. He walked to a quiet part of the lounge and pulled a compact satellite phone from his pocket. "Yes, Charlie."

"I understand congratulations are in order." Bakewell's voice came clearly.

"It was a close thing. We barely positioned the ship and dropped the reflector shield before the convergence occurred. Where are you now?"

"I'm here at the Joseph Marmon Volcanic Observatory in Auckland, New Zealand. I have an update for you from their staff of geophysicists. Their most recent analysis of the sound ray energy's impact on Gladiator Island isn't very encouraging."

"Can they compute the repercussions?"

"I'm sorry to say the predicted magnitude is worse than I originally thought," answered Bakewell. "The two volcanos on the island, I've since learned, are called Mount Scaggs and Mount Winkleman, after two survivors from the raft of the *Gladiator*. They're part of a chain of potentially explosive volcanos that encircles the Pacific Ocean known as the 'Ring of Fire' and lie not far from a tectonic plate similar to the ones separating the San Andreas Fault in California. Most volcanic activity and earthquakes are caused by a movement of these plates. Studies indicate the volcanos' last major activity occurred sometime between 1225 and 1275 A.D., when they erupted simultaneously."

"As I recall, you said the chances of them erupting from the convergence impact was one in five."

"After consulting with the experts here at the Marmon Observatory, I've lowered the odds to less than even."

"I can't believe the sound ray traveling toward the island has the strength to cause a volcanic eruption," said Sandecker incredulously.

"Not by itself," replied Bakewell. "But what we neglected to consider was Dorsett's mining operations making the volcanos most susceptible to outside tremors. Even a minor seismic disturbance could trigger volcanic activity from Mounts Scaggs and Winkleman, because years of excavating diamonds has removed much of the ancestral deposits containing the gaseous pressure from below. In short, if Dorsett doesn't stop digging, it's only a matter of time before his miners uncork the central conduit, releasing an explosion of molten lava."

"An explosion of molten lava," Sandecker repeated mechanically. "Dear God, what have we done? Hundreds of lives will be lost."

"Don't be in a rush to confess your sins," said Bakewell seriously. "There are no women and children known to be on Gladiator Island. You've already saved the lives of countless families on Oahu from certain extinction. Your action is bound to wake up the White House and State Department to the threat. Sanctions and legal actions against Dorsett Consolidated Mining will occur, I guarantee it. Without your intervention the acoustic plague would have continued, and there is no telling what harbor city the next convergence zone might have intersected."

"Still . . . I might have ordered the reflector shield to divert the sound waves toward an uninhabited landmass," said Sandecker slowly.

"And watch it surge through another unsuspecting fishing fleet or cruise ship. We all agreed this was the safest path. Give it a rest, Jim, you have no reason to condemn yourself."

"You mean I have no choice but to live with it."

"What is Dr. Ames' estimate of the sound wave's arrival at Gladiator?" inquired Bakewell, steering Sandecker away from a guilt trip.

Sandecker glanced at his watch. "Twenty-one minutes to impact."

"There's still time to warn the inhabitants to evacuate the island."

"My people in Washington have already tried to alert Dorsett Consolidated Mining management of the potential danger," said Sandecker. "But under orders from Arthur Dorsett, all communications between his mining operations and the outside have been cut off."

"It sounds almost as if Dorsett wanted something to happen."

"He's taking no chances of interference before his deadline."

"There is still a possibility no eruption will happen. The sound ray's energy might dissipate before impact."

"According to Dr. Ames' calculations, there's little chance of that," said Sandecker. "What is *your* worst case scenario?"

"Mount Scaggs and Mount Winkleman are described as shield volcanos, having built gently sloping mounds during their former activity. This class is seldom highly explosive like cinder cones, but Scaggs and Winkleman are not ordinary shield volcanos. Their last eruption was quite violent. The experts here at the observatory expect explosions around the base or flanks of the mounds that will produce rivers of lava.''

"Can anyone on the island survive such a cataclysm?'' asked Sandecker.

"Depends on which side the violence takes place. Almost no chance if the volcanos blow out toward the inhabited part of the island on the west.''

"And if they blow to the east?''

"Then the odds of survival should rise slightly, even with repercussions from enough seismic activity to bring down most if not all of the island's buildings.''

"Is there a danger of the eruption causing tidal waves?''

"Our analysis does not indicate a seismic disturbance with the strength to produce monstrous tidal activity,'' explained Bakewell. "Certainly nothing on the magnitude of the Krakatoa holocaust near Java in 1883. The shores of Tasmania, Australia and New Zealand shouldn't be touched by waves higher than one and a half meters.''

"That's a plus,'' Sandecker sighed.

"I'll get back to you when I know more,'' said Bakewell. "Hopefully, I've given you the worst, and all news from now on will be good.''

"Thank you, Charlie. I hope so too.''

Sandecker switched off the phone and stood there thoughtfully. Anxiety and foreboding did not show on his face, not a twitch of an eyelid, not even a tightening of the lips, but there was a dread running deep beneath the surface. He did not notice Rudi Gunn approaching him until he felt his shoulder tapped.

"Admiral, there is another call for you. It's from your office in Washington.''

Sandecker switched on the phone and spoke into it again. "This is Sandecker.''

"Admiral?'' came the familiar voice of his longtime secretary, Martha Sherman. Her normally formal tone was nervous with excitement. "Please stand by. I'm going to relay a call to you.''

"Is it important?'' he asked irritably. "I'm not in the mood for official business.''

"Believe me, you'll want to take this call,'' she informed him happily. "One moment while I switch you over.''

A pause, then, "Hello,'' said Sandecker. "Who's this?''

"Good morning from Down Under, Admiral. What's this about you dawdling around blue Hawaii?"

Sandecker was not the kind of man to tremble, but he trembled now and felt as if the deck had fallen from under his feet. "Dirk, good Lord, is it you?"

"What's left of me," Pitt replied. "I'm with Al and Maeve Fletcher."

"I can't believe you're all alive," Sandecker said as if an electrical surge was coursing through his veins.

"Al said to save him a cigar."

"How is the little devil?"

"Testy because I won't let him eat."

"When we learned that you were cast adrift by Arthur Dorsett in the path of a typhoon, I moved heaven and earth to launch a massive search, but the long arm of Dorsett frustrated my rescue efforts. After almost three weeks with no word, we thought you were all dead. Tell me how you survived all this time."

"A long story," said Pitt. "I'd rather you brought me up-to-date on the acoustic plague."

"A story far more involved than yours. I'll give you the particulars when we meet. Where are the three of you now?"

"We managed to reach Gladiator Island. I'm sitting in Arthur Dorsett's study as we speak, borrowing his telephone."

Sandecker went numb with disbelief. "You can't be serious."

"The gospel truth. We're going to snatch Maeve's twin boys and make our getaway across the Tasman Sea to Australia." He said it in such a way as to sound like he was walking down the street to buy a loaf of bread.

Cold fear replaced Sandecker's earlier anxiety, but it was the shocking fear of helplessness. The news struck with such unexpectedness, such suddenness, that he was incapable of words for several seconds until Pitt's inquiring voice finally penetrated his shock.

"Are you still there, Admiral?"

"Pitt, listen to me!" demanded Sandecker urgently. "Your lives are in extreme danger! Get off the island! Get off now!"

There was a slight pause. "Sorry, sir, I don't read you—"

"I've no time to explain," Sandecker interrupted. "All I can tell you is a sound ray of incredible intensity will strike Gladiator Island in less than twenty minutes. The impact will set up seismic resonance that is predicted to blow off the volcanos on opposite ends of the island. If the eruption takes place on the western side, there will be no survivors. You and the others must escape to sea while you still can. Talk no further. I am cutting off all communications.''

Sandecker switched off his phone, capable of nothing but the realization that he had unknowingly and innocently sealed a death warrant on his best friend.

54

The shocking knowledge struck Pitt like the thrust of a dagger. He stared through a large picture window at the helicopter sitting on the yacht moored to the pier in the lagoon. He estimated the distance at just under a kilometer. Burdened by two young children, he figured they would need a good fifteen minutes to reach the dock. Without means of transportation, a car or a truck, it would be an extremely close timetable. The time for caution had flown as if there had never been such a time. Giordino and Maeve should have found her sons by now. They had to have found them. If not, something must have gone terribly wrong.

He turned his gaze first toward Mount Winkleman, and then swept the saddle of the island, his eyes stopping on Mount Scaggs. They looked deceptively peaceful. Seeing the lush growth of trees in the ravines scoring the slopes, he found it hard to imagine the two mounts as menacing volcanos, sleeping giants on the verge of spewing death and disaster in a burst of gaseous steam and molten rock.

Briskly, but not in a hurried panic, he rose out of Dorsett's leather executive chair and came around the desk. At that instant, he halted abruptly, frozen in the exact center of the room as the double doors to the main interior of the house swung open, and Arthur Dorsett walked in.

He was carrying a cup of coffee in one hand and a file of papers under an arm. He wore wrinkled slacks and what had once been white but was now a yellowed dress shirt with a bow tie. His mind seemed elsewhere. Perceiving another body in his study, he looked up, more curious than surprised. Seeing the intruder was in uniform, his first thought was that Pitt was a security guard. He opened his mouth to demand the reason for Pitt's presence, then stiffened in petrified astonishment. His face became a pale mask molded by shock and bewilderment. The file fell to the floor, its papers sliding out like a fanned deck of cards. His hand dropped to his side, spilling the coffee on his slacks and the carpet.

"You're dead!" he gasped.

"You don't know how happy I am to prove you wrong," Pitt commented, pleased to see that Dorsett wore a patch over one eye. "Come to think of it, you *do* look like you've seen a ghost."

"The storm . . . there is no way you could have survived a raging sea." A flicker of emotional repossession showed in the one black eye and slowly but surely grew. "How was it possible?"

"A lot of positive thinking and my Swiss army knife." My God, this guy is big, Pitt thought, very glad he was the one pointing a gun.

"And Maeve . . . is she dead?" He spoke haltingly as he studied the assault rifle in Pitt's hands, the muzzle aimed at his heart.

"Just knowing that it causes you great annoyance and displeasure makes me happy to report she is alive and well and at this very moment about to make off with your grandsons." Pitt stared back, green eyes locked with black. "Tell me, Dorsett. How do you justify murdering your own daughter? Did one single woman who was simply trying to find herself as a person pose a threat to your assets? Or was it her sons you wanted, all to yourself?"

"It was essential the empire be carried on after my death by my direct descendants. Maeve refused to see it that way."

"I have news for you. Your empire is about to come crashing down around your head."

Dorsett failed to grasp Pitt's meaning. "You intend to kill me?"

Pitt shook his head. "I'm not your executioner. The island volcanos are going to erupt. A fitting end for you, Arthur, consumed by fiery lava."

Dorsett smiled faintly as he regained control. "What sort of nonsense is that?"

"Too complicated to explain. I don't know all the technicalities myself, but I have it on the best authority. You'll just have to take my word for it."

"You're bloody insane."

"O ye of little faith."

"If you're going to shoot," said Dorsett, cold anger glaring from his coal-black eye, "do it now, clean and quick."

Pitt grinned impassively. Maeve and Giordino had yet to make an appearance. For the moment he needed Arthur Dorsett alive in case they had been captured by security guards. "Sorry, I haven't the time. Now please turn around and go up the stairs to the bedrooms."

"My grandchildren, you can't have my grandchildren," he muttered as if it was a divine statement.

"Correction, Maeve's children."

"You'll never get past my security guards."

"The two at the front gate are—what's the word?—incapacitated."

"Then you'll have to murder me in cold blood, and I'll wager everything I've got that you don't have the guts for it."

"Why is it people keep thinking I can't stand the sight of blood?" Pitt touched his finger against the trigger of the assault rifle. "Get moving, Arthur, or I'll shoot off your ears."

"Go ahead, you yellow bastard," Dorsett lashed out, pronouncing it as *bahstud*. "You already took one of my eyes."

"You don't get the picture, do you?" White-hot anger consumed Pitt at seeing Dorsett's arrogant belligerence. He raised the rifle slightly and gently squeezed the trigger. The gun spat with a loud pop through the suppressor and a slice of Dorsett's left ear sprayed the carpet. "Now, head for the stairs. Make a move I don't like and you'll get a bullet in the spine."

There was no hint of pain in the bestial black eye. Dorsett smiled a menacing smile that sent an involuntary shiver through Pitt. Then slowly, he put a hand to his shattered ear and turned toward the door.

At that instant Boudicca walked into the study, majestically

493

straight and handsomely proportioned in a form-fitting silk robe that stopped several centimeters above her knees, not recognizing Pitt in the guard's uniform, and not realizing her father was in immediate danger. "What is it, Daddy? I thought I heard a gunshot—" Then she noticed the blood seeping through fingers pressed against his head. "You're hurt!"

"We have unwelcome visitors, Daughter," said Dorsett. Almost as if he had eyes in the back of his head, he knew that Pitt's attention was focused briefly on Boudicca. Unwittingly, she didn't fail him. As she rushed toward him to assess the damage, she caught sight of Pitt's face out of the corner of one eye. For an instant her face reflected confusion, then abruptly her eyes widened in recognition.

"No . . . no, it's not possible."

It was the distraction Dorsett had prepared for. In a violent twisting motion, he whirled around, one arm striking the gun barrel and knocking it aside.

Pitt instinctively pulled the trigger. A spray of bullets blasted into a painting of Charles Dorsett over a fireplace mantel. Physically weakened and dead on his feet from lack of sleep, Pitt's reaction time was a fraction longer than it should have been. The strain and exhaustion of the past three weeks had taken their toll. He watched in what seemed slow motion as the assault rifle was torn from his hands and sent flying across the room before smashing through a window.

Dorsett was on Pitt like a maddened rhino. Pitt clutched him, struggling to stay on his feet. But the heavier man was swinging his huge fists like pile drivers, his thumbs gouging at Pitt's eyes. Pitt twisted his head and kept his eyes in their sockets, but a fist caught him on the side of the head above one ear. Fireworks burst inside his brain, and he was swept by a wave of dizziness. Desperately, Pitt crouched and rolled to his side to escape the rain of blows.

He jumped in the opposite direction as Dorsett lunged at him. The old diamond miner had sent many a man to the hospital with only his bare hands, backed by arms and shoulders thick with muscle. During his rough-and-tumble youth in the mines, he had prided himself on never having to resort to knives and guns. His bulk and power were all he required to put away anyone with the nerve to stand up to him. Even at an age when most men turned to flab, Dorsett retained a body as hard as granite.

Pitt shook his head to clear his sight. He felt like a battered prizefighter, desperately holding on to the ropes until the bell for the end of the round, struggling to bring his mind back on track. Few were the martial-arts experts who could put down Dorsett's irresistible mass of sheer muscle. Pitt was beginning to think the only thing that would slow the diamond merchant was an elephant gun. If only Giordino would charge over the hill. At least he had a nine-millimeter automatic. Pitt's mind raced on, adding up viable moves, dismissing the ones certain to end with broken bones. He dodged around the desk, stalling for time, facing Dorsett and forcing a smile that made his face ache.

Pitt had learned long ago after numerous barroom fights and riots that hands and feet were no match against chairs, beer mugs and whatever else was handy to crack skulls. He glanced around for the nearest weapon.

"What now, old man? Are you going to bite me with your rotting teeth?"

The insult had the desired effect. Dorsett roared insanely and lashed out with a foot at Pitt's groin. His timing was off by a fractional instant, and his heel only grazed Pitt's hip. Then he leaped across the desk. Pitt calmly took one step back, snatched up a metal desk lamp and swung it with strength renewed by wrath and hatred.

Dorsett tried to lift an arm to ward off the blow, but he was a fraction slow. The lamp caught him on the wrist, snapping it before hurtling on against the shoulder and breaking the collar-bone with a sharp crack. He bellowed like a stricken animal and came after Pitt again with a look of black malevolence heightened by pain and pure savagery. He threw a vicious punch at Pitt's head.

Pitt ducked and jammed the base of the lamp downward. It connected somewhere below Dorsett's knee on the shin, but the momentum of the flying leg knocked the lamp from Pitt's hand. There was a clunk on the carpet. Now Dorsett was coming back at him almost as if he were completely uninjured. The veins were throbbing on the sides of his neck, the eye blazed and there were dribbles of saliva at the ends of his cracked, gasping mouth. He actually seemed to be laughing. He had to be mad. He mumbled something incoherent and leaped toward Pitt.

Dorsett never reached his victim. His right leg collapsed, and he crashed to the floor on his back. Pitt's swing of the lamp base had broken his shin bone. This time Pitt reacted like a cat. With a lightning move, he sprang onto the desk, tensed and jumped.

Together, Pitt's feet hurtled downward, ramming soles and heels into Dorsett's exposed neck. The malignant face, single eye gleaming black, yellowed teeth bared, seemed to stretch in shock. A huge hand groped the empty air. Arms and legs lashed out blindly. An agonized animal sound burst from his throat, a horrible gurgling sound that came through his crushed windpipe. Then Dorsett's body collapsed as all life faded away and the sadistic light in his eye blinked out.

Pitt somehow managed to remain standing, panting through clenched teeth. He stared at Boudicca, who strangely had made no move to help her father. She looked down at the dead body on the carpet with the uncaring but fascinated expression of a witness at a fatal traffic accident.

"You killed him," she said finally in a normal tone of voice.

"Few men deserved to die more," Pitt said, catching his breath while massaging a growing knot on his head.

Boudicca turned her attention away from her dead father as though he didn't exist. "I should thank you, Mr. Pitt, for handing me Dorsett Consolidated Mining Limited on a silver platter."

"I'm touched by your sorrow."

She smiled boredly. "You did me a favor."

"To the adoring daughter go the spoils. What about Maeve and Deirdre? They're each entitled to a third of the business."

"Deirdre will receive her share," Boudicca said matter-of-factly. "Maeve, if she is still alive, will get nothing. Daddy had already cut her out of the business."

"And the twins?"

She shrugged. "Little boys have accidents every day."

"I guess it isn't in you to be a loving aunt."

Pitt went taut from the bleak prospects. In a few minutes the eruption would occur. He wondered whether he had the strength left to fight another Dorsett. He remembered his surprise when Boudicca had lifted and crushed his body against the wall on her yacht at Kunghit Island. His biceps still ached from the memory of her grip. According to Sandecker, the acoustic wave would strike the island in minutes, followed by the eruption of the volcanos. If he had to die, he might as well go out fighting. Somehow being beaten to pulp by a woman didn't seem as frightening as being cremated by molten lava. What of Maeve and her boys? He could not bring himself to believe harm had come to them, not with Giordino present. They had to be warned of the coming cataclysm if there was still any chance they could escape the island alive.

Deep inside him he knew he was no match for Boudicca, but he had to act while he had the slight advantage of surprise. The thought was still in his mind when he sprinted forward, head down, across the room, crashing shoulder first into Boudicca's stomach. Boudicca was caught off guard, but it made little difference, almost no difference at all. She took the full force of the blow, grunted from the sudden shock, and although she reeled back a few steps, she remained standing. Before Pitt could recover his own balance, she clutched him with both arms under his chest, swung around in a half circle and threw him against a bookcase, his back shattering the glass doors. Incredibly, he managed somehow to remain erect on wobbly legs instead of crashing to the floor.

Pitt gasped in agony. His whole body felt like every bone was broken. He fought off the pain and charged again, catching Boudicca with a bruising uppercut with his fist that drew blood. It was a blow that should have knocked any woman unconscious for a week, but Boudicca simply wiped away the blood streaming from her mouth with the back of one hand and smiled horribly. She doubled her fists and moved toward Pitt, crouched in a boxer's stance. Hardly correct posture for a lady, Pitt thought.

He stepped in, ducked under a savage right-hand slash and hit her again with the last of his remaining strength. He felt his fist drive home against flesh and bone, and then he was pounded by a tremendous blow that caught him in the chest. Pitt thought his heart had been mashed to pulp. He couldn't believe any woman could hit so hard. He had hammered her with a punch that had more than enough momentum to break her jaw, yet she still smiled through a bleeding mouth and repaid him with a driving backhand that drove him into the stone fireplace, forcing all the breath out of his lungs. He fell and lay there grotesquely for several moments, engulfed in pain. As though in a fog, he pushed himself to his knees, then came to his feet and stood swaying, gathering himself for one final move.

Boudicca stepped in and brutally caught Pitt in the rib cage with her elbow. He could hear the sharp snap of one, maybe two ribs cracking, and felt the stabbing pain in his chest as he crumpled to his hands and knees. He stared dumbly at the design in the carpet and wanted to hold onto the floor forever. Perhaps he was dead and this was all there was to it, a floral design in a carpet.

Despairingly, he realized he could go no further. He groped for the fireplace poker, but his vision was too blurred and his movements too uncoordinated for him to find and grasp it in his hands. Vaguely, he saw Boudicca lean down, take him by one leg and hurl him crazily across the floor, where he collided with the open door. Then she walked over and picked him up by the collar with one hand and smashed him a hard blow in the head just above the eye. Pitt lay there, teetering on the edge of unconsciousness, swimming in pain, sensing but not really feeling the blood flowing from a gash above his left eye.

Like a cat toying with a mouse, Boudicca would soon tire of the game and kill him. Dazedly, almost miraculously, drawing on a strength he didn't know he possessed, Pitt somehow struggled slowly to his feet for what he was certain would be the last time.

Boudicca stood there beside the body of her father, smirking with anticipation. Complete mastery was etched in her face. "Time for you to join my father," she said. Her tone was deep, icy and compelling.

"There's a nauseating thought for you." Pitt's voice came thick and slurred.

Then Pitt saw the malice slowly fade in Boudicca's face and felt a hand gently ease him aside as Giordino entered the Dorsett family study.

He stared at Boudicca contemptuously and said, "This fancy maggot is mine."

At that moment Maeve appeared in the doorway, clutching a pair of blond-haired little boys by the hands, one on either side of her. She looked from Pitt's bleeding face to Boudicca to her father's body on the floor. "What happened to Daddy?"

"He caught a sore throat," muttered Pitt.

"Sorry I'm late," said Giordino calmly. "A couple of servants proved overly protective. They locked themselves in a room with the boys. It took me a while to kick in the door." He didn't explain what he did with the servants. He handed Pitt the nine-millimeter automatic taken from John Merchant. "If she wins, shoot her."

"With pleasure," Pitt said, his eyes devoid of sympathy.

Gone was any display of confidence in Boudicca's eyes. Gone too was any anticipation of merely hurting her opponent. This time she was fighting for her life, and she was going to use every dirty street-fighting trick she'd been taught by her father. This was to be no civilized boxing or karate match. She moved wolflike to position herself to deliver a killing blow, mindful of the gun in Pitt's hand.

"So you came back from the dead too," she hissed.

"You never left my dreams," Giordino said, puckering his lips and sending her a kiss.

"A pity you survived only to die in my house—"

A mistake. Boudicca wasted the half second with unnecessary talk. Giordino was on her like a cattle stampede, legs bent, feet extending as they came in contact with Boudicca's chest. The impact doubled her over with a gasp of agony, but incredibly, she somehow retained her stance and clamped her hands around Giordino's wrists. She hurled herself backward over the desk, pulling him with her until she was lying, back against the floor, with Giordino face-down on the desktop above her, seemingly defenseless with his arms stretched out and locked in front of him.

Boudicca looked up into Giordino's face. The evil grin came back on her lips as she held her victim helpless in a steel grip. She increased the pressure and bent his wrists with the intention of breaking them with her Amazon strength. It was a shrewd move. She could render Giordino disabled while shielding herself with his body until she could retrieve a revolver Arthur Dorsett kept loaded inside a bottom desk drawer.

Pitt, waiting for a signal from his friend to shoot, could not line up the automatic on Boudicca under the desk. Barely conscious, it was all he could do to keep from collapsing, his vision still unfocused from the blow to the forehead. Maeve was huddling against him now, her arms clasped around her sons, shielding their eyes from the brutal scene.

Giordino seemed to lie there immobile, as if accepting defeat without fighting back, while Boudicca kept bending his wrists slowly backward. Her silk robe had fallen away from her shoulders, and Maeve, who stared in awe at those massive shoulders and bulging muscles, having never seen her older sister unclothed, was stunned at the sight. Then her gaze drifted to the body of her father sprawled on the carpet. There was no sadness in her eyes, only shock at his unexpected death.

Then slowly, as if he'd been conserving his strength, Giordino pulled his wrists and hands upward as if curling a set of weights. Incomprehension followed on the heels of shock in Boudicca's face. Then came disbelief, and her body quivered as she exerted every trace of strength to stop the relentless force. Suddenly, she could grip his wrists no more, and her hold was broken. She immediately went for Giordino's eyes, but he had expected the move and brushed her hands aside. Before Boudicca could recover, Giordino was across the desk and falling on her chest, his legs straddling her body, pressing her arms to the floor. Held immobile by strength she had never expected, Boudicca thrashed in frantic madness to escape. Desperately, she tried to reach the desk drawer containing the revolver, but Giordino's knees kept her arms effectively pinned against her sides.

Giordino flexed his arm muscles, and then his hands were around her throat. "Like father, like daughter," he snarled. "Join him in hell."

Boudicca realized with sickening certainty that there would be no release, no mercy. She was effectively imprisoned. Her body convulsed in terror as Giordino's massive hands squeezed the life from her. She tried to scream but only uttered a squawking cry. The crushing grip never relaxed as her face contorted, the eyes bulged and the skin began turning blue. Normally warm with a humorous smile, Giordino's face remained expressionless as he squeezed ever more tightly.

The agonized drama lasted until Boudicca's body jerked and stiffened, the strength drained out of her and she went limp. Without slackening his hold around her throat, Giordino pulled the giant woman off the floor and draped her body across the top of the desk.

Maeve watched in morbid fascination and shock as Giordino tore the silk robe from Boudicca's body. Then she screamed and turned away, sickened at the sight.

"You called it, partner," said Pitt, his thoughts struggling to adjust fully to what he beheld.

Giordino made a slight tilt of his head, his eyes cold and remote. "I knew the minute she socked me in the jaw on the yacht."

"We've got to leave. The whole island is about to go up in smoke and cinders."

"Come again?" Giordino asked dumbly.

"I'll draw you a picture later." Pitt looked at Maeve. "What have you got for transportation around the house?"

"A garage on the side of the house holds a pair of minicars Daddy uses—used for driving between the mines."

Pitt swept one of the boys up in his arms. "Which one are you?"

Frightened of the blood streaming down Pitt's face, the youngster mumbled, "Michael." He pointed to his brother, who was now held by Giordino. "He's Sean."

"Ever flown in a helicopter, Michael?"

"No, but I always wanted to."

"Wishing will make it so," Pitt laughed.

As Maeve hurried from the study, she turned and took one last look at her father and Boudicca, whom she always thought of as her sister, an older sibling who remained distant and seldom displayed anything but animosity, but a sister nonetheless. Her father had kept the secret well, enduring the shame and hiding it from the world. It sickened her to discover after all these years that Boudicca was a man.

55

They found Dorsett's island vehicles, compact models of a car built in Australia called a Holden, in a garage adjoining the manor. The cars had been customized by having all the doors removed for easy entry and exit and were painted a bright shade of yellow. Pitt was eternally thankful to the late Arthur Dorsett for leaving the key in the ignition of the first car in line. Quickly, they all piled in, Pitt and Giordino in the front, Maeve and her boys in the back.

The engine turned over, and Pitt shoved the floor shift into first gear. He pressed the accelerator pedal as he released the clutch, and the car leaped forward.

Giordino leaped out at the archway and opened the gate. They had hardly shot onto the road when they passed a four-wheel-drive open van filled with security men traveling in the other direction.

Pitt thought: This would have to happen now. Somebody must have given the alarm. Then reality entered his mind when he realized it was the changing of the guard. The men bound and posed inside the archway office were about to be relieved in more ways than one.

"Everybody wave and smile," directed Pitt. "Make it look like we're all one big happy family."

The uniformed driver of the van slowed and stared curiously at the occupants of the Holden, then nodded and saluted, not sure he recognized anyone but assuming they were probably guests of the Dorsett family. The van was stopping at the archway as Pitt poured on the power and raced the Holden toward the dock stretching out into the lagoon.

"They bought it," said Giordino.

Pitt smiled. "Only for the sixty seconds it takes them to figure out that the night-shift guards aren't dozing out of boredom."

He swerved off the main road serving the two mines and headed toward the lagoon. They had a straight shot at the dock area now. No cars or trucks stood between them and the yacht. Pitt didn't take the time to look at his watch, but he knew they had less than four or five minutes before Sandecker's predicted cataclysm.

"They're coming after us," Maeve called out grimly.

Pitt didn't have to look in the rearview mirror to confirm, nor be told their run for freedom was in jeopardy because of the guards' quick reaction in taking up the chase. The only question running through his mind was whether he and Giordino could get the helicopter airborne before the guards came within range and shot them out of the sky.

Giordino pointed through the windshield at their only obstacle, the guard standing outside the security office, watching their rapid approach. "What about him?"

Pitt returned Merchant's automatic pistol to Giordino. "Take this and shoot him if I don't scare him to death."

"If you don't what—?"

Giordino got no further. Pitt hit the stoutly built wooden dock at better than 120 kilometers per hour, then jammed his foot on the brake pedal, sending the car into a long skid aimed directly toward the security office. The startled guard, unsure which way to jump, froze for an instant and then leaped off the side of the dock into the water to escape being crushed against the front grill of the car.

"Neatly done," Giordino said admiringly, as Pitt straightened out and braked sharply beside the yacht's gangway.

"Quickly!" Pitt shouted. "Al, run to the helicopter, remove

the tie-down ropes and start the engine. Maeve, you take your boys and wait out of sight in the salon. It will be safer there if the guards arrive before we can lift off. Wait until you see the rotor blades begin to turn on the aircraft. Then make a run for it.''

"Where will you be?" asked Giordino, helping Maeve lift the boys out of the car and sending them dashing up the gangway.

"Casting off the mooring lines to keep boarders off the boat."

Pitt was sweating by the time he pulled the yacht's heavy mooring ropes from their bollards and heaved them over the side. He took one final look at the road leading to the Dorsett manor house. The driver of the van had misjudged his turn off the main road and skidded the vehicle crosswise into a muddy field. Precious seconds were lost by the security men before they regained the road toward the lagoon. Then, in almost the exact same instant, the helicopter's engine coughed into life followed by the crack of a gunshot from inside the yacht.

He sprinted up the gangway, fear exploding inside him, hating himself with the taste of venom for sending Maeve and her boys on board the boat without investigating. He reached for the nine millimeter, but then remembered he had given it to Giordino. He ran across the deck, muttered, "Please, God!" tore open the door to the salon and ran inside.

His mind reeled at the shock of hearing Maeve plead, "No, Deirdre, no, please, not them too!"

Pitt's eyes took in the terrible scene. Maeve on the floor, her back against a bookcase, her boys clutched in her arms, both sobbing in fright. A blood-red stain was spreading across her blouse from a small hole in her stomach at the navel.

Deirdre stood in the center of the salon, holding a small automatic pistol aimed at the twin boys, her face and bare arms like polished ivory. Dressed in an Emanuel Ungaro that enhanced her beauty, her eyes were cold and her lips pressed tightly together in a thin line. She stared at Pitt with an expression that would have frozen alcohol. When she spoke, Deirdre's voice took on a peculiarly deranged quality.

"I knew you didn't die," she said slowly.

"You're madder than your malignant father and degenerate brother," Pitt said coldly.

"I knew you'd come back to destroy my family."

Pitt moved slowly until his body shielded Maeve and the boys.

504

"Call it a crusade to eradicate disease. The Dorsetts make the Borgias look like apprentice amateurs," he said, stalling for time as he inched closer. "I killed you father. Did you know that?"

She nodded slowly, her gun hand white and as firm as marble. "The servants Maeve and your friend locked in a closet knew I was sleeping on the boat and called me. Now you will die as my father died, but not before I've finished with Maeve."

Pitt turned slowly. "Maeve is already dead," he lied.

Deirdre leaned sideways and tried to examine her sister around Pitt's body. "Then you can watch as I shoot her precious twins."

"No!" Maeve cried out from behind Pitt. "Not my babies!"

Deirdre was beyond all reason as she lifted the gun and stepped around Pitt for a clear shot at Maeve and her sons.

White rage overcame any shred of common sense as Pitt leaped, hurling himself toward Deirdre. He came out fast, saw the muzzle of the automatic pointing at his chest. He did not fool himself into thinking he could make it. The distance separating them was too far to bridge in time. At two meters, Deirdre couldn't miss.

Pitt hardly felt the impact from the two bullets as they struck and penetrated into his flesh. There was enough loathing and malice inside him to deaden any pain, forestall any abrupt shock. He pounded Deirdre off her feet with a crushing impact that distorted her delicate features into an expression of abhorrent agony. It was like running into a sapling tree. Her back bowed as she toppled backward over a coffee table, pressed downward by Pitt's crushing weight. There was a horrible sound like a dried branch snapping as her spine fractured in three places.

Her strange, wild cry brought no compassion from Pitt. Her head was thrown back, and she stared up at Pitt through dazed brown eyes that still retained a look of deep hatred.

"You'll pay . . ." she moaned wrathfully, staring up at the growing circles of blood on Pitt's side and upper chest. "You're going to die." The gun was still locked in her grip, and she tried to aim it at Pitt again, but her body refused to react to her mind's commands. All feeling had suddenly gone out of her.

"Maybe," he said slowly, looking down and smiling a smile as hard as the handle on a coffin, certain her spine was irreparably fractured. "But it's better than being paralyzed for the rest of my life."

He dragged himself off Deirdre and stumbled over to Maeve. Bravely, she ignored her wound and was consoling the little boys, who were still crying and trembling in terror.

"It's all right, my darlings," she said softly. "Everything will be all right now."

Pitt knelt in front of her and examined her wound. There was little blood, just a neat hole that looked like nothing more than a slight stab wound from a small object. He could not see where the plunging bullet had expanded inside her body and torn through her intestines and a labyrinth of blood vessels before penetrating the duodenum and lodging in a disc between two vertebrae. She was bleeding internally, and unless she received immediate medical treatment, death was only minutes away.

Pitt's heart felt as if it had fallen into a chasm filled with ice. He instinctively wanted to cry in bitter grief, but no sound came from his throat, only a moan of sorrow that rose from deep inside him.

Giordino couldn't stand the delay any longer. Dawn had arrived, and the eastern sky above the island was already glowing orange from the sun. He jumped from the helicopter to the deck, ducking under the rotating blades as the van carrying the security guards raced onto the dock. What the devil had happened to Pitt and Maeve? he wondered anxiously. Pitt wouldn't have wasted an unnecessary second. The mooring lines were hanging slack in the water, and the yacht had already caught the outgoing tide and had drifted nearly thirty meters away from the dock.

Haste was vital. The only reason the guards had not fired on the helicopter or yacht was because they were afraid to damage Dorsett property. Now the guards were only a hundred meters away and closing in.

Giordino was so engrossed in keeping his eyes on their pursuers and his mind on what was delaying his friends that he failed to notice the sound of dogs barking from all parts of the island or the sudden flight of birds ascending and flying in confused circles in the sky. Nor did he sense an odd humming sound or feel the quivering on land and see the sudden agitation of the lagoon's waters as the sound waves of staggering intensity, driven by an immense velocity, slammed into the subterranean rock of Gladiator Island.

Only when he was within a few steps of the door to the main salon did he glance over his shoulder at the guards. They were standing transfixed on the dock whose planking was curling like waves across a sea. They had forgotten their quarry and were pointing to a small cloud of gray smoke that had begun to rise and spread above Mount Scaggs. Giordino could see men pouring like ants from the tunnel entrance in the volcano's slope. There seemed to be some activity inside Mount Winkleman as well. Pitt's warning about the island going up in smoke and cinders came back to him.

He burst through the doorway of the salon, stopped dead and expelled a low moan of emotional agony at seeing the blood oozing from the wounds in Pitt's chest and waist, the puncture in Maeve's midriff and the body of Deirdre Dorsett bent back almost double over the coffee table.

"God, what happened?"

Pitt looked up at him without answering. "The eruption, has it started?"

"There's smoke coming from the mountains, and the ground is moving."

"Then we're too late."

Giordino immediately knelt beside Pitt and stared at Maeve's wound. "This looks bad."

She looked up at him, her eyes imploring. "Please take my boys and leave me."

Giordino shook his head heavily. "I can't do that. We'll all go together or not at all."

Pitt reached over and clutched Giordino's arm. "No time. The whole island will blow any second. I can't make it either. Take the boys and get out of here, get out now."

As if he had been struck by a bombshell, Giordino went numb with disbelief. The lethargic nonchalance, the wisecracking sarcasm, fled from him. His thick shoulders seemed to shrink. Nothing in his entire life had primed him to desert his best friend of thirty years to a certain death. His expression was one of agonized indecision. "I can't leave either of you." Giordino leaned over and slipped his arms under Maeve as if to carry her. He nodded at Pitt. "I'll come back for you."

Maeve brushed his hands away. "Don't you see Dirk is right?" she murmured weakly.

Pitt handed Giordino Rodney York's log book and letters. "See that York's story reaches his family," he said, his voice hard with glacial calmness. "Now for God's sake, take the kids and go!"

Giordino shook his head in torment. "You never quit, do you?"

Outside, the sky had suddenly vanished, replaced by a cloud of ash that burst from the center of Mount Winkleman with a great rumbling sound that was truly terrifying. Everything went dark as the evil black mass spread like a giant umbrella. Then came a more thunderous explosion that hurled thousands of tons of molten lava into the air.

Giordino felt as if his soul was being torn away. Finally, he nodded and turned his head, a curious understanding in his grieved eyes. "All right." And then one last jest. "Since nobody around here wants me, I'll go."

Pitt gripped him by the hand. "Good-bye, old friend. Thank you for all you've done for me."

"Be seeing you," Giordino muttered brokenly, tears forming in his eyes. He looked like a very old man who was shrouded in solemn and heart-wrenching shock. He started to say something, choked on the words and then he snatched up Maeve's children, one boy under each arm, and was gone.

56

Charles Bakewell and the experts at the volcanic observatory in Auckland could not look into the interior of the earth as they could the atmosphere and to a lesser degree, the sea. It was impossible for them to predict the exact events in sequence and magnitude once the acoustic wave traveling from Hawaii struck Gladiator Island. Unlike most eruptions and earthquakes, these gave no time to study precursory phenomena such as foreshocks, groundwater fluctuations and changes in the behavior of domestic and wild animals. The dynamics were chaotic. All the scientists were certain of was that a major disturbance was in the making, and the smoldering furnaces deep within the island were about to burst into life.

In the event, the resonance created by the energy from the sound wave shook the already weakened volcanic cores, triggering the eruptions. Catastrophic events followed in quick succession. Reaching up from many miles beneath the island's surface, the superheated rock expanded and liquified, immediately ascending through fissures opened by the tremors. Hesitating only to displace the cooler, enclosing rocks, the flow formed an underground reservoir of molten material known as a magma chamber, where it built up immense pressures.

The stimulus for volcanic gas is water vapor transformed into red-hot steam, which provides the surge that thrusts the magma to the surface. When water enters a gaseous state, its volume instantly mushrooms nearly a thousand times, creating the astronomical power needed to produce a volcanic eruption.

The expulsion of rock fragments and ash by the rising column of gas provides the plume of smoke common to violent eruptions. Though no combustion actually takes place during eruption, it is the glow of an electrical discharge reflected from incandescent rock onto the water vapor that gives the impression of fire.

Inside the diamond mines, the workers and supervisors fled through the exit tunnels at the first ground shudder. The temperature inside the pits climbed with incredible rapidity. None of the guards made any attempt to turn back the stampede. In their panic they led the horde in a mad rush toward what they wrongly assumed was the safety of the sea. Those who ran toward the top of the saddle between the two volcanos unwittingly gained the best chance for survival.

Like sleeping giants, the island's twin volcanos reawakened from centuries of inactivity. Neither matched the other in their violent display. Mount Winkleman burst to life first with a series of fissures that opened along its base, unleashing long lines of magma fountains that welled up from the ruptures and spurted high in the air. The curtain of fire spread as vents formed along the fissures. Enormous quantities of molten lava poured down the slopes in a relentless river and spread like a fan as it devastated any vegetation that stood in its way.

The ferocity of the sudden storm of air pressure lashed the trees against each other before they were crushed flat and incinerated, their charred remains swept toward the shoreline. Any trees and undergrowth that escaped the rolling inferno were left standing blackened and dead. Already, the ground was littered with birds that dropped out of the sky, choked to death by the gases and fumes that Winkleman had discharged into the atmosphere.

As if guided by a heavenly hand, the ungodly ooze swept over the security compound but bypassed the Chinese laborers' detention camp by a good half a kilometer, thereby saving the lives of three hundred miners. Horrendous in scope, its only redeeming quality was that it traveled no faster than the average human could run. The gushing magma from Mount Winkleman wreaked terrible damage, but caused little loss of life.

But then came Mount Scaggs' turn.

From deep within its bowels, the volcano named after the captain of the *Gladiator* gave out a deep-throated roar like a hundred freight trains rolling through a tunnel. The crater hurled out a tremendous ash cloud, far greater than the one belched by Winkleman. It twisted and swirled into the sky, a black, evil mass. As ominous and frightening as it looked, the ash cloud was only an opening act for the drama yet to come.

Scaggs' western slope could not resist the deep-rooted stress ascending from thousands of meters below. The liquified rocks, now a white-hot mass, hurtled toward the surface. With immeasurable pressure it ripped a jagged crack on the upper slope, releasing an inferno of boiling mud and steam that was accompanied by a single, thunderous explosion that scattered the magma into millions of fragments.

A gigantic frenzy of molten lava shot from the slope of the volcano like a cannon barrage. An enormous quantity of glowing magma was purged in a pyroclastic flow, a tumultuous compound of incandescent rock fragments and heated gas that travels over the ground like liquid molasses but at velocities exceeding 160 kilometers per hour. Gaining speed, it avalanched down the flank of the volcano with a continuous roar, disintegrating the slope and throwing a fearsome windstorm in front of it that reeked of sulphur.

The effect of the superheated steam of the pyroclastic flow as it relentlessly swept forward was devastating, enveloping everything in a torrent of raining fire and scalding mud. Glass was melted, stone buildings were flattened, any organic object was instantly reduced to ashes. The seething horror left nothing recognizable in its wake.

The horrifying flow outran the canopy of ash that still cast an eerie pall across the island. And then the fiery magma plunged into the heart of the lagoon, boiling the water and creating a mad turbulence of steam that sent white plumes billowing into the sky. The once beautiful lagoon quickly lay under an ugly layer of gray ash, dirty mud and shredded debris swept ahead of the catastrophic flow of death.

The island used by men and women for greed, an island that some believed deserved to die, had been annihilated. The curtain was coming down on its agony.

Giordino had lifted the sleek British-built Agusta Mark II helicopter from the deck of the yacht and reached a safe distance from Gladiator Island before the spray of blazing rock fell over the dock and the yacht. He could not see the full scope of the devastation. It was hidden by the immense ash cloud that had reached a height of three thousand meters above the island.

The incredible twin eruptions were not only a scene of hideous malevolence but of awesome beauty also. There was a sense of unreality about it. Giordino felt as if he were looking down from the brink of hell.

Hope flared when he observed the yacht suddenly come to life and charge across the waters of the lagoon toward the channel cut in the encircling reef. Badly wounded or not, Pitt had somehow managed to get the boat under way. However fast the yacht could fly over the sea, it was not fast enough to outrun the gaseous cloud of flaming ash that scorched everything in its path before plunging across the lagoon.

But then any hope vanished as Giordino watched the uneven race in growing horror. The inferno swept over the yacht's churning wake, closing the gap until it smothered the craft and blotted it from all view of the Agusta Mark II. From a thousand feet in the air it appeared that no one could have lived for more than a few seconds in that hellish fire.

Giordino was overcome with anguish for being alive when the mother of the children strapped together in the copilot's seat and a friend who was like a brother were dying in the holocaust of fire below. Cursing the eruption, cursing his helplessness, he turned from the horrendous sight. His face was drained white as he flew more on instinct than experience. His inner pain, he knew, would never fade. His old surefire cockiness had died with Gladiator Island. He and Pitt had traveled a long road, with one always there to save the other in times of peril. Pitt was not the type to die, Giordino had told himself on numerous occasions when it looked like his friend was in the grave. Pitt was indestructible.

A spark of faith began to build inside Giordino. He glanced at the fuel gauges. They registered full. After studying a chart clipped to a board hanging below the instrument panel, he decided on a westerly course toward Hobart, Tasmania, the closest and best place to land with the kids. Once the Fletcher twins were in the safe hands of the authorities, he would refuel and return to Gladiator Island, if for nothing else than to try to retrieve Pitt's body for his mother and father in Washington.

He was not about to let Pitt down. He had not done so in life and he wasn't about to do so in death. Strangely, he began to feel more at ease. After figuring his flight time to Hobart and back to the island, he began talking to the little boys, who had lost their fear and peered excitedly out the cockpit window at the sea below.

Behind the helicopter, the island became an indistinct silhouette, similar in outline to the one it had offered the emaciated survivors aboard the raft of the *Gladiator* on another day one hundred and forty-four years before.

Seconds after he was sure Giordino had lifted the helicopter off the yacht and was safely in the air, Pitt pushed himself to his feet, wetted a towel from the sink in the bar and wrapped it around Maeve's head. Then he began piling cushions, chairs, every piece of furniture he could lift over Maeve until she was buried. Unable to do more to protect her from the approaching sea of fire, he stumbled into the wheelhouse, clutching his side where one bullet had plunged into the abdominal muscle, made a small perforation in his colon and lodged in the pelvic girdle. The other bullet had glanced off a rib, bruised and deflated one lung and passed out through his back muscles. Fighting to keep from falling into the black, nightmarish pool clouding his eyes, he studied the instruments and controls of the boat's console.

Unlike the helicopter's, the yacht's fuel gauges read empty. Dorsett's crew did not bother to refuel until they were alerted that one or more of the Dorsett family was preparing for a voyage. Pitt found the proper switches and kicked over the big Blitzen Seastorm turbodiesel engines. They had no sooner rumbled to idling rpms when he engaged their Casale V-drives and pushed the throttles forward. The deck beneath his feet shuddered as the bow lifted and the water behind the stern whipped into foam. He took manual control of the helm to steer a course toward the open sea.

Hot ashes fell in a thick blanket. He could hear the crackling and the growling of the approaching tempest of fire. Flaming rocks fell like hail, hissing in clouds of steam as they hit the water and sank beneath the surface. They dropped endlessly out of the sky after having been thrown a great distance by the tremendous pressures coming out of Mount Scaggs. The column of doom engulfed the docks and seemed to take off in pursuit of the yacht, rolling across the lagoon like an enraged monster from the fiery depths of hell. And then it was on top of him in full fury, descending over the yacht in a whirling convoluted mass two hundred meters high before Pitt was able to clear the lagoon. The boat was pitched forward as it was struck a staggering blow from astern. The radar and radio masts were swept clean away, along with the lifeboats, railings and deck furniture. The boat struggled through the blazing turbulence like a wounded whale. Flaming rocks crashed on the superstructure roof and decks, smashing the once beautiful yacht into a shattered hulk.

The heat in the wheelhouse was searing. Pitt felt as if someone had rubbed his skin with a red hot salve. Breathing became agonizingly difficult, especially so because of the collapsed lung. He fervently prayed that Maeve was still alive back in the salon. Gasping for air, clothing beginning to smolder, hair already singed, he stood there desperately gripping the helm. The superheated air forced its way down his throat and into his lungs till each intake of breath was an agony. The roar of the firestorm in his ears combined with the pounding of his heart and the surge of his blood. His only resources to resist the blazing assault were the steady throb of the engines and the sturdy construction of the boat.

When the windows around him began to crack and then shatter, he thought he would surely die. His whole mind, his every nerve was focused on driving the boat forward as though he could by sheer willpower force her ahead faster. But then abruptly the heavy blanket of fire thinned and dropped away as the yacht raced into the clear. The dirty gray water went emerald green and the sky sapphire blue. The wave of fire and scalding mud had finally lost its momentum. He sucked in the clean salt air like a swimmer hyperventilating before making a free dive into the depths. He did not know how badly he was injured, and he did not care. Excruciating pain was stoically endured.

At that moment, Pitt's gaze was drawn by the upper head and body of an immense sea creature that rose out of the water off the starboard bow. It appeared to be a giant eel with a round head a good two meters thick. The mouth was partially open and he could see razor-sharp teeth in the shape of rounded fangs. If its undulating body were straightened out, Pitt estimated its length at between thirty and forty meters. It traveled through the water at a speed only slightly slower than the yacht.

"So Basil exists," Pitt muttered to himself in the empty wheelhouse, the words aggravating his burning throat. Basil was no stupid sea serpent, he surmised. The enormous eel was fleeing his scalding habitat in the lagoon and heading for the safety of the open sea.

Once through the channel, Basil rolled forward into the depths, and with a wave of his huge tail, disappeared.

Pitt nodded a good-bye and turned his attention back to the console. The navigational instruments were no longer functioning. He tried sending a Mayday over both the radio and satellite phone, but they were dead. Nothing seemed to function except the big engines that still drove the yacht through the waves. Unable to set the boat on an automatic course, he tied the helm with the bow pointed west toward the southeastern coast of Australia and set the throttle a notch above idle to conserve what little fuel remained. A rescue ship responding to the catastrophe on Gladiator Island was bound to spot the crippled yacht, stop and investigate.

He forced his unsteady legs to carry him back to Maeve, deeply afraid of finding her body in a burned-out room. With great trepidation, he stepped over the threshold separating the salon from the wheelhouse. The main salon looked like it had been swept by a blowtorch. The thick, durable fiberglass skin had kept much of the heat from penetrating the bulkheads but the terrible heat had broken through the glass windows. Remarkably, the flammable material on the sofas and chairs, though badly scorched, had not ignited.

He shot a glance at Deirdre. Her once beautiful hair was singed into a blackened mass, her eyes milky and staring, her skin the color of a broiled lobster. Light wisps of smoke rose from her expensive clothes like a low mist. She had the appearance of a doll that had been cast into a furnace for a few seconds before being pulled out. Death had saved her from life within an immovable body.

Uncaring of his pain and injuries, he furiously threw aside the furniture he had heaped over Maeve. She had to be still alive, he thought desperately. She had to be waiting for him in all her pain and despair at once again losing her children. He pulled off the last cushion and stared down with mounting fear. Relief washed over him like a cascade as she lifted her head and smiled.

"Maeve," he rasped, falling forward and taking her in his arms. Only then did he see the large pool of blood that had seeped down between her legs and spread on the deck carpeting. He held her close, her head nestled against his shoulder, his lips brushing her cheeks.

"Your eyebrows," she whispered through a funny little smile.

"What about them?"

"They're all singed off, most of your hair too."

"I can't look dashing and handsome all the time."

"You always do to me." Then her eyes went moist with sadness and concern. "Are my boys safe?"

He nodded. "Al lifted off minutes before the firestorm struck. I should think they're well on their way to a safe shore."

Her face was as pale as moonlight. She looked like a fragile porcelain doll. "I never told you that I loved you."

"I knew," he murmured, fighting to keep from choking up.

"Do you love me too, if only a little bit?"

"I love you with all my soul."

She raised a hand and lightly touched his scorched face. "My huckleberry friend, always waitin' round the bend. Hold me tight. I want to die in your arms."

"You're not going to die," he said, unable to control the fabric of his heart as it tore in pieces. "We're going to live a long life together, cruising the sea while we raise a boatload of kids who swim like fish."

"Two drifters off to see the world," she said in a low whisper.

"There's such a lot of world to see," Pitt said, repeating the words to the song.

"Take me across Moon River, Dirk, carry me across . . ." Her expression almost seemed joyful.

Her eyes fluttered and closed. Her body seemed to wilt like a lovely flower under a frigid blast of cold. Her face became serene like a peacefully sleeping child's. She was across and waiting on the other shore.

"No!" he cried, his voice like a wounded animal baying in the night.

All life seemed to flow out of Pitt too. He no longer clung to consciousness. He no longer fought the black mist closing in around him. He released his hold on reality and embraced the darkness.

57

Giordino's plan for a quick, turnaround flight to Gladiator Island was dashed almost from the beginning.

After using the Agusta's state-of-the-art satellite communications system to brief Sandecker on board the *Glomar Explorer* in Hawaii, he contacted air-and-sea rescue units in both Australia and New Zealand and became the first person to announce the disaster to the outside world. During the remainder of the flight to Hobart, he was continually besieged with requests from high-level government officials and reporters from the news media for accounts of the eruption and assessment of the damage.

Upon approaching the capital city of Tasmania, Giordino flew along the steep foothills bordering Hobart, whose commercial district was located on the west bank of the Derwent River. Locating the airport, he called the tower. The flight controllers directed him to set down in a military staging area half a kilometer from the main terminal. He was stunned to see a huge crowd of people milling about the area as he hovered over the landing site.

Once he shut down the engine and opened the passenger door, everything was accomplished in an orderly manner. Immigration officials came on board and arranged for his entry into Australia without a passport. Social services authorities took custody of Maeve's young sons, assuring Giordino that as soon as their father was located, they would be placed in his care.

Then as Giordino finally set foot on the ground, half starved and exhausted almost beyond redemption, he was attacked by an army of reporters shoving microphones under his nose, aiming TV cameras at his face and shouting questions about the eruption.

The only question he answered with a smile on his face was to confirm that Arthur Dorsett was one of the first casualties of the holocaust.

Finally, breaking free of the reporters and reaching the office of the airport's security police, Giordino called the head of the U.S. consulate, who reluctantly agreed to pay for the refueling of the helicopter, but only for humanitarian purposes. His return flight to Gladiator Island was again delayed when Australia's Director of Disaster Relief asked if Giordino would help out by airlifting food and medical supplies back to the island in the Agusta. Giordino graciously gave his consent and then impatiently paced the asphalt around the helicopter while it was refueled and passenger seats were removed to make more room before the needed provisions were loaded on board. He was thankful when one of the relief workers sent him a bag full of cheese sandwiches and several bottles of beer.

To Giordino's surprise, a car drove up and the driver notified him of Sandecker's imminent arrival. He stared at the driver as if the man were crazy. Only four hours had passed since he'd reported to Sandecker in Hawaii.

The confusion cleared away as a U.S. Navy F-22A supersonic two-place fighter lined up on the runway and touched down. Giordino watched as the sleek craft, capable of Mach 3+ speeds, taxied over to where he had parked the helicopter. The canopy slid back, and Sandecker, wearing a flight suit, climbed out onto a wing. Without waiting for a ladder, he jumped onto the asphalt.

He strode straightway over to the startled Giordino and locked him in a bear hug. "Albert, you don't know how glad I am to see you."

"I wish there were more of us here to greet you," Giordino said sadly.

"Useless to stand here consoling ourselves." Sandecker's face was tired and lined. "Let's find Dirk."

"Don't you want to change first?"

"I'll shed this Star Wars suit while we're in flight. The Navy can have it back when I get around to returning it."

Less than five minutes later, with two metric tons of badly needed supplies tied down in the passenger/cargo compartment, they were airborne and heading over the Tasman Sea toward the smoldering remains of Gladiator Island.

Relief ships of the Australian and New Zealand navies were immediately ordered to the island with relief supplies and medical personnel. Any commercial ship within two hundred nautical miles was diverted to offer any assistance possible at the disaster scene. Astoundingly, the loss of life was not nearly as high as first suspected from the immense destruction. Most of the Chinese laborers had escaped from the path of the firestorm and lava flows. Half the mine supervisors survived, but of Arthur Dorsett's eighty-man security force, only seven badly burned men were found alive. Later autopsies showed that most of the dead suffocated from inhaling the ash.

By late afternoon, the eruption had substantially diminished in force. Bursts of magma still flowed from the volcanos' fissures, but had dwindled to small streams. Both volcanos were mere shadows of their former bulk. Scaggs had nearly disappeared, leaving only a wide, ugly crater. Winkleman remained as a massive mound less than a third of its former height.

The canopy of ash still hovered over the volcanos as Giordino and Sandecker dropped toward the devastated island. Most of the western side of the landmass looked as if a giant wire scraper had scoured it down to bedrock. The lagoon was a swamp choked with debris and floating pumice. Little remained of Dorsett Consolidated's mining operations. What wasn't buried under ash protruded like ruins from a civilization dead for a thousand years. The destruction of vegetation was practically total.

Giordino's heart went cold when he saw no sign of the yacht carrying Pitt and Maeve in the lagoon. The dock was scorched and had sunk in the ash-blanketed water beside the demolished warehouses.

Sandecker was horrified. He had had no idea of the scope of the catastrophe. "All those people dead," he muttered. "My fault, all my fault."

Giordino looked at him through understanding eyes. "For every dead inhabitant, there are ten thousand people who owe you their lives."

"Still . . ." Sandecker said solemnly, his voice trailing off.

Giordino flew over a rescue ship that had already anchored in the lagoon. He began decreasing his airspeed in preparation for setting down in a space cleared by Australian army engineers who had parachuted onto the disaster scene first. The rotor's downwash raised huge billows of ash, obscuring Giordino's view. He hovered and slowly worked the collective pitch and cyclic control in coordination with the throttle. Flying blind, he settled the Agusta and touched down with a hard bump. Drawing a deep breath, he sighed as the rotors wound down.

The ash cloud had hardly dissipated when a major in the Australian army, dusted from head to toe and followed by an aide, ran up and opened the entry door. He leaned in the cargo compartment as Sandecker made his way aft. "Major O'Toole," he introduced himself with a broad smile. "Glad to see you. You're the first relief craft to land."

"Our mission is twofold, Major," said Sandecker. "Besides carrying supplies, we're looking for a friend who was last seen on Arthur Dorsett's yacht."

O'Toole shrugged negatively. "Probably sunk. It'll be weeks before the tides clean out the lagoon enough for an underwater search."

"We were hoping the boat might have reached open water."

"You've had no communication from your friend?"

Sandecker shook his head.

"I'm sorry, but chances seem remote that he escaped the eruption."

"I'm sorry too." Sandecker stared at something about a million kilometers away and seemed unaware of the officer standing by the door. Then he pulled himself together. "Can we give you a hand unloading the aircraft?"

"Any help will be greatly appreciated. Most of my men are out rounding up survivors."

With the assistance of one of O'Toole's officers, the boxes containing food, water and medical supplies were removed from the cargo compartment and piled some distance from the helicopter. Failure and sadness stilled any words between Giordino and Sandecker as they returned to the cockpit in preparation for the return flight to Hobart.

Just as the rotors began to rotate, O'Toole came running up, waving both hands excitedly. Giordino opened his side window and leaned out.

"I thought you should know," O'Toole shouted above the engine exhaust. "My communications officer just received a report from a relief ship. They sighted a derelict boat drifting approximately twenty-four kilometers northwest of the island."

The distress in Giordino's face vanished. "Did they stop to investigate for survivors?"

"No. The derelict was badly damaged and looked deserted. The captain rightly assumed his first priority was to reach the island with a team of doctors."

"Thank you, Major." Giordino turned to Sandecker. "You heard?"

"I heard," Sandecker snapped impatiently. "Get this thing in the air."

Giordino required no urging. Within ten minutes of lifting off, they spotted the yacht almost exactly where the captain of the relief ship reported it, wallowing dead amid the marching swells. She rode low in the water with a ten-degree list to port. Her topsides looked as if they had been swept away by a giant broom. Her once proud sapphire-blue hull was scorched black, and her decks wore a heavy coating of gray ash. She had been through hell and she looked it.

"The helicopter pad looks clear," commented Sandecker.

Giordino lined up on the stern of the yacht and made a slow, slightly angled descent. The sea showed no sign of white, indicating a mild wind factor, but the yacht's roll and its list made his landing tricky.

He reduced power and hovered at an angle matching that of the yacht, timing his drop for when the yacht rose on the crest of a wave. At the exact moment, the Agusta flared out, hung for a few seconds and sank to the sloping deck. Giordino immediately applied the brakes to keep the aircraft from rolling into the sea and shut down the engine. They were safely down and their thoughts now turned to fear of what they might find.

Giordino jumped out first and quickly fastened tie-down ropes from the helicopter to the deck. Hesitating for a moment to draw their breath, they stepped across the charred deck and entered the main salon.

One look at the two inert figures huddled in one corner of the room and Sandecker shook his head despairingly.

He briefly closed his eyes tight, fighting a wave of mental anguish. So awesome was the cruel scene, he couldn't move. There was no sign of life. Grief tore at his heart. He stared motionless in sad bewilderment. They both had to be dead, he thought.

Pitt was holding Maeve in his arms. The side of his face was a mask of dried blood from the injury inflicted by Boudicca. The whole of his chest and side were also stained dark crimson. The charred clothes, the eyebrows and hair that had been singed away, the burns on his face and arms, all gave him the image of someone horribly maimed in an explosion. He looked like he'd died hard.

Maeve seemed as though she had died not knowing her sleep would be eternal. A waxen sheen on her lovely features, she reminded Sandecker of a white, unburned candle, a sleeping beauty no kiss would ever awake.

Giordino knelt down beside Pitt, refusing to believe his old friend was dead. He gently shook Pitt's shoulder. "Dirk! Speak to me, buddy."

Sandecker tried to pull Giordino away. "He's gone," he said in a saddened whisper.

Then with such unexpectedness that both men were frozen in shock and disbelief, Pitt's eyes slowly opened. He stared up at Sandecker and Giordino, not understanding, not recognizing.

His lips quivered, and then he murmured, "God forgive me, I lost her."

PART V

THE DUST
SETTLES

◇ BASIL ◇

58

The tension that was present in the Paris conference room during the previous meeting could not be felt this time around. Now the atmosphere was relaxed, almost cheerful. The directors of the Multilateral Council of Trade were more congenial as they met to discuss the latest of their international behind-the-scenes business dealings.

The chairs were filled around the long ebony table as the chairman paused, waiting for murmured conversations to die down, before he called the meeting to order.

"Gentlemen, much has happened since our last discussion. At that time we were faced with a threat to our international diamond operations. Now, thanks to a whim of nature, the scheme to destroy our diamond market has been brought to a standstill with the untimely death of Arthur Dorsett."

"Good riddance to bad rubbish," said the chief executive of the diamond cartel, laughing. He could scarcely believe the triumph he felt, and his elation at having a menacing threat fortuitously eliminated without a costly fight.

"Hear! hear!" came a chorus of voices around the table.

"I'm happy to report," the chairman continued, "the market price of diamonds has risen dramatically in the past few days, while prices of colored gemstones have suffered a substantial drop."

The gray-haired man from one of America's richest families and a former Secretary of State spoke from the other end of the table. "What's to stop Dorsett Consolidated Mining's directors from going ahead with Arthur's program of discounting diamonds throughout his vast chain of jewelry stores?"

The Belgian industrialist from Antwerp made a gesture with his hand as he spoke. "Arthur Dorsett was a megalomaniac. His dreams of grandeur did not include others. He ran his mining operations and sales organizations without a board of directors. Arthur was a one-man band. He trusted no one. Except for occasionally hiring an outside adviser and then squeezing the man or woman dry for whatever expertise he could absorb before throwing them into the street, he ran Dorsett Consolidated alone with no one else at the top."

The Italian cargo-fleet owner smiled. "I'm tempted to climb the volcanos that wiped out Arthur Dorsett and his evil empire and pour a bottle of champagne into their craters."

"The Hawaiians do that very thing at the fire crater of Kilauea," said the American.

"Did they find his body?" asked the Japanese electronics magnate.

The chairman shook his head. "According to Australian officials, he never got out of his house, which was directly in the path of a lava flow. His body, or what's left of it, lies under twenty meters of volcanic ash and lava rock."

"Is it true all three of his daughters died too?" asked the Italian.

"One died in the house with Arthur. The other two were found dead on a burned-out hulk of a yacht. Apparently, they were trying to escape the holocaust. There is, I might add, an air of mystery about the affair. My sources inside the Australian government claim one daughter died from gunshot wounds."

"Murdered?"

"The rumor is they were self-inflicted."

The head of the Japanese electronics empire nodded at the director of the diamond cartel. "Can you tell us, sir, now that

Arthur Dorsett is out of the picture, what the future outlook is for your market?"

The fastidiously attired diamond authority from South Africa returned a genuine smile. "Couldn't be better. The Russians have turned out to be nowhere near the threat originally predicted. Their attempts to run roughshod over the market have backfired. After selling much of their hoard of rough stones to diamond cutters in Tel Aviv and Antwerp at discounted prices, but still substantially higher than what Arthur Dorsett intended, they have outrun their production. The upheaval of Russian industry has brought their diamond production to a virtual standstill."

"What about Australia and Canada?" asked the Dutchman.

"The mines in Australia are not as extensive as originally predicted, and the Canadian diamond rush is vastly overblown. They are not showing diamonds of any quality or quantity. At present there is no plan to build a large commercial diamond mine in Canada."

"Do the sweeping changes in South Africa's political structure have any effect on your operations?"

"We have worked closely with Nelson Mandela right from the beginning of the downfall of apartheid. I can safely say that shortly he will introduce a new tax system that will be most advantageous to our earnings."

The sheik representing the oil cartel leaned across the table. "This all sounds encouraging, but will your profits enable you to assist in carrying out the Multilateral Council's goal of a one-world economic order?"

"Rest assured," replied the South African, "the diamond cartel will meet all commitments. The demand for diamonds worldwide is rising ever higher, and our profits are expected to soar for the first ten years of the new century. There is no doubt that we can carry our share of the monetary burden."

"I thank the gentleman from South Africa for his report of confidence," said the chairman.

"So where does Dorsett Consolidated go from here?" asked the sheik.

"Legally," replied the chairman, "the entire business passes into the hands of Dorsett's two grandsons."

"How old are they?"

"A few months this side of seven years old."

"That young?"

"I didn't know any of his daughters were married," said the Indian real-estate developer.

"They weren't," said the chairman flatly. "Maeve Dorsett bore twins out of wedlock. The father comes from a wealthy family of sheep ranchers. My sources say that he is an intelligent and reasonable man. He has already been named to act as guardian and administer assets of the estate."

The Dutchman stared down the table at the chairman. "Who has been named to handle the boys' corporate affairs?"

"A name you're all well familiar with." The chairman paused and smiled sardonically. "Until the grandchildren come of age, the day-to-day business activities of Dorsett Consolidated and its subsidiary divisions will be managed by the Strouser family of diamond merchants."

"There's retribution for you," said the American elder statesman.

"What plans are in place should the diamond market collapse on its own? We can't control prices forever."

"I'll answer that," said the South African. "When we can no longer maintain a grip on diamond prices, we turn from natural stones excavated by expensive mining operations to those produced in a laboratory."

"Are fakes as good?" asked the British publisher.

"Chemical laboratories are currently producing cultured emeralds, rubies and sapphires with the same physical, chemical and optical properties as stones mined from the ground. They are so perfect that trained gemologists have difficulty detecting any distinction. The same is true with laboratory-created diamonds."

"Can they be sold without disclosure?" asked the chairman.

"No need to deceive. Just as we educated the public into believing diamonds were the only stone to own, so can cultured stones be advertised and promoted as the most practical to buy. The only basic difference is that one took millions of years for nature to create, the other fifty hours in a laboratory. The new wave of the future, if you will."

The room went silent for a moment as each man considered the potential profits. Then the chairman smiled and nodded. "It would seem, gentlemen, that no matter which way the pendulum swings, our future earnings are secure."

59

Pitt had been lucky, as every nurse on the floor of the hospital in Hobart, Tasmania, never ceased telling him. After a bout of peritonitis from the perforated colon, and the removal of the bullet from his pelvic girdle, where it had made a nice dent in the bone, he began to feel as if he had rejoined the living. When his lung reinflated and he could breathe freely, he ate like a starving lumberjack.

Giordino and Sandecker hung around until they were assured by the medical staff that Pitt was on the road to recovery, a fact attested to by his requests, or rather demands, for something to drink that wasn't fruit juice or milk. Demands that were mostly ignored.

The admiral and Giordino then escorted Maeve's boys to Melbourne, to their father, who had flown in from his family's sheep station in the outback for Maeve's funeral. A big man, Aussie to the core, with a university degree in animal husbandry, he promised Sandecker and Giordino to raise the boys in good surroundings. Though he trusted Strouser & Sons' business judgments in their management of Dorsett Consolidated Mining, he wisely retained attorneys to watch over the twins' best interests. Satisfied the boys were in good hands and that Pitt would soon be ready to return home, the admiral and Giordino flew back to Washington, where Sandecker received a tumultuous welcome and a round of ceremonial banquets as the man who fought a one-sided battle to save Honolulu from a tragic disaster.

Any thoughts the President or Wilber Hutton might have had of replacing him at NUMA quickly died. Word around the capital city was that the admiral would be at the helm of his beloved National Underwater & Marine Agency long after the current administration left the White House.

The doctor walked into the room and found Pitt standing at the window, gazing longingly down at the Derwent River flowing through the heart of Hobart. "You're supposed to be in bed," said the doctor in his Australian twang, pronouncing bed like *byd*.

Pitt gave him a hard look. "I've laid on a mattress a three-toed sloth wouldn't sleep on for five days. I've served my time. Now I'm out of here."

The doctor smiled slyly. "You have no clothes, you know. The rags you were wearing when they brought you in were thrown out in the trash."

"Then I'll walk out of here in my bathrobe and this stupid hospital gown. Whoever invented these things, by the way, should have them stuffed up his anal canal until the strings in the back come out his ears."

"I can see arguing with you is wasting my other patients' time." The doctor shrugged. "It's a bleeding wonder your body still functions. I've seldom seen so many scars on one man. Go if you must. I'll see the nurse finds you some decent street clothes so you won't be arrested for impersonating an American tourist."

No NUMA jet this trip. Pitt flew commercial on United Airlines. As he shuffled onto the aircraft, still stiff and with a grinding ache in his side, the flight attendants, women except for one man, stared at him in open curiosity, watching him search the overhead numbers for his seat.

One attendant, brown hair neatly coiffed, eyes almost as green as Pitt's and soft with concern, came over to him. "May I show you to your seat, sir?"

Pitt had spent a solid minute studying himself in a mirror before he caught a cab from the hospital to the airport. If he'd auditioned for a movie role that called for the walking dead, the director would have hired him in an instant: the livid red scar across his forehead; the vacant, bloodshot eyes and gaunt, pale face; his movements like an ninety-year-old man with arthritis. His skin was blotched from the burns, his eyebrows were nonexistent and his once thick, curly black hair looked like a sheepshearer had tried styling it in a crewcut.

"Yes, thank you," he said more out of embarrassment than appreciation.

"Are you Mr. Pitt?" she asked as she motioned to an empty seat by the window.

"At the moment I wish I were someone else, but yes, I'm Pitt."

"You're a lucky man," she said smiling.

"So a dozen nurses kept telling me."

"No, I mean you have friends who are very concerned about you. The flight crew were told you would be flying with us and were requested to make you as comfortable as possible."

How in hell did Sandecker know he'd escaped the hospital, left directly for the airport and purchased a standby ticket to Washington, he wondered.

As it turned out, the flight attendants had little to do for him. He slept most of the trip, coming awake only to eat, watch a movie with Clint Eastwood playing the role of a grandfather, and drink champagne. He did not even know the plane was approaching Dulles International until the wheels thumped down and woke him up.

He came off the shuttle bus from the aircraft into the terminal, mildly surprised and disappointed that no one waited to greet him. If Sandecker had alerted the airline's flight crew, he certainly knew when the plane was scheduled to arrive. Not even Al Giordino was waiting at the curb when he walked haltingly toward a taxi stand. A clear case of out-of-sight, out-of-mind, he told himself as his mood of depression deepened.

It was eight o'clock in the evening when he exited the cab, punched his code into the security system of his hangar and walked inside. He turned on the lights that reflected in the mirrored finish and chrome of his collector cars.

A tall object that nearly touched the ceiling stood in front of him, an object that hadn't been there when he left.

For several moments, Pitt stared in rapt fascination at the totem pole. A beautifully carved eagle with spread wings graced the top. Then, in descending order, came a grizzly bear with its cub, a raven, a frog, a wolf, some type of sea creature and a human head at the bottom that remotely resembled Pitt. He read a note that was pinned to the ear of the wolf.

> Please accept this commemorative column in your honor from the Haida people as a token of their appreciation for your efforts in removing the disfigurement on our sacred island. The Dorsett mine has been closed, and soon the animals and plants will reclaim their rightful home. You are now an honored member of the Haida.
>
> Your friend,
> Mason Broadmoor.

Pitt was deeply moved. To be given a masterwork of such eminent significance was a rare privilege. He felt grateful beyond measure to Broadmoor and his people for their generous gift.

Then he walked around the totem and felt his heart stop beating. Disbelief clouded his opaline green eyes. Then astonishment was replaced with emptiness followed by sorrow. Directly behind, sitting in the aisle between the classic cars, was the *Marvelous Maeve*.

Tired, worn and the worse for wear, but there she sat in all her sea-ravaged glory. Pitt could not imagine how the faithful boat had survived the eruption and had been transported thousands of kilometers to Washington. It was as if someone had performed a miracle. He walked over, and reached out his hand to touch the bow to see if he wasn't hallucinating.

Just as his fingertips met the hull's hard surface, people began emerging from the back of the Pullman railroad car parked along one wall of the hangar, the rear seats of the automobiles and from his upstairs apartment, where they had been hiding. Suddenly, he was surrounded by a crowd of familiar faces shouting "surprise" and "welcome home."

Giordino embraced him gently, well aware of Pitt's injuries. Admiral Sandecker, never one for emotional display, warmly shook Pitt's hand, turning away as tears welled in his eyes.

Rudi Gunn was there, along with Hiram Yaeger, and over forty of his other friends and fellow employees at NUMA. His parents were there to greet him too. His father, Senator George Pitt of California, and his mother, Barbara, were shocked at his gaunt appearance, but bravely acted as though he looked healthy and fit. St. Julien Perlmutter was there, directing the food and drink. Congresswoman Loren Smith, his close and intimate friend for ten years, kissed him tenderly, saddened at seeing the dull, world-weary look of pain and exhaustion in his normally glinting eyes.

Pitt stared at the little boat that had performed so faithfully. He turned without hesitation to Giordino. "How did you ever manage it?"

Giordino smiled triumphantly. "After the admiral and I flew you to the hospital in Tasmania, I returned to the island with another load of relief supplies. A quick pass over the eastern cliffs revealed that *Marvelous Maeve* had survived the eruption. I borrowed a couple of Aussie engineers and lowered them into the ravine. They secured the boat to the cable from the helicopter. I hoisted it to the top of the bluffs, where we disassembled the hull and outriggers. The operation took some doing, but the parts we couldn't load inside the helicopter we attached underneath the fuselage. Then I flew back to Tasmania, where I talked the pilot of a commercial cargo plane that was headed for the States into transporting the beast home. With the help of a team from NUMA, we put it back together barely in time for your arrival."

"You're a good friend," said Pitt sincerely. "I can never repay you."

"It is I who owe you," Giordino responded devotedly.

"I deeply regret that I was unable to attend Maeve's funeral in Melbourne."

"The admiral and I were there along with her boys and the father. Just as you requested, they played "Moon River" as she was lowered into the ground."

"Who gave the eulogy?"

"The admiral delivered the words you wrote," said Giordino sadly. "There wasn't a dry eye in the house."

"And Rodney York?"

"We sent York's logbook and letters to England by courier," said Giordino. "York's widow is still living by Falmouth Bay, a sweet little lady in her late seventies. I talked to her by phone after she received the log. There is no expressing how happy she was to learn how York died. She and her family are making plans to bring his remains home.''

"I'm glad she finally knows the story," said Pitt.

"She asked me to thank you for your thoughtfulness."

Pitt was saved from misting eyes by Perlmutter, who put a glass of wine in his hand. "You'll enjoy this, my boy. An excellent chardonnay from Plum Creek Winery in Colorado.''

The surprise over, the party took off in full swing until after midnight. Friends came and went until Pitt was talked out and fighting to stay awake. Finally, Pitt's mother insisted her son get some rest. They all bid him a good night, wished him a speedy recovery and began drifting out the door for the drive to their homes.

"Don't come to work until you're fit and able," counseled Sandecker. "NUMA will struggle along without you."

"There is one project I'd like to pursue in about a month," said Pitt, the old devilish buccaneer gleam briefly flashing in his eyes.

"What project is that?"

Pitt grinned. "I'd like to be on Gladiator Island when the water clears in the lagoon."

"What do you expect to find?"

"His name is Basil."

Sandecker stared, puzzled. "Who in hell is Basil?"

"He's a sea serpent. I figure he'll return to his breeding ground after the lagoon is free of ash and debris."

Sandecker placed a hand on Pitt's shoulder and gave him a look usually reserved for a child who has claimed to have seen the bogeyman. "Take a nice long rest, and we'll talk about it."

The admiral turned and walked away, shaking his head and mumbling something about no such things as sea monsters as Congresswoman Loren Smith came up to Pitt and held his hand.

"Would you like me to stay?" she asked him softly.

Pitt kissed her on the forehead. "Thank you, but I think I'd like to be alone for a while."

Sandecker offered to drive Loren to her townhouse, and she gladly accepted, having arrived at Pitt's welcome-home party in a cab. They sat in reflective silence until the car passed over the bridge into the city.

"I've never seen Dirk so dispirited," said Loren, her face sad and thoughtful. "I never thought I'd ever live to say it, but the fire has gone out of his eyes."

"He'll mend," Sandecker assured her. "A couple of weeks of rest, and he'll be champing at the bit again."

"Don't you think he's getting a little old to play the daring adventurer?"

"I can't think of him sitting behind a desk. He'll never stop roving the seas, doing what he loves to do."

"What drives him?" Loren wondered aloud.

"Some men are born restless," Sandecker said philosophically. "To Dirk, every hour has a mystery to be solved, every day a challenge to conquer."

Loren looked at the admiral. "You envy him, don't you?"

Sandecker nodded. "Of course, and so do you."

"Why is that, do you think?"

"The answer is simple," Sandecker said wisely. "There's a little of Dirk Pitt in all of us."

After everyone had left and Pitt was standing alone in the hangar amid his collection of mechanical possessions, each of which had in some way touched his past, he walked stiffly to the boat he and Maeve and Giordino had built on the Misery rocks and climbed inside the cockpit. He sat there a long time, silently lost in his memories.

He was still sitting there in the *Marvelous Maeve* when the first rays of the morning sun brushed the rusting roof of the old aircraft hangar he called home.

CLIVE CUSSLER'S life nearly parallels that of his hero, Dirk Pitt. Whether searching for lost aircraft or leading expeditions to find famous shipwrecks, he has garnered an amazing record of success. With his NUMA crew of volunteers, Cussler has discovered more than sixty lost ships of historic significance, including the long-lost Confederate submarine *Hunley*. Like Pitt, Cussler collects classic automobiles. His collection features eighty examples of custom coachwork and is one of the finest to be found anywhere. Cussler divides his time between the deserts of Arizona and the mountains of Colorado.

POCKET
B O O K S

WATCH OUT FOR CLIVE
CUSSLER'S FIRST NON-FICTION
BOOK - THE STORY OF THE TRUE
LIFE ADVENTURES WHICH HAVE
INSPIRED HIM TO WRITE THE
DIRK PITT® NOVELS:

THE SEA HUNTERS

For the millions of fans of the Dirk Pitt
novels, THE SEA HUNTERS is Clive
Cussler's own dramatic account of more
than a dozen of the most fascinating and
important shipwrecks he's searched for
and discovered. Having read about
shipwrecks and underwater adventures in
SHOCK WAVE Clive's fans will delight in
reading the true stories that inspired
those adventures, as only Clive can tell
them.